STRYKERS

K. M. Ruiz

THOMAS DUNNE BOOKS
ST. MARTIN'S GRIFFIN
NEW YORK

This is a work of fiction. All of the characters, organizations, and events portrayed in this novel are either products of the author's imagination or are used fictitiously.

STRYKERS: MIND STORM copyright © 2011 by Katrina M. Ruiz and TERMINAL POINT copyright © 2012 by Katrina M. Ruiz. All rights reserved. Printed in the United States of America. For information, address St. Martin's Press, 175 Fifth Avenue, New York, N.Y. 10010.

Design by Jonathan Bennett

www.thomasdunnebooks.com
www.stmartins.com

ISBN 978-1-250-03846-3 (trade paperback)

St. Martin's Griffin books may be purchased for educational, business, or promotional use. For information on bulk purchases, please contact Macmillan Corporate and Premium Sales Department at 1-800-221-7945, extension 5442, or write specialmarkets@macmillan.com.

First Edition: December 2013

10 9 8 7 6 5 4 3 2 1

Praise for K. M. Ruiz

Mind Storm was named one of the best
science fiction releases of 2011 by *BN.com*

"K. M. Ruiz powerfully explores what happens when rogue humans with mind powers set out on a plan to enslave 'normal' humans and control the world after a cataclysmic nuclear war. This is not an X-Men comic book. The books are full of action, intrigue, and graphic violence. It's adult ESP science fiction with a kick. . . . The buildup is impressive, and there is plenty of action to go around." —*Examiner.com*

"*Mind Storm* hurls you three hundred years into a ferociously possible future where the mind has long since escaped the cage of the body and roams free and wild and dangerous. Total, delicious immersion into a world rendered startlingly real by white-hot writing skill."
—Whitley Strieber, bestselling author of
The Day After Tomorrow

"To term *Mind Storm* a thriller, even a post-apocalyptic thriller, doesn't fully describe the novel, because it's also a study in psychological deception and self-deception in a devastated future Earth where the greater the power one has, the greater the deception required, making the book both unsettling and a parable for our time."
—L. E. Modesitt Jr., bestselling author of *Legacies*

"A fast and furious vision of a very dark future . . . one of the best reads of the year." —Nate Kenyon, award-winning author of
Starcraft: Ghost—Spectres and *Sparrow Rock*

"*Mind Storm* crackles with pent-up energy, fresh ideas, and crisp dialogue. It flies like a bullet!" —William C. Dietz, author of the
Legion of the Damned series

CALGARY PUBLIC LIBRARY

APR - - 2014

"Mutants, martyrs, and mayhem—this book has it all and leaves you craving yet more of this broken and battered world."

—Rob Thurman, author of the Cal Leandros series

"It's like X-Men, only more brutal." —*SF Signal*, 4.5 stars (out of 5)

"Kaleidoscopically intricate shifting alliances and relationships, terrifying mental tortures, and near-death experiences and resurrections drive this saga of revolt and renewal and leave plenty of room for future installments." —*Publishers Weekly*

To my father, Michael Ruiz, for everything,

and my mother, Barbara Ruiz

[ACKNOWLEDGMENTS]

All my thanks to my friends and family for supporting me and my writing through the years. You guys mean the world to me. Thanks also to my editor, Brendan Deneen, and my agent, Jason Yarn, for helping me bring these stories to life.

STRYKERS

BOOK ONE
MIND STORM

PART ONE
CONTACT

SESSION DATE: 2128.04.19
LOCATION: Institute of Psionics Research
CLEARANCE ID: Dr. Amy Bennett
SUBJECT: 2581
FILE NUMBER: 346

"Lucas wants to know if they're worth it," the girl says as she colors outside the lines. "If what's left of humanity is worth the future I can see."

"And are they?" the woman who sits across the table from her asks, both of them centered in the camera. The room they are in is sterile and white, no color anywhere except on the yellow dress the child wears and the crayons she wields so carelessly.

"He wants the truth, but I don't even really know what that means anymore." The girl looks up and smiles at the doctor, the charm in her tiny child's face an almost alien expression beneath the faint exhaustion. "I'm not lying, Doctor."

The doctor marks something on her notes, shoulders tense. The girl, hooked to half a dozen machines by way of wires and electrodes attached to her skull, spine, arms, and hands, only hums. She is young, four years old, and seems content to stay where she is.

"*Who,* exactly, is this Lucas you are talking about, Aisling?"

"You don't know him," she says, discarding one crayon for another. "He's not born yet."

The EEG and supporting machines spike almost off the grid, the readings nothing like the human baseline they are layered over. The doctor's expression becomes strained.

"Aisling, can you tell me when the war will end?"

"If I tell you, it'll only make things worse." She bites her lip, brow furrowed in concentration as she turns her head, bleached-out violet eyes staring right into the camera. "We're psions. You have to remember that, okay? We can't survive a human lifetime when we die so young. I don't really want to anyway."

3

[ONE]

Al passengers, please remain seated. For your safety, the protective shutters will be coming down as we pass through Las Vegas. Vidfeed will be available on the train's public stream. All passengers, please remain seated."

The computer repeated its modulated tones over a static-filled comm system. Threnody Corwin cracked open one blue eye and watched as the thick protective shutters slid down the graffiti-covered windows on the outside of the maglev train, locking into place with the soft squeal of hydraulics. The heavy seal blocked out sunlight, her view of the dry, dead land beyond the windows, and the lingering radiation that still covered most of the country.

"Don't even think about opening that vidfeed," her partner said from the seat beside her. "If you've seen one deadzone, you've seen them all, and I want to sleep."

"Then sleep," Threnody said around a yawn. She stretched in the thinly padded seat and shoved straight black hair out of her eyes. In her mid to late twenties, she was built long-legged and lean, which made contorting herself to fit inside the limited travel space difficult. "We've got time before we reach California."

Quinton Martinez merely grunted, brown eyes narrowed down to slits as he scratched at the stubble on his chin. He wore the same type of outfit as Threnody, a black-on-black battle dress uniform, and boots that had walked across three continents. Taller than Threnody, with muscles corded thickly against his bones, Quinton's skin was a deep brown,

5

scarred lightly over the knuckles and the back of his hands from the fire he could control as a Class III pyrokinetic.

Fire wasn't something he could create, not without external help. That's what the thin, malleable biotubes containing compressed natural gas were for. The biotubes were grafted along the metacarpal bones in his hands, radiating up his forearms where skin and muscle biomodifications held them in place. The skin at the tip of each middle finger and thumb had been replaced with razor-thin pieces of metal. Quinton had given up on keeping track of how many times he'd lost his hands and arms to fire. He'd seen the inside of a biotank for regeneration too many times over the years for it to matter anymore.

"The Rockies, then down to the Slums of the Angels," Quinton said, thinking of all that was really left of civilization on the West Coast since the bombs fell, a mirror for the rest of the world. "Chasing a blip on the grid into a goddamn warzone."

Threnody rubbed at her forehead with careful fingers, wishing her skin didn't feel so new. "You didn't have to come, Quin. You're salvageable, according to the psi surgeons. They would have transferred you if you asked."

"And like a good dog I should have asked, right?" The smile Quinton gave her was thin and hard with anger. "You're my partner, Thren. The only family I've got. I go where you go. End of story."

Two failed missions back-to-back: Madrid, and then later Johannesburg, where she had opted to let unregistered humans and potential psions live instead of killing them in the face of threats from higher-Classed enemy psions. Their current mission was simply punishment for past failures.

The Strykers Syndicate contracted out enslaved psion soldiers for high-risk jobs. Death was a known and accepted by-product of those contracts, and the dead needed to be replaced for the company to turn a profit. Those children with psion potential she let go were resources she had no right to touch or lose. Insubordination had only gotten them a stint in medical and a black mark on their records. Quinton could have argued his way out of it. She was the one in charge, after all; it had been her decision, not his. Except they were partners, now and always, and he'd opted to come with her once again. One last mission to prove her loyalty. One last mission to prove she deserved to live.

The government owned her, as they owned every psion. Her independence, according to the ruling World Court, had become a problem.

Never could learn to come to fucking heel, Threnody thought bitterly as she reached over and touched a sensor on the side panel of her seat.

A hologrid snapped into existence before her, projected through the air from overhead, the logo for TransAmerica MagLev Inc. spinning slowly before blending seamlessly into the welcome menu. She dragged her finger over the public-stream option and was treated to a view of the stark, polluted ruins of a lost American city. Just a skeleton of a time abandoned generations ago, of a world no one even remembered. The ruins were similar to all the ones in the many deadzones they had been pushing through since departing from what was left of Buffalo, New York.

She reached out to shift the feed to something different. Only this time, when her fingers touched the hologrid, the data flickered, wavered into colored lines, then sizzled into sparks that shocked her. Whatever pain or irritation Threnody experienced, it was drowned out by the frustration she felt at her lack of control. It wasn't something she could afford.

Quinton yanked her hand away before anyone noticed, reaching over to press the control screen on her seat's arm panel that would shut down the hologrid.

"Don't," he said, mouth pressed close to her ear. "You're not ready. Johannesburg was a mistake and you're still recovering. They shouldn't have discharged you from medical."

Threnody rubbed her fingers against her knee, the shock of the charge nothing more than a tingle beneath her nails when it shouldn't have been even that, not for a Class III electrokinetic. Her power, like that of all electrokinetics, was limited to conduits that she could touch and feed. An involuntary reaction to a machine simply meant Quinton was right. That didn't change a damn thing.

"Can't fight orders, Quin."

"Then we do what we can to work around them. Why do you think I registered our route via train instead of an air shuttle?"

She gave him a sharp look. "Did you even look at shuttles to get us out here?"

"I looked. They didn't interest me." Quinton settled back in his seat, closing his eyes against the dim interior lights of the train. "Go to sleep, Thren. We won't get much of it once we hit the West Coast."

She knew that. She knew the details of this mission better than he did. That didn't make working through it any easier, not when they had to travel across radiation-tainted land to a state that was still being fought over by the government and drug cartels beneath the glitz of seedy glamour. The tension wasn't over the gold California had once been known for—most of the Sierra Nevada had been strip-mined bare decades before the first bomb dropped—but over the government-owned and government-protected towers of SkyFarms Inc. that filled the southern part of the Central Valley. The farming and agricultural company that kept the world fed with its heavily shielded towers of limited produce and animal pens would always be worth dying for.

The world was a different place ever since the first bomb fell in 2124 somewhere in the old Middle East, beginning the worldwide nuclear genocide known as the Border Wars. Five years of bombing hell across nearly all the continents had practically annihilated the human race. The fallout from that time still lingered in a toxic environment, still showed up too many generations later as genetic mutations that caused physical deformities and incurable disease. Since 2129 when the Border Wars finally ended, people hadn't been living, they'd only been surviving.

What cities had managed to survive the Border Wars and rebuild themselves into some semblance of society again were where most of the world's population remained. Linked by way of maglev tracks built as a way to jump-start a broken global economy, or government-built air shuttles designated for the educated rich, countries remade their borders accordingly around deadzones. Travel wasn't promoted or always permitted, but humanity would never give up the urge to explore.

Two hours later the train finally pulled free of the Central Valley, wending its way toward their destination in Southern California. Sunlight burned into Threnody's eyes, burned through sleep, as the protective seal finally lifted well beyond the old state line.

Quinton was already awake, even if his eyes were closed. He felt different to her fine-tuned senses when he was conscious. She knew better than he did the electric song his nerves sang at any given hour. Every person gave off an individual charge. Like the mind, it was as unique as a person's DNA, and DNA was the only thing they had to stand on out here in a place ruled more by street law than judicial opinion. Psion power would always have an edge over guns.

"Time?" Threnody asked.

"Thirty-five and counting."

She nodded, pushed herself up, and made sure her single bag was still stowed securely beneath her seat. They had a forward row in a middle car with enough space to breathe in, but that was about it. Anyone with enough credit to mean anything traveled by air shuttle, and they definitely didn't travel to the West Coast of the United States of America. Elite society held stock and coveted living space in pockets down the East Coast of Canada and America or in Western Europe. The only things left in Australia were deserts and firestorms. What remained of South America was overrun by drug cartels, and most of Asia had turned into a toxic graveyard generations ago, its barrenness rivaled only by the desert Africa had become.

Threnody could feel the maglev train begin to decrease its speed from 320 kilometers an hour to a full stop when they finally pulled into the only platform still servicing the outer edges of the Slums of the Angels. Ceiling lights blinked their arrival as the doors slid open with a crack that shook every car. Quinton helped Threnody to her feet and made a path for them through the Spanish-speaking crowds of people that were pitching themselves off the train, breathing smoggy air for the first time in days. The pollution stung the back of her throat, made her eyes water. What sky they could still see above through the ruins was pale gray from polluted clouds, the wind gritty, and the heat was like a weight against her skin.

It didn't compare to the presence that slid into her mind as they headed for the exit stairwell.

Down on the street, a cautious mental voice with a heavy Scottish accent said. *We've been waiting awhile already. Guess HQ wasn't lying about you guys coming out here. You going to be able to handle this mission?*

Shouldn't that be my question? Threnody asked as Kerr MacDougal pulled her and Quinton into a psi link with his telepathy.

I'm not the one who spent half a month in medical getting their nervous system put back together.

I'm not the one whose shields are slipping.

Touché.

I'm walking. That tell you anything?

That you're a stubborn bitch and your file doesn't do you justice. Over here.

They had reached the ground below the platform, and her gaze zeroed in on two men standing at the taxi zone with heavy-duty bags at their feet. Threnody schooled her expression into one of polite neutrality and swallowed her pride as they approached the team they were assigned to work with. From the top of the list to the very bottom. From being the best to being a problem. It was a strange feeling to know that the standing she and Quinton had fought so hard to attain and keep in the Strykers Syndicate could so easily be wiped away. People only got assigned partnership with this team as punishment. No one liked working with dysfunctional psions, and that's all these two would ever be.

Kerr was a head taller than she was, whipcord thin, and not carrying the weight he should have with his height. The closer they got, the darker the circles beneath Kerr's teal-colored eyes became. His partner, Jason Garret, stood silently beside him, chewing on the filter of a half-smoked cigarette.

Kerr was the Strykers Syndicate's only Class II telepath, with mental shields that never stayed up. Kerr should have been able to make his own, but even the best geneticists hadn't been able to categorize all the quirks that showed up in the DNA and RNA of psions on the human accelerated regions of the human genome. His shields were unstable and his telepathy put him at risk of losing his mind in a maelstrom of the world's thoughts. Riding along behind someone else's shields was a stopgap procedure. It worked for now, but nobody back at headquarters was sure how many years he had left until it stopped.

Jason was Kerr's patch, his temporary fix, a Class V telekinetic that could teleport, making him a dual psion with average reach and strength. He was also the only Stryker in their entire ranks —their entire history— with intact natal shields that had never fallen. Psychically bonded at a young age by a psi surgeon telepath, Jason's shields were Kerr's only saving grace when Kerr's own shields would fail him. The two weren't lovers, despite the bond. They weren't compatible that way. They considered each other family, and while Jason preferred men, Kerr didn't like anyone.

"Threnody," Jason said with a sharp smile, hazel eyes cool in their assessment of her, but warmer when they focused on her partner. "Quinton. Never thought we'd ever get the pleasure of working with you two."

"Apparently you're not doing as good a job as you should be and they sent us to sort you out," Quinton replied with a steady look. "It's amazing you haven't been terminated after so many failures."

Jason only shrugged as if he'd heard that accusation many times before. Threnody resisted the urge to touch the back of her neck where all psions got a neurotracker grafted to their cranial nerves and brain stem the moment they were brought to the Strykers Syndicate. Government control wasn't just lip service, and removing that collar was a death sentence.

"The Strykers need me," Kerr said quietly. "Which means they need Jason. The fact that you two, their favorites, have fallen this far means that they don't need *you*. Not as badly. Maybe you should think about that."

Quinton looked as if he wanted to argue, but Threnody caught his eye and shook her head. "We're all on the same side. We have a job to do and a target to find. If we fail this time, then we'll all be terminated," she reminded them. "Let's just get where we need to be."

Jason stepped away to hail a taxi, the car pulling away from a long line of other service vehicles as he fed credit chips into the pay meter. Down here, credit chips were hacked to be untraceable, and they were all anyone used to purchase things, from transportation to pleasure to murder.

They climbed into the taxi and got settled, bags at their feet and silence among them. Jason told the driver where to go in Spanish. It took an hour to get to their destination, driving down damaged streets in a car that had long ago ruined its shock system. They felt every hole the patched tires rode over in the streets that led to an old expressway, the main artery into the wreckage that existed in the shadows of the environmentally sealed city towers that made up Los Angeles. It was the only part of the city that the American military had managed to save during the Border Wars.

Cars outnumbered the air shuttles that cast quick shadows from above. Threnody stared at the city towers, built high with neon bright adverts scrolling down their sides, until she couldn't see them anymore as they drove into the murky depths of the Slums of the Angels.

Like most of the world, the West Coast of America had once been a thriving, living place. That was before the Border Wars. That was before the deadly radiation and acid storms that filtered over all the continents, before the earthquake of 2167 that devastated the surviving population of the three coastal western states of America. The only pocket of civilization in the West, settled between large swaths of deadzones, to survive the 2167 quake was Los Angeles, but it lost half a dozen city towers when the land shook itself to pieces. The majority of the ruins were never dealt with, couldn't be dealt with. They simply became something different.

What replaced the infamy of Los Angeles and the tech-driven north were South American drug cartels running through the Latin Corridor and Mexico, eager to cater to those who didn't care if their addictions damaged their DNA. The Slums of the Angels became a hole in the world that people with no identities fell into, where a person could buy and sell anything, but the only way out was by death or sheer, mind-boggling luck.

Or power.

Something that the four Strykers had plenty of.

The taxi driver dropped them off a good fifteen kilometers into the Slums, at a corner braced by a building written over with warring gang signs. He seemed glad to leave them behind.

Where are we? Threnody asked as they stood on the crumbling sidewalk.

We need a cover to get us deeper into the Slums, Kerr replied. *Jason and I had orders to build one. This is it what we were able to buy.*

A cartel soldier came out of the building and into the grimy sunlight. He spat between them, military-grade gun held steady in his hands as three more soldiers came out behind him, fanning out on the sidewalk. Their presence had the few people scattered around the street ducking out of sight.

"Ident," he snapped.

Jason spread his hands and offered up a slick smile. "Carlos, you know it's us. We paid good money to get clearance from you."

"*Ident.* You don't get no special treatment just because you got credit."

Jason shrugged and stepped forward, body loose and expression bored as a soldier came close enough to scan his eyes. The portable bioscanner fit neatly in the soldier's hand. The infrared light protruding from the tip scanned the identity of the iris peels Jason had been wearing since he and Kerr were assigned this mission weeks ago.

"Clear," the man said in heavily accented English as he stepped back.

"You got our way in?" Jason demanded.

"I got it." Carlos's gaze swept over the group, skipping over the pair he knew, lingering a little on Quinton, before finally settling on Threnody. His mouth curved into a leer. "She's new. *La gringa* looking for some fun?"

They have orders to kill us, Kerr said through the psi link.

Guess we didn't pay up to scale, Jason said.

Threnody smiled invitingly at the soldier. "Come a little closer and find out."

The soldier's buddies whistled sharply at him as Carlos approached her. Rubbing at his chin, Carlos let his gaze drift up and down her body in an assessing manner, mouth curling up in a hard smile when it became apparent that none of the men with her were going to interfere.

"You'd make more money lying on your back than playing at being a man," Carlos said with another leer as he reached out and squeezed her left breast hard.

"Whores don't keep the money they make down here," Threnody said coolly as she grabbed his wrist and tapped into the bioelectricity that the human body ran on.

Threnody's own nerves sparked as electricity exploded out of her and into him, their bare skin the bridge she needed to work with. Her power coursed through the soldier's body faster than his brain could process and he was dead before he hit the ground; skin blackened, burned and cracked.

Before any of the other three humans could react, Kerr was in their minds and burning them out. A telepathic strike that hard, backed by his phenomenal Class II strength, had them dead in seconds. Humans didn't have the genetic capability to defend against what a psion could do. They weren't built that way. Their minds winked out on the mental grid, that vast psychic plane full of a world's thoughts that all 'path-oriented psions functioned on. Tied into Kerr's mind through the psi link, Threnody could feel through his power the holes those deaths left behind on the mental grid.

"Get our clearance," Threnody ordered as she peeled the dead man's charred skin off her bare fingers.

Quinton rifled through the pockets of the dead for the passes they had paid for. Kerr's telepathy could wipe a person's mind clean of their presence, but he couldn't touch machines, and all checkpoints down in the Slums had extensive security. Quinton found what they needed on the second body, pulling out four thin, transparent pass cards.

"Blanks," he said. "We need someone to program them."

Jason nodded. "Give them to me."

Quinton tossed the pass cards to Jason, who caught them with his telekinesis. Jason dug out a slim datapad from his pocket and jacked the first pass card into the portable computer. He was one of the best hackers in their ranks, one of the reasons why he and Kerr hadn't been terminated yet. The faint gleam in Jason's eyes told Threnody his implanted inspecs were running through the data, connected to it by a wire plugged into the neuroport on his left wrist, as he hacked his way through the pass key's minimal defenses.

Threnody looked at Kerr. "Are we clear?"

The telepath cocked his head to the side, eyes focused on some distant place. "Building is empty inside. Got human peripherals getting curious. I'll take care of them."

"Do it."

She bent down, snagged the collar of the nearest dead soldier, and hauled the body into the dirty office. Kerr followed her lead, pulling one dead man by the arm while Quinton dealt with the last two.

Inside, against the far wall, was a terminal with a single wide vidscreen displaying dozens of security feeds. Threnody glanced at the images as she approached the control console and took a seat in the abandoned chair. She was a brilliant tactician, but a piss-poor hacker. Her body couldn't take most of the biomodifications that a quarter of the remaining population had grafted to their nervous system. All the delicate biowiring that was required to directly uplink with various computer systems wasn't compatible with her body. That didn't mean she was useless.

"Nice of them to leave it accessible," Threnody said as she dragged her fingers over the controls and started pulling up command windows. "Some of it, at least."

Quinton peered over her shoulder. "You going to fry it?"

"Soon as Jason wipes us from the system."

It took her half a minute to find the home feed that showcased the corner right outside the office. She pulled up the log for the past hour, getting all the basic information ready for Jason to parse and do what he did best, outside of flinging things around with his mind. Three minutes later he was there, taking over her spot. He jacked into the system through two neuroports and hacked into the feed, hiding the murders they had committed by wiping the system clean.

"Not even going to bother with a loop. Their server farm is on-site, so the damage needs to go deep, Threnody," Jason said as he pried the wires out of his arms when he finished. "It's all yours."

He shoved the chair back and got out of the way. Threnody leaned over and pressed a hand to the console of the terminal. She took a deep breath, steadied herself for the burn, and pushed her power into the electric heart of the system before her. Not the same as burning it through a human body, but electricity was electricity, and enough of a surge could kill anything, especially a machine.

The system crashed. Circuits melted to slag and the vidscreen went dark. Threnody pulled her hand away and clenched her fingers down tight against the heat that tingled across her palm.

"Are you feeling that?" Quinton asked sharply.

"Some." She couldn't lie to her partner when it might cost them later on.

"I *told* you they should have given you more time. If we had argued, Jael would have allowed it."

"And I told you we had our orders." She looked pointedly at Kerr. "What's our destination?"

Kerr's eyes were closed where he stood in the doorway, hands pressed against the frame, head bowed. Sweat dripped down the skin of his face, falling off the point of his chin. "South. Target's broadcasting twenty klicks away. So far I'm not sensing any Warhounds in the field."

"For once," Jason muttered. "Even if this is their territory."

Threnody ignored him. "We'll use that SUV around the corner to get there. The soldiers won't miss it. Or their uniforms."

Jason nodded at the bags he and Kerr had been carrying. "We've got supplies in there if we need them."

"Good."

They stripped the dead for clothes to create the illusion of cartel coloring over the standard black that should have meant neutral, except no one was neutral in the Slums.

Kerr pulled on a flak jacket, buckling it tight over his chest as he glanced at Threnody. "No Stryker has ever discovered the identity of the target since it showed up on the grid two years ago. Jason and I, we've been tracking it off and on for the past few months and have never gotten close."

"I know," Threnody said as she added extra ammo to her belt pouch for the gun she carried on her hip.

"What are your exact orders?"

"We can't have a high-Classed psion running around unchecked. The government hates when we're not leashed or dead. We've been ordered to find out who it is and bring them in. If retrieval is impossible, we've been ordered to terminate the target."

She didn't bother with the rest of the order, about what would happen if she failed. Everyone in the Strykers Syndicate knew about their demotion, this sanctioned death sentence. Threnody stared at Kerr, daring him to say something, anything, in the face of her situation.

Those strange teal eyes of his searched her face for a few seconds before he said, "You belong to one of the best teams we've got this generation. Why are they wasting your life like this?"

"It's not your business," Quinton said.

Threnody thought otherwise. She didn't experience a traumatic flashback to their last mission. The psi surgeon in charge of putting their minds back together over and over was better than that, but the memory of it was difficult to ignore.

"There was a school," she said, voice steady, even if her thoughts weren't. "An illegal one, run by unregistered humans. There were children. I wouldn't—"

Her nervous system remembered that nightmare better than her head. She could still feel that Warhound's hand around her throat, his electric power cutting past her defenses and into her body. It was pure damn luck that Quinton had reached her when he did to save her.

"Everyone deserves a chance." Threnody swallowed tightly. "Even those without identities."

The Border Wars made this world 250 years ago, and they all survived in the long shadow of that nuclear aftermath. Education was the privilege of the registered elite, not meant for the gene-damaged masses. Population was regulated because there were only so many resources to go around, but laws would always be broken.

Threnody thought about those unregistered children and the handful born with psion potential. She should have killed them to prevent the Warhounds from keeping them, but she was getting old for a psion. She could afford to question their superiors when others would simply obey. She'd lived long enough that the punishment didn't sting as much as it might have if she had more years left to her. Strykers were taught to value human life, or at least the lives of those who belonged to the Registry. The government didn't care about unregistered humans, but Strykers did. She did.

Threnody's body still twitched, even now, from that last remembered electric shock before the Warhounds had disappeared with the children in a teleport.

Kerr pushed the memories aside for her.

They're alive, Kerr said. *If you can't think about the good somewhere in that, then think about the mission.*

It was, after all, what they lived for.

[TWO]

JULY 2379
SLUMS OF THE ANGELS, USA

The Cathedral of Our Lady of the Angels had seen many decades come and go since the ground it stood on was broken and blessed. It survived the upheaval of land and society when so many other structures had not. Perhaps by the grace of God, or so the priests still taught in thinned-out Sunday schools.

While it still stood in all its grimy, gang-marked glory, with its alabaster windows long covered in mold and the bronze on the door stripped and pitted, it had not seen the light of day for over one hundred years. The adobe-colored walls had turned gray over time, marked in layers of ink and grainy pollution that stained the exterior. Generations of gangs had scrawled their call signs on the skeleton of the place even before the city towers were erected over that lonely piece of God's land.

A tiny amount of dim sunlight filtered down through the cracks of metal and the smog-filled air, covering the street just meters beyond the dry expanse of bare earth that once held grass and now only held vagrants. The entrance to the cathedral was located on the south side of the building, overshadowed by a crumbling cement cross that jutted out from the cathedral's wall. The light inside that fifty-foot effigy had burned out before the turn of the century. It had never been relit. Electricity down on the ground was expensive, even back then, and even more so now.

Bishop Michael Santos had spent nearly his entire life in the Slums of the Angels. The only time he had ever left it was when he completed his seminary studies at the Vatican's fortress in the Swiss Alps and earned the right to wear the collar of a priest. The world was in need of men and women who gave their time and effort toward bettering the lives of others. In this secular, technology-filled society driven by desperation and greed, faith burned only in the background, in the cracks, with the forgotten. It wasn't easy living life with faith, but he did it, one breath at a time.

Bishop Santos stared up at the worn and cracked image of Christ on the cross that hung on the wall of the chancel and smiled. *"Otro día, mi Señor."*

No one was in the cathedral except for himself and a handful of Sisters. Mass was only offered on Sundays, confession had to be scheduled in advance, and he was tired of presiding over funerals. Bishop Santos sighed, running a hand through thinning gray hair. He'd been offered other posts over the years, because the pope believed in furthering the education of the faithful, but Bishop Santos didn't believe in neon-colored crosses and biosculpted personalities that preached on vidscreens. Most days of the week he preferred his cracked and dying cathedral to the top of the city towers. But some days he wanted more. Some days he sinned.

It's human nature. Or so it has been said for thousands of years.

Bishop Santos jerked around in response to the voice that echoed in his ears—amused, with a faint English accent—but he didn't see anyone in the vast emptiness of the cathedral.

I never did understand why people would believe in something so limited.

It took Bishop Santos several long moments to realize why that voice seemed so odd as he reached up to touch the side of his head. He wasn't hearing it in his ears, but behind his eyes, in the middle of his brain. Brown eyes darted from side to side, squinting through the sparse brightness that the lights provided.

"Who's there?" he called out, voice rough from years of breathing pollutants.

No one was in the nave. Bishop Santos would have bet his eternal soul on that. Between one blink and the next, a tall young man appeared in the front pew, long legs stretched out in front of him, one elbow propped on the back of the pew so that he could rest his head on his fist. He was dressed all in black, claiming no cartel color when everyone always claimed a side down here on the ground.

Bishop Santos didn't know how the young man had made it into the cathedral without someone discovering his presence. The doors were locked and alarmed for a reason, and he didn't like the faint, mocking smile on the stranger's face.

"The cathedral is closed today," Bishop Santos said. "I don't know how you got in here, but I'm going to have to ask you to leave."

"You can ask all you like. I need to be here."

Bishop Santos bit the underside of his lip, unable to deny that request. Some distant instinct told him he should, but the warning was ignored. "If you've come for confession, you missed the designated day. Tuesday is when the booths are open, and they are booked through the end of summer."

"I have nothing to confess, at least not to you."

"Everyone has something to confess, my son."

That smile got wider. "Your sense of morality is severely misplaced. You're wasting your time trying to convert me. Your God isn't what I believe in. Your God isn't why I am here."

Bishop Santos watched as the young man pushed himself to his feet and brushed past the bishop on his way up to the marble altar and the table that sat in the chancel on the small dais. He stood there, back to the bishop and the empty cathedral, and stared up at the larger-than-life crucifix for a long moment. Then he picked up the metal tin on the table that housed the thin, expensive wafers used in Communion, pulled a few out, and ate them. The shock that Bishop Santos knew he should be feeling never came. The stranger turned around to face him again.

If this is all you have to offer your followers, no wonder they prefer cartel drugs.

Bishop Santos wrestled with the uncomfortable feeling that something wasn't right. Only when his eyes latched onto that smile, to that mouth that had not moved to speak, did he realize that he could still hear the stranger's voice.

I need this place, this last surviving Los Angeles landmark, for something far more important than evening Mass. Dark blue eyes that Bishop Santos *knew* should mean something to him didn't blink and he could not look away. *Just think. You've spent a lifetime praying for your God to send his son to save you.*

The stranger poured all the remaining Communion wafers on the floor and ground them into dust beneath his bootheel. He spread his arms wide.

Here I am.

His mouth didn't move and still he talked. Bishop Santos flinched. He could feel the blood drain out of his face as the stranger's voice filled his mind.

"Demonio," Bishop Santos whispered in a voice that had never shook in the face of countless guns, countless bodies, and countless threats in all his years working in the Slums. But it shook now because understanding wasn't coming to him. He didn't know if this was a test from his Lord or from the devil himself.

Demon? I'm no demon, human.

Bishop Santos blinked, or thought he did. One second the stranger was on the dais, the next he was standing before the bishop, intruding in his tiny bubble of personal space. He tried to run, but found that the only order his body obeyed was one the stranger gave. Bishop Santos watched as the young man raised a hand, palm to the ground, then slowly lowered it again. Bishop Santos's knees bent of their own accord and he slammed down onto the floor in a kneeling position. Crying out in pain, he looked up with panic-stricken eyes.

"Please!" he gasped out. "I don't—"

Understand. Yes, yes, I know you don't. Just like all the children you fucked didn't understand how you could betray their trust. One long-fingered hand reached out to touch the bishop's wrinkled face, tracing over the lines of age. *You are something I will never be, Bishop Santos. You should be thankful for that. I know I am.*

Knowledge finally came to him, too late to mean anything in the face of a disease and a power he had always preached as unholy. "Psion."

They say your life flashes before your eyes when you die. It doesn't, not really. It was only the neurons in Bishop Santos's head forcibly overloading. Just his mind exploding in a novalike burn that rippled across a small pocket in the mental grid, hidden beneath strong telepathic shields.

Maybe he thought about the years he had lived, the people he had led, the God he had served. Maybe he thought about the precious pool of pure, clean water he'd bathed in before being vested with a bishop's robe years ago. Maybe he thought about a lot of things—things that didn't matter any longer—but Lucas Serca made him forget.

Lucas Serca made him die.

Bishop Santos didn't feel a thing when he fell to the steps leading up from the nave to the chancel. Nothing was left of his mind, no life was in those unseeing eyes. His heart still beat and blood still ran through his veins, feeding a body of cells that had nothing to live for anymore.

Lucas stared down at the man lying at his feet. He had never understood the religious, how they prayed for a way out of hell, but couldn't be bothered to find it themselves. The idea of mindless service to a higher power was anathema to his way of thinking—Sercas ruled, they did not serve. Tapping into his power, Lucas finished what he had started.

Telepathy had turned off the bishop's mind; telekinesis stopped his heart.

If there was a heaven, maybe the bishop was there.

[THREE]

JULY 2379

SLUMS OF THE ANGELS, USA

The shuttle came in over the Pacific, cutting across air traffic with priority clearance, dropping down out of vertical. The pilot adjusted the shuttle's vector as it approached the landing docks that stuck out like sharp spokes along the sides of every remaining city tower that made up Los Angeles. With a rush of air, the buzz of gyros and buffers, the shuttle settled firmly into the anchoring arms of a restricted docking cradle at the top of the tallest city tower. It locked in with a shudder and the anchor lights went from green to red.

No one disembarked.

On a midlevel work zone in the tower below, three people appeared in an all-white room, the faint crack of displaced air muffled by sound-proofing.

"I hate cleanup duty," the man in the lead said irritably.

Jin Li Zhang was someone who couldn't be ignored. In his early thirties and close to the end of his short life as a Class II electrokinetic, Jin Li was tall, with black hair and brown eyes. He wore black BDUs similar to the style that Strykers used, designed that way to promote confusion between the government-controlled psions and the Warhounds, rogue psions secretly owned by the Serca Syndicate.

Jin Li chewed on the cigarette clamped between his teeth as he walked down the hallway, the cigarette nearly burned down to the filter, smoke blending into the air around him. The first office he found was empty; the second was not. Two people looked up as the door slid open. Recognition came hard and fast, and the one sitting behind the workstation stood up on shaky feet, all the blood leaving his face.

"Sir." The man swallowed. "I wasn't aware you were coming."

Jin Li drew in a lungful of smoke and let it out slowly, wisps of it twisting behind him as he approached the workstation. The man and his assistant, a woman in a neat business suit, scrambled to get out of Jin Li's way.

"You had your orders to keep us appraised of the situation," Jin Li said as he tapped command codes into the system that overrode every security feature present, shutting it down. "You didn't. We don't appreciate failure."

For a moment, the only sound in the room was the businessman's loud, ragged breathing. Finally he said, "It's difficult to track someone in the system who has the ability to hide from bioscanners."

Jin Li's mouth curled up around his cigarette. "I hate excuses. Come here."

It was painfully obvious that the man didn't want to obey. Sweat had broken out all across his face in a bright sheen, pupils dilated wide from fear. Repeatedly licking his bottom lip, the man took a few scuffling steps forward until he was within arm's reach of Jin Li.

Jin Li wrapped his hand around the man's bare wrist and forced him to his knees. Electrokinetic power burned through human nerves with frightening ease. The man screamed, the sound choking off only when Jin Li released him.

"You were supposed to get a lock on the target. You didn't. The Serca Syndicate requires obedience and results from its employees. You're going to have to work on that," Jin Li said, glancing over at the man's assistant.

The woman took a few steps back, face pale and eyes wide. She let out a little shriek when she ran up against someone she hadn't known was there.

"Humans," a disgusted soprano said. "You're really only good for breeding and menial tasks."

Jin Li spared a glance for the person who was leading this mission. The tall, slim teenager standing beside the woman in the middle of the room was dressed in the same streamlined BDUs as he was, her attention focused firmly on her father's best enforcer.

Samantha Serca was eighteen years old, beautiful, and extremely powerful; attributes courtesy of her genes. Her dark blond hair was pulled back away from her face, opaque glasses hiding the dark blue eyes that were the signature trait of the Serca family. No amount of gene splicing could legally re-create this deep, solid shade of blue outside her family. Anyone who followed the founding family of the Serca Syndicate would know who she was by her eyes alone. Which was why for this endeavor she wore the glasses and strips of synthskin lined with translucent bioware over the facial recognition points of her bone structure.

Standing a step behind her, with hands gripping the buckles of his flak jacket and wearing an identical pair of glasses, was another teen with the same distinctive eyes, the same dark blond hair. Twins; but Jin Li had always liked Gideon Serca more than his older sister. Gideon preferred killing over conversation most days of the week, and as a Class II telekinetic, he was very, very good at it.

"When they initiated a bioscan through security checkpoints in the Slums, they found jack shit and gave up," Jin Li reminded Samantha. "We got that report from HQ on the flight over."

She shrugged. "I'm not surprised. Lucas is almost as good as Nathan when it comes to reading as baseline human on the grid. You're not a telepath, you can't scan for him."

Samantha, however, *was* a telepath, a Class II with the genetics and training that made her capable of tracking their current target. Jin Li's lip curled up, but he stood his ground when she closed the distance between them, her attention focused on the man kneeling before the electrokinetic. The arrogance in the way Samantha held herself was impossible to ignore. So was the strength of her power when it slid into a static, human mind that didn't have the capability to handle such a strong telepathic intrusion.

The man's head snapped back, body twitching as Samantha sifted through his memories, looking for the faint scars that would signify psionic interference. She didn't find any in his mind and released him, sliding her power into his assistant's mind instead.

The woman stumbled from the pain, clutching her head and begging for Samantha to stop as the telepath dug deeper. Samantha found what she was looking for at the bottom of the woman's mind, just a faint dip in her thoughts that a lower-Classed psion wouldn't pick up. Samantha almost missed it. The only reason she didn't was because Lucas had meant for her to find it, some hint of what he was doing, but not why.

Piecing the memory back together proved aggravating, not because it wasn't difficult—it was—but because what she finally found only pissed her off.

The woman had been made to forget the memory Samantha pulled out of the recesses of her mind. The thing about memories was that they were fluid. The brain stored them over a person's life, and unlike humans, telepaths spent their entire lives tearing through other people's thoughts. Samantha knew how to find things most people forgot they even knew. She recognized the mocking tenor voice in that memory, recognized the face of the person she had grown up with. His idea of amusement was something she never appreciated.

It's been a while, Sam. Let's see if you have better luck in the Slums than you did back in London. You do *remember London, don't you?*

Her first failure as a full Warhound at the age of sixteen was something she'd never forget, nor the punishment she received after she failed to keep Lucas from leaving. Samantha flinched away from her own memories. She couldn't, however, escape the woman's memory of her older brother's knowing laughter, or of Lucas walking into this branch however long ago as if he owned it.

I left something behind for you. Find it, and you'll know where to find me. You know I never like to make things easy for you.

Two years on the run, Samantha thought as she wrenched her power out of the woman's mind, not caring about the permanent damage she'd caused. Two years when it was just her to face their father's sadistic wrath outside the glare of press cameras, because Kristen was unregistered and unknown, and Gideon had become the favorite Nathan used now. Gideon wasn't Lucas, despite her twin's sycophantic tendencies. Lucas had a spine, something Gideon still lacked, but Gideon was becoming adept at being cruel.

Samantha was beginning to hate her twin more than was considered healthy by the empaths in her father's Syndicate. She hated Lucas more for putting her in this situation.

"He's in the Slums," Samantha said, ignoring the seizing woman at her feet. "He stopped here first to make sure we would follow him through an implanted message. He left something behind in this branch. I want it found."

"Lucas isn't careless," Gideon said as he shared a look with Jin Li. "We all know that. He hasn't left anything behind in any of the rest of the cities he's run through, so why start now?"

"He's not careless, no. He just likes to play games. In that, he is very much like Nathan." With a crooked, little smile, Samantha toed the dying woman's body. "Have someone clean this mess up. She's bleeding all over my floor."

A puddle of blood was forming around the woman's head as her body still continued to seize. Her boss was only capable of watching her die from his own position on the floor, mouth forming protests he dared not speak, but Samantha heard him anyway.

"How predictable," she said as she turned on her heel and headed for the door. "He wishes he could kill us."

The man flinched when Jin Li dragged his fingers over the back of his neck. Samantha never saw Jin Li move; she felt it when the human died, a sharp white shock against her shields on the mental grid as Jin Li took care of rectifying the man's poor work ethic.

Nathan could get new humans to fill the vacancies in an instant, that wasn't a problem. Neither was covering their tracks. The problem was that she still wasn't sure what Lucas wanted or why he had left the Syndicate in the first place.

The psion in charge of this Syndicate branch was a Class VI psychometrist who went by the name of Jessica Frist. Samantha barely glanced at the screen detailing the woman's company rank—director of this pigsty—before she was palming open the door and walking inside. The spacious office was full of high-grade work terminals overseen by a slim woman. Jessica looked up from the vidscreens that surrounded her, inspecs glowing in her brown eyes, her face the only part of her not covered by a full-body skinsuit.

"Sir," she said, gloved fingers going still against the controls.

"We're cleaning house," Samantha informed her. "You'll get a new set of qualified humans by tomorrow. Their incompetence regarding the job assigned them doesn't excuse yours. The report HQ forwarded us is unacceptable. You had better have something more for me."

"We got a hit within the last thirty minutes in the grid," Jessica said, discomfort and fear making her stutter ever so slightly. "I thought it prudent to stay and monitor the system before I uploaded a second report."

"The humans said you hadn't been able to find Lucas's location."

"This isn't Lucas."

Samantha's mouth curled up viciously. "Strykers."

"Yes."

"This is our territory and they know it. Who's on the grid?" Jessica handed over a small datapad and Samantha took it, studying the information. Shaking her head, Samantha put it down on the desk. "They just don't know when to quit."

"It makes for an amusing way to pass the time," Gideon agreed as he came into the office. "The humans are dead. I teleported their bodies into the Pacific. Someone else needs to deal with the blood on the floor."

"Sir," Jessica said, inclining her head at the order.

Samantha focused on Jessica. "Take us to the servers. Lucas was here and I want to know why. You're scanning that room for any evidence that can give us that information and you're doing it now."

Jessica managed to physically hide her flinch, but Samantha could still feel the recoil in the other woman's thoughts. Jessica disengaged herself from the system, locked it down, and led her superiors to the server room at the back of the moderate-size office. The lights snapped on as the door slid open, revealing two terminals that hummed on standby power.

Samantha eyed Jessica after they stepped inside, not impressed with the other woman's hesitation. "Well? Get on with it."

Jessica moved around Gideon, peeling off her elbow-length gloves. She tucked them into her pockets and steeled herself for what was to come as she pressed both hands to the console, long practice helping her tamp down the fear of the unknown beneath her fingers.

Every psi power in existence affected the brain in ways modern science still couldn't quantify. Afflicted with an incurable disease born out of the ruins of a vicious nuclear war fought 250 years ago, psions were the people that the rest of society feared.

A psychometrist's power worked through tactile contact. Skin was the focal point of their power, and touch activated it. Psychometrists lived with the constant and brutal knowledge that anything and anyone they touched could and would suck them under into memories that weren't their own.

Jessica sank into the flashes of memories that had been imprinted over the years, sliding her hands through hundreds of moments as she ran her fingers over the edges of the workstation. The past sought to carve out space in the present through her Class VI power. It made her head spin as she followed that glittering line to the one bright moment purposefully embedded in the terminal.

One touch to that memory and the trigger Lucas had left behind in Jessica's mind broke her. Or seemed to. She sucked in a ragged breath, yanking her hands off the terminal as if she'd been burned as a hole she never knew was inside her mind filled up.

In her mind, Lucas smiled at her.

She remembered trying to pull away, but he didn't let her go. Hadn't let her go yet.

It won't be enough, you know, Lucas said to her as he turned her head this way and that, his power eating into her thoughts a week ago. *I still expect my sister to try. So let's make this chase interesting, shall we?*

The image of a broken-down, timeworn cathedral filled her mind. It wasn't complete. Pieces of the picture were purposefully missing, and their absence would make teleportation difficult, if not outright impossible.

Here is where I will be. They shouldn't have any trouble finding it. Enjoy your headache when you remember this.

Jessica opened her eyes, breathing raggedly. She tucked her hands close against her body, refusing to touch anything else around her in an instinctive reaction to keep her sanity safe.

"What did you see?" Jin Li demanded from the doorway.

She lifted her head to look at her superiors, hating the words that came out of her mouth. "It's me. He—Lucas left it all in me."

A sick feeling was already in her stomach, pain in her head. Samantha made it all worse as the telepath cut through Jessica's shields, the psychometrist unable to drop them fast enough. Samantha's telepathy, so different from Lucas's cool interference, filled her mind and drove her to her knees. Where a human was incapable of surviving psionic interference if the psion in question wasn't careful, psions themselves were genetically built for it. That didn't mean it was easy to handle, just that they could. The repercussions were still painful.

"I am getting sick to the back of my teeth with the bloody games he plays. He's almost worse than Nathan," Samantha said, biting off the words as she shared the acquired memory with Gideon. "Can you piece that together enough to 'port us there?"

"Maybe. If you get me a clearer picture from someone else's memory," Gideon said after a short pause. "Unless you want to risk being a smear of atoms in the smog?"

"We don't have the time to wait. I'll get you a better memory, you work on getting a stable avenue of teleportation." Samantha tapped the fingers of one hand against the edge of a terminal even as she skimmed her power over the minds of everyone around them until she found what Gideon needed and shared it with him. "You have any ideas on why Lucas would want cartel contacts? It's the only possible reason why he would be here in the Slums, since drugs are really all we handle out of Los Angeles."

Gideon closed his eyes. "He can't possibly hope to cut into the support Nathan's built up over the years. The drug cartels won't switch their loyalty that easily, not until Nathan formally hands over power to Lucas. Which he won't. Now let me work."

"Lucas needs to be killed," Jin Li said, watching as Samantha walked around the two work terminals, running a finger over the console edge on each one.

"That's your opinion. It's not our orders," Samantha said.

Jin Li scowled. "It's going to come down to Nathan. He's the only one with the strength to pull Lucas back into the fold."

"Nathan hasn't lived this long by being stupid, Jin Li." Samantha gave him a sharp look over the top of a vidscreen. "He won't risk himself to hunt Lucas down. He'll risk us. You'll accept our father's orders, or have you suddenly found a way to save yourself from Nathan's attempt at living longer than a human's average lifetime?"

"Fuck you."

"I thought not. Stop hoping for something that won't happen. You're in the same predicament as we are. If we die trying to bring Lucas in, then we die. At least we'll have worn him down."

"Your mother would be so proud of your human sensibilities."

Jin Li was picked up and slammed into the nearest wall, held there by Gideon's telekinesis. The younger twin glared at him. "Don't insult us."

Jin Li just smiled. Gideon let him go after a moment of warning pressure. Once Jin Li had his feet back on the floor, the electrokinetic straightened his uniform. "Lucas is your brother, Samantha. Out of all of us belonging to the Warhounds, you would know best why he decided to leave."

Samantha grimaced. "I've never been deep into Lucas's head. That's Nathan's prerogative, not mine."

"Some prerogative."

It wasn't, not really, not for those who had to live through it. Nathan's and Lucas's arguments had always happened privately and always ended bloodily, but Nathan inevitably won. The only time Lucas came out the winner was two years ago. Lucas had been eighteen when he'd walked away from the Serca Syndicate, from the Warhounds, leaving Nathan to deal with the fallout of his absence right when their father could least afford it. Samantha still didn't know how he had done it.

Samantha turned her attention to where Jessica was still huddled on the floor. "Put your gloves back on and clean this place up."

Jessica nodded, already yanking on her gloves, and stumbled out of the room. Gideon rocked back on his heels, eyes still closed and fingers tapping against his thighs as he concentrated on visualizing the teleport. "I need five more minutes."

"Then hurry the hell up. We have our orders."

Gideon opened his eyes, the light in the room skimming over the irises, turning them black. "Why the rush? Lucas will see us coming."

"Lucas always sees us coming. It doesn't change anything. It never will."

[FOUR]

JULY 2379
SLUMS OF THE ANGELS, USA

They ditched the SUV two kilometers from their destination.

The streets of the Slums were shrouded in darkness, the ruins beneath the city towers like miniature mountains of rubble. People worked their entire lives down hard-cleared alleyways and never left the cartel territory they called home. Electricity was patchwork at best, always expensive and never reliable, even with backup generators.

Kerr's telepathy kept people from looking at them twice as they made their way down the crowded street in a small group. They had already used up the pass cards after a dozen checkpoints, deep enough now in cartel territory that telepathy was the only thing they could rely on. The target pulsed on the mental grid on the other side of a raucous street market teeming with people who moved out of their way with brief mental nudging.

Kerr had everyone shielded beneath his power, so when the psi signature that he recognized from previous missions pinged off the mental grid, he only hoped they hadn't been sensed here on the ground. Even as Kerr began to build up telepathic walls between the Strykers and the Warhound telepath, that mind winked out. Not dead, because Warhounds could drop off bioscanners with a thought and read as human on the mental grid when it mattered. It was a trick no Stryker had yet learned to imitate. A trick they hadn't been *allowed* to learn. Those who tried were terminated. The government liked to keep tabs on their dogs at all times.

"Warhounds," Kerr warned as they shoved their way through a line of people waiting impatiently for their weekly allotment of vitamins and supplements. "This will probably get ugly."

"Hell," Threnody said. She took a sip of distilled water from her water bottle before re-clipping it to her belt, next to the pouch containing her filter-capable skinmask. "We got further than I thought we would. Psi signatures?"

Kerr pulled his mind out of the masses. "I got enough from the initial touch. Class II telepath, female. You know what that means."

Quinton glanced at Threnody and grimaced. "There's only one Class II telepath in the Warhound ranks."

"Brilliant. I always wanted to die at the hands of someone I'll never see coming," Jason said, voice a little garbled as he cupped his hands around a cigarette and lit it. "Never knew this target was such a prize. Two years and the strongest members of the Warhounds still haven't been able to catch it either. Maybe we should just attempt to take *them* out rather than this target."

"We'd have to be able to identify them, which no one has, but they aren't why we're here. It's not our place to question orders, Jason."

"And look where that's got you."

Threnody reached out and grabbed Quinton's arm before her partner could put his fist through Jason's face. "Not the place," she snapped. "I want to know how often you come across Warhounds when tracking this unaffiliated psion."

Jason pocketed his lighter. "Often enough. If not this set of psions, it's some other Warhound. Neither side has gotten close to retrieving the target."

Threnody didn't say anything. She didn't need to be reminded of how impossible this mission was.

"Still think it's worth it?" Kerr asked.

"Guess we'll find out, won't we?" She glanced at him. "How's your mental balance? We're going to need you to hold steady."

Kerr bristled, offended. "Don't worry about me."

"I'm not. I'm worrying about myself."

Conversation died, both physical and mental, as they picked up the pace. The crowd didn't ease up, becoming thicker the farther they walked. Only when they rounded the corner did they figure out why. Between them and a crumbling landmark cathedral was a veritable tenement of ragged tents and lean-tos. The stench of so many people was worse here than in the streets behind them.

"Is it Sunday?" Jason wanted to know.

"Would it matter?" Quinton said as he reached for his gun, pulled it free, and thumbed the safety off.

"Kerr?" Threnody said. "The target?"

A brief pulse of telepathic power and then: "Still on the mental grid." Kerr sounded surprised.

"Let's do this."

The four of them walked through the dirty crowd, Kerr's telepathy clearing them a way to the locked doors of the cathedral. Threnody placed a hand on the control panel just to the left of the doors and used her power to short-circuit the locking mechanism. Jason hauled the doors open telekinetically, just enough for them to slip inside, before closing the doors.

They came into a space that had dirt on the floor, dust in the air, and lights that were only half on. They noticed the emptiness first, the body second. The corpse was sprawled on the steps leading up to the chancel, white and crimson-edged vestments fanned out around it.

Quinton caught Kerr's eye and the two of them approached the body, Jason's telekinesis wrapped firmly around them in a shield. Quinton rested his finger lightly against the trigger guard of his gun as he kept an eye on their surroundings while Kerr knelt down beside the corpse. Kerr lowered a few of his mental shields, reaching out with his telepathy.

There were no physical wounds, no blood, to mark the bishop's passing. It took heavy, extensive trauma to the mind for the wounds to translate to the body. When they did, they showed mostly above the neck. Kerr studied the dead man's twisted face as he withdrew from the edges of the gaping hole that existed where personality had once resided.

"Six hours," he said. "Judging by the echo left behind on the mental grid, his mind was ripped apart from the foundation outwards. Hard telepathic strike."

"I thought we were dealing with a telekinetic, not a telepath?" Quinton said slowly. "One strong enough to teleport. That's the only explanation we were given for how the target has managed to appear and disappear so quickly from one place to the next across continents."

"Sometimes the mental grid can be made to lie."

Quinton stared at Kerr. "That takes a lot of strength and a psionic power that's *not* telekinesis."

"What about the Warhounds who just arrived?" Threnody asked as she and Jason approached.

Kerr shook his head. "This wasn't them. This is—the wound's too deep. A Class II telepath didn't do this. *Couldn't* do this."

Threnody, trained to have a tactician's mind, snapped through all the possibilities in seconds, coming up with the only one that made any sense. It left her cold, breathing too fast, as she turned to face Jason.

"Get us out of here. *Now.*"

Jason didn't bother to second-guess her order, just tapped into his telekinesis, visualized the 'port out of there, and let his mind carry the weight of them all out of the Slums.

Or tried to.

The world shifted in an instant, their kinesthesia stretching past the point of stability for a long millisecond before snapping back into the same reality they were trying to escape. The backlash ricocheted through their minds, the worst of it burning hard and fast through Jason's mental channels as they all hit against a telekinetic wall that he couldn't break through.

Jason doubled over, falling to his knees as a crippling headache nearly blinded him. The rest of them struggled to get their balance back even as a voice filled the silence of the cathedral.

Rude of you to leave so soon when it's taken forever to get you here.

A tall young man, with dark blue eyes and a messy tangle of white-blond hair, appeared on the dais above them. They recognized him instantly. It was who he was, and what he *wasn't* supposed to be, that shocked the Strykers into silence. Four pairs of eyes were riveted on a face many had only seen in news streams over the years, a young boy growing into adulthood with the world at his feet, the poster child for the privileged elite.

Where's a fucking precog when you need one? Threnody thought in some distant, bitter corner of her mind as she tried to struggle, but couldn't, in the Class I telekinetic grip Lucas Serca had her in.

Usually dead, Lucas said telepathically for all of them to hear. *Personally, I consider them a pain in the arse.*

Kerr's telepathic shields slammed up between them and Lucas as he readied for an attack, but it was a useless gesture. Kerr didn't stand a chance against the man who would one day run the Serca Syndicate, he only knew that he had to try.

Lucas's smile stretched wider.

Psions were ranked for a reason, the various mental powers assigned by tenths of strength of conscious Brain Power Used on the Class scale. Class X were straight humans with 10 percent of BPU, and Class IX were those humans who had a fair amount of sixth sense, the sort that let them survive in a harsh world when other humans would merely die. Class VIII through I were psion ranks, and of them all, Class I was the rarest, most powerful rank.

A Class I triad psion was born only once every other generation, if that. They burned bright and fast, dying off young if they constantly used the powers they were born with, a risk every psion took.

This generation there were two.

Lucas, born with telepathy and telekinesis strong enough for teleportation, cut through Kerr's telepathic attack with a brutality that sent Kerr's power snapping back through the Stryker's brain. The backlash sent Kerr's mind almost to the breaking point, his shields skittering against their mental foundations, his control slipping away. Swearing, Kerr struggled to get his telepathy under control through the agony he was feeling.

Lucas ran a hand through his hair as he eyed the four in front of him. "This is not how it's supposed to go."

"You're a Serca and a *psion*?" Jason asked incredulously.

Lucas arched an eyebrow. "Now, really, how else did you think we keep our Warhounds in check?"

All four Strykers flinched at the admission of whom the Warhounds belonged to. The government and Strykers had known the Warhounds were organized; they simply hadn't known they were *owned* by anyone, much less by one of the world's oldest, most prestigious human families. Only not so human, judging by what Lucas could do, by what he really was.

"What do you want?" Quinton asked in a stiff voice.

"Not any of you dead, Stryker. I'm not here to kill you."

"Do you really expect us to believe that?"

"Belief is subjective. I've already had this conversation once today, I'm in no mood to have it again. You're here for me, Stryker. Or did you honestly think that you were targeting an unaffiliated psion?"

Quinton clenched his teeth, muscles standing out in his neck. He turned his head to stare at Threnody, keeping her in view. Threnody kept her attention on Lucas, knowing all she needed was just one touch to take him down; knowing that she would never get that chance.

"I've got a proposition for you," Lucas said. He leaned back against the table and gripped the edge of it with both hands as he looked at Threnody.

"We don't negotiate with Warhounds," Threnody said automatically.

"I bet I can change your mind. I won't even need telepathy to do it." Lucas turned an indulgent smile on her. "Let's even up the odds, shall we? You've got five seconds."

In reality, it was more like two. Threnody blinked and nearly missed the arrival of three Warhounds as they teleported into the middle of the cathedral. Threnody felt Lucas's telekinesis disappear and she moved instantly, the other Strykers doing the same, because to stand still meant certain death, and shock at the revelation of Sercas as psions wasn't enough to cripple their responses.

Jin Li immediately tossed a dozen small, round electric surge anchors in Gideon's direction. The Class II telekinetic caught them with his power and scattered them around the cathedral with a thought, wires linking all of them together. Jin Li twisted the surge anchor in his hands, activating it and all the others. Electricity flowed through the device, powered by Jin Li, a barrier that was a dangerous extension of himself. The surge net took that power and multiplied it ten times over until the entire place burned with it, electricity crawling across the floor and walls and high, arched ceiling, looking for conductors.

Jin Li's power found it in bodies.

Jason struggled to bring up a telekinetic shield, but he was still suffering from being yanked unexpectedly out of a teleport and wasn't quick enough to block the first wave completely. It shocked through him like lightning, curling through his nervous system and brain. His control skipped just out of reach and his shields wavered.

Hands grabbed his arm and shoulder, dragging him behind the precarious safety of a pew. Kerr focused his power on Jason, looking into those bloodshot hazel eyes, and snarled, *"Shields."*

With Kerr's help, Jason wrenched his power back into place, managing to slide his telekinesis around them both. The sudden absence of electric burn left both of them gasping for breath and reaching for their guns. Together, they took aim at Jin Li. Neither of them were surprised when all the bullets missed. A distraction only, and not a threat; both sides had telekinetics to shield against bullets.

Across the aisle Threnody had her hand pressed firmly to the back of

Quinton's neck, her power regulating both their nervous systems against Jin Li's attack. She was still recovering from the last time she had pulled this maneuver in Johannesburg against Jin Li and it was a strain, her power barely able to cope.

"Jason," Threnody said. "Get a shield around Quinton."

She could handle Jin Li's power on her own. Quinton was a drain on her reserves that she couldn't allow. Seconds later, she felt invisible power hardening between her fingers and Quinton's neck, a telekinetic barrier that would let him live. She pulled away, blue ribbons of electricity arcing from fingertip to fingertip, sliding up her arm and through her body. Quinton took aim with his gun at Samantha and fired, the weapon the only thing Jason wasn't shielding. When the gun was wrenched out of his hands, nearly breaking his trigger finger, Quinton realized that Gideon didn't much like people targeting his twin.

Jason looked up, eyes sweeping over the cathedral's interior to visually tag everyone's position. His inspecs were dead in his eyes from the electrical surge, leaving only the human spectrum for him to work with, and eventually even that threatened to shut down as a massive telepathic blow pounded against his mental shields. The surprise that leaked from Samantha into his mind when they didn't break wasn't comforting.

You can't keep those up forever, Samantha said as she began to bear down on his mind.

They keep themselves up, Jason shot back even as he dialed back on the strength of his telekinetic output to focus on the telepathic strike that was carving mental canyons into the outer edges of his mind. Canyons that were then filled by Kerr's power, a burning challenge that Samantha was forced to reckon with.

Get the fuck out of his mind, Kerr said.

The twins had spent their entire life learning how to wield their powers simultaneously in a merge, like the dual psion they resembled, but weren't. Kerr and Jason didn't have the twins' expertise, but that didn't mean they weren't up to the task of protecting themselves against a pair of Class II psions. It just meant they would be the first to falter.

Nearby, Threnody had emptied an entire clip at the Warhounds, the bullets going everywhere except into bodies. Ejecting the empty magazine, she looked over at Quinton and said, "Burn it the fuck down."

He didn't answer her in words. The air down in the Slums was heavy, thick, and hard to breathe at the best of times. It trapped heat and caused the temperature to rise higher than the regulated environment in the city towers of Los Angeles. It was already sticky hot in the cathedral, mere degrees cooler than the suffocating heat that burned outside.

Quinton made it hotter.

He couldn't create fire, but he could control it, use it, make it grow. Quinton clenched his hands into fists, the biomodifications in his limbs releasing the natural gas from biotubes in his arms. He snapped his fingers, the metal tips sparking the gas into fire that crawled through the air and expanded around where he stood. The red-orange flames flickered in the air until it was like an inferno that he sent roaring down the middle aisle of the cathedral toward the Warhounds.

Gideon's telekinesis saved the Warhounds as fire engulfed them. It blinded them from any physical attack even as Gideon reached out with his power and grappled with Jason's to get to Quinton. Quinton's attack still bought them seconds, precious time for Threnody to lunge for the nearest electric surge anchor, get her fingers around it, and slam her power through its electrical field. The surge net broke beneath her power, circuits frying as she overloaded its limited system faster than Jin Li could counteract it, bringing down the barrier separating the two groups.

In retaliation, Jin Li targeted her first, as he had in Johannesburg, electricity sparking across his fist as he aimed for her face. She knocked aside his first attack and dodged an elbow to the throat, Jin Li's blow connecting with her shoulder instead. They fought their way down the aisle toward the back of the cathedral, a pitched battle that was as much fists as it was power. Threnody was fast, but Jin Li was faster, and he caught her in his grip, slamming her up against the wall. His hands were around her throat, just as they had been the last time when he almost killed her. Right now, he meant to rectify that failure.

Threnody planted her hands against his chest, fingers digging into the bare skin near the hollow of his throat, and shoved her power into him before he could off-load into her. She needed to stop his heart if she was going to kill him. She almost did.

Electricity ripped through both of them, frying their nervous systems and pushing their hearts to the breaking point. Their screams mingled over the roar of the fire, over the rush of blood to her head as telepathy that wasn't Kerr's swallowed her mind.

Come with me, Lucas said. *You know you don't have any other choice.*

Threnody gasped for air as her skin got hotter and hotter, her nerves seeking to burn right out of her body. The world bled colors brought on by extreme stress from Jin Li's power, a disconnect caused by a nervous system out of whack, synapses not firing correctly. The neuroplasticity of the brain freezing up, just for a nanosecond.

She didn't answer him.

You can die here or you can die when the government flips the switch to fry your brain through their collar. Or all of you can come with me and live. Make your choice, Threnody Corwin.

What do you want?

The same thing you do—a chance.

Threnody saw bleached-out violet eyes inside his mind, the image of a little girl in some sterile white room frozen in his memory. A cascade of orders, of actions, that couldn't be a hallucination, not when it came from Lucas Serca, of all people.

The shock of that shared memory propelled Threnody to say, *Yes.*

Or maybe it was Jin Li's hands choking the life out of her that made her reach for a way out.

It didn't matter.

They disappeared. Lucas teleported out of that cathedral with four Strykers, leaving behind his siblings and Jin Li to the quiet darkness of a broken place of prayer.

PART TWO
RETRIEVAL

SESSION DATE: 2128.01.15
LOCATION: Institute of Psionics Research
CLEARANCE ID: Dr. Amy Bennett
SUBJECT: 2581
FILE NUMBER: 1

She sits alone at the table, young and small, with feet that do not touch the floor. Paper drawings are scattered across the tabletop and the floor around her. She has stayed silent for over three hours, the chrono marking time in a corner of the feed, amused by the pad of drawing paper and the crayons provided her. Only now, when she is out of paper, does she go still. The machines she is connected to click and whine like a disharmonic orchestra.

"Don't sulk, Marcheline," Aisling says as she frowns at the camera. "I'm trying to help you."

As if summoned by her voice, the door to the white room slides open and a doctor steps inside. The woman is thin and dark skinned. She ignores the camera.

"Hello, Aisling," the doctor says. "Do you know who I am?"

Aisling tilts her head away from the camera, attention on the woman. "Hello, Dr. Bennett. I saw you months and months ago."

"Did you? Fascinating." The woman sits in an empty seat, places her documents and a deck of white cards in neat piles on the table. "Do you know why you're here, Aisling? You're here because you are a very special little girl."

"Mama thinks I'm sick."

"Your mother is concerned about you. She was right to bring you here."

Aisling shrugs and slouches in her chair, something like resignation settling on her face. "You always say that, Doctor."

Behind her, the high-pitched sound of the EEG machine is louder than that of all the rest, loud enough to force the doctor to cover her ears.

FIVE

JULY 2379
THE HAGUE, THE NETHERLANDS

The crowd of personal aides, lobbyists, military soldiers, and reporters jostled for view of the vidscreens that lined the walls of the International Court of Justice, known in the vernacular as the World Court.

The heavily fortified Peace Palace was an old building residing over the bunkers that had protected the only seat of power to survive the Border Wars. It was the world's premier functioning government, the place that all remaining countries with viable populations looked to for guidance and obeyed in the face of continuous societal decline. Its fifteen justices held office for life, whereas they had once been restricted to term limits. In these trying times, so the saying went, justice needed a long eye.

It still wouldn't be long enough to see the future. Humans didn't have that power. Neither did the woman who strode down the main hall. She had been born a Class V empath, not a precog.

Her face—oval-shaped, with a straight nose above a full mouth and wide brown eyes—was well documented on news streams. It needed to be. As the officer in charge (OIC) of the Strykers Syndicate and one of the few psions that the World Court had allowed to go fully public, Ciari Treiva was not a woman most people were willing to tangle with. At forty-one years of age, she was the de facto leader of the government's psions and had held that position for over a decade. It still left a sour taste in her mouth, even after all these years.

Ciari traveled light, accompanied only by a single aide. Keiko Nishimoto was the Strykers Syndicate's only Class II telekinetic, a slim Japanese woman in her early thirties who was chief operating officer (COO) of the company. As Ciari's direct subordinate, Keiko was just as well-known to the public. Both women wore the standard black-on-black BDUs of Strykers, though they carried no weapons. Ciari's brown hair was pulled back in a slick knot, hands loose at her side as the crowd, immediately aware of her presence, fell away from her.

The government's dogs didn't come to the world capital all that often. Business with the Strykers Syndicate occurred behind locked doors. A stigma was still attached to doing business with someone who possessed unclean DNA.

Ciari had clearance, higher than most, that got her through the public domain of the Peace Palace to the restricted wing without so much as a pat down. She didn't need one. If the current president of the World Court felt that she was a danger, he had the code that would activate the implanted neurotracker in her head and terminate her. Almost every OIC died by that neurotracker. The Strykers Syndicate didn't offer retirement to its permanent employees. It only offered a grave. The threat of death didn't mean that Ciari wasn't incapable of independent thought. It meant she was better at hiding her contempt than most people for the man who effectively ruled the world.

When they arrived at their destination, the executive assistant who guarded the door along with a set of quads knew better than to keep them out and simply announced their presence through an uplink to the man they wanted to see.

"I didn't summon you," Erik Gervais said as he studied the hologrid displayed above his antique wooden desk, inspecs glittering in his brown eyes.

"Consider this visit one of preemption," Ciari said, her soprano voice empty of all emotion as she walked into the office and approached his desk. Keiko remained by the door. "We need to talk, sir."

Erik looked at her through the data on the hologrid before it winked out. The World Court's president justice was a tall, lean man, whose black robes of office were perfectly tailored and only left his shoulders in the privacy of his own home. Like anyone who held a government position, or who could afford the cost in the private sector, his brain was wired with a bioware net that constantly monitored the baseline readings of his mind. Any psionic interference—if any Stryker would be foolish enough to do so—was tagged on the grid and the offending psion killed. If it was a Warhound, then that was another problem entirely, and the Strykers were expected to die for the humans they protected.

Unless legally instructed to, Ciari never directly touched Erik's mind. His emotions, however, didn't just exist on the mental grid. Emotion was physical as well as mental, and she tapped into the physical aspect that afternoon. She could read bodies as well as the emotions of a target, and for all that Erik was a judge well schooled in the art of a neutral expression, he couldn't hide what he felt from a psion. Not completely, no matter the technology he had grafted to his brain. Ciari could read him; she simply didn't have the freedom to twist what he was feeling into something useful to her without dying.

"Your predecessor was never one to give orders," Erik said as he leaned back in the chair made for his specific contours alone, eyeing Ciari speculatively. "Perhaps you should follow in his footsteps."

"I know my place." Ciari's mouth quirked slightly into something that might be called a smile if one was generous. The by-product of being an empath of any Class meant that she was a stone-cold bitch when it mattered and utterly ruthless when it didn't. Emotions were her forte; that didn't mean she had the luxury of succumbing to them.

"Really. Because I don't see you on your knees."

Ciari made a tiny throwing-away gesture with one hand from where she stood. "My loyalty is the same as it has always been."

"Then why are you here?"

"Your docket today encompassed the Serca Syndicate and their proposed Act."

"I don't see how a case that has been pending for the past ten months merits you storming in here."

"You ruled in their favor. That merits a lot of things."

"If I didn't know any better, I'd accuse you of professional jealousy. But then, your professionalism extends only so far as we allow it. You should remember that."

The look in Ciari's eyes was flat. "We Strykers obey the directive of the World Court. That doesn't mean we can afford to go about it blindly. What law you allowed the Sercas to author, and which you legalized, will affect how we do our job."

"Please tell me that you aren't seriously accusing one of the premier companies and families of being dangerous to the government?" Erik arched an eyebrow, the twist to his mouth condescending. "The same family that authored and helped implement the Fifth Generation Act, which set the requirements needed for a person to be accepted into the Registry with clean DNA? The Serca family was one of the first elevated out of the trenches of mutation after the fifth-generation benchmark passed. They continue to work toward the betterment of humankind, and I'll be damned if you'll belittle their accomplishments, so choose your next words carefully, Ciari."

Ciari paid lip service to the order, but the silence lasted only a few seconds. "Allowing them an autonomy you've refused all others in this venture the World Court has spent generations hiding from the public view won't end well. It can't. You have a right to keep your secrets, and it's our duty to guard them, but we can't guard what we aren't allowed to see. We need to know what the Serca Syndicate is working on in order to protect you."

"Trade secrets are granted exceptions from the laws that govern us. The Sercas have more than earned their right over the years to retain the cornerstone of their company. What they intend to pursue is integral to the survival of all of us."

"What about oversight?"

"It will be taken care of." Erik studied her through slightly narrowed eyes, his calm tone belying the annoyance his microexpressions were projecting. "You don't need to concern yourself with the how or the why, just that it will be done."

Ciari's own expression was remote and cold as she said, "By letting the Sercas dictate this human trial for however long it takes won't result in the findings that you think will be uncovered, sir. Genetics, especially since the Border Wars, have never been easily harnessed or explained. I and those like myself are living proof of that."

They were psions, people born with a disease caused by mutated genes that could be traced back to the Border Wars. Humanity had spent over two centuries trying to eradicate that taint in their own genetic groups. Ciari knew it was a wasted effort.

"The Serca Syndicate has the capability to discern who is and isn't worthy to be on the colony lists we are building out of the Registry. Their results are the only thing I and the rest of the World Court care about."

"Then what of us Strykers? Will you give up all our identities to satisfy their scientific hunger? You have to know that if you do that, you're going to strip yourselves of the privacy we've fought to give you. Then what? There will be too many humans fighting to reach a launchpad or gain access to a city tower's collection of air shuttles in order to reach France. Even if you put every Stryker between unregistered humans and those on the colony lists, you still won't be able to stop all of them."

Erik reached for the glass of water that sat near the edge of his desk, ice half-melted in the expensive liquid that had been distilled and filtered to remove any and all pollutants and heavy minerals. Water that clear was hard to come by. He drank half of it before setting the glass aside again.

"What's the worth of unregistered humans compared to those on the Registry lists? I'll tell you what they're worth. Nothing. Absolutely nothing." The smile he gave her was chilling in its intensity. "You forget that *your* place in this world is to protect those of us who have worked long and hard to clean our genetics of nuclear taint. If unregistered humans ever discover what we've built in the Paris Basin, then you and the rest of the Strykers will be on that wall, Ciari. And you will kill whoever attempts to climb it, be they human or psion. Do I make myself clear?"

"Of course, sir."

"You've overstepped your bounds, Ciari. Don't come here again until I call for you. Just because you're the face of the Strykers Syndicate doesn't mean you are exempt from the rules every psion must follow." His fingers stroked over a thin, familiar remote on his desk. "Remember that."

The burn at the back of her skull was a reminder that she didn't really need, Ciari didn't let her discomfort show as she turned to leave, the pain magnifying with every step she took until she couldn't stand anymore. She almost made it to the door before she fell to her knees, fire ripping through her brain.

"Ciari." Cool fingers gripped her neck, a startling counterpoint to the heat beneath her skin. "As much as I appreciate your concern for humanity's continued survival, I think I liked it better when you knew how to hold your tongue. Your place in this world is to serve."

"Sir," she gritted out, feeling blood slide out of her nose and down the rigid line of her mouth.

Over the roaring in her ears, she heard Erik sigh, the cluster of his tangled emotions battering against her shields. Ciari carefully kept her defenses passive until the pain receded to something more manageable as the World Court's president took his finger off the remote and let her live.

"You make an excellent OIC, Ciari," Erik said. "Learn how to be a better dog and I might not be so harsh in my punishments next time."

He wanted a reaction out of her, some hint that what he had put her through was as humiliating as he thought it should be. She could feel that. Except Ciari had spent approximately thirty-five years of her life as a government dog and six years before that surviving in the ruins of New York in America as a child before she was picked up by the Strykers. Psions, no matter the Class rank, held on to their memories longer than humans ever could. Ciari remembered what it took to survive in the sprawling mess of a city that made up Buffalo on the polluted banks of Lake Erie. Much more strength than it took to survive in the glass cages of the government's prison, bound by the collar in her head.

So when Ciari said, "Sir," as if her life depended on it, she meant what she said.

It was her duty as the OIC to take the punishment, after all. She bowed to Erik in order to protect the Strykers beneath her. She always would.

He took his hand away and another helped her up. Keiko held Ciari with a firm grip as she escorted the older woman out of Erik's chambers. The door slid shut behind them and both ignored the armed quad, a group of four soldiers, that still remained in the hallway. The humans always feared for their leaders when psions walked through the seat of government.

"Your orders?" Keiko asked.

Ciari lifted a hand to wipe the blood off her face. She ended up smearing it across her skin in a vivid crimson streak as she let her thoughts expand beyond her mental shields to the edge of her public mind in a pointed request to the person who she knew was telepathically listening in. *We need to talk.*

To Keiko, she said, "Stay calm and walk with me."

Keiko followed where she went. Before they even made it down the hall, the two women were teleported out of the Peace Palace and into a shuttle that had yet to leave the government's private airfield. The man who had initiated the teleport at Ciari's request raised a glass of champagne to them, a cold smile their only welcome.

Nathan Serca was a brand first, a man second, and made no apologies for his family's place in history. At fifty-one, he was as long-lived as psions came, with the physique of someone who had grown up with access to clean water and food that wasn't grown in poisoned ground. He kept his blond hair cut short and his eyes were that signature Serca dark blue. His life as psion masquerading as a human was the ultimate sleight of hand. That the Strykers helped ensure his family's success was something no one in the government could ever know.

"Ladies," Nathan drawled as he took a sip of champagne. "Have a seat."

"No thank you," Ciari said, voice cool, calm. "We won't be staying long."

"Just long enough to congratulate me? You shouldn't have. Really."

Nathan's voice was dry, the smug superiority on his face difficult to ignore. As he was a Class I triad psion with telepathy, telekinesis, and teleportation his to command, Ciari knew it was a superiority she had no hope in matching.

Not often could a human brain handle the BPUs required for the control of two psi powers. One power was *always* a lower-Classed level when they existed together, and the main power was almost always telepathy. The more common dual psions that were a steady, if small, presence in their short history were telepaths and telekinetics on the low end of the Class scale, as well as telepaths and empaths. Telekinetics who were a Class V or higher and capable of teleportation were labeled dual psions as well.

Triad psions were something altogether different. They *should* have been impossible, but the Serca family had proven that wrong. There were theories—there were always theories—on psi powers and the brain that housed them. It was possible for that combination to exist, the Sercas were living proof, but a Class I for all *three* powers? The brain shouldn't be capable of holding that much power, but the Sercas could. They were the only psions ever to be labeled triads.

Ciari supposed Nathan had a right to be smug.

"Your family has illegally recorded the DNA of unregistered humans over the course of generations," Ciari said. "The Genome Privacy Act you won out of the World Court today was granted retroactively and grandfathers in your family's previous work. Why request legality now when the World Court was willing to continue turning a blind eye to your efforts, Nathan?"

"My timetable isn't yours." Nathan set aside his glass and leaned back in the shuttle seat. "I have the information I want. The government knows the Serca Syndicate works fast. I'll have a list for them by the end of summer at the latest and they will have to accept it."

"They will never accept unregistered humans."

"Who said anything about them being unregistered?" Nathan waved his hand disdainfully at her. "My family helped create the Registry in preparation for the fifth generation after the Border Wars. Do you really think I *don't* control that information? I have no intention of giving up the power we've worked toward finally owning. I am in the position to make my own future. You are nothing more than the government's bitch."

Keiko took an angry step forward, but Ciari gestured for her to back down. They would lose in a direct confrontation with Nathan, and a fight wasn't the reason why Ciari had asked for this meeting.

"There isn't enough time for me to give you who you need from the Stryker ranks," Ciari said.

"That's your problem, not mine."

Everyone knew there were rogue psions. The Sercas had never been owned by the government, and most of the Warhounds they took in never had either. Psion children, when discovered, were either retrieved by the Strykers or the Warhounds, whoever managed to track them down first, or they were terminated. Usually the Strykers came out ahead, but whereas the Warhounds' numbers were equal to half the total psions in the Stryker ranks, they had more of the stronger psions. Some within the Warhound ranks, at least a sixth of their fighting force, were Strykers saved from government termination, but only those that the OIC of the Strykers Syndicate deemed worth saving and that the Serca family needed.

The Silence Law was a twofold rule. A small group of top officers in the Strykers Syndicate helped keep the Serca family's secrets, and those same few officers were the only Strykers who made sure that the willful, purposeful setup and escape of Strykers tagged for government termination was never discovered. The Sercas only took the best when they deigned to retrieve Strykers at all. Which was why Ciari had these conversations with Nathan on his terms. The survival of her people was worth the humiliation of begging.

Sometimes it simply wasn't enough.

"Give me a little more time to save my people," Ciari asked.

Nathan looked her straight in the eye. "You and your predecessors have had more than enough since the Border Wars. I am through being generous. Now leave. I've got a schedule to keep."

Ciari turned to look at Keiko. "Take us back to headquarters."

Keiko wrapped her telekinesis around the both of them, visualized the office they had left barely an hour ago, and stretched her power halfway across the planet. A long-distance teleport required more power than one that simply took a person across a city. She was traveling across continents. No one else in the Stryker ranks could bridge that distance in a single teleport, and Keiko only did it when it was necessary.

The world shifted in a way it wasn't meant to as they left Nathan's shuttle under psion power. Keiko's teleport brought them to Toronto, Canada, their sudden arrival in Ciari's spacious executive office met by two Strykers. Keiko sucked in a deep breath once her feet hit the floor, a pinched expression of pain crossing her face briefly. She'd need a few hours of downtime to settle her mind and recover from two straight teleports of such long distances. She didn't really want her brain to start hemorrhaging or her heart to burst anytime soon. Recovery was something all psions needed, it just wasn't something all psions got.

"Keiko?" Ciari asked.

"I'm fine. Just a bit of a headache."

"Looks like Erik had fun with you," Jael Dawson said, hazel eyes assessing their damage with a critical look. "What did you say to him this time?"

"Would it matter?" Ciari asked as she walked behind her desk and activated the biometric log-in. "I was breathing. What do you want?"

The Class III telepath and chief medical officer (CMO) set two thin hyposprays filled with painkillers on the desk as Ciari activated the office's jamming defenses. The government liked to listen in on their conversations, and the Strykers Syndicate officers had long ago learned to work around that intrusion for very short periods.

"One for each of you," Jael said as Keiko reached for the closest hypospray and put it to use. "Though you need something more than medication to fix what I can feel past your shields, Ciari."

Ciari ignored the hypospray for the moment, knowing her mind would eventually compensate for the trauma she had just experienced. "It can wait. The World Court is granting Nathan's request to retain the Serca Syndicate's anonymity, at least when it comes to the newest Act they got the government to pass. Which means no one is going to have any sort of clearance to see just who the hell they're choosing for the colony lists. The government won't share that information with us."

"They still don't know?" Jael's expression was one of disgust. "About the Serca Syndicate?"

"We're just as much to blame for their ignorance as they are. Our Silence Law still holds when it comes to the Warhounds."

"Nathan's as charming as always," Keiko added.

"You saw Nathan?" Jael pointed her finger warningly at Ciari. "You need a scan and psi surgery. No telling what that bastard did to you."

"He didn't do anything," Ciari said as she waved off that demand for the mental procedure that telepaths were uniquely capable of administering on wounded or subverted psions. Psi surgery had grown out of instinct and into a field of medicine that only psions were capable of using.

"You don't *know* that."

"Nathan isn't interested in breaking my mind, Jael. He's got other things to worry about."

"Hell." Jael bowed her head as she squeezed the bridge of her nose, the thin dreads of her black hair swinging to hide her dark face. "Times like this I wish we had a chance at stopping what the Sercas are planning."

"You don't think we do?"

"Being optimistic isn't in my job description. I put minds back together, not lives. That's your job."

"Then tell me we have some information on the target that's been holding steady on the West Coast."

Ciari was looking at the man standing next to Jael when she asked the question. Aidan Turner was the Strykers Syndicate's chief administrative officer (CAO), a Class IV telepath, and the last living member of a three-person team that hadn't made it to the age of thirty on the field. He had got past the bitterness and pain of survivor's guilt only by a severe application of psi surgery. Telepaths were the most numerous psions, but the majority were a Class V or lower. The Strykers Syndicate needed him, and it needed him sane.

It did not need the report he delivered.

"We lost contact with Threnody and Quinton in the field," Aidan said. "Jason and Kerr dropped off the mental grid as well."

Ciari's expression didn't change. "When?"

"There was a spike around the same time you left for The Hague. The psi signatures were that of Nathan's twins." Aidan hesitated a moment before continuing, "The target's psi signature changed into that of Lucas Serca's."

Those three were the best murderers on the planet aside from their father, psions that could read as human on the mental grid and you'd never know they were there until they were killing you. Only the OIC and her top supporting officers knew of the Sercas' true nature, a truth that complicated everything.

"Did you give the Warhounds our Strykers, Ciari?" Jael asked sharply.

"You know I didn't," Ciari said as she looked each of her officers in the eyes. "None of us granted those four a reprieve, and Lucas has never been assigned retrieval duty. He's been missing from the field for two years."

Keiko frowned, rubbing fingers over her left temple. "Which begs the question of why?"

Lucas Serca's absence in the media and by his father's side had been noted. Whatever game Nathan was playing, they were far behind on knowing his goal. There wasn't a chance in hell that Threnody and Quinton could be alive, not after the last two escapes. The third time was never the charm, not in this world. Kerr and Jason might have a chance, with Jason being a telekinetic and able to teleport, but Ciari doubted it.

Was it worth it? Ciari thought. She reflected on the government's decision, at her urging, to cut Threnody loose for a suicide run because the electrokinetic cared more than she should for the humans she had been indoctrinated to protect. Threnody had never been one to swallow propaganda whole without choking on it. All Strykers were like that, most were just better at hiding it.

"Get a team together," Ciari said, her face devoid of all emotion. "Bring back the bodies. The World Court always requires proof when Strykers die. It's so damn difficult to make them believe anything without a corpse."

[SIX]

JULY 2379
LONDON, UNITED KINGDOM

New York City had been a crater since the Border Wars, the remains swallowed by the Atlantic Ocean and worn down by acid rain. The world's financial center had been transplanted perforce to London once the fallout dust settled, because London still stood, thanks to the fanatical service of long-ago RAF pilots. The metal clock hands on Big Ben's face remained stuck at 3:27, a historical testament, a reminder, to the arrogance of the human race.

The main city towers that spanned both sides of the sluggish Thames River cast long shadows over the crowded city below. Downstream, the Thames Barrier stood like a silent sentinel, an engineering feat something that only the educated, registered humans understood and were allowed to operate. The streets themselves teemed with unregistered humans who would never find themselves removed from obscurity and written into the safety of the Registry. Their genetics hadn't passed muster when the time came to prove themselves clean of radiation taint and mutation. At least, not any mutation that was profitable. They would never join the ranks of the educated to better their lives save through illegal schools that would mean their death if found out. The government cracked down hard on those who disobeyed the directives that had separated society into what it was now.

Freedom, with all its various connotations, was one of the first casualties of survival.

Nathan was used to his sort of freedom and getting his way, even if the humans—registered and unregistered alike—weren't exactly aware of how he did it. The problem was that he hadn't been getting his way for two years and it had left him in a foul mood for just as long. Nathan was excellent at hiding his displeasure, though, especially in front of the cameras.

The pressroom of the Serca Syndicate was filled to capacity, everyone jostling for the clearest read on the man whose sheer presence up on the speaking stage was enough to capture everyone's attention. Nathan smiled at his audiences, both the one present and the one beyond the cameras, as he stepped behind the podium, and he meant the expression for what it was—a means to an end.

"Ladies, gentlemen, it's always a pleasure to have something to celebrate," Nathan began, his voice carrying through the room. He cut a striking figure behind the microphones, with the shine of a hologrid at his fingertips. All the reporters leaned forward, eager for what one of the most prominent figures in their society had to say.

"The government, in its righteous duty to further enable the survival of the human race, has a difficult balance to keep when it rules on issues that come before the World Court. My family, as you know, has had a unique relationship with the ruling politicians that seek to keep us alive in a world our ancestors made. Not everyone has or will agree with the Fifth Generation Act my predecessors campaigned and fought for, but it was necessary at the time. It remains necessary today, despite its detractors.

"This year marks the two hundred and fiftieth anniversary since the last bombs fell inside China, ending the Border Wars that held the world prisoner for five long and terrifying years. We nearly annihilated ourselves through shortsightedness and greed. The fallout of that time was so much more than radiation sickness and a ruined planet, so much more that we have had to live with and survive through over the past two and a half centuries.

"In 2179 we set a benchmark year to ensure our survival so that those who could prove five generations' worth of clean DNA would be allowed full rights as registered citizens when the time came. Was it a draconian law at the time? Of course it was, but it was needed. And when, one hundred and fifty years later, we reached that finalization point, there were those of us who had made efforts to keep the integrity of our DNA intact. My family never set down in stone how one should go about achieving that goal, just that one *should*."

Nathan offered up a faint smile, the pride in his family's accomplishments unmistakable. "The Border Wars gave us many and varied problems to deal with, not the least being the psions we seem unable to cleanse from the population. The government, thankfully, has the problem under control. Which is why I went about my proposal to the World Court the way I did. You see, I've come to the conclusion that psions will not be purged from our society anytime soon, if at all. Their genetics are too complex, and we still have yet to discover what the Border Wars changed in *us* to make *them*.

"The Serca Syndicate has pursued the Genome Privacy Act for the past few decades since the first clean generation was granted approval by the government to join the Registry in 2329. Those of us who have been lucky enough to remain free of mutation in any form have a duty to save the less fortunate. We must strive with everything we have to better the lives of those who still suffer from our past failures. To do that, we must first study where we went wrong, and the psions are the most prominent mistake that we have.

"The World Court ruled in favor of the Serca Syndicate today. They gave this company the approval to keep our work private for the sake of the average citizen. We all have our secrets, some more than most, and while we are a people now who uphold truth above all else, sometimes there is a need for secrecy. That is why this Act was granted, to allow those who never got the government's approval to join the Registry an answer to a most pertinent question. What, after all this time, taints their DNA, but not others? It is a question that everyone knows better than to ask, because some things are just too personal for public consumption."

Nathan leaned forward a little, the shine in his dark blue eyes that of reflective camera glare, not inspecs. "What's not personal, and which will be presented once we have solid findings, is our results. It may take ten years, twenty, another generation or even two, before we figure out how the psions are being born and why some people remain immune to the mutations brought about by the Border Wars and others do not. But rest assured, we *will* find out. To spare those the stigma that comes with being unregistered in our society, participation in this project will remain private. It has to if we are to have any chance of getting enough people to help us find the answers we are all looking for. Now, I will take some questions."

"Sir," a tall reporter called out as he stood up. "Where will you be getting the samples? Are you restricting your company to just one or two continents, or all of them?"

"There will be a broad representation of subjects pulled from every continent that carries survivors, both registered and unregistered," Nathan answered. "They won't just be from the livable areas. We'll send excursions into the areas around the deadzones as well."

"Sir," another reporter asked. "Where will the psions factor into this?"

"We're still coordinating with the government on that."

"What about the rumors that your eldest son doesn't approve of the direction you're taking the Serca Syndicate and that you've heavily restricted his access to all your current projects?"

Nathan's expression didn't change as he looked at the reporter who had asked that question, a slim Chinese woman of slight stature. "My family is off-limits."

"Lucas Serca hasn't been seen for two years."

"Contrary to rumor, my eldest is currently helping gather the samples we'll need to perform this research and has been for many months now. His appearance before your cameras is unnecessary. Next question."

The ten agreed-upon questions passed quickly, Nathan's answers memorized rhetoric. Once the last question was asked and answered, Nathan left the podium for the side door, ignoring the clamoring behind him for more of his attention. Coming out into a secured hallway, he was quickly joined by his bodyguards and last two functioning children.

Neither Samantha nor Gideon met his eyes as they fell into step behind Nathan. They had changed out of their BDUs into sharp designer attire for the press conference, even though they hadn't been allowed before the cameras. Appearances were everything, especially in the public domain.

I despise failure, Nathan said into all their minds, the incredible force of his Class I triad strength peeling apart their shields like rotten fruit. *You know better than to return empty-handed.*

Lucas has never been an easy target, Samantha said carefully as they were escorted down the hallway to the private lift. *He knew we were coming.*

I do not tolerate excuses, Samantha.

Sir.

Lucas left the Slums with Strykers, Gideon said as the door to the lift slid open and the group stepped onto the platform.

Nathan's face was impassive as he pressed his hand against the control panel. The computer read his biometrics and granted him access to the tower levels restricted to the Serca family alone and the people they owned. The lift began its ascent.

I'm beginning to think that Lucas doesn't want to live, Nathan said.

It was just the three of them and two Warhounds in the guise of bodyguards on the ride up. One of them was biting on an ever-present cigarette, the smoke curling up toward the ceiling. Areas of Jin Li's skin still carried bruises that looked like burns, imprints from someone else's power his body had barely been able to counteract. He hadn't gone through medical yet because they'd been ordered to attend Nathan immediately upon their arrival back in London.

"Do we finally have a kill order, boss?" Jin Li asked.

The lift came to a stop and Nathan's answer, while without words, was unmistakable. Already in their minds, Nathan drove his power deeper between one heartbeat and the next as he stepped off the lift.

The agony of the intrusion drove all three to the floor, the last bodyguard stepping out of the lift and standing at attention with a distant look on his face that every Warhound learned to master by his or her first year in the ranks. Punishment was handed out indiscriminately. Warhounds learned to ignore it when it happened to the person next to them and suffered through it silently when it was their turn. Protesting was considered a waste of breath. So was screaming.

Samantha felt her head hit the floor, the dull ache of it distant and irrelevant against the immediate presence of Nathan deep in her mind. Instinctively, she tried to gather her power into some semblance of defense, but Nathan broke her control with a single thought. Her mind caved beneath his, as it had so many times before. Samantha could do nothing but stare blankly at the open doors of the lift, feeling the coolness of the metal she was lying on seep into the skin of her face as Nathan took from all of them memories of the events he felt he needed.

She could feel the channels in her mind where her power flowed begin to bleed through where they shouldn't. She took in a shaky breath, tasting blood in the back of her throat. Beside her, writhing just as desperately, Gideon and Jin Li struggled to breathe.

Lucas will learn his place, Nathan said as he walked away. *Unfortunately, I can't be the one to drag him back to his knees. I can't afford the damage it might cause to my health and to our political position. I expected more from all of you. It seems my faith in all my children was misplaced.*

Oddly enough, Samantha felt shame; shame that she hadn't been enough, that she never could be, because she hadn't been born that way. She wasn't what Nathan needed; never would be. Lucas hadn't been his answer either, but he'd been close, and that's why they still hunted for him. Samantha was just an afterthought, and not a good one. She, Gideon, and Kristen still performed their duties because their being alive meant Nathan could delegate. It meant he could live just a little longer. One of these days, if Samantha was lucky, she was going to wake up and he would be gone, dead, mind burned away by his power and body broken. It was how all psions died, she just hoped she lived long enough to see it happen to him.

I see your filial piety is as touching as always, Samantha.

She felt it when Nathan exited her mind, like the shattering of glass. Only she knew she could put the pieces back together, given enough time. Pressing her hand against the side of her skull, she sniffed wetly, sucking up blood through her nasal passages. Carefully, she wiped it away on the sleeve of her crisply pressed gray blouse.

Get up.

They stumbled to their feet, staggering out of the lift and into the private space that belonged to the Serca family. Five levels of residential rooms and offices and five more above that no lift could reach, because those levels were accessible only by stairs.

The Serca family had always been a buffer between the rest of the world and the Warhounds, more so here in that psion group's unofficial headquarters than anywhere else. The Serca Syndicate was a human endeavor, founded and controlled by psions who masqueraded as human in the public eye because that's what everyone expected. A prestigious company owned by a family with a prominent place in history wouldn't dare harbor rogue psions. People who discovered or were offered the truth were simply mindwiped until they were useful, or killed.

Samantha and Gideon collapsed gingerly into the available seats in Nathan's office once they arrived. Jin Li, used to Nathan's lashing out viciously, propped himself up against the credenza. Nathan's desk terminal was keyed to his biometrics alone, and it snapped on at the first touch of his fingers as he sat down behind it. He said nothing, simply brought everything online, images and data drifting across the opaque console attached to ancient wood.

The door to his office slid open and a static, human mind pressed up against Samantha's shields. She swallowed her disgust and it tasted like blood. Samantha had never cared for the humans Nathan showed special interest in, especially the ones he fucked.

"You're late, Dalia," Nathan said.

"Apologies, sir," the brunette woman said as she crossed the office to take the last seat.

Dalia would never be described as pretty, but she was striking given the right identity to inhabit. Right now she was wearing the drab uniform of an Eastern European bond worker, someone who would take any job, so long as it paid. The stretch of surviving countries that once belonged to Russia weren't wanted by Western Europe and were shunned by what remained of their former mother country. Shantytowns outnumbered civilized city towers, and people survived in those places only through the skin trade, be it labor, sex, or the sale of body parts and organs. The deadzones there were nearly as bad as the ones the Middle East had become.

Dalia, however, was not a bond worker.

She met Nathan's gaze unwaveringly when few people could. She was human, a static mind to his vast senses, but what she lacked in mental capacity she more than made up for with her hacking skills and Syndicate loyalty. She was Nathan's pet, yes; a decent fuck on the side; but more important, she was his way into the inner sanctum of the government-controlled scientists. Bioscanners could differentiate between a psion and a human, and no official in the world would knowingly let a psion into government-restricted areas.

Dalia pulled a data chip from the pocket of her uniform and slid it across the desk to Nathan. "We have a problem."

He picked it up telekinetically and loaded it into his terminal with a flick of mental power. The hologrid that snapped into view between them hung heavy with a security feed that showed Lucas, in a bond worker's uniform, infiltrating the plant that Dalia had been sent to six months ago. The plant developed the Serca Syndicate's software and hardware, some of which had been held back from public use not because it wasn't ready, but because the Serca family hadn't been willing to give it all up. Nathan's mother had bargained with the government quite a bit when she'd been alive. Thanks to her persistence, the World Court wanted those computer programs, and Marcheline had made them pay for it. Nathan refused to let his family's success be marred by anything.

In the security feed, Lucas tipped his head back, looked directly into the recording device, and smiled, as if he wanted to be seen, before disappearing in a teleport. A visual *fuck you* that wouldn't go over well with the public if that feed got out.

Nathan stared hard at the image of his son, letting the feed replay three times before he finally leaned back in his chair. "When was this taken?"

"Last week," Dalia said. "I've deleted the file from every available hard drive and from the servers supporting that particular security grid."

Nathan's gaze settled heavily on his other children. "This is exactly why I want him brought back."

Samantha willed herself not to look away from her father's gaze. "It's been two years and your Warhounds have employed every known method to retrieve him. We are *trying*. Sir."

"Then apparently you need to open up that mind of yours and try harder. Lucas is planning something and he's spent at least two years laying down the groundwork for it." Nathan gestured at the vidfeed. "This isn't the first time he's infiltrated our satellite branches and stolen data. I am getting *tired* of waiting for Lucas to show his hand when *our* goal is to cut off his head. We can't afford interference, not when we're so close to the launch date."

"What would you have us do?" Gideon asked.

Nathan was silent as he watched the vidfeed one last time. "Two years of teleporting around the planet, interacting with Warhounds and Strykers alike, and only now he takes hostages? The Strykers didn't give up those psions, whoever they were. Ciari didn't request a retrieval. I want to know which Strykers Lucas took and I want that information as soon as it's been confirmed, along with an updated report on everything Lucas has taken from this company. Gideon, that is your task. Dalia, we're going to stage two of our plan. I want the agents you've been working with terminated. You can find new ones."

Dalia inclined her head in silent acknowledgment of that order.

Nathan's heavy gaze settled on Samantha. "I'm sending you to Spain for the oil transfer that the government has scheduled. You're taking Kristen as backup."

Kristen, his youngest child, was sixteen, a Class III empath, unregistered and insane. She was a mistake that Nathan kept around because she was still useful. Crazy, vicious, and difficult to control, but useful.

"She needs to feed."

Samantha knew better than to argue and merely nodded, careful to keep her thoughts as neutral and settled behind her cracked and damaged shields as she could.

"Jin Li," Nathan continued. "We leave for Japan shortly. Prep the shuttle. I have to maintain the *illusion* of living as a human. Dismissed."

The four of them got to their feet and left Nathan to the task of spinning this latest victory for the Serca Syndicate. Once out of sight, Gideon teleported away immediately. Samantha didn't bother to hide the disgust on her face at her twin's eagerness to please. The remaining three took a lift four levels up to the last public level of the Serca Syndicate. Getting farther than that required passing through a host of biometric security features before they could take the stairs to the first restricted level of the Warhounds' headquarters. Samantha left Jin Li and Dalia once they arrived in that brightly lit place.

The top of the city tower that the Serca Syndicate was located in had been built with no real windows to look out and see the polluted sky. Instead, hologrids flowed over every outer wall, detailing scenes of blue skies that no one had actually seen in the past few generations. Samantha didn't notice them as she worked her way to the top floor of the tower, passing through a few security checks on the way up. The last door she walked through led into a short sterilization corridor. Every possible speck of contaminant was stripped from her body in the time it took her to cross that short space in four strides.

Samantha came out into a level that was all white, bright lights shining down on everyone. The medical level was geared solely to psions, and she made her way to the special room assigned to her younger sister. Samantha ignored everyone she passed, just as she ignored the headache that was pounding out a rhythm against her skull. Faint traces of blood had dried around her nose and chin. She scraped them off with one hand, pressing the other against the control panel to a heavily secured door.

It took biometric measures to open that medical room, and only six people in the entire Warhound ranks had access to the person who lived behind that door. Samantha was one of them by right of blood. The door slid open and Samantha shored up her shields as well as she could before stepping inside.

"Been a while, Sammy-girl," a rough, amused voice said from the corner.

At sixteen, Kristen Serca didn't weigh much more than forty kilos, and the specialized skinsuit that she wore was as much her prison as her clothing. With built-in bioware that could monitor her status at all times, it acted as a leash for those with the controls. The skinsuit had the ability to short-circuit Kristen's nervous system and keep her in check when sanity slipped from her, which was often enough for the dysfunctional Class III empath to be a problem for everyone else.

"Hello, Kristen," Samantha said, her voice leached of all emotion.

The girl lifted her head, face full of sharp angles and that ever-present smile, which was her default expression, a rictus grin of happiness. Lank, straight blond hair barely touched her shoulders. A sick silver sheen radiated outward from her pupils and dark blue irises, giving her a vacant, almost dead gaze that most people believed meant she was incapable of paying attention to the world around her. Samantha knew otherwise.

She couldn't ever recall a point in her life where Kristen didn't need the death of another person to keep her mind from falling apart. Maybe it had something to do with all the genetic altering Nathan had done to each of his children, trying to make them into something that none of them were. Kristen hadn't been born this way, mentally unbalanced and always looking for a little bit of sanity. She had Nathan to thank for her predicament, for her need to model her shields and her thought processes on another person's mind in order to try to stabilize her own. It never stuck long.

When she managed some semblance of sanity, the empath knew exactly what she was doing. Outside of those moments, it was anyone's guess what was going on in Kristen's mind.

Samantha eyed the deep scratches on Kristen's face, which were covered with the distinctive shine of a quick-heal patch. Kristen tore herself up just as often as she tore up everyone else. She didn't register the pain for what it was; her empathy didn't let her. Pain was both physical and mental, and while Kristen understood that her body and mind were connected, that understanding got lost in the ravages of her power. She could feel nothing, produce no emotion of her own except a twisted, maniacal glee when given someone to kill. The emotions of other people, however, were easy enough for her to tamper with. There was something to be said for instinct, after all.

"Hungry?" Samantha asked, staying exactly where she was.

The brightness in her sister's eyes matched the spike on the mental grid. Kristen pushed herself up on surprisingly steady feet and approached Samantha with grasping hands and a needy mind. Samantha, still reeling from Nathan's punishment, didn't bother to be gentle when she sent a driving telepathic spike straight into Kristen's mind. The empath grunted, falling to her knees, but she was still smiling as a faint trickle of blood slid out of her nose. She licked it off her lips.

"You taste good," Kristen slurred.

Samantha turned on her heels and left. "We've got a briefing to attend. Keep your mind to yourself, Kristen. Or I'll stick you back in that cell of yours."

The soft laughter that followed Samantha down the hall was cheerful. The gaping, raw need for the kill tainting the mental grid was too dangerous to ignore, and Samantha kept her shields up high and tight as Kristen closed the distance between them.

[SEVEN]

You're sure?" Ciari said, staring at the face on the vidscreen. The connection wasn't the best coming out of the Slums, but it had still been picked up by a communications officer. "You didn't find anything?"

"Not a single body," the Stryker in the field said, her voice thick with a Portuguese accent. "Emilio and I searched a wide area once we teleported in from Brasília. The cathedral is a mess, but we found no remains."

"Thank you, Imenja. I appreciate your efforts."

"We can extend the search if that's what you want. Move into a different cartel area. I don't know if it will make a difference, though. We've spent twenty-four hours here already."

"That won't be necessary. Return to your posts in Brazil."

"Sir."

The connection was cut, leaving silence behind in Ciari's office. She hesitated a long moment before tapping out a request for an uplink. It took ten minutes for it to go through, for her code to be screened by two separate communications officers in two cities, before Erik's face appeared before her on the vidscreen.

"Ciari," Erik said. "I'm heading into session within the hour. You have five minutes."

"Preliminary reports from the team in the field confirm that the four Strykers we sent into the Slums are missing, sir."

"Can you confirm that they're dead?" Erik asked, gaze cool.

"Negative. We've found no bodies."

"Then we're going to presume they're somehow still alive and MIA."

"Did you want to initiate a hunt or kill order?"

"You know the law as well as I do. There are enough rogue psions in the world as it is. We can't afford to add more to the mess we're still fighting."

"That's a Class II telepath you want to terminate, sir. I realize you don't much care about the rest of them, but—"

"That's a *dysfunctional* Class II telepath I'm telling you to terminate," Erik interrupted sharply. "There's a difference between a psion that is worth something to me and one that hasn't proven useful in all the years we've let him live."

"Permission to speak freely, sir."

"If you're going to try arguing for their lives, then no. Terminate them."

The screen went blank, Erik having cut the connection on his end. Ciari rubbed a hand over her face, mouth twisting slightly before the expression smoothed away. She hated this part of her job.

Getting to her feet, Ciari left her office for the lift beyond her doors, taking it down to the busy command level. It was a maze of hallways, offices, and command rooms, full of humans and Strykers alike monitoring Strykers out in the field on contract and those within their headquarters. All Strykers showed up on the government's security grid through bioscans from the signal that their implanted neurotrackers transmitted, a precaution that was law. If they dropped off the grid, they were either dead or attempting an escape, the latter of which resulted in the former.

There was no way out of the Strykers Syndicate except by death. Everyone knew that.

Ciari made her way silently to a room where a Stryker and a human were still struggling to locate four missing Strykers and having no luck. When she entered, the Stryker stood as a sign of respect. The human remained seated. Ciari didn't take it as an insult.

"Contact Jael," Ciari said. "Tell her to report here for a termination."

The Stryker bit back whatever protest he wanted to voice and did as Ciari ordered. He was a telepath, as was Jael, so in seconds Ciari felt the other woman's mind pressing against her mental shields.

You can't be serious, Jael protested. *That's one of our strongest teams and our strongest telepath you want to terminate.*

It's the order Erik gave. I need you as a witness and to sign off on their deaths.

For all that the World Court owned the Strykers and had control of their lives, their capacity for justice paled in the face of their cruelty. That wasn't a popular opinion, but most people weren't psions, beholden to a tangle of delicate, devastating bioware in the back of their head capable of killing them. Rarely did the World Court terminate Strykers themselves. They gave the order to do so.

The OIC initiated the punishment at the World Court's command in situations like this. The act was a punishment in and of itself. A reminder of who was really in control.

Jael arrived some minutes later, her white scrubs spattered here and there with blood. She'd been doing rounds when Ciari had summoned her. Ciari knew the other woman would prefer to be there and not here, but they both knew how to do their job, as distasteful as it was sometimes.

"Ciari," Jael said, her voice flatly neutral.

"Dismissed," Ciari said to the pair of handlers. The Stryker and the human left in silence. Ciari knew word of this termination would spread through the ranks within the hour.

Hate, when projected by several hundred people directly at her, always gave Ciari a migraine, despite her shields.

The door slid shut, leaving her and Jael alone in their personal hell. Jael stepped forward, her eyes flickering over the data on the hologrid before them, a map of what was left of the world prominently displayed.

"I hate this part," Jael said through clenched teeth.

"Me, too," Ciari said quietly before raising her voice. "Computer, mission override. Authorization code Sigma Two Seven One Zeta. Request termination sequence."

"Voice identification confirmed. Ciari Treiva, Officer in Charge," the computer's voice announced in a gratingly pleasant tone so at odds with what they were doing. "Initiating termination sequence."

Jael let out an explosive sigh. "Chief Medical Officer Jael Dawson present as witness."

"Medical authority present, witness acknowledged," the computer responded. "Request Stryker files."

"Pull entire files of the following Strykers," Ciari said, her voice curiously calm. "Threnody Corwin, Quinton Martinez, Kerr MacDougal, and Jason Garret."

"Acknowledged. Files found."

Four dossiers opened, laid atop the world map on the hologrid. Four faces frozen in holopics stared out at them. Four lives were written out in reports of strengths and weaknesses, missions accomplished and missions failed. Numbers, words, that didn't fully encompass the lives Ciari was being forced to cut short. They never did.

"Location of targets?" Ciari asked.

"Location unknown."

Ciari's gaze never wavered as she pressed her hand down on the biometric scanner. The computer read her print in an instant. She formed the word reluctantly. "Terminate."

Their network was fully integrated into the government's security grid that spanned the world, enabling them to track Strykers anywhere on earth. With these four Strykers, Ciari was hoping it wouldn't work, but recklessly hidden or not, neurotrackers would always respond to their programming, even if the person was already dead.

Four sharp spikes on the bioscanners that monitored baseline readings erupted somewhere on the east coast of Russia. The computer magnified the area five times, satellite feed finally pinpointing an area in Magadan, Magadan Oblast, as the final resting place of *someone*. They just weren't Strykers.

The baselines terminated by those neurotrackers were human.

Jael took a step forward, surprise filtering through her voice. "Ciari?"

"Acknowledge the results, Jael," Ciari said, never taking her eyes away from the hologrid.

Jael swallowed tightly before saying, "It is my assessment as the Strykers Syndicate's CMO that the four baselines on record do not match the ones which were terminated."

"Confirmed," the computer said, recording Jael's report for the record.

"This doesn't make any sense," Jael said.

Ciari tilted her head to the side. "No, it doesn't."

They stared at each other, both of them reading between the lines of what they were saying and what was showing up on the grid.

"Computer, save files and shut down," Ciari said.

It took less than a minute for the computer to obey Ciari's command. Only when the terminal went dark did Ciari turn to look at Jael, easily reading the uncertainty in Jael's troubled expression.

"Contact Keiko," Ciari said. "Tell her to report to my office in twenty minutes."

Ciari left Jael behind and returned to her office with determined strides, where she followed protocol and contacted Erik once again. She sent the request red-lined as priority, and he answered more quickly than she thought he would.

"We have a problem, sir," Ciari said when the connection was made.

"It hasn't even been half an hour, Ciari. It takes less than a minute to fry a psion's brain. What could *possibly* be the problem?" Erik said.

"The neurotrackers were activated. The kill results are inconclusive. They spiked as human on the grid."

Erik stared at her. "That's impossible. A psion's baseline is nowhere close to a human's."

"Those are the results, sir."

"I want the results changed. Immediately."

"Of course, sir."

It was just like him to want the impossible.

The connection cut off and Ciari leaned back against her chair. She let out a long sigh, thinking about everything that had gone wrong just now and what had gone right.

Keiko walked into her office ten minutes later, expression neutral, even if her tone of voice wasn't. "Jael told me what happened. Your orders?"

"I'm sending you to Russia. The World Court wants answers."

"I'll see what I can find."

PART THREE
NEGOTIATION

SESSION DATE: 2128.06.02
LOCATION: Institute of Psionics Research
CLEARANCE ID: Dr. Amy Bennett
SUBJECT: 2581
FILE NUMBER: 514

A nurse holds her arm gently, carefully extracting yet another vial's worth of blood as the doctor looks on. When the nurse is finished, she leaves with what she came for, and it is only the two of them again. Aisling carefully touches the small bandage that covers the hole in her skin.

"You won't find what you're looking for," Aisling says, glancing up at the doctor. "You think you can stop the wars by trying to make me better, but you can't."

"I think you need to share with us exactly what you know," the older woman says as she taps her fingers against the table in a steady rhythm. "It's been months, Aisling. The bombs are still dropping."

"They've been dropping for years."

"You can stop it."

"It doesn't stop here." Aisling kicks her feet and sighs, sulking. "You're like her, you know that? Threnody thinks I know everything, too."

"Again with this Threnody," the doctor says in exasperation. "You've mentioned her exactly twenty-three separate times now."

"She's my favorite imaginary friend."

"Aisling," the doctor says as she crouches down beside the girl's chair. "You know what you see isn't imaginary."

"I know," Aisling whispers, sounding scared as she curiously tilts her head to the side, wires brushing her face. "I almost wish it was, though. I just don't want to worry you."

[EIGHT]

Jason came awake to a roaring, screaming pain in his head that made it impossible to think. For once, the pain wasn't caused by his power, just his actual *skull*, and that was enough to drive the unconsciousness away.

Blinking slowly down at the dirty gray floor stained liberally with blood, Jason realized that he could see clearly in all the human visual spectrum, along with the overlay of data in his eyes. His inspecs were back online, which was impossible without surgery, and this sure as hell wasn't the medical level back at headquarters.

He tried to move and became immediately aware that was impossible. The power clamped down on him was familiar, a telekinetic strength that he recognized and couldn't break. Bent forward, spine arched, Jason could sense someone behind him, even if he couldn't see the person. He couldn't feel a damn thing at the back of his skull, but the rest of his head was feeding him pain. He could feel the blood that was trickling down his back. He could smell it, too.

"Interesting dilemma, you know," that vaguely familiar tenor said through the hum of a sterility field, and thank fuck for that, because this place didn't look clean at all. "Your natal shields never fell. You're going to feel this more than the rest of your team since I can't get very far into your mind to block the pain. First time *that's* ever happened."

A pair of scuffed, all-terrain black boots stepped into his sight, but even when he rolled his eyes upward, Jason couldn't see the person's face. Not that he needed to. Even doped up on drugs, it was difficult to forget the shock he had felt when they'd learned that a Serca was a high-Classed

79

psion. Difficult to forget those eyes. Made him wonder about the rest of that famous family and if Lucas was merely an anomaly or *normal* for the Sercas.

"What have you done with them?" Jason managed to get out through clenched teeth. He didn't bother to correct Lucas's assumption that the four of them were a team. At the moment, he really only cared about Kerr, but he could worry about Threnody and Quinton. Especially Quinton. He kind of liked the way the other man looked.

Lucas's tone was amused. "They're recovering, even if everyone's pissed that they can't use their powers. I have them blocked. The doctor's almost finished with you."

"What?"

More blood trickled down his back and Jason squeezed his eyes shut. He didn't know what was going on behind him, not until something clattered on the floor an indeterminable amount of time later. He opened his eyes and stared at the tiny, oval-shaped device with six short spikes and six long filaments of bioware wet with his blood that had been tossed near his feet.

Jason didn't need to ask what it was. He knew, just as every Stryker knew, about the neurotracker one was implanted with upon joining the Stryker ranks. He also knew that removing it should have instantly killed him. Any tampering sent out an immediate signal to the government as a red alert. Standard operating procedure was to terminate. At the very least, the Strykers would know—*should* know—that he wasn't wearing it anymore. Which meant—

Jason laughed, the sound desperate. "I thought you said you didn't want to kill us, because you just did."

The neurotracker lifted off the floor and was drawn upward by invisible telekinetic power, settling into Lucas's hand. He crouched down in front of Jason, focusing on him. No apologies were to be found in his gaze.

"Its programming is active. The signal, while blocked right now, still functions. When the time comes, it will send through the government's security grid, even if it's no longer in your head," Lucas said. "They'll be implanted into some desperate bond worker attached to the skin trade. This procedure is one that my side has done before."

Jason swallowed drily. "And when the government flips the switch, your chosen little carriers will be dead instead. Do *they* know that?"

"Of course not. They just think they were paid for a body transfer over international lines. You should really be happy about being taken off your leash, Jason. Most of you Strykers are when we pull you off the field before you're terminated."

Jason squinted up at him. "What the fuck are you talking about?"

"Nothing that matters at the moment, since I'm no longer a Warhound. I haven't been for many years."

"I doubt that."

"Lucky for both of us I don't care what you think, just what you can do."

Lucas stood up and walked away. Jason had no other choice but to stay where he was, listening to a strange, rough voice mutter behind him as this doctor, whoever he was, grafted pieces of his skull back together and closed his skin inside the safety of the makeshift sterility field. Whatever drugs he'd been given were beginning to wear off quickly, and Jason could feel *exactly* what had been done to him. He squeezed his eyes shut and tried to breathe through it all.

Eventually it was over. The operation complete, Lucas lifted the telekinetic hold he had on Jason. Able to move, Jason straightened up in the seat and immediately regretted it. Nausea came, swift and brutal, and he puked stomach acid onto the floor while Lucas kept him from falling over with a hand on his shoulder.

Jason lifted one hand to the back of his skull, feeling the small area of shaved hair there, the sealed skin, and the hardness of a quick-heal patch. His bones ached.

"I can give you more drugs," Lucas said. "Except you know as well as I do that a psion's metabolism will burn through them in less than thirty minutes. Still want them?"

"I'll manage," Jason rasped as he spat bile-coated saliva onto the floor.

"Better than most, I suspect. Come on. Your team captain seems to think I'm torturing you, even though I already proved that I wasn't after putting Quinton and Kerr through the same procedure. She got to go first."

"We aren't a team. She's not my captain."

"I know. But it irritates her to be called that."

Lucas hauled Jason to his feet, watching critically as the Stryker struggled to stay upright. The doctor shuffled around the operating area, and Jason nearly lost control of his stomach again after getting a good first look at the man's face.

The doctor had no eyes and half his skull had been replaced by metal plating. In place of organic material was bioware designed to process images to the brain in microscopic layers that traditional human eyesight could never hope to attain. Glittering wires frayed out of the man's eye sockets around tiny optics, twining back inside his body through his temples, feeding into his brain. Everything about the doctor's appearance was illegal, and Jason felt contaminated just looking at him.

"Korman is one of the finest transplant surgeons on the black market," Lucas said, sounding almost cheerful as he steered Jason out of the room. "The best part is that he did all of this for free."

"Only because you altered his mind," Threnody said as they stepped out into a cluttered living space, if one could call the mess livable. Her voice, Jason noticed, was slurred just a little.

"You say that like it's a bad thing."

The faint sound of displaced air came from the makeshift operating room. Jason glanced over his shoulder, seeing that the doctor had disappeared. "Warhound?"

"No," Lucas said calmly. "Mine. I teleported him somewhere else to finish the transfer."

The three Strykers were sitting around a rickety table in various stages of recovery. Jason's eyes settled on Kerr, and the telekinetic moved over to his partner as quickly as he could, sitting down heavily on the bench there.

"You're bleeding through your shields," Jason said, studying the familiar pain lines on Kerr's face that weren't all just because of the surgery. "Get behind mine."

Kerr's face twisted just a little. "Jays, you just got out of *brain* surgery. I can't—"

"That wasn't a goddamn request, Kerr. Just do it."

Jason pretended that Lucas wasn't watching them, that he didn't have his telepathy anchored tightly in their thoughts, allowing what needed to be done only after Jason glared at him. Kerr burrowed through the bond that linked him to Jason, transferring as much of his power behind the thick natal shields that stood out in stark relief against Jason's mind as he could. The pressure in Kerr's own mind eased, leveled off, as Jason's shields took up the task of protection that he was incapable of providing himself.

"Interesting." Jason glanced over at Lucas, not liking the calculating look in those dark blue eyes. Lucas just smiled, the expression remote as he crossed his arms over his chest. "I'm sure all of you have questions."

"You think?" Threnody's voice was caustic. "You condemned us to rogue status."

"I saved you," Lucas corrected. "And if you want to know why, you'll follow me outside."

"Here's not good enough?"

"These walls have eyes and ears that I don't trust. Camden Market is safer."

It wasn't, not really, but Strykers thought differently from Warhounds. Threnody stared at Lucas, details clicking into place about what they now knew of the Serca Syndicate, and what they knew of the Warhounds. Camden Market was in London, and London was dominated by the Serca Syndicate as much as it was by the government.

"You brought us to the Warhounds' home turf and you think this is *safe*?" she demanded.

"What better place to hide you than here in plain sight?" Lucas reached up and tapped the side of his head before sliding a pair of dark glasses over his eyes. "I've got you all off the mental grid under my power. You read as human, just like I do, and I can make all of you disappear completely if I need to."

"How?" Kerr asked.

"Today's not the day you learn that trick. Now let's go."

They left the back-alley surgery room for the pipe dreams and broken promises of Camden Market because they had no choice. Quinton kept a hand on Threnody and both eyes on Lucas, while Kerr helped Jason up the rickety stairs to the street. The silent looks the four shared were mirrored by the thoughts in their heads. If there was even a slim possibility at escape, could they take it?

You won't get further than the thought of it, Lucas promised. *So don't bother trying.*

Threnody stumbled on the way up, swearing as Quinton caught her before she hit the crumbling cement steps. Her arms and legs were shaking ever so slightly, and it wasn't just because of the operation.

"Can you feel?" Quinton asked her as he took more of her weight.

"I'm not paralyzed," Threnody said.

"That's not what I asked."

"There's some numbness." Threnody bit her bottom lip and struggled the rest of the way up. "I've lost some muscle control."

"We need a real medical center with a biotank and nanites. The disconnect you're experiencing is going to be lethal in another day or two if we don't get you fixed up all the way."

"I know."

It was more than just knowing that she was dying from the inside out. Jin Li's power had short-circuited her body just as it had in Johannesburg. Only back then, she'd been at her best. This time, she'd been patched. Her nervous system was breaking down, a slow, uncontrollable death that would eventually trickle down from the voluntary functions to the *in*voluntary functions of her body. Quinton didn't want to watch her drown with air in her lungs.

You'll be all right, Lucas said into her mind alone as they reached a heavily secured door. He opened it telekinetically. *Korman fixed what he could after pulling out the neurotracker. He's done the same sort of operation on other Strykers over the years. Your power will do the rest on its own. Aisling said today isn't your time to die. Neither is tomorrow. You'll recover.*

Who the hell is Aisling?

You'll find out soon enough.

His promise wasn't one Threnody would ever trust. Lucas just laughed off her fear as they stepped outside.

Camden Market shone with the glitter of hologrids against the evening sky, neon light edging their faces as they joined a crowd looking for an escape that would never be found in the gutters. Not here, not in the place that was the world's entertainment and pleasure center, built on the back of the skin trade.

The streets teemed with people looking to sell, looking to buy, looking to forget, areas of London carved into territories by gangs who would never live longer than their next adrenaline rush if they were lucky. Whores sold themselves with a look, on their knees no matter their gender so long as the price was right. Addicts looked for their next fix, hands curved into the signs of their individual requests, begging for the next possible high. And all through the miscreants roamed the gray-uniformed quads of military soldiers, their pulse-rifles set to kill, never to stun. They were the only law down here, but it was anyone's guess on who lined their pockets this hour—the government or those on the streets.

Lucas led the Strykers with telepathic and telekinetic chains that replaced the collars the eyeless doctor had cut away. His power guided them to an outside pub that was all counter and nothing else. Aside from the watered-down beer—the vidscreens behind the barkeep advertised a dozen different drafts, but only two ever poured out at any given time— the place also doled out protein meals. Plastic bowls full of GMO rice and cubes of colorless protein that had no flavor would never be their first choice, but it was calories, and they needed that almost as badly as they needed answers.

The Strykers practically fell on the bowls Lucas passed out to them at the far end of the long bar, space provided to them by a subtle telepathic nudge. The beer was stale and warm, but it was distilled enough that it didn't taste too acidic. Lucas watched them eat over his own bowl, dark blue eyes still hidden behind his glasses.

"Does your entire family consist of psions?" Threnody asked around a mouthful of food, ignoring how much it hurt to chew while she watched a heavily armed quad walk past their position. She hunched her shoulders a little and turned her face away from the four soldiers.

"We can trace our lineage back to the Border Wars" was all Lucas said.

"Fuck," Kerr muttered. "I'm going to take that as a yes."

"Why didn't you kill us?" Threnody wanted to know.

"I needed you alive," Lucas said. "A rebellion can't consist of just one person if everything is going to get accomplished."

He was looking at Threnody when he said it, the twist of his lips almost a smile. A flash of bleached-out violet eyes flickered through her mind again. The memory wasn't hers and it hurt after the operation she had just gone through. She reached up to press one hand against the side of her already aching head, as if she could press the pain way by sheer will alone.

"Stop it," Threnody said.

"Thren?" Quinton said, glancing between her and Lucas. When Lucas ignored him, Quinton reached out and gripped his partner's shoulder. "What's wrong?"

"I'm making a point," Lucas said.

Quinton glared at him. "Get out of her head."

Threnody grabbed hold of Quinton and kept him in his seat by digging her fingernails into his skin. Quinton didn't move. Lucas stayed in her mind.

"Aisling makes it difficult to believe in her." Lucas took another bite. *Always has, though the results are worth the effort.*

His telepathy flared up in their minds, reminding them that he was, and would remain, there in the back of their thoughts until he chose to let them go. If he ever did.

"Who?" Kerr finally asked for all of them.

"Not who," Lucas corrected. "What. She's the reason why I'm doing this. She's the reason why I need all of you."

Kerr frowned. "When do we meet her?"

"You don't."

"So, if you're not going to kill us, and we don't get to meet some girl, when are you going to mindwipe us?" Jason said, mouth twisting with disgust. "Or have you done it already?"

"As of right now, I need you all with minds and personalities intact. Though I'll have to find time to fix what your side never bothered to diagnose. You Strykers never cease to astound me with your stupidity. Two wrongly Classified psions active and in the field. You were both accidents waiting to happen."

"What are you talking about?" Threnody said. "And can you do it more quietly? Someone will hear you."

"Everyone's ignoring us because I'm telling them to. They won't remember a thing. What I'm talking about is the mess that are those two." Lucas took another bite of food, chewed, swallowed it, then pointed his fork at Jason and Kerr. "Or didn't you know both are dual psions and that Jason hasn't reached his full potential yet?"

Jason and Kerr stared at Lucas as if he were absolutely crazy. "You don't know what you're talking about," Kerr said flatly.

"Fuck you," Lucas said with a bark of laughter. "I'm a Class I triad psion. I know the human and not-so-human mind better than any Stryker ever will. I know what you are, Kerr, and I know what Jason should be."

"I'm a Class II telepath."

"Also a Class IX empath, something your side apparently missed when giving you your Class rank."

The look in Kerr's eyes was glacial. His tone was just as cold. "That's impossible. A Class IX is a baseline human ranking and I think I *know* my own mind."

"A Class IX still has traces of psion power. It's the gradient Class, the one where people are either mostly human or mostly not," Lucas explained in a tone one reserved for a small child. "Your telepathic strength overshadowed your secondary power by a huge margin, and there's no one Classed higher than you in the Strykers Syndicate to ferret out that channel of empathic power. *You* might not have known your empathy was there, but your *mind* did. Over the years, it tried to compensate for it. The result is that you're a fucking mess and your shields always fall because you can't gear mental shields solely toward one power when you've got two."

Lucas looked at Jason. "And you. A Class V telekinetic with natal shields that have never fallen. Didn't it *ever* occur to anyone in your Syndicate that our first shields need to fall in order to release our powers, or haven't you ever wondered about what your mind is still holding back?"

Jason recoiled from Lucas as if he'd been burned.

"Scientists can reverse engineer pretty much any technological equipment on the planet given enough approval from the government," Lucas said. "I can reverse engineer the process of the human mind. You need access to all your power, Jason. I just need to figure out how to make that happen."

"That's impossible," Jason said. "My shields won't break. People have tried."

"Not hard enough. If the government can rebuild space shuttles for a launch into space, then I sure as hell can find a way to break your shields."

"What are you talking about?" Threnody said sharply. "What launch?"

Lucas signaled the barkeep for another bowl of food. He had hardly touched his beer. "I suppose if I said that I wanted all of you to trust me, you wouldn't believe me."

"We're Strykers," Quinton said. "We don't trust anyone."

"Then you'll have to believe in ulterior motives, and not just my own." The barkeep placed the requested bowl in front of Lucas without really seeing him. Lucas mixed the food all together before starting in on it. "How good is your history?"

"Regarding what?" Kerr said.

"Everything. Specifically, what started the Border Wars."

"A launch command" was Quinton's sardonic answer as he took a swallow of his beer. "Several thousand of them."

Lucas smiled humorlessly. "Yes, but over what?"

"Who knows? Resources, probably. Everyone back then was fighting over what their neighbors had, same as they are right now."

"Depends on the neighbors. Countries blew each other up because no one could launch a nuke to Mars and hope it would hit the colony there."

All four Strykers gave Lucas their undivided attention at that announcement, staring at him with a mixture of disbelief and confusion in their eyes.

"What are you talking about?" Threnody asked slowly.

"It's not common knowledge. The government didn't want it to be." Lucas shrugged his opinion on that. "They couldn't wipe out the fact that the Border Wars happened because we're living with the aftermath still, but they were able to make people forget the reason *why* it all started. Everyone wanted an escape to Mars from a dying Earth, and in the end, no one got it. The world population was small enough after the war happened, and people were desperate enough, to accept the dictates of the World Court as the new government so long as they were saved. Funny how things haven't really changed."

"That's crazy," Jason said. "A colony on Mars? Our ancestors practically destroyed Earth over *Mars?*"

"Mars was in the process of being terraformed. The colony there was half a generation old already, according to the reports I've been able to find, and it was growing. They already had an energy source from giant solar panels in geosynchronous orbit around the planet and at two Lagrangian points between the sun and Mars. They were working on getting a viable atmosphere when the Border Wars happened. Communication died after that. So did supply runs by the ship that's still cold-docked on the other side of the moon."

"A ship," Quinton echoed.

"A *colony* ship, to be precise. The government calls it the Ark." Lucas glanced up at the night sky, which could just be seen past the tops of the buildings that surrounded them. "Bloody thing still has a functioning system, even after all these years. The government got it completely back online about twenty-five years ago. *That* was the mission of the World Court's first manned space launch."

"We lost the capability for space flight after the Border Wars. It killed off most of the population and nearly all the scientists and engineers," Threnody said. "The closest vehicle we've got to a space-faring one are atmospheric shuttles, and they've got limits. They're still earthbound and only registered humans have the right to use them."

Lucas cocked his head to the side as he stared at her. "Humans hate limits and the government hates the limits of this planet even more. The *government* never forgot what the Border Wars were fought over. The *government* never forgot about Mars and the colony there. Neither did my family. Why do you think the Serca Syndicate pushed for the Fifth Generation Act and the Registry? Not everyone can leave Earth for Mars, and not everyone will. The government is going to make sure of that. They're going to leave behind everyone who's not on the Registry, and I've got it on good authority that not everyone in the Registry is going to make it into space either."

The four Strykers were silent in the face of that confession, staring at Lucas and each other as they struggled to swallow a history that made too much sense for it not to be the truth.

"The government thinks Mars is the answer, a new beginning for the human race. *Just* the human race," Lucas said. "Psions aren't human, according to their laws. You Strykers are all going to be dead come the final launch date. Termination is scheduled for the week the space shuttles launch, and Ciari knows it. There's nothing she can do about it."

"They wouldn't kill all of us," Jason protested. "They need us."

Lucas gave him a pitying look. "The World Court isn't going to allow psions on Mars, which is ironic, considering the Serca Syndicate has had berths reserved since before the Fifth Generation Act was passed. And as you all know now, even if the government doesn't, the Warhounds belong to the Serca Syndicate."

Lucas's words tumbled through Threnody's mind as she struggled to make sense of what he was telling them. "Does Ciari know about you Sercas?" she asked.

"Every OIC does."

The betrayal was like a sucker punch to the gut. Threnody stared at Lucas, a bleakness in her eyes that hadn't been there seconds ago. "Then why doesn't she report what she knows to the World Court?"

"I would think you'd be happy that your former masters are going to get a rather bloody comeuppance."

"You're going to kill them." Threnody clenched her hands into fists.

"Everyone who gets on those space shuttles—if there even *are* space shuttles—your family and your Warhounds are going to kill them."

"Oh, there are space shuttles. Platforms of them above the wastewater in the Paris Basin. All those explosions in that area over the years? It hasn't been leftover unstable nukes going off like the government warns in the press. It's not space debris falling from the junk orbiting Earth. And, no, my family doesn't want to kill the humans. My family wants to rule them in the same fashion that the government has owned you Strykers."

"Is that supposed to make us happy?" Quinton asked. "Some half-assed attempt at revenge?"

Lucas leaned forward, staring at the Strykers over the rims of his dark glasses. "It's misguided, not revenge. The Border Wars created psions out of the mutated population left behind. All the humans in the Registry are clean of mutation and disease. No mutation means no psions, not the higher Classes at least. We can breed, but we breed low on the scale. Every psion a Class IV and higher has come straight from the unregistered human population. We go to Mars, we psions die as a people."

"Good riddance," Threnody said around numb lips. "It'll just be you Warhounds."

"You're forgetting the fact that you Strykers will be dead. We fucked up this planet, we've got an obligation to fix it if we want to own it. It's difficult, but not entirely impossible." Lucas pushed aside his empty bowl and half-finished beer. "The means of doing so is standing right there."

He was pointing at Jason as he spoke, focus sharp and unwavering. Jason just shook his head in denial. "You're crazy. Yeah, maybe parts of what you've said make sense, but we still don't know who fed you this information, and I don't know what you want with us. There are other Class V telekinetics out there, not just me."

"When I break your shields, you won't be a Class V," Lucas told him. "You're going to be a Class I if you're lucky, more likely a Class 0."

"Jason isn't a precog," Kerr said, standing a little straighter and putting himself between Lucas and his bonded partner. "Precogs are the only ones who get labeled a Class 0, and there hasn't been one on either your side or ours for over a hundred years. They're the rarities, not telekinetics."

"Microtelekinetic," Lucas corrected. "Power enough to work on the atomic level. And you're right. There haven't been all that many precogs because the use of their power burns out their brains after only a few years of living. I'm offering you a guaranteed way out of hell, it just comes with a price. Question is, are you willing to pay it this time in order to save everyone and not just the registered elite?"

Threnody opened her mouth to answer him when she felt the hard edge of a gun barrel press against her spine. "Running away, dog?" a man's voice growled. She glanced over her shoulder and caught a glimpse of the quad that had passed them earlier, their faces obscured by protective helmets.

Three other weapons were aimed in their direction, and the people at the bar scattered, leaving a swath of empty space around the group. Threnody focused her attention on Lucas.

"I thought you said they couldn't find us," she said.

Lucas waved a hand at the soldiers. "Those are quads, not Warhounds, which means it's the government who located you. Human effort, not psionic. Facial-recognition software is embedded in the security feeds around here and I can't affect machines with my power."

Threnody glared at him. "You knew they'd find us."

"I'm making a point, Threnody. Honestly, did you really think the government was just going to let you *go*?"

None of them got a chance to answer as the quad pulled the triggers on their guns, the bright flare of energy darts striking against Lucas's telekinetic shield, not flesh. The blasts flared dangerously wide and ricocheted backward to hit the soldiers and whoever was still stupid enough to be sticking around, knocking them to the ground. Everyone who had been hit screamed, their voices mingling with the sudden sound of alarm. One of the quad members had tripped the security system for reinforcements.

Casting about for a distraction, Lucas poured his power into the minds of the people around them, starting a riot. Then he telekinetically tossed the members of the quad directly into the path of the suddenly rampaging crowd.

His attention, for the most part, was still focused on the former Strykers.

Lucas pulled the glasses off his face, dark blue eyes bright and fierce with something that might be madness. "This is your one and only chance."

"A bit of an extremist, aren't you?" Threnody said as she shoved away from the side of the bar.

"More of an opportunist." Lucas smiled again, showing all his teeth. "Yes or no?"

She thought about what Lucas had said, they all did. For a vital few seconds, they weighed the words of a Warhound against the edicts of their government, and all of them came away with the same realization.

None of them wanted to die a slave.

"Get us out of here," Kerr said as the noise of people fighting, of people dying, mingled with the shrill alarm of unrest that echoed up and down the street, summoning quad reinforcement.

Lucas teleported out of London, pulling them along with his vast telekinetic strength into the unknown.

[NINE]

AUGUST 2379
TORONTO, CANADA

News of the termination spread quickly through the Stryker ranks. Three days since the two Stryker teams had gone missing, and the World Court hadn't thought anything about giving the kill order. The OIC of the Strykers Syndicate had no choice but to obey. That Ciari became the focus of everyone's fear and hatred was nothing new. That she let herself feel it? *That* was new.

"It's terribly illegal, I know, to want to murder him," Ciari said tiredly, thinking about Erik. "But it would make me feel better."

"You don't like to feel," Jael said as she looked at where Ciari stood in front of a wall filled with vidscreens all streaming different programs in the OIC's office. "You prove that fact over and over again. Why are you choosing today to keep your shields down?"

Jael was angry. It was in the burr of her voice, pressing against the power of Ciari's mind, difficult to ignore. She had every right to be, Ciari thought as her eyes tracked over the dozen or so news streams before her. Every right, and then some. It still didn't mean anything to her despite her empathetic power.

"I knew he would ask for their deaths," Ciari said. "Threnody made too many mistakes during the last few missions. She was on the watch list after Madrid and the botched transfer."

"She and the other teams working with her still got back the stolen crude oil, got it off the trucks, back onto the train, and on its way back to the processing plant in Andorra."

"They lost half of it."

"They still salvaged the rest."

"Doesn't matter. It was still enough of a commotion that the press got wind of it and the government had to do some heavy spin duty to make them look the other way. Propaganda is all well and good, but the government doesn't control *every* news stream."

Jael shook her head, disgust making her voice sharper than usual. "You set Threnody up for failure with this current mission. That blip on the grid turned out to be a Class I triad psion—a rarity—and there's no one in our ranks capable of handling someone like that; not and actually survive the encounter intact."

"The target never previously read as a Class I in all the time we tracked it. It never read as Lucas Serca."

"That's a piss-fucking-poor excuse if I've ever heard one and I've heard many. You *knew* the target had to be dangerous if none of us could pin it down."

Ciari finally turned to face her subordinate, gaze cool. "Everyone in this world is dangerous to someone, Jael. We needed what Threnody could possibly get us, suicide mission or not."

"And what would that be other than two dead teams?"

"A chance. Keiko brought back human bodies from Russia carrying neurotrackers assigned to the missing four."

"I know. I did the autopsies, remember? Best-case scenario is that our Strykers were killed elsewhere, which is better than being tortured. Worst-case scenario is that they're hostages of a rogue Class I triad psion, either being tortured or reprogrammed. You pick."

Over the decades, the Sercas had mastered the skill of hiding their presence on bioscanners and the mental grid, able to project themselves as something they weren't when they had to, which meant their ability to murder unsuspecting Strykers made them formidable enemies. They had passed on that skill to every psion that joined their ranks as a War-hound who had the power to uphold the charade. Ciari had no way of knowing if Lucas Serca was still within the Slums of the Angels or even in Russia. She had no way to confirm if her Strykers were truly dead. The Strykers in the field were still searching in America and Russia for answers, as well as scouring London as discreetly as they could since the government had contacted them about the riot. It was anyone's guess if they would ever know the truth.

"Why let this happen, Ciari?" Jael asked quietly from behind her. "You have the means to work around problems like this. If we had coordinated with Nathan before this happened—"

"No." Ciari cut her off. "We had no other choice."

"I think you're lying."

Ciari let out a low, tired chuckle and carefully raised her shields. "You think?"

"All right, I *know* you're lying." Jael stepped up beside Ciari and looked at her instead of the vidscreens. "You usually appeal every kill order handed down to you, just to have it on record, and it takes a while. It doesn't change a thing—it never has and never will—but it's a sick tradition every OIC has kept. You didn't with these four. Why change the way you do things now?"

Ciari kept quiet long enough that Jael knew she wouldn't get an answer. Letting out a frustrated sigh, Jael turned away from the other woman and headed for the door.

"I'll add their names to our list of the dead," Jael said.

"Don't." Ciari glanced over her shoulder. "Not yet."

"They deserve that much, if not more."

"I know. I'm not saying they don't, but if you put their names on that list, we close out their lives. We can't do that until we've got something to report to the World Court."

"Give us our fucking right to *grieve,* Ciari."

"You only get that right when we've got bodies to burn, and even then only with the government's say-so. They're alive, Jael, and we need to find them. Until we do, they will be listed as rogue status in our records and that won't change. It *can't* change, do you understand me?"

"Perfectly," Jael bit out.

"Good."

Jael strode out of the office, leaving Ciari alone with her thoughts and the twenty-four-hour news stream. Rubbing at the back of her neck, she sighed and turned away from the vidscreens. Retreating to her desk, Ciari dug through the data chips that cluttered one corner, finally finding the one she needed for her next meeting. In her searching, one fell off the desk, and she bent to retrieve it.

Holding it between two fingers, Ciari peered at each side of the data chip. It wasn't shaped like the government chips that they normally used. Clear, with no file number of any sort written on the outside, it was unusual in its blankness. She was never sure when these particular data chips would appear on her desk, but she never questioned their arrival. She'd been getting these data chips at intermittent intervals over the last five years. They always made for a better read than any orders the government sent her.

She put it in her pocket.

Hours later, when she found the time to read the information it held, on a datapad that wasn't synced to any system or acknowledged by the grid, the heavily encrypted message would only be two sentences long: *You know that chance I took? It's paying off.*

The encrypted reply she saved to it was even shorter: *Good.*

In the morning, the data chip was gone from her desk. Ciari didn't question that, either.

TEN

AUGUST 2379

SAPPORO, JAPAN

There was a phrase in this country's language for what Nathan was doing: *nemawashi*. Formally confirming what had informally been proposed, even if it was still all under the table until the press report went out. Corporate mergers never really came as a surprise to the public. The reason behind every single one was always neatly detailed for anyone to read, though it was the oral agreements that really mattered. Those were the deals that were never recorded. Every businessman and woman seated around the long conference table had come for just such a promise. Nathan Serca's word was better than that of most. His family had spent decades making sure that they were indispensable to the world's needs. This was no different.

Jin Li stepped into the windowless conference room, wearing a severe business suit that wouldn't hamper his movements at all, and a single gun on his hip. Casing the room with a glance over the top of his dark glasses, he pulled a small gray sphere out of his pocket and walked over to the only empty seat at the long table. He pressed two buttons on the side of the sphere, activating it. A green light blinked on and the jamming sequence cut off all vidfeed coming from the security points built into the wall and all recording devices scattered around the table.

"We said no records," Jin Li said, voice flat and dangerous as Nathan finally stepped into the conference room.

"Apologies," said Sydney Athe, the venerable old man rising to his feet with the use of a heavy, ornate cane. "This room is set automatically for recording every time it's in use. I did not think to check that it had been deactivated."

97

Nathan offered the head of the Athe Syndicate a polite smile as the man's grandson and successor, Elion Athe, stood to help his grandfather sit back down.

The Athe Syndicate was much like the Serca Syndicate in its survival of the Border Wars to become what it was today. The family had been trapped in Sapporo on a business trip during that horrific time, and of all the islands that belonged to Japan, only Hokkaidō had managed to survive partly intact. The Athe family had made themselves indispensable to the survivors of the country and learned to thrive. Elion's father, Travis, was a member of the World Court, and for that alone they would have been allowed into the Registry. Additionally, their genetics were clean, which was a bonus, and their success in aeronautics and space science was worth the delicate dance the Serca family had done with the Athe Syndicate for the past four generations.

"Ladies, gentlemen," Nathan began as he took his seat at the head of the conference table. "Mistakes happen. Just be aware that I do not tolerate them more than once. Our business tonight is far too important to allow our final decisions to fall into outside hands. None of us desires the spotlight for this little addendum of our merger."

Sydney nodded agreement. "The announcement is set to hit the news in the morning. The Athe Syndicate will become a subsidiary of the Serca Syndicate, but I will retain the position as CEO with the understanding that all final decisions will be left up to you, as we agreed."

"As it should be, for what we've offered you," Nathan said. "The additional berths on the Ark we've agreed to sell you means that when the time comes, you will support us on Mars."

"Of course," Sydney said, looking Nathan straight in the eye when no one else would. It wasn't the Japanese way to get straight to the point, but Sydney still retained some of the mannerisms of his Western ancestors. "A deal is a deal, Nathan. My family will be whatever you need us to be, so long as you take us with you."

It was funny how desperation could make anyone willing to sell his soul. Nathan spread his hands over the datapad he had brought with him, keying in his biometrics to open it. Files appeared beneath his fingertips and he tapped at the only one he needed. The executed merger agreement filled his screen, and Nathan perused all the signatures that had brought him here.

"There will be a meeting for all the subsidiaries of the Serca Syndicate at the beginning of September. Keep your calendars clear. I will send you the confirmed date once I've met again with the World Court." Nathan looked up, his gaze sweeping across the table, capturing everyone's eyes. "I expect the transfer to run smoothly."

"Do you anticipate any difficulties?" Elion asked, his green eyes startlingly odd in a face whose features were predominantly Japanese.

"I plan for all possible avenues, which means you will be ready. If you are not, you forfeit the seats you asked for and I will sell them to someone else. Whoever you hope to bring with you will be left behind. As you know, there are only so many seats available, and my Syndicate is in control of at least half. Not every registered human is going to be on those ships."

"But enough will," Sydney said. "And you are more than capable of keeping everyone in line."

Nathan's smile was indulgent. "Always."

Sydney banged his cane down once on the floor, nodding at those who worked for him. "Leave us. You have your assurances."

All the men and women around the table except Elion got to their feet and bowed, first to Sydney, then to Nathan, before filing out past Jin Li. None of them bothered to hide their disgust for Nathan's bodyguard, and it had little to do with his slouching against the wall.

During the Border Wars, China had fared worse than most countries outside of Africa and the Middle East. Already saddled with a near impossible population density living off hugely strained natural resources and with a toxicity level that was already dangerous before the first bomb fell, China spiraled into devastation faster than most other countries. Like the rest of the world, it wasn't the radiation poisoning that killed off most of the population. That would be the starvation, the disease, and the mass deaths in the countryside that surrounded the craters most major cities had become.

The survivors had no choice but to relocate, and the Chinese numbered more than their neighbors, even after the last bomb fell. Southeastern

Asia still had pockets of ethnic minorities from the countries they had once been, but they were ruled by the Chinese now. Japan had patrolled the East China Sea for over 150 years, refusing any and all refugees looking for port that came out of what China had become. No love was lost between the two countries and Jin Li knew it.

Jin Li smiled at every person who walked out the door, then spat on the floor behind the heels of the last woman out. The door slid shut before any of them could voice their anger.

"Your children have better manners than your guard," Elion said coolly as he eyed Jin Li from where he sat.

"Jin Li has his uses, or don't you remember the last time we came calling?" Nathan arched one pale eyebrow. Elion swallowed his anger with appropriate swiftness as he recalled the businessman whom Jin Li had summarily executed after Nathan discovered his treachery. Corporate spies were annoying, and that one hadn't been worth the effort of reprogramming.

"I see that you do," Nathan said. "It's always refreshing to deal with people who know when to keep their mouths shut."

"What more do you require from us?" Sydney said slowly.

Nathan leaned back in his chair and touched the screen of his datapad with one finger. Another list, this one detailing every known city and company Lucas had hit in the past two years. The Athe Syndicate numbered high on that list, beneath all the Serca-owned branches his son had gone to.

"Your Syndicate built the satellites that the World Court sent out fifty years ago to Mars," Nathan said. "I want you to go through your security records for the past two years and do a facial recognition search. You will be looking for Lucas."

Sydney frowned. "For what reason?"

"Because we psions cannot hide from machines and I want to know what he was searching for."

"Why would your son have broken into our Syndicate?" Elion asked.

"Lucas is no longer my son."

This telling response caused Elion and Sydney to share a brief, sharp glance. Nathan knew what they were thinking, and he allowed them to think it. This was a calculated dispersal of information, seeds that needed to be sown. Nathan's own mother had disclosed the Serca family's true nature to the heads of the Athe family years and years ago to make them think that the Sercas needed them. Sometimes secrets were the best bargaining chips when used appropriately.

"Two years of security feed," Sydney said. "Give us a week to do a thorough review of all our holdings. I will send Elion in person to London with the results once we have them."

"That is acceptable." Nathan pushed himself to his feet. "The launch date may be moved up, depending on certain timetables that the World Court is relying on. If it does, you and your family will personally be brought to London. I can promise you that."

"I thank you."

"I don't do it out of need or some sense of generosity." Nathan offered Sydney a mocking smile. "I do it because I can. Your family is useful. Continue to be useful and maybe you will survive another generation."

The men Nathan left behind were smart enough to heed this warning. Their ability to bend was part of the reason why Nathan had chosen to bring them under Serca control through this merger and why Nathan kept them there. The Athes had always been useful to someone.

Jin Li followed Nathan out of the conference room and down the ornately decorated hallway of the Athe Syndicate's executive suite. A security guard bowed as they stepped into a lift that went to the roof, where their shuttle sat on the landing platform, engines on standby and guarded by Gideon.

"You're not supposed to be here," Nathan said pointedly to his son after Nathan and Jin Li climbed into the shuttle beneath the morning sunlight.

"No one saw me arrive when I teleported into your shuttle," Gideon assured him. "And this needed to be reported in person."

"I take it you finally have what I told you to find?" Nathan shook his head as he sat down in his seat and buckled on the harness. "Three days late."

"I wanted to be sure." Gideon took a seat opposite Nathan and hooked himself into the harness there. "I found something of interest."

Nathan narrowed his eyes. "Get to the point."

"You asked about the Strykers that Lucas picked up out of the Slums." Gideon pulled a data chip from his shirt pocket and passed it over to Nathan telekinetically. "Jin Li fought two of them in Johannesburg thirty-four days prior to the skirmish in the Slums. Threnody Corwin is a Class III electrokinetic. Her partner, Quinton Martinez, is a Class III pyrokinetic."

"That's not unusual."

"She ordered her partner and the teams she commanded in Johannesburg not to pursue Jin Li when he escaped with the children we had targeted at the school there."

"Occasionally Strykers *do* think, Gideon," Nathan said as he uploaded the data chip on his datapad. "They were outmatched in that venture and they knew it."

"Maybe. Those two joined up with a second team for the mission in the Slums. You'll see on that data chip that our records for the Strykers Syndicate's only Class II telepath, Kerr MacDougal, aren't very informative."

"He's dysfunctional. We discovered that when he was first put in the field."

"His partner, Jason Garret, is an anomaly."

"A Class V telekinetic is nothing out of the ordinary."

"Samantha fought him, sir. It was the first time she's faced off against those two. She said the telekinetic had mental shields that were impervious to her strongest telepathic strike."

Nathan looked up from the information on his screen. "Samantha is capable of getting through most shielding. I taught her myself. A Class V of any kind of psion should have been relatively easy."

Gideon shrugged, having to raise his voice over the sound of the engines starting up in order to be heard. "I asked her about it. She said his shields wouldn't even crack. She bruised his mind, but she couldn't break his defenses. And there was something else. The shields? They weren't like any that Samantha's ever felt before."

Nathan scrolled through the brief file they had on Jason Garret before casting his telepathy outward across the world for his daughter's mind.

Her psi signature sparked brightly above all the rest of the humans on the mental grid, and he sank into her thoughts with ease.

This telekinetic you fought in the Slums, he said. *What was so different about his shields?*

Samantha didn't hesitate in answering. *They were anchored in a way I've never seen before. They went deeper than I thought shields could ever go.*

Show me.

Samantha opened up her memories to his perusal, letting him dig again through those moments in the Slums where she had attempted to break into the telekinetic's mind. This time he took more than just her memories, he took her thoughts, her reasoning at the time of the fight. Nathan drew back after a few seconds, faint surprise coloring his thoughts.

Nathan's reaction was enough for Samantha to say, *Sir?*

That doesn't make any sense.

What doesn't?

Those shields you tried to break. They're natal shields.

Samantha's confusion matched his own, but Nathan didn't let her sense it. *That's impossible. How can he access his power if his natal shields are still standing?*

How indeed?

Nathan dropped the psi link, pulling back into his own mind. He opened his eyes, meeting his son's gaze. Gideon was waiting patiently for whatever order would come his way. Gideon waited, when Lucas would already have been suggesting action. Nathan wished Gideon's ability to know and obey his betters had bred true in Lucas.

Nathan had raised his children under the personal bylaws that governed the Serca family, following a long tradition of grooming the next generation for the fight for power. Psions never lived all that long, and the Serca Syndicate's goals needed to be maintained over generations. Nathan had survived longer than most psions only because he'd never used his power enough for it to kill him—yet. Nathan's decision to use his children first before he used his own powers had come at the direct order of his mother, Marcheline, when she had ordered him to risk the next generation for a reason she had never explained. His mother had been a singularly manipulative woman who died in her forties. No love had been lost between Nathan and his mother. Only hate was left between himself and his children.

"I want Lucas found," Nathan said. "I want him brought back to me before autumn, as well as the Strykers he took, if they're still with him and alive."

"Why the Strykers?"

"Lucas wanted them. I want whatever Lucas has."

The shuttle had reached that high cruising altitude where the sky was dark with the edge of space above and the clouds were ugly wisps below them. Nathan undid the straps of his harness and got to his feet.

"Return to London without me," he said, before teleporting away.

[ELEVEN]

AUGUST 2379

THE HAGUE, THE NETHERLANDS

You're late."

The aggravated tone of Sharra Gervais's voice floated down the hallway of their bunker suite. Erik looked up from where he stood in the foyer, shrugging out of his robes of office. His wife walked toward him with a glass of expensive wine in her hand, the stiletto heels of her shoes sinking into the plush carpeting that lay atop the hard metal floor of their home. Sharra was tall, blond, and blue-eyed, a Nordic beauty with her name in the Registry and a ring on her finger given to her by one of the most powerful men in the world. Any man in his right mind would have loved her.

"It can't be helped," Erik said as hung his robes in the wide closet by the front blast doors. The small bunker city carved below the rubble above was still more lived-in than any other building aboveground. By law, the members of the World Court had to reside in the safety of these underground hallways and homes.

"You say that every time. Pick another excuse." Sharra glared at him over the rim of her wineglass. Lipstick had transferred a perfect imprint of her mouth to the delicate, clear glass. The color looked like waxy crayon, which meant this was not her first, second, or even third glass of wine.

Erik stepped closer to kiss Sharra on the cheek. He hated the taste of her drunk on his tongue.

"I take it Lillian has already gone to bed?" he said.

"It's midnight. Even the bunker guards have gone to bed except for a skeleton crew." Sharra spun on her heels and left him where he stood for the mess the dining room had become.

When Erik finally joined her there, he saw that the ribbons and balloons from the party were still up, the half-eaten cake still fresh beneath the preservation cover, and the wrappings from all the presents scattered across the floor. Sharra sat her wineglass down on the table and leaned her weight against the wooden edge of it.

"I asked for one thing from you, Erik," she said in a low voice. "Just one."

"I give what I can. You know that." Erik looked around at the remains of his daughter's birthday party and felt no regret for missing it. He'd had other matters to attend to. "Lillian is young. She'll hardly remember I wasn't here."

"Lillian is *five,* you son of a bitch," Sharra snarled. "She'll remember that her father wasn't here, just like you weren't there for the other four."

"She's a *child,* Sharra." The irritation in Erik's voice was thick after a sixteen-hour workday. "I have no use for children until they're old enough to understand what it is I expect from them."

The laughter that came out of his wife's mouth was strained. "The sad thing is that she has use for *you,* Erik. You're her father. At least one day this year, couldn't you have bothered to *act* like it?"

The headache that had been pounding through his skull since before noon became worse at the shrill tone in his wife's voice.

"I'm not doing this," Erik told her as he walked out of the room. "I've had a full schedule today and it's only going to be worse tomorrow as we run down the clock to the launch. You're impossible to reason with when you're like this."

He left her standing alone in the dining room, with its bright lights and carefully chosen decorations; with the mess on the floor and the mess in her head and tears of frustration in her eyes. She was forty-three years old with the face and body of someone half her age. She should have been *enough,* Sharra thought as she picked up her wineglass and drained it in two quick, long swallows. She should have been more than enough to hold his attention.

Sharra knew Erik wasn't cheating on her. The press would have a field day with that story, but more than the threat of social humiliation for Erik, she *knew* he didn't have the desire to cheat on her with another woman. She'd paid enough for that promise; she just hadn't seen all those years ago that politics was a bed her husband would wallow in more than her own.

"Mama?"

Sharra set the wineglass down and carefully wiped at her eyes with a fingertip. She blinked back the tears, steadied herself despite the alcohol in her system, and turned to face her daughter, pasting a smile on her face that not even the best politician could have seen through for the lie it truly was.

Lillian was a tiny slip of a thing, with her mother's wide blue eyes and her father's dark hair. Wrapped up in her favorite blanket, with her small feet peeking out beneath her nightgown, she was hopeful in the way that only children could be in this world, before they learned their history. The ones who had their names in the Registry since birth, clean air, clean water, and a future paid in full.

"Sweetie, you should be asleep," Sharra said as she carefully bent down to pick up her daughter. "It's very late and the party has been over for hours."

"I thought I heard Daddy."

The taste of wine on Sharra's tongue turned rancid as she looked into her daughter's hopeful eyes. Cradling her close, Sharra walked on surprisingly steady feet through the hallways of their large living quarters, carrying her daughter back to her bedroom.

"Your daddy's still at work," Sharra lied. "I'll send him in to say goodnight when he finally gets home."

"Oh."

The sound of disappointment was thick in the little girl's voice, and Sharra gave her an extrahard hug before tucking Lillian back into the soft bed, which was still warm from when she'd crawled out of it. Sitting beside her, Sharra smoothed her daughter's hair out of her eyes and smiled down at the little girl.

"In the morning, I'll make you breakfast. But only if you go to sleep."

"Pancakes?" the girl asked, knowing she usually got her way.

"Pancakes. With chocolate chips." An expensive dish, about as expensive as the wine Sharra drank. Cacao plants were grown in only one Sky-Farms cluster somewhere in Brazil. Only the very rich in the Registry had ever tasted chocolate. Lillian had a terrible sweet tooth.

Lillian smiled up at her mother, her small teeth shiny and white in the light coming from the hallway. Then the girl squeezed her eyes shut and flopped on her side, pretend snores coming out of her mouth. Sharra leaned down and pressed a kiss to her daughter's cheek, careful not to breathe. She didn't want her daughter knowing what a drunkard her mother was, not yet at least.

She left Lillian's room, but didn't immediately retreat to the one she shared with Erik. Half a bottle of wine left in the kitchen still needed to be finished. Waste wasn't tolerated, even in the households of registered humans. When she finally made it to the kitchen, she found the wine being poured down the sink.

Sharra jerked to a shaky halt on her high heels as she glared at the man standing in the kitchen. In her drunken state, he could have been a hallucination, but even when she was sober, he'd always been real, even when she wished he weren't.

"*What* are you doing here?" she demanded in a low, frantic voice.

"Erik won't wake up," Nathan said as he set aside the empty wine bottle and turned to look at her. "He never does when I'm here."

"You don't *know* that."

"When I put someone under, they *stay* under, Sharra." Nathan came over to her and wrapped a hand around her upper arm, guiding her with learned politeness to the nearest seat. Stiff with panic and fear, Sharra followed like a wooden puppet and sank into the chair. "You need something a little stronger than wine."

A small crystal tumbler appeared on the table in front of her. An eye-blink later and a bottle of aged Scotch joined it. Sharra stared at both as if they were bombs.

She swallowed back bile. "What do you want?"

"I got what I wanted from you years ago." Nathan smiled at her, the expression as cold as his voice. "Right now, I'm more interested in what Lucas wants from you, if he wants anything at all."

"I don't speak to your children, Nathan."

"They're half yours, or don't you remember what it cost to get where you are today?"

Sharra closed her eyes, the wine in her stomach souring into something that wanted to crawl up her throat. A woman of her stature, with a life lived on a mountain of lies. A woman with her name in the Registry, a ring on her finger, and five children to her name. She didn't care about Nathan's. She only cared about her daughter.

That didn't mean her children wouldn't come looking for her, and Nathan knew it.

"He hasn't been here," Sharra said, opening her eyes. "Why would he? I've nothing he could possibly want."

They had their father's eyes, but her straight nose, shades of their blond hair. The rest was all a mixture of DNA—hers and Nathan's, and whatever was in her human genome that could make Nathan's psionic attributes breed true. She was useful, and Sharra knew from personal, painful experience that being useful was the only way to survive. Her current position—her marriage, her *human daughter*—were the results of producing four embryos for the Serca family. In return, she'd been promised certain survival.

Nathan stared at her from where he stood, tall and perfect in his business suit, with power at his fingertips that Erik could never hope to harness. Psion power that no one ever saw because Nathan was a master at being just human enough that no one looked beyond the veneer.

"I've kept your secrets," Sharra whispered bitterly.

"Because you can't speak a word of them to anyone. We made sure of that," Nathan said. "You will notify me if Lucas comes calling. I will know if you don't."

Sharra reached up instinctively to touch the side of her head, thinking of the bioware net that spanned the entirety of her brain and how fucking *useless* it was in the face of psionic power.

Nathan's smile was slow and dangerous as he noticed the motion of her hand. "When has that ever stopped me before?"

It hadn't, and the systems that monitored the bioware nets for those on or related to those on the World Court never showed psionic interference. Nathan and his Warhounds were amazingly adept at circumventing human technology when they needed to.

"Why don't you simply kill us all?" Sharra asked, the alcohol in her system making her braver than she could ever be sober.

Nathan let his fingers stroke through her hair and Sharra drew in a strangled breath.

"Humans live long enough to be useful" was Nathan's calm answer. "Our one evolutionary shortcoming is your gain."

"You've lived nearly two lifetimes, Nathan."

"Yes. Only because I'm killing our children in order to do so, but that isn't a guaranteed cure. If I used my power even half as much as I order them to use theirs, I would be dead. And, oh, you would enjoy that, wouldn't you, Sharra?" Nathan's hands settled heavily on her shoulders, a weight that always pulled at her. "I will live long enough to see Mars Colony. I will live long enough to rule there in the open instead of here behind closed doors. I want that new world, not this mess our ancestors left us. I deserve better than that."

Sharra closed her eyes and breathed through her nose. "I hope to God you die out in space."

Nathan laughed, the sound low and amused, his breath blowing over the shell of her ear. "I want the latest launch information by the end of the week."

"I don't know if I can get that for you."

"Then I suggest you find a way, as you've done all the times before, or your daughter will grow up without a mother. Or perhaps you will grow old without her." He squeezed her shoulders. It felt as if he squeezed the life out of her. "When I tampered with Erik's mind all those years ago to make sure he saw you and only you as a possibility for his wife, you knew the cost of that deal."

She didn't say, *Erik doesn't love me.* She didn't need to. Nathan picked the thought straight out of her mind with an ease that still frightened her, even after all these years of him doing it.

"I never promised you something as useless as love. You got safety. I get information. You have a week." He pulled his hands away from her and she could breathe again. "Good-bye, Sharra."

He disappeared in that disturbingly alien way that teleportation encompassed. Sharra shivered, suddenly cold, and hunched over in her seat. Pressing hands that shook to her mouth, she breathed slowly, trying desperately not to get sick there on her kitchen floor.

In the end, she chose Scotch over sleep, Nathan over her husband, because for all the vows they'd spoken at their wedding, she owed Nathan everything and Erik only the appearance of fidelity.

[TWELVE]

AUGUST 2379

TARRAGONA, SPAIN

Spain was a wasteland cut apart by deadzones and desertification that had swallowed half the country over a century ago. Madrid was a crater, bombed over and over again during the Border Wars, like most of the major and not so major European cities. Barcelona, east of Tarragona on the Iberian Peninsula, was nothing more than a wide bay of water, the newest coastline addition to the Mediterranean Sea.

Tarragona was half-underground to escape the radiation taint that fallout had spread across the country during the Border Wars. Nuclear winter had lowered the planet's overall temperature, but only for a short time. Warmth eventually returned, and with it, massive, deadly storms that swept periodically over the world: hurricanes and tornadoes, sandstorms and derechos, monsoons and whiteout blizzards. Pollution was still a problem, climate change had altered the region even before society nearly blew itself up, and Tarragona had no city towers for registered humans, only segregated bunkers.

The military-grade shuttle flew just above the low-hanging cloud cover in the night sky, lights off, stealth mode up and running. The engines were barely a hum in Samantha's bones as she peered over the pilot's shoulder through the flight-deck windshields. A hologrid shone in the air between the pilot and the navigator, a ground map with precise details of the maglev train gunning toward Spain's largest surviving city. With a population around 146,000, Tarragona was second only to London in population in Western Europe.

"Speed?" Samantha said.

"Two hundred twenty and decreasing," the pilot said as he lightly adjusted his grip on the stick. "Your orders?"

Samantha pushed away from the seat. "Descend. We'll take it from here."

The pilot nodded, attention already focused on the route his navigator was building. Samantha walked back into the cargo bay of the shuttle, letting the hatch close and seal shut behind her. She steadied herself as she felt the shuttle beginning to change its angle of flight for the descent, feeling a telekinetic touch brace her body and give her additional support. She nodded her thanks to the Warhound who had reached out to her.

"We're descending," she told everyone in the cargo bay. "Telekinetics, be ready for assault. Telepaths, you're with me in merge."

"How many Strykers do you think are down there?" Genevieve asked as she checked the clip in her assault rifle and slung the strap across her shoulder, bracing the weapon against her bent legs. The twenty-five-year-old

Class III telekinetic was the best train hijacker in the Warhound ranks. Samantha still wished she had her twin by her side.

"Several teams, at the very least." Samantha dragged herself back to her assigned seat and strapped into her harness. "Fuel transport trains always have heavy defenses."

"Hungry," Kristen said from beside her. The empath was strapped into her harness, fingers tapping out a soft rhythm against the armrests of her seat.

"Not yet." Samantha pressed her power against her sister's mind, skimming it over those jagged broken shields. "You feed on my say-so."

"Sure, Sammy-girl." Kristen's smile got so wide that the corners of her mouth cracked and bled. "On your say-so."

Which, in Kristen's demented way of thinking, could be whenever Samantha opened her mouth or 'pathed out an order. Samantha offered her sister a sharp look and a warning telepathic probe before sliding out of Kristen's mind.

It had taken five days to track the oil shipments coming through the Suez Canal to the Mediterranean Sea and up to Europe's southern shores. Previous generations had nearly depleted the Middle East oil supplies, but the regional governments in control at the time had placed trade restrictions on exports to save some of the fossil fuel for their own people. What the World Court had slowly been siphoning out of the surviving storage bunkers wasn't headed anywhere except to the Paris Basin, to be transported to Mars, or so they thought.

Samantha clenched her hands into fists until her knuckles popped. Warhounds had stolen a quarter of those shipments over the past thirty years, ransoming it back to the government at ridiculously high prices. Her grandmother—may Marcheline's sadistic soul never rest—had begun the credit buildup that the Warhounds would need for their bottom line once they got off-planet, and Nathan was continuing that effort. They would need that monetary leverage when all the functioning parts of society were transplanted to someplace better. Humanity, what they would allow of it into space, was worth its weight in gold.

The shuttle picked up speed as it descended. Samantha pushed those thoughts aside and focused on the scene around her. Genevieve and her telekinetics were out of their seats, held stable in the shuttle's unsteady course by their own power as they pulled on the oxygen helmets attached to the small tanks buckled to their backs. They didn't need safety lines, not when they had the option of teleportation and the anchoring grasp of telekinesis. The six telekinetics ranged from a Class V to a Class III. More than enough telekinetic power to grab those fuel tanks off the back of the train and 'port them out of human reach.

The only problem with that plan, Samantha mused as the shuttle took evasive maneuvers against ground-to-air missiles, was that the humans employed Strykers.

Open the cargo doors, Samantha ordered.

Wind whipped through the interior of the shuttle as hydraulics opened the rear cargo doors, the cabin pressure falling. The telekinetics were lined up in pairs at the very edge, gravity and air pulling at their limbs. Genevieve didn't wait for Samantha's order; she had more experience than Samantha at leading these kinds of missions. The telekinetics wrapped themselves in their power and jumped out of the shuttle, dropping in a controlled fall toward the speeding train below.

Samantha closed her eyes, struggling to breathe; easier to concentrate in darkness than the brightness of the shuttle. The roaring of the wind faded as the cargo doors closed back up, the pressure equalizing again. Samantha dropped her shields, slid her power into the minds of her fellow Warhounds, and started to build the merge.

This was something that the Strykers still didn't know how to duplicate, or simply weren't allowed to learn. The layered strength that came with three telepathic minds coming together meant that they had that much more power to draw from. Samantha took up the apex position in the merge and sent their minds skimming over the mental grid toward the bright spots that burned like fire.

"Leaving me out in the cold," Kristen murmured from beside her.

Samantha felt her sister's bitten-down nails dig into the skin of her left wrist. She ignored the pain that skittered up her arm, the majority of it empathically created.

Ready to break, Samantha said into Genevieve's mind, her mental voice echoed by the other three in the merge.

Genevieve's answer was calm. *Missiles are diverted.*

Samantha couldn't hear the explosions on the ground below; didn't need to. She could hear the panic in the human thoughts of the workers that rode the train as clearly as if she were standing in the cars with them. Samantha felt her mouth curve into a smile, but it was a distant expression.

The merge spread like a net across the mental grid where they fought, telepathic power pressing down like a heavy load onto the Stryker and human minds below. Only when the Warhounds had their positions set did Samantha drop most of her shields, letting her telepathy ram into the minds they had surrounded.

The government had opted for a full squad of Strykers, eight teams, at a pair apiece. Sixteen Strykers of varied types, varied Classes, but none of them could counter a merge backed by her Class II strength. They didn't have the resources available to them, just their orders, and those would get them killed tonight. They would still go down fighting.

Shit, Samantha said, tapping into Genevieve's thoughts. *They're going to blow the train.*

Getting desperate, Genevieve replied. *That's a fucking waste of perfectly good oil. We're working on getting a grip on the weight. We need a few more minutes.*

She was asking Samantha to buy them time.

Samantha did one better.

She reached with the strength of the merge for Kristen's mind, her sister greedily reaching back. The jagged, deep holes in the empath's power bit into Samantha's mind with a viciousness that made her physically flinch. Kristen's mind was a starved thing, twisted into swollen knots as her empathic power fed on itself in a continuous state of desperate survival. Samantha shunted Kristen's mind through the merge, beneath their shields, the other telepaths helping her to control Kristen's descent, as they forced the girl to obey their chosen course of action.

The merged telepathic strike, braced by Kristen's malignant empathic power, broke through the Strykers' defenses with a ferocity that left two Strykers dying immediately of critical psi shock. The rest didn't have the ability to defend against Kristen's need to feed, and the teen had never discriminated between the minds of registered and unregistered humans, nor the distinctive burn of psions who weren't fast enough to escape. They all tasted the same to her.

The mental grid got darker, minds winking out as Kristen's empathy fed on the emotions and thoughts around her. Her power simply ate through the defenses thrown in her way, transferring the foundations of her victims' sanity into her own. Her sanity was makeshift, nothing more, and everything she stole would disintegrate within days, leaving behind yet another hole in her mind.

Samantha left Kristen to her fun, but kept fingers of her power at the edge of her sister's mind even as she checked in with Genevieve.

Forgot how she wrecks everyone's concentration, Genevieve said tightly. *We need some shields, Samantha. These tankers are heavier than the last shipment we stole.*

Can you 'port them? Samantha wanted to know even as she erected a telepathic shield between Kristen's swath of mental devastation and the knot of concentration that was the Warhound telekinetics.

It's a matter of distance and weight. Genevieve's mind dipped heavily against Samantha's, power burning through the psi link they shared as she tapped into her telekinetic strength. *We'll get it done before the train crashes.*

We still need the maglev platform to remain intact.

Train still has to crash. Trust me. I know what the fuck I'm doing.

Samantha didn't have any doubt. Looking through Genevieve's eyes from where the telekinetic was crouched on top of the train's engine car, all she could see was progress. The line of tankers following behind were slowly disappearing.

"Military jets are scrambling," the pilot said over the comm system, splitting Samantha's concentration. "ETA five minutes."

Break away, Samantha ordered. *We're finished here. Genevieve, you've got five minutes before the government's fighter jets are on you.*

We can finish in two.

The shuttle banked hard, throwing Samantha against the straps of her harness and the seat with bruising force. She felt metal bite into the meat of her shoulders, the edge of her cheek. She could feel the shuttle pick up speed as the pilot sought to put distance between them and the jets that appeared on their radar.

Pulling out of Genevieve's mind, Samantha blinked open her eyes, staring hard at the gray wall of the shuttle's interior to ground herself as she untangled her mind from the merge. Something warm slid down her wrist, and she looked down to see that Kristen's nails had cut into her skin, leaving crimson crescent-moon marks across the ridge of her tendon. She flexed her hand, watching the play of muscle beneath her skin.

"I'm not your anchor," Samantha said as she wiped the blood away on her uniform.

"Of course not," Kristen replied calmly, sanity creeping into the tone of her voice, cutting through the gleam of her eyes. They both knew this was a temporary state. "Mine left."

"Lucas isn't coming back."

Kristen's smile tempered itself into a smirk as she lifted bloody fingers to wipe them over Samantha's throat before the older girl could stop her.

"So little faith, Sammy-girl."

Samantha reached out and slammed her sister's head against the cradle of her seat. "Keep your hands and mind to yourself."

Kristen laughed low in her throat. "Never gonna happen. Can't happen. *Won't*."

Samantha's mouth curled up in disgust as she pulled back. "I don't know why Nathan hasn't killed you yet."

"For reasons exactly like this." Kristen licked her lips and shrugged one shoulder. "He still needs me. Same as he needs you."

"Maybe I'll get lucky and he'll leave you behind when we ship out to Mars."

A cheerful "Maybe" was Kristen's opinion on that as her mind evened out some. With the death of all those humans and Strykers on the ground, Kristen was gaining back some shred of mental balance.

In the depths of Kristen's twisted mind, at the bottom where her damaged power stemmed from, the psi link that Lucas had buried in her insanity years ago when she was just a toddler switched on at the barest trace of sanity.

Hello, Kris. Lucas's telepathic power flowed through the swirling madness that was, for a brief moment, dimmed. Controlled. *How was dinner?*

Kristen stared at her sister until Samantha looked away, the contempt between them an emotion that Kristen didn't bother to brush aside.

Delicious.

Why don't you tell me all about it?

On the flight back to London, high in the atmosphere, Kristen did exactly that.

PART FOUR

ALLIANCE

SESSION DATE: 2128.09.22
LOCATION: Institute of Psionics Research
CLEARANCE ID: Dr. Amy Bennett
SUBJECT: 2581
FILE NUMBER: 879

"I want to go home," the girl says, sounding tired and hoarse, sitting slumped in the same seat as before. She is thinner than she was at the beginning, drawn brittle by time that is running out.

"You know you can leave if you just tell us what we want to know," the doctor says.

"You want a second chance on Mars." The girl wrinkles her small nose at the doctor and shakes her head. "But you should want Earth."

"I think you should tell us how to stop this war."

Aisling blinks at her slowly, bleached-out violet eyes set in a hollow face. "I'm tired. I want to sleep."

"Do you know," the doctor says, voice gone ragged and harsh, "how many countries have been lost to this madness?"

"Yes," Aisling says softly as she picks at the electrodes on the back of one hand, the machines spiking on a high-pitched whine. "I saw them all die. But don't worry, Threnody. It's going to be okay in the end."

THIRTEEN

AUGUST 2379

BUFFALO, USA

Buffalo was where the survivors fled during and after the Border Wars. It was where their descendants remained, locked into underground bunkers and sealed city towers.

In the local parlance, it was a sprawl as opposed to a slum, but it had its borders, it had its limits. Pocketed between the deadzones of the Midwest and the inner areas of the East Coast, with a little slice of toxic water named Lake Erie on one side, Buffalo was sanctuary and hell all in one.

City towers stabbed into the sky in the northeast, a shrewdly built wall between the masses and the closely guarded SkyFarms. A detoxification plant hugged the shores of Lake Erie, the make of it different from that of the combo-detox plants that were built into ocean waters. No desalination was needed here, but the price of clean water, which was worth dying for some days, was still high.

Overhead, shuttles winged through the sky to lock in on anchor docks jutting away from the city towers, never settling to the ground. Maglev train platforms spiked away from Buffalo in half a dozen different directions, turning the city into a distorted fat insect when seen from above. The ancient train tracks made of iron and wood from before the Border Wars were no good anymore. They were either completely broken or ran straight through deadzones with radiation levels still high enough that no amount of shielding attached to the maglev trains could block it.

In the sprawl of Buffalo, people got around by foot more than by car or bus, using underground tunnels before risking the open air. The electrical grid that powered everyone's lives only had so much to spare for the ground vehicles that kept humanity lurching forward from one day to the next. Acid storms tended to eat through even the best-protected wires, and the salvaged steel homes of unregistered humans got lower priority than transportation. First priority went to the SkyFarms, second to the city towers of the registered humans. The government controlled the hierarchy in Buffalo, but people still fell through the cracks, just as they did everywhere else in the world.

It was into one of those cracks that Lucas teleported them.

The small warehouse at the city limits was empty when they arrived. The teleport sent all but Lucas sprawling to the ground, the Strykers still shaky on their legs after illegal brain surgery. Lucas was used to the pain that came from a teleport, which bridged the distance between continents. That didn't mean pushing himself like this was a good thing. Sniffing up blood, ignoring the throbbing pain right behind his eyes, Lucas squinted through the dust that drifted in and out of sunbeams pouring through a line of windows on one side of the warehouse. It was like an oven inside these four walls, the environmental systems off and the air almost too thick to breathe.

"Security feed?" Threnody gasped out as she shoved herself to her hands and knees.

"Not here," Lucas said as sweat dripped down his face, soaking into the collar of his shirt. "The scavengers I deal with don't like the government watching their every move. This place is off the government's grid, but the scavengers will know we've arrived."

"Scavengers," Quinton said, the only one who seemed unbothered by the heat in the warehouse. "Those crazy bastards who dig around in the deadzones without protection? Tell me you're joking."

"I don't joke. About anything."

Lucas moved away from the Strykers, who were picking themselves off the ground. He activated the control panel by the warehouse door, tapping out a code that didn't require biometrics for input. With a heavy grinding sound the door unlocked and a long line of light appeared at its bottom. The door jacked itself up slowly, the sound grating on their ears. It stopped at head height for Lucas. A breeze rolled into the warehouse, hot and heavy, clearing out the stagnant air.

Walking into the afternoon sunlight, Lucas spun around in a slow circle, taking in any changes since his last visit. He still had his dark glasses on, his black clothes soaking up the sunlight uncomfortably. More sweat beaded on his skin, streaking through dirt as it slid down his face and arms. He lifted a hand and offered up a mock salute at the nearest security feed monitoring the area.

You coming? he sent across the mental grid, skirting down the psi link he'd implanted in that obnoxious woman's mind years ago, knowing she was keeping a lookout for them.

Your scrawny ass needs more weight on its bones, that raw voice sent back. *You going to put it there?*

The laugh echoed down to him; amused, revolted. *You psions are too expensive to feed. Who're the riders?*

Needed. Just get down here.

He broke contact, turning to watch the Strykers stumble out of the warehouse. They still had that shocky look to them, a fear at the back of their eyes that came from being unleashed from the government. The freedom might have been a lie, but it was heady.

Except they weren't free of Lucas. He still had his power threaded through their minds. He'd know their intentions before they even thought them all the way through, and their powers were his until he decided otherwise.

"Where are we?" Threnody said.

"Buffalo," Lucas replied. "New York."

In sync, all four Strykers looked north toward the city that they couldn't see, not behind jagged teeth of buildings and towers and hazy pollution. Toronto was too far away to be anything but a dream, and they were too smart to believe in something so out of reach.

Jason grimaced and reached up to touch the back of his neck where the quick-heal patch had yet to dissolve. "Why?"

"We made a bargain, remember? You help me do what needs to be done and you'll have your freedom." Lucas tucked his hands into his back pockets and bent backward some. His spine cracked softly as he stretched. "You can have Aisling's word on it, since none of you trust mine."

"You're going to have to introduce us to that girl someday," Kerr said in exasperation.

Lucas pointedly ignored them as he wandered back over to the side of the warehouse, sitting down on the dirty and cracked ground with his back against the building. "We've got a while to wait. Get comfortable."

Three of them would have argued, except Threnody obeyed Lucas's order with a faint shrug, sitting down on the ground with at least a meter's space between the two. Quinton joined her after a moment, with Kerr and Jason following their lead. Kerr helped Jason sit down, the telekinetic still pale in the face. The initial drugs that the doctor had pumped into him for surgery had long ago worn off, and Jason's shields prevented Lucas from manipulating the pain. It hurt Jason to move his head and neck, hurt to walk. He needed more than a quick-heal patch over sealant, and Kerr knew it, could feel it through their bond.

Lucas, Kerr said. *Let me help him.*

He was surprised, to say the least, when he felt the shift of that formidable telepathic strength in his mind, opening up one of Kerr's channels for use. Telepathy flooded through his mind, a rush that Kerr tried desperately not to crave as he sent his power down the bond he shared with Jason. It took a little more effort than he would have liked, but Kerr tricked Jason's mind into ignoring some of the pain. Jason didn't say thank you, just squeezed Kerr's arm. It meant the same thing.

Lucas blocked Kerr's power again.

"Back in London with the quads," Threnody said after the silence became too much, "we all know how they found us. The government has that same facial recognition software here. You can keep us off the mental grid, but they'll still be able to find us if you don't give us what keeps you hidden as well."

Lucas smiled a little at the accusatory tone in her voice. "Smart woman. Still not smart enough to realize that I needed that little scene at Camden Market."

"You like pissing Nathan off that much?" Quinton asked, voice hard. "Use someone else next time you want to get his attention."

"I've got you four. I don't need anyone else just yet." Lucas stretched out his long legs and tilted his head back. "The scavengers will bring the supplies that I need."

He was right.

They heard the cars before they saw them, the harsh growl of engines a distant buzz that grew. The Strykers were the only ones to get to their feet, reaching for weapons they no longer had and powers that were no longer readily available to them. Lucas remained where he was as two rusted and dented SUVs rounded a nearby building, patched tires kicking up dust as they braked to a halt. The handful of men and women who got out were heavily armed. The last person out ordered everyone to remain by the SUVs while she approached the psions.

The middle-aged black woman had short, graying hair and wore her street armor like a second skin. Illegal cybernetics showed in the lines of her hands where sharp metal cut through synthskin provided for other's sensibilities, not her own. She carried a military-grade rifle on one shoulder like an extension of her arm, the weapon clean and well cared for; illegal in civilian hands, but scavengers didn't care about laws.

"Hangman comin' down from the gallows," she said in a rough voice around an unfriendly smile. "Give me one reason why I shouldn't shoot your ass."

"Because I always make you miss," Lucas said as he finally got to his feet. "Matron."

"Lucas." Her dark eyes settled pointedly on the other four. "They ain't unregistered. I don't like surprises."

"How is this a surprise when I told you five years ago what was going to happen?" Lucas offered up a slick smile. "Trust me, Matron. When have I ever not come through?"

"You want that answer in bullet points?"

Lucas laughed as he reached out to clasp her hand, an easy greeting between the two that was still tempered by wariness on Matron's part. The woman wasn't stupid. She hadn't lived this long by ignoring threats, despite Lucas's promises. She knew exactly who and what Lucas was, even if almost no one else in her scavenger group did. Telepathy could work wonders on the human mind.

"I've got kits in the vehicles," Matron said, looking past Lucas at the four he'd brought with him. "Let's get you people hidden."

The Strykers remained where they stood, in a line behind Lucas shoulder to shoulder. One of Matron's scavengers pulled a bag out of the nearest SUV and dropped it at her feet. She knelt down and dug through it, coming up with two different traveling cases. The first one had tiny containers full of iris peels loaded with false identities. She picked four at random and handed them over to Lucas, who flicked them out of her hand telekinetically and slapped them into the Strykers' palms. Threnody and Kerr looked at each other before prying open the cases and inserting the iris peels into their eyes. Following their lead, Quinton and Jason did the same.

The second box had thin strips of clear synthskin woven through with translucent bioware. Matron peeled the first few strips out of the cool gel that kept them active. She walked over to the Strykers and adhered the strips to their faces, making sure to hit as many main recognition points over their bone structure as she could. The government's security grid would read them as someone else long enough to get them past the security checks.

"Do this often?" Jason asked as Matron none too gently pressed a strip over his forehead, aggravating his headache.

She grinned at him, revealing metal teeth. "It ain't none of your business."

She walked away, packed up the bag, and shoved it toward her people with a kick from one dusty boot. Lucas was already heading for the nearest SUV, climbing into the backseat. It was telling that no one tried to stop him.

"You trust him?" Threnody asked Matron as the woman made a quick hand gesture at her people, sending one person to lock the warehouse and the rest back into the vehicles.

"I'm alive because of him."

"You didn't answer my question."

"Get in the fucking car, Stryker."

Matron said it low-voiced, more breath than sound, her eyes on her people and her distance from them rather than the four beside her.

Threnody twitched, just a faint jerk of her shoulders, but it was enough of a reaction that Matron saw it out the corner of her eye.

"Did he tell you what we are?" Threnody said, her voice soft and careful.

"Lucas didn't tell me he was bringing you people into my territory. I know government lapdogs when I see them. I don't appreciate it, but I'm not going to fight him on it. Now *move*."

Threnody and Quinton got in the SUV with Lucas while Jason and Kerr climbed into the one behind. They buckled up as the doors were shut. The noise the engines made as they started up was almost too loud to talk over.

Lucas leaned forward on the middle bench, grabbing on to the front passenger seat where Matron sat for balance. He raised his voice so that he could be heard over the engine. "Are we on schedule?"

"Close enough," Matron said, voice just as loud as she passed back a handful of ration bars that Lucas split between himself, Threnody, and Quinton. "We need to charge the engines, do a few diagnostics runs. The last set of codes you brought us got the hive connection online, but it still needs some work. We can hack the grid to get us over the arctic circle, so long as we've got someone jacked in. We still need to do a test flight."

"The arctic circle is a no-fly zone," Threnody said loudly from the back of the SUV. They had all the windows down despite the dust, making the engine sound even louder. The air-conditioning didn't work and it was too hot without the gritty breeze from outside.

"Ever wonder why?" Lucas asked over his shoulder, leaning back against the seat he shared with another of Matron's scavengers, chewing on his food.

"Wasn't our business."

"It is now."

They drove away from the outskirts of Buffalo, heading southeast along the outside ring of tenement-housing blocks, many just entrances to the tunnels and bunkers below. The skyline of Buffalo was low and knobby until it got to the city towers in the distant north. Haze sat heavy and thick close to the ground, a hot blanket between them and the clouds that moved sluggishly through the sky. They were putting distance between them and what passed for society, and Threnody didn't much care for the kilometers that ran out behind them.

How did you meet Matron? Threnody asked Lucas, wondering if anyone else could hear her through the psi link.

Like I met everyone else. Through Aisling, Lucas said.

Threnody was quiet for half a minute. *I find it difficult to believe you defected from your family and your Syndicate on the whims of some child.*

And yet, you followed me when I offered you a way out. We are very much alike in the ways that matter, Threnody.

You were never a slave. Don't fucking patronize me.

You never lived my life, Lucas said, quiet menace seeping through his words. *It's not as easy or as glamorous as you think.*

Come cry to me after you've had a neurotracker implanted and used on you for the first time.

What makes you think I haven't? Threnody gave him a sharp look from where she sat. He didn't turn around to look at her. *Nathan has always been creative in his punishments.*

That's just sick.

And you wonder why I listen to some child. Lucas's thoughts shifted against hers, but he shared no memories with her again. *Aisling has a way of making people do her dirty work for her.*

Like you?

Not like what she asks for is any different than what I did for Nathan. The killing, at least. The lies. The scope is a hell of a lot bigger.

Threnody couldn't hide the surprise that colored her thoughts. *Nathan doesn't know about her?*

No, Nathan doesn't know about Aisling. His generation wasn't one she talked to.

But she talked to others in your family? Threnody asked with dawning horror at the thought of what they were throwing their support into.

Aisling talks about a lot of people. She only talks to specific individuals. Guess which group you belong to?

Threnody pulled her thoughts together, trying to make sense of something that was out of her control. *I find it hard to believe Nathan never knew what you were doing.*

Marcheline took care of that after Aisling spoke to her. I'm alive because of the actions both of them took. Nathan can't find what he doesn't know how to look for, or what he can't comprehend or see.

Threnody jerked in her seat so hard that Quinton reached out to steady her. She nodded her thanks, closing her eyes to hide her shock. *A mindwipe? On Nathan?*

Or something. Nathan doesn't know half the things I've done on Aisling orders, Lucas said. *I never took to his form of mindwiping, Aisling made sure of it. What I learned about survival—the important parts—I learned from her.*

From a child?

She died that young. Doesn't mean she lived that briefly.

It was such a simple explanation. Such an easy admission that choked the very breath out of her lungs.

Don't worry, Threnody. You'll still get to meet her.

She got a flash of his memories that her mind balked about believing. Precognitives never lived long, but they lived long enough to be useful.

Threnody sat there, in the back of that SUV on a road somewhere in Buffalo, with her whole world going to pieces.

She realized she could do nothing but let it break.

[FOURTEEN]

AUGUST 2379
TARRAGONA, SPAIN

The wreckage of the maglev train was scattered over the surrounding area, tossed aside like the pieces of a child's broken toy. Oil was a slick sheen on the ground where it wasn't fuel for the fire burning through the remains of the train. The engine car was crumpled where it had been flung far from the rest of the cars, broken into pieces. The air was thick with smoke, making it hard to breathe.

There were no bodies to retrieve, no closure. A fire like that wouldn't even give up ashes at the end.

Ciari frowned behind the skinmask she wore, the filters sucking in near her mouth. Standing beside the intact maglev platform, she gazed at the mess and wondered how much this was going to cost them, in money and in blood.

"No one's going to be happy about this," Keiko said from where the telekinetic stood beside her, hands gripping the buckles of her flak jacket. Around them, working diligently to try to contain the fire and salvage what they could, were government soldiers grouped in quads and first responders from Tarragona. All of them gave the two Strykers a wide berth.

"Of course not," Ciari said calmly. "We had a contract. We failed in meeting the terms."

"Eleven Strykers are dead. Seven barely managed to teleport out, coming back with mental burnout. Jael had a mess on her hands in medical, dealing with all of them. You really think the World Court will ask for their termination?"

"Erik isn't that wasteful. He'll want compensation, but I don't think he'll kill them."

Keiko swore softly behind her skinmask. "We did what we could against Warhound interference. The humans have an unregistered shuttle on record out here for the hijack. Our surviving Strykers gave testimony as to who was on that shuttle."

Ciari gave Keiko a warning look. "Warhounds. Rogue psions."

Keiko's expression didn't change. "Of course."

They all—Strykers and Warhounds alike—still abided by the Silence Law, even after the past few centuries of slavery of psions by the human race. Incalculable damage could be done to society if word got out that some of the most powerful, free people in their history since the Border Wars were, in actuality, psions. Some secrets were meant to be kept at all costs, and it was the OIC's job to ensure that happened.

The World Court had enslaved psions since their initial discovery and trained them over their short generations to believe that humans were the only thing in the world worth worshipping, worth saving. That harsh indoctrination resulted in soldiers that the government loaned out for anything from protection to murder. Strykers turned a pretty profit when they weren't dying for humanity.

"No, I want answers!" a disgusted voice shouted in Spanish from behind them. "This train was supposed to make it to the transfer point. It *didn't,* and I want to know why. Rogue psions aren't a good enough fucking excuse. Not for *this.*"

Telepathic implants for language translation allowed both Ciari and Keiko to understand what was being said and the ability to communicate. The two women shared a brief look before they turned to face the man who had just arrived. The shuttle that had ferried him out of Tarragona was powering down to standby mode while the man himself was a flurry of emotion. Fear and anger, yes; possibly something else. Ciari didn't actively try to read his emotions. He had a bioware net attached to his brain, as all high-ranking politicians did, but the mental grid surrounding his mind was saturated with his emotions and those she could read.

The president of Spain—a position monitored by the World Court to ensure its laws were enforced—was a short, stocky man with dark hair, dark eyes, and light brown skin that didn't see the sun all that often. Alfonso Rodriguez's lips were pulled back from his teeth in a furious scowl behind the clear skinmask that he wore. He wasn't thinking straight; Ciari could feel that through her empathy. When he lifted a hand to strike her, she wasn't surprised at all, nor was she surprised at Keiko's reaction.

Keiko slammed a telekinetic shield down between Alfonso and Ciari. The president walked straight into it and nearly fell to the ground. Only the quick actions of the quad assigned him saved him from making a total fool of himself.

"You have *no right* to attack," Alfonso said, the words coming out harshly.

Ciari just stared at him, the cold blankness on her face and in her eyes difficult for any of the humans to look at for long. "Mr. President, that wasn't an attack. It was simply a defensive reaction by my subordinate," Ciari said in the same language.

"Call her off."

"I think not, Mr. President."

"Your contract is with *me, psion.* You will do as I demand and pay for your failure."

"The contract you bought was negotiated through the World Court," Ciari reminded him. "If you have a problem with my Strykers dying for your shipment, then lodge a complaint with the government."

Keiko didn't drop her shield as the quad surrounding Alfonso reached for their guns. Neither did she ask for permission to interfere. She merely reached out with her power to keep their handguns firmly anchored in their hip holsters, finding it slightly amusing how long the soldiers struggled to remove their weapons before they realized what was going on.

"Get your fucking power off us," the man in charge of the quad demanded as he took a step toward them.

Keiko anchored the man's feet to the ground. "We don't take orders from you."

"Then *you* will take them from *me,*" Alfonso said.

"Our orders come from the World Court," Ciari said. "They have already been informed of what happened here. What punishment, if any, is up to the judges."

"They will hear of this, psion." Alfonso spat between them. "If you dogs can't accomplish what you are paid to do, then you should be punished accordingly."

"Then ask to pull the trigger. That *is* the entire reason why you flew out here, isn't it?" Ciari gazed at him unblinkingly, brown eyes flat and cold. "To demand satisfaction?"

Alfonso went white, then red in the face. "Get out of my head."

"I'm not in it."

"Then tell the bitch beside you to get out of my head."

"It's a wonder that you people never take the time to figure out what you buy when you sign contracts with the Strykers Syndicate." Ciari reached up to tap the side of her head. "Empathic, Mr. President. I don't read thoughts, I read emotions. Keiko here is a telekinetic. She doesn't read minds at all. Check your baseline readings when you return to Tarragona. You'll find no interference."

"Fuck you."

Ciari's smile was pure politeness, her tone sweetly acid. "We don't contract out for sexual exploits, Mr. President. Please remember that."

The space between them was filled by the invisible strength of Keiko's telekinetic shield. Even without it, Alfonso and his people wouldn't have crossed that line to strike at them. Strykers were government property, despite their segregation, and an attack on them was an attack on the World Court itself.

Ciari turned her head so she could see the ongoing cleanup and not the furious expression of a man who wasn't as powerful as he thought he was.

"We'll need your records from the military base on the attack," Ciari said.

"No."

"That order comes directly from the World Court, Mr. President. If you do not give them to us, then you can make your excuses to the judges yourself. We'll gladly teleport you before the bench to save you the cost of a shuttle flight to The Hague."

The silence between them was heavy with hatred. Finally, Alfonso snapped out an order to one of the soldiers, who peeled away from the quad and headed back to the shuttle at a quick jog.

"We'll deliver the records to you," Alfonso said. "Encrypted."

Ciari shrugged her ambivalence to that petty decision and said nothing. Keiko kept her undivided attention on the group in front of them, keeping up a light telekinetic shield around herself and Ciari. Only after the soldier had returned with the data chip and handed it over did the group move away to confer with those in charge of the cleanup. Ciari rolled the tiny data chip between her fingers as she stared at the fire in the distance.

"Should we send for a psychometrist?" Keiko asked softly a few minutes later.

"No," Ciari said. "Anything that would have held any shred of memory is burning."

"We could try the tracks. Desperation and fear are strong enough emotions to embed in the maglev platform."

"Not worth the effort, Keiko."

The telekinetic sighed and reached up to knuckle one eye. "That's six tankers stolen, Ciari. Two burned. The Warhounds are no doubt going to ransom the oil back to the government."

"Typical."

"We still don't know why." Keiko pitched her voice lower, the expression on her face never changing. "They can't be planning a secondary launch with extra supplies. Can they?"

"No." Ciari blinked rapidly as the wind changed direction, blowing smoke and dust into their faces. She turned her head to the side to escape most of the grit. "They won't do that. It's not conducive to their plans. Nathan hasn't once gone after the shuttle fuel stored in Paris, which means he isn't interested in tampering with what will get them to Mars. He's more interested in what he can use on the colony once they arrive, hence the oil."

"Can you be sure?"

Ciari pressed a hand to her stomach, knowing that what she did now might not be enough to save what she carried. "Yes."

She wondered, when the time came, if anyone would ever forgive her.

"Should we report back?" Keiko said. "The military looks like they have this well under control, and no one has asked for Stryker assistance."

Ciari blinked and turned her attention back to Keiko. "At this point, they wouldn't. They'll blame us for this fiasco and the insurance company will cover their loss. Our job right now is to figure out what can be used in our favor to grovel appropriately before the World Court."

Keiko gnashed her teeth. "I hate begging."

"It keeps us breathing." Ciari pocketed the data chip. "Take us back to Toronto."

In the blink of an eye, they were gone. No one save the quad noticed the departure. The military was beginning to regroup, preparing to leave. They couldn't do anything more than they already had.

The fire would burn itself out, just like all the ones before.

[FIFTEEN]

The first thing Quinton did when they made it to the tenement that Matron's scavengers called home, past the outskirts of Buffalo, was to shave.

He stripped, disposing of the filthy clothing he'd been wearing since the Slums and used the tiny bit of grudgingly rationed water to clean up. They didn't have razors here, but he had a knife, and the sharp scrape of the blade over his face and jaw was comforting. He bled a little, and the water stung in the cuts, but he didn't care.

He would have given anything for a shower, but he wasn't going to get one. He wasn't a Stryker anymore, he didn't have the government picking up his bill. Staring at himself in the small cracked mirror of his borrowed room, Quinton wondered why he didn't look different, feel different, without the collar still wired to his brain.

"Well, this looks less rat-infested than the room Kerr got," Jason said as he came inside without knocking and dropped his bag on the floor by the bed that had Quinton's gear spread out all over it. "Guess I'm taking the floor."

Quinton turned around. "What do you think you're doing?"

"There's not enough space in this building for everyone. People were doubled up before we got here. Lucas said he needs to work on Kerr's mind, so they're sharing a room." Jason's expression was viciously annoyed. "I didn't even get a say in that and Kerr's my partner. Fuck that shit. Matron gave Threnody a room to herself and told me to find you. We're sharing."

"I'll bunk with Threnody."

"Your partner has a room half this size. Two won't fit in that closet. Just don't step on me when you wake up."

Quinton watched through narrowed eyes as Jason stretched out on the floor by the bed, using the thin blanket roll he'd been given as a pillow. The telekinetic was lying on his side, hazel eyes closed, pain lines drawn tight over the skin of his face.

"You need any medication?" Quinton asked after a moment.

Jason wriggled his fingers in Quinton's direction. He didn't open his eyes. "You're cute when you pretend to be worried."

"Just about my own skin. I trust Strykers, not scavengers."

"We're not Strykers anymore, Quinton."

"I've been a Stryker for most of my life. That mentality isn't going to change just because we've gone rogue."

"Something tells me Lucas expects it to."

Quinton reached for his shirt and pulled it back on, not caring that it wasn't clean. He just wanted to get out of there. "I don't give a fuck what Lucas wants."

Jason huffed out a tired little laugh that held no humor. "Now you're just lying to yourself."

Quinton left the room without responding to that pointed remark. Letting the door close behind him, he went in search of Threnody. A scavenger sent him in the right direction and he knocked on the door to her room, waiting for her okay to enter.

"It's open."

The doors in this place were old, manual, with knobs that needed to be turned. Jason had been right, Quinton decided. The room Matron had given Threnody wasn't even big enough for the door to open all the way. He slid inside carefully, eyes focused on where Threnody lay on the small bed that was more a pallet than anything else. She didn't seem to care. He noticed, almost immediately, the way her arms and legs twitched, little spasms that rolled through the lines of the muscles he could see.

"Is it getting any better?" Quinton asked as he settled on the floor beside her. Reaching out with one hand, he smoothed her hair off her forehead, tucking it behind one ear.

Threnody barely stirred. "Getting there. Lucas was right. That doctor did enough that the rest of my system is building off of the surgery. The reboot kind of sucks, to be honest."

"Still think you need a biotank."

"Won't find one here. Can't go to where we know they are." She sighed softly. "It'll keep."

Quinton wrapped his hand around hers where it was tucked beneath her chin. She was lying on her side, curled up around whatever pain she was feeling, but she still gave his hand a squeeze back.

"You're not allowed to die on me, Thren. I can deal with Jason's attitude, but I don't want to deal with Kerr's breakdowns. I don't have the patience for that shit."

"They're all we've got to rely on. Them and Lucas."

"Yeah, about that." Quinton leaned his head back until it hit the wall. He closed his eyes. "What were you and Lucas talking about on the drive here?"

"What makes you think we were having a conversation?"

"Don't pull that shit with me," Quinton growled. "I'm your partner. *Family,* Thren. I deserve better than that."

"You do," Threnody said after a brief pause. "I'm sorry. That was wrong of me. I don't even know why I said it."

"Yeah, you do."

"Can you fault me for wanting to protect you?"

They'd been partnered when he was nine and she was eight, almost two decades' worth of training and fighting, bleeding and surviving together on the field. So many years where he followed where she led, building up a reputation that kept them both safe from the threat of termination, only to see them lose that safety in the face of someone else's interference. Quinton knew that survival now meant hiding from Warhounds *and* Strykers as much as it meant relying on Nathan Serca's oldest son.

"Shut up and get some rest, Thren. I've got this watch."

She didn't argue, just settled into a restless doze beside him. Quinton wasn't sure how many hours passed before the door to the room was opened, but he knew it wasn't long enough to make a difference to their exhaustion.

"If you want to eat, better get down to the cafeteria," Lucas said as he leaned into the room. "Meals are offered only twice a day in this place."

"Are they that short on supplies?" Threnody asked as she rolled onto her back and stretched out her legs, hissing as blood rushed back into stiff muscles.

"They're unregistered and they're scavengers. They're always short on everything." Lucas disappeared, but they could still hear him talking. "I did a brief run into the city while you slept. I brought back enough supplies for us that we won't eat too badly into their allotment. Matron wouldn't appreciate that."

"Help me up, Quin," Threnody said, reaching for him.

It took both of them to get her to her feet. She leaned heavily on him for a moment, hands clenched tightly on his shoulders, breath coming raggedly. Her nerves burned off and on, hot and cold, numb and full of feeling as her system struggled to readjust through the damage she'd inflicted on it. She sighed, momentarily resting her head on his shoulder.

Quinton gave her a brief hug. "How long do you think until you're fully stabilized?"

"Maybe another day or two. Possibly longer," she said. "I wouldn't mind a painkiller right now, though. One that actually *works*."

"Come on," Quinton said, helping her out of the room. "I don't know about medication, but let's get some calories into you."

Psions had a higher metabolism and burned through energy faster than a normal human ever would. The government was the only one who employed psions because only the government could afford their upkeep.

The tenement the scavengers occupied was three levels tall, practically ancient, with few upgrades and only those that would keep the building standing. The cafeteria and kitchens took up half the second floor, one long, open room full of tables and chairs. Quinton and Threnody queued up with the others waiting for their dinner, and neither complained when the cooks filled their plates with GMO rice, strips of dried vegetable substitution, and cubes of protein. The last serving cook in the line deposited two ration bars on their trays when no one else got extra. Threnody and Quinton didn't question being singled out; they just took a beer from the drink area and joined the long table where Lucas, Kerr, Jason, and Matron were already sitting.

"My second," Matron said, jerking her head at the blond man beside her. "Everett."

He had as much illegal cybernetics as Matron did in his hands and arms, with a glitter in the back of both brown eyes that weren't inspecs, but cybernetic ocular nerves. The wiring done to his eyes was top-notch, none of it showing outside his body. Threnody wondered how he'd been able to afford it.

"Psions," Everett said, his tone revealing that he knew what they really were outside of the obvious.

"Got a problem?" Kerr asked, voice cool.

"Nah. Lucas always pulls through when it matters, even if it does take months." Everett shoveled a bite of food into his mouth. "In this case, years."

"Years," Jason echoed, looking down the table at Lucas.

Lucas methodically demolished a plate holding twice the food of anyone else's. "You don't really think I was in the Slums by chance, do you?"

"Lucas has a way of getting people to do what he wants," Matron said, sounding only vaguely bitter.

"Willingly?" Quinton wanted to know.

"Most of the time." Matron's dark eyes were focused on Lucas. "He means well."

"Choke on your words, Matron," Lucas said. "Finish up. We've got places to be."

It was telling, Threnody decided, that Matron did as Lucas ordered without argument. So did Everett. Threnody took another bite of food, forcing herself to finish what she had been served, even as her stomach kept twisting into knots.

They finished their food before anyone else. Matron got to her feet and left her tray on the table. Lucas followed her lead, but he was the first one out of the room. They took the stairs at the end of the hallway down one floor. Matron led them to a back room, the only place in the tenement with modern security. It was locked, but Matron's biometrics opened it. The entrance that room protected was also locked and physically guarded.

The second door was set in the middle of the floor, braced by steel and concrete, anchored into the very foundation of the building. It was an old design, a holdover from when the threat of nuclear attack was always imminent and people had needed a place to go to ground.

Two scavengers sat at a single terminal, monitoring a dozen different security feeds. Threnody spared them a glance only when Matron pointed at her and said warningly, "You don't touch shit in this place without my say-so."

Threnody shrugged minutely, unapologetic for the ability she had been born with.

"Open her up," Matron ordered.

The scavengers entered a set of codes into the computer, unlocking the blast doors in the floor. The doors opened smoothly, almost silently, revealing sturdy-looking stairs that led into pitch-blackness.

"What, no lights down there?" Jason asked as Matron and Everett handed out flashlights.

"We're off the electrical grid on the best of days," Matron explained. "We've got generators we use on a strictly rationed basis. When the time comes, we'll have to hack into the government's electrical grid."

Kerr knelt by the entrance, letting his hand rest against the side of one of the blast doors. "How'd you find this place?"

"You really think we're going to tell you everything?" Everett said.

"We always have this argument, Everett," Lucas said as he spared the scavenger a brief, annoyed look. "You always lose."

Everett spat between them as he tossed Lucas a flashlight. "I don't like giving up our secrets to people like you."

"It's the people like me who made sure you and yours didn't die from radiation poisoning." Lucas pressed his thumb over the sensor on the slim metal flashlight, activating it. The light coming from the tip was sharp and painfully bright. "Or don't you remember that I was the one who 'ported you to a doctor that replaced your arms?"

"Don't ask me to thank you."

"I could just force it out of you. Now shut up and let's go."

The seven of them descended two flights of stairs into cool darkness. Their footsteps echoed against metal.

"Smells like clean air," Jason said as they walked through a tunnel that could fit three people across.

"First thing we did when my ma claimed this territory as hers," Matron said without looking back at them. "Fixed up the environmental system in this place. Cost a fortune on the black market for the material and even more for government agents to look the other way."

"How long did they stay off your back?"

"Until we killed them."

"Typical."

"You say that like someone who's always had access to the best that the government offers."

"You think walking around with a death switch in our heads is fun?" Threnody asked sharply.

"It ain't there anymore." Matron glanced over her shoulder, the shadows cast by their light source unable to hide the contempt in her eyes. "Quit your bitching, girl."

Threnody clenched her hands into fists, telling herself it wasn't anger, but to prevent the next little wave of tremors that rolled through her arms.

"Here," Quinton said as he passed over a ration bar to her. "Eat this. It should help."

"I'm fine," Threnody said, but she took the little packet anyway, tearing it open with her teeth. She was still hungry, even after the previous meal.

Quinton tucked one hand beneath her elbow, letting her lean on him just enough to give her support. Jason and Kerr were between them and the other three, so no one else saw that brief moment of weakness. Threnody's body wasn't fully healed yet, wouldn't be for a while, not unless Lucas could pull a high-tech biotank and medical support system out of his pocket somehow.

She'll live, Lucas said into Quinton's mind. *I need her alive.*

I don't put much faith in what you say.

That would be hysterical if you hadn't already done exactly that.

I followed Threnody here, not you.

Lucas's laughter was low and tired-sounding in Quinton's head. *You'll have to come to terms with what's going on someday. Might as well be today.*

Let us access our powers and maybe I'll start listening. You're as bad as the collars we used to wear.

Really? Pain spiked heavy and sharp through Quinton's brain, causing him to miss a step and stumble a little. Threnody glanced at him worriedly, but he didn't acknowledge her. *If it comes down to me killing you, at least you'll know why. That's more than the government ever gave you.*

Lucas pulled out of Quinton's mind, the psi link cutting off. Quinton doubted that he had been left completely alone. Lucas had a way with mental monitoring that not even the best Stryker psi surgeons were capable of matching. Quinton chewed on the inside of his lip, keeping the flashlight in his hand trained on the ground. Even with a kind of freedom, it was proving difficult to give up the culture he had come from. His hatred for the Warhounds, even for one who had saved them, hadn't abated.

It was a full kilometer to Matron's destination, a metal tunnel set with half a dozen blast doors between their destination and the questionable sanctuary behind them. Walking through the last set of blast doors, they came into an underground hangar, lights snapping on as the control panel embedded in the wall read Matron's biometrics.

"You're early," a rough voice said. A figure stood up from a work terminal a few meters away. "Next check-in was supposed to be three days from now."

"Novak," Matron said by way of introduction. "He's the best hacker we've got."

"I'm the only hacker left that ain't had his brain fried yet, is what you mean."

Novak was stocky and scarred, body carrying illegal cybernetics like the rest of Matron's scavenger group. He was dark-skinned, with inspecs in his eyes and wires cutting through his temples. His head was shaved, revealing black lines of tattoos inked over his skull. All around the neuroports in his wrists were burns, stretching over his knuckles and palms. He was as makeshift as they came, but makeshift had gotten Matron's scavengers pretty damn far.

How far they'd come was sitting on the launchpad, systems off and metal cold.

"This isn't a shuttle class I've ever seen before," Threnody said as she walked closer to the first of three large shuttles that the hangar housed, each shuttle modified for stealth.

"Course not," Matron said as Novak handed over a datapad. "These were salvaged from deadzones."

Threnody came to a hard halt. "Have they been sterilized?"

"Had to be. Lucas here wants these babies for a specific flight. There's no trace of radiation in those shuttles or this space."

"Did you lose your skin in deadzones?" Jason asked, eyeing the trio from where he stood by Kerr.

Matron raised one hand to show him her middle finger, metal gleaming through the synthskin. "I don't question your physiology and disease, psion. Don't fucking question mine."

"Like father, like son," Threnody said as Lucas walked over to her. "Not willing to do all the dirty work yourself? You just had to get other people to do it for you, didn't you?"

"The people who make up scavenger groups in any settlement were never going to have clean enough DNA when the fifth generation finally came upon us." Lucas slanted her a look. "Just because they're unregistered doesn't mean they're useless. They're good at what they do, even if it kills them quicker than most."

"Are they the only ones you've saved?"

"I save who Aisling wants me to save."

"And how many do you have left before she's satisfied?"

His answer was for her alone when he said, *Everyone.*

Lucas approached the nearest shuttle where it was propped up on its landing gear, walking a wide berth around the wings and attached thrusters.

"The shuttles are in better condition than the last time I saw them," Lucas said, raising his voice.

"Yeah, because they're not all in *pieces,*" Matron retorted. "I told you it was going to take time."

Lucas ignored her as he walked around the shuttle to check out the other side. "How are the cold-storage units holding up?"

"They're holding. There's more space for cargo than there is for crew."

"Cold-storage units?" Kerr asked. "What are you guys hoping to transport?"

"We," Lucas corrected as he stepped back into view. "What are *we* going to transport. This is a heavy pickup mission when we finally go wheels up. We're dealing in tonnage, not kilos."

"Just what the hell are we transporting?"

Lucas didn't answer, either vocally or telepathically, as he walked back to the group. His attention was on Jason, who watched his approach warily.

"You were one of the best hackers in the Stryker ranks," Lucas said. "Which means you're the best hacker we've got now. I'm going to need you to get familiar with the hive connection that we've installed in the shuttles."

"Thought you had everything all set up."

"Novak is the only hacker who survived the job. He helped start the process, but his code is lacking. We need something less fragile, and you know how to write government code quicker and better than he does. Your shift starts now."

"And everyone else?"

Lucas let his dark blue eyes slide sideways, his gaze catching Kerr's. "Your partner and I have some reconstructive psi surgery to begin."

"Hell no," Jason said, stepping into Lucas's personal space. Lucas was taller than he was, but that didn't matter. "Whatever you're going to do to him, I want to know."

"You're a telekinetic, Jason. You can't do shit for him."

"I'm his *partner.*"

"Yes, and I can't help but wonder if that permanent link has caused more damage than benefit. Hiding behind your shields, strong as they are, hasn't helped his mind deal with the problem of his shields collapsing. You're his crutch."

As Jason opened his mouth to argue, a heavy telekinetic hold picked him up and slammed him to the floor. Gasping for breath, Jason stared up at Lucas with anger and not a little bit of fear. Lucas knelt down and grabbed a fistful of Jason's hair, jerking him to a semi-sitting position.

"You're forgetting your place, psion," Lucas said, annoyance twisting lightly through the tone of his voice. "Aisling needs you alive, but there are many definitions of *alive*. We need the power locked up inside your head. That doesn't necessarily mean we need *you*."

Jason felt his heartbeat kick up, but he chose to ignore the adrenaline pumping into his veins. "We'd all be useless to you if you mindwiped us."

"Your idea of a mindwipe is so limited. I'm used to dealing with insanity. We need your power, not your personality."

Lucas let Jason go, and the telekinetic fell back to the floor with a hard thump. Lucas straightened up and looked over at the other Strykers and scavengers. "Anyone else want to argue?"

No one said a word.

Lucas curled his fingers at Kerr as he walked toward the doors they'd come through. "We're going."

Kerr helped Jason to his feet first, giving his partner's shoulder a brief squeeze. "Keep your mouth shut," Kerr said quietly. "I still need you."

"Yeah," Jason muttered as Kerr turned to follow Lucas out of the hangar.

"You really are stupid, aren't you, boy?" Matron said, looking and sounding unimpressed. "If me and mine can trust Lucas with certain things, you Strykers can as well."

"He's a Warhound," Threnody said. "Why do you trust him when it's his family that's helped segregate the world's population? And don't give me that crap about how he saved your lives. He saved ours as well, but it hasn't helped us any."

"See, now, that's where you're wrong." Matron dug into her back pocket and pulled out a pack of cigarettes. She stuck one in her mouth and lit it up. "What Lucas has planned? It's gonna save everyone."

"I find it hard to believe he's shared his plans with a mere human."

"And I find it hard to believe he brought you narrow-minded Strykers into the mix." Matron spat between them. "If *we* believe in what he's trying to do, then you people can."

"Why should we?"

Matron blew smoke out of her nose and smiled, showing her metal teeth. "Other than the fact that he's got his power so far deep in your brains that you can't piss without his say-so? Tell me, what do you know about the arctic Svalbard archipelago?"

"The what?"

"Exactly."

[SIXTEEN]

AUGUST 2379

BUFFALO, USA

C an you be," Kerr asked, struggling for politeness, "a little more careful with him?"

Lucas didn't open his eyes from where he lay on the other bed. "You actually sound like you care."

"He's my partner."

"Shut up and lie down, or you're going to hit the floor with your face when I break open your mind."

Kerr stared at the other man for a few more seconds before carefully lying down on the bed that had been assigned to him. Stretching out, he put an arm over his eyes to block out the room, even if he couldn't block out the relentless presence of Lucas in his mind.

I'm touched you think so highly of me, Lucas said. *Drop your shields.*

Kerr went against everything inside him that was saying no and did as he was ordered. Lucas's power filtered down through the layers of Kerr's mind, his own shields wrapping around the both of them on the mental grid with such strength that they burned like beacons in Kerr's thoughts.

Just like you Strykers to make a mess of things.

I've survived.

I'm still not sure how.

That was the last thing Kerr remembered. The mental grid dipped under the sudden disappearance of Kerr's presence, Lucas holding the other man's mind in his power.

Sometimes I wonder about what you ask of me, Aisling, Lucas thought to himself as he decided where to begin.

The first thing Lucas needed to do was permanently destroy Kerr's shields. The Class II telepath had gone twenty-five years without acknowledging the empathy he carried in his mind. All of Kerr's deeply ingrained thought processes weren't going to be reversed in a single night, but they had to be factored in for this psi surgery.

There was no point in trying to keep up a shield geared solely toward telepathy when empathy kept undermining the process. There had to be acknowledgment of that secondary power, and Kerr had to weave both into the framework of his shielding. There was no getting around that, unless he wanted his shields to continue falling apart.

What had been clear-cut and obvious to Lucas upon a single dip into that mind had apparently been unintelligible to the Stryker psi surgeons. Even a lower-Classed psion had ways to diagnose problems in the minds of those ranked higher. This whole mess could possibly have been avoided, except this was what Aisling wanted. Collusion between previous Stryker OICs and Serca CEOs had only helped along the inevitable.

Digging his telepathy deep into the crevices and canyons of Kerr's mind, Lucas let himself be lost in the problem, allowing his power to bleed carefully into Kerr's. Lucas hadn't been lying, back in London. Scientists could reverse engineer pretty much any technological equipment on the planet with government permission. Lucas could reverse engineer the processes of the human mind only because he'd had his own torn to pieces over and over since his birth by Nathan.

Lucas didn't want anyone else to have that skill. Not that he wouldn't wish that pain on anyone—because there were many people that he *would*—but he wasn't willing to let anyone else have the knowledge that came with it. Marcheline, under orders from Aisling, had helped him gain control, but he'd been the one to build his mind into the weapon that Nathan had thought was his. Lucas hoped it had come as a shock to his father when he walked away from the Serca Syndicate two years ago.

This was the purpose Lucas had worked toward for all of his life: all the different people, all the different pieces, all the various powers that could come out of human DNA. It was hope for a different world that Aisling had instilled in him for the two decades she had seen him grow up. It was the belief in her promise that he was meant for so much more than the prison of his life, for however long he had left.

Ambition was what drove members of the Serca family to attempt the impossible, among other things.

Lucas let himself be lost in the processes of the human mind and felt, vaguely, at ease. When he opened his eyes hours later, he wasn't at all surprised to find Threnody sitting on the floor between the two beds.

"How is he?" Threnody asked, her face turned toward Kerr's unconscious body.

"He's not your partner," Lucas said.

"He's a Stryker."

"We've gone over this, Threnody."

"Getting the collar taken off me doesn't make me any less a Stryker. It never will." She turned her head to look at Lucas. "What have you done to us?"

He sat up slowly. His senses shifted with the migraine-strength headache he was suffering from after performing a long and complicated psi surgery on Kerr, not to mention everything else he'd been orchestrating to get to this point. The physical and mental toll on his body wasn't something he could escape. Growing old wasn't in his genes.

"I actually thought it would be Kerr who would ask that question," Lucas said as he rubbed at his face with both hands. "Him being the telepath and all."

"Before or after you screwed with his head some more?"

Lucas let out a harsh little laugh. "Oh. I like you, Threnody. You actually *think*."

"Can't say I feel the same about you."

"I figured as much." Lucas moved to put his feet on the floor, leaning forward as he studied Threnody. He wiggled his fingers at his head.

"You're wondering why everyone's not as pissed off as they should be. Why everyone is just going along with what I want when all of you should be fighting me tooth and nail."

"Something like that."

"Mental suggestion. I implanted it when all of you were under during your brain surgery back in London. I needed you four to trust me."

"Trust isn't something you *suggest*. It's something you *earn*."

"Since when have rank-and-file Strykers ever trusted Warhounds outside of an ordered suicide mission?"

"What do you mean?"

"Ah." Lucas nodded to himself. "So you *weren't* scheduled for retrieval. Even better, because it means Nathan doesn't know about any of you."

"What the hell are you talking about?"

"Sometimes I think your OIC keeps more secrets than my family does." Lucas lifted a hand to rub at the back of his neck, fingers digging into the knotted muscles there. "We're the ones you rogue psions run to when the government wants you terminated and the Strykers still need you alive. Your OIC asks and we retrieve. I've always thought the Silence Law was more favorable to my side. We've been doing things with psion powers that none of you have even been allowed to *think* about, for fear that the government will lose control of its favorite dogs. It's a bargain, if you will. Your silence for my family's freedom."

Threnody recoiled sharply from him, disbelief thick in her voice. "You and your Warhounds aren't something I would ever willingly run to."

"Lucky for us, those Strykers we're sent to retrieve never get a choice in the matter, either during the transfer or after, when we mindwipe them for loyalty. Technically, I suppose that doesn't apply here. I'm not a Warhound the same way you're no longer a Stryker. Keep your title, if you want. If it makes you feel in control. Just know that you're not. That you never will be."

"Neither are you."

"I know what my sacrifices will gain me," Lucas said as a thin trickle of bright red blood slid down out of his nose. "I know *exactly* what I will get at the end, if we pull it all off this time. And I will do absolutely everything and anything to achieve what Aisling promised my family. What she promised *me*."

Threnody's gaze followed that slow-moving line of blood until it dripped off the edge of Lucas's jaw and fell to the floor. "Even if it kills you before you turn thirty?"

"Try twenty-three."

Threnody met Lucas's gaze without blinking, a slight tick twitching at her jaw. Nerves, but not the emotional sort. Synapses that still weren't healed, but better than they had been. Lucas leaned forward, using his telekinesis to keep her still while he curved his hand over her chin. He tilted her head from side to side, ignoring the fury that came into her blue eyes.

"You need to understand something," Lucas said, voice quiet, tired, the set of his shoulders tense. "We're what the future turns on, you and I. We're the ones who have to do what Aisling says if any of us are going to survive humanity's belabored attempt to reclaim Mars. Everything changes, Threnody. Without mercy, without exception, without pause. The best we can do is change the future into something better. If psions are ruling on Mars or ruling here, what does it matter? We'll all still be alive as a people."

"Don't touch me."

Lucas released her, lifting a hand to his own face to wipe at the blood there. Threnody watched as he studied the red smear on his fingertips, mouth pulled slightly off-center in a dissatisfied frown.

"What's in the Arctic?" Threnody said.

Lucas sighed. "Matron doesn't know when to keep her mouth shut."

"That free will you let some of these scavengers keep, kind of annoying, isn't it? Why didn't you just mindwipe them?"

"Because that's not always the answer."

Threnody shrugged dismissively. "The Arctic. What's so important about it?"

"There's a Norwegian island in that archipelago. Spitsbergen. Pretty much everyone except those on the World Court and my family have forgotten it exists." Lucas pushed himself to his feet and stretched until his bones cracked. "A lot of people died during the bombing years of the

Border Wars. The majority of the world population died afterward, from disease and starvation and environmental change. Every country that exported food to the masses was targeted and destroyed. Agriculture as we knew it back then became impossible on radiation-tainted soils. That's where the deadzones came from."

"I know that. Everyone does."

"Then ask yourself how the SkyFarms came to be. Clean soil? A decent selection of foods and farm animals that could feed the remaining population that the World Court just *happened* to have at their fingertips? Please."

Threnody opened her mouth to argue, but paused, thinking hard. After a long moment, she said, "If the world was so polluted and damaged from nuclear war back then, where did uncontaminated food supplies come from? That's what you're asking, isn't it?"

"Glad to see that the government didn't fry all the synapses in your head every time they flipped that switch of theirs."

Threnody waved off his insult, brow furrowed in thought. "You said we left terraforming machines on Mars. Did we have any here before the Border Wars for our own use?"

"Terraforming machines were expensive. Governments couldn't agree on where to begin here on Earth, which is why they focused on Mars."

"You didn't answer my question." She looked up at him, understanding dawning on her face seconds later. "The SkyFarms. They were built with terraforming machines, weren't they?"

Lucas just smiled.

Threnody dug her fingers into the durable synthfabric of her black BDUs. "What's on that island, Lucas?"

"Machines," Lucas answered after a moment. "Machines and the Svalbard Global Seed and Gene Bank. You don't really think the government is willing to leave without the supplies that feed us, do you?"

Threnody could feel her heart beating against her ribs, the blood rushing in her ears.

"Aisling wants us to save the world, Threnody. It's a little more complicated than simply inciting rebellion."

"I—" Threnody swallowed thickly, her mouth gone suddenly dry. "I'm beginning to understand that."

"Reasoning. Better than a mindwipe any day of the week." Lucas headed for the door. "I'm done with Kerr. His shields will stay up now."

"And Jason? Are you going to work on him?"

"I've been in his head and tested his shields."

"Meaning?"

"I'm going to need a little help breaking them open and Kerr isn't going to be enough."

"So who's going to help you?" Threnody said, suspicion creeping into her voice.

Lucas didn't answer, and then he was gone. Threnody wasn't surprised at his silence. Sighing, she turned her attention back to Kerr's unconscious form, half her thoughts on Lucas's words.

PART FIVE
SUB ROSA

SESSION DATE: 2128.03.15

LOCATION: Institute of Psionics Research

CLEARANCE ID: Dr. Amy Bennett

SUBJECT: 2581

FILE NUMBER: 249

"She thinks there's another way," Aisling says as she peers into the camera, her image larger than usual due to her proximity to the camera. The glue that keeps the electrodes attached to her skull has left her skin red and raw in places. "There are, you know. Lots of them. They just don't work."

Aisling pushes away from the camera and wanders back to her seat and sits down. She is alone in the room, a bright spot of yellow in the whiteness. The machines she is connected to hum with results that are off every reliable scale. The fingers of one hand curve over one knobby knee and tap out a rhythm that matches the pulse of her heartbeat.

"It's so hard to find the right one." Aisling tangles one small hand in her hair and the wires there, gently yanking at both. She squeezes her eyes shut. "You wanted a better half-life. You wanted a better future for everyone."

Aisling tilts her head to the side as if she is listening to something no one else can hear. "You always say that. Every time you get this far and fail, you blame me."

The little girl sighs and opens her eyes. She stares at the camera and peels an electrode off her forehead. "What's wrong, Ciari? Don't you like your present?"

SEVENTEEN

AUGUST 2379

THE HAGUE, THE NETHERLANDS

The old doors to the Deliberation Room closed with a quiet click, the jamming technology that was activated at the start of each session coming online. The fifteen robed men and women surrounding the long, rectangular conference table knew their privacy was assured. Those whose job it was to man those programs knew if they failed at their position, death would be a hoped-for punishment, not necessarily one they would ultimately receive.

"I call this Court into session," Erik said as he struck the gavel he held in one hand on a small tablet of old, lacquered wood. The antiquated gesture had been repeated thousands upon thousands of times before this. He would give it up if he could, but it was tradition. Some things even the World Court couldn't be rid of. "We have work to do, Justices."

The fourteen other men and women nodded, their voices ringing from deep bass to high soprano as they stated agreement. They were different in age and nationality and gender; the one solid thing they had in common was clean DNA.

"The launch date has been moved up to the end of September. We're beginning to prep registered citizens for swift transfer to the Paris Basin. Where do we stand on those totals?" Erik said.

Travis Athe, in his late fifties, tapped decisively at the screen of his datapad. "We have solid readiness from the United Kingdom, the European Union, the East Coast of America, the Canadian Territories, the South American Coalition, Japan, China, and the Southeastern Asian Territories. The numbers are sufficient so far."

"Registered dissidents?" Anchali asked, looking down the table at the president. The elderly woman who was Thai in name only and culturally Chinese was the oldest serving member of the World Court. She was also Erik's strongest conservative supporter as the vice president. That didn't mean they always saw eye to eye.

Erik gestured expansively with one hand. "We've quietly tagged those we believe to be a problem through the security grid. Quads are monitoring their movements. They will be rounded up at the slightest hint of defiance and contained well before the launch date."

"What of the hijacking in Spain?" Cherise Molyneux said. "Those tankers were en route to the Paris Basin when they were stolen and the rest destroyed."

"While we don't know where those rogue psions retreated to, we have enough oil to supply our endeavors once we arrive at the colony. They've never targeted the shuttle fuel transports, and the shuttles on the launchpads remain fully operational. That shipment was simply a precaution."

"I'm more worried about rogue psions knowing our plans." Cherise leaned forward, the beautiful Frenchwoman glaring at Erik. She was the youngest judge on the World Court, with aspirations that would get her killed, sooner or later, if she continued antagonizing him. Erik rather hoped she did. Her dissenting opinions over the past few years had been quite annoying.

Erik leaned back in his cushioned leather chair and stared at Cherise. "Are you questioning our position, Justice? I can assure you that this has been decades in the making and we have been vigilant in keeping it secret. Unless you doubt your own work?"

A faint hint of red stained Cherise's face, but faded in moments. She lifted her chin slightly in defiance. "I don't doubt our accomplishments, Erik. I'm stating a fact that *all* of us here worry about. The Strykers and these Warhounds have been fighting for what seems like forever. The rogue psions are not leashed as they should be. What if they *know?*"

"Do you doubt the protection that our dogs provide us?" Erik said, brown eyes steady as he looked at her.

"Through what constitutes slavery," Travis said from down the table. "Which is never a guarantee."

"Since when has that bothered you and yours?" Erik arched an eyebrow. "When our ancestors hunted down psions after the Border Wars, we saw their uses and hobbled the threat. They obey us because they know little else, we make sure of that. For every generation we humans live through, psions go through two. If they reach thirty or beyond, it's a miracle. Genetics play as much a role in keeping them in check as we do. In the grand scheme of things, psions are useful up to a point, but they're an evolutionary dead end."

"The fact that they are slaves doesn't bother me," Travis said slowly. "What concerns me is that they are more dangerous than the average slave, and for all that we control the Strykers, we don't control *all* the psions in the world."

"Would you rather have all of them free to use their powers against us rather than just some? The Strykers Syndicate was created for a reason. The Strykers live to obey and serve humanity. They have their orders. These Warhounds will not have access to the Paris Basin, nor to the shuttles that wait there. No psion will follow us into space. That directive still stands, and the OIC knows to keep that fact classified until it's time to inform the rank-and-file Strykers about the launch."

"For how long?" Travis gestured sharply at nothing. "If we kill them all before we launch, we lose our protection against the Warhounds. If the Strykers live right up to the launch, we risk them realizing that they have no seats on those shuttles, no berth waiting for them in the colony ship. Their retaliation might be quick enough to damage enough of the shuttles that they will not launch and too many of the needed gene pool will die."

"We need the Strykers," Erik agreed. "We need them to continue to believe that they need us. They are the wall that will stand between us and everyone else when we launch. The OIC will inform the rest of the Strykers when the time arrives for them to do their duty. If only half are alive to do it? It's a shame, but they'll still get the job done."

"And the Warhounds?" Anchali asked coolly. "Surely they won't take our leaving so easily."

Erik's smile pulled thinly at his mouth. "We integrate loyalty into the training of our dogs, and their loyalty is tied to us. The Strykers will be more than enough to hold back the Warhounds when we launch. The Warhounds number less than the Strykers after all. A great many less."

"You sound certain of that fact."

"You don't."

Anchali shook her graying head and reached for her water glass. "I have never trusted in the people whose leashes we hold. They are not *human*, Erik. They do not think the same way we do, they do not feel as we do. Their loyalty is a fabrication built up through indoctrination. Such programming can be undone. There have been instances in the past of Strykers escaping termination to join with the Warhounds. Where do you think the Warhounds came from?"

"We have become adept at putting down rabid dogs."

"Being proficient in killing psions is beside the point. I think it's fair to question if the Warhounds know."

Faint nods of agreement came from around half of the table, an admission that irritated Erik. He didn't let it show on his face or in his voice. "If we stayed rooted in the fear of the unknown and refused to take a chance, then this launch wouldn't be happening. We will be gone from this planet in a month's time. The preparation team is already on the Ark, working to bring the colony ship fully online. We are in the final hours of this countdown after decades of waiting. We shouldn't be looking at the past. We need to be focusing on the future."

"Considering that our past begot this future, I think it's imperative we remember how we arrived here," Cherise argued. "Too many cultures, too many nations, are nothing but deadzones because of our ancestors' actions during the Border Wars. We are effectively doing the same to this world by leaving it behind. We are responsible for the survival of the human race. How can we know for certain that the psions will remain on Earth?"

"The same way that we knew the Fifth Generation Act would work. If we apply the rules to everyone, then no one can claim favoritism. The psions are a product of the Border Wars. Their mutation is a direct block to them being registered. Their *duty* is to serve and protect. Their final act of loyalty will be to die. Who here does not approve of that?"

Erik's gaze swept the length of the table, meeting every set of eyes looking his way. One by one, the judges dropped their gazes in silent agreement to the president's demand. Fifteen strong personalities, each with his or her own set of people to protect, meant that disagreement was a way of life. Compromise was what they fought for.

The World Court collectively owned the Strykers Syndicate in equal shares, but the president alone had the right to give the Strykers their orders. That right only came from unanimous agreement. Killing them only took a single vote.

"I believe we are in agreement," Anchali finally said in her rough voice.

Erik reached for his gavel. "All in favor of continuing on this present course of action?"

"Aye," fourteen voices said without hesitation.

Erik hit the wooden tablet with his gavel once again. "It is so ordered."

Chairs pushed back from the table and everyone stood, gathering up datapads. The judges left in groups of twos or threes, with only Travis and Erik remaining behind.

"A word, Erik," Travis asked, as the doors clicked shut.

Erik gestured with one hand, studying several new messages on his datapad. "Yes, what is it?"

"The Warhounds won't be left behind so easily." Travis paused, studying Erik's profile. "Will the Strykers really be enough?"

"They've been enough since we collared the first one. They will be enough until we kill the last." Erik glanced up at the other man. "You've used them before, you know what they're capable of."

"I know. That doesn't stop me from worrying."

Erik shrugged as he locked his datapad and tucked it into the inner pocket of his dress robes. "It's a little late for you and your Syndicate to second-guess your actions."

Travis frowned. "My family made this possible for everyone. I trust in the science that we rebuilt. I simply don't trust psions."

"No one in their right mind does." Erik offered him a slight smile as he guided Travis out. "Walk with me. I need to give these court minutes to my assistant before we can break for lunch."

They left and the technicians responsible for monitoring the judges turned off the jamming sequence in the Deliberation Room, breathing soft sighs of relief. For all the machines that were built to protect the World Court's privacy, there was no blocking the signal that the bioware nets gave off.

All the judges' baseline readings never deviated, even with Nathan listening in through Travis's mind.

When he managed to extract himself from the delicate, incredibly light psi link that was implanted in Travis's mind, Nathan lifted his head and blinked his office in The Hague back into sight. Even for a Class I triad psion, it took effort to work through a human's mind beneath the bioware net without damaging the human or triggering an alert on the baseline readings. It was complicated enough, and the risks were high enough, that Nathan rarely initiated such a link. Nathan was determined, he simply wasn't stupid, which was one of the reasons he had lived so long.

"Sir?" Dalia said from where she sat in front of his desk, the human woman wearing the identity of an executive assistant this time instead of a bond worker. It suited her better.

Nathan focused his gaze on her. "What is it?"

"We're nearly finished rounding up the bond workers you ordered to be terminated. We're keeping the scientists alive, unless you want them killed as well. Gideon thought you might want to keep them. He thinks they might be useful for the next step, but that's up to you."

"When I said get rid of them, I meant it." Nathan offered her an irritated look. "Gideon's suggestions are useless for my timetable. There are government scientists on our payroll who know how to use what we've created. I want everyone else dead. I hate repeating myself, Dalia."

The human flinched against the threatening presence of Nathan in her mind. "My apologies, sir," she said quickly. "I was only thinking of what might help you."

"I don't pay you to think." Nathan pointed at the door to his office. "Get out."

Dalia got to her feet and left, quick strides taking her out of his office. The door slid shut behind her and Nathan grimaced. Finding good help was getting harder and harder. It was getting to the point where he couldn't even rely on his own family, which was unacceptable. He might not love his children, but they were extremely useful at helping him stay alive by doing nearly all the needed psionic work.

Perhaps that was why Lucas had fled. Dying for other people wasn't nearly as satisfying as dying for oneself.

[EIGHTEEN]

AUGUST 2379
BUFFALO, USA

Lucas knew the location of every Serca Syndicate branch, every Warhound hideout in the world. He knew how personnel were rotated through, how unregistered humans were recruited. He knew how his father operated everything because the company would have been his one day.

Funny how the demands of a single child could change so much.

Lucas walked through the front doors of a manufacturing warehouse in Buffalo with his face bare of synthskin and bioware, no iris peels in his dark blue eyes, and no dark glasses to filter out the security grid's probing identity searches. Lucas went in as himself and that was enough to incite war.

Fifteen unregistered humans died in the first three seconds, collateral damage to the telepathic strike Lucas sent out to deflect the attack coming from a Class IV telepath. The Warhound died instantly, mind fried from the burning strength Lucas carried with such ease.

An alarm sounded as Lucas dropped some of his shields, allowing his presence to register on the mental grid. The workers at the plant knew never to question the sharp sound that pierced their eardrums. Instinct had them racing for the exits, fleeing the warehouse in droves. Lucas let them live. He had more important things to deal with than escaping humans who would come back first thing in the morning for their next shift. A little unscheduled murder wouldn't be enough to make them give up their paychecks.

Lucas walked across the warehouse floor, his worn and scuffed boots taking him past the work area and packing machines. This warehouse only dealt in parts, not the finished product. The environ filters were finished only by registered humans in the city towers.

He focused his telepathy on the mental grid, counted out five, eight, ten Warhounds Classed from IV to III, a mix of 'path-oriented and 'kinetic-oriented psions. They weren't teleporting out. Lucas smiled as he confirmed that, the expression caught by a multitude of security-feed sensors embedded in the walls around him as he took the metal stairs up to the second level. He wasn't in a hurry, which didn't bode well for anyone's survival.

We have orders to kill you, one of the remaining Warhound telepaths said.

Oh, please try. I need the workout, Lucas replied on a wide public 'path.

Warhounds knew never to disobey the ruling Serca. That Lucas had, at one point, been their superior didn't stop the ten from trying to kill him. They knew the odds; dying by Lucas's hands would be quick. Nathan would kill them slowly, if he killed them at all.

The fire that exploded around Lucas's layered telekinetic shields was hot enough to suck out all the moisture in the air. Feeling sweat evaporate off his skin, Lucas teleported out of reach of that burning bubble. Appearing elsewhere, Lucas lashed out with his telekinetic strength, breaking the spine of the attacking pyrokinetic. The fire left behind began to expand, burning out of control.

The telepaths gathered in a merge, striking out at Lucas's mind. Telekinetic pressure bore down on his shields. Defending on two fronts took strength, which Lucas had but couldn't afford to deplete.

Lucas's shields—both telepathic and telekinetic—were solid walls that the Warhounds could not breach, smooth and without the chinks found in lower-Classed psions. The telepaths didn't have a chance, even with their power swelled by three minds. Lucas had been taught by his father, descended from a family who had produced more Class I triad psions in their short history than any other.

The telepaths survived the bright, novalike burnout Lucas inflicted on them. They did not survive sane.

The pair of telekinetics found their minds bent beneath the strength of Lucas's power until they broke, their control shattering to pieces.

If you're finished with this whole pathetic mess, I've got a message for you, Lucas telepathically sent to every remaining Warhound in the building.

You'll kill us, the psychometrist said.

I need some of you alive. You can be that percentage. Choose now.

The surviving telekinetic agreed first, followed by the remaining Warhounds. Lucas watched as they slowly came out of their positions, military-grade guns in the hands of the psychometrist and electrokinetics, the others with their powers held sharply at the ready in their minds.

Lucas rocked back slightly on his heels and smiled at them, the expression malicious and cold. "At least some of you are intelligent."

"We've got standing kill orders," the psychometrist said, her voice flat. "Start talking."

Lucas raised a finger and slammed her into the wall with his telekinesis. He stripped off her gloves with a thought, pressed her bare hands to that old metal structure, and broke her shields. He took away her control and left her with everything that her power could feel in the memories left behind in the warehouse. Her screams echoed long and loud as the memories in that wall overloaded her power in seconds, choking out a mind stripped of all defenses.

"I give the orders here," Lucas reminded them. "Anyone want to argue that?"

The Warhounds stayed silent and stayed where they were, long accustomed to obeying a Serca, no matter which one it was.

Lucas nodded his approval and let the psychometrist fall to the ground. She curled into the fetal position and pressed her hands to her chest, fingers digging into her body as her mind shut down, becoming catatonic.

"Your kill orders are useless without the right people," Lucas finally said, his eyes roving from face to face. "If Nathan wants me, he can come himself."

"You know he never will," an electrokinetic said with careful respect.

"I'm counting on it." Lucas sounded almost cheerful. "Tell my siblings I'll be waiting for them here in Buffalo. Three against one sounds like fair odds, don't you think? I'd even settle for two."

The Warhounds were silent in the face of his mockery, but their thoughts were crystal clear. He picked through their minds with ease, deducing their hierarchy of rank now that he'd killed a third of the integrated teams. With a thought, Lucas teleported into the personal space of the electrokinetic who hadn't yet spoken, the only Class III in the group. She was young, nineteen or so, reaching what psions considered middle age, and smart enough to show fear even as she held her ground.

Lucas let her live for that compliment.

"They have two days," Lucas said, searching her brown eyes with his own dark blue as he implanted the challenge and memory straight into her mind. She doubled over in pain from the transfer. "They won't pass it up."

The electrokinetic nodded, wiping at the blood that was leaking from her nose. "I'll report," she gasped out. "Sir."

Lucas let her go. "You do that."

He teleported out, arriving back in the place he'd left barely twenty minutes ago. It was a small, one-room building thirty kilometers outside Buffalo, built right up against a tall, derelict signal tower. The government had abandoned it years ago; scavengers took the leftovers.

Matron was sitting in front of the building's only control terminal, feet propped on the console, a knife in her hand carefully cutting a small green apple into pieces. She didn't look up at his arrival. "You finish whatever you needed to get done?"

"I wouldn't be here if I hadn't."

"Good. I'd hate to think you failed. I like your bribes too much." Matron popped a section of the expensive fruit into her mouth. The look of bliss that settled over her face stemmed from genuine pleasure. "This is why I believe in God. Or what passes for that negligent asshole."

Lucas huffed out a small laugh as he sprawled in the only other chair in the small control room of what Matron considered to be her property. She had built it up five years ago on Lucas's orders, piggy-backing off the government's official signals to retrieve weather data. It was rarely used by her scavengers, so its sporadic resurgence was never picked up by anyone in Buffalo. The government had other things to worry about than a broken weather station.

Lucas rested his head against the back of the chair and closed his eyes. A headache was creeping across the breadth of his skull, a warning he acknowledged, but couldn't heed. Finishing the mission came before his own health.

"Two days," he said. "If that."

Matron continued to eat her apple. "You're taking a risk, running everything up against that acid storm. Its spine is a derecho. It's gonna be the worst weather Buffalo has seen in a decade. Maybe two."

"This is how it goes."

Matron hummed her agreement; maybe her dissatisfaction. It was impossible to tell. "I have been all things unholy," she whispered as she licked the bright green peel and tasted the sweet tartness of dreams. "'And yea though I walk through the valley of the shadow of death, I will fear no evil; for thou art with me.'"

"Why is it you humans always look outside yourselves for answers?"

"Why is it you psions can't believe in anything but yourselves?"

Lucas stretched out his fingers, filled the space between them with his power until it was difficult for the both of them to breathe. Matron didn't flinch.

"We are your gods," Lucas reminded her. "You made us to save you."

"I didn't make shit." Matron looked up at the faint warning beep coming from the computer as the weather Doppler-radar grid shifted, moving from green to red somewhere over the Midwest. The projections that the computer spit out weren't pretty, bow echos and rain across the vidscreen, across the country; a radar line of storm clouds. "Do I call you Noah now?"

Lucas turned his head and opened his eyes to look at her, this woman he had saved years ago. "Two by fucking two, Matron. Two by fucking two."

Matron bit down on the core of her apple and chewed slowly. She spit the seeds out into her hand and tucked them into her pocket for safekeeping. Things like that should never be wasted.

Somewhere in the far distance, several states to the west, a storm was brewing, moving quickly in their direction. They watched it fill the screen, the only sound in the small weather station their quiet breathing and the crunch of an apple between Matron's metal teeth.

[NINETEEN]

AUGUST 2379
LONDON, UNITED KINGDOM

Nathan was in the Netherlands, securing his political relationships over the latest Act he had pushed through the World Court. Which meant it fell to Samantha to extract the memory from the electrokinetic who had been stationed in Buffalo.

Lucas never failed to piss her off.

Standing in her office, arms crossed over her chest, she glared furiously at the electrokinetic crouched at her feet, letting her older brother's challenge tumble over and over through her mind.

"We shouldn't give him what he wants," Gideon said from where he sat behind Samantha's desk.

"Of course not," Samantha spat out. "The only question is what the fuck does he *really* want? Us there or not there? It's a fifty-fifty chance, and no matter what we choose, you can fucking *bet* Lucas will compensate for it."

"He always asks for you." Gideon gestured at the Warhound on the floor, teleporting her out with the casual use of power that came as naturally as breathing. "Perhaps you should stay behind."

"You wouldn't be able to find him." Samantha shook her head. "I want him *dead,* Gideon."

"So does Nathan." Her twin shrugged. "Unless Nathan goes after Lucas, we'll never be able to bring him back. You know that, every Warhound knows that. It's death to believe otherwise. Nathan doesn't because he *can't*. Not and risk everything we're working toward."

"Then what the bloody hell are we *doing*?"

Gideon gave her a level look. "Obeying."

Samantha ground her teeth, tongue pressed hard against the roof of her mouth. Bending her head, she closed her eyes and easily drew her brother into a psi link that she sent skimming over a sea and a continent to where their father was.

Sir, they said together on the outskirts of Nathan's mind.

After a moment, Nathan dropped his shields and allowed them into his mind. His attention, while solid, was focused elsewhere. That didn't mean his power couldn't hurt them. Samantha steeled herself and dropped the report directly into Nathan's mind. His anger seeped through their thoughts.

An ultimatum? Nathan asked slowly. *Does he never learn?*

It's a trap, Gideon said. *He wants us there.*

Nathan's disgust was thick enough that it translated into an actual taste on Samantha's tongue. *Of course he does. Lucas can't bargain without witnesses.*

Your orders?

Nathan was silent for a long moment. *We're too close to the launch date. We can't afford any interference.*

Sir? Samantha this time; alone. Gideon was a silent presence in her mind that she resented with everything she had.

I want him dead, Nathan said, echoing his daughter's desire. *I don't care about the cost. Our mission is Mars Colony. Lucas is a distraction that needs to be stopped. Do what needs to be done, Samantha. I'll leave the decision of how to go about killing him in your hands. I trust I won't have to tell you what will happen if you fail.*

Samantha buried her anger deep, because it wouldn't help her here—only obedience would. Gideon was right. *Sir.*

Nathan pulled away, cutting the connection, needing all his attention on manipulating the humans. Samantha opened her eyes, raised her head, and found herself staring into her twin's face. Gideon's expression was calm, almost triumphant, as if this were all he'd ever been waiting for, this chance to prove himself to the few who mattered. Samantha was pretty damn certain that she didn't matter, not for this.

"I'll go," Gideon said. "You should stay here."

"No," Samantha said as she clenched her hands into fists.

"You failed to stop Lucas when he left London." Gideon reached out and wrapped his hand around her wrist, the look in his eyes disapproving. "You've failed all the times since when ordered after him."

She tried to twist out of his grip, but she couldn't break free of his telekinesis. "So did you, Gideon."

"I'm not the one who consistently comes up short. That's you." He gave her a little shake, some shred of emotion filtering across his face. It wasn't real, even if he believed it was. "Let me do this for you. For us. You know I can do this for us."

They were twins, born mere minutes apart, she with telepathy and he with telekinesis that was strong enough to incorporate teleportation. Neither of them were a triad psion that Nathan had hoped to control. Hell, they weren't even close to being what he really wanted. They were simply and only functional mistakes that he pitted against each other again and again because it *amused* him. Samantha didn't want the post that Nathan was making them fight for now that Lucas was gone. She didn't want what Gideon would bleed and scream and kill for, though neither her twin nor her father would ever truly believe her, even with her thoughts as proof, not after Lucas's escape.

She didn't want the Serca Syndicate.

She wanted Lucas.

Dead or alive, she wanted her older brother to pay.

"No," Samantha said, backing up her words with her telepathic strength. "Kristen and I will go. You're a telekinetic, Gideon. You'd need a dozen telepaths to help you find Lucas. I can find him by myself."

"Only if he lets you, which is something you can't count on," Gideon said. "When you find him, what will you do? How will you save yourself?"

"Kristen."

Gideon's contempt filtered through to her as he let her go. It was his arrogance, however, that annoyed her. Samantha peeled apart her shields, let her telepathy drag him into the psi link they'd shared since they were born.

You want what Nathan promised Lucas, she said, her mental tone dripping with false comfort. *I don't.*

She let him see how much she simply *did not care* for what Nathan had to offer. Oh, she was a Serca to her core and always would be. She had never understood how Lucas managed to walk away from everything he knew, as if he'd had the opportunity in his restricted existence to learn something different. Samantha's loyalty was carved with blood into her father's Syndicate and it always would be. This was her life, this dual existence of psion and human that she led. She understood that. She knew she had been born to serve, like all Warhounds.

You want it more than I do, Samantha said. *You always have. Lucas would have killed you the second he took that post and you know it. I will always be loyal.*

Her twin's thoughts were bright and hot in her mind, the psi link like scar tissue somewhere deep inside her. Gideon let who he was twist into what Samantha knew she only pretended to be. They were twins. They would always be bound to each other by genetics and Syndicate loyalty, but she was losing faith in that connection. She was losing faith in him.

If you ever betray me, I will kill you, Gideon promised her.

Samantha never doubted it. Just as she had never doubted Lucas when he said, *I will be waiting for you,* two years ago as he left the Serca Syndicate and the Warhound ranks.

She had never told anyone about his promise and forgot it more often than she remembered it. Samantha didn't know where that rebellion stemmed from, where it went when Nathan was searching for betrayal, just that it was a part of her for that one instant. Gideon missed it, because he wasn't a 'path-oriented psi. Samantha broke their merge with a gasp, panting heavily against the back of her hand as she tried not to be sick.

"Nathan doesn't believe you are completely loyal," Gideon said after a long moment as he looked at her. "I know differently. I've *fought* for you, Samantha. Doesn't that count for something, anything at all?"

No. No, it didn't. His subconscious spoke to her more clearly than he did. She knew the truth.

"I need to do this," she said, not answering his question.

"If you fail this time, you'll die. There is no coming back here without Lucas's body. That is the only result Nathan will accept."

"Then I won't fail." Samantha flashed him a wicked, proud smile as she pulled away. It felt like a lie.

Their bond was something that could be broken, but Nathan had never severed it. He called their psi link useful. Samantha thought it was limiting.

Maybe that's why Lucas always worked through Kristen.

The empath understood all the pieces of the puzzle that made up her older sister's carefully broken and reassembled mind better than Samantha herself. Hours later, when Samantha opened up the door to her medical cell, Kristen just *grinned* at her with that same vicious smile she gave everyone.

"Feeling all right, Sammy-girl?" Kristen asked as she pushed herself to her feet. She used the walls to steady herself in the corner she had been curled up against, the skinsuit she wore lining the bones of her body.

Samantha stared at her crazy, empathic little sister and said, "You will follow my orders, Kristen."

"Last chance for you, eh? Always wanted to see what was on the other side," Kristen drawled as she skipped out of her cell, tripped over her own feet, and crashed into the human nurse standing next to Samantha.

When Kristen's power started to eat through the human's mind, Samantha didn't try to stop her. She simply waited while the woman screamed and doctors walked by with hurried steps, pretending not to see the woman dying on the floor.

The mental grid dipped beneath the ferocious strength of Kristen's damaged empathic power, pulling clarity out of the dying woman's mind for Kristen to use. It tasted like memories, like life, a breath that Kristen held in her lungs until her vision grew dark with bright black spots.

Sanity was such a delicate, tentative state of being.

Samantha reached down and curled her hand over Kristen's chin, jerking her head up so she could look her sister in the eye. Kristen's smile eased to something almost sane, the nurse dead beneath the younger girl's white-knuckled grip.

"We have a job to do," Samantha informed her.

"I know," Kristen said cheerfully. "You only bring me along when it's time for a killing spree, Sammy-girl. I get so *hungry* waiting for those moments."

Samantha dragged Kristen to her feet by her neck, pulling the girl down the hallway. In Samantha's mind, through their bond, Gideon was saying, *You really want her instead of me?*

Nathan said it was my decision. He would approve.

Nathan wants you dead. He just hasn't found a reason for killing you yet.

The same could be said of her twin. The day he came to terms with that was the day she'd never see him coming. *Eventually, Gideon. Eventually.*

Samantha pressed her mouth into a hard line as she stepped into the lift at the end of that long hallway, Kristen by her side. The younger girl wrapped her spindly arms around Samantha's waist and pressed her forehead against Samantha's shoulder. She licked sweat off her upper lip and let the salty taste of it spread through her mouth.

"It'll be all right," Kristen muttered against the synthfabric of Samantha's uniform, her smile bleeding onto the material. "This isn't the end, you know?"

Samantha didn't.

She would find out soon enough.

[TWENTY]

AUGUST 2379
THE HAGUE, THE NETHERLANDS

Elion Athe was admitted into the office that Nathan kept at The Hague by way of Jin Li, who didn't offer him anything more than an unimpressed look. Elion spared the man a single glance before walking to Nathan's desk and taking a seat in one of the chairs there.

"You're late," Nathan said, not looking away from the hologrid that flickered images and data between them. "I hope you have something of use."

"Of course," Elion promised as he placed a data chip on Nathan's desk.

He thought it odd that Nathan actually reached over and picked it up with his fingers instead of using his telekinesis, but only for a moment. This was humanity's seat of power. There could be no hint of psionic interference in this ancient building atop an underground city.

Nathan jacked the data chip into his computer and navigated its files with faint motions of his fingers. The information that the Athe family had gathered for Nathan's perusal nearly filled the data chip.

"Interesting," Nathan said after ten minutes of studying the overview report. "My son does seem to get around. Jin Li? Send in Victoria. We'll need a bit of privacy. See to it."

Jin Li set his hand against the control panel by the door before he left, activating security measures that were patently illegal in The Hague, but standard by Nathan's way of thinking. The jamming frequency would ride under the frequency that The Hague used and couldn't be picked up by the government at all. Nathan's office would only show an extremely detailed loop in the system, an interference that would take an expert hacker to detect, and only if the hacker knew what to look for. Elion knew how Nathan conducted business and so relaxed minutely in his chair.

"My father said to tell you that if you require more proof of our endeavors, he would gladly give you our billable hours," Elion said.

Nathan waved aside the suggestion. "That isn't necessary. This is what I was expecting."

"What will you do with the information?"

"It's none of your concern."

Elion bit back on the automatic retort that rose to his lips. He was used to being the one in power, not the subordinate, but was smart enough to realize when to keep his mouth shut. Nathan seemed to appreciate Elion's control and closed down the hologrid to focus on him.

"I have it on good authority that the World Court is beginning to initiate the transfer preparations of its selected people to the pickup points in the major surviving cities," Nathan said.

"I haven't heard."

Nathan's smile was condescending. Elion told himself not to be insulted by it. "Of course not. They wouldn't advertise something they've been keeping secret for generations."

Elion managed not to clench his hands into fists. "We'll be told soon, I presume?"

"Within the week or so. Your family still has the seats promised you."

"We bled enough for them, in blood *and* money."

"Don't be so dramatic, Elion." Nathan gestured at nothing in particular. "Your family enabled our escape off this planet. Even if you had no money left, your reputation would be enough to pay its way onto the colony ship."

"We will do what you require of us."

Nathan's expression didn't change. "I'm so glad to hear that."

Elion wondered if this was what his father felt like, small and unimportant in the face of this man's dangerous attention. Meeting and holding Nathan's gaze took strength. Elion knew what resided in that mind. He knew this was the only course of action.

Aren't you glad your family chose the right side all those years ago? Nathan asked, his mouth not moving one centimeter. *Come now, Elion. You're going to live. Indentured servitude is a small price to pay for your own survival.*

At any other time, Elion would have said yes. Sitting here in Nathan's domain, staring into that man's face and knowing Nathan would be the one that humanity owed their survival to, Elion could only think about what would happen if they stayed on Earth instead.

The office door slid open, allowing Jin Li to reenter. He was followed by a slightly built redhead carrying a heavy black case. At twenty-eight years old, Victoria Montoya had survived well past the median age of a psion and was on a steady trek toward dying. She was the Warhounds' CMO, a Class III telepath who was exceptional at her job, whether it was putting psion minds back together or taking human ones apart.

"Victoria," Nathan said, leaning back in his chair. "I presume you brought everything we need?"

"Of course, sir," Victoria replied as she approached his desk and set the case she was carrying down on the empty chair beside Elion.

Elion watched as she opened it up and pulled out sealed and sterilized operating tools, as well as a portable sterility field device. That last item caused Elion to rise to his feet in alarm, eyes snapping from Victoria to Nathan.

"What is the meaning of this?" Elion demanded, pointing at the medical tools.

Nathan just offered up a smile as he lifted one hand. "I'm covering all my bases, Elion. You don't think you're the first of your family to undergo this procedure, do you? Your father doesn't remember when my mother performed it on him. You won't remember this either."

Nathan clenched his hand into a fist, his telekinetic power immobilizing Elion. All Elion could do was breathe as Victoria worked around him, setting up an operating space on Nathan's desk.

"If you could position him, sir?" Victoria asked, nodding at where she had the sterility field up and running, the quiet hum of the medical machine destroying any and all contaminants within its designated area.

Nathan moved Elion's body like a puppet, forcing the man to sit back down in the chair, then to lean forward with his head resting on the desk within the sterility field. Elion's eyes were blinking rapidly, vocal cords frozen in terror, as Victoria slid an operating cover across his shoulders and around his neck. The last thing he saw was the hypospray that she stabbed against his throat, shooting him full of sedatives. The drugs pulled him under.

Victoria picked up her laser scalpel. Holding it at an angle over Elion's left temple, she cut into his skin and peeled back his scalp, continuing into muscle and bone. He bled down his face and neck as she worked at opening a tiny hole in his skull to reach a viable point of access in the bioware net. Brain surgery was never easy, but this was more a wetware hack than an extraction.

She took her time while Nathan focused on his work. He trusted Victoria to make sure that the wire jacked into Nathan's personal work terminal was connected with precision and with no interference to the bioware net in Elion's brain. When she had the connection, Victoria pulled her hands away from her patient.

"Is HQ uplinked?" she asked.

Nathan glanced at the vidscreen. "Uplinked and hacking. You're clear, Victoria."

She took a step back. "Then he's all yours when they finish."

Bioware nets were a unique form of technology that the Sercas had invented, sold to the World Court generations ago, and subsequently learned to work around over the years. The device was the sole reason why no Serca had ever risked joining the World Court. Too many people had too much access to the servers and networks that monitored the baselines that the bioware nets produced. Better to work outside of that system than to risk it all collapsing due to recorded psionic interference.

Getting around the security system of a bioware net required a strong uplink, a back door in the system, hackers at an off-site location—and the human. Transferring the bioware net signal into Nathan's computer, where the hackers embedded it and kept the signal alive, took less than an hour. Making sure Elion's new baseline readings would copy over the old ones took a little more time, as it involved hacking the Registry through a separate back door that the Serca Syndicate had built into that particular system. The Registry was just one of their many creations, and they never completely gave up what they believed to be rightfully theirs.

Only when they had confirmation that the signal was set in the system did Nathan put aside his datapad and lean back in his chair. Closing his eyes, Nathan reached out with his telepathy for the static human mind before him. He wrapped his power through those muted, limited thoughts and twisted Elion into what Nathan needed. Mindwipes, at least ones that didn't leave humans obviously damaged, were always such a delicate, devious psi surgery.

Elion had walked into Nathan's office with a mind of his own and the ability to choose his own future, as limited as his choices were. Hours later, when he left The Hague—cleaned up and in one piece—he left under Nathan's control, the changes in his personality and mind so subtle that no one would ever notice. His changed opinions, however, would suit Nathan's needs now and forever. With his baseline readings globally replaced in the Registry and through all viable systems that humans used, Elion's conversion was complete.

It left Nathan with a throbbing headache and an ache in his chest, by his heart, small reminders that he was well past the age that a psion was supposed to die.

Nathan turned his attention to the information at his fingertips, gathering up a half dozen datapads from across his desk. Victoria was already long gone and on her way back to London, the mess she had made cleaned up.

"Is my shuttle ready, Jin Li?"

"Ready and waiting, sir."

"Good." Nathan stood up. "I've a schedule to keep."

Jin Li nodded as he followed Nathan to the door. "What have you got planned for the cartels?"

"Nothing they're expecting."

[TWENTY-ONE]

AUGUST 2379

BUFFALO, USA

Jason didn't know what the plan was, all he knew was that it *sucked*.

"If I had a functioning uplink, this might work," he argued with Novak. "If I had a working jack-in system, we might get further than *Canada*. This? This will crash us into the Great Lakes if we're *lucky*."

Novak chewed on his bit of tobacco and just grinned. "Luck ain't got nothing to do with it, Stryker. I did what I could, on top of everyone else finishing what *they* could before dying. Quit your bitching and figure out where we start."

Jason glared at Novak from where he sat in the pilot's seat of the largest shuttle in the underground hangar. "We might need better code than what we've got in this system to support the electronic countermeasures if we're going anywhere near government airspace and not detouring through deadzones."

"So write it."

"I can't go in and rewrite code for every separate program in this damn shuttle. We've been working on upgrading the firmware for the hive connection for days already and we're running out of *time*." Jason leaned forward and stabbed his finger at the hologrid stretched over the wide flight-deck windshield, showing new data that had been downloaded just that morning. "See that? That fucking storm is going to eat us *alive* and you're crazy if you think we can launch through it safely."

Novak spit black saliva onto the metal flight deck of the shuttle, pieces of synthetic tobacco stuck in his teeth. "Lucas says we will."

Jason groaned loudly and pressed his hands over his eyes, hard. "Fucking *hell*. We're taking orders from a man who listens to a goddamn *child*. We're all going to die."

"Shut up, Jason," Lucas said as he stepped into the flight deck of the shuttle, sounding annoyed. He looked paler than usual, with bruises pressed heavily beneath his dark blue eyes. "Tell me the hive connection is ready?"

"I want to say yes." Jason dropped his hands away from his face and leaned forward. "I do. If I had a system up to the grade I'm used to dealing with, possibly. If I had another week, I could be absolutely sure."

"You have two days to finalize everything."

"Two—" Jason choked on his next words and simply resorted to swearing. Novak seemed impressed with his repertoire.

"Two days," Lucas repeated. "More than likely less, so see about doing it in one. The Warhounds are going to start arriving here in Buffalo in force, which will definitely bring in the Strykers. They'll make a nice distraction. The storm is going to hit anywhere between twenty-eight and thirty-six hours from now. Depending on the winds, it could hit earlier."

"You want these shuttles ready for stealth against military jets in *one day*?" Jason shook his head. "That's impossible. You're going to get us all killed if we don't have time to do a dry run on everything."

Lucas walked up to Jason, wrapped his hand around the telekinetic's throat and slammed him face-first down against the flight-control panel. Lucas held him there more by the strength in his arm than by the power in his head.

"Would you fucking be careful with that?" Novak shouted, pointing at the panel. "You break it, we don't got extra!"

"Listen to me, you annoying piece of shit," Lucas said as he leaned in low to whisper into Jason's ear. "The only reason why I haven't broken open your mind yet is because I need a little more power than I've got available. That doesn't mean I'm not figuring out the most painful way to turn you into someone else. We need these shuttles to be flight-ready. Everything about them is solid except the hive connection. Your job is to fix that."

"With three shuttles? I need more *time*," Jason spit out, still trying to breathe.

"Try three dozen." Lucas's grip didn't lessen any as he leaned his weight against the other man. "This isn't the only underground hangar with long-haul shuttles. I'm not stupid enough to pin everything on such a low number. The hive connection will be installed into all the others once you're done here. Novak should have told you that by now."

Jason's gaze cut over to the human hacker. "He hasn't told me shit."

There was the sound of a body hitting a bulkhead and the harsh gasps of someone choking on his own blood. "Novak," Lucas said easily enough. "You know what's at stake. Remember that I can replace you. If you want to keep breathing, play by my rules, or I will feed you to the Warhounds when they arrive. I'm expecting them soon."

Jason glared up at Lucas from where he was pinned to the control console, face pressed against the sensors. "You fucking bastard. You led them here on purpose, didn't you? I thought you wanted to get the fuck out of here unnoticed?"

Lucas tilted his head, dark blue eyes expressionless. "Try to understand something, Jason. This mission isn't just to piss off your side *or* my side. It's about saving everyone the World Court wants to leave behind. That should be easy for you to understand as a former Stryker. Now get the job *done*."

Lucas let him go with a hard shove and stepped back. Jason, gasping for air, reached up to touch his throat. His skin was hot and bruised where Lucas's fingers had held him.

"You only showed us three shuttles," Jason rasped. "What the hell am I supposed to think if you keep lying to us?"

Lucas crossed his arms over his chest, watching impassively as Jason got to his feet. "What you perfect here will be applied to the rest, which is why I need you to finish this sooner rather than later. We're minimizing the risk by containing it to the first three shuttles."

"You just made my fucking job *harder*."

The telekinetic didn't seem to care that he was pissing off one of the most powerful men in the world as he got in Lucas's face. His anger was driving his reactions quicker and faster than logic. Lucas wondered if he had the time to spare to change that.

"Stop it. Both of you."

Jason's gaze jerked away from Lucas in an instant, some of the anger leaving his face as he caught sight of the figure stepping over Novak's unconscious body and coming into the flight deck. Kerr looked as if he'd been dealing with psi shock for the better part of a month, not the handful of days he'd been lying unconscious in that borrowed room. It wasn't a good look for him.

Jason shoved past Lucas, reaching Kerr and putting his shoulder beneath the other man's arm. Kerr nodded his thanks for the support, even as he leaned most of his weight against the bulkhead. As bad as Kerr looked, his mind was stable. His shields were a solid barrier that weren't going to skid out from under his control anytime soon. Lucas eyed him, satisfied to see that the trick he had taught Kerr in reading as human on the mental grid was working.

"You're finally awake," Lucas said.

"I puked on the floor between our beds," Kerr said evenly. "Matron said you get to clean it up."

With Kerr's shields solidly raised, Lucas couldn't tell if he was lying. It was progress. "Your mess, your problem. I'll take another room. Not like we'll be here long enough for me to need it."

Kerr wasn't impressed. "I think it's time you give us a full briefing, Lucas. You owe us that much."

"I owe you nothing."

"Please."

Jason heard the need in Kerr's voice and didn't like it, his mouth twisting in anger. But he kept quiet. It would be years before Jason stopped thinking of Kerr as the one in charge of their two-person team, if he ever did.

"Get the others," Lucas finally said as he reached out and nudged Novak into solid wakefulness with his boot and his telepathy. "Matron is in the weapons room. Bring her here. She hates when I 'port her around without warning."

"Do it yourself," Novak groaned. "You're the damn psion."

Lucas simply stared at him until the other man quickly looked away. It took two tries for Novak to get to his feet, but the hacker finally managed it. He stumbled out of the shuttle on shaky legs, Jason watching him go while Kerr focused on some distant point that only he could see as he tapped into his telepathy.

"They're coming," Kerr announced, blinking solid awareness back into his eyes.

"Good," Lucas said as he walked past them, telekinetically stealing a few cigarettes and the lighter from Jason's pocket. He left the shuttle with quick strides, going to sit on the open cargo ramp beneath the bright lights of the underground hangar.

Above him, the launch silo was dark. It wouldn't come online, the blast doors wouldn't open, until they were ready to fly the hell out of here. Lucas figured that time couldn't come soon enough.

Thirty minutes later, everyone started to trickle into the hangar. He was almost done with his second cigarette when Matron, Everett, and Novak finally got there, the last to arrive. They made a ragtag little group, these five psions and three humans, every single one with a part to play. Lucas wondered, yet again, what Marcheline was thinking years ago before she died when she had convinced him to go along with this craziness. Her expectations had been impossible to ignore. So were Aisling's orders.

"Your boy here," Matron said as she pointed at Quinton, "I like the way he shoots."

"He's a crack shot," Lucas said as he stubbed out his cigarette on the cargo ramp he was sitting on. "Of course you would."

"I need a replacement for the one you got killed."

"You can't have me," Quinton said irritably.

"Stop arguing," Threnody said, giving Quinton a sharp glance and a silent warning not to start a fight. "What do you want, Lucas?"

"It's not what he wants." Jason gestured among them all. "It's what we need to know. Did he tell you that these aren't the only shuttles?"

Quinton's expression became stony. Threnody didn't look surprised, and Jason narrowed his eyes at her. "Did you know?"

"I guessed." Threnody shrugged. "We had a talk the other day after he was finished working on Kerr. I needed confirmation on something Matron had told us."

"You've been keeping secrets an awful lot lately," Quinton said, unable to keep anger out of his voice.

"I'm sorry." Only she wasn't. Lucas could read that in her mind, if not in her face, in her voice. Threnody stared at him. "Jason's right, though. We need to know the full extent of your plans, Lucas. We need access to our powers again if you want us to actually help you."

"Four against one," Jason muttered.

"It wouldn't be enough," Kerr said. "And I won't fight him."

Jason's expression was one of betrayed surprise. *"What?"*

"Neither will I," Threnody agreed quietly.

Quinton stared at her, a tight, wounded expression on his face. Jason caught his eye when he looked away. "You and I, Quinton. We're the only sane people in this group."

Threnody rolled her eyes. "It's not about sanity, Jason. It never was. It's about doing what's right."

"How is joining forces with Lucas Serca, *right?*" Quinton demanded.

"Because he's the only one willing to save the human race. Mars isn't the answer. We can't just pick up and leave like none of this ever happened, like we didn't ruin this planet. Maybe everyone who launched the bombs all those years ago knew that as well." Threnody lifted her chin a little, squaring her shoulders like the soldier she wasn't supposed to be anymore. "Tell them what's in the Arctic, Lucas. Tell them what you told me."

Lucas looked at the expectant faces of the Strykers, the bored stances of Matron, Everett, and Novak. Getting to his feet, Lucas stepped off the cargo ramp and onto the launchpad.

"Threnody's right about the shuttles. Don't blame her because she's smarter than all of you combined," Lucas said. "There's an island in the Arctic that holds a seed bank that survived the Border Wars. The World Court knows of it—hell, they've *used* it. How do you think we got the Sky-Farms to feed everyone after the fact? The world was too polluted, too *dead,* to grow anything in the aftermath of the Border Wars. The World Court is going to take all of that with them when they leave Earth— every last seed, every last frozen embryo of all the species we drove to extinction over the centuries, and all the ones we lost in the Border Wars. They'll take it with them and leave us with *nothing.*

"They're only taking registered humans to try and stop the spread of psions. They're taking with them everything that lets us survive on this planet and leaving us behind to die." Lucas shook his head, his accustomed expression of sarcastic amusement and disdain slipping away. "What they want isn't going to fix their lives how they think it will. We destroyed the future we should have had with the Border Wars. This is the one we have to survive in. This is *all we've got.* We owe it to the next generation to build a better world."

"Thought that was supposed to be Mars," Novak said.

Everett smacked him upside the head. "Shut up."

"If Mars was meant to be livable, it would have stayed habitable," Lucas said. "It died out long before humans walked on this planet."

"That doesn't explain the Warhounds," Jason said in a frustrated voice. "Or why you're purposefully bringing them here."

"They've got someone in their ranks who can break through your shields. We need what's in your head, Jason. More than you realize."

"You can't do it yourself?" Jason's mouth curled into a sneer. "I thought triad psions were capable of anything."

"Just because I'm a Class I doesn't mean I'm always going to be the right person for the job or that I will have the required strength. Why do you think I brought all of you together? I had to wait for the Strykers to demote Threnody and Quinton, had to wait for them to be paired up with you. It's going to take all of us to make sure those left behind survive."

"Wait," Quinton said. "You mean you *don't* want to stop the launch? I thought that was the whole point of us working with you?"

"Let them go to Mars. We'll keep Earth. We just need half of what they're going to take with them. Half the seeds. Half the embryos. Half the people. Half the psions, once we ensure the Strykers' survival. We can build something new with all of that."

Lucas was staring at Threnody as he said it, seeing steely agreement in her eyes.

"The government is gonna fry all your brains before they launch into space," Matron said. "Even *I* know that."

"There's a way to reprogram the neurotrackers," Lucas said. "How do you think the Warhounds managed to keep all the defected Strykers alive long enough to remove the bioware?"

"There's twelve hundred of us in the Strykers Syndicate," Kerr said. "How are you going to stop the kill sequence for that many psions?"

Again, Lucas looked at Jason. The telekinetic just frowned. "I'm not *that* good of a hacker."

Lucas shook his head. "It's not your hacking skills we'll need."

"Fucking great. Why do I have to be your crux?"

"Not the crux. The linchpin." Lucas walked over to where Jason and Kerr were standing, then reached out and pressed a finger to Jason's forehead. Jason knocked his hand away and took a step back. "I said it before. You were misdiagnosed, Jason. You're not an average telekinetic. All that power inside your head means you're something more. Our natal shields *always* break. They have to if we're at all able to access our powers. But your shields are still up and you can still use your telekinesis to a certain degree. You're strong enough to teleport."

Jason gave a derisive little snort. "So, what, you're saying that just because my shields never broke, I'm a Class 0?"

"Yes."

"Bullshit. The only psions who reach that rank are precognitives. I don't see the future. I'm not whatever it is you think I'm supposed to be."

187

"Microtelekinetic," Lucas said as he brushed past him. "You are what Nathan failed to produce in me, Jason. The Strykers got lucky when they picked you up. So did the world."

Lucas twisted his telepathy through their minds. He broke the mental blocks he had erected around the areas in their brains that bridged the synaptic distances between conscious thought and the powers they had been born with. Control came back in a heady instant, making the four light-headed.

We're either not human enough to leave, or we're too human to stay, Lucas said into all their minds. *It can't be about who is more deserving anymore. That's what got us here in the first place.*

They watched him walk away, none of them saying a word. What broke the silence was the faint hiss of gas, the scrape of metal on metal, and the crackle of fire as Quinton let tiny flickers of flame twist around his fingers. Clenching his hand around the fire, he put it out with a thought, skin hot to the touch.

"I'm in," he said, glancing over at Threnody and giving her a nod. He watched as some of the tension drained from her shoulders, loosening the rigid way she held herself.

Jason threw his arms up in the air as he went back into the shuttle. "You're all fucking crazy. Now leave me the hell alone so I can work in peace."

[TWENTY-TWO]

AUGUST 2379

TALLINN, ESTONIA

They threw the bodies into the toxic burn pits.

Dug deep into the limestone cliff that ran through the remnants of the capital city, kilometers from the Gulf of Finland, the burn pits were mostly full, but they still smoldered.

Dalia panted through the filter of her skinmask, believing that she could taste the dead on her tongue. She couldn't, not really. Didn't stop her brain from trying to tell her nose that she *should* be smelling the dead. Perception was so easily messed with.

"Is this the last of them?" the telepath beside her asked.

Dalia looked at the small group of bond workers and scientists that were huddled together as if that solidarity could save them. They were dressed in worn-out work uniforms or lab clothes, faces full of terror, unable to run. Transferred here from farther inland, these were the people that had been assigned to her warehouse for a job that couldn't be on record. Which meant they could not be on record.

"Yes," Dalia said as she reflexively touched her front pocket, feeling the multitude of data chips safe in her possession. Schematics enough to liberate them all. "Nathan wants no witnesses."

A telepath to turn off their minds.

A telekinetic to toss them into the burn pits.

Dalia licked her lips and tasted nothing but her own sweat. She had long ago gotten over the guilt for being a murderer. The government wouldn't miss their stolen data, just as they wouldn't miss the dead. Nathan, she knew, would be pleased that his orders had been so perfectly executed, here and in all the other places across the world like this. Those who weren't wanted would be left behind and forgotten.

There was no place in the stars for the useless.

PART SIX

CONVECTION

SESSION DATE: 2128.02.27

LOCATION: Institute of Psionics Research

CLEARANCE ID: Dr. Amy Bennett

SUBJECT: 2581

FILE NUMBER: 196

"Where's Matthew, Mama?"

"Your brother's not here, sweetheart," a dark-haired woman says as she crouches down beside the table, peering beneath it at the girl hiding in the only darkness that exists in the room. "He made it out of the country, remember? But he's watching over you. Just like you wanted."

"Good, good," the girl mutters, picking at the lace on her white socks as she glances at the camera. "I miss him."

"I know you do, but if you're really good—"

"Maybe I'll get to see him," Aisling interrupts, the frustration in her young voice impossible to miss. "You always say that."

The woman goes still. "No, I don't."

Aisling raps her knuckles on the floor so hard the skin splits. "Here. You always say it *here*."

"Stop it." The woman reaches out and pulls the girl into her arms, several wires pulling free because of the sudden movement. An alarm sounds, coming from one of the machines. "Stop hurting yourself."

"What if I'm wrong? Mama, what if I got it wrong?"

The woman slides her fingers through her daughter's dark hair, touching more wires than anything else. She hesitates only a moment before she grips a handful and yanks them off the girl's head, setting off a multitude of alarms.

"I should never have brought you to this place," she whispers as the door slides open and a nurse comes in. "You're not God, baby girl. You can't save us, no matter what they say."

"I know, Mama." Aisling wraps her small arms around her mother's neck and holds on tightly. "I can't save you here. I'm sorry."

TWENTY-THREE

AUGUST 2379

TORONTO, CANADA

"Miss me?"

Ciari didn't bother to look away from the hologrid above her desk displaying all the recently gathered data from field Strykers. "You shouldn't be here, Lucas."

"You always say that. Notice how I never listen."

This time Ciari did look up, watching the person who sat across from her through the colorful sharpness of the hologrid. The smile on Lucas's face hadn't changed a bit in the five years she'd known him. It was still as challenging as ever.

"One of these days they'll find out."

"Yes," he agreed. "Sooner than you or I would like, but that's the cost of success."

"*Are* we succeeding?"

He looked away from her to stare at the ceiling. "*Success* is such a dangerous word. Everyone's definition of it is different."

"I'm only interested in yours."

"You aren't the only one." Lucas glanced back at her, the smile on his face twisting into something unreadable as he rose to his feet. "There won't be time after today for us. Not for a while yet."

"There's never been time for us," Ciari reminded him as he came around her desk and stopped behind her chair. "You showed me that when you revealed those old files showing Aisling and what she wanted. Disagreeing never got me anywhere."

"What have I told you?" He leaned down to whisper the words into her ear even as one hand curled over her chin to turn her head toward him, the other settling over her stomach. "You can argue about what Aisling wants all you like, it's not going to change a damn thing."

"It could."

"Oh, Ciari." He pressed his mouth against hers, the pressure just a ripple in her mind. "There's a reason why she told me to include you. I've lived my entire life trusting in the veracity of details. Aisling is the devil in all of them. You can't fight her, so stop trying."

Lucas.

"Ciari?"

The space behind her was empty, her mind just as barren. Just a memory, of some moment before this. Sucking in a soft breath, Ciari turned her head to acknowledge the pair of Strykers that had entered her office. "What is it?"

Aidan and Jael shared a brief look before both telepaths focused on their OIC. Aidan stepped forward to set a data chip on Ciari's desk. "We've got incoming reports from Buffalo of Warhound arrivals on the mental grid. Some of their shields slipped a little and we got confirmation of two psi signatures that match Samantha and Kristen Serca."

Ciari gave them both a surprised look. "Kristen? Are you sure?"

Aidan nodded. "It's her."

"She hasn't been seen in years. I thought Nathan had her put down." Ciari shook her head. "Kristen being alive complicates things."

"We'll warn the Strykers that a dysfunctional psion has entered the fight." Aidan shrugged. "I'm not sure if that warning will do any good, though. Everyone who's ever gone after Kristen has always ended up dead."

Ciari minimized the hologrid with a wave of her hand. "It doesn't matter. If those two are in the field, then that means Lucas has to be as well. Did the scans find any evidence of our missing Strykers?"

"No. That's not to say they aren't with him, if he is there."

"Or dead," Jael added.

"It's been a while since we lost the four in the Slums." Ciari frowned. "If Samantha is leading the Warhounds in Buffalo, then most likely that is where Lucas is."

"We still don't know if Lucas is aligned with them or not," Aidan said.

"I vote not," Jael said sharply. "Two years on the run, being hunted by Strykers *and* Warhounds? Looking back at the information we've accumulated on that outlier blip that we now *know* is Lucas Serca, there's not much evidence to the contrary. He was integral to the Serca Syndicate's image while growing up as Nathan's successor. Now it's the twins. Lucas is no longer with the Serca Syndicate, nor the Warhounds. I think it's time we let the Strykers Syndicate know that blip is still alive."

"And have everyone worry that we've got a *third* psion group coming into play?" Ciari grimaced as she pushed her chair back and got to her feet. "The World Court would blame us for allowing that to happen. The punishment would be severe. Not to mention the Silence Law is still in effect."

"They're just going to kill us all anyway," Jael argued. "What's a few weeks early?"

"Jael," Aidan said, giving the CMO an admonishing look. "Remember who you're speaking to."

"I do." The petite black woman lifted her chin and glared stubbornly at Ciari. "The one person who has the power to argue our existence to the World Court. How's that going, Ciari?"

Ciari's expression didn't change. If she was angry at Jael's accusation, at her bitterness, she didn't show a single shred of it. "I'm not the one who's going to save us. That's someone else's task."

"Really." It was hard to ignore the ugly hatred in Jael's tone. "Care to explain what you mean by that?"

"I'm not obligated to explain anything." Ciari shrugged. "But I'm a Stryker, Jael. No matter what happens, my goal is our continued survival. Give me some credit. I'm too close to the World Court to be able to effectively do everything that needs to get done. Every OIC has always relied on others for the more delicate work we do. You know that."

"Then who's your scapegoat if you're ours?"

"You'll know soon enough." Ciari turned her attention to Aidan. "I'll review what you gave me within the hour. Begin a callback of Stryker teams that we can afford to remove from the field for an immediate emergency transfer."

"What are you planning?" Aidan said.

"What needs to be done. You have two hours to get me a list of teams that we can ship into Buffalo."

"What's our limit?"

"This is a Class I triad psion we're going up against. You don't have a limit."

Aidan nodded and turned to leave the office. Jael remained behind. Leaning against her desk, Ciari gazed at her CMO and offered up a half-smile.

"Do you even know what you're doing?" Jael asked, reeling in some of her anger.

"I know what needs to be done."

"That doesn't answer my question or ease my worry at all, Ciari." Jael came around Ciari's desk to stand by the other woman, looking out through the window wall that lined half of Ciari's office. Jael could see the horizon, where Lake Ontario was still and placid in the summer heat beneath the haze of lingering pollution. "Unlike almost everyone else in our ranks, I've got full access to Stryker records. It may take me a while, but eventually I realize when something doesn't add up."

Ciari didn't bother to correct Jael's misunderstanding of her own knowledge. She'd let the telepath believe what she wanted if it would keep the peace for just a few more weeks. "Aidan doesn't question me. Perhaps you still have something to learn from him."

"Aidan doesn't see the wounded, the dying, and the dead on a daily basis" was Jael's flat response. "I do. We Strykers in command positions know about the launch date. Some of us just know, same as you do, that we won't be on those ships when the engines trip over into full burn."

"No, we won't."

Frustration bled out through Jael's shields, thick enough for Ciari to almost taste it. "Then why aren't we fighting to free ourselves? We have a right to *live,* Ciari."

"The World Court doesn't think so. Luckily"—Ciari held up one hand to forestall Jael's instant argument—"I've never believed that. I know what I'm doing, Jael. I know what's at stake. So I'm asking you—*asking,* not ordering—to give me a little more time."

It was ironic, Ciari thought, that she was asking for the one thing that none of them had if she didn't play this game *just right*. Jael meant well, but her desire to save people just made Ciari's own job harder. Just as the World Court had decided that not everyone could have a seat on those shuttles, a berth on that colony ship, Ciari knew that not all of her Strykers would survive. It was just the way this particular world worked.

That was the way it *had* to work.

Jael shifted her gaze away from the skyline, turning her head to stare at Ciari. "You haven't looked as hard as you could have for Threnody's and Kerr's teams. Is this why?"

Ciari managed to give the other woman an actual, genuine smile that made Jael's skin crawl. Real emotion never looked right when empaths used it for themselves, but it was all the answer that Ciari gave her.

That, and "Trust me."

Looking at her right then, Jael thought that not even the gods some humans still believed in would trust Ciari. Jael supposed it was a good thing she wasn't human.

"It's not like I've got a choice," Jael said, hazel eyes narrowing ever so slightly in her dark face. "You're all we've got standing between us and the World Court."

No, I'm not, Ciari thought. "Go coordinate with Aidan on the teams. I want them transferred as soon as possible once we have that list."

"How do you hope to explain this to the World Court?"

"That's not for you to worry about."

Hearing the dismissal in Ciari's words, Jael left.

"Computer, initiate lockdown," Ciari said as she sat in her chair, hearing the chime signaling that her verbal order had been obeyed. Sighing, Ciari reached for the data chip that Aidan had delivered, unsurprised to find a second one resting beside it, clear, with no markings whatsoever to show whom it had come from or even where it had been manufactured.

Ciari scooped them both up, holding the tiny squares in the palm of her hand, trying not to think about everything else that she couldn't hold on to.

[TWENTY-FOUR]

AUGUST 2379
BUFFALO, USA

The hypospray hissed softly against his throat as Jason jammed his thumb against the release button. Adrenaline shot through his veins, sharpening his senses to an almost dangerous degree. He pulled the thin cylinder away from his body with a ragged gasp.

"That's your sixth injection in the past twenty-one hours," Quinton said from the hatch behind him, almost sounding worried. "You're going to burst your heart if you use any more."

"Can't be helped," Jason rasped as he tossed the empty hypospray onto the floor of the flight deck. "I have to be able to think."

"Why not get one of the telepaths to keep you awake? Turn your mind permanently on for a few hours, or however much longer this will take."

"Doesn't work on me." Jason craned his head around to give Quinton a strained smile. "My shields don't allow for very much psionic interference. Always wondered why, before Lucas said I'm supposed to be something other than a regular old Class V telekinetic. Anyway, I burn through this stuff so quick that I have to keep it in my veins with continuous injections. You know how it is."

Quinton stepped into the flight deck and watched as the younger man sat himself down in the pilot's seat. Jason's hands skimmed over the control terminal, prying hardwires out of the console and connecting them to the neuroports in his arms. Hologrids sparked into existence all around him, the light turning his skin a sickly gray.

"Kerr can't do anything for you?"

"Kerr can only go so deep in my head, even with the bond," Jason explained as he dragged his fingers through the readout, most of his attention on the program. "He needs to focus on his own mind right now. I'll be fine. Something tells me Lucas won't let me die before I finish this hive connection. The hackers they used didn't know government code as well as I do."

Quinton grunted soft agreement.

"Why are you still here, Quinton?"

"Threnody was worried about your limits. I'll tell her you've got none."

It drew a strained laugh out of Jason, making him glance over his shoulder at Quinton. The inspecs in his eyes were bright spots in his pupils. "Oh, I've got limits, but Lucas doesn't care about them. I'm all out of hyposprays. Bring me another one in three hours. I'm going to need it."

Quinton shook his head as he turned to leave. "Just don't get dead, Jason. We still need you."

Quinton walked through the cargo bay and down the open ramp of the cargo door to the launchpad. The area, which had been empty when he'd gone into the shuttle, was now filled with large metal supply trunks, courtesy of Lucas, who was looking a lot worse for wear. After ten straight hours of constant teleportation between underground hangars, ferrying supplies, Quinton figured anyone would.

"What's in these?" Quinton asked.

"Insulated skinsuits," Lucas said as he kicked one of the trunks with his boot. "We're going to need them when we hit the Arctic. It might be summer, but it's still cold as fuck."

"Where do you want them?"

"Cargo hold. Three in each. I'll leave you to it."

He teleported out and Quinton swore tiredly. Just a fucking stevedore, that's all he was right now. Quinton retrieved the hoverlift that was sitting idle past the launchpad and dragged the trunks one at a time into the shuttles, because more than just skinsuits were in those huge containers. The weight had carefully been calculated by Matron, things that they would need for and after the Arctic. Lucas hadn't said as much, but everyone knew they weren't going to stay on Spitsbergen. They couldn't. The World Court would wage a quick and dirty war with them if they tried to, and the psions would lose.

The thing was, Quinton thought as he guided the second set of trunks into the next shuttle, Lucas was damned good at keeping them all in the dark. Whether it was psionic interference or just a slick mindwipe, Lucas only gave out enough details to get the results he wanted. Didn't matter how many lives he took or ruined, the only thing that he cared about was a final goal he shared with no one.

"Where's Jason?"

Quinton glanced up as he finished anchoring the latest supply trunk beside one of the massive cold storage units bolted to the deck of the shuttle. Threnody stood at the bottom of the open cargo ramp, a tense expression on her face.

"In the other shuttle," he said.

"Kerr just informed me that he picked up Warhound and Stryker psi signatures on the mental grid."

Quinton grimaced. "They're early."

"Or they're right on time." Threnody climbed up into the shuttle, peeling open a ration bar. She had two in her hands and offered the unopened one to Quinton. "Depends which schedule we're running on. That's not all of it. Matron said the acid storm out west caught the polar jet stream. It's going to hit here sooner rather than later. We don't have much time left."

"How soon?"

Threnody chewed hard on the bite of ration bar she'd taken before saying, "Three, maybe four hours. We can predict the weather, but we can't control it."

Quinton took in a careful breath. "Guess that's why Lucas just teleported out."

"We've got sixteen underground hangars to prep for launch in less time than we thought we'd get. That's what I need to tell Jason. He needs to get these shuttles online *now*."

Quinton finished securing the last trunk before following Threnody to the shuttle Jason was working in. The telekinetic was hunched over the console, wires streaming out of both arms and inspecs running at high capacity as they parsed out the downloads that were coming through the bioware in his brain.

"Jason," Threnody said.

"Busy" was his absent-sounding answer.

"Not as much as you're going to be." Threnody leaned over his chair and put a hand over his eyes, forcing a physical connection he had to deal with instead of the hologrids in the air around him and the data being downloaded into his brain. "That storm is going to hit within the next few hours. We've got Strykers and Warhounds on the ground in Buffalo. We need these shuttles flight-worthy."

Jason swore, finished what he was working on with a few quick commands, and started the compiler. Then he pulled her hand off his face and twisted his head to stare at her.

"Are you *kidding?*" Jason asked, voice dry. "How long?"

"You've got two hours to finish this, Jason. That's it."

"Or we're all dead, I *know.* You're lucky I've already installed all the firmware on the rest of the shuttles." He refocused his attention on the data before him. "You did your duty by me, now start warning everyone else."

Quinton and Threnody left the shuttle side by side, hurrying back to the tenement where Matron had kicked her scavengers into high gear hours ago. There were fewer scavengers than when they'd first arrived in Buffalo. Matron had been sending them out in small groups to the other hangars over the last few days.

"This is it people, we're at the endgame," Matron shouted over the buzz of conversation as a multitude of bodies worked around her. "You know your places. I want you all there before that acid storm hits. Keep your head down, stay off the grid, and stay the hell away from the quads."

Matron saw the Strykers approaching and nodded in their direction. When they got close enough, Threnody said, "Jason knows. He's going to have the hive connection fully up and running in two hours."

"You sure about that?"

"He was one of the best hackers the Strykers Syndicate had. He'll get it done."

Matron grunted as she continued to separate out weapons on the table she was standing at. "Novak's at his assigned hangar with Everett. I've got reports in from half my crew, the ones that are already at the other hangars or on their way. They're worried about being discovered by you psions."

"Lucas and I have their minds shielded," Kerr announced as he slipped through the crowd to plant himself next to Matron. "Don't worry about them."

"Yeah, the last time Lucas said that, I ended up with a third of my crew dead." Matron scowled, lips pulled back over her metal teeth. "How many is he going to let die this time?"

"You'll survive." Kerr shrugged as he reached for a gun and hooked the weapon to his belt. "Isn't that the only thing you're worried about?"

"Stay the fuck out of my head."

"I'm not in your mind."

Kerr nodded at Threnody and Quinton before disappearing back into the crowd with his own set of orders to follow.

"Fucking psions," Matron muttered as she loaded yet another gun and set it aside for someone else to claim.

Quinton joined her at the table, sorting through the stash of weapons with familiar ease. Threnody positioned herself on the other side of the room, helping a trio of scavengers destroy the accumulated data the tenement held, which meant burning out everything electrical they handed her until it was just slag.

Based on Matron's orders and the way she was giving them, Threnody knew that Matron wasn't going to return to Buffalo anytime soon, if ever again. She was covering her tracks in a methodical, almost brutal, way, stripping the tenement down to its bones. Threnody had a feeling that the other sites around Buffalo the scavengers owned were going through the same strip-and-burn scenario.

"What about the hangars?" Threnody asked as she placed her hand on yet another hard drive and sent her power through it. "You're not going to leave them for the government to dig through, right?"

"That's why we've got the C-4," Matron said. "Don't worry your pretty little head, girl. I've been doing this for longer than you've been alive."

The tenements that Matron's scavengers used as their base of operations were off the electrical grid most of the time, but not for this mission. Matron was savvy, in the way most survivalists were. She didn't have a permanent hard connection to the rest of Buffalo, but her restricted system could still uplink through a secondary one. It ran under the connections that the government used, but Matron considered information and secrecy more important than credit and following the law. Always had; it's what enabled her to survive. Right now, they needed to be connected to the government's grid.

The vidscreens in the building switched on all at once, the emergency stream that appeared flickering red around the edges. A reporter for Buffalo, a pretty brunette press anchor set up high somewhere in the city towers, smiled at the masses.

"People of New York. Please do not be alarmed. Curfew has been enacted for your personal safety. It has come to the government's attention that rogue psions have infiltrated Buffalo. The government advises everyone to remain in their towers or in their bunkers. Strykers are on the ground for your protection against the rogue psions. Adhere to the curfew or face a heavy fine."

The average citizen didn't know that rogue psions were a well-organized group, just that they were a dangerous enough threat to make people think twice about venturing outside the bunkers and the sealed city towers. The government didn't want their problem spun any which way but dead, which was why they mentioned the Strykers.

The broadcast repeated itself a second time before the stream went to standby mode. Like all emergency streams, it would be repeated every few minutes. Matron turned her head to look at Threnody.

"How's that notoriety feel?" the woman asked.

Threnody clenched her hand around the latest hard drive she was holding, electric lines of power crackling from her fingers to the small machine in her hand as it became nothing more than slag.

"They aren't revealing our identities," Threnody said. "Which means the government doesn't want the world to know that Strykers have gone rogue."

"Most rogue psions are Strykers who defect."

"That's not common knowledge outside of highly classified reports." Something Threnody had only recently learned. "And *most* is a little too high a count."

Matron's mouth curled up in disgust. "Fucking sheep."

Threnody chose not to feel insulted. Matron's disgust only lasted for a few seconds, or as long it took for the lights in the tenement to flicker and die out, only some coming back online with the whine of generators a few seconds later when they were *supposed* to be tapped into the main electrical grid.

Matron's teeth clacked together loudly in the sudden silence. "That ain't good."

Threnody followed her gaze to the nearest dark tracts of lighting. "I thought we were already running off the generators?"

"We normally are, but how do you think we're going to open fifteen launch silos?" Matron shook her head. "One would drain all my generators. Fifteen isn't possible. We've been tied into the government's electrical grid since Jason started his hack."

"And now?"

"Now we're fucking *not*." Matron spun around. "Someone get me an uplink! I want to know what the fuck just happened here!"

She rushed off, barking out orders as she went. Threnody was still needed for a few more minutes of disposal work, so she jerked her head at Quinton in a silent order. Weaving his way through the crowd of scavengers who were busy gathering up what they would need to get them to the other launch sites, Quinton kept doggedly on Matron's heels.

The two ended up back in the room that guarded the blast doors to the underground hangar. Matron was leaning over the chair in front of the control terminal, fingers stabbing at the hologrid that hovered in front of the vidscreen. A map of the Buffalo sprawl was sketched out in the air, rapidly expanding and decreasing, depending on Matron's order. It was feeding her data through the neuroports in her cybernetic limb, a wireless feed that wasn't as stable as a wired connection.

"Coincidence?" one of the scavengers in the room asked, sounding hopeful.

Lucas teleported in, saying, "*Coincidence* is a word used only by liars and fools."

"You would know," Matron snapped. "Come look at this."

Lucas paced forward and watched as Matron zoomed out from the street view of Buffalo to the citywide view, bright blue dots pulsing where their launch silos were and an overlay of green from the electrical grid that was steadily blacking out over the entire city.

"What about the main bunkers?" Quinton asked tightly.

"They have environmental systems that run on backup generators located all over the city," Lucas said. "For a lockdown like this, people can last a day, maybe two, with the environmental systems running at full before emergency restrictions would have to be enacted."

"You don't think it'll take that long, do you?" Threnody said as she came into the room.

"I think a lot of people are going to die under a government-sanctioned power outage with an acid storm riding a derecho spine about to hit." Dark blue eyes flicked her way. "The storms always do damage, that's expected. The government never shuts off the power just because the weather's bad. They're doing it this time to find us. Warhounds are spreading out through the city, so are Strykers, and they're all hunting for us. Kerr and I have already deflected search scans through human minds. We're linked to every scavenger, but that's a network that can be found more easily than a single mind, despite the precautions we've taken."

"So what are you saying?"

"I'm saying that we need the power plants to be turned back on—at least one of them."

"Can't you mindwipe those workers to change it for you?" Quinton demanded, not liking where this conversation was going.

"No," Lucas said, voice firm. "The second I start altering minds, my sister will pick up on it. Samantha's on the ground here and she was trained by Nathan, just like me. She knows the same tricks I do. If she finds out what I'm doing, she'll want to know *why* we want the generators on when

I could just as easily teleport everyone out of this place. It won't take her very long to figure it out."

Threnody's gaze was steady when she looked at him. "You need us to turn the electrical grid back on for you."

"I need *you* to turn it on." Lucas turned his head and reached out for the map, dragging his fingers over the hologrid to zero in on one of the two power plants that kept the city running. "You're a Class III electrokinetic. You can override whatever lockdown they've got on the power plants and jump-start the grid."

"That much power in those places will fry her nervous system," Quinton said, voice hard. "That's suicide."

"Not necessarily. It'll take time for her to make her way to power plant two, and by then, the storm will have hit."

"The other power plant is closer."

"The other one feeds only into the city towers. We need the one for everyone else." Lucas pushed away from the chair he was leaning on to face the Strykers. "If you want to go with her, then fine. Take Kerr along as well. You'll need the coverage a telepath can provide."

"What about you?" Threnody asked. "And Jason?"

"Jason's working on the shuttles. He's not going anywhere until we launch. As for me? I'm going to be the bait." The smile Lucas gave them was tired, but every bit as dangerous as the ones he'd offered up before. "The Warhounds are looking for me because I called them here. The Strykers are just an additional bonus. I'll draw their fire and let them take each other out."

"And if you die?"

"This isn't where I die. I'll be there at the end to pick you up, as long as you get the job done."

"What if we don't?"

"Then Aisling was wrong."

Threnody pressed her mouth into a hard line. She swallowed and said, "I'd rather she wasn't."

"Kerr's getting a vehicle ready right now." Lucas nodded at the door. "Get your gear and get out of here. That curfew is already in effect and quads are going to be on the street."

"You'll want to hit the underground entrance about six kilometers north of here," Matron said as she hurriedly downloaded the city map into a data chip. "You'll need to travel underground half of the way to the power plant on the maglev trains, if they're still running. If not, take a pedestrian tunnel. The rest of the way in, when you get closer to the power plant, it's gonna be all aboveground travel. The government likes to see people coming."

"I'm guessing the security grid is still up and running through the backup generators," Quinton said.

Matron gave a hollow little laugh as she tossed the loaded data chip and a datapad to Quinton. "You'd guess right. Get the fuck out of here. You've only got so much time."

Quinton and Threnody left without arguing. Threnody was hell-bent on this mission and Quinton knew better than to try to change her mind. It was too late to back out now.

"Hope you know what you're doing," Quinton said as they finally made it to the garage, the doors winched wide-open and wind rushing inside. "You're still not fully recovered."

"Then you better hope that Lucas packed some decent medical supplies in those trunks you were loading onto the shuttles," Threnody said as they wove their way to where Kerr was checking over the SUV that would get them back to the city.

Kerr tossed a bag at each of them. "Our old uniforms," he explained. "I figured they might get us a little further than civilian attire if we alter them enough."

He was already wearing his, the black-on-black BDUs overlaid with bits and pieces of protective armor. Threnody and Quinton stripped right there in the garage, everyone ignoring them. The uniform felt strange after so many days wearing borrowed clothing. This wasn't who they were anymore, not completely, and Threnody couldn't help but wonder if the changes would show up on a feed.

They still had the strips of bioware on their faces, iris peels coating their eyes. False identities that might get them into the city without being detected, but if the security grid was running on full, Threnody had a feeling the precautions wouldn't get them far enough. They were the hunted this time, not the hunters, but they knew how Strykers thought. Maybe that would help.

Then again, maybe not.

Quinton packed extra ammunition into a case hooked to his belt before slinging a military-grade rifle over one shoulder. A separate hard pack that hung securely from his belt was a match for the one that Threnody wore as well: a field med-kit, specifically decked out to deal with loss of limbs. Quinton tended to lose parts of himself in the field while using his power if the fighting got bad enough.

"We good to go?" Kerr asked as he climbed into the driver's seat and started the engine.

The other two Strykers got into the SUV, Threnody in the back and Quinton riding shotgun. The side windows were all long-since broken and the windshield was cracked. It didn't seem to bother Kerr and it wouldn't impede Quinton's cover fire.

"Let's get the hell out of here," Threnody said. "Quinton, you got our way in?"

Quinton held up the datapad Matron had given him. "Just start driving. I'll navigate."

"Fine." Kerr revved the engine and shifted the SUV out of park and into drive, gunning it forward.

They drove out onto the dusty, barren road for Buffalo. They'd been inside for so long that they hadn't seen the change in the weather. They couldn't see the sun where they knew it was positioned in the western sky. Dark thunderclouds stretched from the city they were driving to all the way to the black line on the horizon that was steadily sweeping over the earth.

The wind picked up, sending dirt flying through the open windows of the SUV. Threnody blinked grit out of her eyes and reached up to tie back her hair as the first tiny drops of acid rain began to fall.

[TWENTY-FIVE]

AUGUST 2379

BUFFALO, USA

The landscape of Buffalo reminded Samantha of broken teeth—worn down, jagged, badly cared for—when they teleported into an empty street of the city. The wind seemed to find every open point of her uniform and blow through it to chill her skin with the damp. As they ran for the blast doors that led to the underground bunkers most of the unregistered humans called home, Samantha looked up at the world that surrounded them.

Broken buildings, broken lives, broken promises. It was the only thing every surviving city had in common.

The acid rain was coming down in sheets, soaking her in seconds as she dragged Kristen after her into the relative dryness of the small receiving building. Samantha swiped at her eyes beneath the dark glasses she wore, ignoring the burn. She tugged Kristen out of the way of the entrance to the far wall.

This entry point was minimally guarded, not meant to handle a huge influx of people going into the bunkers. The quads who had manned this post were already dead, bodies stacked against the other wall. A Warhound electrokinetic in the first wave had fried the security feed, and a hacker was busy writing it back into the main system on a different signal. They needed a place to act as their ground base for communications. The warehouse wasn't viable, not anymore. Lucas had already hit it once; he'd hit it again given half the chance. This would have to do.

"Tastes like fire," Kristen muttered as she licked at her wet lips, watching through half-lidded eyes as the other Warhounds in their squadron came hurrying inside.

"Shut up," Samantha said.

Kristen hummed against her side, and while she didn't open her mouth again, Samantha highly doubted that her order would be obeyed for long.

A tall figure broke free from the crowd and jogged over to them. Jin Li offered Samantha a casual two-fingered salute and a sharp smile. "Every other team's in position. We're the last. Ready to move out?"

"Been ready," Samantha said. "Let's go."

Jin Li gave her a sarcastic little bow. "Lead the way."

The blast doors rolled shut after the last Warhound came through. A skeleton team would remain behind to cover for them. This entry point wasn't going to be accessible to anyone but Warhounds from here on out. The humans still rushing around outside after curfew in this section of the city were going to have one hell of a hard time getting below before the quads discovered their presence.

The long stairs leading down were new, replaced every decade or so after countless feet had trod upon them until they cracked. The stairs led deep into the ground, to a metal tunnel that was big enough to house a maglev train, except it didn't. A quarter of the space that made up Buffalo were tunnels for straight foot traffic, or ground vehicles where it was viable. Another quarter were tunnels for the maglev trains that serviced only a handful of spots in the city, both below- and aboveground. The other half wasn't tunnels at all, but huge bunkers carved deep into the ground, the heart and soul of a city that had died centuries ago.

That's where they were heading, into Bunker East, along with hundreds of humans who had finally heeded the curfew call in the face of an approaching acid storm, late though they were getting down below. The storm above was just the leading front, a supercell that churned above them, a mere precursor for the derecho spine that hadn't yet hit.

Samantha tucked a wet piece of hair behind her ear as she stretched out her telepathy to sink into the human minds all around them. She let the humans believe that the people in the black uniforms were just as human as they were, strangers with faces they would never remember.

Are we hacked into the security feed yet? Samantha wanted to know.

We've got hackers working on it from the city towers, Jin Li said. *They're*

coordinating with the ones in the field. We won't be recognized by the gov-
ernment, if that's what you're worried about.

That's only if the Strykers don't interfere.

Here's hoping they do.

Jin Li would want a challenge. Samantha only wanted this mission to
be over.

The lights that lined the tunnels were at half-power, the dimness difficult to see through with her glasses on. She didn't have the option of
taking them off. Samantha risked being identified without them, and
Kristen wasn't even *in* the Registry, but only a blind person would miss
the color of her eyes and not know what family she belonged to. They
couldn't be made because that would break all of Nathan's carefully laid
plans more thoroughly than anything the Strykers could come up with.

Warhounds peeled away at every cross-tunnel intersection they came
to, telepaths pairing up with various other psions as they spread out for
the hunt. Samantha, Kristen and Jin Li continued on through the main
tunnel, followed by two telekinetics. Samantha didn't have Gideon with
her down here, and they needed psions with telekinesis to counter what
Lucas could throw at them.

Glancing down at the bioscanner in her hand, she couldn't find Lucas
on it, but she could place the Strykers if she narrowed down the search.
Strykers were incapable of hiding completely on the mental grid, and the
government always had them tagged into the system. Government dogs
needed to be watched over in case they turned rabid.

It took them an hour to circumvent the Strykers, all the while march-
ing through the tunnels for Bunker East. Just because Lucas wasn't
showing up on the bioscanner didn't mean he wasn't flickering on the
mental grid. He wanted to be found, Samantha could read that in the
way he stayed in one place. Whatever trap he was building, it wasn't
going to be pretty, not for him, not for the Warhounds, and certainly
not for the Strykers drawn to his mental presence.

Lucas was definitely Nathan's son, and Nathan never did anything
by halves.

The Warhounds came out of the main tunnel into a wide underground space that was like a minicity, all steel-gray metal and walled-off

habitation, the whine of generators cutting through the sounds of human life. Straight down the center of that huge space, the size of an old stadium, was an empty maglev platform, the line of it lit brighter than anywhere else.

The unregistered humans with the most corrupted genetics called Bunker East home. It was closest to the deadzone that took up half of New York State. Even with shielding against radiation, the people here were never going to scrape their DNA clean. They were never going to escape what their ancestors had left for them.

Kristen moved away from Samantha to the railing that separated the crowd from a short fall to certain death on the maglev tracks below. She leaned over that point of separation to look down at the maglev platform, the tracks and the humans waiting there for a train that wasn't going to arrive anytime soon.

"Bet they'd all taste so good," she said around her smile.

Jin Li clamped a hand on her shoulder and pulled her back into the group. "Start walking, girl. You've got a bigger target to find."

The bioware that lined her skinsuit flickered a warning, which she ignored. Kristen didn't care about the prison she wore, just about her chance at survival that she could taste beyond her shields.

Samantha curled her fingers around the back of Kristen's neck and squeezed down warningly. "We're not here for them."

"Of *course* not, Sammy-girl," Kristen drawled as she reached up and squeezed Samantha's fingers tighter around her own throat.

Even down here, the world wasn't much different from the one above: still a mess of people, of poverty, of the dying looking to forget. Holo-grids rolled adverts over every conceivable surface, interrupted here and there by the government's curfew reminder. They weren't enough of a distraction.

Samantha felt it when Kristen started to engage her empathy, Kristen's power bleeding through her shields. It weighed down the mental grid in a way few other powers could, because a mental dysfunction was hard to correct and even harder to hide. Samantha had her own shields wrapped around Kristen's mind, forcing the other girl to work beneath a veneer of human static, but the shields just barely held and their cover didn't last.

They made it to one of the lower levels of Bunker East at the same moment as the Strykers. It didn't really matter to Samantha how they were found out as a telekinetic blow leveled everyone flat between the Warhounds and the team of Strykers coming at them, just that they were.

The attack hit hard against the telekinetic shield that surrounded the Warhounds, and Samantha reached out to pull Kristen up against the wall, trying to make them less of a target. Grabbing her gun, Samantha fired on the Strykers, the two Warhound telekinetics letting her attack get through. The bullets never hit their target. She didn't expect them to.

Kristen, go, Samantha ordered even as she dropped her shields.

A hole opened up on the mental grid, pulling everyone into the manic swirl of insanity that was Kristen. The mental grid buckled beneath the Class III strength made all the more dangerous by her insanity. It washed over human and psion minds alike. The only reason that her power didn't begin to eat through everyone immediately was the solid telepathic shield that slid between Kristen and her next meal.

"Not *fair*," Kristen spat out, dragging herself to her feet to glare at her oldest brother, where he leaned up against the railing, standing between them and the Strykers and the quickly scattering humans.

The security feed, Samantha sent out on a broad 'path. *Shut it down!*

Whether or not their hackers obeyed her in time, she would never know. Lucas wasn't bothering to hide his identity. She could have killed him for that callous thoughtlessness.

"I hear you've been looking for me," Lucas said, his voice barely audible above the screaming and the sharp, shrill sound of the alarm as people ran for a safety that couldn't be guaranteed.

Tension snaked through everyone on both sides of the fight, Lucas the line no one could cross. He knew it, they knew it, and the smile he gave his sisters was both condescending and cruel.

Kristen offered her own in return as she slid her power up against his shields. "Oh, I've missed your games. Nathan's not happy, but come play with me anyway."

"What else is new?" Lucas said as he raised a hand at the Strykers.

The Strykers amassing behind him were bowled over by a line of telekinesis that cut through their defenses hard enough to break bones. Lucas wasn't there for the Strykers. He was there for the Warhounds, for his sisters. The Strykers were just a complication he had dragged here because he needed the distraction. He'd had two years to perfect how to play the role of bait, and getting people to follow him had never been difficult. Digging into three of the Strykers' minds, he broke their shielding and altered their way of thinking, a quick and dirty mindwipe that would leave them unable to differentiate between their teammates and the enemy.

Then he let them go, let them attack humans and psions alike, because even Lucas needed backup sometimes. The results were bloody, but he couldn't regret the deaths of civilians down here, not when the rest of the world needed saving.

Samantha fell into merge with the two telekinetics, their strength together enough to counteract most of what Lucas could possibly throw at them. Maybe. She briefly regretted leaving Gideon behind, so used to her twin fighting alongside her.

The roar of energy darts rained down from above with sudden brutality, smashing into telekinetic shields and ricocheting every which way without finding a single target. Quads, military soldiers. They'd drawn the attention of the government, and that was never a good thing.

Don't worry, Lucas said into her mind. *The humans here won't remember us at all.*

Liar, Samantha said.

His laughter echoed in her mind, the psi link thin enough and precise enough that she knew they were the only two tied together in it. *I never lied about saving you.*

The world shifted, crumbling at the edges of her vision as Lucas's telepathy roared through the mental grid, slicing through everyone's thoughts with a ferocity Samantha could barely counter. She dug in with her own telepathy, slamming her shields up high and tight around her mind, around Jin Li's, around the two telekinetics who lashed out with their combined power at where Lucas stood. She left Kristen alone. Kristen was more than capable of taking care of herself.

The railing Lucas was leaning on cracked, the metal shearing off in large chunks. He lurched backward, catching himself before the spot he'd been resting against fell off onto the maglev platform below.

Fire exploded in the air around him, around the Warhounds, an inferno that scorched the area they were standing in. A Stryker pyrokinetic, because they didn't have a Warhound with that particular power in their current group. Samantha grabbed Kristen by the collar of her skinsuit and dragged her in close when she would have run forward. The girl never did care about her own skin. The telekinetics strengthened their shields and stood their ground. Jin Li took a few steps forward, eyeing Lucas with a feral look on his face.

"Nathan wants you dead," Jin Li said.

Lucas spread his arms wide; offered up a slick smile. "Go ahead. Try. I'll even let you get close enough to touch me."

Jin Li wasn't stupid enough to agree to something like that, at least, not alone. Linked to the telekinetics by Samantha's telepathy, Jin Li was teleported within striking range of Lucas, shielded down tight except for his hands as he reached for Lucas's throat. Lucas reacted like any well-trained Warhound would—with exponential force.

The ground he was standing on *cracked,* the air burned as his telekinetic blow slammed Jin Li into and *through* the support wall of the building they were fighting next to. Jin Li survived only because the Warhound telekinetics with them were well-trained in their power. They managed to cushion Jin Li's landing as best they could. Jin Li fell to the ground across from Kristen, half-conscious and bleeding from his nose and mouth, but mostly whole and alive.

Kristen turned her face in Lucas's direction, the smile she gave him stretched to its limits. "Try," she echoed, then wrapped her power around his mind in ways that not even Nathan could achieve.

The solid, mentally corrosive barrier she erected around her brother skewered his attention for only a few seconds, long enough for Samantha to dig her telepathy into his shields, to scorch her power over his. It was followed, incongruously enough, by two telepathic strikes from the Strykers.

It wasn't a merge. The Strykers didn't know *how* to merge, and

Samantha was alone in her attack because no one merged with Kristen and walked away alive. But a Class I, for all his or her strength, still had *limits*. Every psion did. Lucas, forced to battle on three separate fronts, remembered that when his top shield cracked beneath the onslaught, crumbling away.

He could sense Kristen's glee, Samantha's determination, and the Strykers' desire to see them all dead. He could also sense the minds clustered in the maglev train that was kilometers away and getting closer, running on the last dregs of power that could safely be siphoned off the generators as it struggled to make a stop on its schedule. He reached for the Stryker telepath he had altered, giving her a different set of orders this time, letting the woman target the soldiers in that approaching maglev train and the quads already here for him now that most of the Strykers nearby were either dead or incapacitated. The effort of fighting against his orders would probably break her mind. Lucas didn't care, so long as the Stryker had a target that wasn't him.

With a wrench that left his ears ringing, Lucas slid his mind away from the psions who wanted so badly to break him and teleported down to the maglev platform. Quads were rapidly surrounding the area, having long since shoved their way through the fleeing crowd for a better position from which to shoot and kill the enemy. They lined the second platform with only one intent, but Lucas knocked the group of soldiers down and out with a telepathic blow that left half of them catatonic and the other half bleeding their brains out their ears and noses.

Left behind on the walkway, Samantha holstered her gun and shoved herself to her feet. *Cover me,* she snarled at the pair of telekinetics, even as she launched herself over the railing.

It was a three-story drop to the platform below; she landed with telekinetic help. Still shielded, her movements jerky from running in step with someone else's power, Samantha raced toward her brother where he waited on the maglev platform.

Why now? she sent at him, layering her shields as Nathan had taught her when she was a child, creating a canyon between herself and her older brother on the mental grid. It wouldn't be enough, but she still had to try. *Why ruin everything when we're so close to being free of this place?*

What if I said this was all just meant to be? Lucas told her from where he stood, tense and waiting before her. *That it was inevitable?*

Nothing's inevitable, you know that. Samantha skidded to a halt, breathing heavily, feeling the telekinesis forced away.

The alarm was still sounding in Bunker East, the lights still dim along the walls and ceiling and floor. The hologrids were dark, any and all extra energy diverted to the maglev tracks, which were beginning to hum. This far underground, the storm couldn't reach them, but they were building their own where the humans had lived for generations.

What if it is?

Samantha felt the mental grid stretch itself thin and tight against her mind, Lucas's power reaching for something inside her that she never knew she carried. Consciousness. Awareness.

Memories.

Hers and not hers.

No. She threw up more and more mental shields, but he tore them all down.

I can't do this alone, Lucas told her, sounding tired. Old. As if he'd lived too long and hadn't died young enough before the bitterness overtook his life when he was only twenty years old.

She didn't feel herself hit the ground, just knew that her skull hit first, then her shoulders. The world spun in a sickening lurch that she felt in her gut, and Samantha choked on her breath the way people choked on water when they drowned. Warm hands pressed the side of her face against the stained metal of the platform that too many feet had walked over, dragging the dirt of the world down to a place where people bled out hope.

"You know what they said when the bombs fell?" Lucas pinned Samantha down against the maglev platform with his physical strength alone, his mind busy tearing hers apart. "Don't fear the end of the world. Fear what comes next."

She fought him with everything she had, but it wasn't enough. It had never been enough. As the maglev train roared into Bunker East, sliding with a hard, telekinetically anchored *stop* against the platform, Lucas leaned down and whispered into his sister's ear, "*We* are what came next, Sam. And I am so much better than what you could ever hope to be."

"I'm not—scared of you," Samantha gasped out as his telepathy curled through her mind and ruined what Nathan had built her into.

She broke; pieces of who she was shearing off, all the scar tissue that she had accumulated over the years just—ripped away.

Breathe. I still need you.

"You should be." Lucas rested his forehead against hers for a moment, just a moment, before he got to his feet and walked onto that train, leaving her a panting, bleeding wreck on the platform. "You really should be."

Panicked humans were struggling to get off the train, those that weren't already dead or dying, brains fried by the telepathic attack that the altered Stryker had aimed in their direction mere moments ago. Just bodies lying one on top of the other, on the floor, on the benches, the stink of bodily fluids filling the air. Death, when it came, always smelled human.

Lucas lifted himself above the mess with his telekinesis as the doors slid shut, looking through the clear plasglass at Samantha as she picked herself up off the ground with shaky effort.

Come after me, he said into her fractured mind. *I'll be waiting.*

Footsteps raced over the platform as the maglev train lurched forward with a hum of power. The lights all through Bunker East flickered dangerously low as the train drew nearly all of the remaining electricity out of the generators that kept everyone breathing down below.

Jin Li reached Samantha's side, dragged her all the way to a standing position, then got her the hell out of there. "That train's going to Bunker North," he said. "By the city towers. We'll get another telekinetic to 'port us there."

"Everyone else?" Samantha asked in a ragged breath as he pulled her into a waiting area on the platform with an overhang, where Kristen had her hand against the temple of the telekinetic that had survived Lucas's show of power. Blood was pouring out of the man's ears, pumping through her fingers. His partner had a halo of red around her head on the floor beside him, life already gone from her body.

The Sercas were the best assassins the Warhounds had. They needed to remember that.

"Dead and dying," Kristen reported cheerfully.

Samantha leaned down, letting Jin Li support her as she pressed her hand over the telekinetic's forehead.

Get us out of here, she said into the Warhound's mind, holding on to his thoughts and power, cognizant that she could barely hold herself together.

She kept him alive long enough for him to teleport them all to the surface.

Kristen devoured his mind as he died, smearing her fingers through the blood and acid rain that greeted them when they arrived in the middle of the storm that had been centuries in the making.

[TWENTY-SIX]

AUGUST 2379
BUFFALO, USA

The lights in the tunnels, already a dim emergency blue, flickered ominously. Some went out, others came back on a little brighter than before. No one still making their way toward Bunker West from Bunker South thought that was a good thing.

They'd made it into Buffalo from the outskirts, then been forced belowground, just as Matron had said. It was a good thing none of them were claustrophobic. Threnody slowed to a stop, pressing up against the curve of the tunnel as a straggling group of humans passed them by. Quinton was right beside her, cradling his rifle, watching their back. Kerr was barely an arm's length away on point, his telepathic shields wrapped tight around their minds, projecting them as human on the mental grid with an ease that he'd never before had. Even Threnody, who was not a 'path-oriented psion, could feel the difference against her own shields.

She peered past the brim of her stolen cap, pulled low over her eyes to shadow her face, as the humans continued straight ahead to the cross-tunnel intersection fifteen meters from where they stood.

"Quinton?" she asked softly.

He checked the datapad in his hand, thumb swiping over the screen to get a new readout. "If we follow them, there's no quick way out of the tunnels for another three, four kilometers. We've got to go aboveground if we're going to reach our target. No way around that now."

"Right or left?"

"Right. That tunnel will spit us out northeast of where we need to be, but closer than the last one."

"And with more problems." Kerr was squinting up at the ceiling. "The lights? That was Lucas being our distraction. He's on a maglev train heading to Bunker North."

"Why?" Threnody asked as they started forward again.

"He didn't say and I didn't ask. The good thing is that the Strykers are beginning to focus their attention on him instead of us."

"Were they getting close?"

"Close enough."

It took less than a minute to reach the latest intersection in the maze of tunnels. They turned right, carefully averting their faces from the security feed that they couldn't completely hide from. The tunnels weren't lined with hologrids, not as the bunkers were. Instead, at intervals every quarter of a kilometer or so the gray metal gave way to an opaque hologrid that could become anything it was programmed to be.

Crimson lines sparked across the hologrid, projecting outward to form a mirror image of themselves. Three dark figures running where they shouldn't, the bioware on their faces and in their eyes difficult for the computer to work around. It still got something, coming up not with their false identities, nor their real ones. Just trouble.

"You are in a restricted area," an automated voice said as they stared at themselves reflected in the hologrid stretched between the walls, facial-recognition software still looking for points to build off of. "All citizens are to obey curfew and return to their domicile in bunkers, tenements aboveground, or city towers. You are in a restricted area."

Threnody reached out with her hand, fingers sliding through the holo, until her skin touched the smoothness of the grid. Electricity danced around her wrist, curling from red into electric blue as she tapped into her power and burnt out the hologrid with a controlled shock. Electricity crawled over it, arcing high around her to the other side with a single thought as she fried the localized system that the hologrid ran on.

"You know that whoever is monitoring the security feeds probably got that on record," Kerr said. "Strykers will start coming down into the tunnels where we are instead of where we aren't."

"We won't be in the tunnels long enough for them to find us." Threnody clenched her hands into fists, the electric spark of her power fading away. She took off her stolen cap and tossed it to the floor. "Let's move."

They ran for it, gear and guns secured tight to their bodies. The tunnels were getting darker the farther away from the bunker they ran, the air hotter. A constant clicking sound that they couldn't locate echoed in the guts of the tunnels.

"We're losing oxygen," Quinton said as they turned at another cross-tunnel intersection. "CO_2 scrubbers aren't working right. That's what we're hearing, according to the computer. I've got a warning feed on the bottom of my screen."

"No shit?" Kerr shook his head as they ran. "I couldn't tell at all, the way my lungs are burning."

"The government is taking a risk," Threnody panted out.

Kerr snorted his opinion on that. "The government enforces policy. Everyone else takes risks."

They kept running, the tunnel snaking out in front of them and on the screen of the datapad in Quinton's hand. They made it to the exit point ten minutes later, breathing harshly as they slowed to a stop.

Strykers aboveground, Kerr said through the psi link.

Do they know we're down here? Threnody said.

We're human on the mental grid, but I've had us blocked completely since you slagged the computer back there.

Threnody looked up at the dark ceiling, dim blue light creating long shadows over her features from the emergency shine a ways behind them. *So they're waiting for us.*

This was the most logical exit route for us to take. Yeah, I'd say they're waiting for us.

Can you tell what we're dealing with? Quinton asked.

Kerr closed his eyes, brow furrowing in the darkness. *Two telepaths, one telekinetic, two pyrokinetics.*

Class?

Class IV and lower.

All less powerful than they were. Threnody shared a look with Quinton. *I've got the pyrokinetics,* Quinton said, pocketing the datapad.

I'll deal with the telekinetic and telepaths, Kerr said. *Threnody, you've got to knock them all out. I don't trust myself not to kill them. My control isn't good enough yet.*

The government had a kill order out on them, they knew that. Defection resulted only in a grave if the escaped Stryker was caught. That was never going to change, but they weren't here to kill their fellow Strykers. That wasn't their goal. Their objective was the electrical grid, the power plants it ran off of, and whatever else Lucas needed.

Threnody snapped her fingers together, creating bright electric sparks that lined her nails. *You sure about this, Kerr? Your head's only just been worked on.*

Lucas does excellent work. Grudging respect was in Kerr's mental voice. *I trust what he rebuilt. I kind of have to because I've got to live with it.*

Good enough for me.

They didn't have a telekinetic for offense; Jason was back at Matron's base, frantically working to get the shuttles online. Lucas was elsewhere, pulling Warhounds and Strykers alike to him. That didn't mean they were at a disadvantage.

They took the stairs up to the surface two at a time, minds sharpening into battle focus as the roar of the storm filtered slowly down to their ears. The closer they got to the top, the slicker the steps became, acid water flowing where gravity led. The air became thick and warm and hideously saturated. Side by side, the three reached the surface, coming up into a small storage warehouse, all the windows broken and the blast doors wrenched wide apart.

They stood there for a moment, listening to the wind howling outside the building, catching flashes of lightning sparking through the sky, feeling thunder rattling the ground.

Now, Threnody thought over the psi link even as she raced out of the building, Kerr's mind a heavy presence in her own.

Quinton stayed by Kerr's side, gas and fire lighting up the air around him as he focused his power, draining a tube in each arm to get the fire big enough, hot enough, to burn through the storm that raged beyond the four fragile walls. Pressure existed beyond his mental shields, the unmistakable biting strength of telepaths going to war on the mental grid. Then his attention was divided, the fire he had built suddenly being carved into pieces by other pyrokinetics hoping to steal what he controlled.

Quinton's dark eyes narrowed. Over his dead fucking body. He grabbed Kerr by the arm and dragged them out of the burning building, through the smoke and fire, into the storm.

Acid rain soaked them in seconds, wind whistling in their ears. Quinton blinked the stinging wet out of his eyes, desperately looking for his partner. He gave up after a few seconds, needing to save his own skin, knowing Threnody could survive on her own. He got off a few shots with his rifle before the weapon was telekinetically torn out of his hands and tossed away. Quinton didn't bother running after it.

He thrust out an arm toward the pair of Stryker pyrokinetics, twisting the fire bigger, hotter, forcing it to burn when the storm wanted to put it out. Fuel came from nearby buildings, the flames crawling up their sides with a furious roar. Quinton struggled to maintain control of the inferno and keep the other pyrokinetics at bay.

Silhouetted against that bright orange glow was Threnody, her lean form moving with lethal intent as she fought to get within touching range of her target. The telepaths were between her and the telekinetic, whom Kerr had brought to his knees, but not before taking his gun. Landing a solid punch to a telepath whose mind was mostly tied up in defending against Kerr's powerful attack, Threnody held on to the Stryker as she bore the other woman's body to the ground. Pressing one hand to the telepath's face, she shocked the Stryker's nervous system as hard as she could.

Electricity crawled over the telepath, the woman seizing for a few long seconds before she went limp on the ground. She was still breathing, but was totally and completely *out* as Threnody moved on to her next target. With one less mind to deal with, Kerr was able to sharpen his focus on the remaining four Strykers.

Two, Threnody thought with hard satisfaction as she brought down the second telepath with a punch to the solar plexus and her hand around his throat.

It was easier because Kerr was in his mind, tearing through it with a telepathic strike that the Stryker couldn't counter, not against a Class II. Threnody's power burned into him with instant, shocking results. He screamed, his voice drowned out beneath the sound of the storm as he fell to the ground.

The telekinetic was still in the game. Threnody discovered that the hard way when she was picked up and tossed across the street to land on the crumbling sidewalk there. Landing hard on her side, Threnody rolled with a pained yell, coming to a stop up against a building that wasn't burning. She spat out a mouthful of mud and blood—she'd bitten through her lip—before shoving herself back to her feet. The world spun sickeningly for a few seconds before her inner ear found balance again.

Blinking burning water out of her eyes, Threnody unclipped her gun and took aim at the approaching telekinetic. Before she could fire her gun, it was wrenched out of her hands. Her body slammed back against the building, invisible pressure nearly crushing her.

Kerr, Threnody said. *I need you to take care of this one.*

On it, Kerr said.

It was simpler, now that the telepaths were out of the fight. Threnody didn't know what Kerr did, but the telekinetic fell to the ground between one step and the next, out cold. The pyrokinetics were next, the fire that all three of them had been fighting over expanding dangerously for a few seconds before Quinton got control over the flame. It was easy to let the fire die, to let the rain wash through it and extinguish the inferno.

The street was suddenly dark, but not silent. Thunder still pounded through the sky above them, but a secondary roar was filling the air now. Like the sound of a steam-engine train, in ancient movies saved to vids long after the fact, the increasing rumble couldn't be ignored.

They couldn't see the derecho hit, but they heard it. They felt it.

There on the street, the three Strykers felt the spine of that long wind-storm slam into them, through them, knocking them to the ground with sideway winds and stabbing acid rain. It screamed over Buffalo, a heavy wall of nature come out of the west; power that humans couldn't fully predict, that psions couldn't control.

Threnody pushed herself up against the weight of the storm, arms shaking and barely able to hold steady in the face of the wind.

The tunnels? Kerr sent into their minds.

No. Threnody stumbled toward where she'd last seen Quinton, the lightning up above not nearly enough to show where her partner was. *We've got to stay aboveground.*

There's a car near my position, Quinton informed them. *It functions, according to the computer.*

Driving through this storm is liable to get us killed.

So's walking. At least this way we'll be a little drier.

Good point.

Kerr showed Threnody where Quinton was on the mental grid. She worked her way to where Quinton had broken into the vehicle and over-rode the controls, headlights barely distinguishable in the heavy storm. She pried open the door and fell into the backseat.

Kerr was struggling to get into the front passenger seat, Quinton al-ready behind the wheel. Kerr was barely able to pull the door shut be-hind him against the strength of the wind. For a moment, the three sat there in the car, the engine running, and the storm the only sound as the wind battered the vehicle.

"Lucas is crazy if he thinks we can fly out through this," Threnody finally said, surprised at how dry her throat was, how rough her voice came out.

"Crazy, yeah, but it might work," Kerr said as Quinton took the car out of park and pressed his foot to the gas pedal. "I don't think we'd have gotten this far if he didn't believe we could make it all the way."

It was funny, Threnody thought as Quinton drove into the storm, just how much faith all of them were putting in someone who was supposed to be their enemy.

PART SEVEN

APERTURE

SESSION DATE: 2128.05.26
LOCATION: Institute of Psionics Research
CLEARANCE ID: Dr. Amy Bennett
SUBJECT: 2581
FILE NUMBER: 487

"We can't go aboveground anymore," the doctor says as she sits rigidly in her seat. "Too much fallout in the air is killing us and the towers aren't sealed yet. I haven't seen the sun for almost three years."

"Don't worry. It's still there."

"Aisling."

She is coloring again, rubbing her crayons to small nubs. "Shh, be quiet. He's talking."

"Aisling."

The girl looks up and frowns at the camera as the machines behind her whine. "I could never promise you *the* world, Lucas. Simply *a* world."

The doctor leans forward. "We need answers, Aisling. Not these disjointed reports of people we can't locate."

"You want what he wants." Aisling sounds frustrated as she slowly slides her crayon off the paper and onto the table, forcibly staining the room with color. "He wants what I want, but they aren't the same thing."

"We need to know when the next bomb will fall."

"Lima, Peru," she says, the tip of her crayon breaking off. "Five, four, three, too late. Can I have another box of crayons, Doctor?"

TWENTY-SEVEN

AUGUST 2379

BUFFALO, USA

The maglev train slid slowly into Bunker North, but no one was expecting anyone on it to still be breathing. Neither were the Strykers lining the platform expecting enemy psions to still be present in any of the cars as they worked their way through the stinking mess left behind.

Shielded tight on the mental grid, wrapped in a telekinetic shield to stave off the soaking wetness of the storm, Lucas was aboveground. Standing beneath a metal overhang of a building that did nothing to keep out the wind and the rain, Lucas ducked his head against the storm and reached through the psi link for Jason.

Tell me you're close to being done, Lucas said.

It's makeshift, but it should hold. Long enough to get us out of here, at least, Jason replied. *I don't know about this storm. You trust Matron's scavengers to be able to pilot through this?*

Enough of them will make it.

What do you mean enough?

Lucas ignored that question. *Get those shuttles prepped for launch, Jason. As soon as Threnody gets the electrical grid back online, those launch silos will activate.*

You better not fucking leave them behind.

I still need them.

It wasn't really a promise. Lucas cut the connection with a thought, the psi link going dormant. Where he was standing, the world was nothing but darkness and sound. Unlike in the tunnels, no emergency lights were shining to show the way on the streets. Closing his eyes didn't really change his situation, but it let him concentrate that much harder as he expanded his power through the mental grid for that one shining mind he would know anywhere. Through the other person's eyes, he got a glimpse of an office in a city tower, wide, familiar. Empty.

He teleported with that visualization firmly in his mind, arriving beside the woman he had first met when he was a child, and later, at the age of fifteen, when he realized he needed her help to change everything.

"Security feed is being blocked," Ciari said as she stared out the plasglass window at the storm that was hitting Toronto the same as it was hitting Buffalo, with only slightly less force. "My Strykers here are busy and the World Court is dealing with the media. They won't interrupt us."

Water slid off the telekinetic shield Lucas still had up, then fell in spatters when he dropped his defenses. "I can't stay long."

"You never do." Ciari turned her head a little, just enough to look at him. "Did you get what you needed from the Strykers you took?"

"More than. They'll be enough in the end, I think." Lucas frowned. "She hasn't been wrong yet."

"Yet," Ciari echoed.

"You gave me the best you had," Lucas reminded her.

"If I could have kept them from you, I would have."

He reached for her, let his fingers curl around hers for a second or two, no longer. "Maybe in some other future you did. We wouldn't be here today if you had."

"I like to think my choices are my own."

"You're not stupid, Ciari. Your life has never been your own and you know it."

Lucas stepped in front of her, blocking her view of the storm and everything they had made together. He was taller than she was, younger, more powerful; everything she hadn't been in years, but she still reached for what he offered. Ciari liked to think that maybe whatever was between them was real, or had been at one point. They used each other to save their own lives, and the taste of his mouth now was so different from the memory in her head.

His hands were cold against her face, grip painful as he explored her mouth with a ferocity that would have spoken of quiet desperation in anyone else. But this was Lucas, and he didn't do desperation. He only took and never gave.

"She told me you'll be carrying a girl," Lucas whispered against her mouth before he pulled back, a faint, mocking smile on his own.

Ciari closed her eyes, refusing to flinch away from his touch. "I shouldn't be carrying anything, much less a child."

It was just a bunch of cells right now, no more than five weeks old, dividing and multiplying along human DNA with incredible psion potential. She was determined to see the baby born free, outside of the collars the government issued and away from the human veneer Lucas had been forced to wrap around his entire existence.

Aisling had promised her that much, at the least, in exchange for the world. Some new future to survive in. Pipe dreams were something Ciari never normally believed in. Maybe it was the hormones.

Trust me, Lucas said into her mind before he disappeared, teleporting out beneath everyone's searching thoughts on the mental grid.

She didn't. She never would.

Opening her eyes to her empty office, Ciari thought maybe that was the reason why Lucas kept coming back to her. She was the product of a way of life that kept his side of this fight free to do what needed to be done. That didn't necessarily mean that each side was in the right, just that they believed in one simple truth.

No salvation was to be found in anything except escape. Maybe their ancestors had it right all those years ago, when countries fought each other for the chance to leave this world behind.

Ciari liked to think otherwise.

TWENTY-EIGHT

AUGUST 2379

BUFFALO, USA

ucas's mental order left a distracting ringing sound in Jason's ears, or maybe it was just the way his own mind acknowledged the tension and worry that was holding his body stiffly hostage. Days of working with too little sleep and too much stress had resulted in the completion and installation of the hive connection among thirty-six shuttles. The program that the scavengers had started, and which Jason had finished, would slave the systems together so the shuttles would hopefully read as a single entity on any scan that might hit them if it got past the jamming technology. In the event that they were captured or shot down, every shuttle's black box could instantly be wiped clean with a single command.

With no time to test the code he had written, Jason needed to believe that it would hold up. He'd hacked through enough pirated and government-sanctioned defenses in his time to know what worked and what didn't when it came to security. He wished that they'd had time to do a dry run on everything, but that wasn't possible. Right now, all that was left was to input their destination coordinates, but that upload wouldn't happen until the electrical grid was back up and running. Lucas had been adamant on not plugging in their route until they were in the air, so at the moment all Jason had left to do was wait.

He hated waiting.

"Did you finish?" Matron said tiredly as she came through the hatch into the flight deck, looking worn-out.

"Yeah," Jason said as he rubbed at his burning eyes, the neuroports up and down both arms swollen and red from overuse. "The hack is good. I told Lucas it should hold."

"Guess he was right to bring you people in on this," Matron said as she squeezed his shoulder. "Now get out of my seat. You ain't piloting this shuttle."

"I'm your anchor," Jason shot back as he got up. "How else do you think you're going to be able to fly through this storm without telekinetic help?"

"Go check on my demolitions, Jason. And lock the blast doors open to take the explosion while you're at it. I'll worry about our flight plan."

Matron promptly ignored him, used to instant obedience. She knew what needed to be done, and Jason had been buried beneath code for the better part of the week. He'd trust her judgment, for now at least.

The air in the hangar was a little too warm, the generators working overtime to keep them breathing. It was still barely enough power, stretched thin from hard use. They needed the government's electrical grid to come back online if they were going to get off the ground.

The three shuttles on the launchpad were slowly powering up to standby mode in preparation for flight, Matron and two other scavengers the pilots for this launch. Matron had handpicked every assignment because she knew her people better than Lucas did, despite all his psionic interference. She was as good as her word, not leaving any of her people behind, but only because Lucas actually did need them all. If that hadn't been the case, Jason knew there'd be more dead bodies than live people, and Matron wouldn't have mourned their passing for even a second.

Jason made sure he still had his comm unit with him, hooked to his belt. It was tuned to Matron's frequency, and the soft hum of the connection followed him out of the hangar, back down the tunnel to the empty tenement, a thin beam of light from his flashlight shining the way.

All were already at their posts, had been for hours, and the building was dark. Every available hertz of electricity was being funneled into the hangars. Every block of C-4, every wireless receiver, was set to green, ready to receive the detonation signal. Once they were in the air and they tripped the detonation codes, this place would blow itself up into debris the size of his hand. The tunnels would buckle and collapse beneath the blast, the hangar following suit, which was Matron's intent. Leave nothing behind. They were cleaning house and Jason was making sure no one had cut any corners.

He climbed out of the tunnel sometime later, the blast doors open flat against the floor of that heavily fortified room. A block of C-4 was encased in stabilizing plastic by the entrance to the room across from him, a lead of the stuff stretching out in one long, uninterrupted line that surrounded the tenement. Every level had the same setup. Jason followed the plastic-coated wiring with his light, checking every receiver he came across and making sure nothing critical had been left behind.

Threnody had slagged every computer in the place. All weapons had been distributed equally among the scavengers, any and all personal effects taken along or otherwise destroyed. For all intents and purposes, the tenement had been abandoned.

The people who knocked down the front door to get inside didn't know that.

Jason cut the light immediately, ducking into the nearest room on the first floor and raising a personal telekinetic shield around himself. He hadn't felt a telepathic probe, which didn't mean an attack wasn't pending. One of the many annoying things about being a telekinetic was that telekinetics were always targeted first. They had the only physically destructive, long-reaching psion power in existence. They could do a hell of a lot more damage to property and fragile human bodies than any other psion, and they were numerous enough to be a problem.

The people coming down the hallway found that out the hard way.

Jason couldn't be sure no psions were in the tenement. He didn't want to break cover, but he had no choice. He was the first line of defense and that meant going in for the kill. Stepping out of the room with a heavy telekinetic shield between himself and the intruders, Jason peered past the light coming from scopes mounted on the guns to see just who the hell he was dealing with.

Humans, Lucas's voice said suddenly into his mind. *Quads. I've got them.*

No, Jason said. *Your telepathy might ping off the mental grid during the attack.*

You're kidding, right?

You've got a lot to handle already, so let me deal with them.

Their conversation lasted no more than a second or two, long enough for the quads to notice Jason. They took aim and fired, the flare of energy darts streaking down the hallway. Jason averted his eyes as the attack hit his telekinetic shield. Tapping into his telekinesis, Jason yanked the weapons out of their hands, wrapped his power around their skulls, and viciously twisted each head. The sound of bone cracking mimicked the thunder that still rolled outside. When their bodies hit the floor, it was with a familiar, distinctive sound.

Is that all of them? Jason asked through the psi link, taking a careful step forward. When Lucas didn't immediately answer, Jason strengthened his thoughts beneath the other man's telepathic shields that turned him human on the mental grid. *Lucas!*

I hear you, I hear you. No need to fucking yell, Lucas said a few seconds later. *Those were it for this section. The only problem now is their check-in times.*

Pretty sure they've got voice-recognition software on their comm units.

Yeah, so don't even bother trying to use them. Their superiors will just hone in on their last known location, which isn't here, but close enough to be a problem.

You think reinforcements will come after them in a city this big?

I think we're running out of time. Hide the bodies, then get below, Lucas said, mental voice distant.

What's going on?

Those aren't the only quads I have to deal with. The place rigged to blow yet?

I'm just checking Matron's work.

That woman never fucks up her bombs. Just get back to the shuttles.

Jason left his position, telekinesis still a strong barrier between himself and the rest of the world. He used it to teleport the two sets of quads out of the hallway and into an abandoned room on the top floor, stacking the bodies against the wall behind a pile of scavenged junk. Out of sight, out of mind.

The lock had been shot off the front door, leaving a hole that acid rain blew through. Jason telekinetically shoved a table in front of the door to keep it shut before retreating back to the tunnel. He checked the position of the blast doors on his way back down, telekinetically holding the flashlight in the air to help him see as he made sure the two main doors in that room wouldn't close. Only then did Jason take the stairs two at a time back down to the tunnel.

We're finished with the hive connection, Jason reported, leaving his thoughts open for Lucas to retrieve.

Good. I'm pretty sure we're only going to have a narrow window of time to get all the shuttles airborne. Lucas sounded tense, power bleeding against Jason's shields. The lack of control was startling.

Lucas, what's wrong?

We haven't been found out, not yet, Lucas said, ignoring Jason's concern. *The quads are pushing through the typical boundaries. They're hitting up the outskirts.*

Jason swore. *The other hangars?*

No one's been discovered yet, but I've got other problems to deal with.

How far along are Threnody and the others on getting the electrical grid back up and running?

Not far enough.

Jason didn't know what to say in response, so he kept his mouth shut and his thoughts to himself as he worked his way back to the hangar. He double-checked that the blast doors were secured in their retractable casings. When he reached the underground hangar, the cargo doors of the Alpha shuttle were the only ones open. He clambered back inside, the doors closing behind him as he made his way back to the flight deck.

Matron was there, busily running through diagnostics of the shuttle. She didn't look at him. "We good?"

"Yeah," Jason said as he sat down in the navigator's seat, staring out into the darkness of the hangar. "For now."

Matron grunted, whispering something under her breath. He had to strain to hear her, but he managed to make out a few words, just enough to realize she was praying.

"That ever work?" Jason felt compelled to ask.

"Does what work?"

"Whatever you just asked your God for."

Matron offered him a sharp look. "Boy, you leave me and my prayers in peace. If I'm gonna get through this sane, I'm gonna need a little bit of guidance of the sort your government never programmed into you. When you find God, then we'll talk."

He didn't bother to tell her that the Strykers already had, in some way, that it wasn't a god they worshipped, but humanity itself. It was why he was still here, still working with Lucas instead of fighting him, because this course of action made more sense than the one the government was determined to take.

Matron rolled her shoulders, trying to ease some of the tension in her muscles. "Make yourself useful and go check what medical supplies we've got back there. I've got a feeling we're gonna need them."

Jason obeyed. Maybe it would keep his mind occupied instead of thinking and worrying about his fellow Strykers in the field.

It didn't.

[TWENTY-NINE]

AUGUST 2379
BUFFALO, USA

She fell.

Telepaths' minds were layers of control and power, memory from birth to now, perfect recall, and a silent plea that the space in their head remained theirs for just a little longer; that their thoughts and who they were remained *them* and not *other*. Control meant keeping that separation intact. Power meant being able to live through the aftermath of when control wasn't enough and everything in their head just broke down.

Pieces of who she was, who she had been, cut into her thoughts.

Samantha swallowed blood and snot, wiping at her nose. It felt as if her brain were leaking out of her nostrils. Just her mind playing tricks

on her, she decided as she studied her bloodstained fingers. Just everything and nothing, because this wasn't what she was supposed to be.

She'd lived nearly her entire life broken. Eighteen years of a *very* slow
mindwipe.

How had she missed that?

Arms wrapped around her waist, and Samantha looked down at her
sister, Kristen's thin face turned upward. Her gleaming dark blue eyes
were hooded, knowing, mouth curved hard in that gleeful smile of hers.

"Shh," Kristen whispered through the noise of the crowd around
them in Bunker North. "It always hurts the first time. When you learn
to think for yourself."

Samantha dug her nails into her sister's shoulder, held on, because the
world was moving without her. Clarity. It was such a fucking bitch.

"I've always thought for myself," Samantha ground out, pitching her
voice low, because she couldn't focus enough to *think,* much less use her
telepathy.

"No. Nathan thought for you."

Truth never tasted so bitter, so bad. Samantha swallowed against the
bile that was crawling up her throat, stomach clenching from pain, nausea making her a little weak. Kristen held her up as they followed Jin Li
away from the maglev platform, a few new Warhounds surrounding them
as they continued the hunt for Lucas. More telekinetics and two telepaths, because she couldn't fully perform her duties anymore.

Do I want to? she thought somewhere inside the mess of her head,
shields barely strung together. Too many minds pressed against her own.
It was difficult to remember why they were here, what they had been
ordered to accomplish. It was difficult to care.

The hardest thoughts to ignore were her sister's. Kristen was a pulsing, sick presence on the mental grid, a deep well of borrowed emotion
and little sanity, despite all the minds she had eaten through that night.
The strange thing was that she wasn't intruding, wasn't trying to pull
apart Samantha's weakness. The empath never gave up an opportunity
to eat her way through someone else's mind; this should have been no
different from all the times before. Only it was and Kristen's distance
wasn't comforting at all.

"We need to get aboveground," Jin Li said, looking over his shoulder at Nathan's children. "Lucas isn't down here."

"I'm searching through the human minds around us," one of the telepaths said. "I'm not sensing any hidden pockets that he's carved for himself. Just—"

She broke off with a frown, dark head turned in the direction of a set of quads behind them who were ignoring the Warhounds through psionic interference.

"What is it?" Samantha felt compelled to ask.

"They're getting a report from their command central. Something about a break-in at the power plant."

Jin Li rocked to a hard halt, ignoring the humans flowing around him as if he weren't even there. "The power plant? Which one? And what the hell is Lucas doing there?"

"Are you sure it's even him?" Samantha said. "Of the three Strykers he took, one's an electrokinetic. The only reason why they could possibly be there would be because they want to turn it back on."

"Want to? Or need to?" Kristen corrected as she chewed on a fingernail until it bled.

Samantha rubbed a hand over her face. They'd lost their identity-protective glasses a while ago, but the bioware was still attached to their skin. They had their hackers working through the security grid to circumvent the feed, all of them knowing that the Strykers were most likely doing the same. She didn't think it would be enough in the long run.

Jin Li focused his attention on the other telepaths in the group. "Can we get a fix on whoever it is?"

They all looked away in order to concentrate, closing their eyes and merging their powers together. The whole group was stretched out in the crowd, pressed close against the side of the bunker's wall on the second level, unnoticed only by way of psionic interference and hackers in the system. Samantha took in a careful, shallow breath and felt another layer inside her head shear off.

Kristen's power seeped into her mind, sliding past her shields with jagged edges. Emotions weren't something that Samantha had the luxury of feeling; Kristen lived them, day in and day out. It hurt, drawing her sister into a link, as if her mind were being torn to pieces all over again.

And again.

Listen. Kristen's thoughts, soft, modulated, backed by a coherence that Samantha had never before felt in that tangled, ruined mess of a mind.

Samantha had spent all of her life learning when to bend so that she wouldn't break. All Warhounds learned that skill early. The Serca children of any generation learned it earlier than most. Samantha raised a shield between herself and her sister, forcing Kristen out of her mind. It left her with an almost debilitating headache, but she'd lived through worse over the years. Compartmentalizing the pain was easy. Ignoring her sister was not.

Kristen leaned up to press her mouth against Samantha's ear, her voice barely distinguishable from the noise of the crowd.

"You're going about this all wrong, Sam."

Kristen's voice, but not her words. Only one person had ever called her Sam.

She would have pushed Kristen away, except the younger girl was holding on to her so tightly that it was impossible to shake her off completely.

Traitor, Samantha thought, shoving the word straight into Kristen's mind, ignoring how it made her own bleed psionic pain.

The empath smiled at her, her psi signature overlaid with Lucas's presence. *Tell me, Sam,* Lucas said through Kristen's mind. *How am I the traitor when I was the one who pieced your mind back together over and over again? You've got those memories back now. Aren't you grateful?*

Not to you.

Still so sullen. We're going to have to work on that. Lucas stretched his power through Kristen's mind, the empath's insanity a barrier between him and the scans that the Warhound telepaths were doing. *You know what Nathan wants. I want something different.*

I'm not on your side.

Remember when I said I would save you? I never said it would be easy. Trust me, Sam. I'm all you've got left. Do you think you can go back to Nathan with your mind the way it is now?

She couldn't. She knew that it would be impossible to return to London, present herself to their father, and leave his presence alive. Nathan would take her changed state of mind as betrayal, and only one punishment fit that crime in the Warhound ranks.

He'll kill you messy and he'll kill you slow, Lucas told her as he drifted away through the cracks in Kristen's mind. *I need you alive. What's it going to be, Sam?*

Kristen sagged against her, done being her oldest brother's conduit. Her head rolled against Samantha's shoulder, the smile on her face unchanging.

"Strykers," one of the telepaths announced, breaking Samantha's precarious concentration. "That's not Lucas in power plant two. It's Strykers."

"Any of them the ones he took with him out of the Slums?" Jin Li said.

"No. Several teams' worth, though."

Jin Li shook his head as he made his way back to where Samantha and Kristen were standing. More like leaning, Samantha thought, curiously removed from everything as she felt the wall at her back. Jin Li stood before her, eyes narrowed into slits.

"I don't give a fuck what you previously decided with Gideon," he said in a low voice. "But he's a Class II telekinetic and we need his ass in the field. Contact him, give him a visual, and tell him to get here. Now."

Samantha glared at Jin Li. "He stayed behind for a reason. One of us needs to be available to Nathan."

"Bullshit." Jin Li tangled his hand into her hair and yanked her closer to him, his fingers brushing over her bare scalp, over her nerves. "The little one-upmanship game you two are playing isn't helping us here and—"

He broke off with a strangled curse, shoving himself away from Samantha as Kristen slammed her empathy through his mind. Much as Jin Li's power could disrupt a person's nervous system, Kristen's disrupted downright everything. He got his mental shields up before she went too deep, but the first layer was already gone, peeled off by Kristen's insatiable hunger.

She bared her teeth at him, smile fixed and threatening as she put herself between Jin Li and her sister. "Naughty boy," Kristen rasped. "We own you, remember?"

Jin Li raised his fist, pride demanding that he retaliate. Except these two were Nathan's children, his blood, Sercas to their very DNA. Even if Kristen would never be acknowledged, even if Samantha would never take control of the Serca Syndicate after Nathan, they still ranked higher than Jin Li did in the grand scheme of things. Much as Jin Li wanted to tear Kristen apart, he didn't dare touch her. He'd crossed a line with Samantha just now. He couldn't afford to do it again.

"Keep your mind to yourself," he snarled. "And you, Samantha, get Gideon down here. We need a functioning Serca."

Jin Li retreated because he had no other choice. He wasn't 'path-oriented, and no way in hell was he going to fight Kristen unless ordered to by Nathan.

"Do it," Kristen said, laughing through the words. "Oh, bring our brother down here, Sammy-girl."

Samantha would have given anything not to, but if they were going to face a contingent of Strykers in the middle of a powerful acid storm, then they would need whatever strength they could get. With Samantha's telepathy pretty much broken, her mind bleeding through psi shock, she didn't have a choice in the matter. Jin Li was right. They needed a functioning Serca.

She closed her eyes against the chaos of the bunker, against the pain in her head. Stripped as she was of everything even remotely resembling control, the only way she could reach her twin was through the psi link that was still intact between them. She shielded as best she could, but Gideon would still know something was wrong.

Gideon, she sent at him, mental voice strained, the psi link between them shaky. *Gideon, we need you on the field.*

What happened? He didn't sound concerned, just curious, and Samantha swallowed her bitterness until she couldn't taste it anymore.

What do you think? She managed a tight, angry little laugh. *I've hit burnout, pushing into psi shock. We need you to lead.*

You wanted me to stay behind.

Now I want your arse here. Samantha opened her eyes, sharing the space she was in with him, the dimness and crowdedness of the bunker. The way it smelled of old metal and human perspiration, the stench of too many years lived beneath the ground. *Do you have it?*

She felt him like a vise inside her skull, in what little area of her power she could spare, the world gone blurry as another pair of eyes looked through hers. *Yes.*

Suddenly, her twin was standing before her, a little smile on his face that was for her alone. It wasn't supposed to be reassuring.

"I told you it should have been me," Gideon said.

Samantha pushed herself off the wall, let Kristen continue to hang off her because her sister's mind was a better barrier than anything she herself could come up with at the moment. "You really think Lucas will let you find him?"

"One wonders why he let you."

They stared each other down, but Samantha couldn't afford to be the one who looked away first. Kristen solved the problem for them, shoving at Gideon with one hand, or at least trying to. Gideon held her in place with his telekinesis, her hand splayed against an invisible shield millimeters above his chest.

"Don't," Gideon warned. "Or I'll break your arm."

Kristen licked her dry, cracked lips and winked at him. She was shoved back against Samantha, Gideon leaving the pair of them behind whole and intact because they needed everyone they could get to take Lucas down. Samantha sucked in a breath and started walking after her twin, Kristen keeping pace with her. The Warhounds with them were grouping together—she counted sixteen of them, herself and siblings included—everyone except Gideon wearing a field uniform. He didn't need one, nor the armor it came with, not with his power wrapped like a second skin around his body.

"Report," Gideon said, now the center of attention, taking control of the mission away from Samantha.

Clenching her hand into a fist, Samantha looked down at her white knuckles, the blood drying on her fingers, and listened as the War-hounds who had obeyed her for the majority of this mission switched their focus and loyalty to her twin.

Kristen wrapped her arms around Samantha's waist, pressed her forehead against Samantha's spine. "What's it going to be, Sam?"

Kristen's voice, Lucas's words.

Samantha didn't answer. Not here in the bunker, not when they arrived in the middle of the acid storm ninety seconds later, teleported within meters of the power plant in question, where Strykers were hunting some of their own. The wind nearly threw them both to the ground. Kristen dug in her heels and kept them upright through sheer will as thunder and lightning crashed above them, the clouds so low, it gave the illusion that if they lifted their arms to the sky, they could touch the storm.

What's it going to be?

A memory. A promise. Lucas seeding rebellion throughout the ranks, throughout her mind.

Trust me.

[THIRTY]

AUGUST 2379
BUFFALO, USA

Threnody couldn't hear anything over the sound of the storm, not even her own ragged breathing as she crouched behind the thick security wall of the power plant, next to the guard building. Quinton and Kerr were directly across from her, on the other side of the front blast doors.

To get past the quads who guarded the area, Kerr had altered their minds and convinced a human to walk with the three of them, in the illusion of a quad, through the power-plant gates to get inside. Once there, Kerr had knocked out every single human. Humans were always easy to control. Dealing with the Strykers who had arrived soon after was something else entirely.

Quinton's power was useless now that the storm had picked up. So were their guns because shooting bullets through wind that was blowing at 320 kilometers an hour was just asking to die. They had Kerr's telepathy and Threnody's electrokinesis, two powers against ten times that on the other side of the doors. Quinton had managed to close them again, but the doors were steadily being peeled apart despite Kerr's psionic interference that blocked 'path-oriented strikes and teleportation. Not good odds.

The one thing they had in their favor was that the Strykers couldn't find them on the mental grid. Lucas's trick of hiding a psi signature until the person in question seemed only human, or not present at all, was keeping them alive. She didn't know how much longer their luck would last. They *needed* to get inside the power plant. Running right now would leave them easy targets without a telekinetic to watch their backs, and the only way inside that power plant was through the front doors. A lot of open space was between them and those doors.

We should have brought Jason, Threnody said in a tense voice through the psi link Kerr had strung between their minds.

Kerr didn't answer her. Someone else did.

He was needed elsewhere. You'll have your chance to make a break for it in thirty seconds, Lucas said as he appeared beside her, stumbling out of his teleport and needing the wall to support his weight for a few seconds. He'd startled her; blue lines of electricity sparked over her hands out of instinct. She pulled her power back in only after she realized who it was.

Threnody glared up at Lucas through the rain, rapidly blinking the stinging wet out of her eyes. *What did you do?*

Twenty seconds. Be ready.

When the Warhounds teleported in, arriving between where they were cornered and where the Strykers were waiting, Threnody felt her stomach clench. Lucas waved a hand at her, the features of his face sharply lit by the brightness of the security lights that burned hotly through the storm on the walls around the power plant.

Now, Lucas told her, head turned toward the doors that had been torn to the ground under telekinetic pressure. *Both of you, run.*

Threnody was already running toward the entrance of the power plant, slipping through the sheet of mud that overlay the cement pathway, bent nearly double against the wind and the rain. Quinton was running in her direction, both of them highlighted by the lights and the storm, presenting perfect targets to everyone behind them.

Except they would have to get through Lucas first.

Kerr, Lucas said, drawing him into a merge. *I'll need your support.*

Kerr didn't understand what was happening, having never had his mind merged into another's before. He didn't try to fight it, as he hadn't fought Lucas when the other man had fixed his mind, knowing that this was the only way they were going to survive. Lucas needed his strength, he could feel that now, because for all that Lucas was a Class I triad psion, the younger man had been pushing himself hard since well before the Slums. Alone, Lucas didn't have the reach he needed to fight nearly fifty-odd Strykers and Warhounds.

The limits of Kerr's mind expanded, his power pushing through someone else's strength and laying down anchor points across their area of the mental grid. A merged Class I and Class II mental wall was built up along the edge of a chasm that cut so deep and so wide it would take everything all the psions outside the power plant had and more to break through their shields. A breach was still a possibility.

It was similar to how Kerr had worked most of his life with Jason, except this partnership went deeper. Kerr could feel the channels of Lucas's telekinesis more clearly than he'd ever felt Jason's. Kerr let Lucas take whatever he needed, their minds weaving together seamlessly, thoughts paralleling as Lucas became the apex of a two-mind merge.

On the mental grid, pockets deepened with individual powers from the Strykers and the clumping knots of power that signified Warhound merges. None of them even remotely approached the strength that Lucas and Kerr wielded.

Telekinesis wrapped around their bodies; a shield also bubbling over Threnody and Quinton as they made it to the rusted blast doors of the power plant. Lucas and Kerr planted themselves on one side of those torn-down doors, clothes soaking wet and skin chilled beneath the sudden barrier against the storm. Two men who were neither Stryker nor Warhound, just human enough to believe in doing the right thing.

Traitor, Gideon said on a narrow psi link between himself and Lucas, riding a Warhound's telepathic power to make the connection.

Lucas didn't sense Samantha in any of the Warhound merges at all, nor did he feel the devastating pull of Kristen's deadly need. A slow smile cut across his face, Kerr the only witness to it.

You seem to think that because I want to survive, I'm a traitor, Lucas said as he readied his and Kerr's shared power behind their shields. *You can have what Nathan's offering. I found something better.*

Lucas's and Kerr's telepathic strike ripped through everyone's mind like an explosion, burning through the shields of anyone who was a Class V and lower, shattering concentrations. People fell to the ground, Warhounds and Strykers alike, minds whiting out in pain. The backlash of that much power caused Lucas's control of the merge to waver, just a little.

Don't kill them, Kerr said, guilt and a lifetime of commitment to the Strykers asking for a reprieve.

Beg elsewhere, Lucas said as he raised their shields and felt the dip on the mental grid that signified an attack from the Strykers, because they had never learned what the Sercas had imparted to the Warhounds about merging.

Telekinetic strength exploded around them as if a bomb had gone off, cracking the ground and the walls, sending debris spinning off into the storm for the wind to catch. Lucas was ready for it, mind braced to deflect the attack. He grunted, rocking back on his heels from the mental strain, muscles drawn tight over bone as he stubbornly held his ground.

Kerr fed him more strength and Lucas absorbed it greedily, fortifying his telekinesis right before they were hit. Lucas's training and knowledge of how Gideon worked on the field was the only thing that let him anticipate his younger brother's attack. The Class II telekinetic had merged seven other telekinetics with his power. Lucas could feel the difference between his brother and the Strykers like a sharp divide. Gideon had been trained by Nathan. His attack was quick, powerful—expected in this instance in the wake of the kill order. The Warhounds had dropped off the mental grid, covered by telepaths in merge, and this time the telekinetic attack happened both outside and inside Lucas's shields.

The power Gideon wielded would have crushed Lucas and Kerr if Lucas's defenses had been even a sliver less than what they were. His shields weren't a single barrier; he layered them at intervals around their bodies and mind. What Gideon's merge broke down was only half of Lucas's defenses, but the damage was more extensive than that. Power broke apart in Lucas's mind, synapses overloading somewhere in his brain at the backlash. Lucas's mind dealt with the damage instinctually, compensating for a bridge that was lost, the merge shifting just enough to steady both minds.

I'll take the telepaths, Kerr said. *You deal with the telekinetics.*

It was the logical choice, and Kerr was used to being a backboard for telekinetic strength. Lucas didn't hesitate to switch his concentration to the telekinetics, holding up his shields while Kerr used his own Class II telepathic strength in an attack that left holes in all lesser-Classed psion minds. Not as deep as Lucas could go, but deep enough to cause damage.

Not even a month ago, Kerr wouldn't have been able to stand his ground in a battle like this. His shields wouldn't have withstood the follow-up attacks. Here, now, his power had a new depth, strength once used fighting his empathy now relegated to controlling it, twisting his secondary power into an attack that affected everyone's emotions.

He had no formal training for his empathy. What Kerr knew now had been imparted through Lucas from the psi surgery, and what Lucas didn't know about the human and not-so-human mind wasn't worth the knowing. Kerr had control of his minute amount of empathy, just enough to push *fear* against the minds that he slammed through until they choked on it.

A Class IX power wasn't really much of anything to be worried about. Kerr didn't think it would make a huge difference, but it left damage in its wake. People forgot, sometimes, why the higher Classes were rare and why most psions never broke past a Class V. The human mind didn't need a lot of power to do a lot of damage. It just needed enough to leave a scar. A reminder.

Kristen understood that better than anyone else because she lived with it day in and day out. Her mind was just scar tissue built on top of scar tissue, layers of damage that would never be fixed because she'd been broken too young and too many times, and no one had bothered to put her back together again. When she dropped her shields, called by the taste of fear Kerr had projected, her presence shook through everyone's mind.

Lucas cut her off at the pass, sliding between Kerr and his sister with a skill that spoke of long practice. Kristen was only a distraction, though, just a threat that they couldn't ignore and had to face down first even as Gideon dropped out of the merge he led, his place filled by a different telekinetic. Lucas couldn't react fast enough and stop them, not and risk letting Kristen find a crack in his own two-person merge and exploit it.

Lucas, Kristen called to him, laughter in her thoughts. *Come play with me!*

In the midst of all that fighting, only one person stood apart from it all, mind bleeding into her bones as she felt Gideon teleport beyond Lucas's defenses with Jin Li by his side. Samantha spat out a mouthful of blood and saliva as the wind howled in her ears. Kristen was a heaviness between herself and Lucas on the mental grid, a barrier that was steadily eating through the thoughts that swirled all around them.

Samantha's shields were paper-thin and full of holes. Her defenses were no better than a human's, which was all the difference that mattered.

For the first time in her entire life, Samantha could *think*.

She used it—that decadent, giddy sense of freedom—to fight.

THIRTY-ONE

AUGUST 2379
BUFFALO, USA

Threnody fried the control panel to the blast doors until its necessary parts melted beneath her power. The blast doors unlocked, but they didn't open.

Lucas, the doors, Threnody said through the psi link.

Focused as he was on not letting them die, Lucas still managed to telekinetically open the blast doors for them. The two slipped inside the power plant, where the lights were running on half-power.

Power plant two, built in the middle of Buffalo, ran on fossil fuels, like the majority of the power plants left in the world. Nuclear power plants were a thing of the past, humanity's absolute fear of nuclear power etched into the backbone of the remnants of society. Renewable energy plants were few and far between, and America's East Coast had relied on fossil fuel power plants for centuries before the Border Wars. The tradition continued through to the present.

This one burned coal, supplies scavenged from cities all along the coast, stored by the ton in tall steel silos that supplied the plant's six pulverizers by way of conveyer belts. Those belts weren't running, stilled in the face of the acid storm and the government's order. The hum that should have filled the power plant had been replaced by the screaming wind and Threnody's and Quinton's own harsh breathing.

The skeleton crew assigned to monitor the power plant was dead. Only when Threnody tripped over a body did they discover that. They stared at the corpse's face twisted in an expression of permanent pain, a puddle of blood outlining the head. The lack of physical wounds had her thinking it was a mental attack. Lucas's doing, or possibly the Warhounds'. Either way, with the scientists dead, anyone who could have helped them bring the power plant back up to full readiness was dead.

"Well, shit," Threnody said as she knelt down to rifle through the dead man's pockets until she found a security card.

Quinton glanced at her. "I figure they'll have biometrics throughout this place."

They looked at the body on the ground. Without a word, Quinton called up fire from some of the remaining natural gas left in the bio-tubes in his arms, snapping his fingers to light it. The fire burned bright and hot, shrinking down to a thin blue line of the hottest heat he could produce. He focused it on the dead man's right hand, just below the wrist, and the fire burned through flesh easily. The stench was foul, something they ignored, having smelled the dead many times before. Only when they started to smell metal did Quinton stop to bend down and pick up the severed hand. It was cool to the touch, the wrist area cauterized.

"Let's go," Threnody said.

She and Quinton hurried down the hall, bypassing the doors that led to the boiler steam drum and the high-powered steam turbines, all abnormally silent. They ran, leaving a trail of wet footprints for anyone to follow. Working their way to the control room, they found it behind layers of protective shielding and fire-resistant paneling. Threnody swiped the card over the security reader as Quinton pressed the severed hand against the screen. The computer read the print, as well as the security card, and the doors slid open. Quinton dropped the severed hand on the floor; Threnody kept the security card.

Inside were more bodies, and they hauled two corpses out of the chairs they had died in. The terminals were still on, access to the power plant's computer network available. Threnody and Quinton slid into seats on opposite sides of the control room, the wide, clear windows providing them with a near 360-degree view of the massive, internal guts of the power plant.

"You ever wish they taught this in a simulator?" Quinton asked as he brought window after window up on the vidscreen, furiously looking for any prompt that would get them further than the public areas of the system. They couldn't get far without viable codes or passwords, not with the entire network so tightly locked down.

"You're a better hacker than I am," Threnody reminded him.

"I'm not that good, Thren. Maybe it should have been Jason after all."

Threnody didn't say anything to that, just continued to demand answers from a computer that was reluctant to give them up, security card or no. She swore after the fifth failed attempt, slamming her hand down in frustration on the terminal.

"Careful," Quinton barked.

"I *know.*"

Frying the main system that controlled this place wasn't in anyone's best interest. There had to be a different way.

Lucas, we need a little help here, Threnody said. *Can you link us to Jason?*

No answer. From the way Lucas and Kerr had been fighting outside, she wasn't surprised. Swearing, she brought up a map of the power plant on the screen and stared critically at every last section of the place. Her gaze lingered longest on the transmission lines and transformers built into the ground outside, some distance away from the cooling tower and the building they were in.

"Think a jump start might work?" Threnody asked as she swiveled her chair around to face Quinton.

Quinton turned his head to look at her, a tight expression on his face. "It'll kill you."

She shrugged, grimacing. "Better here than under the government's control."

"Threnody—"

"*Quinton.*"

She got to her feet and crossed the distance between them in a few quick strides. A bittersweet, ruined smile curved across her mouth. She hid it against the top of Quinton's skull; a brief caress, a thank-you, for all his years of loyalty.

"I'll come back if I can," Threnody said, promising no more than that.

Quinton pressed his hand to the small of her back, pulled her into an embrace that lasted only a second. "Go," he said, voice low and gravelly. "I'll keep trying to contact Lucas or Kerr."

She left the control room and didn't look back. Quinton didn't watch her go. This was how they worked, how all Strykers learned to work with their partner or their team. You did what had to be done for the good of everyone else, for the mission. Personal desires were never, ever allowed.

Quinton put all his focus on the terminal before him and calling out through the psi links for their only telepaths. Distracted, he missed Gideon and Jin Li's arrival. He didn't miss their presence when he was telekinetically slammed face-first into the wall.

His nose broke; so did a few of his teeth. Quinton spat out blood and shattered enamel, the front of his face feeling as if it were on fire.

"Jin Li, go after the other one," Gideon ordered as he flipped Quinton around onto his back against the wall.

Quinton wrenched his eyes open at that command, blinking through the swollen heat that encompassed his face in time to see Jin Li leave the control room.

Lucas! he shouted through the psi link. *Kerr!*

Silence, the psi link empty of any support. Held immobile against the wall by that strong Class II telekinetic grip, Quinton could only stare as Nathan's third child approached the terminal he had been working on, studying all the open command windows on the vidscreen he'd been struggling to break through.

"You're not a hacker," Gideon stated. "Not a good one. I don't know why Lucas allied himself with you Strykers if you don't have the proper skills to get the job done."

Quinton didn't say a word. Gideon was a telekinetic, not a telepath, which meant unless he brought in a Warhound telepath, he wasn't going to be able to pry a damn thing out of Quinton. Mentally, at least, and Strykers had died for less.

Gideon glanced up at him, the intent in his dark blue eyes different from the pair Quinton had been staring at for the past few weeks or so. "Why do you want the power plant turned back on?"

Quinton kept his mouth shut. Gideon was unsurprised at this silence. His gaze settled on Quinton's bare arms and the shadow of biotubes beneath his skin. "Pyrokinetic. You can make this easy on yourself if you open your mouth and start talking."

Quinton couldn't risk a fire here, not in a place that they needed. It didn't matter anyway, not when he couldn't create the very thing his power controlled. Gideon had him held fast, the weight of his telekinesis slowly crushing Quinton up against the wall.

Gideon started with Quinton's fingers first, breaking every bone from nails to knuckle with each refusal to answer his question. Eventually, Gideon moved up to the bones and biomodifications that spanned Quinton's palms and the carefully placed tubing there. Quinton didn't scream, just squeezed his eyes shut and ground his broken teeth together, trying to breathe through the agony of the slow torture as Gideon telekinetically tore his body apart.

"I'm sorry," a new voice said an indeterminate time later through the pain he was feeling, sounding raw and broken and so, so determined.

The power holding Quinton prisoner abruptly disappeared. He fell to the ground, gasping for air around the blood in his mouth, vomiting when his shattered hands touched the floor. This time he screamed, unable to choke it back, the sound mingling with the high tone of Gideon's own voice.

Lying on the floor of the control room, Quinton stared in disbelief at the sight before him. Samantha Serca had both her hands pressed against Gideon's temples, eyes narrowed in concentration, lips pulled back in a snarl as she focused all her telepathic strength on frying her twin brother's mind. The effort left the tendons standing out in her arms and throat, sweat pouring down her face, mixing with the blood that was dripping out of her nose.

Gideon, though, Gideon was rigid in her grip, mouth opened wide and the expression on his face one of shocked betrayal as his twin overrode his thoughts and his power. She sent him spinning down into psi shock with the last of her strength. Gideon fell to the ground first, Samantha less than a second behind him. But while Gideon was unconscious from the massive psionic overload, Samantha wasn't, and her dark blue eyes focused on Quinton's bloody, broken face.

Behind her, a skinny form slid into the control room. Quinton could only stare in shock as the girl approached him, the smile on her face cracked and bleeding, her eyes that signature Serca dark blue. He didn't need to be a telepath to recognize the distorted pressure against his shields as that of a dysfunctional mind.

Lucas, you fucking bastard, he thought muzzily through the pain. *You never said anything about this.*

"Shh, shh," that girl whispered as her fingers touched his forehead, stroking over his hot skin.

With every motion of her fingers, she wiped away the pain.

His brain ceased to acknowledge the agony that existed from his elbows on down in each arm, the sudden absence of it leaving him lightheaded and queasy. The pain in his face faded until it was just a distant ache that was hard to breathe through. Quinton's brown eyes snapped open and he stared up in shock at the smiling teenager who knelt beside him, a psion who could only be an empath after that little show of power.

"Promises to keep, Stryker," she cooed at him. "Promises, promises."

"Wha—?" The word came out messy, garbled. Spitting blood, coughing to get air into his lungs, Quinton tried again, concentrating on what he was saying so that he could be understood, even with a broken face. "What?"

"You aren't the only person Lucas needs," Samantha said as she dragged herself into the nearest seat. "Kristen, get him up."

Instinctively, Quinton jerked away from that crazy empath's touch, wishing for the first time in a long while that he had even a sliver of 'path-oriented power in his genes. The knowing look in Kristen's gleaming dark blue eyes told him that his fear hadn't gone unnoticed. Still, for such a small girl, she had a lot of strength; enough to help Quinton get his feet back underneath him. Once vertical, Quinton shrugged her off, stepping away from her grasping, clinging hands.

"Kristen," Samantha said sharply.

"You're no fun, Sammy-girl," Kristen complained as she stepped over Gideon's still body and back to her sister's side.

"Is he dead?" Quinton asked carefully after a few seconds.

"No." Samantha sounded as if the word hurt her. "I don't have enough strength left in me to kill him."

Maybe she did, maybe she didn't. Maybe her reluctance was due to the nine months they floated together in an artificial womb and the eighteen years since that they had stood side by side beneath Nathan's judging eyes. It didn't matter. This was where her loyalty ended—with Gideon still breathing.

Quinton leaned against the other chair, staring at Lucas's sisters while blood dripped down onto the floor from his fingers and his face. "What are you doing?"

"What you couldn't," Samantha explained as she worked her way through the power plant's control system using access codes instead of a hack. "I stripped everything we'd need to bring this place back online out of the minds of the engineers and scientists before killing them."

"You do it on Lucas's order?"

"It doesn't matter."

"The hell it doesn't. Why isn't he here?"

"Because he and that other telepath are busy holding off what's left of the Strykers and Warhounds that are still on the field. We've got maybe five minutes, if we're lucky, to lock in the codes before the military reaches this place."

"Jin Li went after Threnody."

"I know. They both have their parts to play."

"What do you mean?" Quinton demanded, jerking himself up straight again. "You're not going to try and help her?"

Samantha didn't look away from the vidscreen. "I can bring this plant online, but it's going to take time to generate the amount of electricity Lucas needs to reach where it has to go. Threnody's an electrokinetic. So is Jin Li. There is a derecho storm raging outside. Do the math, Stryker."

Quinton didn't need to. He was already staggering out of the control room on shaky legs, heart pounding in his chest as he raced against time, knowing it was already too late even as the first hint of sound started to come from the machines around him.

The power plant was starting to come online again.

[THIRTY-TWO]

There was a service door—locked, of course—that she had to fry before she could shove it open. It took all her strength against the crushing weight of the wind to move it. Threnody stood in the doorway, braced against the fury of the storm while acid rain lashed her body.

The transformer and transmission lines weren't housed in a separate building. They were outside, maybe twenty meters from the door and farther than that from the cooling tower. Located in the back, far from where the Strykers and the Warhounds were fighting Lucas and Kerr, they were cold, most of the city running off strained backup generators during the storm. Even if they weren't running at full power, they were still capable of transmuting electricity, of carrying it forward.

"I must be losing my mind," Threnody muttered under her breath as she stepped out into the storm.

Getting soaked wasn't new. The ground between the main building and the tall transmission towers was covered in cement, rain flooding the place. It sloshed over her boots, making it slippery to walk, much less run, as she made her way to the bulky transformer.

After the Border Wars, when many of America's and the rest of the world's electrical grids had been destroyed, rebuilding them had been a top priority for the survivors. They were limited, though, built specifically to support small pockets of survivors and expanding no farther than that. The government had controlled the output of electricity back then and still did now, because controlling the resources that everyone needed kept the population in check.

A wire fence surrounded the transformer block, more for safety than to keep anyone out, but it was still a restricted space. The door was locked, the mechanism easy to fry to gain entrance. Shoving the door open as wide as she could, Threnody stumbled toward her goal.

The transformer block was a three-phase system, with heavy wires pulled taut between the transformer and the transmission tower that they fed into. Even with the light coming from the single spotlight focused on the area inside the fence, it was almost impossible to see where those transmission lines disappeared to in the storm.

Swiping water out of her eyes, blinking against the sting it left behind, Threnody maneuvered her way back around the transformer block to the front, running through her options. Walking around that last corner, she came face-to-face with Jin Li. Threnody jerked back out of instinct, her feet nearly sliding out from beneath her. Jin Li followed her with electricity sparking in long arcs between his fingers.

"Your partner's being torn to pieces by Gideon," Jin Li shouted over the noise of the storm as Threnody twisted around the corner.

"He knew the risks," Threnody yelled back. "We all did."

"Those risks are gonna get you dead, girl."

Jin Li lunged forward, aiming his fist at her face. Threnody ducked, twisting her body against his attack and the wind. Her hand hit the ground for balance as she lashed out with a sharp kick to Jin Li's knee that he avoided by jumping out of reach. Threnody hauled herself back to a standing position, sliding her feet farther apart for balance as she tapped into her power.

Blue electricity wrapped around her fists, a match for the power that sparked around Jin Li's. He grinned at her, face eerily lit by the lightning exploding through the sky above them. Threnody could feel the charge in the air, could feel it in her skin all the way down to her bones. Her body practically hummed with the power that the derecho storm was generating.

Jin Li moved over the slick surface of the ground, one hand stabbing forward. Electricity danced through the air between them, crackling against Threnody's power, over her skin. She returned the gesture with a wide arc of electricity that cut through his attack and slammed into him.

Blue sparks lit up the air around them, tiny Vesuvius flares that would have blinded anyone who didn't have their power.

It wasn't often that electrokinetics fought like this, electricity cutting through the air from body to body like lightning did from sky to earth, cloud to cloud. Their power wasn't meant to function like that; they needed a conduit to keep the electricity flowing. The storm above had charged the very air they breathed enough to be that bridge.

This wasn't like Johannesburg. It wasn't even like the Slums. Threnody knew what she was fighting for this time and she couldn't afford to lose. That desperation drove her forward, forcing her inside Jin Li's defenses to take the blows he gave her and pound her own against his body. They used their fists, feet, and knees, the crackling burn of their power, but when it came right down to it, Jin Li was a Class II and she wasn't. He would always have the upper hand, and Threnody still wasn't fully recovered from everything she'd gone through over the past few months.

His foot caught the edge of her knee in a hard kick, knocking her legs out from under her. Threnody grunted as she fell, pain stabbing up her left thigh. Jin Li pinned her to the ground, his weight heavy on her chest, but not as heavy as the hands around her throat. Threnody wrapped her own hands around his wrists, choking against the pressure of his fingers and the bright sparks of his power.

"Lucas was never worth shit," Jin Li said around gritted teeth, electricity crawling over his face in sharp lines that had no pattern. "You chose the wrong side, Stryker. All that's left for you to do is die."

Black spots ate into her vision, the brightness fading. She couldn't breathe, lungs burning beneath her ribs and her heart beating so fast that she could feel its speed. Threnody stared up past Jin Li's determined face, at the swirling blackness of the storm, and thought about everyone in the underground hangars, waiting to launch in scavenged shuttles. About the people who would be left behind when the government chose only those they considered worthy to be human enough to leave this world. She thought about Lucas and Aisling, and wondered how that little girl had died, if she had died like this, with the life choked out of her as the world went to hell.

No, Threnody thought as lightning cut through the sky.

She was a Stryker, a psion. A Class III electrokinetic. Threnody Corwin at your fucking service. But more than that, at the most basic level, she was a living, breathing *battery* with a brain. It's what her power was, it's how her body functioned, charged from the inside out.

She let Jin Li's wrist go, lifting one hand past his head for the sky above them. Electricity sparked dully at her fingertips, the world narrowing to tunnel vision that was all black clouds and white lightning. She could feel the charge in her nerve endings, the way it set her hair standing on end. The smell of ozone as the world got suddenly brighter, a blinding whiteness that exploded through her, running down her arm into her body, through Jin Li's hands, and straight into him.

Jin Li screamed when the bolt of lightning hit them, propelled backward from the harsh shock of a near system overload. Threnody forced herself off the ground. Electricity was jumping between them, flowing over the water-soaked ground and across the metal fence, the transformers, *everything,* flinging back through her and him in a loop that would kill them both soon enough. She wrapped her burning, bleeding hands over Jin Li's shoulders and pushed the momentarily stunned man backward with all her strength until he hit the side of the transformer.

His brown eyes had a blue-white sheen over them when they focused on her. He spoke, but Threnody didn't hear what he said. She doubted he heard her either.

"You're never getting off this planet," she promised.

Threnody kept her eyes wide-open, the world becoming a flash image in her brain as she sucked up every last bit of electric power into her body and channeled it through Jin Li's, forcing it farther into the transformer behind him. The smell of burning flesh reached her nose; her nerves never noticed the damage. Threnody held on, driving the electricity farther, down coils and wires, through conductors, and into the transmission lines, up into the towers that sparked and popped beneath the sudden heavy load.

The power had no place to go except out.

Threnody pried her fingers off Jin Li long seconds later, the man still connected to the transformer by way of burned and melting flesh, his body still jerking from the electricity that was running through him, killing him by quick degrees. Threnody left all the skin of her fingers and palms on his shoulders, blackened strips peeling off as she collapsed to the ground.

Lying there, in the hot water beneath the storm, with acid rain pelting her body and her heart beating jaggedly in her chest, Threnody let the world fade away.

The electricity she had called down out of the sky still burned through the transformer, funneled with precision through the transmission lines as it scattered to the substations that existed throughout Buffalo. It only took seconds for that power to reach through kilometers of power lines and feed a city starved for energy.

That night, Buffalo lit up as if it were on fire for the first time in decades, in centuries, a brightly glowing sprawl that burned defiantly beneath the storm.

PART EIGHT
DELIVERANCE

SESSION DATE: **2128.07.13**

LOCATION: **Institute of Psionics Research**

CLEARANCE ID: **Dr. Amy Bennett**

SUBJECT: **2581**

FILE NUMBER: **638**

"We know you have the answers," the doctor says as she picks up a white card from the deck on the table. One side is blank, the other side holds a shape viewable only by the doctor.

"They aren't your answers. Purple star," Aisling says as the EEG and supporting machines click and whine, spikes reading across the screen. She is kneeling on the chair, attention elsewhere, yellow dress twisted around her legs.

The doctor places the card down and marks something in her notes before picking up another. "Your track record for being right is unmatched."

"With the cards? Orange square."

Another card gets set aside. "With where the bombs fall."

"They're not done falling. I've told you that. This is reeducation on a worldwide level. This is how we start over. Everyone will say the same thing eventually."

"By killing ourselves?" The expression on the doctor's face is angry, but the grief in her voice is what makes the girl finally glance at her. The look in Aisling's bleached-out violet eyes is startlingly adult.

"You kill us without regret. You're killing me."

"Aisling, we're not . . . we're not *killing* you. You've just been a little sick, that's all. We're treating you for it."

"No, you're not," the girl whispers, shoulders slumping. "You can't fix me and I can't see the world how you want me to."

For once, in a long, long while, the machines are quiet.

THIRTY-THREE

AUGUST 2379

BUFFALO, USA

The lights in the hangar snapped on with a startling, loud hum, blinding everyone who had been sitting in the flight decks of the shuttles. Jason leaned forward, jerked out of the middle another diagnostic test, and stared at the hangar.

"Fuck, they did it," Jason said as he cut the diagnostics short. He started to upload the destination coordinates that Lucas had given him hours ago into the corresponding shuttles through the hive connection in the computer.

Beside him, Matron opened an uplink on her terminal even as she started to kick the shuttle into full flight readiness. "Alpha shuttle to Beta and all others, do you copy, over?"

She got a multitude of responses, all calling in their status as she strapped into her flight harness. When all thirty-five shuttles came back with positive identification, Matron said, "Do you have power at the launch sites, over?"

More affirmatives.

"Then get the hell into the air, out." Matron cut the uplink and turned her head to look at Jason. "You ready?"

"Already powering up the launch silo," Jason said, his hands flying over the controls in front of him.

Outside the confines of the shuttles, the control terminals to the side of the launchpad were picking up Jason's signals. Computers switched out of power-save mode into full activation as Jason plugged in the commands remotely. Above them, in that wide, round launch silo, lights came on in a continuous line. The blast doors at the top of that long open space responded to the orders currently driving its system and began to open. A hole appeared high above, quickly getting larger, allowing rain and mud to drop down onto the shuttles below.

In Alpha shuttle, Jason was trying to contact Lucas or Kerr telepathically, but no one was responding on the shared psi link. Swearing, Jason shook his head. "They're not answering my call."

"They dead?" Matron asked.

"No. I'd have felt the psi link sever if that was the case. Hurts like a bitch when it happens."

"We can't wait here. Not for much longer." Matron switched to an uplink with the other two shuttles in the hangar with them. "Grady, Torrance, get the hell out of here. We're holding for the main cargo, out."

Jason ground his teeth and dropped his head into his hands. *Lucas, Kerr, I need a response, damn it.*

The roar of the first shuttle activating its vertical-takeoff-and-landing (VTOL) function nearly drowned out Jason's thoughts and the faint, telepathic voice that finally crawled through the psi link.

We need a pickup, Lucas said, mental voice strained and distant, almost fractured. *At power plant two. Teleportation isn't possible.*

Understood.

Jason opened his eyes in time to see the first shuttle launching out of the silo and the second already lifting into the air. "They need a pickup."

"Fuck," Matron swore as she stabbed a finger at Jason. "Blow the charges."

Jason picked up the remote detonator from the control panel and unlocked the device. He gripped it tightly as the second shuttle cleared the launch silo, and then it was their turn. Matron was a scavenger, born and bred, part of a people who possessed any number of skills in order to survive. That she could pilot a shuttle wasn't surprising; he just hoped she was good at it. Matron activated the VTOL, and Jason felt the shuttle shake as it lifted into the air. It rose higher and faster through the launch silo, the storm rushing down to meet them.

They cleared the blast doors and Jason pressed his thumb down hard on the detonator's red button. It sent out a limited-range signal, picked up by the receivers far below. The charge coursed through the C-4, and the resulting explosions rocked the stormy air, buffeting the shuttle with shocking intensity. Despite the wind and the rain, the fire they left behind wasn't going to go out anytime soon.

Matron was already pulling away, banking hard to the left, struggling to keep the shuttle steady in the face of turbulent winds. When she spoke, she sounded almost in awe. "Holy mother of God."

Below them, every street filled with light, was the city of Buffalo. The sprawl stretched from Lake Erie all the way to the east, where it faded into emptiness. The city towers were like burning fingers to the north, a misguided crowning glory.

"Never saw it like this before," Matron murmured, her sharp eyes studying the shuttle's instruments as well as the view.

"Never going to again," Jason said as he plotted a course and uploaded the vector onto Matron's hologrid for her to see.

On their radar, they were picking up thirty-five other bogeys—shuttles scattered around the southern edge of the city—and about a hundred more coming out of Toronto.

"Fuck." Jason leaned closer to the vidscreen and everything that was showing up. "Matron, the military scrambled their jets earlier than expected."

"Shit," Matron said as she accessed the uplink again, getting a chatter of voices coming from all the shuttles. "Crew, this is your boss. We're detouring for the main cargo. Get the fuck out of this airspace. We've got incoming, out."

She kept the connection open, the chatter filling the flight deck to replace the sound of their breathing. Jason was focused on his half of the controls, and Matron was struggling to fly the shuttle through the derecho, forced lower than she would have liked by heavy downdrafts and the thick cloud cover that made it almost impossible to see. The shuttle cut through the storm.

"Never fucking doing him a favor again," Matron decided as she held tight to the stick with both hands and felt the drag of the shuttle in her arms.

The storm wreaked havoc on their instrumentation, giving them hope that it was interfering with the military's as well. They couldn't be sure, and the military had better stealth capabilities than Matron and her scavengers had been able to salvage from the deserted cities of America. What the military didn't have sitting in the cockpits of those jets were psions.

The storm dragged them off course for a precious few minutes. Matron struggled to guide them back in the proper direction. They were almost to their destination when a red warning line filled the bottom of every active vidscreen.

"They've got a lock on us," Jason snapped.

"I see it, I see it!" Matron said, one eye on the red warning cutting across her controls and another on the sky outside the shuttle. She yanked hard on the stick, maneuvering the shuttle into a sharp dive out of the clouds to clear, if rough, skies below.

They were uncomfortably close to the ground, flying over tenements and near-empty streets. A heat-seeking missile, locked onto them, came streaking out of the storm clouds. Jason saw it, on the screen and in the air, and he reached out with his telekinesis, struggling to wrap his power around the fast-moving weapon. He finally caught hold of it. Anchoring his power to that long, dangerous missile, Jason wrenched it around onto a new trajectory.

The military jet that dove out of the clouds could pull all the evasive maneuvers it wanted. That missile was backed by living human thought, not a computer, and Jason sent it straight into the belly of the jet as it rolled. He let go at the very last second so his power didn't block the explosion.

The jet fell in fiery pieces to the city below. Jason didn't have time to worry about the damage the debris would cause. Five more jets were dropping out of the clouds and coming straight at them, requiring his attention, firing a volley of missiles that he didn't have time to grab for independently. Jason erected a wide telekinetic shield between them and the missiles, watching as they exploded in midair. A headache blossomed in the back of his head, but he ignored it.

Some of the jets managed to bank fast enough to get out of the way.

Some of them didn't, their technology incapable of identifying a teleki-netic shield. Most crashed at full throttle into Jason's shields. Jason was thrown forward against his flight harness, a physical reaction to the sud-den mental agony ripping through his mind. He dropped his shields, gasping for air as his entire head throbbed from the impact of jets against his power.

"You still with me, Jason?" Matron snapped at him, her harsh voice cutting through the painful ringing in his ears.

"Yeah," he ground out, forcing his eyes open. Jason scanned the sky and the shuttle's instrumentation, searching out those last few jets.

They popped back up on radar, coming from behind. Jason focused on the rearview camera feed to guide his telekinesis. It hurt, but he ground his teeth against the pain as he telekinetically ripped the wings right off the fighter jets. They fell to earth, no longer a problem.

Matron let out a breath and guided their shuttle ever lower as the jets disappeared from the radar. So did several of the dots that were identi-fied as transport shuttles, caught in the cross fire of enemy missiles. She tried not to watch the numbers dwindle.

"There," Matron said. "Down below. *Finally*."

Jason opened his eyes, squinting through the brightness as he realized that the open space Matron was aiming for surrounded a large power plant with steam blowing out of the single cooling tower. Bodies were scattered on the ground, some wearing uniforms that Jason recognized all too easily. Matron landed the shuttle close to the broken doors, the vertical landing sending hard vibrations through the shuttle. Jason wrapped a telekinetic shield around the shuttle even as he undid the straps of his flight harness.

"Stay here," he ordered tiredly as he steeled himself for a teleport. Ja-son arrived near the first set of doors by the security walls and erected a telekinetic shield around himself for protection as he quickly scanned the area.

He didn't know if those lying on the ground were dead or alive and couldn't care. Moving forward, Jason climbed over the downed doors. He was halfway to the power plant's main entrance when someone ex-ited the building. Kerr was a familiar and welcoming sight. Jason was damned glad to see his partner walking on his own two feet, but he could have done without the person that Kerr was helping outside.

Samantha Serca had one arm slung over Kerr's shoulder, limping along beside the other telepath. Jason wrapped a telekinetic shield around the pair as he hurried as fast as he could through the wind to reach them.

"*You're* who Lucas needed?" Jason asked in a disbelieving voice.

Samantha's face was covered in blood from the nose down, her dark blue eyes half-lidded and full of pain. "Fuck you," she slurred.

"The others are inside," Kerr said, jerking his head back the way they'd come, expression strained. "The shuttle?"

"Out front. Hold on."

Jason wrapped his power around them, pictured the shuttle's cargo bay in his mind, and teleported the pair inside the safety of the shuttle. He continued forward, using his power to wrench the second set of blast doors open wider, despite the throbbing in his skull. He swallowed thickly in fear once he got a good look at the group huddled just inside the power plant.

Quinton's arms were a mess, broken to fleshy pulp, white bone sticking out of his skin. His face wasn't much better, but he didn't seem to notice, kneeling as he was beside where Lucas was sitting with Threnody's mostly burned body in his arms. Standing over them was someone Jason had never even known existed. The girl smiled at him, the rictus look pulling at the skin of her face.

"Calvary has arrived," she announced cheerfully, throwing her arms up into the air victoriously.

"Shut up, Kris," Lucas said as he dragged open his eyes.

Jason stared in shock at the girl's gleaming dark blue eyes, the eerie resemblance she had to Lucas. "Holy shit," he breathed. "There's *four* of you fucking Serca kids?"

Lucas glared at him. "Get us to the shuttle, Jason."

He didn't need to be told twice.

Jason teleported them into the shuttle's cargo bay, where Kerr had already strapped Samantha into one of the seats, the girl fully unconscious now.

"Your sister's mind is a broken mess, Lucas," Kerr said, not looking up from where he was administering a sedative to Samantha, the hypospray pulled from their first-aid supplies, along with a portable IV that he strapped to her arm.

Lucas shrugged minutely. "She'll live. She's used to it."

"Matron, get us the fuck out of here," Jason yelled through the open hatch. "What the hell *happened,* Lucas?"

"Kris, help Quinton strap into a seat. Kerr, you've got another patient," Lucas ordered even as he telekinetically hauled a supply trunk over to his side and began to dig through it. "Threnody's alive, but not for much longer."

"I'm not leaving her side," Quinton said.

"I don't need you yet," Lucas said bluntly. "And you're useless to her right now, so stop arguing. Let Kerr see to your arms and face."

Quinton wouldn't move, so Kristen did it for him. The empath touched his arm above the elbow and altered the emotional blocks she'd implanted in his mind, just enough to remind him of the agony his body was keeping from his brain. Quinton's knees buckled and the only reason why he didn't collapse face-first to the deck was because Jason caught him in time.

"Fucking hell," Jason said as he hauled Quinton over to the nearest seat, refusing to let that crazy empath within reach of either of them.

Quinton tried to fight him, but the pain blocks were gone and there was no moving if a telekinetic didn't want you to move. Jason strapped him down and left him to Kerr's tender mercies even as Matron took them into the air again. Jason telekinetically anchored himself to the deck so that he didn't go slamming into the side of the shuttle. He kept Kerr upright as well. Lucas wasn't moving, neither was Kristen, the pair of them anchored around Threnody's too still body. But he could see her chest moving, albeit out of rhythm and far, far too slowly.

"What happened?" Jason asked again.

"She jump-started the electrical grid before the power plant came online," Lucas said without looking up from whatever he was doing. "She was the only one who could."

Because she was the only electrokinetic they had in their group. Jason swallowed, not sure how she could still be *alive* after that stunt. So much of Threnody's skin was bubbled up red and black, following the lines of her damaged nervous system beneath her uniform like burned circuitry.

"I'm keeping her alive, but just barely," Lucas said even as he ripped the sterile plastic off a med-kit item and withdrew a hypospray full of viscous gray matter. "Her mind wants to shut down."

"Is it my turn?" Kristen asked, tugging on the sleeve of Lucas's shirt. "Is it?"

The shuttle gave another violent shake as Matron guided them back into the storm, everyone in the cargo bay held steady by telekinetic anchors. Lucas looked at where Jason was standing over them and held up the hypospray for him to see.

"You're the only one that can save her," Lucas said, dark blue eyes bloodshot in a too pale face, blood dripping out of his nose, trickling from his ears.

"I'm not a medic," Jason said.

"Shut up and listen to me. You're a microtelekinetic behind those shields of yours. At *minimum,* a Class I psion. Your power has the potential to work on the atomic level. This hypospray holds a regulated amount of nanites that I stole sixteen months ago. We don't have a biotank on this shuttle, which means you're going to have to be the driving force behind getting this stuff to work on Threnody."

Jason stared at him. "I don't understand."

"You will soon enough. Kris?"

Lucas's sister perked up. *"Finally."*

The empath reached for Jason, but he shoved her away telekinetically. Kristen stuck her tongue out at him. "Don't touch me," he said hoarsely. "Lucas—what the *hell?"*

Lucas reached out with his own shaky telekinesis, dragging Jason close enough for him to look the other man straight in the eye.

"Listen to me, you fucking selfish piece of shit," Lucas snarled. "Threnody still has a part to play. If she dies here, then it was all for nothing. Everything I've given up and risked—it's all worth *nothing* if she dies, do you understand? You're no one's messiah, Jason. You're just a weapon, and I'm taking the safety switch off of you. You're the only one who can save her, and Kris is the only one who can break through your shields. We don't have *time* for this bullshit!"

Behind them, Quinton said, "Jason. *Please.*"

In the end, it didn't come down to Lucas ordering him or Quinton begging him. It came down to Jason owing them all as much as they owed him. Loyalty could be bought and it could be sold, but the only kind that mattered was the sort gained by way of blood.

Kristen's hands, when she touched him, were cold.

Her mind, as it entered his, was not.

"You taste so good," she whispered into his ear as her empathic power started to eat through Jason's thick natal shields.

Jason screamed with the first bite she took out of his defenses and didn't stop for a long, long time.

[THIRTY-FOUR]

AUGUST 2379

LONDON, UNITED KINGDOM

The last cartel drug lord—mindwiped to within a synapse of a new personality—was escorted out of Nathan's office in a city tower of Brasília. Nathan leaned back in the chair, closing his eyes against the pain of too many psi surgeries in too short a time. Promises were easily broken and wiped away, but it had taken more effort than he would have liked. He'd had to hunt through old memories and thoughts for every last person who could possibly have been involved in holding oil stolen from the government for the Warhounds. The cartels had been useful, and still were, but Nathan had never intended to give them berths on the *Ark*.

Removing every last shred of detail about the Serca Syndicate had taken a toll on him. Coming off the delicate psi surgery he had performed on Elion, adding in all the ones he'd done in Brasília, Nathan knew he had probably lost another year or two of life. Not exactly what he wanted, but so long as he lived to see Mars, these instances when he relied on himself and not his children would continue to happen.

Nathan opened his eyes and got to his feet, the night sky outside the windows dark. The door to the office opened again and Dalia walked in, still in her identity as an executive assistant.

"The shuttle is ready," she told him, hands clasped behind her back.

"We're done here," Nathan said.

They took the human way to the landing docks that lined the length of the city tower, walking out of the Serca Syndicate branch with a group of Warhounds that doubled as bodyguards to human eyes. Nathan didn't bother to hide his departure, even if he had hidden the arrival and departure of the cartel lords. He was known as a hands-on CEO, which meant surprise visits were inflicted on his subordinants.

When they came to the docking area, the computer guided them down the walkway to the correct shuttle, where their pilot was waiting. Teleportation would have been quicker; however, it wasn't an option at the moment. Nathan hated the veneer of humanity he had to keep up at all times, to pretend to be something he wasn't, but the survival of his company required it.

It also required that he have a successor, a position that never seemed to stay filled.

Sir, a telepathic voice said sometime later into his mind when they were halfway across the Atlantic Ocean, heading for London. He recognized Victoria's psi signature immediately. *We have a problem.*

What now?

The report was dumped straight into his public mind, the woman's tension making her thoughts sharp-edged. Nathan jerked up straight in his seat as he realized what had happened.

"Sir?" Dalia asked.

Nathan ignored her, teleporting straight out of the shuttle and into the tense atmosphere of the Warhounds' command center at the top of a city tower, ignoring the warning twinge in his mind from the effort. Nathan had been receiving field reports over the past few hours, but the emergency evacuation was just starting. The wounded coming off the field required Victoria's specialized skills in the arrival room used for teleportation. That's where Nathan found her working on his son. Victoria looked up at Nathan from where she was kneeling on the floor, both hands cupped over Gideon's temples.

"They found him in the power plant," Victoria said as medics worked to stabilize Gideon's vitals, a hover-gurney waiting close by to transport him to medical.

Retrieval teams were bringing back the living and the dead. Nathan's gaze swept the large arrival room with cold precision. Everything must have gone straight to hell and worse in Buffalo in a short time, otherwise he would have been informed earlier of the problem. Nathan cataloged the dead, his eyes coming to rest at last on a charred husk of a human-shaped body, the only thing identifiable about it.

Victoria noticed where he was staring. "Jin Li," she said quietly, looking away. "A nurse ID'd him through a biometrics scan using dental records. There wasn't enough viable tissue left for the process."

This was not how Nathan thought he would lose his best soldier.

His rage coated every thought that crossed his mind as he stepped closer to his one remaining son. Nathan wasn't gentle as he slid his mind past Victoria's and into Gideon's, into those of all the Warhounds that had returned to headquarters. He wanted—*required*—answers.

Samantha and Kristen were not in any of the returning groups. Warhound coming back knew where they were and reported such to Nathan's demands. Only when Nathan pried open Gideon's damaged mind did he find the answers he was missing.

She did this to me, she did this to me was the repeating, wounded mantra that spun through Gideon's thoughts, a memory of Samantha's betrayal of the Syndicate, of her twin, the most prominent thing in his mind.

Nathan did not take the betrayal well.

As Nathan retreated out of the mind of the only child left to him, he felt the mental grid bend in a way it never before had, a precursor to something terrible. He instantly raised his shields, as did every psion in the Warhound ranks. Everyone felt the novalike explosion that ripped through the mental grid. Such power was in that blast, a psionic strength that Nathan had never before encountered, that it scorched across every psion's mind the world over. A person he hadn't known existed—and somehow Lucas *must* have known.

You deceiving little bastard, Nathan thought, something that resembled disgusted awe coursing through his mind as he reached out with his telepathy, struggling to follow that stranger's mind back to its core. *You knew this power existed, didn't you, Lucas?*

The mind winked out on the mental grid before he could reach it, sucked back into a hole that was impossible to find, no matter how hard he searched. Nathan eventually drew back his power, raising all his formidable mental shields once again. He doubted that unknown psion was dead. Lucas took after Nathan too much, whether he liked to admit it or not, and Lucas never took a risk unless he knew he would win. Losing had never been an option for Nathan's eldest child.

Nathan was only now beginning to realize that.

[THIRTY-FIVE]

AUGUST 2379
CANADIAN SHIELD, CANADA

The world opened up in layers, bright filaments of energy, atoms, the connectivity of a living system that nearly broke him.

Jason found it almost impossible to breathe as Kristen ate through his shields with a ferocity that no one else could have matched. She was insane, with a power that operated through murder, and she almost killed him during that psi surgery monitored by Lucas as Matron flew them through the stormy night sky. Kristen tore down every last piece of that mental block, pulling Jason's mind apart to create a hole for all the power he hadn't known existed to come pouring out.

Every single synapse in Jason's brain turned *on* at once when that power connected with the rest of his mind, the overload having no place else to go except down the bond, the psi link that tied him to Kerr. A bridge that Lucas desperately kept blocked with what was left of his telepathic strength while Kerr screamed at him, *Get out of the fucking way.*

It can't be you, Lucas said in a strained mental voice. *It can't be you, Kerr. It has to be Quinton.*

Jason's the only family I've got, Kerr yelled, his Scottish accent getting deeper with every telepathic word he slammed into Lucas's mind. *I'm not going to abandon him!*

You will, eventually. Just not yet.

Enough with your cryptic bullshit, *Lucas! You're* killing *him!*

No. You are. Lucas pulled at the other telepath through the last shreds of the merge that existed between them, gaining just a little bit of mental traction. *You don't need him anymore. Not like this. And he can't need you. Let it go, Kerr. Let him go.*

Fuck you if you think—

You'll kill them both if you don't break the bond and let me attach it to Quinton's mind. You'll kill us all. I can't break it, not right now, but I can keep him from bleeding into you, and then we're all fucked. This is how it's supposed to be, so let it fucking be.

Kerr was silent for a heartbeat, his mind a ball of tension and agony, a swirl of emotion that leaked through his shields into Lucas's ragged thoughts.

Blame me for it when he wakes up, Lucas said.

Oh, I will, Kerr said in a quiet, deadly voice. *Fucking count on it.*

It won't make you feel better.

Fuck you, Lucas. Fuck you.

Carefully, unflinchingly, Kerr severed the bond that had linked him for so long to his partner, to his brother, to the only family the Strykers had ever allowed him to have beneath the shadow of the government. The link had saved his life, his mind, his *sanity,* for so many years. That he had lived this long was a testament to Jason's strength. That it felt as if he were cutting off his own arm told Kerr how much he had grown to rely on the telekinetic, a reliance he would never regret and would always, always miss.

Kerr broke the bond on his side, unable to get past Lucas and into

Jason's mind. It left a gaping, raw hole in his mind where Jason had once resided, the ragged ends of the bond unraveling too fast for him to keep hold of. Left him feeling empty and alone, completely bereft.

Let me, Lucas said. *Just—hold on.*

He was holding back an immense amount of power. Kerr could feel that, could feel the surge in Jason's mind that was burning through the layers of telepathic shields that Lucas had placed around the telekinetic's mind, the protective casings simply being eaten away. Kristen was somewhere inside that mess, steadily taking down Jason's shields, the only one who could do it and survive the overload. Lucas was right, they were running out of time, but that didn't make the transfer any easier.

Why me? Quinton demanded to know as Lucas pulled the pyrokinetic into the psi surgery.

Does it matter? Lucas said tiredly. *He needs another mind, Quinton. He's carrying too much power for one person to contain and live with. Your power is kinetic-based, a better match than Kerr ever could be.*

If it had been anyone else lying in Lucas's arms, Quinton would have refused. And he could have, he knew that. Lucas was worn too thin, carrying too much, to be able to fight on a dozen different fronts right now. But his refusal would kill Threnody, would kill Jason, and that wasn't something Quinton could ever willingly allow and be able to live with himself afterward.

Quinton dropped all of his shields. He had no other choice. Lucas entered his mind, going down deep to the very bottom where the channels that his power stemmed from were located. There, Lucas anchored the bond to Quinton's mind with Kerr's help, tying him to Jason more permanently than the Stryker psi surgeons had been able to tie Jason to Kerr. It hurt, as if Lucas were digging out pieces of who Quinton was and discarding them all, carving out space in his mind to make room for someone else in a place that should have only held him.

Ready? Lucas asked.

No.

It didn't matter.

Lucas removed the block, dragging Kristen out of Jason's mind as she tore apart the last barrier. He threw up a mental shield around them both, around all of them, as Jason's mind exploded.

No thoughts. Just power. A white-hot burn that turned the world inside out and fought for space, for room, for the body that housed it to breathe. It ricocheted down the bond, straight into Quinton's mind, burning through the synapses in his skull and changing everything that he was into whatever Jason needed him to be in order to survive.

An anchor. A shield.

A victim.

Quinton screamed, the sound brief. His eyes rolled up into his skull and he passed out where he sat strapped into his seat. On the deck of the shuttle, Jason lay sprawled beside Lucas and Threnody, bleeding out of his ears and nose. The world was so much *clearer* than it had ever been before as awareness returned in slow, painful increments.

Lucas gripped the hypospray in his hand and injected Threnody with nanites, his mind in hers, forcing her to keep her heart beating, to keep her lungs moving.

You know how to do this, Jason, Lucas said. *Aisling said you would. It's all instinct at this point. It always is.*

Jason turned his head, his power filling the shuttle like a heavy, unwanted pressure. He closed his eyes, his mind in pieces but still being guided by Lucas's implacable will.

Deeper.

The walls of the shuttle. The burned skin of Threnody's body.

Deeper.

The charred lines of her muscles. The hot flow of her blood.

Deeper.

The nanites that swam there, with their ability to coax cells toward the regeneration of the human body, waiting for their orders.

Deeper.

The feel of his microtelekinesis pulling at Threnody's DNA.

THIRTY-SIX

The order came at 0600 hours, on a weekday. It came through the usual channels, and Ciari took the uplink in her office, a twenty-second demand that Erik delivered in a quiet, emotionless voice at odds with the furious expression on his face.

"We require the OIC of the Strykers Syndicate to present herself before the World Court to explain the actions taken in Buffalo."

No more and no less, but the threat was there; the anger and the hate.

The world press was already reporting on the fighting that had taken place in Buffalo, streaming eyewitness accounts of what had happened in the bunkers and aboveground. The most downloaded image from that stormy night was a holopic taken by a military jet, of the sprawl that made up the city burning like a star, running on full power for the first time in generations.

Not the sort of thing the World Court needed to be dealing with when they were so close to the launch.

Pirate streams were already cutting into main media downloads, impossible to ignore. The government was having a difficult time containing everything. Ciari could feel the quiet shift of a city's emotions moving from fear into something much more difficult to deal with—suspicion. Resentment. A mob mentality, when it encompassed the majority of a population, couldn't be ignored.

Ciari dressed with care that morning, in her best uniform, not a hair out of place. Appearances were everything, and she had to look the part she played down to the shine on her boots. She walked with measured strides to Jael's lab two floors below, where the CMO was busy dealing with the wounded Strykers under her care who had survived the field operation in Buffalo. She didn't take kindly to being interrupted.

"I need to speak with you," Ciari said. "Privately."

Jael, having heard about Ciari's summons from Keiko, kept her attention on the datapad in her hands and the Stryker on an exam table. "It can wait."

"No, it can't."

Jael arched a dark eyebrow at the steely tone of Ciari's voice before she sighed and ordered a nurse to take care of her patient. Then she silently led Ciari to an empty exam room, which was harder than it sounded, since most of the rooms were occupied. She watched as Ciari went to stand beside the exam table, showing something Jael might have called regret if it had been anyone else.

"There's something I need you to do for me," Ciari said. "And we have very little time to do it."

"What's going on?"

"I'm pregnant."

In the years after that she survived, Jael would point to that moment, to those words, as the start of it all, of the beginning of the end.

[THIRTY-SEVEN]

AUGUST 2379
ARCTIC CIRCLE

Lucas," Matron said over the comm system, sounding tired, voice raspy and dry. "You should see this."

He blinked open eyes more red than blue, exhaustion, pain, and stress carving deep lines into his face. Blood was dried in streaks over the lower half of his face, his mouth, his throat. Dark, brown-red stains that flaked off as he moved, hands fumbling with the straps of his flight harness, the portable IV and tubing strapped to his left arm catching a bit on the edge of his seat. Everyone except Matron was hooked up to one of them, the IV fluids barely enough to keep them all stabilized. His head ached in a way it never had before, body weakened due to mental damage.

Lucas hit the audio on the control panel of his seat and said, "On my way," out loud instead of telepathically. His mind was so badly strained, teetering between the edge of psi shock and something dangerously deeper, that *thinking* hurt. A psi link was out of the question.

He spared a glance for the people around him as he levered himself to his feet. His sisters, slumped together in a sprawl two seats away from him, tied down by individual harnesses and strong support restraints. Threnody, who was strapped down across a row of flight seats in the center of the cargo bay, hooked up to a portable IV they had secured to the seatback near her hip and a trauma kit to monitor her vitals. The nanites in her veins were still struggling to fix damaged organs, to turn burnt flesh into new, pieces of her skin sloughing off in slow, slow increments.

Quinton, sitting on the opposite side of the cargo bay, his arms and face slowly becoming whole again courtesy of the nanites Lucas had injected him with and Jason's power. Kerr had set Quinton's broken bones as much as he'd been able to. Jason was seated next to Quinton, one hand wrapped around Quinton's wrist, face so white that Lucas could see the veins beneath his skin, power like an inferno behind the new secondary mental shields his mind had created. Kerr sat on Jason's other side, with the ravages of his fight and his loss pressed deep into his body, still unconscious.

All of them a mess. All of them half-dead, it seemed.

Lucas stumbled his way to the hatch, unable to stand up straight, and pressed his hand against the control panel to open it. The flight deck was marginally warmer than the cargo bay. Lucas took the navigator's seat, collapsing into it with little grace.

"Got a total," Matron said, not looking at him as she passed over a hypospray. "Roll call puts us at nine."

Lucas took the hypospray and shot himself full of painkillers. It was a momentary relief that wouldn't numb him long enough to be useful. Closing his eyes, he scratched at the dried blood on his face. Nine shuttles out of thirty-six had survived the launch out of Buffalo and the derecho that was still blowing its way toward the Atlantic. Nine shuttles, which was more than he'd thought they'd actually come away with.

"Take a look at that."

It took effort to open his eyes again, to focus his blurry, tired vision on what Matron wanted him to see. The surviving shuttles were flying in a jagged line over the Arctic Ocean, almost too low to be safe as they struggled to stay beneath whatever security measures the government had up here. Which would be enough, but not too much, because the World Court couldn't afford to draw attention to what they hoarded.

On the horizon, in the constant daylight of an Arctic summer, a black dot could be seen, growing larger with every kilometer they put behind them.

Spitsbergen.

The Svalbard Global Seed and Gene Bank.

Matron's voice came out softly, barely stronger than a whisper. "Your orders?"

"Get us down without them noticing us," Lucas said, curling his hands over the edge of the seat, light from the midnight sun biting into his dark blue eyes. "We've got a world to steal."

PART NINE

PROLOGUE

SESSION DATE: 2128.10.02

LOCATION: Institute of Psionics Research

CLEARANCE ID: Dr. Amy Bennett

SUBJECT: 2581

FILE NUMBER: 921

She sits listlessly in the chair, a tired, wilted shadow of herself. The wires that connect her to machines are a heavy weight she has long since given up fighting against.

"Aisling," the doctor says, desperation and fear coloring her voice as she leans over the table, body shaking ever so slightly. "Please. You have to help us."

The girl turns her head slowly, looking at the camera. She blinks, the bruises beneath her bleached-out violet eyes darker than her irises. "Are you listening? I can see it, Matthew. It's going to be okay."

The door to the white room slides open. Two more attendants in lab coats rush into the room, mouths open in half-formed screams that the camera is barely able to pick up through the static that cuts across the screen.

"It's going to be—"

BOOK TWO
TERMINAL POINT

PART ONE
DEPRIVATION

SESSION DATE: 2128.05.07
LOCATION: Institute of Psionics Research
CLEARANCE ID: Dr. Amy Bennett
SUBJECT: 2581
FILE NUMBER: 418

She is young, only a child, bent over the table and coloring furiously. The wires attached to her hands, arms, back, and head shake with the motion. The crayon she is rubbing down to nothing is red, the black one tossed away. The paper she is using is covered with a shapeless picture. It's the only color in the white room, save for the yellow dress she wears.

The doctor sits across from her and touches a finger to the waxy residue on the large drawing paper. "Is this how you see the world?"

"This is how the world is now," Aisling says, pushing a trailing wire out of the way.

"You could change that," the doctor says. Her hand beneath the table is shaking. "You could tell us how to stop the wars."

"No, I can't."

"You are being a very selfish little girl, Aisling."

The girl looks up, her bleached-out violet eyes wide and unblinking as the EEG and supporting machines she is connected to whine shrilly behind her. "Am I in trouble?"

"Not if you help us. Not if you save us."

When Aisling speaks, she sounds mournful. "I can't do that."

ONE

AUGUST 2379

SVEAGRUVA, NORWAY

They flew east into Bellsund, the arctic waters below mostly free of ice floes. The group of shuttles descended into the Van Mijenfjord beneath the government's security grid, light from the midnight sun shining down on their wings. They stayed locked in tight formation, all nine following a route uploaded on another continent. The whine of the engines echoed eerily across the vast emptiness of the island they were approaching.

The Van Mijenfjord began to narrow after the first forty or so kilometers, the lack of airspace noticeable, but not dangerous. Skimming above the still arctic waters between ragged shorelines, the shuttles sped toward their destination.

Sveagruva was a mining settlement abandoned long ago, located some distance from the head of the Van Mijenfjord. A dilapidated airfield sat at its edge, where the nine shuttles finally came to ground, landing gear sliding dangerously on uneven terrain. Less than half a kilometer away were the remnants of Sveagruva, the dormitories and the supply center long since iced over and eaten away by the elements.

The shuttles switched to standby mode, only their environmental systems running at full. Inside Alpha shuttle, the pilot leaned back in her seat and looked at her navigator.

"Well?" Matron asked. "Now what?"

Lucas Serca didn't answer. He stared out the forward windshield, dark blue eyes red from burst capillaries. Bruises pressed beneath his eyes and dried blood clung to the skin of his face, his ears, his neck. As a Class I triad psion, Lucas possessed one of the most powerful minds born in this generation, and it was killing him.

"Lucas."

"We need a day," Lucas finally said, glancing at the leader of the scavengers. "Can the shuttles' stealth systems handle that?"

Matron pressed her lips together, brow furrowing. The exhaustion on her dark face was impossible to miss. "They got us here, so they should be good for it. Let me check with Novak, since he was the only one jacked into the system."

Lucas levered himself out of the seat, his lean frame rigid with pain. "You do that."

He stumbled back into the cargo bay. It was warmer in the main guts of the shuttle than on the flight deck. Lucas leaned his back against the cool metal of the hatch, letting it hold him up as he surveyed their passengers.

Threnody Corwin, a Class III electrokinetic, was pale-faced and sitting up, a vast improvement from the beginning of this trip, when she couldn't even breathe on her own. Wrapped in several thermal blankets, the former Stryker was carefully peeling off blackened skin from one hand, revealing healed pink flesh beneath the damage. She was still hooked up to an IV and trauma kit, her blue eyes glassy, but she no longer looked mostly dead.

Sitting beside her, one hand gently pressed to the back of her neck, was Jason Garret. The only Class 0 microtelekinetic in existence wasn't looking at either of them. Jason's attention was focused on where his partner, Kerr MacDougal, sat slouched in a seat against the bulkhead beside Quinton Martinez. Both men were unconscious with exhaustion. The IVs hooked to their arms were almost empty and would need to be replaced soon.

"Should you be moving?" Lucas asked.

"Felt the landing," Threnody rasped. "Jason took off my restraints."

"She's doing better than she was even an hour ago," Jason said. "Though she still has a long way to go."

Lucas studied Jason. The microtelekinetic looked better than the rest of them, but that didn't mean he wasn't in pain. Jason's power now let him work on the subatomic level, let him manipulate DNA in order to heal, to create. It's what he was doing right now, still leaning on the nanites in

Threnody's body to help heal her since he didn't trust his new strength alone yet.

Jason's upgraded Classification didn't come without cost. His mind had been violated by Lucas's youngest sister, Kristen Serca, a dysfunctional Class III empath, in order to give him access to his full power. The psychic bond Jason once shared with Kerr was severed after Kristen broke his nearly impenetrable natal shields. Lucas permanently reset the bond into Quinton, and the link between the pair was still raw. It had saved Jason's life, yes, but at what felt like the cost of Quinton's.

"We make it?" Jason asked in a low voice. He moved his head a little, tipping it back until he exposed his throat. Lucas could see the rise and fall of his Adam's apple as the older man swallowed.

"To Sveagruva, yes," Lucas said. His English accent got thicker with every word he spoke, exhaustion heavy in his voice. Lucas shoved himself away from the hatch tiredly.

Jason frowned, blinking slowly as he turned his head to look at Lucas. "Thought it was supposed to be Longyearbyen? Those were the coordinates you uploaded."

"We'll get there soon enough. In a day or so." Lucas crossed over to where his sisters sat slumped together on the other side of the cargo bay. "We need a day to recover."

"We need more time than that."

Lucas said nothing as he looked down at Samantha and Kristen. Of the three siblings, Kristen came away from the fighting in Buffalo with the least amount of damage, not surprising when one considered her default damaged state. Most psions tried to keep insanity at bay; Kristen reveled in it. His sixteen-year-old sister destroyed the minds of others in her search for a balance she would never find. Kristen's dysfunction made her dangerous, yet also powerful. Even at full strength, Lucas was hard-pressed to keep her in check. Kristen was the only person who could have broken Jason's formidable mental shields and survived. If they were lucky, maybe she had learned how to build sanity out of Jason's neural pattern.

Lucas wasn't going to hold his breath.

Reaching out with a steady hand, Lucas stroked his fingers over Samantha's tangled blond hair, cradling her head. The eighteen-year-old

Class II telepath didn't stir at his touch, her mind a mess that Lucas didn't bother to reach for. He could feel her wounds through his shields, those she sustained at his hands and also at her own. When Samantha severed the bond she once shared with her twin and Lucas's brother, Gideon, it nearly broke her. Lucas didn't attempt to heal her mind. She knew how to fix herself.

"Why didn't you take your brother?" Jason asked. "If you're saving your family from your father, why not save them all?"

"Aisling has no use for Gideon," Lucas said as he pulled his hand away from Samantha. He returned to the center row of seats where Jason and Threnody sat.

"What about you?"

"Family ties mean little to Sercas and their Warhounds."

"I find that hard to believe after you dragged your sisters into this mess."

Lucas laughed, a dry, hacking sound. "They chose the lesser evil. That's all. We don't love each other. We don't even like each other. They're going to need to be reminded that this course of action is the right one, or the minute we turn our backs they'll try to kill us."

"Your family is really fucked-up."

"Says the man who was leashed and collared like a dog not even a month ago."

"I still had people I could rely on," Jason countered as he lifted his other hand to press it against Threnody's sternum beneath the blanket. His careful, gentle touch was at odds with the raw anger in his voice. "I still had Kerr."

The loss was still too recent for the emotion to just be swept aside. Lucas didn't need to be an empath to understand that the twist to Jason's voice was fury, grief, and pain.

"You know, Lucas, I could probably kill you right now," Jason said, his eyes locked on Threnody's face.

"I may be suffering from psi shock, but trust me when I say I'd survive whatever you tried to throw at me. Then I'd have to mindwipe you, and there goes all my hard work," Lucas said evenly. "How is Threnody?"

"I'm not a psi surgeon."

"No. You're something better."

Jason didn't argue. It was the truth, whether he liked it or not. He sucked in air around his teeth, looking for a balance he wasn't sure he would ever get back. It was different, reaching for his telekinesis now that nothing held it back. The depth of his power, the strength, was frightening. He could no longer trust his control or any of his childhood training in the Strykers Syndicate. Most of that training didn't apply, not when he had the power to see the atomic makeup of cells. Channels he never knew existed were now accessible, areas of his mind geared to see the world on a completely different level all synced up now.

Maybe telekinetics who attained Class V strength and could teleport had the potential to become what he was now. Jason didn't know. All he knew was that he didn't want to be the only person who could do this.

Jason tapped into the wealth of power in his mind and let it pour out of him. He slipped through Threnody's skin down to her bones. An echo of her damage crawled across his own nerves, countless pinpricks of heat and sudden scar tissue that was being absorbed back into her body at an accelerated rate. The new nerve endings created through cellular regeneration were going to take time to rewire, even with Jason able to control the nanites.

"Ow," Threnody said, grimacing. "That feels—weird."

"Does it hurt?" Jason asked, gaze blank.

"Not exactly." Threnody frowned, feeling the muscles in her face move stiffly. She peeled skin over the top of her finger and tossed it away. "It feels like my insides are being moved around."

"I had the nanites target your organs first. I think they're still working on them." Jason adjusted the placement of his hands. "The reason you lived long enough for me to help you was due to your electrokinesis. You'd be dead if you were any other kind of psion."

"That makes me feel so much better. Really." She flexed her fingers carefully. "How did you fix me without a biotank?"

"Take a wild guess."

The lightning strike that seared through Threnody's body and jumpstarted the power plant back in the sprawl of Buffalo had fried her entire body. When Quinton finally found her, he hadn't been sure she was even alive, but her electrokinesis had preserved her brain and central nervous system from total destruction. It shut down her body, then shocked it back to life over and over again, a dangerous cycle that her system had struggled to overcome. Only when Lucas arrived to keep her heart beating to a steady rhythm with his telekinesis did Threnody start to stabilize.

Jason did the rest. He was still doing the rest.

The amount of power Jason carried now left him seeing the world—literally—through new eyes. His optic nerves shifted through spectrums of vision that should have been impossible for any human or psion to process without biomodifications. It made him nauseous, especially when magnification was thrown into the mix, allowing him to see the microscopic with the naked eye.

The nanites were doing their job. Threnody was alive and healing. For now, that was enough.

Jason carefully pulled his power out of her body, letting every last cell and nanite go, until he could no longer even visualize the layers of skin cells and capillaries that made up his eyelids. His head felt heavy. He watched as Lucas changed out Threnody's IV bag. The soft, constant beeping of her cardiac rhythm was almost lulling.

Jason shifted his focus to Lucas, sinking his power into the younger man's body. It showed Jason the dark spots in Lucas where trauma had left ugly pools of damage beneath his skin.

"I can feel you," Lucas said as he finished securing the IV bag. "Get your power off me. Now."

"You've got bleeding in your brain."

"I'm handling it."

"Not well enough. That subdural hematoma isn't going to fix itself. Let me do something about it."

"You finally get full access to your power and suddenly you think you can do the impossible."

Jason arched an eyebrow as he pushed himself to his feet. "That *is* why you were after me, right?"

"I'm not the only one," Lucas said as he went to toss the used bag in the head's disposal system. "Not anymore."

Jason grimaced. "Nathan."

Nathan Serca, the oldest psion alive at the age of fifty-one, was a Class

I triad psion that Lucas rivaled in power, if not cruelty. Lucas's father had no equal when it came to cruelty.

Lucas came back out, nodding at Jason's answer. "And every last Warhound at his disposal, so remember to read as human on the mental grid, at least until the launch, or you'll get us all killed."

Unlike Warhounds, Strykers were never taught how to match their psi signature to a human's, reading as human on the mental grid, that vast psychic plane of the world's thoughts. But Jason wasn't a Stryker anymore, and Lucas had taught him how to shield on the flight over, literally dumping the information straight into Jason's mind and letting the microtelekinetic sort through the overload on his own. There hadn't been time for subtlety, but Jason still got his shielding right.

Jason looked over his shoulder at Samantha and Kristen. Three of Nathan's children were turning their backs on their heritage, but Jason still didn't trust them. One of the founding families of the society that survived the Border Wars, the Serca Syndicate they owned was well-known for its forays into politics and government-restricted sciences. Genetic manipulation and segregation were just the beginning. The Sercas were the ones to force the Fifth Generation Act on the world, beginning the long cleanup of tainted and mutated human genetics. The Act went hand in hand with another Serca creation, the Registry, a list of people whose genetic makeup was clean and utterly human. The Sercas had placed themselves on top of the list, though they were far from human.

The Sercas had freedom and they wanted to remake humanity on Mars Colony, with themselves ruling atop society. The World Court and their chosen elite contemporaries were planning to inherit what the world's ancestors had left them—Mars Colony. They dreamed of a utopia and a chance to start over. Caught in between were the Strykers, psion slaves bound to a paramilitary company, who only wanted to save what was left of the world and their own skins. The whole mess of false fronts and alliances was the reason why they were here, on Spitsbergen, following Lucas. Jason owed him for more than just removing the neurotracker that was once grafted to his brain, but that knowledge was a bitter pill to swallow.

"Sit down," Jason said flatly. "Let me fix you."

Lucas seemed amused by Jason's temerity. "Do you honestly think Nathan hasn't inflicted worse on me before? I'll be fine."

"Don't compare me to Nathan." Jason scowled, but his gaze held steady. "I'm not going to kill you. Now sit the fuck down and let me take a look at your brain. We still need you, Lucas. Even I know that."

"How altruistic of you."

"Just take a damn seat."

"You should listen to him," Threnody said. "He does okay work for being such an obnoxious pain in the ass."

"I'll take that as a compliment because I'm not arguing with someone in your current state." Jason eyed her. "You should lie down, Threnody."

With Jason's help, Threnody once again stretched out on the row of seats that was her berth, wrapped securely in thermal blankets and modified harness straps to keep her stable. Once Jason saw to Threnody, he headed over to Lucas, picking up a hypospray half-full of nanites from a case as he moved through the cargo bay. They couldn't afford weakness, and all of them were damaged in some way. Recovery was going to be slow for some, quicker for others, but even Jason knew that if they wanted to survive what was coming, they would need Lucas at full strength.

"Get the bleeding stopped," Lucas said as he sat down beside Samantha and let Jason inject him in the throat with a dosage of nanites. "The rest will keep."

Jason braced himself over Lucas with one hand, his other curving carefully over the left side of Lucas's skull, pale blond hair beneath his fingers a dirty mess. Jason closed his eyes, bent his head, and let his power seep into Lucas's skull. Down through the blood-brain barrier, down to the dura mater, into the brain itself with its swollen tear, just a few centimeters long. Jason could feel where Lucas had picked at it telekinetically, struggling to ease the pressure there with a power that couldn't compete with the one Jason now wielded.

"Messy," Jason muttered.

"I don't need your opinion on how I keep myself alive."

Jason dug his fingernails into Lucas's scalp. "Be still."

Jason saw capillaries and cell structure, flash images of hemoglobin and plasma, as he worked through nanites to carefully reattach torn capillaries. Blood flow returned and the swollen tension in the cells around the area began to fade. Jason spread his microtelekinesis through Lucas's skull, helping the nanites chase down stray blood cells that were shifting into clots and teleporting them out of Lucas's body. Tiny drops of red splattered intermittently to the shuttle's deck until Jason was certain he'd done enough to ensure that Lucas wouldn't keel over and die from an aneurysm right when they needed him most.

Jason retracted his power, opening his eyes. The layers in the world wavered and it took effort to fix his vision. He wondered if he would ever get used to this, to the way he could see things, feel things, through his power.

"I never wanted to be this."

"This is what you were born to be," Lucas said, satisfaction curling through his voice. "I'm not the only one the world needs."

Jason's answer to that was a twisted smile that reminded Lucas of Kristen. Lucas found little comfort in the expression. They stared at each other for a moment, the only sounds in the cargo bay the quiet hum of the environmental system and everyone's soft breathing.

"You're awake" came Matron's rough voice a few seconds later. She stood in the open hatch with her arms crossed over her chest, tapping her foot. "Get your ass up here, Jason. Novak needs some help with the hack."

Jason straightened up, but didn't move. Lucas smiled tightly at him. "Go."

"All right." Jason left the cargo bay for the flight deck.

"How come you're the only one not bleeding out their eyes?" Matron asked as he took over the navigator's seat.

Jason reached for a wire embedded in the controls. "I don't know."

His fingers brushed over faint flecks of blood on the console, his power momentarily slipping free of his control. It seeped into the blood, and the only DNA he could identify in the fluid was Lucas's. He grimaced, clenching down hard on his control.

The world looked, and felt, strange.

It always would.

[TWO]

The seed bank is going to be difficult to get into," Lucas said. He studied the map on his datapad that showed the surrounding terrain of Longyearbyen and the airfield a kilometer away. A bright red dot identified where the Svalbard Global Seed and Gene Bank was located. "It's going to have layers of security, and the first layer we're going to have to take down is the one that breathes."

"Distraction? Make it a two-group feint, but only one group goes in and the rest draws their fire?" Threnody said, rubbing at her mouth and scratching at her skin. "Everyone's going to have to pull their weight and we're all in crap condition, but we could try a head-on attack. Or maybe something more subtle might work?"

"We don't have time for subtle."

Quinton prodded at his teeth with his tongue. They weren't broken. Neither were the bones in his face or the ones in his arms. The scattered burns on his hands resulting from his being a Class III pyrokinetic were gone, as were the biotubes. All he felt was their absence when he pressed his fingers down over skin and muscle. The tips of his middle fingers and thumbs no longer had the thin plating of metal needed to spark natural gas into fire. For the first time since being extracted from a cartel drug lord's training camp as a child by Strykers, Quinton's arms were wholly flesh and bone.

"I'm going to need something more than a lighter if you're hoping to work my power into your plan," Quinton said, raising his head to look at Lucas. "I'd do better with a gun."

"We've got grenades if you need to make fire," Matron said, staring down at a list of supplies on her datapad. "Otherwise, I've got guns, but they won't be military grade. Lost most of those when the rest of my shuttles blew getting out of Buffalo. You'll be shooting with bullets, not energy darts."

"I can work with that."

Everyone in Alpha shuttle was awake and huddled in the cargo bay, pretending the chrono wasn't ticking away seconds that they needed. Lucas rubbed at his forehead, unable to get rid of the ache building there. "I don't care which weapon you use. This part is going to be a straightforward hit-and-run."

"You can't have my scavengers for your suicide run," Matron said. "I only have enough left to pilot the shuttles and you need them for that."

Lucas waved aside her worries. "When we arrive in Longyearbyen, we'll need to make sure none of the quads manage to send out a signal for help. I wouldn't put it past Nathan to have Warhounds up there."

"He placed two teams there last month," Samantha said. "We'll be dealing with both psions and humans."

"And none of us can even stand up straight," Threnody said. "Great planning, Lucas."

"I kept you alive," he reminded her.

Threnody shrugged, the motion a little stiff. She was wearing an insulated skinsuit beneath her clothes now like everyone else, but still looked as if a good wind would knock her over. Ten hours since landing and Jason had already worked on her twice more. She was healing at a pace that outstripped the regular cellular rate, but was on par with a biotank. It was a tiring process, for both her and Jason.

"I won't be any good at shielding," Kerr said, his teal eyes bloodshot. He cleared his throat, words riding a heavy Scottish accent. "You'd do better to put me on offense. I can handle a few quick and dirty strikes. I can't hold up any shields right now but my own."

"What about your empathy?" Jason asked.

"If you want an empath, use Kristen."

Kerr was a dual psion with Class II telepathy and Class IX empathy and was worn down like everyone else. His empathic power was newfound, but nowhere near Kristen's level. The younger girl graced him with a teeth-baring grin. Her dark blue eyes had lost some of their sick silver sheen with the dubious onset of borrowed sanity.

"Is that admiration you're feeling?" Kristen asked.

"Hardly."

Jason eyed Kristen contemplatively. "If we can get her inside, she'll get everyone else outside for us. We can handle the quads and Warhounds better if we can see them rather than wondering if they're trying to call for reinforcements. It'll be a bloodbath, and we can't let the fight get drawn out, but the odds are in our favor if we keep the element of surprise."

"They're in our favor even if we don't," Lucas said. "We aren't failing here."

"Do we know how many targets there are?" Threnody said, scratching at peeling skin on the underside of her jaw. She couldn't seem to sit still. "Any previous reconnaissance records to extrapolate off of?"

"The World Court posts five quads up here at any given shift," Samantha said. "Regular check-in happens at oh six hundred every day."

"So we hit them ten minutes after. Plenty of leeway for them to finish checking in, and we've got hours after that to break into the seed bank. What's the terrain like?"

"The ruins are overrun with sparse vegetation, but there are a few buildings that the government has taken care of. It'll be a clearer line of sight than what we had when we fought in the bunkers," Lucas said. "The mountain isn't habitable and they've got a weapons system surrounding it for defense. It'll be cold, but no major radiation risk."

Threnody nodded, brow furrowed. "Our best bet is to drop down right on top of them. We'll have to go in shooting, so to speak."

"That's a brilliant way to die," Samantha said. "We're all burned-out. How do you expect us to function when our range is so limited?"

"Do you have a better idea? No? Then shut up until you can give us something useful."

Samantha glared at Lucas. "Are you going to let her talk to me like that?"

"Yes" came his calm reply. "I am. You've never organized a plan of attack on this scale. You only led them on Nathan's orders. Threnody is better at this than you are."

Samantha abruptly stood and went to the only place for privacy in the shuttle—the head. The door closed behind her with a faint hiss and she locked it. Leaning against the sink, she took in a deep breath and struggled to calm her nerves. With slightly shaking hands, she turned the cold water on and used a little to wash her face and ease her dry eyes.

Her skin itched everywhere the acid rain had touched it back in Buffalo. That annoyance would fade, given time. The swirling nausea in her gut would probably stay with her for a little while longer. Pressing a fist to her middle, Samantha stared at herself in the tiny mirror above the sink and gave her reflection a smile that was more snarl than anything else.

The door to the head slid open.

"That was locked," Samantha said flatly.

"I know the override," Lucas said. "Are you regretting your decision already?"

"Sercas don't do regrets."

"Glad to see you've kept the arrogance." Lucas stepped inside and let the door slide shut. His presence made the space feel even smaller.

Samantha turned her head fractionally to keep him in her sights. "What else did you let me keep?" she demanded, voice harsh. "Sanity, obviously, but you function like Nathan at your most basic level, Lucas. You use people the same way he does. You're just better at rationing our lives."

Lucas pinched the bridge of his nose, eyes half-lidded as he gazed at her. "You're alive. Be grateful."

"You haven't given me a reason to be."

Lucas smiled. It was the only warning she got. Lucas's hand wrapped around her throat too fast for her to block, then he was slamming her head against the mirror. Samantha choked on a scream, biting it back. The edge of the sink bruised her hip. Lucas had a death grip on her throat.

Agony ripped through her skull. "I won't beg for you."

"I don't want you to beg," Lucas said. "I want you to work with me. If we're going to survive at all, I need you on my side, Sam."

"My mind should be my own."

"You're a Serca. Your mind belongs to whoever inherits the Syndicate."

"Gideon won't accept me after what I did."

The loss still hit like a sucker punch, that emptiness in her mind where her twin once resided through their bond. It was as if she still had a body, just no vital organs to make it live; a hole at the bottom of her mind with no way to fill it.

Lucas eased his grip, letting her go. Samantha shoved him away, putting as much distance between them as she could. It wasn't enough to make her feel safe. She curled her hands over the edge of the sink and glared at him. Lucas didn't seem bothered by her animosity.

"You knew when I ripped apart your mind in Buffalo that you had no other options but this, but me," Lucas said, flicking his fingers at his chest. "I expect you to obey, Sam."

She raised her chin, defiance in every line of her body even as she licked her lips. "And if I don't?"

"Then Kris can change your mind for me. Or at least your loyalty."

"She was always yours, wasn't she?" Samantha said, remembering those moments in Buffalo when Lucas spoke through their youngest sibling.

Lucas nodded. "Always."

"How did Nathan never know?"

"If Nathan fears anything other than death, it's insanity. He feared losing himself in hers. I never did." Lucas shrugged. "Kris was the perfect tool. I wielded her as needed."

"And me?"

"I needed you sane and I need you to be on my side. I saved your mind over the years because I can't do what needs to be done alone."

"What if I refuse?"

"We've gone down that road many times before. It never ends well when you choose Nathan over me." Lucas's gaze was steady. "There's too much at stake, Sam. We both know that. Surviving this fight starts here."

She looked away, seeing their reflections in the mirror. They were both a mess, but still alike in their resolve.

"What's in it for me?" Samantha said.

"Your life and the ability to live it in a changed world."

"Never knew you were such a humanitarian."

"We aren't human, Sam." Lucas passed his hand over the control panel to open the door at his back. The sound of everyone else's conversation filtered inside. "I won't be anything less than what Aisling promised."

"And that would be?"

Lucas didn't answer as he stepped out, but she didn't need him to. If the Sercas had one thing in common, it was their belief in themselves and what they could accomplish. Samantha lifted a hand to scratch off a tiny flake of dried blood she had missed in her washing. She flicked it off her finger, wondering how much blood she would end up losing to reach her brother's goal.

[THREE]

AUGUST 2379
LONGYEARBYEN, NORWAY

Longyearbyen lay north of the arctic circle, a frozen graveyard of a time when almost every last coastline in the world had communities thriving with people, even a tiny, wintery archipelago. Currently, the town center was surrounded by buildings eaten away by the cold and disuse, time having made inroads on a place only twenty people inhabited on any given day. Richard Cuellas had spent the past five years on sentry duty in the far north, drinking his way through gallons of coffee and whiskey. It was a lucrative, if boring, post.

Richard was one of those who didn't mind the isolation, along with the rest of the people assigned with him in the north. Up here at the top of the world, there was space to stretch out, land that wouldn't kill you if you stayed too long in one place, and air that smelled better than in any other place on earth. Their mission was to monitor bioscanners and a security grid that encompassed a quarter of the island. The computers could do this well enough on their own, but the government still required a human mind to interpret the data that ran across the vidscreens.

Sipping at steaming black coffee, Richard tilted his chair back on two legs, balancing there as he called up the log for the past ten hours. It was shift change, and despite its being a post where nothing ever happened, they stuck to protocol. The government expected full protection of what was buried in the ice and volcanic rock of Plataberget. Neither he nor his compatriots knew what was so important up here, and they weren't stupid enough to ask. Their mission was to guard Spitsbergen. In the entire time that the government had manned the island—250 years and counting—no unauthorized person had ever set foot on it.

That morning, the long-standing record was broken when Richard saw the image of a civilian girl on one of the security feeds in a place she shouldn't be.

Choking on his coffee, he let his chair fall back to the floor and swore as some of the hot liquid splashed over his bare fingers. He set the cup aside and reached for the controls to magnify the security feed, but the girl had disappeared. Richard swore again, wondering if the madness that came from being cut off from society was finally getting to him after five years of duty. He commed the rest of his quad.

"Graham, get your ass up here, I need a second sign-off," Richard said as he leaned forward and squinted at all the various angles he could call up on the security feed.

He found no sign of the girl, and replays of the feed didn't show him a damn thing. It was as if she'd never been there. Five seconds was a long time for it to be a glitch, and he knew for a fact that the last shipment of entertainment bodies had all been dumped in the water a month ago. It wasn't some government-supplied whore.

The door behind him slid open a few minutes later. Richard looked over his shoulder at the man who came into the control room, his second-in-command, bundled up against the cold. The environmental system kept the place warm, but heat could stand up against the elements for only so long before the arctic chill seeped into everything.

"I'm on break," Graham said irritably.

"Yeah, and I don't care." Richard stabbed a finger at the vidscreens. "Got a glitch. Security feed showed some blond-haired girl outside."

Graham frowned and leaned over the console to bring the feed up in a quick loop, showing him every angle of their tiny settlement. All he saw was barren land and decrepit houses that were once part of the ancient town. The airfield a kilometer away was empty and the waters of Isfjorden were placid against the icy shore.

"You drink too much at last night's poker game, Rick?" Graham asked as he let the security feed revert to its default circulation mode.

Richard scowled at him. "Do I fucking look hungover? Do a recon of the area with the others. I want it cleared by a live report."

"You're kidding, right?" Graham laughed. "Hell, there's no one up here but us."

"If there's no one here, it shouldn't take you long to confirm that fact, right? Now get out there."

"Asshole."

Graham left the control room. Richard didn't doubt that the other man would follow orders, but Graham was a lazy son of a bitch who'd been packing on weight over the past two years. He'd take his sweet time getting it done.

Sometime later, Richard could see Graham and some of the other soldiers posted up here wandering around outside on the security feed—along with a shuttle that dropped down out of vertical, coming within camera range nearly on top of the small outpost. Richard didn't recognize the make, and it was completely off schedule. He flipped open the plastic cover that protected the emergency button and slammed his hand down on it to trigger the alarm. The piercing sound nearly ruptured his eardrum, catching everyone's attention in the connected buildings.

"We've got a breach!" Richard yelled into the system's local comm frequency before moving to switch it into an outgoing uplink.

The press of a gun barrel to the back of his head made him freeze.

"No bioware net." The voice sounded young, her words riding on a soft laugh. "They should have given you one. Hands up. Turn around."

Richard complied. He came face-to-face with a tall, thin teenage girl who smiled wide enough to show all her teeth. Her bony face was dominated by gleaming dark blue eyes, and her smile made Richard's skin crawl. The girl stared at Richard over the barrel of her gun, and Richard thought about reaching for his own weapon, but he couldn't remember why he needed it. Standing there, breath coming in rapid bursts, he tried to remember his duty, but it was difficult to think around the fear flooding his body.

"Who—," Richard choked out, one hand clutching at his chest. His heart was beating so fast it felt as if it were going to beat right out of his body.

She lowered the gun, smile still in place. *"What."*

Scared to death wasn't how Richard wanted to die, but Kristen didn't give him a choice. She dug her power into his emotions, twisting them beyond anything he'd felt before. Fear, yes, but also pain, both of which incited panic. The body could be made to feel anything, and what Kristen made Richard feel stripped him of all control. His heart burst seconds later, the sound a muffled pop in his chest.

Kristen pulled the body off the chair. Taking the dead man's place, she spun around a few times in the chair before finally settling down to face the monitors. The security feed was framed in every vidscreen, showing her the entire outpost. Empathically, she could sense everyone's position, and she put faces to psi signatures using the security system.

Outside in the cold morning air, Threnody's body was already regretting this plan of action. Breathing heavily, she took shelter behind a crumbling foundation wall slick with moss, teeth clenched against the pain she was feeling.

Stay low, Quinton said through the psi link. It was a tenuous connection, all that Lucas could provide. *I've got your back.*

He lay on top of the shuttle, teleported there by Jason and spared the heat from the fuselage by a thin telekinetic shield. Rifle in hand, aiming through the sight scope, Quinton shot once to get a read on the air current, purposefully missing his oncoming target, watching where the bullet hit to check wind speed and distance. He adjusted the angle of his rifle slightly, curled his finger over the trigger, and pulled it between one breath and the next.

The soldier was thrown backward to the ground, blood spraying out of his chest as the bullet hit home.

Go, Quinton told Threnody. *I don't see anyone in that hallway.*

She scrambled to her feet, throwing herself forward, eyes on the door the soldier had come out of. Threnody skidded inside, glancing up at the security feed embedded in the wall.

I'm your eye in the sky, Kristen said cheerfully into her mind on the psi link. *Two soldiers coming your way at fifty meters and closing, second intersection down the hall. One is a Warhound.*

Class? Threnody said.

That would be telling.

Lucas, your sister is a rude little shit.

That Warhound is a Class VI telekinetic, Lucas said. *You'll have to handle what she throws at you, Threnody. I can't get to you yet. And, Kris?*

Yes? Kristen said.

Don't piss me off.

All that filtered down the psi link from the girl was a sense of sullen discontent. Threnody kept running, using her teeth to pull the glove off one hand. The buildings here were old and patched, metal threaded through the structures everywhere. Threnody took a chance and fell to her knees as the footsteps got louder. She slammed one hand against the metal wall, looking for a conduit, and brought her gun up to bear right as two people came hurtling around the corner.

Bullets cut through the air over her head. She felt telekinetic pressure on her bruised ribs, but her power was already arcing up into their bodies. Threnody's vision tunneled out, a roaring sound filling her ears. For one long moment, she didn't know if she was even breathing, then a sharp pain spiked through one side of her face. Spiked harder on the other. She blinked, vision coming back to her in time to see Jason's hand descending for another slap. She made a wordless noise and he stopped in midmotion.

Threnody was lying on her back, staring up into Jason's face, his hazel eyes wide and worried. He let out a harsh breath. "Shit, Thren, don't go undoing all my hard work."

It was strange hearing the familial diminutive of her name come out of his mouth. Threnody struggled to sit up. Jason helped her out, bracing her with one arm behind her back as she caught her breath. "My hand."

Jason looked down at the limb in question, finding red lines spanning across her skin like circuit wires. "Nerve damage. Guess you aren't as healed as I thought you were. I think you might have fried the nanites in your veins, too."

"Wonderful." Threnody grimaced. "Help me up."

Jason got Threnody to her feet. She checked her gun and they got moving again. The faint mutter in the back of their minds was everyone else's conversation on the psi link as they cut through the outpost section by section. Overlaid across that was Kristen's heavy, intense presence that was blocking the Warhounds' ability to teleport away or telepathically get a warning out. Her psionic interference scratched against their shields. Kristen didn't care about harming the Strykers if it meant the humans died, and Lucas was too busy right now to make her see reason. Kristen's help was needed but it was difficult on their end to deal with it.

The sound of an explosion nearby pulled them up short. "That came from outside," Threnody said.

Was that us or them? Jason sent out along the psi link.

Us, Quinton answered. *Samantha just blew up part of a building. We've got fire.*

Joining the fray?

No. I'm staying put.

"We need to get to the control room," Jason said as they started moving again. *Kerr, sitrep.*

You aren't feeling the headache I am, came Kerr's pained reply. *Remaining Warhounds are in merge. Lucas and I are picking their minds apart, but I'd rather put a bullet in their brains.*

And the quads? Threnody asked.

None in your section. Go knock some sense into Kristen and tell her to stop biting at my shields.

Kerr's mental voice faded. Threnody and Jason were still methodically careful on their way to the control room, but Kerr was right. They didn't find any more quads on their way to Kristen's position, and she greeted their arrival with a soft and raspy "All clear."

Jason hauled Kristen out of the chair and took her place. She immediately draped herself over the back of it. Threnody eyed the girl, keeping a finger on the trigger guard of her gun.

"Maybe you should go find your brother," Jason said as he yanked connecting wires from the console and plugged them into the neuroports in his arms and wrists. "I don't like having you at my back."

"I know," Kristen said. "It's why I'm staying."

"I'm not leaving," Threnody said evenly.

Jason switched on his inspecs, data rolling across his vision, merging with the hologrids that snapped into the air. "I remember your psi signature from a few years ago, Kristen. Every Stryker died trying to get close to you. No one managed a solid ident."

"You wouldn't have," Kristen said. "We Sercas are supposed to be human, remember?"

Jason shrugged his opinion of that. "You've fooled the world. Don't expect anyone to be happy about that."

"You Strykers never are. You should see the faces of the ones we keep when they meet with old teammates. So many tears. So sad."

"What are you talking about?"

"We retrieve select Strykers for our own purposes and make them loyal to us. We can make them forget where they came from, but we can't make those they left behind forget who they lost." Kristen stood up on her tiptoes to peer over the seat at Jason. "Your rank and file keep secrets better when dead."

Her empathy rolled through them, brushing up against their shields, but went no further than that. Lucas's previous warning was enough to make Kristen stay her hand this time, just not her mouth. Pointedly, neither Threnody nor Jason engaged her in that conversation.

Jason set to work breaking through encrypted software, inspecs streaming data over his sight. Lucas arrived several minutes later, looking tired and tense. He pried Kristen off the chair and pitched her toward the hallway.

"Go back to the shuttle, Kris," Lucas said, not watching to see if she left.

"Maybe you should go with her," Threnody said. "Make sure she doesn't try to kill everyone else."

"Kris knows what will happen if she tries."

"You're in no condition to stop her."

"Doesn't mean I won't." Lucas gave Threnody a hard smile before addressing Jason. "Give me an update."

"That damn mountain is surrounded by artillery," Jason said as he moved his hands through the hologrid, searching out leads for the hack. "Most of it is still active."

"I want you to keep anything from coming online when we get up there," Lucas said. "That's all we need."

"It's going to take a while. The security up there runs on a different system than the one we hacked flying in."

"You've got two hours."

Jason grimaced. "I doubt I can do it in two. It already took us a day to fly to this island and hack the outer security. This is going to take longer."

"We have less than twenty-four hours to finish this. I'm moving everyone to the airfield that services Longyearbyen. I want you to set up five days' worth of future communications to be sent out during the required status check-in time. The quads up here had a standard security code. I'm sure you can falsify it."

Lucas left and Threnody followed after him. Jason started hacking into everything the government had built up in Longyearbyen. Novak couldn't help him with this, the scavenger having burned through most of the wiring in his brain and body already. Jason knew the feeling, knew the heat of burned wires before they cooled, the tiny surges making sections of his body go numb. He wasn't looking forward to going through that again.

Two hours later, Jason had to resign himself to the inevitable: he wasn't going to meet Lucas's timetable. Jason rubbed at his eyes, inspecs bright against the darkness. "Shit."

He was tired. Staring at command windows and the framework of a security grid he had no hope of breaking would exhaust anyone.

Right on schedule, Lucas commed him. "Finished?"

"I finished the communications you wanted, but we've got a problem."

"That's not what I want to hear."

"I managed to hack the security feed around here earlier only because it was tied into the same system Novak hacked on our flight over the Atlantic. I got lucky with the artillery, but I can't hack this last system, Lucas. It's completely separate, half of it is tied into biometrics on-site, and I'd need a week, at minimum, to build a back door."

The comm hummed softly with static. Jason winced as Lucas implanted an image directly into his mind for a visual. "Get back here."

Jason extracted himself from the hack and closed out before teleporting back to the shuttles sitting on the airfield a kilometer away. Alpha shuttle had its cargo doors open, metal ramp digging into the dirt. Lucas was standing at the edge of the ramp, bright blots of red dripping from his nose to the metal beneath his feet. Lucas might not have been hemorrhaging anymore, but nosebleeds were common while suffering through psi shock. Jason was surprised the younger man was capable of walking, much less pulling off an attack on a government outpost.

Shaking his head, Jason jerked his thumb over his shoulder in the direction of Longyearbyen. "Security grid for the island is set. The artillery on the mountain is dormant now, but the security system tied into the seed bank is something else."

Lucas wiped at the blood dripping from his nose, flicking it off his fingertips. "If we jacked Novak into the hack?"

"He's burned through all his neuroports."

"We could strip new ones onto different nerves and modify the ones in his brain."

Jason stiffened. "That will kill him."

"Most likely." Lucas turned his head to stare south at the flat-topped, small mountain that rose into the sky nearby. It was mostly white near the peak, the rest dark rock and dull green moss. "If you can't hack it, we only have one option."

Lucas headed back into the shuttle, Jason on his heels. Matron and Kerr were huddled near some of the cold-storage units, with Samantha and Kristen sitting nearby, watching them. Jason didn't see Threnody or Quinton.

"Did you scan the terrain?" Lucas asked Matron as they got closer.

"This place don't get tectonic shift like other continents," Matron said, glancing up from the readouts on the unit's control screen. "That road is stable enough, but I wouldn't want to land a shuttle on it. Lucky for you, two of the shuttles that survived are carrying the gravlifts. We'll be able to transfer whatever Jason can't teleport."

"I take it I'm the stevedore," Jason said with a heavy sigh.

Matron smiled at him, showing a line of metal teeth. "You know you're worth more than that, so stop complaining."

"Is the hack finished?" Kerr said.

Jason shook his head. "No."

"Then how the hell are we getting inside that mountain?"

"Better question would be how are we doing it without tipping off the government?" Matron said.

"They won't know what's happened up here until it's too late," Lucas said, heading for the flight deck.

"You sure about that?"

"We'll be in Antarctica by then."

"We'll be *where*?" Jason said. "What the hell, Lucas? You want to go from polar day to polar night? There are other places in the world we can go to ground that are less extreme."

"And that's exactly where the government would think we'd go, except we won't be in Norway, Greenland, or Canada. There's no other place to match the Arctic except the south pole. Antarctica wasn't worth the trouble for the government to excavate after the Border Wars, which means they won't be searching for us there." Lucas glanced over his shoulder at them as he palmed open the hatch to the flight deck. "The seeds need to be kept frozen. These shuttles won't run forever."

Matron snorted. "Tell me about it. We're gonna have to refuel somewhere between here and there. Hope you've got a place in mind."

"Just stick to the plan and don't ask questions, Matron. You'll live."

"You keep saying that. I keep not believing it."

Lucas ignored her in favor of Quinton's sharp gaze. "I need Threnody."

"No." Quinton stood up from the navigator's seat. Threnody was curled up in the pilot's seat, seemingly asleep, but at the sound of Lucas's voice, she opened her eyes. She looked worse than she had before the fight.

"You don't have a choice."

Quinton put himself between her and Lucas. "She can't handle whatever it is you need her to do."

"She survived a focused lightning strike. She can survive this. Move."

Quinton's fist smashed against Lucas's jaw hard enough to knock the other man on his ass. Pain stabbed through Lucas's skull from the blow, blood trickling over his tongue from where he bit it. Black dots edged his vision, telepathy slip-sliding against his shaky shields. Lucas sucked in a deep breath, taking a few seconds to anchor his shields before anything else. Then he propped himself up on one elbow and glared at Quinton.

"You're starting to annoy me, Stryker."

"Quinton," Threnody called out, pushing herself out of the seat. "Lucas—*don't*."

Telekinesis yanked Quinton forward, slamming him onto the deck beside Lucas with enough force to knock him briefly unconscious. Lucas used those few seconds to roll over until he was crouched over Quinton, hands on either side of the pyrokinetic's head.

Wake up.

The older man's eyes jerked open as that harsh mental order stabbed into his mind. Blood dripped out of Lucas's nose, falling onto Quinton's cheek.

"Still a bloody telepath, even with psi shock," Lucas said, voice low and flat as he moved one hand to Quinton's throat. "I'm not powerless here."

"Fuck you," Quinton forced out between lips that barely moved, telekinesis holding him down.

"We don't have time for a hack. Threnody is the only one who can get us into the seed bank. And she will. You don't get a say in the matter."

Lucas pressed his hand down hard against Quinton's throat, feeling the ridges of the other man's trachea roll against his palm. Quinton choked from the pressure, incapable of fighting back.

Cool, shaking fingers pressed against the back of Lucas's neck. He felt a faint, warning electric tingle against his skin. "Let him go, Lucas."

Be grateful Aisling needs your life, Lucas said into Threnody's and Quinton's minds. *I would eradicate you if given the choice, Quinton.*

Lucas stood up, his telekinesis shifting off the other man. Quinton dragged in a ragged breath of air, shoving himself to a sitting position. Lucas bared his teeth at Threnody around a split lip. "Ladies first."

Threnody shook her head and walked away from him. Quinton got to his feet and followed Threnody to the cargo ramp. Lucas tracked their movement, watching as Quinton supported Threnody with a care he showed no one else.

"Matron," Lucas said. "Pick half your crew to come with us up the mountain. The rest can stay here and organize the shuttles for loading."

"You psions up to the task?" Matron said, eyeing them.

"Worry about your own people."

Matron knew better than to argue and took herself out of the shuttle, yelling for Everett and Novak. Lucas focused his attention on his sisters and the other two Strykers as Quinton and Threnody argued in whispers near the cargo ramp.

"Let's go," Lucas said.

"Are you sure about this?" Kerr asked, glancing from Lucas to Threnody. "If all she's doing is frying the system, won't that trigger an alarm somewhere?"

"The alarm would have to reroute through the outpost first, and Jason has done enough damage that it won't get very far. No one outside of the highest reaches of the government knows about this place, and the government is busy dealing with the mess in Buffalo," Lucas said. "The Strykers were never informed of this location, so a teleport can't happen. The World Court won't send a team by shuttle until it's too late and we'll be long gone by then. It's still a calculated risk, but we're taking it."

"And is using Threnody up a calculated risk?" Quinton asked harshly.

"We're all taking a risk here," Threnody said. "Let it go, Quin."

Jason shook his head. "I don't know if I can save Threnody again, Lucas. My first few attempts apparently didn't take."

"Keep her breathing until we reach Antarctica, that's all I need," Lucas said. "I've got someone there who can help if it comes down to it."

Surprise flickered over Jason's face. "Don't tell me you've got black-market surgeons stashed all over the world?"

"When I find useful people, I keep them."

"I've always liked your collections," Kristen said as she skipped past them for the cargo ramp. Everyone followed her outside.

Matron and ten of her scavengers were busy hauling three gravlifts off two shuttles. The machines were capable of carrying heavy loads on the flatbed, with lifts that could deposit the cargo on any given surface. Their max was half a ton, and they would be utilized as much as Jason's telekinesis.

"These are good," Matron called out to Lucas as she hauled herself up into one of the gravlift control seats. "No damage on the flight out."

"You know how much of whatever's in those vaults you want to load?" Everett asked as he climbed onto another gravlift. He sported a quick-heal patch over his left temple, having taken a minor beating on the flight out of Buffalo.

"Half or more of everything the World Court is hiding in there," Lucas said.

"Yeah, you better hope we've got room."

"If we don't, you stay behind." Lucas climbed up onto the flatbed behind Matron and settled in for the ride. "Your scavengers need a refresher course on how to take orders."

Matron glanced at him over her shoulder. "I lost more'n half my crew getting your ass out of the fire back in Buffalo. Leave them alone."

The Strykers and Lucas's sisters climbed up onto the flatbed, finding handholds along the edges where straps were coiled into shallow recesses. Kerr helped Quinton get Threnody on board, the two men working in silence to steady her and help her get comfortable. When they were ready, Matron started the gravlift and steered away from the airfield to the rarely used road.

The incline wasn't that steep, and the long, winding road seemed stable. The wedge of metal sticking out of the mountainside was covered in moss and seemed like part of the landscape. When they reached the level part of the road, they passed by the remnants of an old-fashioned gate off to one side, the rusted metal still visible. Up ahead, the dirt road curved until it cut parallel to the entrance of the metal wedge. The gravlifts were locked into a hovering line behind Matron's lead when they arrived, the engines a soft hum in the chilly air.

A faded logo could be seen on the side of the metal wedge: The Svalbard Global Seed and Gene Bank.

"Why can't we teleport inside?" Everett said as everyone started to climb off the gravlifts.

"Teleporting requires a visual," Kerr said as he watched Quinton and Jason help Threnody get her feet on the ground. To his eyes, she wasn't looking too steady on her legs. "You can't teleport to some place you've never been, not unless you want to end up embedded in a solid object."

Lucas took a careful step forward, letting the rusted support ramp that linked the road and the entrance take his weight. The metal creaked, the sound a grating echo in their ears, but it held. He assumed the government had replaced it a few times over the years. Lucas looked over his shoulder. "Threnody."

"Front and center, yeah, I know," she said.

Quinton had her by the elbow as they walked across the ramp slowly, trying not to jar her too much. Jason was right behind them while everyone else waited on the road. Threnody leaned heavily against Quinton, staring at the control panel.

She swallowed thickly. "I don't know if I can do this. I don't know if I'll be fast enough."

"I can have Kris turn off the pain," Lucas said.

"No. I'll lose myself that way."

"Then I'll anchor you."

Stepping forward, Lucas carefully pressed one fingertip against her temple. Threnody flinched from the pressure, skin still sensitive. She needed a biotank, but he didn't have one here to put her in. Lucas closed his eyes and concentrated on pulling his telepathy together. He hadn't lied about his ability to recover. That still didn't mean it was easy. Psi shock made it difficult to focus, and Threnody's mind was disturbingly quiet when he dipped into it.

We fixed your body, but I forgot about your mind in the aftermath, Lucas said, his words ghosting over the shadow of her thoughts. *I wasn't in any shape to fix it.*

Meaning?

You blocked out a good chunk of what happened in Buffalo and your mind is still reorganizing those memories.

Psions don't forget.

This isn't you forgetting. It's you rebuilding. We just need you to do it faster. I think if you have those memories as a template, you'll know how far you can push your power.

He bypassed her shields, coiling his telepathy around the pulse of her personality, thoughts, and memories buried deep beneath the shock of trauma that still lingered. He dragged Threnody's mind into full awareness, steadying her as she reconnected with the memories of her fight at the power plant.

The pain wasn't something Lucas could block, and it drew a ragged sound from her, like an animal's. Quinton closed his eyes, holding himself perfectly still even though he obviously wanted to shield her from Lucas's implacable drive and their current desperate need.

"Thren," Quinton whispered.

She didn't seem to hear him, face screwed up in pain, hunching in on herself when she should have been resting in Alpha shuttle.

Threnody, Lucas said. *The doors.*

She remembered lightning. He felt the protest in her thoughts, in some distant, primal memory that came from the mind knowing the limits of the body, but she was a Stryker and Threnody knew how to follow orders. She knew the cost of disobedience. She was here with Lucas because of it.

Blue eyes cracked open, dark with pain. Breathing harshly, she lifted one hand to the panel. Faint sparks popped around her fingers, tiny electric lines emerging from her skin. She was mere centimeters away from touching it when she stopped, hand curled like a claw.

"It's not enough," she panted. "I don't have enough power in me to do this."

"You will," Jason said.

Threnody's breath came in shallow, painful gasps as she pressed her hand against the control panel. Threnody was a Class III electrokinetic, and her power was the only option in light of the failed hack. Electricity sparked along the tips of her fingers. The surge she was readying wouldn't be enough to do the damage they needed to fry the system before the alarm triggered.

Jason fixed that. Fixed her.

He saw how her nerves were still a mess, synapses unable to talk correctly to each other, electrical impulses dying before they bridged the distance between nerves. He let his power bleed into her body. The connection was there, her body knew it, she just couldn't find it on her own.

Microtelekinesis coursed through her instantly. The shock of the shutdown and reboot lasted for half a millisecond, if that. The results were all that mattered. Threnody's power snapped together inside her body, her baseline stabilizing. Electricity ripped through her limbs and out of her skin, surging through the control terminal with a blinding burst, the same way it had surged through Jin Li in Buffalo.

Jason and Lucas withdrew their power. Quinton was the only one holding Threnody up as she shuddered through the aftereffects.

The doors jerked in their casing, unlocking. Lucas telekinetically pulled them apart, breaking through decades of built-up ice and debris. Cold, stale air filtered out of a place no one had walked into since the government's SkyFarms Inc. agricultural towers first went online in the last major cities.

Lucas strode into the ancient seed bank and didn't look back.

[FOUR]

AUGUST 2379
THE HAGUE, THE NETHERLANDS

The ache in Ciari Treiva's gut had nothing to do with nerves or emotion.

It was a physical reminder, one the Class III empath hadn't fixed before leaving Toronto. It grounded her in a way she knew nothing else could. As the officer in charge (OIC) of the Strykers Syndicate, it was imperative that Ciari maintain her health. Like every other Stryker, she didn't own her body—the government did. And what better way to prove that ownership than to appoint a psion as the liaison between the government and the Strykers Syndicate?

"This is not going well," Keiko Nishimoto said. The Class II telekinetic and chief operating officer (COO) for the Strykers Syndicate kept a sharp eye on the set of quads stationed in the hallway with them. "We've been waiting for hours."

"The morning session for citizens comes before our punishment," Ciari said quietly. "Erik likes having an audience."

Keiko ducked her head, hiding her grimace from the security cameras embedded in the walls. She had teleported Ciari to The Hague as ordered. They'd been told to wait outside the courtroom doors in the Peace Palace, which held the International Court of Justice, called the World Court by most people on the planet.

To be kept waiting after the rush to arrive wasn't a surprise, simply annoying. They had no right to argue about anything, not when the neurotrackers implanted in their brains could kill them so easily. Every Stryker who didn't die in the field or from overuse of his or her power died with the flip of a switch, victim of a government termination order. Perhaps the wait was psychological on the part of the World Court, but the two Strykers accepted it as part of the job. The government's dogs, as they were so often called, could do nothing but obey.

They weren't the only ones going about their business in the hallway. Aides, lobbyists, and politicians walked the halls, most of them hurrying past the two women without a second glance. Most humans, registered and unregistered, didn't trust psions. Too many people had died at the hands of rogue psions since the Border Wars ended for trust to ever be more than political lip service.

Despite their disease and danger, psions were useful, lucrative, and rare enough in the world's surviving gene pool that the government kept them around for business and security reasons. Contracts brokered with the Strykers Syndicate pulled in a lot of money, and the government wasn't willing to give up a ready source of income.

The World Court beat obedience into their dogs. The failure of government indoctrination and the escape of formerly subordinate Strykers were the reasons why Ciari was here.

The door to the courtroom finally opened an hour later and a legal clerk stepped into the hallway. "The World Court will hear your case."

He didn't look at them. Out of fear or disrespect, Ciari didn't know. Probably both. The Peace Palace was owned and operated by humans, by the only government that had survived the Border Wars. Psion power, unless explicitly permitted by the World Court, was illegal here. Bioware nets spanned the brains of all the politicians and registered humans who could afford the technology, constantly monitoring for outside manipulation. Any deviation from the baseline resulted in psion deaths. When it came down to it, though, the World Court didn't need an excuse to kill their dogs.

Ciari and Keiko stood, tugged their uniforms straight, and walked into the public courtroom. The grand, rectangular place had old wood paneling and stained-glass windows that had survived the relentless bombings. Ancient, beautiful crystal chandeliers hung from the ceiling. The rows of seats between the door and the long bench set high on a raised dais beneath the windows were full. So was the balcony that extended halfway into the room.

Open session, Ciari thought as she and Keiko walked down the center aisle. *This won't end well.*

They came to a stop between the tables of opposing parties at the front of the courtroom; both were empty. Arrayed before them along the judicial bench were fifteen seats filled by the most powerful humans on the planet. The occupant of the center seat was the only one who mattered to Ciari.

Erik Gervais, president and justice of the World Court, stared at her. Ciari met his gaze without blinking. The faint narrowing of his brown eyes showed annoyance, but only to her. Erik had built his life around political aspirations that required him to be unreadable for the sake of legal neutrality. But the government was never truly neutral, especially when it came to their dogs. Years of reading the microexpressions of bureaucrats and politicians had saved Ciari's life many times where psion power would have gotten her killed instantly. She wondered if that skill would be enough this time.

"Sirs," Ciari said, dipping her head in rote respect to the fifteen judges before her. Keiko did the same.

The crowd around them wasn't completely silent. Registered humans, the elite of society, shifted in their seats. The rustling of personal items and the soft buzz of cameras from reporters sitting in the press box filled the air like static.

"Are you prepared to give your report?" Erik said.

"Yes, sir."

"Then begin your statement. If we like what we hear, we might be persuaded to show leniency."

Ciari didn't blink at the threat. It meant nothing to her. She lived with a death switch in her brain; words were merely sound.

"A month ago, we lost four Strykers in the Slums of the Angels. They were in pursuit of a rogue psion targeted for retrieval. We believe the target took them. When we carried out your orders to terminate the Strykers, the results from the neurotrackers were inconclusive. The baselines spiked as human on the security grid through bioscanners." Ciari paused for a moment, letting the information sink in. "We have no witnesses to the events in the Slums. Human bodies were eventually retrieved from Russia with the missing neurotrackers. When that same target from the Slums appeared in Buffalo, I initiated a full-scale field transfer of Stryker teams to deal with the threat."

"You've had two years to retrieve or terminate this rogue psion," Anchali said. The vice president of the World Court was its oldest member and one of its shrewdest. "Transferring that many Strykers to Buffalo was a mismanagement of resources and a failure on your part."

Ciari met her gaze as calmly as she had Erik's. "Other rogue psions were on the ground in Buffalo aside from the target. I felt it prudent to take action against them."

She was careful to refrain from numbers, from names. The public knew about rogue psions. They didn't know about Warhounds unless one believed in the stories downloaded into pirate streams. Truth could be found in those conspiracy theories, even if most people didn't have all the facts.

"So you initiated a full-scale field transfer, taking Strykers off prior contracts and sending them to Buffalo without authorization?"

"It wouldn't be in anyone's best interest if the target slipped away during such a blatant attack on the government," Ciari said. "My orders are to protect. We did."

"And yet, the target still escaped," Erik said.

There was no way out of the punishment she could hear in Erik's voice. Ciari could never admit that she knew the identity of that seemingly unknown target. All Strykers who held the OIC position and those of the company's highest officer ranks obeyed a hidden law, and it had nothing to do with human legal wrangling. The Silence Law gave and took, but above all, it saved. Some might argue that the cost was too high, but Ciari never had.

Despite everything that was going on, she wouldn't betray her people. Her life wasn't worth theirs. She stayed silent.

Erik leaned forward slightly and rested both hands flat against the old wooden tabletop. "You are not justifying your case, Ciari. Silence is not an acceptable defense."

She could have spoken for days straight and it wouldn't have mattered. The judgment had been decided prior to her being summoned before the bench. This was merely a formality and a showcase of control.

"We announced the presence of rogue psions in the city as required by law," Ciari said. "It served to explain the large numbers of Strykers on the ground and resulted in the deactivation of the electrical grid. We thought the reduction in power would help us flush out and corner the target."

Travis Athe raised a single finger. "It didn't."

Ciari shook her head. "No, sir."

"How could you think that frightening human citizens was a good idea?"

"We acted in accordance with the laws in order to save them."

"That is debatable."

"Is this a debate, sir?"

"You overstep yourself, Ciari. Much as you overstepped yourself in Buffalo."

"We did what we thought was correct in the face of rogue psions and an unknown threat. We only ever had the well-being of humans in our thoughts."

It was a lie, they all knew it, but one every Stryker learned to tell.

"Your actions produced failures that resulted in this mess," Erik said. "That is unacceptable."

Ciari couldn't argue that statement. "We did what we could with the information we had. It was my decision."

"Do you stand behind your decision?"

Ciari looked him straight in the eye. "Yes."

In a world full of deadzones and toxic gene pools, with a population barely at a million and a quarter strong, Erik created order with the strike of a gavel. The World Court's efforts over the years had resulted in hundreds of secretly built space shuttles waiting to be filled in the Paris Basin, poised to leave the planet for a distant promised land. Earth meant nothing to the elite descendants of those who survived the Border Wars and managed to clean up their DNA by the fifth generation and join the Registry.

Erik embodied that mind-set, as did everyone else seated in judgment before her. This fact hadn't changed in all the decades the World Court had been in power.

"You've been such a model psion to those beneath you in the Strykers Syndicate over the past eleven years, Ciari," Erik said.

"I train my people as you require me to, sir."

"And therein lies the issue. They are not yours. They have never belonged to you. We own them, as we own you."

Ciari expected the pain, the flip of that switch. For one crystalline moment, she thought she could feel the hum of the neurotracker implanted in the back of her head as it processed the order for punishment. Perhaps she did, but it was drowned out by the searing agony that burned through her brain, pressing against the interior of her skull and spiking down her nerves.

She screamed when it became too much, too hot, knowing that to hold it all in would just drag it out longer. The sound of her voice echoed in her ears. It was the only thing she heard, the only thing that made any sense as she writhed on the floor, both hands clutching her head, incapable of making the pain stop. When it became too much, when it seemed as if the agony were too big for her skin to contain, Ciari clung to the self-inflicted pain in her gut to differentiate between the real world and the threat of insanity that began to crawl through her mind.

I want, Ciari thought through the fiery feeling of having her brain torn apart. *I want you—*

She tasted blood on her tongue, smelled metal all along the inside of her nose and mouth. She swallowed air and couldn't breathe, her nerves following the dictates of a machine and not her own body.

It went on and on and on.

FIVE

What the hell is *Cinnamomum verum?*" Kerr said. He held up a silvery foil packet to the fluorescent lights bolted to the ceiling of the vault, squinting at the faded text printed over the front of the packet.

Jason telekinetically added another box of seed packets and clear glass vials to the top of a pile. The entire stack teetered precariously near the entrance to the storage vault they were ransacking. "Hell if I know."

"Cinnamon," Kristen piped up from where she had climbed one of the storage racks and was methodically handing boxes down to a scavenger for loading. When he didn't move fast enough for her tastes, she dropped the boxes on the floor. "Spice out of Sri Lanka."

"Right," Quinton said as he hefted a box onto a gravlift. "What's Sri Lanka?"

"It was an island country in the Indian Ocean. Rising sea levels swallowed half of it. The Border Wars destroyed the rest."

"Huh." Kerr turned the packet in his hands from side to side, wondering what the seeds would look like. "Guess whoever built this place had the right idea. You know, I never did believe those conspiracy theories on the pirate streams about the government hiding supplies. Wonder if anything else they talk about is true."

"Most of those people are dissidents repeating false information," Lucas said. "They don't know any better."

Quinton eyed him. "You said most. What about the rest?"

Lucas smiled slightly, but his only answer to Quinton's curiosity was "You don't need to worry about the rest."

"If we can't trust government history, and pirate streams don't have the entire truth, how do you know all this stuff?" Jason said, warily eyeing Kristen where she clung to a metal shelf.

"Government history is fairly accurate," Lucas said as he entered information into his datapad. "But only if you sit on the World Court or know how to pry it out of the server farm that handles the data traffic for The Hague."

"Why didn't the governments from before the Border Wars use what was up here to save their people? The terraforming machines alone could have saved billions," Kerr said.

"Who would have gotten the right to use them first? Third-world countries? First? In the face of declining resources, overpopulation, and environmental change, the ruling classes thought Mars was the better option for them, just not for everyone."

Kerr shook his head and put the packet back into the box. He resealed it before handing it to the nearest scavenger. He reached for another one, ignoring the twinge of sore muscles all across his back and down his arms. Everyone was past the point of exhaustion, but they kept going. The only person excused from doing heavy lifting was Threnody. She was back in Alpha shuttle, sleeping off the exhaustion of opening the seed bank. Jason checked up on her once every hour or so. She hadn't woken up yet and wasn't getting any better.

The temperature in the three storage vaults was set at -18 degrees Celsius and needed to remain that cold to keep everything viable. They methodically worked their way through each of the vaults, taking half of everything: seeds, cell lines, DNA samples, frozen embryos, and everything else in the inventory. Aside from the boxes of seeds, the frozen zoo would hopefully repopulate empty continents and oceans one day through cloning. None of them expected they would live to see that miracle.

Lucas wanted more than what they were stealing, but two days was all they could risk on Spitsbergen; one day of recovery, one day of work. Then it would take hours to fly to Antarctica. The environmental systems on the shuttles had been prepped at a near-freezing temperature to handle the cargo. Each was equipped with a limited amount of cold-storage units, and they had to factor in space for the disassembled terraforming machines, but not all the stolen goods would fit in cold storage.

Looking up from his datapad, Lucas nodded to Jason. "This stack is ready. Get it out of here."

"Right," Jason said. He wrapped his telekinesis around the stack of boxes and teleported out. Appearing outside a shuttle in the marked-off arrival zone, Jason waved tiredly at Everett as the other man came down the ramp.

"How many more?" Everett said as he eyed the pile that Jason had brought out.

"We're barely halfway done," Jason said. "You can expect two more loaded gravlifts in about fifteen minutes."

Everett frowned. "We're full up on three of the shuttles already, and one of the shuttles needs to carry the terraforming machines."

"Lucas needs to check if those are still in working order. It's been a few hundred years since they were taken apart and stored."

"Tell him to hurry it up then. We need to know in order to calculate volume and weight."

Jason shrugged and teleported away, carrying Everett's concerns with him. Lucas didn't even look up from the datapad in his hands as Jason finished reporting. "Everything will fit. If we need to make space for the weight, we'll leave people behind."

Jason stared at him. "You said we couldn't risk leaving any evidence of our passage."

"No one will think to look for bodies in the water. Get back to transporting these things to the shuttles. Matron has a stack ready for you in the second vault."

Jason left. He knew better than to argue with the man who still had an iron grip on their lives.

It took hours of nonstop cataloguing, transferring, and pure grunt work to get the job done. Seeds were infinitesimal in weight, but with the amount they were transporting, it quickly added up. Toward the end, they ripped open boxes, taking just one or two packets of the remaining seeds, or just one vial of DNA, one stored embryo. For the more important items—such as algae and countless tree seeds and grains—the amounts were never reduced.

Only when the last cargo door closed and everyone was settled in for the flight did Lucas strap himself into the navigator's seat in Alpha shuttle. Matron was piloting again, and Threnody was laid out between them, unconscious and liable to remain that way for hours. The flight deck was set at a higher temperature to accommodate her.

Matron yawned through the preflight procedure. After the fifth yawn, she picked up a hypospray nearby and pressed it against her throat, dosing herself with a shot of adrenaline. A minute or so later, Lucas could feel the engines start up through the soles of his boots.

"Didn't think we'd make it this far," Matron said as she settled her hands on the stick and activated the vertical takeoff and landing.

"Get us in the air," Lucas said.

Matron did as she was told in silence, launching the shuttle and feeling the weight of the cargo in the jerk of the stick. They had a heavy load in the shuttle's belly, one more precious than anything her scavengers had ever discovered in the broken, abandoned cities of America. For all the credit that the government issued, for all the elite perks that one could have by gaining entrance into the Registry, clean DNA wasn't worth anything compared to what nine shuttles ferried out of Spitsbergen one late-August morning.

Behind them, its doors shut but not locked, the Svalbard Global Seed and Gene Bank was just as silent, just as cold as it had been for centuries.

They flew north, climbing over the Arctic Ocean, heading for the Pacific. The midnight sun guided their way, a constant bright circle beyond the clouds.

PART TWO
COGNIZANCE

SESSION DATE: 2128.03.18
LOCATION: Institute of Psionics Research
CLEARANCE ID: Dr. Amy Bennett
SUBJECT: 2581
FILE NUMBER: 251

The doctor watches Aisling play with a deck of cards. The child's small hands spread the plain, white rectangles across the table in a shapeless mess. She picks cards at random and lays them before her in a line.

"You never ask how I do it," Aisling says as she pushes the cards together. "Why?"

"Would you tell us if we did?" the doctor replies.

The girl tucks a piece of dark hair behind one small ear, studying the cards. "No."

"That's why, Aisling."

"But you're a doctor. Doctors should ask questions."

"We do."

"Not the right ones." Aisling smiles as she flips over a card, revealing a crimson red square on its face and nothing else. "Pick a card, any card. I can tell you the future."

"Would it be the right one?" The doctor leans forward to catch the child's gaze with her own. "Would you help us survive?"

Aisling flips more cards over, one at a time, until a line of shapes and symbols lie before her. She picks a card seemingly at random, holding it up beside her bleached-out violet eyes, the color of the shape a deep, dark blue. "My brother has eyes like this."

"Where is Matthew, Aisling?"

Aisling scoots the card as far across the table as her small arm will stretch. "You can't have him."

[SIX]

Beneath the Peace Palace lay a city of underground tunnels and bunkers. Its protective warrens once housed thousands of people during the Border Wars and still held their descendants today. The most well-guarded bunkers were reserved for those who served on the World Court. The business of ruling, however, was always conducted aboveground.

Sharra Gervais was blond-haired, blue-eyed, and gorgeous, human down to her very registered DNA. She was Erik's wife, his perfect piece of femininity; a woman who spent the majority of her time raising a daughter that he rarely saw or interacted with unless for a public event. The world press adored those family moments; Sharra hated the lie she was living. But she knew her role and played it well, portraying the good wife the world expected her to be. She sat in the area reserved for the families of those serving on the World Court, hands clasped in her lap, looking at her husband as he stood before the cameras of the world press.

He still wore his robes of office, the black synthfabric soaking up the glare from the cameras. Beneath the robe, Sharra knew he wore a perfectly tailored business suit in charcoal gray and pinstripes, the crisp whiteness of his hidden shirt a match for her dress. She smoothed her hands over the synthfabric resting against her thighs. White was such an expensive color to keep clean.

"I admire your husband's resolve when it comes to the safety of society," Fatima Omar said softly. The much younger woman sitting to Sharra's left wore a far less fashionable outfit, one that covered nearly every centimeter of her body. The long skirt and blouse were modestly cut, her hijab a demure black with little adornment save for a tiny amount of embroidery along the edges. Her husband, Mohammad, was a justice who stood in solid support of Erik.

"Yes," Sharra said absently, her attention focused on the spectacle before her. The reporters took up much of the area inside the renovated pressroom, with its small stage and guarded section for families and dignitaries who didn't merit a place before the microphones of the world press.

"—cannot condone what happened in Buffalo," Erik said. "The families of those who lost their lives during the cowardly attacks by rogue psions will be compensated, as is the law. The Strykers Syndicate is reviewing how they organize and initiate their missions. This will not happen again. Punishment has been administered to those responsible for the break in the chain of command."

Killing dogs makes people happy, Sharra thought, feeling the corner of her mouth tick minutely upward. *But it doesn't solve the problem, Erik.*

Politics wasn't her place, so she kept her opinion to herself as she always did. Sharra understood society's fear of psions better than most, but she also knew that psions were a cog that couldn't easily be replaced. The Strykers Syndicate kept rogue psions in check, but they also kept Sharra in couture fashion, clean food and water. Selling soldiers to the highest bidder under strict contractual terms had made those who sat on the World Court very, very wealthy over the years. Slavery was profitable, even if certain people considered it immoral. Sharra wasn't religious in the least, though she made a good show of bowing her head in prayer every Sunday.

"The Strykers Syndicate is well under our control. There is no need to fear government psions when science has produced ways to keep them in check," Erik said, gesturing faintly toward his head and the bioware net everyone knew was wrapped around his brain. "Society has nothing to fear from them."

Of course not. Sharra had to bite down on her bottom lip to keep from grimacing. *Oh, Erik, you are such a fool.*

She loved him, or thought she did. More and more as the years passed, she began to believe it was the idea of love that she adored, not the man she had married when she was young and incapable of seeing the loneliness that came with marrying a man of his social standing. They both kept secrets, and the one true thing they shared now was their daughter. Dinner needed to be scheduled in advance. Sleep was preferable to sex.

She regretted. It was an odd feeling.

Before her, the reporters were beginning to ask questions, and Sharra realized she had missed much of Erik's calculated apology in favor of her own thoughts. She already knew the gist of it. Being the wife of the most powerful human in the world had its perks.

Sharra gave a good show for the news when it was all over, standing beside her husband and smiling proudly at him. Only when they were in the back hallways of the Peace Palace, where the judges separated into their fractious little groups and went their separate ways, did Sharra speak.

"How is killing the OIC of the Strykers Syndicate conducive to everything we've worked for?" Sharra said, her voice a low hiss as they walked back to Erik's office. Behind them trailed a quad for security, the four soldiers keeping an eye on their charges.

Erik shot her a steely look. "Ciari Treiva isn't dead."

"She might as well be after what you put her through."

"Is that compassion for a dog I hear coming out of your mouth?"

"Hardly" was her clipped response. "You know exactly what I'm talking about."

Sharra bit back the rest of her argument until they were within the confines of his office and the jamming sequence for privacy was activated. She tossed her small purse on his desk in a fit of pique.

"What have I said when it comes to speaking in public of things you know nothing about?" Erik asked in a cold voice as he went behind his desk.

"For our daughter's sake, I'll pretend you didn't just say that," Sharra snapped as she headed for his bar.

"Starting early today, I see."

Sharra uncorked a bottle of merlot and poured herself a glass of the expensive drink until the red liquid reached the thin crystal rim. "Not early enough."

"Don't get drunk. I don't want you to make a mess of your clothes."

Sharra took a long swallow of her wine before she toasted him with bitterness on her tongue. "You know me so well, husband."

"I know your vices," Erik said as he unsealed his robes. Draping the clothing over the back of his leather chair, Erik sat down and studied his wife. "I mean it, Sharra. The world press is camped out everywhere right now and the last thing I need to deal with is you falling down drunk."

"I would think you'd be more worried about the problem with the missing psions than how I can embarrass you."

"I don't need your attitude right now."

She shrugged elegantly, every centimeter the supposedly perfect woman he had married. She'd come to her alcoholism late, needing something to drown out the pain and regret she lived with. "I can't decide if it's stress that's making you act so heavy-handed or merely the lack of sleep. Since you haven't slept in our bed in over a week, I'll assume it's the latter."

"I'm not cheating on you."

"I know you're not." Sharra took another sip of her wine, choking it down along with the laughter that threatened to pass her lips. "You're too busy setting up the launch and burning out our enslaved protectors to find someone else to fuck."

"I am doing this for our daughter. I am doing this for you. For *us*."

If he were a better man, if she were a less cynical woman, she might have believed him. Except Sharra knew otherwise, knew secrets of his business associates that he had no concept of. She scraped her teeth over the edge of the glass and drank down more wine, one arm crossed over her chest. "Honestly, Erik. For a judge, you're a terrible liar."

The flash of anger in his eyes told her she'd hit a nerve. Like any man, Erik took pride in his work and his ability to wield power. She watched him get to his feet and approach her, a hard expression on his face. Sharra held on to her wineglass, a flimsy barrier between them.

"I'm not the one who refuses to believe I have a problem," he said, voice low and flat as he stared at his wife over her glass.

Sharra licked a wet film off her teeth and smiled at him, mouth tinted red. "I am aware of my faults."

In the entire time they were married, he had never hit her. But some days, Sharra thought abuse would be preferable to this war of words.

"I don't have time to pander to your pathetic needs," Erik said, the tension between them almost painful. "Drink your wine, drink the whole damn bottle, but you don't leave my office until you're sober. Kindly shut your mouth and stay out of my way while I prepare for my next meeting."

"So it's the good, silent wife you want," Sharra murmured, licking her lips. "Darling, why didn't you say so?"

Her mockery made his temper rise higher, but Erik had already spent too much emotion this morning debriefing a woman he considered beneath him to expend any more on his wife. Sharra pressed a finger to his mouth, watching as he jerked back, as if he couldn't stand her touch. Her own mouth twisted into a thin, brittle smile.

"For our daughter's sake, I won't make a fool of you," Sharra promised.

Lillian was the one good thing she'd ever done with her life, and Erik was a decent father to the five-year-old child that she loved. The same could not be said for how he felt about his wife. Their private lives went much like this of late, fighting with every ounce of spite they had over everything.

Erik took Sharra at her word and retreated to his desk. She remained by the wet bar and steadily drank her way through the bottle of wine. She opened up a second one right before Erik left, smiling at the disgust in his eyes.

Sharra set the wine bottle aside after she was certain he wouldn't return and went to his desk. She grabbed her purse, pulling out an unmarked data chip as she sat down. Erik's terminal was wide-open for use, trust between them something carved deep into his mind, beyond the capacity of his bioware net to detect. Psionic interference perpetuated by the Sercas had worked wonders on his mind all those years ago. She still hated the results, though there were days she loved them. Loved him.

Their anniversary was coming up, the beginning of December. Erik had promised her the stars this year.

"I would rather have nothing," Sharra said softly, thinking of her daughter and what they would suffer through after the launch. The inevitability of a contract with Nathan she could not rationally escape.

She jacked in the data chip and uploaded the program meticulously created to bypass the World Court's security. Sharra knew her place. It wasn't by her husband's side.

She got up to pour herself another glass of wine.

[SEVEN]

AUGUST 2379
TORONTO, CANADA

The crack of displaced air from a teleport caused Jael Dawson, chief medical officer (CMO) for the Strykers Syndicate, to jerk her head up.

"Jael! Ciari needs you!" Keiko shouted.

Jael was already moving, having been on standby since being notified by a nurse that Ciari and Keiko were on the news streams. Keiko was crouched worriedly over Ciari's still form on the arrival platform. Jael swore, her thin, black dreads swinging around her face as she ran to aid them.

"Get me a gurney," Jael snapped to one of the nurses. "And prep OR three."

They had been dealing with the fallout of Buffalo for hours, even before Ciari was ordered to The Hague. The medical level was full of wounded, dying, and dead Strykers, with a handful still unaccounted for. Teams who hadn't been transferred to Buffalo for the initial fight now hunted for the missing in bunkers of that city, looking for bodies. Jael hated retrieval.

She knelt beside Ciari, dropping several layers of her mental shields to see what kind of mess she had to deal with. The Class III telepath swore loudly as the mental trauma of a mind raked through physical torture battered against her own. Jael, the best psi surgeon in the Syndicate, wrapped telepathic shields around Ciari's mind to try to stabilize her.

"We need to move her," Jael said, glancing up at the crew of medical personnel that swarmed around them. "Let's go, people, we don't have much time."

Keiko telekinetically lifted Ciari off the floor of the medical level's arrival room and onto the hover-gurney. Ciari's face was streaked with blood and tears, her lips bitten through and teeth flecked with pink-tinged saliva. Her eyes roved beneath her eyelids. When Jael brushed against Ciari's mind, all she got was a tidal wave of emotion. Jael flinched.

"The OR," Jael said. *"Now."*

Everyone rushed to obey, the medics and nurses working to stabilize Ciari's physical form as they hurried to the operating room. Keiko followed in their wake, the telekinetic pale-faced and angry, a futile emotion, Jael thought.

Don't die on me now, Ciari, Jael thought grimly as she let her crew pull the hover-gurney into the operating room. *We still need you.*

Jael thought for a moment of a time just hours ago when she'd had Ciari on her operating table for a different sort of procedure. Shaking aside that memory, Jael spared a moment to look over at Keiko, the telekinetic standing just outside the tiny sterilization room. "Do you need medical attention?"

"No," Keiko said, voice tight. "They didn't touch me."

Jael nodded. "Then wait outside. I've got work to do."

The door slid shut and Jael continued through to the operating room. She still had to scrub in, standing shoulder to shoulder with some of her nurses and assistants. For all that this was psi surgery, a physical operation was involved as well.

"Marguerite," Jael said. "Deal with the bleeding. I'll deal with her mind."

Jael's second-in-command nodded and began barking orders. A nurse cut off Ciari's uniform, another hooked her to an IV and other machines to monitor her vital signs. Electrodes were adhered to her skull, pulling up Ciari's chaotic mental readings on an EEG machine and overlaying it with the baseline in her medical records. Jael closed her eyes against the organized chaos of the operating room as she curled a hand around Ciari's own lax one. She dropped all but a single mental shield and sank her telepathic power into Ciari's traumatized mind.

A maelstrom of agony greeted her on the mental grid, jagged edges cutting into her own mind, psionic pain bleeding through her power. Jael worked to hold on to her own sense of self. She let a little of the pain seep in, needing to know where it stemmed from. The brain was a link between the body and the mind. The neurotracker that every Stryker carried was capable of doing enough damage that sometimes death would have been the preferable option.

Jael focused her power, splitting it through the burned-out pieces of Ciari's psyche. She went deep, letting herself be drawn into the other woman's subconscious mind. Jael knew that Marguerite would be putting Ciari under with as many drugs as her battered body could handle. Consciousness would be a slippery thing to grasp right now, and sometimes healing worked better as a suggestion than as an order. Sometimes it didn't.

Ciari, Jael said, piecing together the woman's shattered sense of control one thought, one heartbeat, at a time. *I need you to turn off the pain.*

Raw emotion flowed over her, no control in the response. Jael struggled to find an answer in a sensory overload where words weren't even an afterthought, but simply forgotten.

Turn it off.

Of all the psions, empaths were the best at altering how they felt pain. It was nerves and tissue, mind over matter, the concept of pain, of an ache that could carefully be denied. Jael used every bit of her power and concentration to guide Ciari into changing how her body felt, so it would change how her mind felt. It was almost a relief when the pain switched off, that all-encompassing drag on Jael's mind disappearing.

"ICP at twenty-one mm's," Jael heard a nurse say. "Scans are showing possible brain herniation, definite epidural hematoma."

"Prep for decompressive craniectomy," Marguerite ordered. "Map out placement of the neurotracker for the operation. We can't take any chances with her."

The hum of a laser saw was a hideous background noise. Conversation was reduced to medical jargon that only a tiny part of Jael's mind bothered to translate. Jael felt Ciari's mind dip sharply beneath hers, sliding away. She gripped the cold hand tighter, a physical anchor point for the one on the mental grid.

No, Jael said, holding tight to the other woman's frayed thoughts. *You don't get to leave us yet.*

They didn't like each other; never really had. They were trained to handle different tasks, to reach different goals. Ciari led Strykers into harm's way; Jael pulled them out. The only thing they had in common was that they actually gave a damn for their fellow Strykers. In this instance, Ciari was just another patient who needed Jael.

With Marguerite handling the physical operation and Jael refusing to let Ciari's mind die, they managed to keep her alive. This took several long hours and the results could be summed up in a single sentence.

"She's breathing," Jael informed Keiko and Aidan Turner, the Stryker Syndicate's chief administrative officer (CAO), outside the recovery room. "On her own. Consider it a miracle. The neurotracker did a lot of damage."

"Erik meant to kill her," Keiko said, looking through the observation window at the still form surrounded by machines and nurses. "Travis Athe wanted her alive. He managed to get a majority vote to spare her life. They appointed me Acting OIC until Ciari recovers."

Jael's mouth twisted. "Travis doesn't have a compassionate bone in his body. Why would he spare Ciari?"

"I don't know."

Possibly because the launch is so close, they can't risk the upheaval appointing a new OIC would cause, Aidan said, the Class IV telepath drawing both women into a psi link.

Keiko's Acting OIC, Jael pointed out.

They can risk me being in the public eye during Ciari's absence, but they made it very clear it was to be temporary, Keiko said. *They need her for the launch.*

Did they give you a time frame for when I'm supposed to have Ciari standing on her own two feet and not in a coma?

Aidan winced at that announcement. *Be honest, Jael. What are her odds?*

Jael crossed her arms, stepping out of the way of a nurse. The nurse, used to the silent, gesture-filled conversations that happened between 'path-oriented psions, ignored them. *She's in no pain, but only because I was able to get her to turn off part of her mind.*

What?

Her system was in overload because of the neurotracker. She's going to need a biotank and regeneration of most, if not all, of her central nervous system. We have her hooked up to an external monitor that's sending impulses directly into her brain to ensure her major bodily functions still continue to work. Jael spread her hands in a helpless gesture, grimacing. *I've got her telepathically anchored, but there's no guarantee she'll want to live. There may very well be damage to her body, to her brain, that we can't treat.*

Erik had his finger on that kill switch for a full five minutes, Keiko said softly, the look in her brown eyes bleak and hateful.

I still sensed coherency in her subconscious mind during the surgery, Jael said.

What about her conscious *mind?*

Jael was silent on that, and Keiko let out a harsh little laugh. "So it's like that."

"It's not like anything." Jael ran a hand through her dreads, pulling the mass away from her face. She sighed tiredly. "I'll keep you apprised of her condition, Keiko. We're setting up a biotank and will transfer her to it immediately once the swelling in her brain has gone down."

"Every six hours. I mean it, Jael. We have to be able to tell the World Court how she's progressing."

Jael didn't argue.

"Keep me updated as well," Aidan said. "What about the Strykers that were in Buffalo?"

Jael knew he wasn't asking about their condition. Less than half the Strykers that were in Buffalo survived. Those that did had all gone through a tiny, discreet mindwipe performed by Jael herself, their memories of seeing Lucas Serca and his siblings on the field erased. The Sercas weren't supposed to be anything other than human, and the high-ranking officers of the Strykers Syndicate were obligated to keep that secret, even at the cost of their own lives.

"They're recovering," Jael said, voice mild. "From everything."

It was enough of an assurance, and the three parted ways. Jael should have gone to her office, where she had space to think that wasn't full of people dying either beneath her hands or beneath her mind. Instead, she detoured into a lab that only had two approved biometric signatures for entry. This, Jael's personal research space, had been used by many CMOs over generations. Jael stepped inside and approached the work area in the back, where an opaque, cylindrical machine sat, surrounded by monitors.

It was securely attached to the countertop, with all readings on the tiny control screen positive and green. Jael checked the numbers, looking for anything out of the ordinary that could possibly harm the growing embryo housed inside the gestational unit. This was going to become a standard part of her routine, a deviation she never foresaw. Caring for Ciari's unborn child could arguably be considered her most important job at the moment.

She grabbed a stool, dragged it over, and reached for the datapad that lay abandoned near the gestational unit. The screen came alive at her touch, and Jael scrolled through the information. It was all preliminary lab work and reports that would need tremendous fleshing out. She wondered if it was worth it to even try. They had a month, maybe less, before everyone died, either by a kill switch, riots, or starvation. She wondered if this was how their ancestors felt during the Border Wars, that five-year span of nuclear hell that gave birth to their current lives; trapped in a situation that had no easy way out.

Stay with us, Jael thought down the psi link that tied her to Ciari for medical purposes as she looked critically at the program decoding a genome. *We still need you. Your baby will need you.*

[EIGHT]

AUGUST 2379
INVERCARGILL, NEW ZEALAND

New Zealand had tried to avoid the conflicts of old, but the shifting tides of war brought Australia's destruction to it just the same. Now it was two long, barren islands, the iron and asphalt skeletons of its cities touched only by the wind and the sea. At the very southern point of the South Island, Invercargill was just a shell.

The silence was shattered by what was left of a rusted metal door on an old river-port warehouse being torn off its hinges and telekinetically hurled down the street. All the broken warehouse windows meant the air inside was as cold and dry as it was outside.

"This way," Lucas said.

He ran past Jason, expecting the others to follow. Jason didn't hesitate in following his lead. Behind them ran Quinton, Threnody cradled protectively in his arms. She was barely responsive, her comalike state the entire reason why they had fallen off course and detoured here. The last two hours had been hellish, with her intermittently suffering through seizures and Jason unable to stop it.

"Is that what I think it is?" Jason asked. "How did you get it here?"

"I don't care so long as it works," Quinton said in a tight voice as he skidded to a halt, eyes flickering across the biotank. "Tell me it works, Lucas."

"I would have risked a teleport to Antarctica that would ruin my own recovery if it didn't," Lucas said without looking up from the control terminals. Wires snaked across the floor to a portable generator. Tubes connected a small storage tank to the holding tank through a pressure system that whined loudly as everything came online.

"How did you know to store this here? And the fuel?" Jason said as he wiped dust and grime off the biotank's top seal with his uniform sleeve.

"How do you think?"

No one mentioned Aisling, the child whose orders Lucas was following, but her name hung heavy between them anyway. They should have hit Antarctica already, but they'd taken the long route south across the Pacific Ocean, flying over an expanse of gray, acidic water and arriving here. They were stopping in New Zealand only because they couldn't risk Threnody's life any longer. Her health since unlocking the seed bank had only gotten worse over the hours. Staying the course meant losing her, and Lucas wasn't going to risk that. They needed a refuel anyway, and Matron was handling that out on the street.

These three had a life to save.

Lucas dealt with the biotank while Jason and Quinton worked to strip Threnody of the blanket she was wrapped in and her clothes. Quinton carefully removed the IV lines sticking out from the back of her hands. He pulled a long hypo out of the bag Jason was carrying and ripped the plastic seal off it with his teeth. Jason carefully turned Threnody onto her stomach with his telekinesis, letting her hover a few centimeters off the ground.

"Hold her steady," Quinton said as he spanned one hand over the jut of Threnody's hip, lining up the hypo against the bone. They didn't have time to administer a sedative, and no one was sure how she would react to the drug in the state she was in.

Jason held her still as gently as he could. Quinton jammed his thumb down on the release button, feeling resistance as the longer, thicker needle of the hypospray pierced Threnody's bone to extract a stem-cell-packed marrow sample.

Quinton passed the hypo to Lucas once it was full. Lucas slid it into the receiver tube attached to the storage tank that held nanites and the regen-therapy fluid integral to biotanks. Mixed together, the concoction would accelerate the healing capabilities of cells in the human body. With a hard stab of his thumb, Lucas depressed Threnody's marrow into the tube, letting the nanites get a preread on her DNA. Clear, viscous fluid was already pumping into the holding tank for oxygenation.

"I hope this works," Jason said as he struggled to find a viable vein in first one of her arms, then the other. The empty tubing floated in the air by way of telekinesis. They didn't have a sterility field here, so Jason was improvising, trying to keep the tube off the ground and free of contamination. "I hope—*shit!*"

He flipped her from her side onto her back so suddenly that Quinton didn't have time to let go of her wrist. His fingers snagged on the needle in her vein, dislodging it with bloody results. Her skin tore, so did the vein, and blood leaked from the wound.

"Jason," Quinton snarled, head snapping up.

"She's not breathing," Jason said, holding one hand down over Threnody's chest. "She's not *breathing.*"

Which meant her heart wasn't beating.

Quinton felt the burn in the back of his mind through their bond as Jason accessed his microtelekinesis. Bright spots filled Quinton's vision, obscuring Threnody. He fumbled for the gauze in Jason's bag, working to clean up the mess her hand and wrist had become and reset the needle.

Jason sank his power into her chest, wrapped it around her heart, and started up a cardiac rhythm. He used his own as a baseline, nearly breaking her ribs from the inside out as he struggled to keep her from dying.

"Lucas, you need to move faster," Quinton yelled over his shoulder. "She's crashing!"

"This can't be rushed" was Lucas's only answer.

"God fucking damn it." Jason's pupils were dilated as he stared blankly down at Threnody. "Okay, I've got her. I've got her."

Quinton pressed two fingers to Threnody's throat, searching out a pulse that was too erratic for his liking. "Slow it down, Jays."

Jason sucked in a deep breath. "I'm trying."

"Try harder."

"The biotank is ready," Lucas said seconds later, voice taut. "Bring her."

The machine's side panels slid far enough apart for Jason to telekinetically lower Threnody inside. He held her down as the thick fluid flowed over her, sliding up her nose, into her mouth, down her throat, drowning her. Even unconscious, Jason could feel her struggling as he telekinetically attached the tubing to the sides of the tank. Lucas tapped in another command, and seconds later a heavy, gray stream of nanites mixed with the regen-therapy fluid began to flow through the tubing into Threnody's body. Dozens of sealed wires extended from the sides of the tank, pressing against her skin to monitor her vitals.

Lucas came around to Jason's side, carrying a handful of wires. He peeled the tape off the tiny electrodes, sticking them to Jason's temples and his chest. A second set of vitals showed up on another screen; Jason's baseline. It eerily matched Threnody's.

Quinton stared at the jagged moving lines representing two heartbeats. "Jason?"

"I've got her," Jason said, sounding distant.

"He's in deep," Lucas said, eyeing Jason critically. "He caught her in time, so maybe this will work."

"Maybe?" Quinton said.

"We're going to be stuck here for a few days, and Jason is going to need to be awake for the entire process." Lucas glanced over his shoulder. "Find me a shot of Adrenalin."

Quinton went for their bags. "You think he can handle it? He dosed himself pretty heavily with that stuff back in Buffalo."

"If he passes out, she dies."

Quinton came back with not one dose of Adrenalin, but a dozen.

Lucas pressed the hypospray against Jason's throat and administered the dose. Jason shuddered, leaning heavily against the biotank. Lucas helped him sit down, back to the machine. He was pale-faced and breathing quickly, sweat beading along his brow.

"Jason?" Quinton said, closing his eyes against the sudden pull at the back of his mind.

"I've got her," Jason repeated like a mantra. "I've got her."

A biotank could force cellular regeneration to happen faster than the human body could do so alone, building off a patient's own stem cells through the persistence of nanites. With enough time and training, Jason might one day accomplish the same on his own in minutes, not hours or days, but he still didn't know what he was capable of. As things stood, he was barely holding Threnody together, his power slip-sliding through cellular levels, chasing after nanites. He tried to recall through remembered agony what he had done on the flight out of Buffalo. Jason forced himself to concentrate on the shape of Threnody's cells to get a feel for her DNA and build off the genetic blueprint of her body.

Quinton looked at Jason, feeling the other man's power pulling at the back of his mind through the permanent bond they shared. He winced at what felt like an itch on the inside of his skull and tried to ignore it. Quinton pressed his hand against the dusty, dirty plasglass and didn't take his eyes off Threnody.

[NINE]

SEPTEMBER 2379
INVERCARGILL, NEW ZEALAND

She took a breath.
Then another. Deeper.
It was cold; wet.
Fluid was in her lungs. In her mouth.

Threnody cracked open her eyes to a world made of light. Fractured light, seen through the heavy, curved plasglass of a biotank and the thick, undulating fluid that breathed for her. She closed her eyes. Opened them again. The world didn't change.

Shadows moved around her outside the biotank. She could hear the soft, constant beeping of a monitor, the sound deep and distant through the fluid. She tried to move her hand, felt her fingers get tangled in tiny wires, so many attached to the length of her body. They didn't hurt.

She did.

Who am I?

Go to sleep, someone answered. The voice was clear, accented, sounding like those who hailed from London. Stretched in a way she felt in her bones. In her nerves.

Who am I?

Threnody Corwin. Now go to sleep. We aren't finished.

She was dragged under by waves of water and light, a riptide of power that took her to the depths of the ocean. Which was impossible, for this wasn't any ocean found in the world.

She slept.

When she regained consciousness, it was to cold air blowing across bare skin and pressure in her chest. She struggled to cough up the thick fluid in her lungs and replace it with oxygen. Strong arms held her steady, a deep, familiar voice filling her ears and not her mind.

"That's it, Thren," Quinton said. "Like that. Keep coughing. It's almost all out."

His skin was dark against her own, his grip solid as she heaved and jerked in his support, coughing out every last minuscule bit of the perfluorocarbons that she didn't remember swallowing.

"Hate this part," Threnody rasped as her body shuddered through the motions.

"I know. You're almost there."

When she was breathing air and not fluid, he picked her up from the cold metal floor and carried her to a portable sterilization tent. The plastic walls smelled too sharp in her nose. She thought she could taste it. Wires were stuck to her skin, in her veins, dangling like long-dead vines made of plastic and metal.

"Ready?" a voice asked.

She opened her eyes, watched as Jason came into blurry focus at the entrance to the small tent.

"Ready," Quinton answered for the both of them.

Jason sealed the inner layer shut, then the outer. The soft hiss of the sterilization process starting up echoed in her ears, vaporizing the viscous fluid sticking to her body. Threnody held one hand close to her face, struggling to focus. Her hand shook, but with no spastic jerk to the movement of her muscles. Just exhaustion, nothing more complicated than that.

"Should be dead," Threnody murmured, letting her head drop onto Quinton's shoulder. Gravity pulled her hand down, arm swinging in the air.

"Go to sleep, Thren," Quinton said, voice rough.

"Did we make it inside the seed bank?"

"Yeah." He swallowed. "Yeah, we made it."

She took a breath, felt air flow into her lungs; sterile and cold. Unconsciousness took her once more. When Threnody woke again, she was lying on a flight deck, wrapped in thermal blankets and clean clothes. It was silent, and the person watching over her this time wasn't Quinton.

"Where are we?" she asked, her voice dry, tongue sticking to the roof of her mouth.

Lucas looked up from the datapad in his hands and whatever report he was familiarizing himself with. The bruise from when Quinton had punched him in the mouth was gone. "New Zealand."

Threnody's eyebrows drew together in confusion, thin creases lining her forehead. "I thought—the Arctic?"

"Mm." Lucas set aside the datapad. "You've been unconscious since frying the seed-bank doors."

"How long?"

"We spent two days in the Arctic. It took half another day to get down here with everything we stole, and we've been here for almost two days since we landed so Jason could work on you. You weren't going to make it to Antarctica, so we took a detour."

"Antarctica," she echoed, fingers curling against her palms. Her skin felt new and it itched, but the burning pain she remembered from the power plant and the seed bank was gone. Threnody sucked in a deep breath, her mind unfolding those memories easily enough. "I feel like I should be dead."

"You don't die here."

"Here is relative."

Lucas smiled at her, the look full of some twisted understanding, as if he knew what secrets she kept. He probably did.

Threnody pushed at the blankets until she was free of them and could sit up, putting her back against the bulkhead. A faint twinge from her right hand made her look down. A small bruise surrounded the entrance point of the IV there. She eyed the tubing that connected her to the mostly empty bag hanging off the pilot's seat.

"So we succeeded in the Arctic. Did everyone make it off Spitsbergen?"

"I love that you distrust me so thoroughly. It's refreshing, to say the least."

Threnody gave Lucas a cool look, blue eyes slightly narrowed. Her black hair was a tangled mess, she needed a shower, and she had no idea what had transpired between the Arctic and now. She wanted answers. "If you're not going to tell me what's going on, I'll find someone who will."

Lucas got to his feet, looking down at her. "Who else would have the answers you need?"

Threnody curled her hands around her knees and glared. "Just give me what I want, Lucas. You already have my support. You don't need me to beg."

"It's so interesting when you do." Lucas shrugged his ambivalence and ran a hand through his pale blond hair. "We didn't leave anyone behind, if that's what you're worried about. None of our people, at least."

"Have our actions been discovered yet?"

"The government isn't going to announce what happened on a news stream. If they haven't discovered the discrepancy by now, then they will within the next twenty-four hours. We can't confirm where they stand right now without risking our position and that's not something I'll do."

Threnody had more questions, but Lucas was already leaving. Before the hatch closed, Quinton stepped inside, scowling faintly at Lucas's back.

Threnody glanced at Quinton, taking stock of how he moved, needing to assure herself that he was all right. Then his attention was on her, some of the worry leaving his brown eyes. She swallowed a sudden surge of relief as Quinton knelt beside her. She dimly recalled moments from her time in the biotank that made no sense to her. Dreams, maybe. Or possibly nightmares. But always, always, he was there.

"Brought you another insulated skinsuit," Quinton said as he set the pile near her knees. "You'll need it where we're going."

"Antarctica, I know. Lucas told me we're still heading there." She slid the IV out of her hand and reached for the skinsuit. "Thank you."

Quinton moved to sit in the navigator's seat. It was habit to take care of each other, the only family they'd had for years. There had never been anything sexual between them, and privacy wasn't something they had ever received. They lost their right to it the moment the neurotrackers were grafted to their brains. When you fought in the crowded streets of dying cities and along the boundaries of deadzones, privacy was a luxury you weren't allowed.

When she finished dressing, Threnody carefully stood. Quinton knew better than to help her, but from the way he held himself, she knew he would catch her if she fell.

The biotank had regenerated her nervous system, fixing the massive, self-inflicted damage she'd caused while fighting Jin Li at the power plant, and the further damage from pushing herself in the Arctic. It couldn't do anything about exhaustion. She stared at her palms and fingers, at the healed flesh that felt too new. Taking a deep breath, Threnody accessed her power and tried not to flinch as it sizzled through her nerves with a new sharpness.

Blue electricity crawled across the skin of her hands, dancing over her fingernails. It sputtered and sparked, tiny lines of power that was all her. It made her a little dizzy, but she had no other way to discover if she could still function as a psion.

A warm hand curved over her elbow, holding her steady as she absorbed that power back into her body. Still a Class III electrokinetic. Still everything she was born to be. Jin Li tried, but he hadn't been able to take that from her.

"Everything working right?" Quinton asked.

"Yeah," she said, even if it wasn't really true. Threnody felt his fingers tighten on her arm. She didn't fight when he pulled her into a hard hug.

"You pull that shit again, I'll kick your goddamn ass."

Threnody let out a strangled little laugh, turning her face against his neck and giving herself a moment—one fucking moment—to be human.

It was a minute or two before they separated. Threnody ran both hands through her hair, irritated when her fingers caught on tangled knots. "Heard we got the seeds and everything else that was on Spitsbergen. Half of it, at least."

Quinton nodded, rubbed at the back of his head, wincing. "Yeah. We got it. Jays did a lot of the heavy lifting both there and here. He's sleeping it off now."

Threnody froze when she heard that familial diminutive come out of Quinton's mouth. Only Kerr had ever been allowed to use it. She thought back to the fight at the outpost in Longyearbyen, the name Jason had called her in that hallway. She and Quinton had spent too many years living in each other's personal space for her not to know when something was wrong.

"Quinton? You've never called Jason by that name before."

He looked away from her, out the windshield over her left shoulder. His silence was unnerving. Threnody sighed and framed his face with hands that shook only slightly, forcing Quinton to look at her.

"Lucas wasn't very forthcoming with details," she said. "Did something else happen in the seed bank? Tell me what I need to know."

The Strykers mind-set would take years to break, years they didn't have. She was in charge, he would always see their partnership that way. When Threnody gave an order, she, like Lucas, expected to be obeyed.

"It didn't happen in the seed bank," Quinton said.

Threnody steeled herself for his report, knowing she wasn't going to like it. "What didn't happen?"

"You were dying. I didn't want to lose you, so I made a deal with Lucas." He pulled her hands away, putting distance between them. "Gideon Serca broke my arms at the power plant. Broke my face. I think he would have broken every last bone in my body if Samantha hadn't stopped him. I wasn't in any condition to save you back in Buffalo."

Threnody's gaze dropped to his hands. She ran her fingers over his forearm, feeling only muscle and not the ridges of biotubes. "Lucas keeps saying that he needs me. He would have saved me anyway without you asking him to."

"It's more than that. It has to do with Kristen."

"I know she's dysfunctional," Threnody said. "I don't know what she does in order to gain sanity. Quinton, what are you saying?"

"She broke Jason's shields. She was the only one who could. His natal shields are completely gone. That's why he was able to save you."

"I assumed it was Lucas's doing, that he found some way to merge with Jason."

"No, it was Kristen. Because of her, Jason's finally got his secondary shields and full access to his power. He—" Quinton broke off, voice cracking a bit.

Threnody didn't even know she was reaching for him until her hand was gripping his shoulder. "Quinton. What happened?"

"You were dying," he said, struggling to speak. "Jason's mind was opening up to all that power. He's a Class 0 now, Thren. Lucas was right. Microtelekinesis all the fucking way, but it was too much. His mind needed more room, which he didn't have."

"The bond," Threnody guessed. "With Kerr."

"Kerr isn't a 'kinetic-oriented psion," Quinton said very, very softly. "He couldn't handle the overload. Their brain patterns wouldn't match."

She stared up into his face, a curious rushing sound filling her ears. "No."

"Lucas made the connection. He took the bond out of Kerr and put it in my mind. It's permanent." Quinton gave her a careful, broken smile as he brushed his knuckles over her cheek. "You lived."

Threnody didn't know what to say. She opened her mouth; closed it again. Shaking her head, she finally found her voice. "I would never have asked that of you. Ever."

"You weren't in any condition to argue."

"Consider yourself lucky." Threnody took in a deep breath and straightened her shoulders, hiding the pain with long practice. "Jason and I need to have a talk."

Quinton blinked at her, startled into laughter. "Even with Jason having all that power, I'd put my credit on you."

The hatch slid open and Matron stepped inside, the older woman eyeing Threnody. "So you're finally awake. You missed all the fun."

"I doubt that," Threnody said.

Matron jerked her thumb over her shoulder. "Go strap in. We're launching in five and I don't need you underfoot."

Quinton put a hand on Threnody's shoulder and guided her out of the flight deck, back into the cold of the cargo bay.

[TEN]

Dawn broke over London, late-summer sunlight piercing through a haze of thin, gray clouds. The air was hot and muggy, the breeze coming from the north only marginally cooler. The people who called the winding, ruined streets home were beginning to wake up and start another day while those who worked the night went to ground. People lived in cycles and this was only one of many.

Main city towers spanned both sides of the polluted deluge that was the Thames River, with others spread out around them. Clustered in the central zone, with foundations anchored deep into the ground, the city towers were covered in hologrids, with adverts that scrolled down their sides. The Serca Syndicate called a main city tower home, and Nathan Serca sat with his back to the view from his office. He'd seen it all before and was more interested in what his own CMO had to say.

Victoria Montoya, a Class III telepath, hadn't slept much in the past few days and it showed in the stiff way she carried herself, the way stress lined her eyes and mouth.

"We lost forty-nine Warhounds in Buffalo," Victoria reported, studying her datapad. "Of the total, Jin Li Zhang was the most critical loss. Fifty-two other Warhounds are currently off the active-duty roster and under medical care ranging from a few days to a few weeks. Most won't be ready for immediate field missions. That's almost a sixth of our total ranks. We still don't know the location of your daughters."

Nathan's expression didn't change as Victoria tallied up their losses. He already knew the few major ones, the losses that involved his children; these numbers made it all worse. His fury at the betrayal of his children was difficult to hide, but he was adept at censoring himself. Nathan was supposed to be human, but as a Class I triad psion, he had more than enough power at his disposal to change an adversary's mind. He rarely used his powers, choosing instead to act through subordinates in order to extend his life span. It was how he'd survived to reach fifty-one when most psions were lucky to reach thirty.

"And my son?" Nathan leaned back in his chair and curled his hands over the armrests. "What about Gideon?"

His youngest son was the only successor he had left. Lucas defected first. Now, with Samantha gone, her absence would cause problems Nathan had never thought he'd have to deal with. She'd been taking on public duties for two years, and her disappearance wouldn't go unnoticed. Kristen had been kept hidden away, never even put into the Registry. The continuing loss of his chosen successors would, however, be impossible to hide.

"Gideon is stable," Victoria said after a moment's hesitation. "Physically, he wasn't hurt that badly. Mentally? It's been rough."

Stable wasn't enough. Nathan required a functioning heir. "Fix his mind, Victoria. I need Gideon conscious for a mission while I attend a scheduled meeting with the Syndicate's subsidiaries."

Going into that meeting alone would raise questions, but it couldn't be helped. Nathan didn't have the time or the tools to cut his way past two dozen bioware nets in a day and alter minds, even with help. Psionic interference would tip too many people off, and at this juncture that was the very last thing he needed.

"When does the meeting take place?" Victoria asked.

"The end of next week unless circumstances dictate otherwise. I'm sending Gideon out before then."

Victoria managed to hide most of her wince, the only sign being a faint tic at the left side of her mouth. It was a difficult task, but she could accomplish it if she disregarded her own health in favor of Nathan's son's. She would, because she, like everyone else in the Warhound ranks, knew that the Serca family was the only thing standing between them and government enslavement.

"He'll be ready," Victoria said, staking her life on that promise.

"Excellent. Now, what of the Strykers that were seen with Lucas? Do we have any eyewitness reports?"

Victoria consulted her notes. "Gideon's memories are intact. He tortured a pyrokinetic Stryker inside the power plant. The electrokinetic partnered with that Stryker was seen entering the power plant, but her condition is unknown. We think she may have been involved with Jin Li's death and with what happened to the electrical grid. The telepath was merged with Lucas and no one saw the telekinetic."

"Do we have any information of what may have caused the near breaking of the mental grid?"

"No." Victoria glanced up. "Sir, do you have any thoughts on the matter?"

Nathan drummed his fingers once against the armrests of his chair, gazing past her. "During her fight in the Slums, Samantha discovered that a Stryker still had intact natal shields, but could use his power."

Victoria's expression became incredulous. "That's impossible. Natal shields always fall within the first two to three years after birth so we can access our powers. If they don't fall, we can't access our powers. That is a documented fact, sir."

"Apparently not for this particular Stryker. Our records indicate that Jason Garret is a Class V telekinetic who can teleport. We can add to them that he has intact natal shields. The question we're left with is what would happen if those shields fell? What are they holding back?"

"Do you think it was him, sir?"

Nathan had been thinking about the question endlessly since Buffalo started running at full power. "I think it's a possibility."

"Will we be looking into it?"

"I will be." Nathan dismissed her with a wave of his hand. "Go finish your work on Gideon."

Victoria left, the door sliding shut behind her. Nathan allowed himself a moment of personal, frustrated bitterness at the position his children had put him in. He hadn't wanted more than one child, but Marcheline had ordered him to create more. His mother died years ago, and Nathan felt he could blame her for this mess. Fighting his own family right now was a distraction he didn't need, not when the only thing that should be occupying his attention was the scheduled launch. Nathan refused to let his ancestors' plan wither and die all because of a few spoiled children who refused to learn their place.

Except their rebellion was undermining his control.

How had Lucas discovered and kept hidden a psion of such incredible strength? Nathan had been in and out of Lucas's mind for years. Lucas shouldn't have been capable of deceit. If the Warhound ranks had a traitor, however inconceivable the thought, then Nathan knew he would never find the person. Like Nathan and all Sercas before them both, Lucas would kill to keep his secrets. Nathan doubted he'd find even a memory of the traitor. Two years of searching had proven that conclusion as fact.

Nathan grimaced. Doubting his powers and his Syndicate right now would be disastrous. He needed Gideon in the field, searching out that new target. Being introduced as the new face of the Serca Syndicate would have to come later. Jin Li's death meant Nathan had a hole in the Warhound ranks that needed to be filled, and quickly. The world press kept demanding a statement from Nathan, not just his Syndicate's official publicist, on what had transpired in Buffalo. Nathan wasn't going to cave to their demands, not yet. There was a lot to do, with little time to do it in, and too few people he could trust to get it done right.

The mental grid dipped beyond his shields, a psi signature sparking bright and high far away on the psychic plane. The presence of another mind brushed against his. Nathan recognized the orderly thoughts of a psion who lacked the impression of a static human mind, which told him it wasn't a Warhound asking for a link. Nearly all Warhounds were shielded as human to some degree in order to hide. Strykers didn't have that luxury.

Aidan, Nathan acknowledged, initiating a psi link between himself and the Strykers Syndicate's third-in-command. *To what do I owe this lovely little chat?*

You already know, Aidan said, voice empty of all emotion. Nathan could still feel the ripple of the other man's mind, how it strained against his own power. *We require a meeting.*

You require? I'd rather you beg.

Nathan. Aidan paused, the pull of his mind weakening slightly as he conversed on a separate psi link with someone else. Finally, the Stryker said, *Please.*

Any other time it would have amused Nathan. Today, it only irritated him, but he had appearances to keep up. *Keiko knows what my office looks like.*

She'd been in it before, ferrying Ciari from wherever the Stryker OIC might have been, on the pretense of negotiating a contract to hide their true reasons for meeting with him. Only in The Hague, when they were in the same city together, did Nathan purposefully keep a mental feeler out, waiting to hear from her. Ciari wasn't with Keiko this time; she had Aidan. It was a mistake on her part, even if she didn't know it. She should have brought an empath.

They arrived before his desk in a teleport, and a red alert popped up at the bottom of the vidscreen. Nathan disengaged it. Security still called in.

"Sir," someone said over the uplink. "Is everything all right?"

"Only some visitors. Nothing to be concerned about."

"Sir."

The connection cut off and Nathan took in the pair's tired appearance with a keen eye. "I expected you earlier than this."

"We're under stricter monitoring by the World Court," Keiko said.

"They're a little behind the mark, don't you think?" Nathan said. "If I'm dealing with you, I suspect Ciari's closer to dead after that little stunt Erik pulled. Such an entertaining show."

"She's alive."

"And yet, she isn't here." Nathan leaned forward and turned off the vidscreen. "I know what the World Court has planned for your people, Keiko. Their salvation has always been the duty of your OIC. Did the World Court change its mind, or are you still the Acting OIC?"

Keiko lifted her chin higher. "I am."

"Congratulations. I doubt you'll live as long as Ciari did in that post." Nathan's eyes flickered from one to the other. "If the World Court knew where your true loyalties lie, they would have terminated you all. I can't have that happen before the launch."

"Strykers are excellent liars, Nathan. We have to be." Keiko paused, weighing her next words. "Things have changed since our conversation weeks ago at The Hague. You know why we're here."

"You came here hoping to bleed off more of your people into the Warhound ranks."

"Yes."

"A wasted effort." Nathan lifted a hand to forestall any argument. "I don't have time to retrieve the amount of psions you want to rescue. What you're asking for would raise the World Court's suspicion in a way I refuse to accept before the launch. That action would get you all killed via mass termination and you know it."

The World Court was ignorant of the Silence Law that secretly tied the two Syndicates together. Only the highest-ranking Strykers Syndicate officers knew that the Serca family wasn't human. Their silence on the matter guaranteed the survival of certain rank-and-file Strykers. Suicide missions handed out by the World Court were altered into Warhound retrievals by the Strykers Syndicate OIC. Those saved Strykers were then reconditioned by the Warhounds for the Serca family's own use.

Those transfers were done with utmost care, the image of Strykers fighting for their lives against the enemy needing to be upheld until they were brought under Serca control. Freedom, of a sort. No neurotracker in their brain, but they were still required to obey strict rules if they wanted to survive under the government's radar. They lived longer in the Serca Syndicate—usually.

"You still need some of us," Keiko said. She took a half step forward, Aidan staying by her side. "You need a wider gene pool than you've got."

"You are less the conniving bitch than Ciari is, so don't think you can bargain where she failed. Our partnership will be terminated at the launch," Nathan said. "You have known that since you took the post of chief operating officer for your Syndicate, Keiko."

"We've kept your family in the clear," Aidan snapped. "You owe us."

Nathan got to his feet, letting his mind weigh heavily against theirs as he approached Keiko. He smiled down at her, his expression all teeth and utter contempt. "The same can be said of you. I am, however, not completely heartless."

Keiko snorted her opinion of that.

"You have people you still want to save. I can admire that, Keiko."

"You admire nothing that doesn't happen on your orders," she said.

"True, but I can make room on the last wave of shuttles if I want. I will give those seats up only to the Strykers that I find useful."

"And those would be?"

"Every kind of psion at a Class III and higher—excluding you officers." Nathan's smile got fractionally wider. "I don't need a rebellion within my own company."

"The question is, will you keep your word?" Aidan said.

Nathan—three Class levels higher and thirty times stronger than the other man—stabbed his telepathy outward and coiled it tight around Aidan's mental shields. Aidan's defenses were good, but he couldn't prepare for Nathan's skill. Nathan might not have the years of use under his belt that other psions did, but his strength was something only Lucas could match.

"I don't like being questioned," Nathan said as he telekinetically forced Aidan to his knees, telepathy ripping through the other man's mind. "You don't rule here, Stryker."

"Let him go," Keiko demanded.

Nathan could feel her telekinesis slam against his own shields, scraping over his defenses. He sharpened his power against her, holding her back. Sharpened his telepathy until it sheared off half of Aidan's mental shields, causing the younger man to shudder, blood dripping from his nose.

"This is my only and final offer," Nathan said, twisting his power through Aidan's thoughts. "Whether or not you accept it, I still expect your silence on the matter of my family."

"So, you live and we die?" Aidan gasped out, shields caving beneath the pressure of Nathan's telepathy. "Is that it?"

"That is how it has always been. Don't fool yourself into believing otherwise. You won't live to see Mars Colony, to take part in what my family has worked to build. Even Ciari accepted that."

"No matter the amount of unregistered humans that you substitute for those who should have a berth on the *Ark*, you won't have enough to breed psions out of them," Keiko said. "Let him go. Please."

"So little faith, Keiko. You're all about filling Ciari's shoes, aren't you?"

Nathan wrenched his telepathy out of Aidan's mind, leaving behind raw mental wounds. "I'll have what I need."

Keiko's lips curled back from her teeth as she bent to help Aidan up. "Fuck you, Nathan."

The smile on Nathan's face got fractionally wider as he felt her pull back her telekinesis. "Your jealousy is showing. Find yourself an empath instead of a telepath next time. I'd have thought you learned something from Ciari other than how to argue futilely. It seems I was wrong."

Keiko swallowed her anger and the desire to strike out. It wouldn't solve anything here. "My loyalty to Ciari was never in question. Her loyalty to the Silence Law has never been in doubt. The only transgressions here are yours." Keiko's mouth twisted as she slung Aidan's arm over her shoulder. "We'll consider your offer."

"An empath, Keiko. You need one. Now get out of my office."

In an eye blink, they were gone.

Nathan returned to his desk, accessing the system again. A new download had come in last night that he needed to deal with. Sharra, given enough incentive, managed to accomplish the impossible some days. Who would have thought a human could be so much more useful than his own children?

Sharra had sent along two files. The first was confirmation of the back door now embedded in Erik's personal computer system, where the most sensitive data on the upcoming launch was stored. Nathan forwarded that to the hackers in his Syndicate, whose job it would be to monitor and retrieve information. The second download was pure data.

He initiated an uplink with the records division of the Warhounds. "Get me everything we have on the Stryker known as Jason Garret. Check Samantha Serca's reports first, then supplement it with nonduplicative files. I want it within the hour."

"Sir."

Retrievals were done at his discretion, no matter how hard Ciari had lobbied for the saving of her people in the past. Nathan could leave Earth without the psion Lucas had discovered, but he didn't want to. The explosion on the mental grid after the fight in Buffalo must have been the breaking of Jason's natal shields. Samantha's last useful act was discovering that Stryker's unique shields, but it wasn't enough to keep her alive now that she had turned traitor.

A window popped up on the vidscreen again, stating that the second download was complete. Nathan opened the file and scrolled through the latest schematics of the *Ark* that lay docked in cold space behind the moon, its decks just waiting to be filled.

[ELEVEN]

SEPTEMBER 2379

PARIS, FRANCE

The Border Wars were instigated by first-world countries, so it was no great shock when they were the first casualties. France was hit hard, situated between countries that suffered just as badly. That nation had owned a stockpile of nuclear bombs at the beginning of the five-year stretch of war, all the excuse anyone needed to attack. Retaliation was inevitable for every country on Earth, in whatever way possible. France was no different in its response, and like many countries, it was wiped off the map by the end of the Border Wars.

Deadzones still covered the European continent, areas where nuclear fallout and lingering radiation made it impossible for life to take back the land. The Paris Basin was a toxic pit, a concentrated mess of pollution and nuclear taint that no one could live in. The Seine, that ancient waterway that carved through France, was a poisonous water route that twisted through and around the ruins of the city. Massive dams that had once graced the banks downriver to hold back the Atlantic Ocean had been destroyed or eroded over time. Salt water inevitably flowed into fresh, seeping deep into dirt to mix with toxic runoff. Pools of water and crawling fog were stained an eerie green.

Paris—flooded, abandoned, and lost—stretched out before Dalia in the early-afternoon sunlight. Dalia was one of Nathan's best spies, a human capable of taking on any identity and owning it for the duration of her mission. She was unremarkable to look at, easily forgotten once she finished a job. Switching identities and appearances to gain information was her life, and Nathan owned all of them.

Squinting through the brightness of a clear, near-autumn day, Dalia scratched at the skin where the collar of her uniform rubbed against her throat. Beneath it, she wore a skinsuit specially tailored to block the lingering radiation in the Paris Basin. Her hard helmet was on the floor by her seat. People could work without a skinsuit, as bondworkers did, but the radiation levels were still high enough to damage DNA. The government's Command Center was specially shielded, but people always took precautions.

The threat of certain death and ruined DNA kept people out of France, or should have. When records of Mars Colony, with its massive enclosed habitat, made their way back into the awareness of the surviving government, getting there became the number one priority. Surviving meant more than simply clawing one's way into the Registry by any means necessary. It meant preparing to take up the mantle of a progressive society once again. The results of that effort stood before her beyond the Command Center, reflecting sunlight.

Platforms, hundreds of them, stood above the wastewater and ruins, all holding space shuttles. Running through the middle of those platforms was a long launch ramp that curved into the sky. Built by government scientists and enslaved bondworkers, shielded against lingering nuclear taint, the shuttles were waiting to be filled by those lucky enough to be in the Registry.

"Shuttle Prime, this is Command, do you copy, over," the government's head of operations said into an uplink where he stood some meters away from Dalia.

"We copy, over," the pilot said.

Dalia trained her eyes back on the vidscreen in front of her instead of the view beyond the large plasglass windows. Her role here was in operations, just one of many bodies contracted out of government-controlled scientific divisions. She'd worn her latest identity as a scientist before, just not here. Studying the vidscreen, Dalia watched the shuttle's system come online, the same information showing on other terminals.

"Weather looks like it's holding. We've got clearance for launch, over."

"Copy that, Command, over."

"Begin preflight calibration and start countdown, over."

The countdown went smoothly, months of practice simulations enabling the crew to launch on time and without difficulty. The shuttle roared down the curved ramp, thrusters burning a bright line through the sky as it launched, smoke and vapor trailing in its wake. This was one of the larger shuttles, capable of carrying three hundred people and supplies. Today, it carried only three-quarters of a full load as it fought gravity and left Earth behind, the shuttle's route rigidly plotted on the vidscreens in the command room.

The crew on that shuttle would begin the final preparations on the *Ark* for its passengers, joining the lead group who launched six months ago. Dalia watched the shuttle until it wasn't even a pinprick in the sky, the smoke trail dragged to pieces by the wind. A soft beep brought her attention back to her console, an arriving encrypted message requiring her attention. She tapped in a few commands, downloading it to a separate folder. A background filter was already running, keeping the download from being discovered by the central command system. She'd crack the file later and retrieve her new orders from Nathan. At the moment, she had other duties to perform.

"Sir," Dalia said to her supervisor. "Preparing for communications with the *Ark* in fifteen hours and counting."

She set the clock, the numbers winding down.

PART THREE
VITIATE

SESSION DATE: 2128.06.29
LOCATION: Institute of Psionics Research
CLEARANCE ID: Dr. Amy Bennett
SUBJECT: 2581
FILE NUMBER: 596

"I'm tired," Aisling says. The nurse taking a vial of her blood for testing doesn't look up.

"We're almost finished, Aisling," the doctor says from where she stands behind the nurse, watching the procedure.

The nurse pulls the needle out of the girl's arm and places a small bandage over the hole in her skin. Aisling leans her head back and stares at the doctor, wires framing her face.

"There's nothing special about my blood," she says.

The doctor waves the nurse out of the room. Only when they're alone does the doctor step closer and stare down at her small patient. "It's not your blood we want."

Aisling slowly nods, the wires swaying with the motion. "You can't see what I see, but you want to. That's why I'm here, isn't it?"

"We have records of people that don't exist and years none of us or our children will live to see because you refuse to help us."

"Everyone has their part to play." Aisling blinks rapidly, the machines changing pitch. "Right, Threnody?"

"What about us?" the doctor asks sharply.

"You're running out of time."

[TWELVE]

They flew straight into the polar night until even the ocean became impossible to make out as darkness filled the sky. They passed over the Ross Ice Shelf, shuttle lights cutting through a blackness lit only by long streaks of green. The aurora australis guided their way from time to time, a brightly glowing ribbon in the sky. Maps drawn across hologrids surrounded the navigator's seat. They showed only two points marked on the continental outline of Antarctica. Twenty minutes later, the shuttles flew over the first point, McMurdo Station an invisible ruin below. It had long since given way to the elements.

"Gonna be a tough flight the rest of the way," Matron said as she stretched in her seat. The sound of metal popping was uncomfortably loud as she rotated her arms in ways real limbs couldn't bend. Her cybernetic replacements were covered in synthskin, but these moments reminded Lucas that she wasn't all flesh and bone.

"Wind is gonna be a bitch. Here's hoping the deicing coat we put on the shuttles holds up after the Arctic." Matron glanced over at Lucas, who was in the navigator's seat. "You want to comm them or should I?"

"When we're past the mountain range," Lucas said as he continued to monitor their route. "Piggybacking off the government's satellites is easier to do farther inland."

"You're the boss."

They kept one eye on their instrumentation and the other on the dark around them. They couldn't see the Queen Alexandra Range as they approached that small subset of the Transantarctic Mountains, which spanned the frozen continent. All they could rely on was the computer as the shuttles flew over snow and ice far below.

Like the Arctic, Antarctica was relatively untouched, only two areas of the continent having been inhabited when the bombs first fell. Most of those eight hundred people had been pulled out by their respective countries at the time due to distrust. The abandonment of McMurdo led to the abandonment of the Amundsen-Scott South Pole Station as well. The domino effect meant no one should have remembered that either place ever existed, but Lucas had a knack for finding abandoned history.

Thirty minutes later, Lucas started an uplink, one with a noticeable lag in sending and receiving. "South Pole, this is Alpha shuttle leading Operation Deep Freeze, do you copy, over."

The uplink hummed for over a minute before someone answered. "Alpha shuttle, this is South Pole. We copy, over."

"We've got nine shuttles en route and our ETA is one hour, over."

"Thought you were bringing more'n that, over."

"This is all we've got. Be ready to transport, out."

Lucas cut the connection.

Matron gestured at her terminal. "Get me a route."

Lucas silently plotted her a vector, and she waved her thanks at him when he finished. Night flying was always dangerous, especially when one needed to land in unfamiliar terrain. They saw the lights of the Amundsen-Scott South Pole Station well before they arrived. The illumination wouldn't make it any easier to land on packed snow in the middle of the polar night.

The spotlights shining through the dark illuminated the improvised airfield. Tiny figures milled about near two half-buried buildings, one in the shape of the letter *E,* but with a fourth little leg added on, and the second, which looked like a dome. Bumps protruded from the icy snow, eroded foundations of buildings that no one could live in anymore. The shuttles landed in careful unison.

Matron stared through the windshield at the group making its way across the airfield. "She's grown," Matron said as she went through the postflight protocol.

"Children do that," Lucas replied. He slid the hood of his insulated skinsuit over his head, sealing the skinmask to it for protection against the dangerous cold.

The Strykers were waiting for Lucas by the cold-storage units when he finally made it into the cargo bay. From a nearby seat, Kristen yawned behind her skinmask, gleaming dark blue eyes tracking her brother's every move. Samantha sat beside her, expression ruthlessly blank. Lucas curled his fingers at his sisters in a commanding gesture, expecting them to follow him out.

The cargo door opened, letting in a blast of freezing air. Even sealed against the elements behind skinsuits and heavy clothing, it was impossible not to feel the cold. Jogging up into the shuttle, leaving wet footprints behind her, came a slim young woman. Behind the skinmask she wore, her face was as black as Matron's, her smile one of vast relief.

"Shit, Ma, took you long enough to get down here," the stranger said as she was pulled into a fierce hug by Matron.

Matron gave herself a five-second reunion before putting her only child at arm's length. "You put on weight, Zahara," Matron said with a decisive nod. "Didn't think that was possible down here."

"You'd be surprised at what the hydroponics lab can produce. None of us starved." The woman turned to face Lucas, jerking her thumb in the Strykers' direction. "They ain't scavengers."

"Like mother, like daughter," Lucas said, a hard smile pulling at his mouth.

Zahara didn't seem to mind his coldness. "You know it. But, hell, if you brought 'em, we'll work 'em." Zahara patted one of the large cold-storage units bolted to the deck. "These the precious cargo?"

"Observant as always, Zahara."

Zahara shrugged, ignoring the glare that Samantha turned on her for the familiar way she addressed Lucas. "It's what you pay me to be. We've got the dome open and snowcats ready for hauling. How much are you gonna be teleporting?"

"None of it," Lucas said, gesturing at the others. "Jason here is your telekinetic."

"For half the load," Jason said. "If that. I need a fucking break."

Zahara eyed Jason before sighing in exasperation. She crooked a finger at him. "Follow me. Let's get you a visual."

"I take it you don't need an explanation on the functions of teleportation."

"Been working with Lucas for years. I know how you telekinetics work."

Jason followed the younger woman outside, sliding through the crowd gathered at the bottom of the ramp. Matron tracked her daughter's path for a second or two before refocusing her attention on her people.

"All right, everyone. Listen up," Matron called out. "Getting out of Buffalo was worse than getting out of DC two years ago. Lost about as many people, but we don't got time to grieve right now. So choke back whatever arguments you've got and get to work. We've got cargo to shift."

Matron expected her people to obey, and she had Everett to help make them toe the line. Lucas watched her call out orders, content for the moment to let her organize the work flow. Quinton came to stand beside Threnody, watching the scavengers.

"You're not up to playing stevedore, Thren," Quinton said, glancing over at all the cargo strapped down in the shuttle.

She bristled at the implication she couldn't pull her weight. "Watch me."

"I have. You're going to undo everything we've done to keep you breathing."

"He's right," Lucas said. "You're not helping with this, Threnody. Get inside the station. Korman needs to look you over."

"Korman?" Threnody said. "That doctor with biomodifications for eyes?"

"The very same."

"I don't need to be operated on again."

"Which is good, since he's probably drunk." Lucas shrugged at Quinton's angry expression. "He'll be coherent enough to run some tests."

Quinton shook his head. "You want me to trust some goddamned drunk with Threnody's life?"

"No. I'm telling you to trust *me*. Now get to work, Quinton. Threnody? Get inside."

Lucas walked away. Kerr drifted over, giving Threnody a sympathetic look. "You can't really argue with him. He got us this far."

"Yeah," Threnody said as she started down the ramp. "Makes you wonder how much further he's going to take us before he finds a reason to discard us."

Kerr nodded. "Come on, Quinton. Let's do this."

As Threnody headed for the nearby station, Quinton and Kerr moved to join the scavengers, all of whom had separated into small groups charged with operating gravlifts and a dozen old-style cargo sleds hooked up to ancient-looking machines with flat tracks in place of wheels. They joined a work queue, adding their strength to hauling out boxes of seeds and other items, and organizing them into piles for teleportation into the dome.

The cold-storage units in every shuttle were unbolted and gravlifts used to pry them out. They were transferred onto cargo sleds, stabilized with heavy metal chains and hooks, then driven down a brightly lit icy path. Kerr rode along with the first load into the snow-covered dome. The entrance looked as if it had been carved into one side of the dome, the road they were on canting downward at a slight incline. They drove through the entrance at the bottom, the way braced by walls of ice whose weight Kerr didn't trust.

Zahara and Jason were still looking the place over, Jason needing to know the dimensions of the dome and the placement of everything inside to form a safe teleport. It looked as if various rooms had once existed inside the dome before the scavengers tore the interior apart to form an open space. Kerr jumped off the vehicle and let the scavengers start unloading the cold-storage unit.

"Are you going to be all right, Jays?" Kerr asked as he approached Jason.

"I'll be fine," Jason said as he squinted up at the geodesic ceiling. "This needs to be done. I can do it quicker than the machines."

"If you're sure."

"What, you don't trust him?" Zahara said, arms crossed over her chest. Kerr stared her down. "This doesn't concern you."

"The hell it doesn't. The South Pole is ours, not yours."

"I'd like to see you use that argument on Lucas."

Zahara scowled, but kept quiet at the pointed reminder of who was really in charge. "You ain't worth the people we lost," she said before walking away. "Hey, Rex! That thing don't go in the damn middle of the dome. Move it to the fucking side."

"She's got a mouth on her like Matron," Jason said as he finally turned toward his partner. "Strong genes."

"There are those who would argue that conclusion," Kerr said.

Jason shrugged. "Let's get to work. The sooner we finish, the sooner we sleep."

Jason wrapped his telekinesis around the both of them, exhaustion forcing him to go slow. Beside him, Kerr watched as Jason struggled for a second to find a balance that had shifted permanently off-center. Kerr swallowed, his mind empty of the solace Jason's shields once gave him through the now-broken bond.

"You okay?"

"I don't see the world like I used to," Jason said. "It's strange."

"I can only imagine."

Jason's power finally steadied, and in the blink of an eye they appeared outside again, off to the side of the airfield so as to not arrive in the way of anything or *in* anything. They fell a few centimeters to the ground, feet hitting against hard snow.

The two separated, Kerr returning to help load up the cargo sleds and Jason moving to the nearest pile of seed boxes stacked haphazardly in the snow. Kristen was leading the work crew nearest him, and it was almost funny how the scavengers were keeping their distance from her.

"Humans are so easy to scare," Kristen said as Jason approached, her voice cheerful. "It gets boring after a while."

"I don't think Lucas would appreciate you killing anyone here," Jason said, eyeing her warily.

Kristen gave him a sly look, her mind briefly brushing against his mental shields. "Lucas doesn't like cleaning up my messes."

Jason didn't know how her damaged power functioned and wouldn't trust her, no matter what assurances Lucas made. The dysfunctional empath rarely left her victims breathing, but Jason was still alive. The mental pattern of his natal shields must have been enough to stabilize her, to show her how to build her own. He wondered how long her sanity would last.

"Stay out of my head," Jason said. He placed a hand on top of a wide stack the scavengers had created in the twenty minutes he'd been gone.

With a slow, methodical wink, Kristen answered, "Maybe."

Jason gathered his power and teleported the boxes of seeds with him to the dome, the first of many teleports. It was less weight than the cold-storage units or the various pieces of disassembled terraforming machines, which was easier for his mind to handle. He'd have to deal with the heavier items eventually.

An hour later, but what felt longer due to Jason's headache, a commotion around one of the shuttles caught his attention. Quinton was yelling instructions at scavengers as they painstakingly shifted one piece of the terraforming machines out of a shuttle's cargo hold. Jason swore under his breath and jogged over to that area, holding his power in reserve.

"You should have called me for this," Jason said.

Quinton shrugged. "You were busy with the seeds."

"Of everything we brought out of Spitsbergen, these machines are pretty fucking important." Jason took a step forward and raised his voice. "Hands off, I've got it."

Telekinesis stabilized the heavy weight of the piece, the final product something he couldn't fully envision. Lucas had the diagrams downloaded and stored in a datapad, stolen from the Arctic. The terraforming machines could be reassembled, but more would need to be built eventually. Learning to reverse engineer that technology was going to be integral to rebuilding the planet. The terraforming machines were capable of cleansing and cloning with the aid of nanites on a level that could jump-start a previously uninhabited planet such as Mars. Fixing Earth came with government interference, and in the past no one had been willing to fight it for the sake of everyone. Even now, it was anyone's guess how long the machines would last.

"Just don't drop it," Novak joked as Jason carefully settled the piece of machinery on the flatbed of the cargo sled.

"Novak, shut the hell up," Quinton said. He followed a step behind Jason, keeping an eye on the telekinetic. He didn't like the strained look on Jason's face. In the back of his mind, Quinton could feel the push and pull of power not his own, and it made him a little dizzy. He wasn't sure when the bond would settle, but he hoped it would be soon.

"You need to find yourself a sense of humor, man," Novak said.

"Give me your lighter and I'll show you what I do for fun."

Novak didn't offer it up.

With a shuddering groan of cold metal, the transfer was complete, and Novak climbed into the enclosed cab of the yellow vehicle, flat tracks rimmed with snow.

Jason bent over to rest his hands on his knees and breathe. "How many of those are left to move?"

"Two more pieces for this set," Quinton said.

"I'll move them, but I won't be able to teleport anything afterwards."

Quinton nodded and watched as Novak started the engine of the snowcat, carefully pulling out into the small road that linked the airfield to the station and the dome, joining the work caravan that was departing and returning in a steady loop. Headlights mingled with taillights while the aurora australis moved across the night sky high above them.

[THIRTEEN]

SEPTEMBER 2379
AMUNDSEN-SCOTT SOUTH POLE STATION, ANTARCTICA

D r. Isaiah Korman was a pockmarked drunk, but he could still see straight when jacked into a system. The biomodifications that had replaced his eyes shifted in his metal-lined eye sockets, their observations fed directly to his brain through neuroports. Korman took a sip from a metal flask and swallowed as he studied Threnody's test results.

"He wants the impossible. Did I say that already? You get stuck down here and you're screwed."

"Are you done yet?" Threnody said from where she sat on the metal exam table. After four hours of tests, she was done with him.

Korman rubbed a hand over his face. His fingers skimmed over the wires that cut out from his eyes and back into his skull through his temples. Half his skull was metal plating, tapering down to his spine. He seemed to have more cybernetic replacements in his body than Matron did.

"Your nervous system is intact. More than intact. If your synapses were talking to each other any louder, they'd be screaming."

Threnody scratched at her bare arm, fingernails moving around the needle stuck into the crook of her elbow. "Doesn't feel like it."

"You said he tanked you?"

"Yeah."

"Huh." Korman took another sip from his flask. "Lucas must have found an upgraded program, because you're healed. Fully functioning body. It's a damn miracle."

"I was nearly dead."

"Well, I can officially upgrade your status to living. Congratulations." Korman let out a bark of laughter that grated on Threnody's ears and toasted her with his flask. "Goddamn it, I could use a biotank like that. It fixed you faster than any of the ones I've got here. I hope Lucas brought it with him."

"It wasn't just a biotank that did this," Threnody said, splaying one hand over her knee and thinking about someone else's power in her body.

"Your psion physiology probably had something to do with it. You've all got complicated genomes. You people can take more damage than us humans and survive it."

Korman tipped his head back and poured what remained in the flask into his mouth. What was left of his skin, already blotchy, got redder. Threnody slid the needle out of her arm. She wasn't going to stay in the presence of someone intent on drinking himself to death. She got to her feet, bootheels touching the floor as the door to the small lab opened.

Lucas stepped inside, gaze moving over the two. "Korman. So glad I caught you mostly sober. Diagnosis?"

"Mostly sober?" Korman snorted and tossed his flask onto the nearby counter. "I took the nanites out of her veins. She's got no lasting damage from trauma. More like she wasn't damaged to begin with. What am I supposed to do with her?"

"Nothing." Lucas walked over to view the vidscreen, assessing the information in silence. "Interesting. Looks like all my efforts saved your life, Threnody. Care to thank me?"

"No," she said.

"Smart girl," Korman muttered. "He's worse than the damn World Court when it comes to torture. Best to keep your mouth shut."

"What's that supposed to mean?"

"The Strykers Syndicate's OIC got terminated on a worldwide news stream the other day. They left her second as Acting OIC."

Korman was telekinetically yanked out of his chair and slammed against the wall. Dangling with his feet off the ground and struggling to breathe against the pressure wrapped around his throat, he clawed uselessly at Lucas's power.

"They did *what?*" Lucas snarled.

For the first time since they'd teamed up, Threnody heard actual, real emotion in Lucas's voice, saw it on his face. Shock and fury drained all the blood from his face, the dark circles beneath his dark blue eyes standing out sharply.

Surprised, Threnody cleared her throat and said, "He can't answer if you kill him."

Abruptly, Korman fell to the floor. Threnody never saw him land, too busy staring at Lucas's shaking hands. She took in all the tiny details of how he stood before turning her head to look at Korman.

"Get out."

The doctor obeyed her in record time, stumbling out of the room and slamming the door shut behind him. Threnody walked over to lock it. Turning, she put her back to it and crossed her arms over her chest. She knew she wouldn't be able to stop Lucas from leaving the room, but judging by the way he looked right now, he wasn't going anywhere until he got himself under control.

"Is this about the Silence Law?" Threnody said, refusing to look away from Lucas's gaze.

"No," Lucas said, taking a deep, steadying breath. Some color started to return to his face. "No, it's not."

"Then why are you worried about Ciari?"

"It doesn't concern you yet."

"Yet." Threnody let out a harsh laugh before moving away from the door to stand in front of Lucas. "We are here because of your goddamn concern, Lucas. Don't lie to me."

For one brief moment, something alien filled his eyes. Alien because Threnody never thought she'd see fear inside Lucas.

"I should have taken her with us when we left Buffalo," Lucas said. "She was only in Toronto. I had time to get her down here and have Korman perform the extraction."

"Why are you worried about her?"

"She's carrying my child."

Threnody felt as if she'd been punched, all the breath leaving her lungs. Shock came first, then the sickening realization that no unborn child would be able to survive what a neurotracker could do to a human body.

"Are you joking?" Threnody said weakly, searching his face. "You're not joking."

"I need to find out what happened to Ciari." Lucas headed for the door, but Threnody's hand on his arm stopped him. "Let go."

"You can't leave the South Pole. We only just got here and Ciari's torture was days ago."

"All the more reason for me to leave."

"And do what? You're in no condition to save anyone right now." Threnody dug her fingers into his arm and moved so he had to look at her. "We need more downtime."

"You don't understand," Lucas snapped, wrenching his arm free of her grip and glaring at her. "My daughter is why I'm doing all of this."

Threnody didn't move, never broke eye contact. "And I'm doing it for everyone else. Your reasons aren't any more or less valid than my own, despite your shitty attitude. So for once, listen to me."

Lucas blinked at her, momentarily thrown off-kilter by her complete lack of obedience.

"Korman said the World Court put the Strykers Syndicate's second officer into the OIC post as *Acting* OIC," Threnody said. "They don't do that unless the OIC is still alive. Which means Keiko is running the Syndicate and Ciari is still breathing. I can't say anything about your daughter, but if Ciari's been helping you all along, betraying both the World Court and Nathan beneath the rules of the Silence Law, don't you think she would have watched out for her own unborn child?"

"Would she?"

Threnody punched him in the same spot Quinton had. Her fist made contact only because Lucas wasn't thinking straight and wasn't up to full strength. Lucas's head snapped to the side and he swore.

Threnody shook out the tension in her hand from the hit. "You goddamn bastard. After everything that Ciari's given up for you, you're really going to ask that? Fuck you, Lucas."

Lucas touched his mouth, fingers skimming over swelling tissue. She hadn't split his lip, and she had half a thought to try again to rectify that mistake.

Don't, Lucas said into her mind, but without the heat of anger.

"The OIC is a position I would never want," Threnody said after a long moment of silence. "Ciari's argued for our lives over and over again and this is the payment she gets for it. For toeing the fucking line and letting you do what needs to be done, she gets her fucking brain fried. And you think she'd risk losing her baby?"

Lucas let his hand drop away and he spat on the floor of the lab. "I need to know what happened to my daughter."

"After the clusterfuck in Buffalo, Ciari had to know she'd be summoned before the bench. She'd have time to do whatever she could to save the baby before that order came. Your daughter is most likely in Toronto. Probably in the medical level of the Strykers Syndicate."

Lucas closed his eyes, but the tension didn't leave his body. "Can you be certain that's true?"

"No, but it's the most logical place. We can't run off and find out just yet." Threnody lifted both hands to rub at her temples, feeling a headache coming on. "We need to be at full strength before we rush into things, otherwise we'll make mistakes and it'll cost us."

"Tomorrow," Lucas said after a moment. "We'll figure out what to do tomorrow."

Threnody could only agree to that compromise, and this time she didn't try to stop Lucas from leaving. He unlocked the door and pulled it open, pausing only long enough to say, "Coming?"

She followed him out.

Lucas led her to a small room barely big enough for a single bed and an old, rickety desk. "Yours," he said. "And Quinton's. I'll let you decide who gets the bed. Cafeteria is down the hall. It's cramped quarters all around, but don't worry. I'll keep an eye on my sisters."

He said it as if they were still a threat and she stared at him. "Should I be worried?"

Lucas didn't answer and started to close the door. Threnody put her hand against it, forcing him to stop. Threnody gazed at him silently for a moment before saying, "Get some rest."

Lucas closed the door. Shaking her head, Threnody went to sit on the bed, wondering if it was worth it to peel out of her skinsuit. Instead, she slid beneath a patched blanket and dozed.

Threnody woke when the door opened again, instincts too fine-tuned to ignore even the slightest of noises. She opened her eyes and watched as Quinton came into the room and switched on the light.

"I'll take the floor," he said tiredly, carrying extra blankets. "Go back to sleep, Thren."

"The cargo?"

"Safely stored." Quinton rolled the blankets out on the floor. "Still needs to be sorted. That's going to take weeks."

It was hard to believe what they had accomplished, stealing from the government for the sake of a world. She swallowed, wishing she had water. "How many seeds?"

Quinton lifted his head and looked at her. Even through his exhaustion, she could see the awe in his eyes. "Millions, Thren. Millions."

She squeezed her eyes shut, the strange feeling curling in her gut almost foreign. Hope always was.

FOURTEEN

SEPTEMBER 2379

AMUNDSEN-SCOTT SOUTH POLE STATION, ANTARCTICA

Kristen found Threnody with Quinton during lunch, when Threnody was shoveling a forkful of rice and actual beans into her mouth. They had a corner table in the cafeteria with their backs to the wall, but they never saw Kristen coming. She was suddenly there across the table from them, chin propped up on her bony hands, psionic interference scratching against their shields. Her permanent smile wasn't inviting.

Threnody paused midchew, meeting Kristen's gaze with a healthy dose of wariness. The teenager used her hands to twist her blond head into a painful angle until it looked as if Kristen might snap her own neck. "Do you know what happens when Warhounds touch Sercas without our permission?" Kristen said, gleaming dark blue eyes never blinking. "We kill them."

"You touch her, I will burn you," Quinton said, reaching for the lighter in his pocket.

"An eye for an eye." Kristen dragged a finger down over her face, scratching a long line of red into her skin. "For what both of you did to my brother. It's only fair."

Quinton cast Threnody a questioning glance. Threnody shrugged and swallowed her bite of food. "We disagreed about something, so I introduced my fist to his face."

"So proud, aren't you?" Kristen laughed, raspy and amused. She stretched out her arms, let her hands slide against the edge of the table as she leaned her weight forward, catching Threnody's gaze. "How highly everyone must think of you. To waste all that time saving you. To let your hands wander like they do."

"What caused me to punch Lucas isn't your business."

That smile never changed, though the look in Kristen's eyes became predatory. "And here I thought all they beat into you dogs was obedience."

"Would we be here if that was the case?"

"You would be wherever it was Lucas needed you to be." Kristen abruptly sat back, lifting both hands to tuck strands of hair behind her ears. Her eyes became half-lidded; the smile never fading. "I can make you be whatever I want you to be."

"Kristen," a sharp voice said. "What did Lucas say about cornering people?"

Threnody looked away from Kristen, knowing that Quinton would keep the girl from going for their throats, and watched as Samantha approached their table. Even in this cramped place at the bottom of the world, Samantha still looked put-together. Built like her older brother, she was tall and thin, gorgeous enough to shine from a news stream, but that wasn't her place anymore. Samantha came to a stop behind Kristen's chair, attention on her sister and no one else.

"Sammy-girl," Kristen drawled, canting her head back to look at her sister. "Did Lucas put you in charge of holding my leash today? How boring."

A malignant pressure slid against Threnody's mental shields, saturated with negative emotion. Quinton must have felt it as well because he was getting to his feet, ready to fight. Samantha placed her hand on Kristen's head, stroking her fingers through straight blond hair. Affection almost, or so Threnody thought. Right up until Samantha gripped Kristen's hair with one hand and slammed the younger girl's head against the tabletop.

Bright red blood splattered across the cracked plastic. Kristen choked on her laughter as the low hum of conversation in the cafeteria faded. The pressure in Threnody's mind disappeared. Quinton remained standing, but didn't intervene.

"Not broken," Kristen said, even as she lifted her head and straightened her crooked nose with both hands, blood dripping down her face. Her skin was starting to swell. She pressed her teeth into the cut that split her bottom lip, sinking the edges into a faint line of red.

"Come along, Kristen," Samantha said, her gaze flicking over to the other pair at the table, gaze icy. "Lucas wants you. All of you."

Threnody picked up her fork and tapped it against her bowl. "When I'm done."

The contemplative look Samantha gave her made the hair on the back of Threnody's neck stand on end, as if the teenager were thinking about how to take her apart in the slowest way possible. "Now, Stryker."

Deliberately, Threnody took another bite. Samantha's expression became remote and Threnody could feel telepathy claw against her mental shields. The vast power of a Class II telepath flowed around her mind, digging hooks into her defenses.

I won't pretend to understand why Lucas chose you. I just know that he did, Samantha said against the outskirts of Threnody's mind. *Stand up, or I will make you. It's a process you will not enjoy.*

I thought Lucas didn't need an enforcer, Threnody said, letting her thoughts sit where the telepath could barely reach them without inciting trauma. *He's done just fine without one all these years.*

Lucas is breaking the world. I'm simply ensuring I remain on the winning side.

Your usual position, yes? Threnody arched an eyebrow and took another bite of her food. *Always second, never first? Unless we're counting your twin. How is Gideon, Samantha?*

Really now, Lucas interrupted as he telepathically put himself between Threnody's mind and Samantha's sharply focused power. *As amusing as this is, I have better things to do than fix the both of you again. We have a meeting. It starts in five minutes. None of you will be late.*

He pulled out of Threnody's mind, taking Samantha with him. The younger girl didn't seem offended at his interference, merely turned her back on Threnody and Quinton with a disdain that no one could miss. Threnody didn't take it personally as she watched the sisters leave the cafeteria, Kristen skipping ahead.

"If Lucas gives her half a chance," Threnody said quietly, "she'll kill him."

"Which one?" Quinton said.

"Take your pick."

Quinton nodded agreement. Threnody took one last bite of her food—her third bowl in the past twenty minutes—before they got up to deposit their dirty dishes in the designated area. Everything was reused down here since they had no way to bring in new supplies unless it was either flown or teleported in. The only shuttles Quinton had seen at the outpost were the nine they arrived in. Lucas had effectively trapped some of Matron's scavengers in Antarctica for over a year. It was a wonder none of them went mad during the long polar day and even worse polar night.

The two were the last into the heated room for the meeting. The only people who looked happy to see them were Jason and Kerr, though the smile Kerr gave Threnody was pained. Despite everything they'd gone through since the Slums, it was hard to reconcile the changes that had happened among the four. Blame was just as devastating as hate and they were struggling not to feel either.

Threnody wouldn't apologize for surviving. Kerr would never believe it if she did. They still stood together, shoulder to shoulder, to face what came next.

The room was cluttered with work terminals. Novak and Everett were hunched over one, muttering to themselves about issues with a hack, while Matron and Zahara watched their progress in silence. Samantha and Kristen huddled in a corner by themselves, far from where Lucas stood next to Korman with three strangers.

Threnody thought they belonged to Matron, but then the tallest man opened his mouth and her attention locked on him. "Now that we're all here, can we upload the damn program so that me and mine can get a flight off this continent?"

The man was middle-aged, with a scar like a second smile curved around his throat. Biomodifications showed in his jaw and neck, his altered voice coming through electronics. The sound was the harsh burr of a reality no one liked to be told about, familiar from a decade of riding the pirate streams that the government could never quite kill.

"In due time, Fahad," Lucas said as he studied the datapad he held. "We have other things to discuss before I let you go."

"Yeah?" Matron asked. "Like what? We got the seeds and everything else. That's what you wanted and it cost us."

"I really don't care how many people you lost, Matron. We've gone over this."

The group shifted uneasily. Matron scowled, her metal teeth scraping together. "Those were good people, Lucas."

"They weren't mine." Lucas set the datapad aside before looking up at everyone. "We're coming up on a week since Buffalo and from what I can tell, the government isn't as settled as it claims."

"Is anyone surprised about that?" Threnody said.

Lucas shrugged. "The fact that they aren't immediately beginning to transfer the people on the colony lists to Paris means we still have time to implement our plans. We need the government to break from its current course. I want them to panic."

"Breaking into the seed bank will go a long way toward meeting that goal," Jason said. "But I don't think you're stopping there."

Lucas nodded. "Fahad will be flying to Johannesburg. Evidence of the *Ark* will be uploaded on a pirate stream from Africa within twenty-four hours, but we need some lead-up time to get things sorted. We aren't risking what we're hiding by having the stream go live on the premises. Matron, you're giving up Novak for the cause. Samantha and Kristen will be in charge of that mission."

"Why don't you just shoot me before dumping me on that shuttle with your sisters?" Novak said with a scowl, jerking his head up. He ran a hand over his tattooed skull, wiping away sweat in a nervous gesture.

Lucas ignored him. "As for the rest of you, we aren't finished stealing from the government yet."

"Don't tell me they have another hidden warehouse full of supplies?" Kerr said.

"No. You Strykers have never been hidden from the public. Your former Syndicate is our next target."

"What do you want with the Strykers Syndicate?" Threnody said.

"The same thing that I got from you four—an alliance, of sorts."

"You really do like fucking with Nathan, don't you?" Samantha said. She had her fingers curled around the collar of Kristen's skinsuit, keeping the other girl close.

"I need to pass the time somehow," Lucas said. "Korman here has spent the past year working on how to program nanites in a controlled environment outside of a biotank."

Korman's expression, moved by muscle and wire, was bitter. "And by controlled environment, you mean human."

"No one misses bondworkers, Korman. They aren't worth your grief." Lucas neatly turned his attention to the next item on whatever internal schedule he was keeping. "Korman will explain what needs to be done on your end, Jason. He produced the same results you got on the shuttle with Threnody using the nanites, only this time they won't be forcing regeneration and they won't need your power."

"I'm no scientist," Jason said. "I don't even know what I did to save Threnody. And you still haven't told us what this mission is."

"You're a psion and a hacker. That is all I require of you." Lucas glanced over at Threnody. "We won't be able to extract the neurotrackers like we do in the Serca Syndicate following a retrieval. What we're doing is simply turning off the kill switch. The signal will remain active. Strykers will continue to show up on the government's security grid, but they won't die. An extraction takes time, something we don't have right now, so we had to get creative."

"Meaning what, exactly?" Threnody said.

"You built a virus," Jason guessed, looking to Lucas for confirmation. "You're going to infect the neurotrackers on a wide scale."

Lucas nodded. "They're bioware with a system that can be hacked, housed in the best biological entity this planet has ever made. The nanites Korman programmed will infect only the neurotrackers with the virus and nothing else. Every other biomodification will be spared."

"Are you sure? Nanites are tricky to program and the neurotrackers have some serious defensive programs built into them."

"My family created this technology. It's why we could unlock the neurotrackers without the government's assistance when we retrieved Strykers." Lucas shrugged. "The government has the code to fully deactivate the neurotrackers, which is different from the code that activates the kill switch for termination. My family knows both. We supply those codes every two years."

"If an encrypted password is the only thing keeping those things in

Stryker brains, why hasn't anyone tried to hack them before this?" Novak asked derisively.

Lucas gave him a cool smile. "The encrypted password for deactivation is two hundred digits long."

Jason whistled. "That would be a problem."

"Not for too much longer. The government might want the Strykers dead, but I don't."

"How are you going to administer this virus?" Quinton said. "The Strykers know we defected and they've got standing kill orders for each of us."

"There are ways around that." None of the Strykers looked as if they believed him, but Lucas didn't care. Pointing at Fahad, he said, "Get your people and your gear. Novak will fly you out of here. You will follow Samantha's orders to the letter."

"About fucking time," Fahad said, shaking his head. "One more week in this place and I'd have gone mad. Been here three months too long."

"You get used to it," Zahara said.

"To the dark, yeah. But to the cold? Never."

Fahad and his two assistants left the room, followed by Novak and Everett. Samantha leveled her brother a cool look as she let Kristen go. The empath trailed after the humans, tapping at her recently set and swollen nose with one finger.

And when we're finished? Samantha said between them alone.

I'll find you, Lucas said.

It was a threat as much as it was a promise. Samantha left without a backward glance. Matron spat on the ground in her wake.

"Your sisters ain't got your back, Lucas," Matron said.

"I have them, which is all I'm concerned about," Lucas replied. "Korman, I want you to consolidate your work on the virus-carrying nanites, then prep your operating room. Jason needs to familiarize himself with the virus, and Quinton is going to need replacements for his biotubes. Matron, go help him."

Korman and Matron left the room. Kerr looked around at everyone who remained and said, "Got something to say you didn't want anyone else to hear?"

No one missed how Lucas glanced at Threnody. Quinton sighed. "Thren, you keeping secrets again?"

"Wasn't a secret Lucas shared until last night," Threnody said.

"Is that where he got the swollen lip?" Jason asked.

"As amusing as this conversation is, we've got business to discuss," Lucas said. "Tomorrow, Jason is going to teleport Threnody and Kerr to the Strykers Syndicate and retrieve my daughter."

Jason gaped at him. "I'm going to—what?"

"You have a daughter?" Quinton said.

"She's not born yet," Threnody said calmly, the only one other than Lucas who wasn't shocked by the announcement. "Lucas, I thought we'd get more time?"

"We can't afford to stay our hand. I want my daughter, Threnody. I trust you to get her for me."

"Who's the mother?" Kerr asked.

"Ciari." All three men glared at Lucas, who only shook his head. "It didn't happen like that. I didn't rape her."

"You wouldn't need to. You'd just have to mindwipe her."

"Shockingly enough, we discussed this issue as adults."

Kerr grimaced. "Ciari got brought before the World Court. How do you even know the fetus is alive?"

Lucas touched a finger to his jaw. "As Threnody so thoroughly pointed out last night, Ciari wouldn't risk her own child. Given the chance to save her, Ciari would take it. I have to believe that."

Maybe it was the quiet way he said the words. Maybe it was the faint hint of uncertainty in Lucas's voice when he had only ever been arrogantly assured. Either way, the Strykers didn't argue. Plans weren't set in stone and even Lucas wasn't immune to chance, despite Aisling's orders.

"We won't kill fellow Strykers," Threnody said.

"You handle this mission as you like, so long as you don't return empty-handed."

"I'm going with them," Quinton said.

Lucas shook his head. "You're getting biotubes put in tonight and you'll need a bit of recovery afterward. Jason can only help so much with that."

"Then put me in a biotank. I'm not staying behind."

Threnody stepped closer to her partner, putting a hand on his shoulder. "Quinton, no. Don't argue. I'm planning this mission, so you don't have to worry about me, okay? Things will work out."

If it were Lucas pressing the issue, Quinton would have argued. With Threnody giving the order, he kept his mouth shut. Shaking his head angrily, Quinton left the lab. Threnody gave the microtelekinetic a pointed look and Jason reluctantly followed Quinton.

Then it was just the three of them. Lucas picked up his datapad. "I need to show you something."

Threnody and Kerr approached with slow steps. Lucas tapped at the datapad for a few seconds before handing it to Threnody. Kerr looked over her shoulder, both of them staring down at the screen with its listing of encrypted files and several hundred names. The one highlighted was her own. The one above hers was Lucas's. More names were listed after hers. Carefully, she tapped the icon beside her name, and a command window popped up, asking for a password.

"What is this?" Threnody said.

Lucas leaned back and braced himself against the table. "Aisling."

Both Threnody and Kerr shot Lucas identical incredulous looks. He met their stares without blinking. Weeks on the run, following where he led, told them this wasn't a joke. Lucas didn't have a sense of humor.

"What's the password?"

Lucas shrugged. "I don't have it. That's your file, Threnody. Only you can unlock it."

"What are you talking about?"

"Type in the password. You know it, whether you realize it or not."

Threnody stared down at the datapad, studying the blank command window. She raised a finger to the keypad image, but didn't touch the screen. "What if you don't like what it reveals?"

Lucas shrugged one shoulder, but the tension in his body was impossible to miss. "It doesn't matter."

"Lucas."

"Threnody. *It doesn't matter.*" When she looked up at him, he held her gaze. "I'm not going to ruin what Aisling started. Maybe someone else will, or did, but it's not going to be me, and it's not going to be here. Not this time. I'll follow what she says, like I always have. Even if I don't like it."

He gave Threnody a strained, lopsided smile. "She told me to find you and you've been a right pain in the arse, Threnody. But I'm listening."

Threnody nodded slowly, then tapped out a string of numbers that represented the date of the first time Quinton was introduced as her field partner. The first time she got someone she could call family after becoming a soldier, even if it was only in the deepest part of her mind.

It was a wild guess, but the encrypted file unlocked. Opened. Began to play.

The camera was focused on a small table in a white room, with a woman on one end and a child hooked to machines on the other. The caption pinned to a corner gave a date and a location that made Threnody swallow hard. Kerr sucked in a sharp breath. In the room, the child turned her head to stare at the camera, and the image magnified on its own until bleached-out violet eyes were staring directly at them.

"Hello, Threnody," Aisling said over the sharp whine of machines.

Threnody almost dropped the datapad, too shocked to make sense of what she held in her hands. Kerr steadied her grip with his own hand, the pair of them looking at Lucas with horror in their eyes. Lucas stared them down, his gaze unwavering.

"She'll tell you what she wants," Lucas said. "And we'll listen."

It wasn't what they expected.

That didn't mean the knowledge hurt any less or that they had the right to walk away.

FIFTEEN

SEPTEMBER 2379
TORONTO, CANADA

A re we really doing this?" Jason asked. He ran a hand through his hair in frustration, shaking his head. "Are we really going to break in to the Strykers Syndicate and steal some unborn baby we can't be certain is even there?"

"I don't like it any more than you do, but it needs to be done," Kerr said. "How's Quinton?"

"He made it through the surgery without any problems. Threnody's with him right now." Jason rolled his eyes. "I told her I sped up the recovery time, but she didn't believe me."

"She believed you. She just wanted to see him for herself."

The two were in the station's small cafeteria, eating one last ration bar before they started their mission. They no longer wore skinsuits beneath their clothing. They couldn't carry any trace of their recent activities with them to Canada. They wore clothes borrowed from Matron's scavengers, all of them black, none of it traceable to a single environment. They carried no physical weapons, forced to rely on their powers alone for this mission.

The amount of downtime everyone had managed to grab wasn't enough to bring any of them up to full strength, but they were healing. Since leaving Buffalo they'd been eating as much as they could, sleeping whenever they got a chance, just trying to mentally heal enough so they wouldn't collapse under the stress. As if being forced to fight Strykers all over again wasn't stressful enough.

"For the record, I still don't like it," Jason said.

"For the record," Threnody said from behind him, "I don't care."

She sat down in a chair and Jason handed over a ration bar without asking. "How'd Quinton take being left behind?"

Threnody tore open the ration bar and took a bite. "He's not happy about it."

"You know he said he'd kill us if you came back with so much as a scratch? After all the effort I went through to boost his healing, that's the thanks I get."

"Thank you," Threnody said, the quiet sincerity in her voice impossible to miss. "I know it can't be easy to work on any of us. How are you holding up?"

"I'm hungry all the damn time and I've had more headaches since my shields came down than I did all last year. At the rate the side effects are growing, I'll need to start limiting use of my microtelekinesis if I want to live through the next few years."

"I told Lucas we needed more rest, but he's right. We're not going to get what we need until this is over, and waiting helps no one."

"Have you decided where you want to go in?" Kerr said, leaning back in his chair.

"Medical level," Threnody said.

"Logical. If Ciari took care of the baby before going in front of the World Court, then she probably had Jael do the extraction procedure."

"Her lab." Threnody kept talking around her food. "That's where the gestational unit has to be. Jael wouldn't risk leaving it unsecured where anyone could tamper with it."

"I can't teleport into her lab. That space changes all the time," Jason said.

"I know. I'll settle for the arrival room on the medical level."

"Her lab is halfway across that floor," Kerr said. "It's going to be a hard run to get there."

"I'm hoping we won't be doing a lot of fighting. It's the medical level. There's bound to be Strykers recuperating from Buffalo. I doubt they're up to our strength right now, crappy as it is, and I doubt everyone else would be willing to fight us around the injured. They don't have Jason and we're not aiming to kill anyone."

"Kind of sick of being the answer to everyone's problems," Jason said. "Kind of sick at the thought of using Strykers as human shields."

"We don't have a choice."

"I know. Briefing over?"

Threnody tossed her wrapper on the table and stood up. "Yeah. It's over."

"Quicker than the meeting yesterday. I like that."

Kerr and Jason got to their feet. Kerr pulled them both into a psi link with his telepathy even as Jason wrapped them in his telekinesis. Taking a breath, Jason visualized a place he hadn't seen in weeks but would never forget, and teleported out.

They arrived in a room that was at once familiar and not, the stark white walls of the place manned by Strykers wearing black-on-black BDUs. A telepath and telekinetic were on duty, nowhere near Kerr's or Jason's strength, but strong enough to shield against both men long enough for one to initiate an alarm.

"Let's go," Threnody said.

She jumped off the platform and ran for the door. It had locked at the first sound of the alarm, but that wasn't going to stop them. Threnody slammed her hand against the control panel, short-circuiting the door with her power. Jason wrenched it open telekinetically, and then they were in a hallway, racing past rooms that housed recuperating Strykers. Nurses, surgeons, and psi surgeons were scattered throughout the hall, none of them knowing what to make of the alarm going off. Only when they saw the three former Strykers marked for death did they figure it out.

An intense telepathic strike rammed into Threnody's mind, deflected by Kerr's shields, but she still felt the near miss reverberate through her thoughts. She stumbled, Jason grabbing for her with one hand to keep her steady.

If you kill even one Stryker, you won't leave this city tower alive, Jael snarled into their minds on a wide public 'path. *Stand down.*

Sorry, can't do that, Threnody said, letting the words sit at the very edge of her public mind for Jael to hear them. *We've got our orders.*

And we have ours.

Behind them came the crack of displaced air from a teleport, one right after the other. What felt like ropes of telekinesis wrapped around the three, searching for a way to hold them. Jason slammed his power through the foreign telekinesis and broke through easily enough, clearing their path.

Up ahead, a heavy security door blocked the way, with two Strykers standing before it. They didn't carry any guns, but they didn't have to.

The fire that burned near one teenager's hand was warning enough. He sent it in a controlled wave at them, blocking their view of the hall as it covered Jason's telekinetic shields completely.

Kerr focused his telepathy on the two Strykers. A telepathic strike cut cleanly through their shields and he knocked them unconscious. The fire faded; their problems didn't. Threnody skidded against the security door, slamming one hand on the control panel. Electricity sparked and popped beneath her palm, frying the system. Jason again telekinetically wrenched the door open.

They immediately got another faceful of fire that couldn't make it past Jason's shields. More 'path-oriented Strykers were gathering, slamming their individual powers against Kerr's shields. They weren't merged, but they didn't need to be. Against anyone else, the initial attacks would have shattered their defense. But the Strykers didn't know that Kerr's and Jason's Classifications had changed.

"We really don't have time for this," Jason said.

Threnody slammed one hand against the wall, electricity arcing outward down its length to knock several Strykers off their feet. Jason slammed his telekinesis forward, his power ripping down the hallway. It hit against bodies, knocking everyone to the ground with enough force to break bones. His power merged with Kerr's telepathic strike meant none of the Strykers in the hallway were getting up anytime soon.

Jason still wasn't used to his strength, however, and several of the Strykers he hit were slammed hard into whatever was at their back. In one case, a young teenage girl rammed her head against the corner of a nurse's desk. She left behind a splatter of blood as she slid to the floor, knocking over a few monitoring machines, and Jason skidded to a stop beside her, swearing.

"Jason!" Kerr yelled.

"Go," Jason said, even as he knelt down among unconscious and semi-conscious bodies. "I'll cover you from a distance."

"Don't touch her," a Stryker said from nearby as he struggled to stand. "You've already hurt her."

"She was in our way," Jason said even as he curled his hand around the back of the girl's head, palm pressed against the bloody wound there.

Jason was still connected to the others through Kerr's psi link, providing telekinetic shielding. Jason dropped all his mental shields, letting his power flood into the girl's body. He didn't care if people could read his intentions in his thoughts. He sank quickly into a world made up of blood and bone, rushing through the soft shadows of tissue and cell shapes into the flaring network of nerves that spanned the breadth of the brain.

He could see blood pooling, black stains in his vision that looked wrong. Jason blinked, felt everything lurch around him as he focused on that buildup of blood. He'd only had a few days of practice using his power like this. It wasn't enough time for him to trust it, but he was getting better at focusing. He teleported the blood out of the girl's brain, letting it splash onto the floor in thick droplets near his knee. She would need surgery, but he'd cleared her of immediate danger.

Jason came back to himself in a rush, the world solidifying into the hard angles of standard human eyesight. The emergency alarm that still shrieked through the air was now almost drowned out by the piercing sound of a bioscanner registering off the scale. He looked down and realized a few wires had tangled around his fingers, the electrodes sticking to his skin.

He glanced at the monitor lying on the floor. One of the nurses—human, judging by her lack of uniform—was staring in shock down at it. The machine didn't recognize the psi signature. It wasn't one the nurse had ever before seen.

"Get her to Marguerite," Jason told the youth who was on his knees now, staring at Jason with an unreadable look on his face.

Jason shoved himself to his feet, reaching for Kerr through the psi link. *I need a visual.*

Kerr gave it to him. Through Kerr's eyes Jason could see the hallway where Jael's lab was located, and the crowd that braced the other two on either side. Keiko was standing shoulder to shoulder with Jael in front of the lab door. Jason teleported into that small space with blood on his hands, automatically strengthening his shields as he arrived.

Jael's mind brushed up hard against Jason's mental shields and her face went ashen. "What happened to you?"

Jason didn't answer her. Threnody did. "Get out of the way."

"You come in here like you did, attacking us, and you think you can give *us* orders?" Keiko said.

"We didn't come to hurt anyone."

"Like hell you didn't."

"No one's dead," Jason said. "Everyone who tried to stop us will live."

Jael's telepathy slid over their mental shields, not attacking. Kerr followed her touch with ease, ready to defend in an instant. Jael could feel the difference in Kerr's power, so attuned as she'd lately been to an empathic touch.

"You're an empath," Jael said, stunned.

"Barely," Kerr said.

"Your shields?"

"Stable. Which means there's no one you can pull up who can match me or Jason."

The emergency alarm was still going off, the lights up above flashing their constant warning. Threnody caught Jael's gaze. "Is Ciari alive?"

Keiko glanced at Jael; whatever telepathic conversation they had was quick. Judging by the murderous look Keiko gave her, Jael disobeyed orders when she said, "Yes. She's alive."

It was all the assurance Threnody needed. *Kerr? Do it.*

Jael's head snapped back from Kerr's attack as he ripped open her shields and pulled from her recent memories the visual of her lab in its latest state. He shared that image with Jason.

Leave me behind, Threnody said when she felt Jason's telekinesis wrap around her.

What? Jason said. *Are you kidding? Quinton will kill me.*

Just do it.

Jason was used to obeying orders, not giving them. The two teleported out, leaving Threnody alone in the hallway with Keiko holding up Jael. Threnody felt Jason's telekinetic touch pull away, leaving her unshielded and surrounded by people who were prepared to see her dead.

We have the gestational unit, Kerr said. *Good luck.*

Then he was gone and she was alone in her mind.

Threnody raised her arms in surrender. She felt Keiko's power slam into her, telekinesis bruising her body. She hit the wall with enough force to feel her ribs crack. Threnody collapsed to the floor, struggling to breathe. Invisible pressure crawled over her throat, choking her into unconsciousness.

[SIXTEEN]

SEPTEMBER 2379
AMUNDSEN-SCOTT SOUTH POLE STATION, ANTARCTICA

"Well?" Lucas demanded.

"Don't rush me," Korman said curtly, carefully plugging in the last wire. The gestational unit's control board that monitored energy levels turned from the yellow of battery power to the bright blue of a solid electrical connection. Korman hummed to himself for a minute or two, the glitter from his optic replacements shifting as he studied the data. "No damage from the transfer. Everything is fine."

"Everything except the fact that you left Threnody behind," Quinton said, glaring at where Jason and Kerr stood on the other side of the lab table.

"She told me to," Jason said. "This was her mission and I wasn't going to argue her orders."

"Now you choose to obey without question?"

"Take this fight outside," Lucas said, not looking up from the readouts on his daughter's health. "Right now."

Quinton headed for the door, expecting the other two to follow. Knowing this conversation wasn't one that could be ignored, Kerr and Jason joined him out in the hallway. Without warning, Quinton grabbed Jason by the collar of his shirt and slammed him against the wall.

"What the fuck were you thinking?" he snarled into Jason's face.

Jason telekinetically shoved him away and Quinton stumbled backward. "I already told you. She wanted to stay."

"I don't care what she wanted. There's no reason for her to stay behind if you had Lucas's daughter."

"Ciari's alive," Kerr said with a shrug. "Reason enough."

Quinton glared at him. "What the hell is that supposed to mean?"

Kerr didn't seem concerned about Quinton's temper. "If Ciari's alive, then there's a chance we can reconnect with the Strykers."

"After today, I doubt that will happen," Jason said with a faint snort. He was staring at his left hand, still smeared with blood, and the expression on his face was pained. "They'll be on heightened alert after this."

Lucas pushed open the door to Korman's lab, coming into the hallway. Quinton focused his attention on Lucas. "We're getting Threnody back."

"That was never in doubt," Lucas said, letting the door shut behind him. "But I needed leverage if we're going to convince the Strykers to let us administer the nanites virus."

"So, you traded Threnody for your daughter?"

"And we'll trade their freedom for Threnody." Lucas met Quinton's glare without blinking. "I'm not leaving her behind, as you inelegantly put it. There is a reason for every single thing I do, and Threnody knows that. She knew what was required of her if Ciari still lived."

"You don't know what they'll do to her."

"I know she's still alive." Lucas tapped the side of his head. "I've got a shield wrapped around her mind, and I doubt your Syndicate officers will immediately hand Threnody over to the World Court. For one, the loyalty you Strykers have for each other is incredibly hard to break. I've mindwiped enough of your fellow Strykers after retrieval to vouch for that. For another, the World Court is going to have far greater problems to deal with than one escaped Stryker. The pirate feed goes live today."

Kerr grimaced at that news. "You're aiming to make the world riot."

"If the dregs of humanity choose to retaliate with violence after learning the truth the government's kept hidden from them, then so much the better." Lucas shrugged, as if the oncoming societal upheaval didn't bother him in the least. "It will make it more difficult for the government to continue with the launch."

"I thought you didn't care if they made it to Mars Colony," Quinton said. "I thought you didn't care if the government left us all behind. We get half the seed bank, they get the *Ark* and some other planet."

"Things change," Kerr said, refusing to look at Lucas, even if he couldn't stop thinking about what a dead precognitive child had said in some old recorded file.

"Yes," Lucas agreed with a faint, twisted smile. "And that's what Jason is going to be doing to my daughter."

Jason frowned. "What?"

"My daughter needs to grow up with your type of power, and you are going to make sure that happens."

"What do you want me to do? Alter her DNA?" Jason gave Lucas a blatantly disbelieving look. "I don't know what I'm doing with this power, Lucas. Do you honestly want to risk an unborn child—*your* unborn child—by having me perform some act which I can't guarantee will work?"

"Psions are born with the genetic ability to control their powers. It's instinct that turns into conscious control. Why do you think Kerr had such problems with his shields? Why do you think you're capable of reading as human on the mental grid after I showed you how to do it once? We're born into bodies that are geared towards supporting our minds."

"That's different than me trying to apply my power to something like this," Jason argued.

"It's worked on all of us at one point or another since we left Buffalo."

"All of you are alive. You aren't some cluster of multiplying cells."

"Which is exactly the best time to do this," Lucas said. "Her DNA is still very malleable. Right now is the only chance you've got to make her into what I need her to be. What *we* need her to be."

Jason glared at him. "You don't know that I can do this."

"Yes, I do." Lucas's voice was implacable, his gaze unwavering as he stared Jason down. "And you will."

"Why? Because Aisling told you I would?"

"Jays," Kerr interrupted. "You stopped to help a fellow Stryker back on the medical level. Do you believe what you did saved her?"

Jason let out a harsh breath. "Maybe."

"That's not an answer."

Jason scrubbed a hand over his face, not looking at any of them. "Yeah, I do."

"Then you need to do this."

After a moment, Jason pushed past Lucas to walk back into the lab, letting the old door slam shut behind him.

[SEVENTEEN]

SEPTEMBER 2379
JOHANNESBURG, SOUTH AFRICA

When Africa died, it took history with it. A continent of deserts and jungles, Saharan plains and winding rivers, teeming with a biodiversity of life that spawned the human race in all its forms, it should have been worth saving. Records existed, Samantha knew, of a time when people tried. Drought, desertification, poaching, and stubborn human greed destroyed it, just as humans destroyed the rest of the world.

Too many places in Africa were bombed to ruins. Johannesburg was no different. The surface was jagged wreckage and displaced melted slag. People lived among the remains if they weren't lucky enough to live in bunkers.

Resources were provided by the government. Johannesburg only had a single SkyFarms tower, heavily guarded by the government. Combodetox water plants desalinized and filtered out toxins from the polluted Indian Ocean before the water was transported inland on maglev trains. The city limits incorporated bunkers, not sealed towers, and the skin trade was a currency most people used in some form or another alongside credit chips. Survival came with a cost and always would.

Samantha touched a finger to the dark glasses that sat on her nose. Translucent bioware woven through clear synthskin was stuck to her facial recognition points, hiding her identity from the government's security grid. Matron's stockpile of the tech was large, most of it top-notch. Samantha had to admit that Lucas's ability to find useful people was on par with Nathan's.

"Smells like lunch," Kristen said. The girl crouched in the dirt just inside the broken entrance to one of the converted ruins, watching the oblivious humans pass them by. The dilapidated building they were in leaned at a precarious angle. Since it hadn't fallen down in the last decade or so, Samantha considered the odds of its staying up to be on their side.

Johannesburg smelled of too many people living in too small of a place, with the harsh scent of toxins rolling over the flat, devastated land on the back of the wind. It was making Samantha sick.

"You only think you're hungry," Samantha said.

"It's waning, Sammy-girl." Kristen canted her head to the side, her own dark glasses sliding down her nose. "Things are falling apart."

It was a warning, plain and simple. Nathan once predicted that Kristen would never live to see the age of eighteen. Judging by how skewed Kristen's mind was, even with a borrowed framework of sanity, Samantha knew Nathan had been right.

"Come along, Kristen."

Samantha grabbed at the collar of Kristen's skinsuit. She was the only one still wearing it; everyone else wore street clothes. It made hauling her around easier and made it more difficult for Kristen to cut into her own skin.

It's a pity we can't attach bioware to it, Samantha thought absently. *Shocking her into obedience was always so much easier than having a row with her.*

Samantha hauled her unruly sister into the depths of the building where Fahad and his assistants had set up a portable work terminal with Novak's help. The media pirate was barking out orders to the men and women around him, ruthlessly running the show, as he had for so long. He gleaned rumors from conspiracy streams and paired them with hard facts from anonymous sources to create a whole picture. The government had a bounty on his head for the information he streamed to the unregistered masses, inciting riots and spreading truth the World Court could ill afford. What he was about to broadcast next would trump all his previous endeavors.

"You just gonna stand there and watch?" Novak said as Samantha put herself and Kristen against the wall, out of the way.

Samantha slid her power through Novak's mind, uncaring of the sudden pain she caused the man.

I am not my brother, Samantha said as she increased the presence of her telepathy in his thoughts to a critical degree. *Speak to me like that again, and you won't live beyond those words. Do I make myself clear?*

"Very," Novak gasped out.

Samantha released him, ignoring the faint trickle of blood that dripped out of Novak's nose. Novak turned his back on the sisters and moved out of physical, it not mental, reach. Kristen watched him retreat with a hungry look on her face. Samantha made sure she had a firm hold on her sister.

Lucas had charged them to oversee this mission with the knowledge that Johannesburg had both Warhounds and Strykers on the ground. Samantha was needed for defense, but was uncertain of her strength. Recovering from the trauma of Buffalo had taken days. For Samantha, it had meant the restructuring of her mind from the bottom up.

In Buffalo, Lucas had ripped out of her mind layers of false thoughts that had seemed real, revealing a mindwipe that had forged her into whatever Lucas needed her to be beneath Nathan's seemingly solid control. Samantha wasn't sure when Lucas had implanted this loyalty in her, she just knew it was there, that it was foreign, and she could do nothing to break it. Odd to sift through one's own mind and not recognize it. Odder still to realize that maybe it was better this way.

What she still couldn't come to terms with was the hole that had been punched in her mind where her twin once resided. Even Lucas couldn't make her forget eighteen years of living with Gideon in her head. If she was grieving for her loss, she didn't know where that grief was.

"We're ready," Fahad said, a satisfied bite to his words. "Let's get this uploaded and begin. I can't wait to see how it all goes down."

Samantha pulled Kristen to her when the girl would have followed Fahad's assistants around the portable work terminals. Hacking into the media streams took effort, but the results were always interesting. Samantha had seen the outline of what Fahad was going to report. That it would be picked up on all conspiracy and public streams meant the government wouldn't be able to keep it hidden, that the information they would be disseminating would never die.

Fahad took his place before the camera, wearing the same sort of street clothes as the rest of them, his face covered by a shapeless headscarf that was lined with bioware to hide his identity and the same sort of dark glasses Samantha wore. Technology wasn't the only detail he employed—a quick retreat was always on the table. Their bolt hole was a squeeze in the back between two collapsed walls, out into a thin alley that linked to a market square always teeming with people.

Samantha loosened her grip on Kristen's shoulder, fingers tapping against the other girl's skinny frame. *Patience.*

Novak finished uploading the program with the help of Fahad's assistants, having worked on the actual hack on the flight over to get faster access to the public streams. They were able to access the backdoor in minutes, not hours.

"We're reporting on the edge," Fahad said, altered voice coming out strong. "If you're hearing this, seeing this, then it's a reminder that the government doesn't own all of us. Here's to the fallen, to the righteous, to Allah, who guides us. The government can't control everyone, but control was never their final goal.

"The World Court has lied to everyone since the Border Wars. The Fifth Generation Act is a long-running con for the rich to buy their way into the promised land. Their hope isn't our hope. What succors them won't succor us. How many people have died, will die, for their greed? The rest of the world, if they have their way."

Fahad gestured off camera to one of his assistants. The woman tapped out a few commands into her console. Fahad continued, "This is a picture of the Paris Basin, where the capital of France once stood. As you can see, it's not all ruins and water. It's not just a deadzone, but a hidden lifeline." The picture switched to a closer magnification, rows and rows of shuttles, waiting to launch on a sleek ramp. "What you see is the government's real plan, their way off this rock to the stars.

"Leftover nukes haven't wrecked this area, no matter the lies the government tells. The truth is that our ancestors didn't own one planet—they owned *two*. A colony ship is docked near the moon waiting to ferry the government's chosen people into paradise."

Another hand wave and Samantha knew the satellite pictures of the *Ark* were being added to the mix. She could see them on the vidscreen over Novak's shoulder.

"But I tell you this, my brothers and sisters, that we—we who have bled and died for want of a better life—*we* have been betrayed, for we will not be on those shuttles. We will never see that ship."

Samantha had seen the *Ark* before, when she was a child and Nathan had shown her what was promised to them. The pixels of a stream did the colony ship no justice, the nongovernment-controlled satellite providing the pictures old and barely functioning. But it still showed the massive scale of the *Ark,* large enough to take many citizens, but not all, to a new life.

It was a new life she had dreamed of once.

"This is the proof people have died to uncover. We deserve more than the government will leave us. We deserve more than scraps and walls and beatings and graves," Fahad said, staring into the camera. "The government talks about laws and resources, as if this world was all we were left with, when they knew of some place better. They say we aren't meant for some distant alien shore. I say, who are they to destroy our future? Who in the gutters will fight for it?"

The connection cut off, the actual feed of the pirate stream barely two minutes long, but it was two minutes that would live in infamy. Samantha knew that better than most. She had played at being human for her entire life and knew exactly how the registered elite would react in the face of such a reveal. The rest of the world, those who had never met the requirements of the Fifth Generation Act, would either take the stream as truth and riot, or do nothing and keep living the only life they knew.

"It's done," Fahad said, yanking off his headscarf and glasses.

A giddy, satisfied smile sat on his face, one born of pride and anticipation. The expression turned to horror as he watched Kristen approach one of his assistants. Kristen pressed her hand to the young man's head and ripped through his mind with her empathy. The man's scream lasted only a second or two, a sound that shredded their ears before it cut off.

"Your words are useful," Kristen said as she turned her head to face the others, gleaming dark blue eyes full of malice. "You aren't. At least, not anymore."

Fahad and his people crumpled before Kristen's unwavering onslaught, the hunger for sanity driving her. Jason's shields hadn't been enough. Nothing would be. The cracks in her mind were widening, and no one could stop her descent back into insanity.

Novak put his back against the wall. Five bodies lay scattered around the area where the pirate stream played in a continuous loop. It would run until someone on the government's end managed to hack it out of existence, which he doubted they could, because the damage was done.

"I knew Lucas was gonna kill us. Matron never listens to me," Novak said, curling in on himself as he hid his face. Samantha tore her gaze from the vidscreen and the loop, to where Kristen was approaching Novak with a dreamy smile on her face.

"Don't kill that one," Samantha reminded her sister, erecting a mental shield between Kristen and Novak's mind.

"Oh, fuck, why not?" Novak asked, head jerking up, eyes wide with fear. His own or Kristen's, Samantha didn't really care.

"We needed a message people would believe in. Fahad delivered it perfectly."

"So you killed him for doing a good job?"

"We have the message. We don't need the messenger, especially not one with traitorous thoughts. Now get up," Samantha said, already stretching her telepathy through the mental grid beneath the shield of static human minds, reaching for Lucas. "Lucas still has use for you, so stop yelling. Kristen won't kill you."

Kristen's smile was wide and vicious. "Yet."

Novak closed his mouth.

Did you finish? Lucas said as he drew Samantha into a psi link, suddenly there in her thoughts.

We're done, Samantha said. *Pirate stream is running, information is uploaded, Fahad and his people are dead.*

Good. Show me the others.

Obediently, Samantha looked at Kristen and Novak. Her vision doubled, the light from the vidscreens wrapping everything in halos as Lucas stared through her eyes. Lucas's telekinesis settled over her and pulled.

In an instant, all three were gone, leaving behind corpses, the voice of a dead man, and evidence of a betrayal that society wasn't strong enough to survive intact.

"They say we aren't meant for some distant alien shore. I say, who are they to destroy our future? Who in the gutters will fight for it?"

PART FOUR
CLARITY

SESSION DATE: 2128.08.13

LOCATION: Institute of Psionics Research

CLEARANCE ID: Dr. Amy Bennett

SUBJECT: 2581

FILE NUMBER: 750

"We can find others like you," the doctor says as she stares down at her notes. "We're learning what makes you different from us. It's in your blood. In your brain."

"In my mind," Aisling concedes. "We're different."

"Not human."

"Human enough." Aisling coils a wire around one finger, never looking away from the doctor's face. "Do you want to know a secret?"

"Of course."

"It never works when those like me are free at the beginning." She raises a finger and presses it to her lips. "Shh. Don't tell anyone."

The doctor folds her hands together over the table, knuckles white. The hum of machines fills the air and echoes on the feed. "Your parents signed you over to us. Did you know that?"

"You told them to."

"Where is your brother, Aisling?"

"You can't have him." The girl smiles; a slow, precise motion beneath bleached-out violet eyes. "You asked me once to save you. This is how I do it."

EIGHTEEN

SEPTEMBER 2379
LONGYEARBYEN, NORWAY

The government shuttle came in from the south, flying across Spitsbergen. Four teams of quads were strapped in for the flight out of The Hague. They escorted a single man into the cold of the Arctic, a man who would have preferred to remain in Japan. For the first time since the government started security shifts after the island was rediscovered, the watch team in the north had missed their check-in.

Elion kept his attention focused on his datapad, glancing up only occasionally at the map on the hologrid to check their progress. He was a politician, not a soldier, and the utilitarian shuttle they were traveling in didn't have the first-class comforts used by elite society. The skinsuit he wore beneath his clothes itched around his joints, but was necessary considering the environment they were heading into.

What the hell could have happened up here? Elion thought to himself. *This post has never missed a check-in, not once.*

Heir to the Athe Syndicate and his father's seat on the World Court, Elion came from a family that prided itself on science over all else and survived the Border Wars because of it. Their contributions to the world that came after were needed, if highly selective. Their forays into space were key to the World Court's plans, but they would never be as highly regarded as the Serca family.

The Serca Syndicate had helped the government establish SkyFarms Inc. after the Border Wars, using forgotten technology and salvaged seeds pulled from the Svalbard Global Seed and Gene Bank. The Athe Syndicate had lost its bid on that project, and the Sercas got the bulk of the credit for those ventures, second only to the government. Elion's family was still bitter about the issue. Elion wondered if the Sercas would get the bulk of the blame this time around as well.

"How much longer?" he asked the pilot.

"ETA thirty minutes."

Less than an hour before they found answers. The communications officer had been hailing the watch team since they took to the air, and not once had he received a response. The lack of contact was worrisome, and Elion wasn't sure what to expect. He was exceptional when it came to anticipating people. He had to be if he was going to succeed his father on the World Court, but he could never have anticipated this.

The shuttle landed not in the airfield west of Longyearbyen, but on the outskirts of the small town itself. A dangerous endeavor, as the ground was uneven and untested, but they didn't have time to waste and no Strykers were contracted for this mission. Teleportation wasn't an option. Looking out the shuttle's windshield through the floodlights, Elion felt as if he were going to be sick.

One of the buildings still used by the government had been blown up, its charred remains an ugly black spot against the steel gray of the rest of the buildings. Bodies were scattered around the area, already bloated from decomposition.

"Let us go first, sir," the most senior quad member told him. Her dark eyes didn't look away from Elion's own green ones. "You should stay here."

"By all means," Elion said around a numb tongue. "I'll remain."

The shuttle's side hatch opened. It was cold outside, the chrono indicating that it was a little after midnight. Elion's sense of time was already thrown off-kilter from being teleported to the World Court out of Sapporo before being flown north. This didn't help.

He'd been hoping it was an electrical problem, a breakdown in the communication system. It was so much worse than that, Elion decided, when the quads returned twenty minutes later, their recon finished.

"Everyone's dead," the woman from before said. "Looks like the attack was quick and brutal. We only saw signs of one shuttle. Security system is a mess. We can't pull anything from it."

Elion stared at the quad blankly before taking in a deep breath. "We're going. Now. Take me to the airfield."

The pilot got the shuttle in the air again a few minutes later and headed for the nearby airfield. They landed and the quads were the first out, doing recon. They found evidence of activity, but no evidence on who might have attacked the outpost. When Elion remotely plugged in the codes to stand down the artillery turrets, he discovered they were already off-line.

Sweat broke out across his face, cold and clammy. He swallowed the taste of bile and led the quads up the winding road to his destination on the mountain. It was a hard slog, but Elion refused to slow his pace, breathing heavily as they climbed.

Getting soft, Elion thought. *I figured I could handle this.*

If the quads were surprised by the metal wedge sticking out of the mountainside, they didn't show it. The ramp that bridged the road and the doors was newly broken in some places, as if a great weight had been applied after decades of neglect. Elion slid forward on careful feet, testing its stability. The ramp creaked and groaned, sounding as if it were about to break, but it held.

The control panel was dead. A few centimeters' worth of space separated the doors.

Elion staggered forward, one shaking hand sliding through that space. "It's unlocked," he whispered. "It's *unlocked.*"

The quads helped him haul the doors open. Lights snapped on, one after the other as they stepped into the tunnel, illuminating a space recently disturbed. Elion pressed his hand against the wall for support.

"Sir?" one of the soldiers said. "Let us canvass the area for your safety."

"*Iie,*" Elion said, the word ripping out of him.

Breathing harshly, Elion pitched himself forward, long legs eating up the distance between the entrance and the next set of doors. Like the first set, this one was unlocked; all of them were. His chest constricted with panic as they reached the first storage vault.

"*Iie,*" Elion choked out as he stared inside. "*Iie! Masaka . . . shinjirannee!*" Ransacked. Gone.

Boxes and packets were strewn across the floor, whole bays empty of supplies. Someone had broken into the most secret and secure place on earth and stolen half the government's most precious assets.

Elion felt sick as he shoved his way through the quads and ran to the next vault, finding the same scene. Hurrying down the rows of storage units and shelves, Elion couldn't think. His mind was a white-hot burn of panic at the realization that everything the government had worked for had become meaningless.

Behind him, one of the quads bent down to pick up a silver-foil packet from the mess near his feet. "What the hell is an *Attalea speciosa*?"

The soldier stumbled over the words, his tongue unfamiliar with the name.

"Hell if I know," a woman said as she kicked at a box.

Elion did. Oh, not the species, but he knew what were in these packets, what had been stored here and stolen, all their careful planning, all their generations' worth of work—gone.

"They're seeds," Elion said, stumbling through the remains. "They're *everything*."

He couldn't breathe in the face of what they had lost. It didn't matter that some of the inventory remained, that they still had two-thirds of the terraforming machines. It didn't matter because someone outside the government had discovered this place.

Elion didn't know how he was going to explain this to the World Court.

[NINETEEN]

SEPTEMBER 2379
LONDON, UNITED KINGDOM

Of his ordeal in Buffalo, Gideon Serca remembered screaming wind and acid rain, a street lit by lights, and two men standing in his way. Remembered his twin and *I'm sorry* and how nothing would be the same again.

When Gideon eventually regained consciousness, he was alone in his mind. Eighteen years of his twin rummaging around in his head, a psi link between them that he thought would never be severed, had skewed his sense of the world. Samantha had carved it out to save some worthless Stryker. Its absence felt like a bottomless pit in his mind and he hated her for that.

Victoria had done what she could to repair his mind. In saving him, she had killed herself through overuse of her telepathy. Gideon's mind continued to build off Victoria's repairs. He needed aftercare, but wouldn't get it. The only person strong enough to halve the recovery time in the Warhound ranks was Nathan, and Nathan wasn't going to coddle him.

Sitting in Nathan's office, Gideon studied his father. Neither of them had spoken while they watched the pirate stream on the vidscreen. The conspiracy-mongers were out in force, downloads crashing server farms across the planet. The world press was trying to contain the information on the government's orders, but they were failing.

"How did he do it?" Gideon finally asked.

Once, Nathan would have ignored his son. He no longer had that luxury. Gideon was Nathan's sole remaining heir and most powerful subordinate. Sharing every last detail with the eighteen-year-old Class II telekinetic who would someday succeed him was now a necessity. He could no longer force Gideon to use his power more than was considered safe to survive. Nathan was going to have to find other Warhounds to take up the slack.

"You remember the Stryker with the natal shields that Lucas took with him out of the Slums?" Nathan said, his attention still riveted on the pirate stream.

"Jason Garret, yes. I've read his file."

"We're still pulling details from the fight in Buffalo out of everyone's memories. I believe that Stryker is more than just a Class V telekinetic."

"I don't know what you're talking about. I fought him in the Slums. He was only a telekinetic, and not a very good one."

It was questionable how Nathan would react to being argued with, but Gideon could no longer remain silent. He'd been third in line to this post, never expecting to hold it, not until Lucas walked away. Samantha, bare minutes older than he was, never seemed to want it, but would have taken the position if offered. If required. It was his now, as the last child Nathan had left, the last Serca that would follow Nathan into space. An heir to whatever Nathan would build out of Mars Colony and the unsuspecting humans who were seeking refuge there. Gideon was determined not to squander his chance.

"The mental grid buckled, for lack of a better description." Nathan tapped his fingers against the hard shine of his desk, command windows popping up with each precise pressure against the touch-sensitive controls of the console. "Tracking him became impossible afterwards. Lucas must have shown him how to read as human on the mental grid."

Gideon frowned. "The mental grid doesn't buckle. It can't."

"It did." Nathan coolly met Gideon's gaze. "Whatever secondary power Jason might have, its strength is off the charts. He can't be solely categorized as a Class V, or even a Class I."

"A Class I has been the highest rank handed out to psions for decades. The only Class higher is a Class 0," Gideon said. "And the only ones ever given that ranking are precognitives. You know how rare those psions are."

"In our entire history, there have only been three precogs. None of them have been dual or triad psions, and all died before the age of five. It's impossible that Jason is a precog."

"Then what do you think he is?"

"What Lucas never was."

Gideon opened his mouth, then closed it. He couldn't hide his surprise, nor the brief spurt of jealousy. Everyone knew Lucas hadn't turned out to be what Nathan needed, no matter the amount of gene splicing that helped form his genetics. Psion DNA was difficult to work with and the results were unpredictable. Lucas was born a triad psion instead of a microtelekinetic, and he'd been living with that failure all his life.

"Can you be certain?" Gideon asked. "How could Lucas have known about this? About any of it?"

"Only Lucas can answer that question. This"—Nathan gestured at the feed, which was repeating itself—"is Lucas's doing. Everything from here on out will be Lucas's doing, and countering it is going to be difficult. Some of the public will believe this information, and there are those who will not. Who *cannot*. Regardless, preparing for the launch just got more complicated."

"What do you need from me?"

"I want Jason Garret," Nathan said flatly. "I want his power for use on

Mars Colony. You will track him down and retrieve him. Which means a visit to the Strykers Syndicate is in order, since Lucas has proven impossible to pin down. They'll have better records than we do on their missing Strykers. Also, I want you to determine whether or not they are dealing under the table with Lucas."

"If I do this for you, will you finally trust me?"

Nathan's gaze cut into Gideon. "That has no bearing on what I require from you right now."

"I think it does."

"Considering the results I've wanted for the past two years, and which neither you nor your sister could provide, you aren't in any position to demand anything from me. If Lucas was dead, things would most certainly be different, and you wouldn't be living in his shadow."

Gideon straightened in his seat. "Then perhaps you should have done it yourself."

"You place a lot of faith in the idea that I won't kill you," Nathan said, sliding behind Gideon's mental shields with a dexterity that belied his age.

"You need me," Gideon said, flinching against the pain in his head, but he didn't look away from his father's face. "You've got no one else to succeed you. I'm all you have left."

"You are not what I require."

"None of us ever were. Now there's a psion out in the world who is, and it's your choice not to hunt him down directly. You want us to use back channels, and I don't know if that will be enough." Gideon lifted his chin, defiance in every line of his body. "I think you could find him, if you really wanted to. But it would cost you, wouldn't it, Nathan? It would cost you in effort and in power and in years. You're too close to your promised land to risk it, so you risk us instead."

Nathan studied his third child, telepathy sliding through thoughts that Gideon didn't bother to hide. "The arrogance of youth has always been annoying. You can't kill me, Gideon."

"I don't want to."

"Yet." The look that settled on Nathan's face could almost be described as pride. "I think you're worth it after all."

Gideon's smile was all teeth. "Thank you."

"Now show me you deserve it and bring back that Stryker."

The pressure of Nathan in Gideon's mind leveled off. "Will anyone in the Strykers Syndicate be expecting us?"

"No."

"I'll need a telepath," Gideon said, wishing he didn't. Working with someone who wasn't his twin was going to be strange.

"Warrick is being briefed."

"I need someone stronger than a Class IV."

"He'll have others in merge with him if things turn out messy." Nathan glanced at the chrono ticking away on the vidscreen. "I have a meeting in two hours and need to prep for it. Keep me updated. You're dismissed."

Gideon left, teleporting to the private levels of the city tower that housed the Serca Syndicate. A faint twinge of pain blossomed in the back of his head at the use of his power, a reminder that he wasn't completely healed yet. If he could have taken another few days to recuperate, he would have. Except Nathan needed him and that need came before Gideon's health.

Gideon stepped off the arrival platform. He headed for a briefing room down the hall and found Warrick Sinclair finishing up with an operations officer. The Class IV telepath was with two other telepaths, Mercedes Vargas and James Olsen, Class VII and Class V respectively. Their lower rankings would bolster Warrick's in the merge. When the operations officer left the room and Gideon stepped inside, Warrick and the other two stood.

"Sir," Warrick said. "Good to have you back."

Gideon nodded at the acknowledgment. "You know we're switching targets. Looking for this Stryker is going to be as difficult as looking for Lucas. Maybe worse. Were you ever assigned to track Lucas?"

"Once. Nothing came of it."

"I've got some defensive tricks we were both taught as high-Classed psions, and I know how Samantha looked for him during her missions. I'll give them to you. We're assuming Lucas shared them with the Strykers he's allied with."

"This Stryker we're after. Is he the one who fucked up the mental grid?"

"That's the working theory. Were you in Buffalo?"

"No, I stayed behind in Toronto until I got called back here. Mercedes was there."

Gideon turned his attention on the slight young woman standing beside Warrick. "Do you have the target's psi signature?"

"No, sir," Mercedes said. "When that power hit the mental grid, it didn't stay static. It changed and kept changing until it was cut off."

"We've got his original psi signature in our files," Gideon said. "And I've got memories of the feel of them from Samantha in my head. See if you can't meld the two with the one that appeared after the fight in Buffalo."

Mercedes pressed her mind against Gideon's shields, her power completely alien to the feel of Samantha's telepathy. With vicious force, Gideon shoved his thoughts and memories of his twin to the back of his mind, compartmentalizing the loss. Regret had no room in war.

He had natal shields? Mercedes asked, surprised. Swiftly, she shared the information with the other two telepaths.

Gideon thought about what Nathan had said, why they'd been assigned this mission, and reached his own conclusion. *Not anymore.*

Warrick stayed linked with Mercedes. *Combining the two will be difficult.*

"We'll have some time to work on that in Toronto before we drop in on the Strykers," Gideon said as Warrick left Gideon's mind. "Get your gear and meet back here in fifteen minutes."

The three telepaths left. Gideon looked down at his hands and only then noticed that both were shaking. It took effort to make them stop.

Samantha was no longer there to remind him. He needed to remember to do it for himself.

[TWENTY]

The meeting of the Serca Syndicate's subsidiaries started precisely at noon. The agenda, however, had changed. Sydney Athe, the patriarch of the Athe Syndicate and family, looked Nathan straight in the eye. Beyond him, the pirate stream played on the vidscreen embedded in the wall.

"Who leaked those shots?" Sydney demanded, not caring that he was nothing more than Nathan's subordinate now and not someone to be wooed.

"It doesn't matter," Nathan said, voice cool. "They were given to the public. The fallout of this will be dealt with by the World Court. I'm sure Travis can handle it."

Anger flashed over Sydney's face at the mention of his son. "It will become our problem once people discover that it was my company which enabled our return to space."

"Your company is owned by mine now. I'll deal with the problem." Nathan smiled tightly. "You're here to be introduced as the newest member and to affirm the schedule that the World Court has laid down. Due to the unfortunate revelation of the Paris Basin, this meeting is now about protecting our investments."

"You promised us berths on that colony ship," a woman halfway down the long table said.

"And those berths remain. Unless, of course, the World Court's requirements force me to pare down my lists." Nathan shrugged. "The launch date currently stands at the end of September and running into October. It was moved up almost a month by order of the World Court. I would be surprised if they don't move it again considering the latest development. Right now, authorized registered citizens are being moved to transport points."

"Do they know why?" Sydney said. His gaze flickered over to the vid-feed of the stream in question.

"No, but they'll figure it out. The average citizen can't reach Paris. That entire country is a deadzone. Physical proof of what's going on will be hard to come by, but it will be found. As much as we would like for the government to keep this and other information hidden, that won't happen."

Of those sitting at the table, only Sydney knew Nathan's true genetic identity. He also knew that Nathan's heir was no longer Lucas, something Nathan hadn't yet publically confirmed. Right now, Nathan didn't need his son to take center stage on any issue, and for all that he was a reluctant supporter of Nathan's goals, Sydney knew better than to threaten with the truth.

"I want all of you to start winding down your individual companies immediately. Try to keep your efforts out of the media," Nathan said, gaze sweeping across the table. He thought about how much easier it would be if he could simply mindwipe everyone into obedience. Unfortunately, all those seated at the conference table with him had a bioware net grafted to their brain, which meant it would take daylong individual meetings with each to perform the necessary psi surgery on them. That was time he no longer had.

"That's going to be difficult given the current crisis," someone said from the far end of the table.

"That is not my problem," Nathan said. "I want it done. Make sure you remind the people cleared for the transport points that if they speak about the launch, they lose their place on the shuttles."

"We'll remind them," Sydney said.

"Good. Let's move on to the next issue."

The meeting should have taken hours. It didn't. They weren't forty minutes into their agenda, the tea and coffee barely lukewarm, when a sharp knock on the conference room door interrupted the conversation.

"Sir," Nathan's secretary said as she stepped inside. "You have an up-link."

"I'm busy," Nathan said. "It can wait."

"Sir, it's from The Hague."

Which could only mean one person. Nathan refused to let emotion show on his face as he excused himself from the proceedings.

"It's a secure uplink on their end," the woman said.

"I'll take it in my office."

It took roughly five minutes for him to make it to his private office, going by lift. He couldn't teleport, not with so many people around. When Nathan finally arrived, he opened the uplink on his desk terminal and then Erik's face was filling the vidscreen.

"To what do I owe this meeting?" Nathan asked.

"We have a problem," Erik said flatly.

"Yes, I've seen the pirate stream. There is—"

"That's not what I'm talking about. The quads up north missed their designated check-in two days ago."

Nathan kept the annoyance out of his voice through long practice. "Why am I only being notified of this now?"

"The World Court doesn't bow to you, Nathan," Erik said, voice cold and vicious. "This didn't become your problem until we had solid evidence that the seed bank was broken into. Half the supplies are gone. *That* is why I am calling you."

For a second, Nathan couldn't breathe. Surprise did not come naturally, as Nathan prided himself on knowing the world's secrets. How he had missed seeing this, knowing this, was beyond him. His team of Warhounds situated in Longyearbyen should have warned him.

Lucas.

Every time his son had infiltrated Serca Syndicate branches and subsidiary companies over the past two years, stealing disparate amounts of information that never added up, Nathan had been left wondering why. Nathan mentally ripped through everything he knew about Lucas's actions during his time on the run. Just a vast sleight of hand when the real goal was so much bigger—a psion with a coveted power and supplies to feed a world. If Lucas wanted to buy his way into power, that would be enough incentive to make anyone agree.

Lucas never had any intention of leaving Earth. He wasn't planning an insurrection on Mars. Nathan could see that now, could see what his son was striving for. The release of evidence about the Paris Basin was merely a distraction. The World Court would have to deal with the fallout of that before pursuing the robbery of the one thing left in the world that was absolutely priceless. The seeds weren't scheduled to be moved until the week of the actual launch to alleviate the risks of transfer from the environment they'd been stored in for so long.

"What do you want from me?" Nathan said after a few seconds of silence.

Erik let out a harsh laugh. "I'm going into closed session with the rest of the World Court to hammer out a new timeline for the launch. We're pushing it up again and it's going to be brutal. *You* are going to Spitsbergen to help Elion with the transfer of everything left up there. I'm sending a small contingent of Strykers as security."

Nathan thought about how easy it would be to end Erik's life. Unfortunately, murder wasn't always the best course of action. Getting rid of Erik now would only bring more chaos, and Nathan had enough problems to deal with already. Later, he could weigh the risk of the president's early death.

"When did you mobilize the Strykers?" Nathan said.

"An hour ago."

"I'm in the middle of a meeting that I can cut short, but the world press has been requesting a statement since the pirate stream showed up. I need to make one."

"Don't," Erik said. "I've already ordered most Syndicates to keep silent on the matter. When the World Court finally comes to a decision on how to handle this fucked-up mess, you'll get your orders."

The uplink cut out, leaving Nathan no option but to play by human rules.

[TWENTY-ONE]

SEPTEMBER 2379

TORONTO, CANADA

The room was white.

For a long moment, Ciari thought she was dreaming, that the colorlessness of the place was due to her mind dying. Recognition came slowly to her, of where she was, who she was.

She couldn't remember why that was important.

"You're a mess," a quiet voice said from nearby. "I can't fix you this time around. I'm sorry."

Ciari moved her head a little, just enough to see the person standing next to her bedside. The petite black woman wore white medical scrubs, thin dreads pulled back away from an angular face.

"Jael," Ciari said, the name sliding through her thoughts. Her voice was rough, tongue dry, as if she hadn't moved her mouth in days, which was probably the case.

"Yes," Jael said as she stepped forward. She carried a tiny cup and proceeded to feed Ciari ice chips until the dryness of her throat faded. Eventually, Jael set the cup aside. "How do you feel?"

Ciari watched as Jael crossed her arms over her chest, fingers digging into her uniform. The skin over her knuckles was ashy and drawn, the expression on the other woman's face ruthlessly neutral. Except—Ciari could see the tightness in her jaw, the way her mouth curved ever so slightly upward at one corner, the way her eyes were just a shade too wide. Tiny details that most people would miss, except Ciari had spent her entire life reading the emotionality of the human body.

Only now, she didn't know what it meant.

"I don't know," Ciari said. "How should I feel?"

Jael closed her eyes briefly, expression twisting enough for Ciari to recognize the look for what it was. It was a struggle to define it, to know it, despite the long association with the other woman.

Pain.

It still didn't make sense to her. Which told her, more than anything else, that something was horribly wrong. She waited for the panic to come, the fear, but it never did.

"Do you remember what happened?" Jael asked, moving to drag a chair over to Ciari's bedside.

Ciari scratched at the IV line connected to the back of her left hand. "The World Court," she said slowly as she pressed her hands flat to the bed and tried to sit up. Jael tapped a command into the controls of the bed, raising it so that Ciari wouldn't have to hold herself up. "Erik. I was—"

She remembered the feel of incandescent fire running through her body, scouring every square centimeter of her being. Ciari touched the back of her head, where the neurotracker was located, and realized that her hair was shaved completely off. The soft skin of her scalp felt smooth in areas, faint pricks of hair follicles snagging the edges of her nails in others. Occasionally, her fingers ran across tacky residue left behind by a quick-heal patch. Being bald didn't matter to her. Whatever damage came from it, physically at least, was mostly fixed. She remembered that Jael did good work.

"Erik meant to kill you," Jael said. "According to Keiko, he kept his finger on the trigger of the kill switch for five minutes before Travis came to your defense. We had to cut out a piece of your skull to give your brain room to swell."

Ciari flattened her hand against the back of her skull, let her fingers splay over the curve of skin and bone. "I remember it burned."

Just facts, not emotions. It was all she could articulate.

"It—the damage to your nerves was easier to fix than the damage to your mind."

"What's wrong?" Ciari said, looking over at the CMO. She let her hand drop back down to her lap, gripping the sheet that covered her.

"A lot of things."

"Tell me."

Jael grimaced, her gaze flicking away from Ciari's face. "I held your mind together as best I could, but in order to keep it from slipping away,

I had you turn the pain off on your own. It was too difficult for me to try without risking your life. I don't have that sort of reach, not when a mind is almost dead. You turned off the pain, but it created a domino effect from that internal order. Once the pain turned off, everything else—every other emotion—was switched off as well. I can't—I can't fix that, Ciari. I can't undo what you did."

Ciari was quiet for a long moment before she said, "You're the best psi surgeon this Syndicate has."

"I don't have the power or finesse to take your mind apart and put it back together again. Not this time."

Ciari stared at her, brown eyes now tinged silver near her pupils. There should have been anger in her gaze, at the very least a sense of horror, but when Jael finally looked at her, Ciari's eyes were empty of anything that might have resembled emotion. The lack of accusation in her face was disheartening.

"We need you," Jael said. "I hoped a medically induced coma would help your mind reset itself, except that's not going to happen. So I woke you up."

Ciari nodded. "Who's in charge?"

"Erik appointed Keiko as Acting OIC." Jael hesitated before continuing, "Lucas sent Threnody, Kerr, and Jason to retrieve your daughter. I'm sorry. We couldn't stop them from taking her, but we managed to take Threnody into custody."

Ciari closed her eyes. Opened them again.

"Tell me," Ciari said slowly, struggling to wrap her thoughts around a concept she no longer understood, "why you need me."

Words flowed over her when Jael spoke, sound that told a story Ciari tried hard to feel connected to. Except that she didn't—couldn't.

In the end, when Jael finally left her alone, Ciari was certain of only three things. She was still a Class III empath; that genetic fact could not be changed. She could still use her power, on others and on herself. She simply had no name for the emotions she could play with and no reason to care why, either about the people she would have to apply it to or the people she was required to lead and to protect.

TWENTY-TWO

SEPTEMBER 2379
TORONTO, CANADA

The pain in her head reminded Threnody of when she peeled burned skin off her hands in the Arctic, how it came free one ragged piece at a time. The way Jael sought to flay her mind felt the exact same way.

The Class III telepath had already stripped most of Threnody's mental shields from her mind, her personal defenses broken down to their foundations. Now Jael contended with the safeguards Lucas had left in Threnody's mind, and for all that Jael was a skilled psi surgeon, breaking past a shield erected by a Class I telepath was practically impossible.

Coughing, Threnody spat out saliva mixed with blood, tasting the coppery tang of iron on her tongue. She kept her eyes closed. "Just ask me your questions," she rasped, the words coming out slow.

Strapped to a chair in an empty cell, Threnody's hands and feet were encased in rubber gloves that stretched to her elbows and rubber boots that hit her knees. Around her throat was a heavy metal neurocollar with tiny needles that cut into the skin of her throat and into her spine. The external device acted like a neurotracker, a precaution against her using the power she'd been born with. A dark bruise discolored the right side of her face from where her head had hit the wall when Keiko slammed her into it. Keiko's brutality had been unexpected, and Threnody wondered how badly things had frayed in the Strykers Syndicate since her defection.

"We aren't interested in your lies," Aidan said, voice flat and clinical.

Threnody forced her eyes open, blinking rapidly to clear her vision. She winced as the harsh light in the cell nearly blinded her. "They wouldn't be lies."

She hadn't set foot in the Strykers Syndicate since July, when she was assigned a suicidal mission to track a target that couldn't be caught. The target turned out to be Lucas, and the mission had brought her full circle to the only home she'd ever known before she tasted freedom.

Threnody managed to smile at that delirious thought as she looked at Jael, the black woman swimming in her vision. "I want to speak with Ciari."

Pain. It ripped through her mind like one of Quinton's firestorms, burning her from the inside out. Threnody's head snapped back and she let out a strangled cry. She only had Lucas's singular shield to hide behind and she wondered, distantly, if it would be enough. He didn't answer her. No psi link connected them, just the faint touch of his power.

"Aidan," Jael snapped out. "I already said that isn't going to work."

"Keiko said she wanted answers when she got back. Staying our hand isn't going to get those for her," Aidan said, sounding frustrated.

"I doubt Ciari wants Threnody dead, and the strength required to break through that last shield would probably kill her."

"She isn't a telepath. How the hell is she holding it up?"

Panting heavily, Threnody felt blood pool in her nose and had to let her head fall forward to let it drain out instead of back into her lungs. It dripped onto her thighs, soaking into the patched clothes she still wore.

"You didn't tag me for retrieval," Threnody coughed out, feeling blood slid down the back of her throat. "'S'okay, Lucas is better than Nathan."

The sudden quiet in her cell wasn't comforting. Nothing about her current position was comforting.

"What do you know about retrieval?" Jael said, the words sounding as if they were pulled out of her by force.

Threnody laughed, soft and low. It made her ribs hurt. Keiko hadn't pulled her power when she telekinetically hit her.

"Ask me your fucking questions." Threnody lifted her head, staring at the two Stryker officers who were still beholden to the whims of their human masters by way of the neurotrackers in their heads. "Or ask Ciari. Either way, get on with it."

Telepathy curled through her bruised mind once again, attempting to cut into the last defense she had against people she once trusted.

[TWENTY-THREE]

Keiko squinted through the lenses of her binoculars, glad for the shade the shuttle wing provided. Her gaze caught on the magnified metal wedge protruding from the mountainside and the road that wound its way up to their eventual destination. The visual was enough for a teleport, but they weren't ready to move yet.

Behind her stood Terrence Finn, a Class V psychometrist. He silently took the binoculars from Keiko when she passed them to him. Born with a power that shared traits from both telepathy and empathy, Terrence could pull memories out of inanimate objects. He'd been on medical leave in Toronto after fighting in Buffalo, making it easy for Keiko to add him to the small team of Strykers assigned this mission.

Only four of them had been ordered out: Keiko, Terrence, a telepath, and a pyrokinetic. They'd flown across the Arctic Ocean to this island on the World Court's orders. Erik had imparted to her the details of the mission and the location of the outpost in person, not trusting an uplink after the current political mess running through the media. Their contact here hadn't bothered to leave his shuttle, and Keiko had stopped trying to get orders out of Elion after the first try.

I wonder if Ciari knew about this place, Keiko thought as she surveyed the dead land that surrounded the abandoned airfield.

They couldn't access the Svalbard Global Seed and Gene Bank yet. Not until the World Court's appointed leader of this mission arrived on a government-charted shuttle. He landed less than an hour later.

We really need to stop meeting like this, Keiko, Nathan said as he stepped off the shuttle. Two Warhounds in the guise of human bodyguards and a quad followed him. Meters away, Elion was disembarking from his own shuttle, coming to join their small group.

Keiko realized right then just how little they knew about Nathan's political maneuverings. Or at least, how little *she* knew. Despite taking over as the Acting OIC, Keiko knew certain details were locked in Ciari's head that could be the difference between living and dying. Keiko wished she knew them. Lifting her chin, Keiko watched the group's approach in silence.

"Strykers," Nathan said when his group got within hearing range, "the World Court has seen fit to give me your contract."

You're enjoying this far too much, Nathan, Keiko said, shoving the words into the public area of her mind.

The expression on his face didn't change. *No, I'm not.*

"Sir," Keiko said, careful not to make the word grate.

"I was told there would be a psychometrist in this group," Nathan said, his eyes resting unerringly on Terrence. "Which one of you is it?"

Terrence took a step forward. "I am."

For Keiko, it was strange to face Nathan with people who knew nothing of his true identity. Nathan lived a brilliant lie, Keiko had to admit. Brilliant and deadly. The Silence Law would dictate their actions here, with she as the psion and Nathan as nothing more than human. It would be a tricky dance.

"I've got a visual on the mountain," Keiko said, looking between Nathan and Elion. "Whenever you're ready, I can teleport us there."

"How many Strykers did you bring?" Elion said, sounding agitated.

"Four, myself included." Keiko tilted her head at the shuttle behind her. "Our telepath and pyrokinetic are monitoring the security grid. We've been waiting for your arrival before we proceeded up the mountain."

"We're here now," Nathan said. He turned his head to stare up at the mountainside. "Teleport us."

Keiko steadied her mind before wrapping her power around everyone. She teleported them up to the road that led to the seed bank's entrance. Elion and the quads stumbled a bit on their arrival; no one else did. People who were used to the quirks of a teleport—where the telekinetics always 'ported a few centimeters or more higher than the ground of their targeted location—didn't stumble.

"The ramp can support our weight," Elion said as quads moved to slide open the doors.

Lights came on, brightening the tunnel in sections. The group moved quickly down its length. When Keiko took her first steps into the long storage vault, all she saw was a mess of scattered boxes holding silver-foil packets and glass vials strewn across shelves and the floor. All she felt was quiet, fragile disbelief.

It was one thing to be told about a place such as this. Actually seeing it in person was almost painful. This place, this vast seed bank, was the whole reason why humanity had survived after the last bomb fell. Keiko knew of the launch; she hadn't known about this.

"We've lost half the inventory," Elion said. "We have everything that we need, just not in the amounts we expected."

"And the terraforming machines?" Nathan asked, dark blue eyes sweeping over the mess before them. He ignored the startled look the rest of the party gave him at that revelation.

Elion's voice was bitter. "A third of those are gone as well. Whoever was behind this didn't seem to care about taking everything, just enough of it."

"Or they simply didn't have the means or the time to finish the job." Nathan turned and headed for the hallway. "Show me the rest of the damage."

Elion led Nathan down the length of each of the three cold-storage vaults, reporting on their losses. Only when Nathan's inspection was complete did he speak again.

"The psychometrist will begin with the main door," Nathan said.

Terrence led them back to the front entrance. The doors were still in their casings, but he wasn't going to work with those yet. Unsealing his left glove, Terrence pulled his hand free. He lost the warmth that the insulation provided, but he ignored the cold. Taking a deep breath, he raised his hand to the cold metal of the control panel and pressed his skin against it. He didn't hesitate, so none of the humans present knew that he feared using his power. The neurotracker in his brain denied him the right to protest, denied him the right to give in to the fear that all psychometrists experienced when using their power.

Terrence dropped his mental shields, pulling memories out of cold metal. Memories that were both old and distant, too faint to catch completely, or shining bright and sharp against the backdrop of the mental grid. Terrence's mind opened wide and swallowed the memories whole, instances, moments, that people unknowingly pressed into the physical world around them.

Tell Nathan he can go to hell, Lucas Serca said into Terrence's mind, the clear message left behind days ago for them to find.

Telepathy that didn't come from the embedded memory slammed through Terrence's mind, meeting zero resistance since his shields were down. The attack happened so quickly that Keiko didn't know Terrence was dead until he hit the ground. She stared at the Stryker in shock, forcing herself to not look at where Nathan stood.

"What happened?" Elion said, pointing at the dead Stryker. "What the *hell* just happened?"

You didn't have to kill him, Keiko said, fury breaking up her thoughts as she dropped to her knees beside Terrence, fingers searching for a pulse that wasn't going to be there.

Nathan's gaze was unapologetic. *I don't have time to deal with a broken Silence Law.*

He didn't know a goddamn thing about the Silence Law. What did he see?

It's not your concern. Out loud, Nathan said, "Yes. Do explain what happened to the Stryker."

Keiko stared at the body beside her. Blood trickled out of Terrence's nose, dripping slowly to the ground.

"I don't know. I'm not a 'path-oriented psion," Keiko said, forcing her voice calm as she pushed herself back to her feet, brushing dirt off her knees. "I'm guessing it must have been a mental trap."

"How is that even possible?" Elion said.

"Please, give me a few minutes to find out." She glanced over at Nathan. *Was it Lucas that he saw?*

Nathan's gaze didn't waver. *Call your telepath, Keiko.*

Keiko shook her head, as if she could shake his mental touch out of her mind. She opened herself up to the psi link someone else had stitched into her mind. *Eva.*

Yes?

I'm bringing you up here. Terrence is dead. Whatever was left in the walls killed him.

Well, shit.

The Class VI telepath gave Keiko a visual of the shuttle for the teleki-netic to find her. Keiko reached for the Stryker over the distance between mountain and shuttle, teleporting the telepath to their position. Eva Collingsworth landed lightly on the road beyond the support ramp. She was a petite woman in her midtwenties; dark-haired, dark-eyed, with heavy scarring over the lower half of her face and throat. Her body didn't have the capability to accept biomodifications, and cellular regeneration had never worked for her. Eva had lost her voice when she was twelve. Telepathy was her only means of communication.

I'm not a psychometrist, Keiko, Eva said, eyes narrowing with emotion that showed nowhere else on her face. *And Terrence is dead. What do you expect me to find?*

Pretend you're trying to get something out of the hole in the mental grid, Keiko said. *See if you can't possibly find out what killed him. Let me deal with the humans.*

Eva inclined her head to the people in charge before closing her eyes.

"Eva is looking for answers," Keiko said, turning to face Elion and not Nathan. "Telepaths aren't psychometrists, sir. Whatever was left behind by whatever rogue psion who was here, I don't know if Eva will find it."

Elion glared at her. "We need answers, Stryker."

"We're trying to get that for you," Keiko said, sounding frustrated. "I don't know what killed Terrence, but if whatever it was is still embedded in these walls, then it's not safe."

"I don't care if you think it's not safe. You're not in charge. Your contract was handed over to us and you have an obligation to obey the World Court."

"I mean no disrespect, but the World Court hasn't issued a kill order for any Stryker here. Let us do the job you brought us here to do in order to keep you safe. Sir."

Elion opened his mouth to argue, or perhaps to threaten to activate the neurotracker in her head, but Nathan interrupted whatever tirade the other man was about to indulge in.

"Elion," Nathan said. "Let them do their job."

Keiko kept her gaze trained on Eva. Her thoughts, however, were elsewhere. *Don't expect me to thank you.*

For interceding on your behalf? Ciari was never one to play that sort of groveling game unless she had someone needing to be saved. I miss her begging. Nathan kept his attention on the two Strykers. *Tell me, Keiko, how is Ciari?*

Keiko had to force herself not to think about the changes in Ciari. *Tell me, Nathan, how does it feel to be backed into a corner by your son?*

My family is of no concern to you.

You say that like I don't know Lucas hasn't been on your side for two years and counting, Keiko said, a grim sort of satisfaction creeping through her mind. *You didn't order him to do this. You wouldn't, if this is what will feed you on Mars Colony.*

What do you think you know about what I and the World Court have planned?

Security for the launch is why the government keeps us alive. You? Keiko's mouth thinned into a bloodless line. *I don't read minds, Nathan.*

Nathan's smile was faint and barely there, missed by everyone except Keiko. She saw it only because she was looking for it. Then Eva pulled her into a psi link, the telepath unaware of Nathan's presence, and Keiko had to focus on the mission.

Massive telepathic overload, Eva said. *Memories don't do that. They can't. This feels more like a telepathic strike. The people who broke in might still be on the island.*

Keiko looked over at Elion, weighing her options. She knew that if she attempted to change the playing field, Nathan would kill her. As a Class I triad psion, he could easily do it. The cleanup afterward—of bodies and mindwipes—would take time, but Nathan was a perfectionist and Keiko didn't doubt he'd find excuses to keep himself safe.

"Our telepath can't speak," Keiko said. "And we aren't authorized for telepathic contact with either of you. Eva confirmed Terrence died from a strong telepathic attack."

"What about the perpetrator?" Elion asked sharply.

Keiko didn't look at Nathan. "Unknown. Possibly the same rogue psions that were in Buffalo, but those particular psi signatures haven't shown up since the fight."

"That is unacceptable, Stryker."

"Unfortunately, it's all we have at the moment. Perhaps the security system—"

Elion let out a short, harsh laugh. "Don't you think we tried? That was the first thing we checked after confirming the breach. The security logs are inaccessible. It would take weeks to hack through the new encryption embedded in everything now. We don't have that long."

Keiko looked down at Terrence's body and wrapped her power around his form. She teleported the corpse into their shuttle for transport.

"We should begin a transfer of everything in the seed bank, sir," Keiko said. "We can't guarantee that the people who broke in won't return to take the rest."

"These seeds and embryos and everything else require a specific temperature in order to survive. They can't be risked," Elion said. "Considering it seems psions are responsible for this mess, I don't trust your involvement."

"The World Court assigned them this job, but I agree with your assessment, Elion. We'll bring in as many cold-storage units as we need," Nathan said. "We will physically transport everything to London."

The better for you to keep it away from Lucas? Keiko asked.

Do you honestly think I'll be protecting it from just him?

Images of the *Ark* from the pirate stream ran through Keiko's mind. She knew that society wasn't going to take such deceit lying down. Everyone's view of the world was changing, and change never came easy.

You'll do what the government requires of you and you'll die for it, Nathan said. *But some of your Strykers will live, so keep your mouth shut.*

"Take us back to the shuttle," Nathan said, the look in his dark blue eyes curiously satisfied.

Keiko decided she should have brought an empath after all. Tapping into her power, she pulled everyone into a teleport.

PART FIVE

FLUCTUATE

SESSION DATE: 2128.03.25

LOCATION: Institute of Psionics Research

CLEARANCE ID: Dr. Amy Bennett

SUBJECT: 2581

FILE NUMBER: 270

Aisling hums again. The sound is an offbeat melody that clashes with the noise the EEG and supporting machines make behind her as she leans over the seat of her chair and stares at the camera. She is alone.

"I can see what it's going to be like and I think that scares them."

Her head hangs down, her hair falling around her face like a curtain. The wires lay heavily across her back.

"It scares me." She kicks her legs a bit, smacking the toes of her shoes against the ground. "Everyone's afraid of me. I don't have any friends here."

Aisling waves one small hand at the camera in a vague gesture before she props herself back up on both hands. Then she sighs and collapses again over the chair. She scratches at a line of electrodes adhered across her forehead and pushes wires out of her face.

"It could have been different, and it is, but then it wouldn't end. Mama said it should end." Aisling glances at the camera, her gaze looking past it. "I don't want Nathan, Marcheline. I need his son."

[TWENTY-FOUR]

T hrenody."

She opened her eyes slowly, staring at her knees. She knew that voice.

Slowly, achingly, Threnody lifted her head enough to see the woman standing in front of her. For a moment, Threnody thought she was dreaming. Gone was the dark brown hair, shaved off completely for the surgery the older woman must have gone through. Harsh red lines still laced the skin of her skull, and her eyes were like empty holes in her face. She wore soft-looking black pants and a gray, long-sleeved shirt. She looked as if she had lost weight.

Ciari looked fragile.

Threnody sniffed loudly. Her nose itched from all the dried blood inside it. "Never saw you out of uniform before."

"I've never seen a Stryker without a neurotracker still breathing," Ciari said.

"Liar." Threnody smiled, the corners of her mouth cracking. Her lips were dry.

Someone had brought another chair into Threnody's cell while she was unconscious. Ciari sat down in it and laced her hands together in her lap. She stared at Threnody with a heavy, unblinking gaze that was hard to meet. Something was off about the way the older woman acted, and it made Threnody uneasy.

"I'm not giving you up to the World Court," Ciari said after a moment.

"That's not really a kindness."

"You took my daughter. It's not about kindness."

Threnody rolled her head from side to side, trying to ease the heavy ache in her shoulders. The motion brought a wave of nausea, but she managed to not throw up this time. She stank enough as it was. She hadn't eaten since being teleported in, but she'd been given some sips of water. It wasn't enough to sooth the parchedness in her mouth. Swallowing, Threnody stopped moving so her stomach would settle. The pressure in her head was all mental trauma, but Lucas's shield was still standing. She assumed it was the only reason she was still alive.

"Her father wanted full custody, not visiting rights," Threnody said. "Sorry."

"Lucas is making a mess of things."

"So, no more pretending?" Threnody let out a heavy sigh, flexing her fingers. The rubber gloves made her skin itch. She couldn't stretch her arms, not with her wrists cuffed to the chair, and her joints felt tight. "I would have kept your secret."

"Jael already knows. She was keeping it safe. How did you find out where we were keeping her?"

"The Syndicate trained me as a tactician, remember? I took the details we had and came up with the best possible scenario."

"Was releasing information about the *Ark* your idea?"

"I'm just a soldier, Ciari. All I do is follow orders."

"No, you aren't. And, no, you don't."

Threnody licked her lips and chuckled softly. "Never was very good at lying about how I felt."

Ciari nodded agreement. "It's what got you into this mess in the first place. I never wanted to send you on that mission to the Slums."

"You were just following orders, right?"

"I won't apologize for my actions."

"I know," Threnody said quietly. "You have nothing to apologize for."

"The world knows about the launch now. About the *Ark*. The World Court is pushing up the launch date, which means we Strykers have only got days left to live."

Threnody stared at her, not liking the toneless way Ciari was speaking. Her voice had no emotion, not even the coldness that came with an empath's rigid control. She was just—empty.

"What can I say that will make you believe there's a way out of this?" Threnody said. "That the Strykers don't have to die like animals?"

"Belief requires faith. I have none."

Threnody flinched. "I learned to."

"You aren't the first to make that mistake." Ciari pushed herself to her feet and approached Threnody. "You won't be the last. But mistakes are what make us human."

Ciari unlocked first one cuff, then the other. Threnody stared blankly down at her freed hands.

"Lie down and get some rest, Threnody. We aren't done fighting yet."

Ciari walked out of the cell without looking back. Threnody slowly pulled her arms free of the cuffs and stretched them, groaning as stiff muscles protested the movement. She peeled off the rubber gloves, tossing them away. Then she leaned over to undo the cuffs around her ankles, hissing as the ache in her ribs got sharper. She pulled the rubber boots off her feet before carefully sliding out of the chair. Her aching ribs protested the movement, but Threnody still lay down on the cold metal floor, fingers of one hand curled over the collar wrapped around her throat, the bioware tipped needles digging deep into her skin and vertebrae. She still obeyed the order given to her.

Threnody closed her eyes to block out the light, and slept.

[TWENTY-FIVE]

SEPTEMBER 2379

THE HAGUE, THE NETHERLANDS

Sharra knew what it meant when the pirate stream hit the world press and society was unable to look away. She paused in front of the vidscreen long enough to watch it all the way through once. Then she retreated to the bunker suite she called home and began to pack.

They were on a schedule that Erik had been keeping to over the past few years. It was easy for her to go through that mental list and see exactly where she was in packing up her life.

"Mama, what are these boxes for?" Lillian asked.

Kneeling, surrounded by heavy cargo trunks, Sharra craned her head around to watch as her daughter walked into the bedroom. "They aren't boxes, sweetie. They're for storage."

"What are you storing?"

Her perfectly human daughter climbed onto a trunk, sitting on the lid. She was dressed in her school uniform, the jacket slung over a chair in the kitchen. Sharra had left Lillian there eating cookies under the watchful eye of a soldier while the movers rattled around the suite of rooms.

Sharra tucked a stray strand of blond hair behind her ear before beckoning to Lillian. "Come here, sweetheart."

The little girl hopped off the trunk and walked over to her mother. She didn't protest when Sharra pulled her into her arms, giving Lillian a hug that almost hurt.

"You know how important your father is," Sharra said, stroking Lillian's dark hair. "Sometimes important people need to make very hard decisions, and that's what I'm helping your father with."

"But all our stuff is going away."

"Yes, well. Your father has been working extrahard to make sure you have a wonderful new home. Not everyone is special enough to live there, and we didn't want to make people jealous, so it was a secret. Unfortunately, that secret got out and now we're going to be moving a little earlier than your father thought."

"What about school?"

In that regard, Lillian was her father's child. Sharra had been illiterate until the age of nine, when she found her way into an illegally run school in London. She could read and write, do basic arithmetic, but any sort of desire for education that Lillian had did not come from Sharra.

"There will still be school where we're going," Sharra promised her.

"And my friends?"

"You'll still have your friends. Don't worry, honey. Everything's going to be okay. Right now, I need you to go to your room and pick out only your most favorite toys. Can you do that for me?"

"Why can't I take them all?" Lillian asked, pouting. In this, she was most definitely Sharra's child.

"Because I said so." She gave Lillian another hug before gently pushing her toward the door. "Now go. Do what I say and there might be cake for dessert tonight."

Whatever anger Lillian might have had, it faded in the face of every child's favorite meal. "Chocolate?"

"Perhaps. You won't know until you begin to sort out your room."

"I'll do it, I promise!"

Lillian raced out of the bedroom. Sharra pressed the side of her hand against her mouth, biting down carefully on the skin there to hold back the sick feeling in her stomach. What she wouldn't give for a glass of wine, but even she knew there came a time for sobriety. For her daughter, she would learn it.

Sharra spent the next few hours mindlessly filling the trunks in her room with what would fit from her life, tearing apart a place that had been home for so many years. If she dropped a vase or two because her hands were shaking, no one said a word, and the mess was ignored. It was pointless cleaning a place they were never going to see again.

Sharra was in the middle of closing another trunk when Lillian came skipping back into the room. "Daddy's home!"

Sharra got to her feet and smoothed out the wrinkles in her pale blue dress. She hadn't thought that Erik would be back so soon. "Come along," Sharra said, reaching for her daughter's outstretched hand. "Let's go say hello to your father."

They found Erik in his office, the first place Sharra knew to check whenever he was home. It was of moderate size, lived-in, with antiques cluttering up the corners and holopics of his family on the wall that she hadn't got to packing yet. Sharra had decorated it for him years ago, and nothing within those four walls had ever changed. Erik never really cared about what surrounded him, only who. His desire for power was similar to Sharra's desire for safety, and they were losing both.

"Daddy!" Lillian shrieked, letting go of her mother's hand to fling herself at her father.

Erik embraced her easily enough, but most of his attention was on the vidscreen embedded in the wall. It was separated into four different news streams, and the latest update wasn't pretty.

Sharra came to stand beside her husband, glancing from him to the vidscreen. "What are they saying?"

Erik shook his head, the tight look on his face evidence enough of his answer. If it had been less of a problem, he wouldn't look so exhausted.

"Nothing good," he said, smoothing back Lillian's hair. "I had to sign off on payment for stolen oil with a terrorist group earlier this week, oil which we need on Mars Colony, and some hacker found the trail of funds. That's just the latest bit of proof the media is using to rip us to shreds."

"Hasn't anyone argued on the government's behalf?"

"People have, but no one's listening to our side of the story. Everyone's only interested in what the pirate streams can dig up. Thank God no one has found out about the seed bank yet, but I doubt that ignorance will last. We've already lost half that inventory to a breach."

That news sent a cold chill running down Sharra's spine. She placed a hand on her husband's arm, holding on to him. "Erik?"

"The Strykers couldn't pull anything from the location. A Stryker died doing recon and they think it's the same rogue psion that orchestrated the mess in Buffalo. I don't have any confirmation, but it's the only logical suggestion offered up so far. Nathan Serca is overseeing the transportation of the remaining inventory to his Syndicate's tower for safety reasons before transferring it to Paris. It's going up on the first wave of shuttles."

Sharra swallowed thickly. "Is London safe enough to house the seeds?"

"Nowhere on this planet is safe right now." Erik pressed a kiss to Lillian's cheek and hugged her a little tighter. "I want you to finish packing within the hour, Sharra. I've got to give a press conference soon to try to buy us a little more time. We're moving up the launch to this week."

Erik went quiet, his eyes locked on the vidscreen and the satellite readout of the *Ark*'s design. "We only wanted to save humanity," he said. "We just can't save everyone."

Only the strongest could survive. Sharra knew that rule more intimately than Erik ever would. Sharra let go of her husband's arm and turned to leave. "I'll finish packing."

The bunker still had furniture and art cramming its walls. Wineglasses were still in the kitchen sink, unopened bottles scattered around the suite. She was trying to be prudent with the packing, only taking what they absolutely couldn't leave behind—holopics of their life here, her collection of jewelry, Lillian's handful of stuffed animals.

Their lives would fit into a dozen cargo trunks, and that was all they would take with them into space. Sharra tried not to think about what they were leaving behind.

[TWENTY-SIX]

SEPTEMBER 2379

AMUNDSEN-SCOTT SOUTH POLE STATION, ANTARCTICA

That's a lot of hyposprays," Quinton said. "Are you sure it's going to be enough for everyone?"

Rows of silver hyposprays stretched out down the long table, each calibrated to give twenty doses of the virus-carrying nanites before needing to be discarded. Quinton picked one up, holding the thin object in his hand. It didn't weigh much, didn't look as if it had the power to change a person's life, but that's exactly what Lucas had created. Korman didn't care to see the value in something that would save psions, not at the expense of the human bondworkers he had tested it on. Quinton didn't let himself dwell on the process, just the results. As horrendous as the process was, it was still saving people.

"It'll be enough," Lucas said without looking up as he packed them into carrying cases. "Your job is going to make sure you use them all."

"I thought we were just dropping them off and breaking Threnody out?" Kerr said.

"I would bet my Syndicate's entire bottom line that Erik is pushing up the launch, which means we need to work on convincing your Strykers that they need our help."

"You ask for the impossible a lot of the time," Samantha said as she closed one carrying case and reached for another. "It's very annoying."

"You want to know what I find annoying?" Matron said, glaring at Lucas. "The way you keep killing off my scavengers. Fahad'd been around a long-ass time. He deserved to see the end."

"He wasn't *your* scavenger and he wasn't as loyal as you think. You're lucky it wasn't me who killed him. Kristen was actually quick for once," Lucas said. "Her version of nice."

Matron opened her mouth. Lucas shut it for her, telekinesis wrapped around skin and metal. He stared at her across the worktable in silence. Matron closed her eyes, hunched her shoulders, and got back to work. One packed carrying case later, Lucas retracted his power.

Jason came into the crowded workroom five minutes later, dragging Kristen behind him telekinetically. The younger girl knew better than to fight his hold, but the second he freed her, she invaded his space again.

"You want me to fix your daughter?" Jason snapped at Lucas. "Keep your sister out of my fucking head."

Lucas rolled a hypospray between his fingers, staring at them. "I sent you to get the rest of the hyposprays, Kris. Not to touch things that aren't yours."

"Little, itty-bitty thing is a Serca," Kristen said. "I just wanted to say hello."

Whatever else Kristen might have said, Lucas cut her off before the thought was even half-formed in her mind. The empath's head snapped back from his telepathic blow, mind cracking a little beneath her brother's strength. Lucas let his telepathy drift through the growing stain of insanity that was creeping back into his youngest sister's mind, familiar holes that were beginning to open all over again. He could sense the places that Jason's stolen pattern had once filled and which were slowly dissolving. Kristen's mind wasn't meant to hold sanity.

She couldn't be fixed; he had always known that.

I never blamed you, Kristen said, her voice soft and achingly sweet in the maelstrom that was beginning to churn once again through her mind.

It wouldn't have mattered if she did.

"Keep a closer watch on her," Lucas said to Samantha.

"She seemed fine" was Samantha's irritated reply, not looking up from her current task.

"That's never a guarantee."

Scowling, Samantha left her spot and went to drag Kristen to the far side of the table.

Jason watched them get settled with the last of the hyposprays that needed to be packed and shook his head. "Please tell me she's not coming with us."

"I'm not leaving my sisters here."

"Take Samantha. Leave Kristen. She's insane."

"Everyone always underestimates her because of that." Lucas looked over at him. "You did, remember?"

Jason didn't bother to argue that fact. "Korman doesn't have any hyposprays left. He didn't trust Kristen to tell you that this is everything we've got to do the job."

All of which could be counted up in carrying cases full of a virus and the hope that they wouldn't get shot on sight when they teleported to the Strykers Syndicate. Lucas pushed away from the table, taking in everyone's attire. "Change out of your skinsuits. If things go badly, I don't want them to have a hint of where we've been."

"If things go badly, we're all fucked," Quinton said, leaving the room.

Jason left with Kerr, the two heading for the room on the far end of the station they'd been sharing since their arrival. The pair stripped out of their insulated skinsuits and dragged on a set of mismatched street clothes that left them shivering a bit in the low warmth of the station. Power was gained by way of three old generators, only two of which Matron's scavengers had managed to get up and running. They had heat; it just wasn't enough without skinsuits to stay warm continuously.

"Think Threnody's still alive?" Jason said as he yanked on a shirt.

"Lucas isn't worried," Kerr replied as he laced up a pair of boots. "Which means she can't be dead."

"I'd hate to be in Quinton's shoes right now."

"You hate what we're doing anyway."

"Can you blame me?" Jason looked over at Kerr as he grabbed the jacket hanging off the chair. "I don't care if Lucas thinks he's going to save everyone. I don't trust his methods."

Kerr leaned forward on the bed where he was sitting, resting his elbows on his knees. "Maybe you should try. He's got a way to save us, Jays."

"At too high of a price." Jason tapped the side of his head. "You're not in my head anymore. Feels fucking weird."

"It's worth it. You know that."

Worth it to not have his shields skidding out from beneath his control, to not be at risk of an insanity driven by a storm of the world's thoughts. Telepaths were born to read minds, but they craved a silence they would never get. Kerr had only ever found silence behind Jason's natal shields, and now those, too, were gone. Both of them were exactly what they were supposed to be, but that didn't make their lives any easier.

"All the times when you were in my mind, did you ever know what I really was?" Jason asked.

"No," Kerr said with a shake of his head. "I couldn't get very far past your shields. I only got far enough to readjust my own and hold them to the pattern that you had. I never knew you were a microtelekinetic, the same way I never knew I had an empathic power. Hell, I never knew your kind of power even existed."

"You and me both."

The two looked at each other, separated now by so much more than the space between them. The severing of their bond was still a wound in both their minds. For Kerr, it was the constant reach for something that was no longer there. For Jason, it was the emptiness in the back of his mind that used to be filled with the hum of someone else's thoughts. He never felt that anymore unless Kerr produced a psi link, but the connection would never again be the same.

"I never said thank you," Kerr said, looking Jason in the eye. "For how you kept me safe and sane."

"Yeah, you did." Jason gave him a faint, bittersweet smile. "Too many times to count."

"Sometimes I never meant it."

"The times you were screaming in my head and wanted me to kill you before you went crazy? I know, Kerr. And I don't blame you for giving the bond up. You didn't need it anymore. You got your mind fixed. That's all you ever wanted, and I'm not a shitty enough person to hold that against you."

"I never wanted to leave you like this."

"Fuck that, man. You can't get rid of family."

Jason had been the volatile one growing up, always ready to defend Kerr in the face of derogatory comments and dismissive attitudes from their fellow Strykers. Jason didn't care that his shields made him an anomaly back then, and he counted the black marks in his old record for fighting for Kerr like honor badges.

A knock on the door brought Kerr to his feet. The door opened and Quinton leaned into the room. "Hey. You two ready?"

"We're ready," Jason said.

The three of them headed back to the workroom, finding Lucas and his sisters already there. Matron was leaning against the table, having sorted the carrying cases into five stacks. Kristen pouted when she wasn't handed any.

"What about you?" Quinton asked the scavenger. "You've been with us since Buffalo. Aren't you coming?"

"Been with Lucas longer than that and I ain't always with him when he goes running off," Matron said.

"You make it seem like I'm the reckless one," Lucas said as he tossed an apple from one hand to the other.

Matron shrugged, rubbing at one shoulder where the metal cybernetics of her arm attached to flesh and bone. The cold made the connecting points ache. "You've always been reckless with everyone else's life."

Lucas only smiled at her. Matron bared her metal teeth in a responding grin. It wasn't the first time that Matron wondered about the faith she was putting in him that wasn't going to her God, but she wasn't going to stop now. "I pray to God you're doing the right thing here, Lucas."

"Your God isn't why I'm doing this. Remember what I told you when I pulled you from the swamps of Chicago?"

Matron snorted. "You think I forgot that? You promised me a garden if I did your dirty work."

Lucas tossed her the apple. Matron caught it easily in one hand. "Keep sorting the seeds."

"I know how to do my job," Matron said, dark eyes wide and opaque, face full of a belief that wasn't for Lucas, but for what he had the chance to make. "Don't forget about us down here."

"Never," Lucas promised. He almost sounded as if he meant it.

Lucas wrapped his telekinesis tightly around his sisters and the other three. He kept the visual in his mind of a white room as he teleported them all across the world in a single 'port. Their feet hit the platform in the arrival room with a heavy sound. This time it was guarded, but Lucas wasn't concerned about that. Beside him, Samantha let out a soft gasp as she recognized a familiar presence that had been missing from her mind since Buffalo.

Lucas slammed his telepathy up through half a dozen levels filled with psions and humans alike, leaving a burning path of pain on the mental grid in his wake. He slid into a cracked mind that was no longer familiar and looked through Ciari's eyes.

[TWENTY-SEVEN]

SEPTEMBER 2379
TORONTO, CANADA

Gideon stared out the window of the suite, squinting through the polluted haze that lingered over everything. He was in a private level that the Serca Syndicate owned in one of Toronto's city towers. It came with a perfect view of the city tower that housed the Strykers Syndicate, its top floors a government-owned prison on the outskirts of the main cluster. Beyond it, Lake Ontario was a dark swath of water against the landscape.

Toronto was nothing like Buffalo. The slums surrounding the city towers were mostly aboveground and sprawled over land that hadn't suffered as badly as other cities during the Border Wars. Buffalo existed mostly belowground, in sealed bunkers and tunnels. That city's towers were far fewer than the count here, limited in numbers because of the deadzone that took up most of New York State.

Gideon was glad for the differences. It made being in this part of the world bearable.

"Have you matched the psi signature yet?" he said. He could see the reflection in the plasglass of the three telepaths who were seated at the conference table, surrounded by datapads.

"No," Warrick said, rubbing at his temple. "We have nothing in our database on who that psion might be."

"There's no match with our target's records or the psi signature from Buffalo either," Mercedes said. "I'm still willing to say it's Jason Garret. It certainly wasn't Lucas, and the way it registered off the scale? Lucas is strong, but this power tops his strength in a very specific way."

One of the Warhound teams on surveillance duty in Toronto had tagged a strong, abnormal psi signature two days earlier on the mental grid. It originated from the Strykers Syndicate, and Gideon refused to believe it could be anyone else.

"I'm not hearing any answers," Gideon said.

"Because there aren't any, sir," Warrick said. "Not with the information we have. The Strykers would have more than we do, especially since that psion was in their Syndicate."

They should have initiated their visit yesterday, but Nathan had informed Gideon about the breach in the seed bank before they left for the Strykers Syndicate, which had delayed the visit by twenty-four hours. Gideon adjusted the tie knotted around his throat. He was wearing a suit for this endeavor. He would have preferred a field uniform.

"Feels like Kristen is in this city," James said.

Gideon turned to give the telepath a sharp look. "I doubt Lucas would make it that easy to find him again."

"It's not your sister, sir. It's her dysfunction that feels similar on the mental grid. Insanity has a particular spike to it."

"Strykers rarely keep dysfunctional psions. The government usually orders their termination at a young age. Most likely it's someone injured from the fight in Buffalo." Gideon walked over to the chair where his suit jacket was hanging and put it on. "Let's go."

They were doing this the human way, restricted from using Gideon's ability to teleport. He knew what the Strykers Syndicate looked like; specifically, their arrival rooms for psions, but Nathan wasn't quite at the point where he could risk their family's secret coming out.

They left the suite of rooms for a shuttle that was locked into one of the landing docks that stuck out like spokes down the side of the city tower, just one of many used by the registered elite. The walk there took them down to a public level, past brightly lit department stores and restaurants, the hologrids that lined every wall showing news streams and not the usual adverts. Residential routes cut away from the public space, leading off to the lifts that would carry people to their homes.

The atmosphere was muted and tense. People walked by with their heads down, looking at no one as they went about their business. The group made it to their assigned shuttle walkway and entered the short, enclosed tube that extended to the shuttle's hatch. Minutes after they strapped in, the pilot disengaged the anchor locks once given the all clear.

The flight to the other city tower and the Strykers Syndicate was short. Gideon had the pilot dock the shuttle on a lower level and the four disembarked, heading for a lift that would take them right to the top. A security system had already scanned their eyes and faces for identities, so when the lift came to a stop and the doors opened onto a sleek lobby, Gideon was greeted by a familiar woman.

"Keiko," he said, stepping out of the lift and into the Strykers Syndicate.

"Sir," she said evenly. "This is unexpected."

"We have business to discuss."

Despite being surrounded by psions and humans, only four people in this Syndicate knew the truth about the Sercas. Keiko wasn't about to break the Silence Law. She didn't argue Gideon's order and simply led him to a lift farther inside that had access to the rest of the Strykers Syndicate's levels.

Keiko took him to the administrative level. She took him to Ciari.

Gideon was surprised to see the other woman conscious. Considering the trauma that Erik had inflicted on her at The Hague, Gideon expected her to be well on her way to dying. Instead, Ciari looked decently recovered. She had Aidan and Jael with her, and while those two acknowledged his arrival, Ciari continued watching a news stream.

The World Court was standing before the cameras again, on trial themselves before public opinion in the face of irrefutable evidence that they still categorically denied.

"This should be interesting," Jael said. It was anyone's guess if she meant the current company or the current news as Gideon crossed Ciari's office to take a seat before her desk.

"I've never cared for your interests," Keiko said.

On the vidscreen, Erik was arguing his case, backed by the other fourteen judges that made up the World Court. Between the judges and the reporters was a line of quads with pulse-rifles, which said more about the situation than anything else.

"We who have held the title of judge on the World Court, all of the previous men and women who have presided here over the past two hundred and fifty years, have only had the world's best interests at heart," Erik said, his voice filling the office. "The Border Wars nearly destroyed Earth, making it impossible to live in all but the most desperate of places. Even now, we are a desperate people, but we have not lost the greatest part of our humanity. We have not lost our capacity to hope for a better life, for a better world.

"The Fifth Generation Act was just one of many plans implemented in order to help society distance itself from its horrific past. Five generations to cleanse our DNA, with the Registry securing the identities of those who succeeded. It had to be done, if only to separate us from the psions that the Border Wars created. The psions threatened and still threaten our own existence to this day, their disease a reminder of what is still at stake—our survival as a people, as humans."

He paused for a moment before the cameras, taking in a deep breath. "Fewer of us are born every year with the ability to live healthy lives. Too many of us are born with genetic defects, caused from leftover radiation taint. Too many of us die young from disease. It is difficult, almost impossible, to heal everyone in the population. It takes time, but we have been *trying*."

Someone shouted a vicious dissent from offscreen, but Erik didn't react.

"Since the end of the Border Wars, the government has been trying to make this world a better place. It's a seemingly impossible task, but we have done the best job we could over the years. Yes, there have been draconian measures taken to ensure humanity's survival, but that's the cost we pay to live. We have come so far since the collapse of the old world and we aren't prepared to stop now. These lies that unregistered dissidents spread are abhorrent and insulting."

"Lies," Ciari echoed. "We could teach him something about that."

On-screen, the crowd of reporters was being jostled by a ruckus out of view of the cameras. More shouting ripped through the audio, and the quads leveled their guns at a crowd that was starting to get unruly. It was mere seconds from becoming a massacre when everyone went suddenly quiet and still. People froze where they stood, the silence in the room difficult to comprehend after that sudden fit of fury.

"Empath," Jael said, arms crossed stiffly over her chest. "Who's on guard duty?"

"Three teams," Keiko said. "The World Court is protected. They authorized psionic interference if necessary."

"You seem to have everything under control," Gideon said. "It's a far cry from the government."

Ciari finally turned her head to look at him, and the deadness in her eyes was shocking. Gideon studied her face and noted the lack of expression.

"Our orders stand," Ciari said. "We've been tasked with protecting the registered elite in the city towers during their transfer to the Paris Basin. We have no choice."

"You always have a choice with us." Gideon offered her a careful smile. "Let's discuss those choices, shall we?"

"I was under the assumption that Nathan wasn't extending us help. As he pointed out, it's too late for retrievals."

"We said we'd take your high-Classed psions and bring them with us into space, but as of right now, we'll only do that if you give us the one we really want."

"We haven't been hiding Lucas from you."

"We don't want Lucas any way but dead." Gideon shrugged. "We want Jason Garret."

He didn't miss the way everyone but Ciari went tense at his demand. Gideon studied Ciari intently. He was not a 'path-oriented psion, but he'd lived eighteen years with one digging through his mind. Something was wrong with the Strykers' OIC.

"That's a bit of a problem, considering he defected," Ciari said slowly.

"He was here during the fight in Buffalo. The Warhounds in this city felt his presence. Don't lie to me."

"I'm not."

Gideon leaned back in his chair. "So you'll risk all your people for the sake of one psion?"

"We can't risk anyone when we don't have the person you're looking for," Jael said. "Jason Garret has been targeted for kill on sight by the World Court since he managed to escape. Do you think we could keep him here when we're scrutinized so closely?"

"The fact that we're having this conversation in your office proves you wrong."

"No, it simply proves we can circumvent the system, but not for long and not frequently," Aidan said. "With what's going on, the World Court has more important things to worry about than watching our every move so long as we obey orders."

"Considering how badly they need you for security right now, I doubt that."

Ciari tapped at the controls on her desk, turning off the vidscreen. "At some point, even we won't be enough. I'm sorry, Gideon. I can't accept your bargain. I don't have who you want."

Gideon looked her in the eye, searching for something he couldn't find, because all he saw was a faint glint of silver in brown depths. "Does Erik know you're awake?"

"Yes."

"Does he know you're going insane?"

The question hit home hard, none of the officers standing around Ciari's desk able to hide their surprise quick enough at his assessment of the situation. Ciari, on the other hand, couldn't care that he knew what was wrong with her.

"Is that a threat?" Ciari asked.

"Can you even tell?"

"Damn you," Jael said, slamming her hand down near the corner of Ciari's desk. "We can't give you what you want, Gideon."

"Prove it," Gideon said, still refusing to look away from Ciari. "Let Warrick here link me to you, Ciari. You can't lie mind to mind, not in the state you're in."

"Absolutely not."

"I wasn't talking to you, Jael."

Ciari slowly tilted her head to the side, studying Gideon. "You remind me so much of Nathan right now. He should have chosen you sooner."

Gideon had to fight back the scowl. "You don't know what you're talking about."

"And you don't know what you're asking for." Ciari flicked her fingers at him. "Do it."

She was still the OIC, even in the wrecked state she was in. Her officers couldn't counter her order, even though they wanted to. Warrick, telepathically merged with Mercedes and James, pulled Gideon into a psi link and reached for Ciari's damaged mind.

TWENTY-EIGHT

SEPTEMBER 2379

TORONTO, CANADA

Gideon was on his feet when the crack of displaced air exploded in the room. Bodies dropped out of a teleport, but he was already stumbling away from Ciari's desk, information cutting through his mind from what Warrick and the other two were able to discover for him. The echoes of Lucas's thoughts in Ciari's mind were like a telepathic punch he had no defenses against.

"You have a *daughter?*" Gideon exclaimed.

You never could learn to leave things well enough alone, Lucas said into his mind.

Then suddenly he was there, in a way Nathan had never been, cutting so deep through Gideon's thoughts that the younger man didn't have a chance at surviving. Not on his own. Gideon had an image of a room burned into his mind, of an escape all Warhound telekinetics never forgot, except he couldn't reach it. His telekinesis couldn't make that final jump into a teleport, and the panic at that realization nearly drowned out the agony from Lucas's attack. Gideon fell to his knees while around him chaos erupted.

The three Warhounds who'd come with Gideon were doing their level best to block some of Lucas's attack against Gideon, but they weren't strong enough to win against a Class I, even in merge. Faced with the daunting odds in Ciari's office, they fought to save their own skins for as long as they could. Their efforts were joined by the Stryker officers, who didn't take kindly to being ambushed.

Kristen was slammed against the far wall by Keiko's initial telekinetic punch. The Japanese woman knew how devastating Kristen's mind could be and needed to preemptively take her out. Kristen would have been severely injured if Jason didn't cushion her landing, ripping Keiko's power off the teenager. Keiko retaliated against Jason even as she shielded Ciari and her fellow officers.

"Shit—we didn't come here to fight this time!" Jason yelled at her.

The three Warhounds were bearing down on Lucas's mind with telepathic strikes, and Jael added her own attack to the mix. She found it deflected not by Lucas, but by Kerr. Her mind, still bruised from the last blow he'd leveled through her thoughts, flinched against the pressure of his touch.

Jael, we mean it, Kerr said. *Don't fight us.*

But both sides knew that they couldn't give any ground, not with everything that was happening in the world. Jael's duty right now was to protect Ciari's mind. She might only be a Class III telepath, but she'd spent her entire life putting minds back together. She knew how to take them apart. Kerr may finally have gained solid shielding, but Jael knew where weakness once resided in his mind, and she attacked those areas with her telepathy. Jael managed to stop Kerr's next strike before it even touched her mind by aiming hard and fast for the bottom of his shields.

A psion mind never forgot, and Kerr instinctively flinched against her attack. His shields held, but Jael managed to bruise his mind. Training demanded retaliation, but Kerr came up short. Jael was the Strykers Syndicate's CMO and they weren't here to murder their former officers.

Fire erupted in Ciari's office, controlled by Quinton as he targeted the Warhounds. Skin burned just as easily as anything else, and the horrific screams of the two men being engulfed in flames rang in everyone's ears. The stench of burning bodies filled the air, making everyone gag. Jason wrapped the Warhounds in a telekinetic shield, limiting the damage Quinton's fire could do to the floor and ceiling. The woman the other Warhounds had come with managed a mercy killing for the two before Samantha broke her mind so thoroughly that she was dead before she hit the floor.

Then it was just Strykers and Sercas, the lines of loyalty blurred beyond all belief. With a sinking sense of anguish, Samantha focused all of her power on her brothers—and stopped Lucas from killing her twin.

The mental grid reverberated with her attack, the backlash slamming against everyone else's shields. Lucas doubled over from the white-hot pain in his mind, swearing loudly, unprepared for her sudden betrayal.

Gideon knelt on the floor, hands clawing at his head. His mouth was open in a soundless scream, agony written in every line of his rigid body, and all Samantha could see was her other half.

I'm sorry, she whispered into the fractured remains of Gideon's mind. Lucas had torn apart every memory that held the information about his daughter and damaged even more than that. Samantha could see what Lucas had done, could see the insidious corruption that was already snaking through Gideon's mind like acid, eating away at everything that made him who he was. The torturous mindwipe could only result in death.

But Gideon still had his power. And, for just right now, he had her.

Go, Samantha said into her twin's mind, pieces of who she was imprinting onto him. She gave him enough balance and clarity to finish the teleport he still struggled to form, a last attempt at an apology he would never accept.

Gideon disappeared.

When Lucas slammed his mind into hers, Samantha wished she could as well.

Why? Lucas demanded.

He's my brother, Samantha said, struggling to hold up her shields. *Same as you.*

Except Gideon was her twin and she owed him more than Lucas. That debt was paid now. Lucas peeled her shields apart and Samantha let him, knowing she couldn't stop him if he wanted to kill her.

"*Stop.*"

Ciari's voice cut through the melee like nothing else could. Everyone obeyed, ingrained training impossible to ignore when the OIC spoke, no matter how long some of them had been gone from the fold. With one final, vicious wrench of his telepathy, Lucas let his sister go and didn't bother catching her when she fell to her knees, forehead pressed to the floor. Samantha laced her hands over the back of her head, as if she were trying to keep her skull from breaking into pieces.

Around them, the mental grid was layered with the minds of those Strykers still within the confines of the city tower, Lucas and Kerr merged and working to hold off their attacks.

Ciari was on her feet, hands flat on her desk. "This gets us nowhere."

Lucas met her gaze evenly. "Is your security loop still running?"

"Since Gideon walked through the door. We have ten more minutes on the clock." She pointed at the three dead Warhounds. "Get rid of those."

Jason teleported the bodies away, dumping them from a distance into Lake Ontario. Quinton doused what was left of his fire, but the smell of smoke and burned human flesh still filled everyone's lungs when Jason collapsed his telekinetic shields. Too many minds in close proximity on the mental grid had Ciari pressing the palm of one hand to her forehead.

"Jael, tell everyone to stand down," she said.

Jael hesitated, but she didn't argue, which was probably why Ciari asked her and not Aidan. *Stand down.*

The Strykers were reluctant, but they listened. With the pressure gone, Ciari straightened up, staring at Lucas. "It's been a while."

Lucas stared at her, dark blue eyes unblinking as he assessed her mental state. "I can't fix what's wrong with you."

"I don't recall asking. Pick your sister off the floor."

Lucas didn't move. Samantha got to her feet with Kristen's help.

Keiko watched them warily, both hands pressed to the sides of her head. The pressure didn't help clear her mind of the pain. "Why are you here? Did Nathan send you?"

"Lucas." Kerr jerked his thumb at the other man. "It was his idea."

"He figured you wouldn't want to die," Jason said.

"As if he has the capacity to care," Keiko said.

"Considering I've gone out of my way to ensure your survival, kindly shut your mouth," Lucas told her as he set about divesting himself of the carrying cases he still held. He tossed one telekinetically to Keiko, and she had to catch it or risk it slamming into her chest. "You're going to need that."

"What is it?"

"A virus capable of reprogramming the neurotrackers. Every last one embedded in your Strykers."

"What?" Keiko said, her eyes riveted on the case in her hands. "That's suicide. Attempting to access the neurotrackers on that scale will get us all killed quicker than if Erik decided to flip every kill switch by himself."

"I see he's already started with Ciari."

"Leave her out of this," Jael said, voice hard.

"She agreed to it," Lucas said, glancing at Ciari. "There's no backing out now."

"You didn't give her a choice."

Ciari tipped her head to the side, face disturbingly blank. "He didn't need to. It was either take this chance and find a way out, or do nothing and die when the government is done using us up. We psions don't live long, Jael. Twenty-five at the most, thirty years if we're lucky. Longer than that if the government deems us useful, but not by much. How many times did you wish you were born free? I want that for my daughter."

"Wait," Keiko said weakly. "Ciari—what are you talking about?"

"The newest Serca," Kristen answered from where she stood beside Samantha. "But Ciari hasn't named her yet."

Aidan's and Keiko's shock was hard to miss, but they'd spent a good chunk of their lives playing with secrets no one else knew about. They took the news in stride, even if it didn't make them happy.

"I really want you to be lying," Aidan said. "But I know you aren't."

Jael took the case Keiko was holding and opened it, staring down at the secured hyposprays. "Nanites. You know this is dangerous. We only ever use them in a biotank and only within strict medical parameters. How do we know you're not trying to kill us all before the launch to get us out of the way?"

"Unlike Nathan, I never had any intention of leaving Earth," Lucas said.

Jael huffed out an angry little laugh. "Of course you didn't."

"Look, I've been the least agreeable since Lucas took us out of the Slums," Jason said, glancing from one group to another. "I don't like Lucas, and he knows it, but I've seen the source code for this virus and it's good. Better than good. While it won't be able to turn off the tracking signal, it will be able to turn off the kill switch without alerting the World Court. It will save us."

"We're scattered all over the planet," Keiko said. "The Strykers are all working to transport registered humans to the Paris Basin as well as fight off attacks by unregistered humans. It's becoming difficult to do both. Everyone wants a spot on those shuttles and a berth on the *Ark*."

Lucas shook his head. "The logistics will be worked out."

"Really? Thought of everything, have you?" Jael said. "I'm not buying it."

"Then read our minds," Kerr told her. "We aren't lying about any of this."

Jael looked from face to face, seeing only determination in their expressions. "Drop your shields."

First Kerr, then Jason and Quinton, dropped their shields and power washed through the mental grid. Jael wasn't going to risk her sanity by trying to read the minds of Nathan's children, so she settled with the soldiers who had once been under her medical authority. Sliding into their thoughts, she came across psychic wounds that were half-healed and deeper ones that might not ever heal. When you lived with something for so long, you got used to its being there, even after it was gone.

Like the spark right before an inferno, she didn't realize what she was falling into until Jason's mind seemed to swallow her whole. Even with his shields down, Jason's power was difficult to quantify. It filled the mental grid around them, his psi signature an imprint Jael had never experienced before.

Oh, Jael said into Jason's mind, her thoughts colored with awe. *No wonder the mental grid almost broke.*

She sifted through their thoughts and memories, skimming over the conscious and subconscious areas of their minds. Jael struggled to stay focused, the vast power that Jason harbored now difficult to work through. She sent her mind twisting down the anchoring bond that tied him to Quinton, letting her telepathy pool in the back of Quinton's mind, feeling the emptiness in Kerr's.

I can't undo this, Jael said almost apologetically to the three of them.

No, you can't, Quinton agreed, sounding resigned. *We're not asking you to.*

It will kill you eventually. I can see what Lucas did, but you don't have the space in both your minds to hold your power in check, Jason.

There's enough, Kerr said. *It's why Lucas used Quinton and not me.*

They still weren't comfortable with the change, she could read that easily enough. It was permanent, a by-product of a fight that wasn't over yet.

Jael retreated from their minds, but she kept her attention on Jason. "What are you?"

"A microtelekinetic." Jason offered her a crooked little smile. "Anyone want to trade places with me?"

In the silence that followed his words, almost no one knew what to say. Quinton, however, had only one concern. "Where's Threnody?"

Jael pushed a few thin dreads behind her ear, getting her hair out of her face. "Alive."

Quinton headed for the door without another word.

"Where are you going?" Ciari said.

"To get my partner. I doubt you've changed the cells in this place since we left."

He was gone before anyone could stop him. Lucas looked over at Jason. "Go with him."

"If her wounds are extensive enough that she needs my help again, we'd be better off with sticking her into a biotank," Jason warned before hurrying after Quinton.

Jason found the other man about to run down a team of Strykers standing guard outside Ciari's office. They were refusing to let him pass. Before things got ugly, Jael came out and joined them, her presence alone guaranteeing their safety.

"I'll take you to Threnody," Jael said. "Follow me."

It didn't take that long to get to where they were holding Threnody, and the Strykers who saw them could only stare. Strangely, they didn't pass any humans. Even Jael seemed surprised until Lucas's telepathy crawled through their minds. *I'm not risking our presence here. The Strykers will do what Ciari says regarding us. The humans assigned here only obey the government. They're guards as much as they are employees of this Syndicate.*

What about the bioware nets? Jael asked.

I didn't touch their minds. Your Strykers are keeping them occupied elsewhere.

Lucas disengaged his telepathy, leaving them alone. When they finally reached Threnody's cell, Quinton wished Lucas hadn't left so quickly. He'd have asked the other man to show the same sort of care Threnody had received to Jael.

Quinton stared through the two-way viewing window at where his partner lay, trying to control his temper. "Open it."

"What happened here was protocol," Jael said unapologetically. "We did what we had to do in order to protect ourselves."

Quinton shot her a murderous glare and shoved past her once she tapped in the code to open the door. Threnody was lying on her back, the clothes she wore filthy with vomit and bloodstains, an external neurocollar locked around her throat. Blood was dried on her face and in her hair, but Quinton didn't hesitate when he touched a hand to her shoulder.

"Thren."

"Took you long enough," she croaked out, but no heat was in her tone.

Jason knelt down on her other side as Threnody opened her eyes. "Thought I told you not to undo all my hard work?"

She managed a tight smile. "Couldn't help it."

Jael leaned over and pressed her thumb to the sensor lock on Threnody's neurocollar. The biometrics read her print and it unlocked. Jael got out of the way so Quinton could carefully pry the restraint off, pulling the bioware-tipped needles out of Threnody's skin and spine as carefully as he could. He tossed the neurocollar aside, hearing it clatter against the floor somewhere behind him.

Jason rested his fingers against the back of Threnody's hand and let his power sink into her body. His vision layered itself to countless degrees of magnification, creating a kind of vertigo that made his stomach heave as he felt the damage in Threnody's body along his own nerves.

"Ribs," he said clinically. "They're bruised and cracked, but not broken. Nothing that would account for the blood."

"You'll need Lucas for that." Threnody coughed. "They broke all my shields. His is the only one I've got left."

"Bastards. All right, hold still. You're lucky I got all that practice working on Quinton's face and arms."

Jason knit bone back together quicker than he had with Quinton. Practice and use was going a long way to showing him how this was supposed to work. It was like building something tangible with his hands, only he was using his mind to reshape cells. Jason didn't have any nanites this time to guide him, but he was beginning to realize he didn't need them.

Threnody finally took in a deep, unlabored breath and turned her hand over to squeeze Jason's. "Thanks."

"Don't mention it."

Quinton helped Threnody to a sitting position, supporting most of her weight. "You need a shower and some rest."

"I *want* a shower and some rest. I *need* to know what's happening." Threnody rubbed carefully at her throat and the small holes leaking blood there. "Get me up, Quin."

Between Jason and Quinton, they got Threnody to her feet. Threnody bared her teeth at Jael in a smile when she saw the other woman. Jael didn't seem bothered by the animosity.

"You should have asked," Threnody said. "I would have told you the truth."

"Maybe you should have let me into your mind," Jael retorted.

Threnody turned her head to look at Quinton. "Take me to Lucas."

TWENTY-NINE

SEPTEMBER 2379

LONDON, UNITED KINGDOM

Nathan stared down at the limp form of his son on the medical bed, studying the stress and agony lines that ravaged Gideon's young face. His mind wasn't much better, a jagged mess of broken thoughts and missing memory. When Gideon had teleported into the Warhound arrival room, Nathan was forced to abandon his job overseeing the last of the seed bank transfers from his Syndicate in London to Paris and help save his only remaining child.

The damage Lucas had done to Gideon's mind was uniquely twisted, but had echoes of Nathan all throughout. Nathan had trained Lucas extensively in the capabilities of a Class I power and he had learned those lessons well. This torture went deep, seemingly cutting out the most recent memories stored in the short term before widening out for days, sometimes weeks past. Nathan wondered about that. Wondered just what his oldest son was trying to hide that Gideon had found out—and now no longer knew.

No answers were to be found in Gideon's mind. Nathan stopped the mindwipe from doing any more damage, but he couldn't fix what was already torn apart. Lucas knew the value in total eradication, and that's what he'd attempted here. It was sheer luck that Gideon managed to make it back to London, luck that had a name: Samantha. Her act of guilty compassion stood out in bright relief in Gideon's mind, the thing he'd clung to in order to escape. It didn't absolve her.

Nathan stood with his hands in the pockets of his suit jacket and closed his eyes, thinking about his options and how little time he had left. The Genome Privacy Act he'd lobbied for weeks ago merely legalized actions taken by his family over decades at the behest of the World Court.

It enabled him to search out unregistered humans without needing to hide his actions anymore.

Nathan was supposed to have weeks left to seed the Registry with targeted, unregistered humans who had unclean DNA. They were essential to his plans for Mars Colony, because high-Classed psions only came from the dregs of humanity. He'd been planning to have Gideon help him coordinate the movements of all those people and the Warhounds to the launch site, but now it fell on him alone, as it always did.

I wonder, Marcheline, Nathan thought, thinking of his long-deceased mother, *if you realized you were throwing everything away when you demanded I breed four children instead of just one.*

She'd forced him to break with tradition, ignoring the personal bylaws that the Serca family ran on. It didn't matter, not anymore. Marcheline died years ago and Nathan was left dealing with the fallout of her orders—three lost children and one damaged heir.

Nathan opened his eyes and dipped his mind into Gideon's to wake him. *I need you to focus, Gideon.*

Dark blue eyes opened slowly, a faint glint of silver staining their depths. Nathan had seen that gleam before, in Kristen, a warning sign of impending insanity. "Father?"

More a question, not really recognition. Nathan grimaced. "On your feet."

Gideon slowly pushed himself to a sitting position before swinging his legs over the edge of the bed. "What happened?"

He didn't know, his mind a jumbled mess of fractured memories. Nathan didn't have the time to help Gideon sort it all out. The blank spots Nathan could feel in Gideon's mind were hard to accept, but he couldn't replace what had forcibly been lost.

"The details are in there," Nathan said, removing a hand from his pocket to point at the datapad sitting on the nearby table. "You can review it later. Right now, we need to move."

Gideon stood up on shaky legs, squeezing his eyes shut as a headache jolted through his skull. He blindly reached for the datapad. "I can't—where's Samantha? I can't feel her."

Confusion filled his voice, but no panic. No sense of the permeating ache Nathan had felt in Gideon's mind since Samantha's defection.

"I'm not concerned about your twin." Nathan looked over Gideon's shoulder at his new CMO, Hu Yin. The Class IV telepath stepped forward and firmly took hold of Gideon's arm, giving him support.

"I have his mind shielded," Hu said, his telepathic presence in Gideon's mind hard to miss. Hu carried a heavy medical trauma kit in his other hand. Trunks were stacked behind him, some bearing the international symbol of the Red Cross, still used by those who worked in the medical field, be they human or psion.

Nathan closed his eyes, blocking out everything.

Sharra, Nathan said, reaching for Erik's wife through an increasingly volatile mental grid. *Open your eyes to me.*

The psi link they shared, thin and tenuous and part of her registered baseline, pulled stronger. Nathan saw the inside of a private waiting room that lacked any adornments and housed only chairs. He sensed people around her, just a few political aides and technicians. More than that, he sensed Dalia, his human spy.

Visual established, Nathan teleported himself, Gideon, and Hu into the room Sharra waited in at the Command Center above the flood of wastewater in Paris. The humans weren't expecting his arrival, but it didn't matter. Nathan telepathically put them to sleep where they sat, Dalia catching the only one who was standing. She dragged the heavier man over to a rickety chair.

"Nathan," Sharra said in a shaky voice as she held Lillian tighter, her daughter suddenly dead weight in her arms. Her blue eyes skated past him, taking in the sight of Gideon and Hu. She'd seen enough wounded psions in her life to know that Gideon was hurting.

"Dalia, lock the door," Nathan ordered.

"Are things that bad out there?" Sharra said as Nathan gestured Hu to take care of Gideon.

"The fact that you don't know means that you simply don't care."

Sharra swallowed and moved to lay Lillian down on the floor, on top of a small blanket that looked as if it came from the child's bed. She smoothed back some of her daughter's hair before straightening up again.

Nathan watched her, the look in his eyes flat. "When is Erik joining you?"

"I don't know. He and the rest of the justices are still at The Hague." Sharra tugged at the collar of her blouse, biting her lip. "The transfers are picking up, but they're still far under the numbers the World Court hoped to move. The launch was supposed to take weeks, not days. They're working to ensure enough of us get out before the riots get out of hand."

"So he's still trying to position himself as the savior of the world," Nathan said contemptuously.

"We wouldn't be in this situation if you had controlled your children."

Nathan reached for her, not with his hands, but with his mind. *I'm of the opinion that this insolence in our children comes from your side of the family.*

He telekinetically slammed her down into the nearest chair with enough force to bruise her tailbone. Biting back a cry of pain, Sharra held herself still. She knew better than to fight, not here.

I got what I bargained for, Sharra thought bitterly as Nathan approached. A bargain between a psion and a human was never really a bargain. She had learned that lesson late in life, but she still learned it.

"Yes, you did," Nathan said, reading her thoughts. "Survival. I know the new timeline for the launch. I was notified when Erik authorized the changes. That infiltration program you set up on my orders proved useful, like yourself."

"What do you want?"

Nathan tilted her chin up with his hand, releasing his power. She could move, but Sharra didn't dare. "You'll be taking Gideon with you on your assigned space shuttle. Remove someone else if you have to, but he is going with you."

Terror filled her mind, worry for her daughter an almost overriding partner to it. Sharra glanced down at where Lillian lay on the ground. She was a small thing, skinny, like her mother. Lillian was going to grow up beautiful, if she grew up at all.

"I wanted a life for her on Mars Colony," Sharra said desperately. "That's all I ever wanted."

"A mother's instinct and a mother's love. I can honestly say I've never felt either."

"That's because your mother was a monster."

Sharra remembered Marcheline only too well, remembered the paralyzing fear that always wracked her whenever the woman entered her prison cell in the Serca Syndicate all those years ago. Freedom from the streets meant wearing a golden collar in a gilded cage. City towers weren't all that much better than the gutter. Mars Colony was supposed to be the answer. Maybe it wasn't.

Gideon had never cared for the human side of his genes. It stood to reason he wouldn't care about his half sister. Sharra didn't want to lose Lillian.

"One of the few things we'll ever agree on," Nathan said. "I don't expect you to care about Gideon, but I know you'll care about your own life. Keep Gideon with your retinue until I get up there. Don't let anyone put you or him into cryo sleep."

"I wasn't planning on going through the procedure until Erik arrived on the *Ark*."

Nathan's smile was slight and condescending. "Keep being that dutiful wife, Sharra."

She jerked her chin up, finding a sense of defiance from somewhere. "I never regretted becoming this."

"No, you just regretted never knowing if Erik loved you. Would you like to find out?"

"Damn you."

She had always wondered—would always wonder—if it was Erik's own feelings or Nathan's psionic interference that existed in their marriage. The kind of courage it took to claw her way out of the streets of London was different from the strength it took to tear apart her carefully crafted second life.

Sharra was brave, but she wasn't stupid.

"Live with what you've made," Nathan said, taking a step back. "And get my son off this planet."

All Sharra could do was obey.

"Dalia," Nathan said. "Make sure they get on the next space shuttle."

The uniformed woman with an unremarkable face only nodded. "Of course, sir."

Nathan teleported out, the only one to leave. Those people rendered unconscious during Nathan's arrival snapped back to awareness, none the wiser of their brief blackout. Neither did they ask questions of the two newest faces in the room, Nathan having erased their curiosity and implanted new memories. Lillian stirred at Sharra's feet, and Sharra bent to pick up her daughter and pull the girl onto her lap.

"I fell asleep?" Lillian asked, yawning through the question. She rubbed at her face with one small hand, looking and sounding grumpy. All her toys were packed away and she was bored.

Sharra tucked Lillian's head under her chin and closed her eyes. "Just for a little while."

She rocked her daughter in her arms, thinking about what it took for her to reach this moment. From the streets of London to the isolated glitter of The Hague. From the launch out of Paris, then the flight to the moon and the colony ship there by way of space shuttles painstakingly reverse engineered from those left behind after the burgeoning age of space was destroyed by bombs.

For far longer than the length of Sharra's life, the government had been making careful forays into space to hone the skills needed for this venture and to bring the *Ark* back online for their escape. So much effort, so much deceit, so much hope placed over the decades for the safety and survival of the human race onto the shoulders of the men and women who ascended to the World Court.

All of it useless in the face of the Serca family's machinations and desire for the same freedom Sharra and those like her wanted.

"Sharra."

She grimaced at her name coming from her son's mouth. "What?"

"I'm not going with you."

She opened her eyes and lifted her head in shock. "But Nathan—"

Sharra never finished her sentence, much less her thought. A foreign telepathic touch invaded her mind, ignoring the risk of being discovered by the bioware net. It didn't matter anymore. Her orders didn't matter because she no longer remembered Nathan delivering them.

Sharra blinked, staring dazedly around the room, wincing against the tension headache that pounded through her head. The woman charged by Nathan to look after them approached and nodded down at Sharra and Lillian. Dalia looked how Sharra felt. "Let's get you on a space shuttle, Mrs. Gervais."

Sharra nodded and stood with Lillian in her arms. It took several minutes for everyone to get organized and leave the room. The small group was met in the hallway by a scientist who took them to the ready room being used for the more important transfers. They were helped into space suits by a dozen workers, bodies wrapped in an enclosed environment that made Sharra feel claustrophobic. She held Lillian's hand tightly in hers and followed every order given to her.

Dalia walked them to the small dock shuttle and helped them get settled before letting the pilot know they were ready. The jaunt to their assigned space shuttle was short. The dock shuttle locked into place against a shielded transport tube and the hatch opened. Sharra took in a heavy breath and undid her harness, then Lillian's. One step, then another, took her closer and closer to an escape she wasn't sure would save them.

"Mama?" Lillian said as they were escorted into the space shuttle by its crew. "I'm scared."

Sharra knelt in front of her daughter and framed the child-size helmet with her hands. She managed to dredge up a smile from somewhere. "I know. But everything's going to be fine. Be my brave little girl, darling. I'll be right here with you."

"Promise?"

"Always."

They were strapped into their assigned seats so tightly it hurt to breathe. Sharra held Lillian's hand in her own as hard as she could and didn't let go.

Erik, she thought. *I'll see you soon.*

Sharra would remember leaving Earth in flashes, not whole memories. How the space shuttle's engines roared in her ears and shook her bones. How the g-forces flattened her body against the curve of her seat. The way her breath was forced out of her lungs as the pressure got worse down the two-kilometer-long, curved launch ramp before they were flung into the sky. The sharp pop of her ears over and over as the space shuttle gained altitude, struggling to break orbit on a one-way trip to a new life. The way she never let go of her daughter's hand.

Left behind on the ground, Gideon watched the space shuttle until he couldn't see even the spark of it anymore. Beside him in the viewing room, Hu watched Gideon with a frown on his face. "You should have been on that shuttle."

Gideon pressed the heel of his palm against his forehead. "I don't need you questioning my actions."

"I shouldn't be doing this, Gideon. Nathan wanted you on the *Ark*."

"Nathan needs to learn I'm the only one he's got to rely on. He can't do that with me in space."

Hu let out a heavy sigh. "Then let's find a private room to wait. It'll give me time to sort out your mind."

Gideon turned away from the window and the view stretched out beyond it, no longer interested in what it had to offer.

PART SIX

SALVATION

SESSION DATE: 2128.04.09
LOCATION: Institute of Psionics Research
CLEARANCE ID: Dr. Amy Bennett
SUBJECT: 2581
FILE NUMBER: 308

"You broke it," Aisling says as she tugs on the short sleeve of her yellow dress. A wire is caught in the fabric and she frees it with careful fingers. She kicks her feet where they dangle in the air.

"We didn't break anything," the doctor replies, not looking up from the datapads on the table.

"Tell that to the people of Río Gallegos."

The doctor's head snaps up, face turned toward the two-way mirror near the door. She makes a gesture with one hand, one she has made before.

"Too late," Aisling sighs. "You're always too late. Bombs away."

The doctor slams her hand against the table, shaking it. "We wouldn't still be in this situation if you helped us!"

"If I could help you, I would, but you would still be in this situation." The girl slides a little in her chair, her small head tilting back. She stares at the ceiling, with its bright lights, and doesn't blink. "Please don't be mad. I'm trying to fix this."

"How? How are you trying? You're not giving us the information we need."

"I'm sorry, but you wouldn't understand."

[THIRTY]

The Strykers Syndicate was pared down to a skeleton crew over the course of hours. Every Stryker was ordered into the field to deal with the escalating riots, including those who were still recovering from wounds incurred in Buffalo or elsewhere. To stay behind meant dereliction of duty and the promise of instant termination. That was the order of the World Court, and Ciari heeded the warning. Their absence meant Lucas's small group had far fewer people to run into and risk tipping off the government.

They gathered in a debriefing room, standing around a large conference table that had the small carrying cases stacked neatly across it. Everyone's attention was on the vidscreen embedded in the wall.

"This isn't going to trip an alarm, is it?" Jael asked.

"I know government code and I learned a few new tricks while on the run," Jason said, never taking his eyes off the vidscreen. "They won't know we're hooked up where we're not supposed to be."

"Will it last?"

"Longer than the measures you've got running in Ciari's office to hide your activities."

The vidscreen showed a view none of them had ever before seen. A hazy, ethereal blue glow seemed to smudge the center, dividing black from a curve of gray-blue. The cloud formations were gray and thin over a murky blue ocean. The darkening shape of a continent moving into night seen from space was unfamiliar. The old satellite they were using didn't have the best focus capabilities after decades of floating through space without upgrades. Still, Lucas knew what was happening when he saw it.

"There," Lucas said, leaning forward, eyes on the grainy picture.

A tiny, brightly glowing dot was lifting off the planet, rising into space. It grew larger, the satellite bringing the shape into focus. It was a space shuttle, the first of many, and no one could look away as it left Earth behind and disappeared offscreen. More space shuttles followed the first.

"That's the start of it," Lucas said. "We'll only have so much time left now. A few days at the most."

"With the amount of people they need to move, I'd think it would be longer," Keiko said.

"The launch site was built to house space shuttles, not people. It's a bottleneck in terms of movement. It's why the government wanted to do this over the course of weeks, not in the middle of a panic. They can't hope to ship thousands and thousands of people into space, then put them all into cryo on the colony ship quickly. Cryo is complicated and there are only so many doctors on board the *Ark* who can oversee the process."

"Which means a lot of people won't make it," Ciari said, staring at the vidscreen.

"If a registered human misses their shuttle to Paris, then there's no chance for them."

"And the ones in space?" Threnody said.

Lucas shrugged. "I've seen the schematics of the *Ark*. It's mostly storage space, bays and bays of cold boxes for cryo sleep and storage units for supplies. Easier to pack bodies in as cargo than as passengers. You use up less space if you don't have to factor in living quarters for anyone but the crew."

"Will that ship make it to Mars in one piece?"

"It's survived over two hundred and fifty years cold-docked in space. It'll survive a few more."

Ciari stared across the table at him. "You don't want it to."

"I thought we could let them go, let them fly to some uncertain future." Lucas ran a hand through his hair, nails scratching against his scalp. "We'd have Earth, which is all I ever wanted, but they would return."

"Are there Warhounds on the space shuttles launching right now?" Quinton wanted to know.

"There will be Warhounds on every single one until Nathan has transferred them all."

It went unsaid that when the *Ark* returned from a failed colonization on another world, it would arrive bearing humans and psions beholden to Nathan, who would fight for his rightful place in society. The world didn't need another war.

"What now?" Kerr said. "You want to stop the launch? How do we do that and save the Strykers as well?"

"Distributing the virus has priority. We're going to need everyone free to help fight, because we won't be enough on our own, even merged," Lucas said.

"Can you be sure they won't run away?" Samantha said, not looking at her brother. She hadn't looked him in the eye since letting Gideon go free. "If I was a Stryker and no longer had a neurotracker in my head, I'd go to ground in an instant."

"When I give an order, Strykers obey," Ciari said. "You weren't trained how we were. Don't believe all of us will abandon our posts. Freedom won't mean anything if we don't have a place to stay and live."

"Speaking of living," Keiko said. "The government only has half the supplies from the seed bank in the Arctic. I helped Nathan organize the transfer of everything left. If that's what they were using to replenish the SkyFarms over the years, we're going to need the rest of it. Where did you take it, Lucas?"

Lucas smiled at the question. "I see someone found my little message in the wall."

"Your damn message got a Stryker killed. Where's the rest of the seed bank?"

"Safe. You don't need to know where."

Keiko opened her mouth to argue, but Ciari interrupted her with "That's all we need to know, Keiko. Leave it be."

Threnody spared a glance at Jael before saying, "If we want the Strykers to believe what we tell them about the virus, they'll need to hear the reason from an officer."

"That's why Keiko will be with Jason and Quinton to administer the virus," Lucas said. He cut off Quinton's protest with a look and a warning touch against the pyrokinetic's mental shields. "I'm sending Threnody and Kerr on a different mission that requires their powers. Aidan will monitor Keiko's progress, and when she returns, I'll teach her the basics of merging."

"What about them?" Aidan said, pointing at Lucas's sisters.

The permanent smile on Kristen's face was half covered by one hand, which she used to prop up her chin. She was seated next to Samantha, tapping her fingers against the edge of the table. "We're going to the City of Lights."

"Where is that?" Jason said. "I've been to almost every city that's left in this world. I've never heard of that one."

"Paris," Samantha answered in a clipped voice. "We're getting Lucas a sitrep on security at the launch site. No one will question us Sercas being there if humans discover our presence."

"Is that safe with the amount of Warhounds that will be around? Not to mention the toxicity of the surrounding area."

"The radiation won't be as high as it was in the past, but it's still intolerable, especially if you're human." Samantha shrugged. "We need to know what's happening in Paris now that we no longer have people providing us inside information."

"It's been so long, you'd think the radiation would fade," Jael said. "But it doesn't. It just gets in your cells and lingers."

"Sounds like everything's been decided," Quinton said, turning his back on the room and the space shuttles on the vidscreen that were still launching. "Come get me when it's time to go into the field."

He left, ignoring Threnody when she called out his name. Sighing in frustration, she shoved away from the conference table, calling over her shoulder to the room at large, "I'll be back."

Jason's careful, meticulous hack of the security system that spanned the Strykers Syndicate had been limited. Quinton couldn't go far. Threnody found him in a room that held rows of empty research terminals, the people who would have manned them currently reassigned. Quinton didn't immediately look up at her arrival.

"Hey," Threnody said, putting her back against the door.

"You could have argued," he said after a moment, letting his hands rest on the edge of a terminal as he glared at her. "You could have done something other than accept everything that comes out of Lucas's mouth."

"Where would that have gotten us? This is the only course of action. If it means we have to work apart, then we work apart."

"You don't know if this is the only way."

"Yes," Threnody said quietly. "I do."

She had faith in a child that no one alive had ever met, that no one ever would except through saved encrypted files. Maybe Threnody didn't trust Lucas, but she trusted in his goal, and Quinton couldn't doubt that, because it meant he'd be doubting her. Quinton shook his head and tried to smile, but it came out wrong, crooked. She saw it for what he meant it to be.

"Damn it," he whispered. "Why can't I ever argue with you?"

Threnody shrugged. "Maybe you should have. I'm the reason why we got sent to the Slums in the first place, remember? Maybe if you reminded me to toe the line growing up, fulfill our contracts without arguing, and do as we were ordered, we wouldn't be here."

"It wasn't my place to tell you how to do your job, Thren. It was my place to follow where you led."

Threnody pushed away from the door and went to his side. She adjusted the flak jacket he wore, settling it more evenly on his broad shoulders. Threnody let her hands rest there, thumbs pressed against the bare skin of his neck. She could feel the electric pulse that ran through his body, a thing she knew just as intimately as she knew her own.

"I'm glad," Threnody said, "that they gave you to me as my partner, Quin. I don't regret that, and I don't regret everything that brought us here to do this. I just hope you won't either."

Quinton splayed one hand against the back of her head, fingers digging through her loose hair. He leaned down to press his forehead to hers, staring into her eyes. Conviction filled Threnody's voice, the same conviction that had gotten them through countless hellish missions over the years. It was a belief that they could survive anything, that they could survive this, and Quinton wondered what he would do without her by his side, shoring him up.

"I don't regret you," he said.

She offered up a tired smile, some of the tension leaving her body. They were family, no matter how hard the government tried to beat that belief out of them. A few years shy of thirty, the two of them, and they had survived so much. Psions had long memories, and forgetting anything that happened in their lives was damn near impossible. The neural pathways linking the intricate relationships of memories meant a lifetime could be recalled with crystal clarity. In that lifetime, they would always have each other.

"Come on," she said, pulling away, eyes clear of everything except determination. "Let's get back to the others."

When they returned to the conference room, they found only Lucas and Kerr waiting for them. The vidscreen was running the satellite feed, but nothing of interest was happening. It seemed the launch was at a lull. Lucas focused his attention on Quinton once the other man stepped inside.

"I don't like disobedience," Lucas said.

"You're going to get a lot of it when you free the Strykers," Quinton said. "If you're hoping to grind us under your heel when this is over, you're not going to like what happens."

Lucas nodded at the door, ignoring the threat. "Go find Jason. He's with Keiko figuring out the best route for teleportation over the continents."

Quinton knew a dismissal when he heard one. He still hesitated, wondering if he could get away with remaining in the room. Threnody shook her head. "Go, Quinton. It'll be all right."

"Watch your back," Quinton said as he left. The door slid shut behind him.

Threnody eyed Lucas. "What now?"

"Everyone has their orders but you two," Lucas said. "I'll explain what needs to be done after we leave tomorrow."

"Why?" Kerr said.

"We need to pick up Novak. You need a hacker and Ciari can't spare one from the Stryker ranks."

"And you can't spare Jason," Threnody said. "When we get Novak tomorrow morning, where are you teleporting us? What do you want us to do?"

Lucas smiled, the expression an echo of Nathan's ruthlessness, Nathan's cruelty. "You're going to steal a bomb."

[THIRTY-ONE]

SEPTEMBER 2379
PARIS, FRANCE

The streets of London echoed with the voices of rioters demanding entry to the restricted area around the city towers. Bodies were strewn in the street near where military defense holed up, but people still struggled forward over the fallen. Segregation based on the cleanliness of a person's DNA had been the norm for centuries, rarely challenged, and always rigidly enforced. Now the government was applying segregation to an extent never before seen in society, and the people who had slipped through the cracks all their lives were refusing to be forgotten.

Unregistered humans weren't the only ones joining the growing worldwide fray. The military, with its scores of quads sent out to police what was left of the world, were made up of a mix of people. Some soldiers came from families that had barely made it into the Registry when the Fifth Generation Act was enacted. Other soldiers called the streets home. City towers refused to have unclean DNA in their midst, and the soldiers who patrolled those areas refused to work in the streets. The military had become as divided as the rest of society. It wasn't any great shock when it began to break apart and soldiers took opposite sides in the fight.

People held their ground in the streets of surviving cities, waves of protesters hitting against the anchor foundations of sealed city towers. In London, it was no different, and in the early light of morning, its streets were crowded.

Lucas's group teleported out of Toronto when it was full dark, arriving in London when the sun was starting to rise over the distant horizon. The air had a faint bite of cold to it, an early warning of the oncoming change of seasons. Dawn filtered through an overcast sky filled with smoke and pollution as their feet hit the roof of a tenement with a hard smack. Lucas was executing this part of the plan through shortened teleports, needing to conserve his strength for the oncoming fights ahead. The brief rest everyone had managed before scattering across the world was only that—brief.

A scan of the tenement proved it was almost empty, the majority of its inhabitants drawn to the riots. Lucas looked out over the city as he sent his mind skimming through the mental grid, tagging the population. People on the streets of London were closer to the foundations of the city towers near the Thames than any other territory. He wondered how long the registered humans would last before security was overwhelmed.

"I really hope they don't burn the city to the ground," Threnody said as she surveyed the area from behind her helmet. "There's less toxicity around here and there's no room in any of the other cities for this population. The bunkers couldn't handle the overflow."

"It will stand for now," Lucas said as he squinted into the dawn. The city tower he once called home was backlit by the rising sun. "Nathan still needs it as a launching point to Paris for his Warhounds. He's not going to risk losing them because of the riots."

All of them wore specialized skinsuits capable of shielding against radiation, with hard helmets instead of skinmasks coverings their heads. The places they needed to go weren't kind to survivors. Samantha adjusted the strap on her shoulder, the metal carrying case also shielded against radiation. It held extra supplies they couldn't risk getting contaminated, items she would need when they got to Paris.

Kristen wandered to the edge of the roof, crouching down beside the crumbling safety wall. "They're all so angry," she said, smiling through the words. She turned her head to glance back at her siblings, the sunlight skating over her gleaming dark blue eyes, turning them silver for an instant. "Are we going to keep it?"

"Don't concern yourself with London, Kris. It's not your problem."

Lucas lifted a hand and gestured at Kristen, telekinetically pulling her back from the ledge. She was deposited back beside Samantha, the older girl looking disdainfully down at her sister.

"I wish you would take her with you," Samantha said, pointing at Kristen. "I can handle Paris on my own."

"Perhaps, but Kris will keep you honest."

Samantha's mouth curled up contemptuously. "Don't trust me?"

They were all three of them Sercas, with complicated blood ties and psi links that bound them together to an impossible degree. Lucas was supposed to one day own their family's Syndicate, and the rest were simply supposed to fall in line and obey. He had learned—eventually—that blind obedience was never useful.

"I trust you more than you could possibly imagine," Lucas said, surprising Samantha with that confession. Then he telekinetically yanked her to his side, Samantha's body cutting through the air until she was eye to eye with him, feet centimeters above the ground. "But don't mistake your freedom for something it isn't."

Samantha stabbed her telepathy into his mind, holding it against his shields, knowing better than to attack any further. That Lucas let her get that far had more to do with his twisted sense of generosity than her skill. Something deep in his mind resonated in her own, and it sparked pain throughout her head.

She closed her eyes for a second or two. "What did you do to me?"

"What had to be done."

He shoved her away, retracting his telekinesis. Samantha couldn't keep her balance and fell, skidding against the grit and old debris on the rooftop. Her teeth bit through the inside of her cheek at the impact. Swearing, she got to her feet, swallowing blood and saliva.

"If this is what having siblings is like, I think I'm glad I never knew mine," Kerr said.

Samantha shot him a dirty look. "A field partner is nothing like a family."

Kerr gave her a pitying look. "Yeah, but I never have to watch my back around them."

Kristen closed the distance between herself and Samantha, wrapping her arms around the other girl's waist and resting her head on Samantha's shoulder. Kristen only had eyes for Lucas. "It hurts here. Can we stay?"

"No," Lucas told her. "We can't."

Samantha extracted herself from Kristen's grip. "She's unstable, Lucas. She's going to make this mission difficult. You really should have left her behind."

"She'll be all right." Lucas glanced in the direction of the city towers before saying, "Hold on everyone."

The next teleport was shorter than the last, taking them to Paris. They arrived on a dilapidated street braced by the gutted remains of buildings survived only by their foundations. Some streets were collapsed into the subways, quarries, and sewers that existed beneath the old city. They could make out a few scraggly trees and bushes nearby, none of which looked healthy.

What they could see of the city around them consisted of hard, discolored dirt in craters that broke up ancient asphalt, and stunted vegetation that crawled over the surrounding ruins. In the distance, a rusted and broken Eiffel Tower clawed for prominence in a sky that was eclipsed by launch platforms built over the dead city. Sunlight was a bit brighter here; they'd lost an hour in that split-second teleport.

Threnody walked a few meters away from the group, slowly turning to take in a rotting city that had been one of the greatest capitals on earth. "Hard to believe millions once lived here. I wonder what it was like?"

"Loud, cramped, and noisy, I would guess," Kerr said. "Like a bunker city, but with sky over your head instead of a metal roof and dirt beyond it."

Samantha looked across the distance that separated them from the launch platforms. Even as they watched, a space shuttle was barreling down the long, curved launch ramp, hurtling itself into the sky. The smoke trails of previous launches left a haze in the air. The hard helmets they wore made it impossible for them to smell the exhaust and stagnant pollution.

Warhounds are scattered all over those platforms, Samantha said at the edge of Lucas's mind. She went to pull Kristen away from a crumbling set of ruins that had caught her attention.

Nathan might be holding them back, Lucas replied. *Probably to coordinate the transfer of their people. I doubt they'll need to get rid of any extrane-*

ous registered humans anytime soon. There's plenty of seats right now for them to take over.

We need to get inside.

I know. I'm looking for the right pair of eyes. Lucas had his own closed in concentration.

Once we have what you need, what then?

I'll bring you back and we stand our ground, so to speak.

Samantha glanced over at him. *You're serious about the Strykers, aren't you?*

Yes. We need them just like we need the humans that are being left behind. More so, since they're going to be our source of power.

You really think they'll bow to you? After so many years dying for the humans, do you honestly think once they've tasted freedom, the Strykers will accept you holding them down again?

I'm the one who made their freedom possible. You'd be surprised what sort of loyalty that can buy.

Samantha's hand tightened on Kristen's shoulder, an involuntary protest to the knowledge that her loyalty hadn't been bought, but forcibly imposed on her.

"Found her," Lucas said, opening his eyes.

"Found who?" Kerr asked.

"Dalia."

Kristen perked up at the name and let out a gleeful little chuckle. "Nathan isn't going to be happy you've touched his toy."

"I'm not going to use her mind. The fact that she's still here means Nathan hasn't arrived yet. She's coordinating shuttle routes."

Lucas didn't use Dalia to get a visual. Instead, he skimmed through the static human minds showing up on the mental grid, dipping in and out of dozens until he found the one he needed. The scientist in question knew the layout of the Command Center, knew the restricted areas that people left vacant for hours. Lucas pried from the man's memory the image of a dimly lit room belowground, surrounded by metal and machines.

It wasn't the best thing to draw from—human memory was so easily broken—but he managed to piece the room together through other people's memories once he knew what to look for. When he finalized the visual, Lucas teleported them into a cramped generator room. They dropped down onto a metal floor, all five of them appearing in the small aisle between machines.

Kerr moved and bumped his shoulder against a safety railing as machines thrummed loudly around them. "Shit, Lucas. Cutting it a little close, aren't you?"

"I know the space I 'port into," Lucas said.

Threnody craned her head around, taking in the loud machinery. "Where are we?" she asked, raising her voice in order to be heard.

"One of the support columns that holds up the Command Center."

"We're surrounded by wastewater? Bloody hell," Samantha said as she undid the helmet of her skinsuit and pulled it off. She scratched around the bioware lining her face to hide her identity. "Is using Dalia an option at all, Lucas?"

He shook his head. "Nathan's been in near constant contact with her. Don't try it."

"She'd be the best source of information on security."

"Which has all been severely altered due to the move-up of the launch. I don't want to gamble on Nathan discovering our presence."

"All right." Samantha dropped her case to the floor. Kneeling, she dug through it for the clothes she and Kristen would wear to disguise themselves and the dark glasses that would hide their distinctive eyes. "Kristen and I will get you what you need. I'll contact you when we're finished for an extraction."

"Don't get caught," Threnody said.

"I know how to do my job," Samantha said without looking up.

Lucas didn't say good luck or good-bye before teleporting out. Samantha didn't expect him to. Their family didn't believe in something as flimsy as luck. Blackmail, torture, and political maneuverings, yes—but not luck.

THIRTY-TWO

SEPTEMBER 2379
THE HAGUE, THE NETHERLANDS

The drug cartels have overridden the barriers around the city towers in Sapporo, sir," an aide said, looking at a point over Erik's shoulder. "Reports coming in state that four of the thirteen city towers have been destroyed by dissident bombings."

Erik half rose from his desk, hands pressed flat against it. *"What?"*

The aide drew in a shaky breath, sparing a glance down at the datapad he held in his hand. "That's all we have at the moment. We're still trying to get numbers on casualties."

"There shouldn't *be* any goddamn casualties!" Erik snarled. "Where were the Strykers when this happened?"

"In the field, sir. The security grid showed that some died during the collapse."

"They died during a collapse that shouldn't have happened. Where was the military? Where were the rest of the Strykers dispatched to protect registered humans?"

The aide swallowed, glancing over his shoulder at the door he'd come through. "The, ah, the OIC of the Strykers Syndicate is here to address that."

Erik froze where he stood, body going tense. His eyes narrowed at that announcement, fury momentarily twisting his face into something ugly. "Bring her in."

The aide scurried out; Ciari let herself inside. Erik studied the bald woman as she approached his desk, her steps careful. Her punishment had left marks etched into her skin. Erik couldn't recall anyone wearing a more empty expression than Ciari wore on her face right now. It was like seeing a dead soldier walking and it should have brought some measure of comfort to him, but it didn't.

"My aide informed me that we lost city towers in Japan," Erik said through clenched teeth. "Explain yourself."

"The Strykers weren't holding the line" was Ciari's simple, easy answer.

"Come again?" Erik said after a moment, disbelief in his voice.

Rather than repeat herself, Ciari stepped closer and offered up the datapad she carried. Erik took it with surprisingly steady hands, the information on the screen making cold sweat creep down his back. He swiped his thumb over the screen, scrolling through the report, some distant hint of panic rising inside him as he studied the changed placement of Strykers.

"Has this been verified?"

"In Japan and elsewhere, but not across the board." Ciari tilted her head to the side, staring at him with unblinking eyes. The weight of her attention made his skin crawl. "We can't reach some of the teams from our end back in Canada. I came to see if perhaps you were giving out orders I didn't know about. I can't do my job, Erik, if you don't let me."

With a sudden, vicious motion, Erik hurled the datapad at the far wall, a wordless shout ripping from his lungs. His atypical reaction didn't seem to faze Ciari.

"You can't do your *job*?" Erik shouted. "Is that why you're here? Because you can't do your fucking job and you want a reprieve?"

"If I begged, would it make a difference?"

"The Strykers aren't doing their job and people are dying, Ciari. *Good people.* Their lives are worth a hundred times as much as you psion dogs."

Erik stalked out of his office. Black spots danced across his vision as he hurried down the halls of the Peace Palace. The building was mostly empty, the mass evacuation of the world capital and the bunker city beneath it having been well under way for hours. Staying longer was beginning to seem like a fool's choice.

He turned a corner blindly and nearly ran into Anchali, the much smaller and older woman catching her balance between her cane and the wall as she pulled up short. "Erik?" Anchali asked, taking in the fury on his face. Her attention jumped from him to the psion who followed obediently at his heels.

"Anchali," Erik said, hands clenching and unclenching near his thighs. "I'm sorry. If you'll excuse me?"

She caught him by the arm before he could walk past, her wrinkled face tilting up to look at him. "No, I will not. What is going on, Erik?"

He didn't turn to look at Ciari, but he could sense her presence. Erik was struck, rather viscerally, by how useless the layers of security that surrounded the Peace Palace were in the face of losing the upper hand. The military wouldn't be enough against Strykers who might have slipped their leash.

"I'm heading for the command information center." He was so careful to keep the fear out of his voice, to look only at Anchali. "Come with me."

Anchali didn't like what she saw in his face, but she wasn't going to leave him. She followed him to the center of the Peace Palace and the lift that would take them below to the barricaded and burrowed heart of the world's military.

Once there in those steel corridors, Erik headed for the area that handled communications with the Strykers Syndicate, to the officers whose sole job was to monitor and control the psions through technology. The Strykers Syndicate in Toronto was saturated with spyware and monitoring equipment, as well as formal programs for government communications. Through the world's security grid, the military could monitor every single Stryker baseline and their location through the neurotrackers in their brains.

"Show me Japan," Erik ordered as he strode into the operations hub.

Soldiers rushed to obey. Despite the world's fracturing, it was nice to know that military discipline was still intact. The vidscreens that circled the walls and terminals soon showcased the pulsing dots of nearly a hundred Strykers scattered across the map of the only inhabited island of Japan. The unique neural pattern of a psion's brain was fed through nerves into bioware, which then translated the information into a signal. The output of that signal was fed into the security grid by the neurotrackers. It was those signals that cut across the screens, solid placement of psion baselines pinpointing locations through satellite connections and bioscans in the security grid.

"Bring up the locations of all Strykers on a world map," Erik said, voice carrying through the buzz of conversation. "Priority given to my order."

His order was executed immediately, the data scrolling across the main command screen.

"Erik," Anchali said in a low voice, "what are you doing?"

"Laying to rest a problem."

It took five minutes to bring up and verify all Stryker positions across the globe, the government's security grid showing up in tiny patches across too-empty continents.

"Positions confirmed," a woman said.

Erik stepped to the nearest terminal, hand hovering over the controls. He turned, just enough that he could see Ciari and the blank expression on her face, but he couldn't find any emotion in her eyes.

"Will you beg now?" he asked, biting out the words. Her silence was answer enough, and Erik pressed his hand down against the sensor. "Initiate full termination sequence."

The soldiers overseeing the security grid obeyed instantly, activating the kill switch in every neurotracker the system was linked to. Anchali watched the vidscreens and the data while Erik refused to look away from Ciari.

"You're wiping them all out," Anchali said, her gaze sweeping across the storm of red that ripped across the map. Solid confirmation of roughly twelve hundred lives snuffed out in an instant.

Only the Stryker with them was still breathing and the signals on the screen were still showing up as active.

Erik staggered against the terminal, legs gone suddenly weak. He pressed his hand against the sensor a second, third, fourth time, but the results didn't change.

Ciari still lived.

"You—," Erik choked out.

Anchali heard fear in his voice for the first time in her life. She turned to see what could cause the president of the World Court to sound like that.

Erik knew that Ciari was only an empath. He had preferred dealing with that kind of psion over one who could read his thoughts. He had never felt that he constantly needed his hand on the kill switch when facing down an empath over contract issues and Stryker transgressions through the years. It struck him suddenly that he only knew the names of maybe a dozen psions in the entire Strykers Syndicate. The rest had always been nameless numbers on the company's bottom line.

They were never people to him. Never human. Erik had trusted blindly in the chains that science had built to contain the disease psions lived with, but technology could always be subverted. Diseases could evolve.

"We were informed of the World Court's decision regarding Strykers and the launch," Ciari said into the sudden silence. "We couldn't fight the orders when you told us to protect you."

The quads scattered throughout the room sensed the threat and moved, aiming their weapons at the enemy. They put themselves between the government and the lone woman who was still perfectly cognizant and alive in the face of people who had only ever used her kind.

Erik stared past the quads at her, voice coming out ragged and harsh. "And now?"

"We won't fight you." Ciari smiled slightly, the expression eerie and wrong on her face. "And we won't beg anymore."

"We *own* you," Anchali snapped out, wrinkled face ashen from shock.

Ciari pressed her fingers against a small, circular bruise that stood out on the side of her throat, the only evidence of Lucas's deceit, even if the humans didn't know it. "We own ourselves now."

"Ciari," Erik said. He thought of the eleven years he'd ordered her to live by his rules and all the rest before that when she'd fought in the hardscrabble streets of the world on orders from the government. Loyalty wasn't found in slavery.

"Stay on Earth, Erik," Ciari said. "If you stay, we can show you a different way."

"Go to hell."

The quads opened fire, but it was too late. Ciari was gone, teleported out to who knew where by some other newly freed Stryker, taking with her Erik's faith in the way the world worked.

THIRTY-THREE

SEPTEMBER 2379
THE SLUMS OF THE ANGELS, USA

Keiko teleported herself, Jason, and Quinton into a safe house buried in the Slums of the Angels. The broken mess of buildings and roads that surrounded the city towers of Los Angeles were where most of the population resided. She stumbled when her feet connected with the ground, and only Quinton's firm grip stopped her from checking out the floor of the arrival area with her face.

"You all right?" Quinton asked.

Keiko straightened up. She swiped at her nose and the faint hint of blood that leaked from it. "Yeah, I'm good."

"I could have pulled this round," Jason said.

"You teleported the last time, and you spent more time in Japan shielding than I did. It was my turn anyway."

They'd been teleporting across continents and oceans during the last sixteen hours without rest. That many teleports, across increasingly longer distances, mixed with the arguments and fights that inevitably broke out with every group of Strykers they met, had exhausted them. Quinton looked marginally better. After the first twelve times, he'd been the one to submit to telepathic verification by other Strykers to confirm the truth of their orders, sparing Keiko and Jason from having someone else mucking around in their minds.

Keiko took a moment to stretch her arms over her head, trying to ease the knotted tension in her body. "At least we've reached North America again. We're almost finished."

They knew they were working under a time limit and had hit the ground running back in Toronto before moving on to Buffalo. They kept going east, teleporting across the Atlantic Ocean to arrive in London and begin the hard task of giving Strykers the virus beneath the heavy presence of the government's security grid.

It had taken long hours to work their way through the Stryker ranks in Europe under the pretense of Keiko checking on their status as the world rioted. They couldn't reach their people in The Hague. Africa had been easier, with less than a dozen surviving cities across the entire continent. They bypassed the Middle East, which, like most of Russia and nearly all of Asia, was full of deadzones. They'd skipped from Africa to Asia's ravaged coastlines along the tip of India and the southeastern swatch of land appropriated by China. Australia was nothing but desert and firestorms, and they'd just come from Japan.

They still had two continents to work their way through, with at least 250 Strykers left that they needed to reach.

"Here's hoping this group doesn't argue like the last one," Quinton said tiredly as he touched the bruise on his face.

Jason snorted. "I can't believe you let her get past your defenses."

"I wasn't going to burn a fellow Stryker. I figured she'd accept Keiko's authority as chief operating officer after picking through my memories. How was I supposed to know she'd have an emotional breakdown?" Quinton shrugged uncomfortably. "She still believed us and didn't question Ciari's orders."

"Telepaths tend to believe more quickly than anyone else," Keiko said as she stepped off the arrival dais in the corner of the large garage. "So let's find one."

They didn't even reach the door before a short, young man was palming it open. Telekinesis slid against their own shields, a heavy weight that made Keiko's headache worse. "Daeng," she said. "We're here on the OIC's order."

Daeng pointed at Keiko's companions. "Sir, you know we've got kill orders for those two."

Keiko managed to dredge up a smile from somewhere. "Orders have changed. We're here to save your life and that of every other Stryker in the Slums."

He hesitated, not quite believing her, but they didn't have time to deal with wasted moments.

"You got a telepath on-site?" Jason said.

"Yes," Daeng said. "Tanya is our senior telepath right now. She's upstairs."

"Call her down here so she can verify our actions and that we're not trying to kill any of you."

Daeng looked at Keiko for confirmation; she gave it. His eyes lost focus for a second or two as he tapped into the psi link he shared with his team. "Tanya's coming."

A minute later, a thin Mexican stepped into the arrival room, wariness in her gaze. "Sir?"

"Link with Quinton," Keiko said. "Ciari's orders."

Strykers knew better than to disobey their Syndicate's officers, especially the OIC. Tanya pulled Quinton into a psi link, taking the memories that he shoved into the forefront of his mind and reviewing them.

"You're kidding," Tanya said, staring at them in disbelief. "That should kill us."

"Hasn't killed anyone we've dosed so far," Quinton said.

"Ciari wants her Strykers to live," Keiko said, her voice cracking from exhaustion. "You will accept her orders and recall in shifts every Stryker in the Slums. We don't have time to waste on petty arguing."

"No," Tanya said after a moment. "I suppose we don't."

"Tanya?" Daeng said warily.

She gave the younger Stryker a lopsided smile, eyes bright. "It's fine, Daeng. We're going to follow their orders."

It took ten minutes for Tanya to telepathically contact all the Strykers assigned to the Slums and coordinate teleportation for everyone. Keiko, Jason, and Quinton left her to deal with the transfer while they went to set everything up.

The Slums were filled with rioters, the buffer zone around the city towers a veritable bloodbath between the military and assigned Strykers holding back the deluge of people hoping to reach a transfer shuttle. The safe house had been ignored only due to psionic interference. The World Court had tasked those Strykers in the Slums to keep everyone down on the ground and out of the city towers. Not that it mattered any longer, with most of the registered humans leaving, but the Strykers still had a job to do and they were going to do it to the bitter end.

That maybe the end wouldn't be so bitter was why no one really fought this procedure. The virus could save them, and no one living with a kill switch in his or her head was going to say no.

Jason rubbed a hand over his burning eyes as he gestured at the first few Strykers who had arrived. "Find a place to sit or lie down. It can't be administered standing up."

Daeng was the first to pick a spot, sliding to the floor with his back against the wall. "What exactly does it do?"

"Turns off the kill switch so the government can't fry your brain. The virus reprograms it around the internal security system. We can't turn off the tracking signal yet. If Strykers started going missing on the security grid in large numbers, the World Court would just fry everyone before we got to them," Jason said as he prepped the dosage. "Took the doctor who wrote the code months to get it right."

"What happened to the doctor?"

"He's still alive." Jason knelt down and pressed the tip of the hypospray against Daeng's throat. "Hold still. This is going to hurt."

"The government won't know?"

That was the fear and the choke hold that all Strykers lived with, the knowledge that if the neurotracker processed even a glitch in its programming, they would die. Jason tapped the hypospray gently against skin.

"It's bioware the code is targeting and nanites are machines." Jason smiled, but it was more teeth than anything else. "We're nothing more than biological machines, when you get right down to it. The virus is going to create a backdoor through our wetware. It'll take a few minutes to complete."

Jason stabbed his thumb against the hypospray button. The soft shushing sound the thin cylinder made as it pressed a dozen tiny needles into skin was echoed by air sucked through Daeng's teeth. Jason moved back and switched the hypospray to his other hand, lifting his free hand to scrape his teeth over the small bruise on his thumb.

He'd pressed that button hundreds of times since leaving Toronto. Those that received the shot came away with a perfect circular bruise on their throat, right over their carotid artery. The rest of the procedure was just as painful, as if the kill switch itself had been flipped.

The nanites, already activated within the hyposprays, followed their programmed orders. Even as Keiko, Jason, and Quinton urged the other Strykers to relax, the nanites were already moving through the internal carotid to where it joined with the arterial circle of Willis. From there, the nanites disseminated through the smaller capillaries and reached the areas where bioware filaments connected to the nerves and brain.

The neurotrackers, when the bioware died, felt as if they took their bodies with them, the way the Strykers thrashed against the agony, nervous systems out of whack and bodies suffering through an unwanted machine's death throes. When it was over, the Strykers remained unconscious for a minute or two as their bodies and brains adjusted to the absence of something they had lived with for most of their lives.

"Breathe," Keiko was saying to another Stryker. The recipient shoved herself up straight in her chair, face pale and bleeding from the nose. "Take a deep breath, it's going to hurt for about an hour."

The Stryker ran her fingers over the back of her head, where the neurotracker sat beneath skin and bone. "Hurt doesn't really cover it." She opened her mouth wide, trying to ease some of the pressure in her skull. "Fuck, that burns."

"You sure it's off? That it can't kill us?" Daeng said from where he sat. His breath was coming quick and fast through his mouth.

"We're sure. Ciari would never risk her people on something that wouldn't work," Keiko said. "The signal is still going strong. Take a minute to catch your breath, then get back to your posts."

Keiko, Jason, and Quinton managed to get through five more shifts of Strykers before the clock ran out. Their luck couldn't last, but that didn't stop Keiko from reaching desperately for the Stryker beneath her hands, who suddenly reared backward, clutching at his head. He started screaming and wasn't the only one. Other Strykers they had yet to dose keeled over screaming, clutching at the back of their necks and heads.

Keiko yelled wordless protests as bodies convulsed around her. She'd seen too many Strykers die like this over the years to not know what was happening. The mass termination was quick, but it was brutally painful to watch, made worse because they could do nothing. They had no way to save the Strykers writhing on the floor as their entire central nervous systems were fried from the inside out.

Keiko didn't know she was crying until she couldn't even see through the tears in her eyes.

"Fuck," Jason yelled, slamming his fist against the wall. *"Fuck."*

"We weren't finished," Keiko said, voice breaking as she stared at the bodies strewn around her. Reflexively, she clenched her hand around the hypospray she carried.

It wasn't just the Slums. They still had cities to pass through, Strykers to dose in the Latin Corridor and South America where they were embedded in cartel territories or the few actual cities that had survived below the equator. Only it didn't matter anymore, because they were too late, and all the remaining doses of the virus-carrying nanites were worthless.

Quinton carefully pried the hypospray out of her hand, wrapping his fingers around hers. "Keiko," he said, voice raw. "Take us back to Toronto."

He was asking her to focus when all she wanted to do was fall apart. Keiko swallowed thickly. "Such a fucking waste."

"I know. But our job isn't finished."

Keiko ran the back of her hand across her nose and took in a deep breath. "Tanya, deal with the bodies. We need to keep a presence in this city and that order comes directly from Ciari."

"We don't have to stay," Tanya said.

"Where will you go?" Keiko asked in a brutally hard voice. "That's what we asked everyone else we've dosed. Where will you be safe in a world that would rather see you dead if not leashed? That's a mentality we need to change, and it won't happen if we go running off to save our own asses or for revenge. It will get us nowhere."

Tanya ducked her head a bit, expression twisting as she stared down at the bodies of her fellow Strykers. "Do you care about the registered humans?"

"Not as much as the people on the street," Jason said, rubbing at his face. "We psions need them to survive, and anyone in the city towers who's not in a shuttle right now is shit out of luck. The World Court has to see the tracking signals are going strong, which means they've got to know most of us aren't dead. They'll push the launch even harder now."

"All right," Tanya said. "We'll hold the line for those on the street and help them fight off the military. We'll wait for Ciari's orders."

"Try to keep the city towers intact," Keiko said. "We're going to need something to live in when this is all over."

Keiko teleported the three of them back to where they started, arriving in Ciari's office back in Toronto. She looked around, realizing that everything in the office but the lights and a single vidscreen showing a map of the world was switched off. The only one to greet them was Jael.

The Strykers CMO's eyes were red. "You're back early."

"We didn't make it in time," Jason said, choking on the words.

"I saw." Jael tilted her head at the vidscreen. "On the monitoring system."

Keiko sucked in a deep breath and turned around to face Jael. "Where's Ciari?"

"She's gone. Left with Lucas for The Hague."

"Just now?"

"About an hour ago." Jael let her attention focus on Jason and Quinton. "Who is Aisling?"

"Fucking hell," Jason said. "What did they say?"

"Only that this is what Aisling wanted. Ciari's words, not Lucas's."

"Aisling," Quinton said, "is who Lucas has been taking his orders from, near as we can tell."

"Where is she? Can you bring her here?"

Jason and Quinton shared an uncomfortable look. "We've never met her," Jason said.

"Are you telling me that Lucas has been following orders from someone that you've never seen or spoken to? And you just blindly trusted in Lucas's word for this?"

"No, we don't blindly trust him. But he's been right every single time, and what he wants—" Quinton broke off to take a deep breath. "What Lucas wants is better for everyone in the long run."

"If I didn't know how many Stryker lives the Serca family has saved for us over the years, I'd be disgusted to know that you believe in their propaganda."

"We weren't scheduled for retrieval."

"Not by us," Jael agreed, a sharp look in her hazel eyes. "I'm thinking Ciari had her own agenda."

"You think?" Keiko said. "Aren't you in her mind?"

Jael sighed and shook her head. "Ciari ordered me to sever the psi link."

"What the hell is wrong with her?" Quinton said.

"You know Erik fried her brain," Keiko said. "She almost died. What you don't know is that the psi surgery went wrong and she lost control of her empathy."

"She turned off part of her own mind," Jael said quietly, looking down at her hands. "I told her to. It was the only way to save her."

The silence that followed that remark was uncomfortable and difficult to fill. Keiko chewed on her bottom lip before asking, "Can we kill the signals in the neurotrackers now that we no longer need to hide our freedom? We don't need the government knowing where we are anymore."

"There's a way," Jason said. "I need access to the government's working satellites, though."

"I can get you that. We should do it now before they try to cut us off." Keiko waved a hand at Jason and Quinton, beckoning them to follow her out of the office. "We'll be on the command level, Jael."

The door slid shut behind them, their footsteps fading away. Jael looked around at an office she had wandered in and out of for years. She wondered what the walls remembered of her, if the history embedded in this place would paint her as something other than a desperate woman trying to survive.

"Computer, activate. Chief medical officer override," Jael said, digging her fingers into her thighs, nails scratching at her uniform. The terminal behind her switched on.

"Receiving," the disembodied voice said. "Voice identification confirmed. Command required."

"Pull up the Registry records. Locate the listing for Lucas Serca and backdate."

"Acknowledged."

The Registry had been put into effect to support the Fifth Generation Act. Every family listed in the Registry was required to submit an intact genealogy that stretched back to the Border Wars. It was viewable to the public, an issue of transparency the burgeoning World Court back then had required. Truth, in that instant, couldn't be locked away. Jael closed her eyes, hoping she was wrong as the computer began to spit out names, dates of births and deaths, the years spinning backward.

[THIRTY-FOUR]

SEPTEMBER 2379
KRASNOYARSK, KRASNOYARSK KRAI, RUSSIA

Threnody's fingers were cold, even through her heavily shielded and insulated skinsuit, but they still found a handhold along the rock face. She hauled herself up, feet scraping against the rough stone, breathing quickly through her nose. One wrong move, one wrong grip, would mean her death. She wasn't afraid of heights, but this place could make her learn to be.

"You know what? Screw Lucas. He couldn't spare us a damn telekinetic from the rank and file once the Strykers were dosed?" She gasped as she pulled herself over onto the flat ledge of rock. "Or do this himself?"

Kerr, already crouched on the ledge, shook his head and helped her the rest of the way up. "He has other things to worry about."

"I don't give a fuck." Threnody moved until she had her back pressed against the rock, careful of her oxygen tank. She was on her second set and they didn't have a third. "He could have at least teleported us up here. I realize he couldn't get us into the holding site, but damn it, we've been trekking through this area for hours."

"Have you seen the security around this place?" Novak said from where he sat nearby. "Even with the codes Lucas gave me, it's difficult as hell to hack. If he dropped us on their doorstep, we'd have been shot before we took a single step. Trying to hack it from anywhere but the system's perimeter would have triggered an alert, no matter how good my skills are. Maybe Jason could have done it, but he ain't available."

Threnody felt sweat slide down the back of her neck and face, but she couldn't wipe it away. Squinting up the last curve of the path before them, she sighed heavily. "We're almost to the top. The sooner we leave, the sooner I'll feel like we're not walking over bones anymore."

"Not like we haven't been doing that since we got dropped off," Kerr pointed out.

Stretched before them lay a vast, empty vista. Not even nature had fully reclaimed the shattered remains of the ruined city they could see, but the glistening ribbon of the Yenisei River still flowed across the land. Krasnoyarsk was an abandoned city, capital to a deadzone, and a place few in their right mind would venture. Radiation still tainted everything, and while no bones or bodies were left, everywhere they walked seemed to have the black, ashy imprint of the dead.

Mountains rose into the sky in the northwest, ruins to the northeast. No sound but the wind existed as it blew across barren plains and the steep mountainsides. It whistled through the countless fingers of rock that surrounded them, the stone thrust up from the ground like ancient pillars. They had pushed through this forgotten reserve for over half a day already, and the bleakness of the scenery wasn't changing.

Threnody got to her feet, brushing off dirt and tiny bits of rock. "Are we still off the security grid, Novak?"

The hacker glanced down at the tiny datapad hooked into the neuroport on his left wrist. "So far. The loop must be holding because I haven't gotten a blip."

"Then let's finish this."

Her sense of time was off and hadn't resettled through four teleports and as many continents. Threnody understood Lucas was delegating more than he liked, that he needed to save his strength for the final push, but she knew he was uneasy giving up control. Regardless, she could have used more people for this mission. Shaking her head, Threnody led the way down a rocky patch to a tiny, lead-lined bunker half-built into rock. They had to pass through a cleared landing area that looked just big enough for a small shuttle to land in.

This was government-owned property, built in the middle of a dead-zone to keep watch over a weapon everyone in his or her right mind feared. Novak kept his attention on his hack and the security loop, walking steadily toward the heavy door bolted into rock and metal.

I'm sensing four people inside, Kerr said into Threnody's mind. *Three are human. One is a Warhound.*

Class?

He's a dual psion. Class IV telekinetic and Class VII telepath.

Threnody frowned as she approached the control panel, pulling out the gun on her hip. *Lucas did say that Nathan always had some of his people on duty here along with the government's. We were hoping they'd all be recalled for the launch, but maybe not. It's possible this one has orders like ours. Can you keep him from teleporting out?*

Kerr nodded. *Yes, but I'll have to stay behind you. I'll block whatever psi link he has in his mind so he can't get a warning out and then immobilize him. I don't want to make myself a target any more than I need to.*

Understood.

Threnody entered code after access code, each one accepted as she went through the entire list Lucas had given her. Since few people knew about this outpost, the codes didn't change that often. He'd stolen this set last spring, and she breathed more easily after the last code processed and the thick, heavy doors slid open.

She went in shooting, feeling the recoil in her wrist as she picked out her targets and kept her finger on the trigger. The first room in the bunker seemed to be the common area, and two men were sitting at a table playing cards. Both were halfway out of their seats when they each took a bullet to the chest, blood spraying out over the scattered cards and credit chips. They fell to the floor, twitching and gasping for breath as they drowned in their own blood. Threnody stepped closer and put a bullet in each of their heads.

She chanced a look through the inner door that led to a short hallway, not seeing anyone. Behind her Kerr came inside the bunker. The heavily shielded door slid closed on his heels. He nodded at her, gaze distant, and she trusted in Kerr to handle the Warhound, which meant the only one left to deal with was human. Moving down the hallway, Threnody reached another door, this one closed and locked. She took up position beside it.

"Here," Novak said as he edged around her, carrying his own gun. "Took a security card from one of the others."

The security card was bloody, but the lock scanned it just fine. The door slid open and Threnody immediately went to her knees as shots were fired chaotically through the open doorway. Novak hit the ground at the same time she did.

"Amateurs," he muttered. "I hate them more than crack shots."

Threnody nodded, shifting her weight and angling her body so she could shoot into the room when the bullets stopped. It was a risk to put herself out in the open like that, but necessary. She saw a woman frantically trying to reload her gun, shaking hands making it impossible to slide the magazine home. A man was sprawled at her feet, blood leaking from his nose and the corners of his half-opened eyes. He wasn't breathing.

Threnody aimed, fired again, and put a bullet into the woman's chest, straight through the lungs. Her second shot missed, but the third clipped the woman in the arm. Threnody took in a steadying breath, aimed one more time, and hit the woman's gut. She collapsed to the floor and didn't move. Threnody got to her feet, approached the bodies, and put a bullet through their brains just to be sure.

Clear, Threnody said through the psi link to Kerr.

He met them at the far end of the main hallway, at a door that looked stronger and heavier than all the rest. "Door is sealed up front," Kerr said as he undid the hard helmet locked around his throat. He pulled it free of his skinsuit. "Air's clean. The environmental system here is built along the lines of a city tower. Place is tightly sealed, filters are working, and my tank is running low."

"Mine, too," Threnody admitted, unlocking her own helmet and pulling it off.

Novak removed his as well. With Lucas's codes having reached their limit of usefulness, Novak began a hack on the door. An hour later found them walking into a high-tech laboratory built around a single object. Sitting behind a thick partition of lead, metal walls, and specially treated plasglass, and perched on top of a work terminal whose base was drilled into rock, was a single weapon. When Novak finally got a good look at it, all the blood drained out of his face. The tattoos inked into the skin of his skull stood out sharply.

"That's—," he choked out hoarsely.

"Yes," Threnody said as she approached the secured casement of something that could, and had, caused so much destruction. "Lucas said Nathan probably wouldn't have removed it yet, or even planned to. What use would he have for something like this on Mars Colony?"

"This is crazy."

Threnody shrugged. "This is our mission. The access codes change every week and Lucas said he was months behind the cycles."

Novak's hands shook as he smoothed them over his face and the curve of his sweaty, tattooed head. "You couldn't just pull the codes out of their minds before you killed them?"

"The scientists didn't know the removal codes," Kerr said. "I pulled that from the Warhound's mind. Only high-ranking government officials have the ability to unlock this system."

"Novak." Threnody tilted her head in the direction of the intricate terminal with its complicated-looking control panel. "You need to get us in."

"What? No. This is anathema to the very way we *live*," Novak said, eyes wide and frantic in his face. "You can't be serious."

"This made the way we live," Threnody said fiercely, glaring at him. "And we suffer for it endlessly. I may not like it or agree with Lucas's methods, but this is the only way we're going to secure our safety."

"Are you even listening to yourself?" Novak pointed at the terminal, eyes wide with terror. "That's a *nuclear bomb* in there."

"Novak," Kerr said, his telepathy pressing down hard on the other man's static human mind. "You don't have a choice. Neither do we. Now get started."

Novak swallowed thickly, shoulders slumping. "This system is going to be difficult to hack."

"Remember what Lucas said? You'll hack it or die trying." Kerr grimaced, not liking the order at all. "You better hope you die after, because right now you're the only one who can do this."

"Why didn't Lucas just get a damn telekinetic to teleport the thing out of here?"

"Pressure plates," Threnody said, pointing at the platform through the view window. "If they're removed without the codes being entered, an alarm is triggered. Lucas said there's always a team of Warhounds on standby ready to teleport in. Considering the state of the world right now, we don't know if they actually would, but we can't risk it. Nathan can't know we're stealing the bomb."

"Great." Novak unsealed his gloves and freed his hands. "Never thought we'd be repeating history."

"For a hacker, you lack imagination," Kerr said. "Lucas is making history, not repeating it."

"Says you." Novak stared bleakly at his task. "This ain't right."

"Stop arguing and get to work. We don't have much time left. We aren't teleporting out and we need to be finished before our pickup arrives."

Novak reached for the controls attached to the work terminal. He pulled out a hard wire and attached it to the neuroport in his left wrist. Taking a deep breath, he opened himself up to the inevitable, inspecs flickering in the back of his eyes as code flowed through his brain.

PART SEVEN

TEMPORAL

SESSION DATE: 2128.07.10
LOCATION: Institute of Psionics Research
CLEARANCE ID: Dr. Amy Bennett
SUBJECT: 2581
FILE NUMBER: 627

When the doctor enters, Aisling is standing in front of the machines, staring at the monitors and the data that moves across them in sharp lines; high peaks and deep valleys dictate who she is. She has one hand pressed against a vidscreen that shows her baseline, the graph far more skewed than a human's.

"Aisling, please step away from there," the doctor says.

"Don't worry. My power isn't the kind that affects machines." Aisling slides her fingers over the baseline reading. "That one isn't born yet."

The doctor takes her seat at the table, and Aisling calmly returns to her own. The wires trail behind her and brush along the ground. She climbs onto her chair and looks at the camera instead of the doctor.

"You know I'm right, Ciari."

"Please focus, Aisling," the doctor says. "Let's stick to what's important."

"She *is* important. They all are down the years, so long as they listen."

The doctor glances up at her. "Will it change anything, these people you dream about?"

"They aren't dreams," Aisling says, scowling. "They're real. And things will change if they listen."

"What if they don't?"

Aisling shrugs. "There are lots of ways this could end, but I chose to only see one."

[THIRTY-FIVE]

SEPTEMBER 2379
LONDON, UNITED KINGDOM

id Gideon make it onto the space shuttle?

D Nathan felt Dalia wince at his telepathic demand, the psi link in her mind an overused ache that she couldn't block or ignore. *Sharra's space shuttle launched hours ago with all passengers accounted for, according to the manifest. By tomorrow morning, they'll have reached the* Ark.

You're certain?

Yes. We've been launching space shuttles all day, but we only have one ramp and only so much space to house people, even if it is temporary. I've transferred all the Warhounds you've sent me into priority boarding, but that's all I can do right now. How many more should I expect?

Half of my Warhounds haven't even left their posts yet. There are supplies and other things that are important to gaining control of Mars Colony that we can't leave without. By tomorrow, you should have close to a quarter of those left behind.

Are you sure that's safe? Dalia's thoughts shook with exhaustion and fear. Nathan clamped down tighter on her mind.

As you said, the government has only one launch ramp and little safe space in Paris for everyone. The launch is going to take days and it's going to be messy. There will be space shuttles still available.

Of course, sir.

Nathan cut the connection, his attention refocusing on the half dozen uplinks spread across his work terminal's vidscreen. Human field controllers loyal to the Serca Syndicate by deep mindwipes and Warhounds whose duties weren't quite done yet waited patiently for his commands.

"Where were we?" he said, bringing the meeting back on track.

It didn't take long. Twenty minutes later, he was cutting the uplinks, the vidscreen going blank. Nathan got to his feet and paced over to the window wall behind his desk, looking out at the dark London skyline. The view was familiar, committed to memory long ago. Back when he was a child, he thought London would remain his home. That he would die here, young and seemingly human, but that was no longer the case. London would only exist in his memories and Nathan found he wouldn't mind forgetting it.

Rioters still fought on the streets surrounding the city towers. Their attacks against the government and registered humans hadn't abated, were in fact becoming more violent with every hour that passed. Shuttle launches to Paris were scheduled to continue for the next few days. It was enough time for everyone not on the colony list to come together and fight for rights long denied them, but it was a fight they would lose.

The world population of highly educated people was dwindling at an alarming rate, with registered humans fleeing Earth for a tenuous promise in the stars. The remains of society would struggle to pick itself up, if anything was left after the first year of abandonment. The brain drain the World Court had engineered would cripple those left behind. Perhaps not into extinction, but close enough that the rot in the world would win. The rioters were protesting their oncoming deaths. Nathan thought it a futile action.

The computer chimed, alerting him to an incoming uplink. Nathan turned around to see that it was tagged with an emergency code. He went over to his desk to accept it. Erik's face filled the vidscreen, pale and frantic.

"Nathan," Erik said. "The neurotrackers failed."

The words froze Nathan, disbelief twisting through his thoughts. It was swiftly followed by a rage that tunneled his vision, and Nathan had to work at showing fear instead of fury. That's what Erik would expect from him, in the guise Nathan lived with. "Did you use the master override?"

"Do you think I don't know how to put down a dog? We can still track some of their positions, but they aren't all *dead*."

"Explain yourself."

"Ciari was here." The woman's name fell from Erik's lips like a curse. "She had some asinine offer that they could save us if we stayed. She didn't die when I issued the mass termination order and was teleported out before we could shoot her. We know that a few hundred Strykers died in the Americas and some here in The Hague, but all the rest were showing live signals on the security grid before we lost contact. I doubt any of those Strykers are dead."

Nathan felt his fingernails bite into the palms of his hands. "I'm to assume your version of using a panic switch is to uplink with me? What do you think I can do about this problem?"

"Your family created this damn technology and sold it to the world when psions were first discovered. I'm hoping you have an override that can fix this problem. You Sercas don't give up anything for free."

It was a rather astute assumption, even if Nathan couldn't outright acknowledge the underhanded way his family functioned. Moving to his seat, Nathan kept his attention on the uplink.

"What are your plans right now, Erik?"

"If you can't give us a way to kill the Strykers, then the World Court is leaving tonight for Paris. We aren't safe anymore if the Strykers decide to rebel and come after us."

"Like the rest of the world?"

"Don't act like you won't be joining us on that shuttle, Nathan." Erik frowned, weariness pulling at his mouth. "Why are you still in London anyway?"

"My Syndicate requires a firm hand to wind it down on such short notice. I'm waiting to hear from the Athes."

"You'll be waiting a long time," Erik said flatly. "The city towers in Sapporo fell. Sydney is dead."

Nathan tapped his fingers against his desk. He'd been so focused on transferring the contents of the seed bank and his Warhounds that he missed the news coming out of Japan. "When did this happen?"

"Within the last few hours."

"I hadn't heard. What about Elion?"

"He's still in Paris. I don't know if anyone's informed him of his grandfather's death. If they haven't, Travis will when we arrive."

"When do you expect to leave?"

"Right now, if you have nothing to give us."

Nathan stared at Erik in silence for a long moment, weighing his options. "I may have something."

Erik let out a deep breath, mouth twisting, despite the relief seeping into his eyes. "Why am I not surprised?"

"My family guards its secrets the same way the World Court guards theirs. We're just better at it. I'll take a shuttle and be at The Hague soon to see what can be done."

"We'll await your arrival."

The uplink cut off and Nathan leaned back in his seat, grinding his teeth, free now to let his true emotions show. He had no doubt that Lucas was behind the failure of the neurotrackers. His son knew the intricacies of the technology, both its strengths and carefully guarded weaknesses, just as well as he did. Releasing the Strykers from the chains that had bound them since their emergence after the Border Wars meant the Silence Law was void. His family's genetic secret was fair game now, and if Ciari was in The Hague, Nathan only had one option left to him regarding the World Court.

He had no qualms about taking it.

Again, Nathan found that the hard decisions were left to him. He didn't regret the decisions that had let him live this long, to see this happen. The only thing he regretted was his family and the way he couldn't use his children to further his own life. Being born a Class I triad psion meant his body was just looking for a way to kill his mind. Dying was slower for him than for most psions because of his social status, but he could no longer expect that to hold true.

Gideon was on his way to the *Ark*, safe from Lucas's machinations, but also out of reach of Nathan. Lucas, Samantha, and Kristen were hidden somewhere on Earth, fighting for a goal that Nathan didn't understand. The one thing Nathan wanted, he could no longer bargain for, not with the neurotrackers disabled and the Silence Law broken. Jason Garret was out of reach now unless Nathan opened his own mind and used his powers to their absolute limits to find the Stryker. The effort would surely kill him.

Nathan wasn't that desperate.

He reached for the controls on his desk, fingers skating over the touch panel. The uplink came through in an instant. "Ready my shuttle."

THIRTY-SIX

SEPTEMBER 2379
THE HAGUE, THE NETHERLANDS

rik stared at the security feed monitoring the defenses surrounding the Peace Palace. He couldn't see the streets beyond the wall, they were so crowded with people. Quads on the perimeter were all that existed between them and the fury of a people that the government hadn't deigned to save.

The Strykers were gone, the World Court's dogs having fully slipped their collars for the first time in 250 years. The bitterness, the fear, was difficult to cope with. The only people left to protect them were human, and there was no guarantee how long the military would continue to believe the lie that they would have a place on the *Ark* to guard the new world on Mars Colony.

"I think it's time we leave," Travis said, eyeing the vidscreen from where he stood with a cluster of other judges. "Enough of those chosen have heeded the transfer orders. If any are left behind, then their failure to keep to the schedule is on them. We gave enough warning for people to muster out. It's not in our best interest to remain any longer."

"I'm inclined to agree," Nathan said. He stood beside Erik in the courtroom before the judicial bench, both men focused on the security feed. "There is nothing I can do about the neurotrackers, not after what failsafes my Syndicate had didn't work. The last of the inventory from the seed bank is being put on a shuttle right now for a launch. The entirety of the supplies left to us will be safely out of reach. The most essential part of this plan is safe."

"They can't be safe if we're missing half of what we were charged with keeping track of," Erik said. "It makes me wonder what happened to those missing supplies. It makes me wonder who betrayed us. The Strykers shouldn't have been able to get free."

"I did warn you, Erik. Our attempts at ownership weren't enough over the years if this is the result," Anchali said from where she sat on a chair, both hands resting on top of her cane. "They bypassed our control and this is the result of our failure to keep them leashed."

"We had humans working all throughout the Strykers Syndicate. We had monitoring systems in place that infiltrated not only every psion office but their own bodies. This should have been impossible."

"Impossible or not, why haven't they tried to kill us?" Cherise Molyneux demanded. "Reports have come in from all over the world that Strykers left their posts guarding the city towers and retreated to the streets, taking half the military with them. They haven't murdered the people who held their contracts."

"Yet" was Anchali's sharp retort. "Their timing, I must say, was perfect. Unfortunately, we don't have the time or the means to track them down and kill them, and thus our only option is retreat."

"This is no retreat, this was planned," Erik said, voice cold.

"Plans never go accordingly." Anchali shook her head, gray hair swaying around her thin face. "We are done here, Erik. We are *done*. Let us go while there is a window of opportunity left and soldiers still loyal to the cause to fly us out of here."

Erik pressed his thumb over the biometric key on the remote he held, dragging it down the sensor. No confirmation of termination came from the hub of soldiers charged with administering termination. Anchali was right. They had done their part, played their roles as saviors. If they stayed any longer, they would play a role of martyr that none of them desired.

Gripping the remote, Erik spun and threw the device with all the strength he had at the ancient, stained-glass windows that spanned the wall over the dais. It slammed through the fragile glass and shattered part of a pane. Tiny shards fell to the ground, thin cracks spiderwebbing across the rest of the picture.

"Does that make you feel better, Erik?" Nathan said.

Erik turned to give the other man a sharp look. "If anyone is to share blame, Nathan, it is you and your family."

"I find that you have little ground on which to blame us for your mistakes." Nathan gave him a cool look. "My family offered up the science to keep humans safe from psions. We offered a way to alter human DNA and clean it up. We lobbied for segregation with the World Court's support for the greater good. You owe me your rank by virtue of the knowledge my ancestors shared."

"Like hell."

"I'm inclined to agree with Nathan," Travis said, gesturing at the other man. "But it doesn't matter anymore who's to blame. Are the shuttles at the airfield ready for us to board?"

"Yes," Anchali said. "Save your male posturing for when we arrive on the *Ark*. We have better things to do than argue which family is more human than the rest."

"A difficult decision amongst you fifteen, perhaps," a familiar voice announced. "Not, I think, for the Sercas."

The door to the courtroom was pushed open, a slim figure stepping inside. Erik choked down his fear as he recognized the uniformed woman striding down the aisle between the rows of seats.

"Someone call the quads," Anchali said, clutching at her cane.

"They are occupied elsewhere," Ciari said calmly.

The last time the World Court had seen her, she'd been writhing in agony and bleeding on the carpeted floor of this courtroom. She had changed, the expression on her face remote. She no longer had a collar to hold her in check. Her gaze swept over the group, judging them as they once judged her.

"We offered you another way and you refused it," Ciari said. "Abandoning this world isn't the answer. Do you really think you'll find a better life on Mars Colony?"

"You don't know what you're talking about," Erik spat out. He stepped backward, away from her.

Ciari touched her neck, fingers sliding over the circular bruise that stood out in stark relief against her pale skin. "I know what I've lost and what I've gained, Erik. Do you?"

"You have gained nothing," Travis said as he pulled an antique gun from a shoulder holster beneath his robes. He aimed at Ciari's head. "I made a mistake when I voted to spare your life if this is how you repay our generosity."

He pulled the trigger, the crack of the gun loud in the courtroom. Travis's aim was true and Ciari stared at the bullet as it spun in place directly in front of her nose. She carefully touched the bullet with one finger. It fell to the floor.

"There are more with her," Anchali said in warning, her voice high with fear.

"Of Strykers, there's just me," Ciari corrected. "Rogue psions? You have only one other here."

"Along with one lost cause at that," a tenor voice said from up in the balcony. "Though, really, you lot are worse off than I could ever hope to be even if I tried."

Everyone's attention was drawn upward, Nathan's head immediately snapping up at the familiar voice that greeted everyone. Lucas stood above them, arms braced against the wooden railing of the balcony. Wearing a black-on-black Strykers BDU and carrying no weapons, he only had eyes for one person in the room.

"Hello, Nathan," Lucas said. "Do you like what I've done with the world?"

It had been two years since father and son last stood face-to-face. Two years of sabotage, of hunting and being hunted. The lies and deceit the two men shared were family secrets that should never have seen the light of day. Yet here they were, stripping themselves bare as they clawed their way to a future that each saw differently, that each believed in differently.

"Lucas," Nathan said, the name falling from his lips in a sharp hiss. "And so the prodigal son returns. What—inconvenient timing."

Lucas offered up a thin-lipped smile. "Am I disappointing you again? I'm not really sorry about that."

"*What* is going on here?" Erik demanded, staring in pale-faced shock up at Lucas. "Nathan, why is your son wearing a *Stryker* uniform?"

"We haven't seen your son in two years, Nathan," Anchali said, rising to her feet shakily. "You will tell us what is going on."

"It's family business that doesn't concern you," Nathan said.

Erik turned angrily to face Nathan. "You don't give the orders here. Tell us what the hell—"

The garbled scream that came out of Erik's mouth was issued around a broken jaw, the sound of bone cracking loud enough to startle everyone. Cupping his face in both hands, Erik screamed and gasped for breath through a mouth that wouldn't close, his lower jaw hanging at an awkward angle from his skull.

"Shut your mouth" came Nathan's icy order. He hadn't moved.

"Mon Dieu," Cherise yelled at Ciari. "What have you done?"

"Nothing. I'm an empath," Ciari said.

"Don't you hate it when they give credit for your work to someone else, Nathan?" Lucas asked, voice calculatingly cheerful. "The seed bank, the space shuttles, the program to bring the colony ship back online. Everything our family has ever done for the humans and they pass most of it off as their own."

"Do you really want to do this now?" Nathan said flatly, refusing to look away from his son.

"When will we have the chance if I don't?"

In the blink of an eye, Lucas teleported down to the courtroom floor. The judges collectively stepped back, fear replacing shock on their faces, none of them capable of speech.

Nathan faced his son, cold anger filling his dark blue eyes. "I will kill you."

"You'll certainly try," Lucas said.

Travis, like most of the rest of the judges, looked from Lucas to Nathan with a growing sense of horror. He was the first to speak. "Did the Strykers buy you off, Nathan? Is that why the neurotrackers don't work?"

Lucas's laughter made their skin crawl. "Buy us off? Hardly. We were their salvation."

"What are you talking about?" Anchali asked, voice strained. "Lucas, what have they done to you?"

"Did you honestly think the Strykers would simply let you slaughter and discard us, over and over again?" Ciari asked. "You had to know we'd find a way to save some of our people, even if it meant giving up control to someone else. We gave up high-Classed psions that were scheduled for termination to the Sercas. The Serca family's Warhounds were always a better option than death, no matter the violations to our minds once the kill switch was removed."

"Warhounds," Cherise said, the word coming out mangled. "Nathan, what is she talking about?"

They were all looking at the owner of the Serca Syndicate, disbelief and horror in their eyes, on their faces, desperately hoping for an answer that would keep their world on an even keel.

Your inability to see things for what they really are is staggering, Lucas said into everyone's mind. *Did you really think you could leave all the psions behind to die? Your entire dream was shored up by my family, and we happen to be some of the strongest psions on this planet.*

Lucas didn't bother to hold back, shoving his power into their static human minds without care. The fifteen judges were unable to handle the intrusion and several of the older ones collapsed.

If this was the point you wanted to make, it won't do you any good, Nathan said, a riot of power surging beyond his words.

Lucas readied his telekinesis for a teleport and felt his shields almost buckle beneath Nathan's powerful telekinetic blow. He stumbled forward a few steps, balance thrown off by the strength of the attack. Lucas lifted his head, glaring at Nathan, hating to reveal even a shred of weakness before his father.

You never did learn to obey your betters, Nathan said. *I blame Marcheline for that.*

The combined telekinetic and telepathic strikes against Lucas's shields were expected. He held up beneath the attack, mind still reaching for the teleport. Lucas could see his destination in his mind, had strength to get there, even through Nathan's power—except it was only enough to carry himself out of The Hague. If he was going to be at all ready to fight later on when his power would be needed, he couldn't fight for anyone's life save his own. Neither could he remain here much longer.

Lucas felt too-warm fingers touch his cheek, sliding down the curve of his jaw. Felt lips brush against his ear. "Save my Strykers," Ciari said, her voice soft. "You owe me that."

He owed her everything. They both knew it.

"Good-bye," Lucas said.

He slammed his power against Nathan's defenses, putting every bit of strength into that one blow. It bought him seconds, enough time to teleport out of Nathan's reach, physically leaving Ciari behind. She briefly closed her eyes, feeling an echo of Lucas in her mind.

Nathan stared at the empty spot where his son once stood, trying to find some reason behind Lucas's actions.

"You can't be a psion," Travis whispered, begging for it to not be true. "Nathan—you *can't*."

"He is," Ciari said, gaze locked on Nathan's face. "Every Serca has been. You've all wondered over the years about who controlled the rogue psions of the world and allowed them to thrive. The Warhounds have been the Sercas' private army since the beginning."

"And for all the psions we saved at your behest and those who held your rank in the past, this is how you repay my family." Nathan gave Ciari a faint, mocking bow. "So glad to know where your loyalties lie."

"With my people" was her answer. "Always with them."

"You'll certainly die with them."

If the World Court thought they could beg, barter, or bargain their way out this time, they were in denial. Nathan heard their pleas, their willingness to do whatever he wanted, pay whatever he asked, if he would only spare them.

Like you spared all the psions you and your predecessors enslaved and killed? Nathan asked, his power fluctuating across the mental grid with deadly force. *I have no use for most of the humans who belong to the Registry. This was planned over generations, over centuries. There is nothing you have to offer me, for I already own everything you thought you would keep.*

For all the arrogance of the World Court, for all the pride that collective government body took in saving the human race, their discriminatory practices destroyed them in the end. Knowledge of what they had unknowingly harbored in the pristine halls of government since the end of the Border Wars—diseased psion DNA in a family that looked so human—left them reeling.

They died, one by one, minds burning out beneath the onslaught of a telepathic strike that had no boundaries. Human minds weren't capable of handling psionic interference. Nathan took them apart, unraveling their lives until nothing was left except empty minds and empty eyes; just bodies with hearts that beat, and then, just corpses.

Ciari watched them die and felt nothing. She raised her eyes to Nathan as he turned to look at her, neither of them bound anymore by the conventions of a life they were born into.

"My son should have saved you," Nathan said as he skimmed his power over Ciari's fragile, broken mind. "His loyalty has always been questionable."

"He didn't come to say good-bye to you."

Ciari smiled as Nathan's mind slid into hers, breaking through mental shields tainted with insanity. Her smile was small, just the faint quirk of her mouth, but it held so much emotion. A lifetime of wanting, of hoping, brought Ciari to her knees, the schemes of a child laying waste to her memories as Nathan cut into her mind. He ripped apart the foundations of her shields, baring her mind to the cacophony of the world's thoughts and emotions, but he hesitated when faced with the irrefutable presence of growing insanity. The hesitation lasted only a moment before Nathan continued his onslaught.

A second telepathic touch flowed through Ciari's thoughts—familiar, cool. She sucked in a quiet breath even as pain began to override her body. She thought she understood it now.

Close your eyes, Lucas said, telepathic fingers sliding over everything that she was, everything that she had lost, hiding all that she knew from Nathan. *I'll take you away from here.*

She did as he asked, his telepathy a barrier that Nathan couldn't cross, no matter how hard his father fought. Ciari's mind was a battlefield between a pair of Class I triad psions, and she didn't have the capacity to survive it. Lucas knew that, had always known that. Somewhere in Ciari's mind, she knew it, too.

This isn't what Aisling promised me, Ciari said as she opened her eyes and looked around at the familiar, twisted landscape of her birth city, Buffalo a tangled mess of forgotten dreams and living nightmares spread out before her. The Hague and the Peace Palace seemed like a lifetime ago. She thought she could still feel the carpet beneath her cheek.

I know, Lucas said, standing by Ciari's side in the street he built in her mind.

Clouds were in the makeshift sky, and a breeze touched Ciari's skin, freezing her by centimeters. Somewhere in the distance, there was thunder, growing fainter with every breath she took.

We tried, Ciari said, tipping her head back to stare at the sky and the storm that was leaving her. *That has to count for something, doesn't it?*

Lucas touched his hand to hers, but she didn't feel the pressure. *It does.*

The air smelled wet, felt shock-edged with potential. Lucas's hand fell away. When Ciari turned to look at him, only emptiness was beside her, around her.

The rain, when it came, fell soft and clean down on a memory blowing through a world that was crumbling away.

Lucas let her go.

[THIRTY-SEVEN]

SEPTEMBER 2379
TORONTO, CANADA

Matron picked them up, flying a familiar shuttle through the gray Russian sky to retrieve them from the rocky outpost. The scavenger took one look at where the three stood at the bottom of the cargo ramp, heavy, hard-backed metal carrying case resting between Threnody and Kerr, and shook her head.

"Just tell me it ain't gonna blow us out of the sky," Matron said.

"So long as you don't roll the damn shuttle, it'll be fine," Novak said in a ragged voice. "Tell me you got painkillers on this piece of junk."

"Stop whining and go dose yourself."

The hacker staggered up the cargo ramp, every step looking as if it hurt. He headed for the med-kit bolted to the deck near the front hatch. Matron watched him go with a frown on her face. "What's wrong with him?"

"He fried half his brain getting us the bomb," Kerr said as he reached down to grab the handle on his side of the carrying case. "You should take him to Korman after you drop us off in Paris."

Matron swore. "Goddamn that boy. Lucas is gonna kill all my scavengers and what the fuck am I supposed to do then?"

"I wouldn't recommend asking."

"Go scrub off in the decontamination tent once you get that thing inside. It's set up in the corner."

Threnody and Kerr carefully hauled the carrying case up the cargo ramp. Matron made sure to keep several meters' worth of distance away from them as the two secured the bomb in the cargo bay. The scavenger was already in the pilot's seat, readying for launch, when Threnody made it to the flight deck. She'd stripped out of her skinsuit and gone through decontamination. The clothes she wore now were from Matron's stores. Threnody sat down in the navigator's seat, strapped herself into the harness, and started pulling up information.

"Didn't know you could fly," Matron said as she put on a pair of reflective dark glasses.

"Most Strykers can pilot a shuttle," Threnody said. "I prefer not to, but you need a navigator and I'm leading this mission."

"With your power, I can't imagine why you'd want to fly."

"It's why I have Quinton." Threnody reached over to toggle some of the controls between them. "Lucas wants us back in Toronto."

"Why didn't he teleport you?"

"Didn't want to risk the bomb."

Matron glanced reflexively over her shoulder, but all she saw was the closed hatch. "Nice how he don't care about our asses."

"Let's get in the air. We need to stay clear of government flight paths."

"I know. Military is shooting down anyone who gets close and don't squawk proper ident. We'll go north, over the Arctic Ocean."

"Again?"

"No one's gonna be flying our route. Everyone's heading for Paris."

They were as safe as they could get with a nuclear bomb strapped in the belly of their shuttle, and that wasn't saying much. But Matron knew the uncharted routes between government security grids better than most people. They made the long, uneasy flight back to Canada beneath a cloudy sky all over again.

Hours later, they pinged against the security grid that surrounded Toronto, but no one on the government channels initiated an uplink. Someone in the Strykers Syndicate did.

"It better be you in that shuttle, Thren, do you copy, over," Quinton said.

Threnody jammed her finger down on the audio control, opening up the line. "Good to hear your voice. We're carrying precious cargo that needs delicate handling, over."

"You're clear for the rooftop landing pad, out."

The uplink cut off and Threnody let out a deep sigh, some sense of calm trickling through her now that she knew Quinton had made it back from his mission alive. Slouching in the navigator's seat, Threnody rubbed hard at her burning eyes. Teleporting across time zones, fighting to complete their mission, then flying back to Toronto had screwed with her inner clock. The chrono on the flight controls said one thing, her body was saying another. The headache pounding through her skull wasn't going to go away anytime soon, and her eyes burned with the need to sleep.

Matron made a soft noise in the back of her throat and Threnody looked over at the other woman. "What?"

"Never been to a city tower before."

"Really?"

"Government don't care for my kind. Not how they cared for yours."

"Given the choice, I would have preferred your freedom."

"It wasn't all that great."

Matron was a good pilot, years spent crisscrossing countries around deadzones and security grids forcing her to be. She landed the shuttle on the rooftop with precision. A small group of people waited for them beyond the illuminated safety lines. Threnody recognized them all.

She got out of her seat and palmed open the hatch. The cargo ramp was already opening, and Kerr was busy undoing the restraints that secured the carrying case in place. Novak was passed out on a row of seats from exhaustion. Threnody left him for Matron to take care of and went to help Kerr with the bomb.

"You got it," Lucas said as he strode up the cargo ramp.

"Yeah, we got it," Kerr said as he kicked the anchor straps aside. "Was like a nightmare flying back with it."

"What did they get?" Jason asked as he came jogging up the ramp, Quinton hot on his heels.

Lucas waved off the question, attention focused on the cargo. "Let's get it somewhere secure first before we talk about what we're doing next."

"You got medical personnel in this place?" Matron said as she helped Novak to his feet.

"Got a whole level," Threnody said with a grunt as she finally pushed the release lever all the way down. The metal clamps used to keep the case in one place released.

"Good. They better work on Novak without complaint."

Jael? Lucas said, linking with the Strykers Syndicate's CMO. *I'm sending someone down for your people to fix. Get him sorted, then come meet us in the command briefing room.*

Give me ten minutes and I'll be there came Jael's response.

Lucas teleported Matron and Novak to the medical level's arrival room before focusing his attention on the Strykers. "Let's get below. We've got decisions to make."

Instead of teleporting, Lucas headed for the stairs. If anyone thought it strange, no one said a word. Threnody and Kerr handled the carrying case with a careful wariness that told Quinton and Jason the cargo wasn't ordinary.

The Strykers Syndicate was filled with a new sense of urgency, with fewer humans manning posts than ever before. On their way through the command level, Threnody noticed the empty terminals first and the Strykers second.

"The virus worked?" she asked as they passed by half-empty monitoring rooms.

"We didn't get everyone," Quinton said tightly.

She heard the guilt in his voice. Threnody tilted her head in his direction as they walked. "Did you get most of them?"

"As many as we could."

"If you're going to dwell on numbers, then focus on the positives, not the negatives."

Easier said than done, and they both knew it.

The command briefing room was as streamlined as every other room in the Strykers Syndicate. The company wasn't about comfort, but about security and making money. Threnody wondered if that would change when this was all over.

Keiko and Aidan were already waiting for them. The two officers were studying a command window of information, the touch screen that filled the entire length of the table filled with a grid map of the world. Threnody didn't know enough to make sense of what she was seeing without being briefed, but she could guess.

"What is that?" Aidan asked suspiciously as Kerr and Threnody carefully placed the carrying case onto the table. Threnody touched the control panel nearby, freezing the local screen and shuffling the data around the carrying case.

"A difficult answer to a difficult problem," Lucas said as he pulled a seat out and sat down. "We'll start when Jael gets here."

Nine minutes later, Jael arrived. "Your hacker is going to need brain surgery, Lucas. What the hell did you have him do?"

"He helped get that." Lucas pointed at the carrying case sitting on the table between Threnody and Kerr. "Sit down, Jael."

She took the seat farthest from Lucas. "Where's Ciari?"

"She's not coming," Lucas said.

"Why not?"

"Because Ciari is dead. So is the World Court. Nathan killed them all in the Peace Palace."

Keiko's telekinesis slammed against Lucas's shields with enough strength to rattle the conference table. Threnody and Kerr both reached for the carrying case, holding on with white-knuckled grips to keep it steady.

"Stop!" they both yelled, the fear in their voices causing Keiko to pull up short.

The Japanese woman was half out of her seat in a rage. Lucas slammed her all the way back into it, leaning forward in his own. "Ciari went to The Hague to die," he said. "She went while she still understood the choice she could make."

"You fucking bastard," Jael said harshly. "You took Ciari there to kill her, didn't you? To get her out of the way so you can take control of the Strykers Syndicate."

"As always, your imagination is impeccable, Jael. But, no, I took Ciari there so she could offer Erik a way out of this mess. He vehemently declined." Lucas pinned Jael with an angry look. "You know her mind was breaking. What you did to save her from that aborted termination broke her. She wasn't going to last much longer, not as the Ciari you knew anyway. She was too old to survive something like that."

"So you put her out of her misery, is that what you're saying?" Quinton said.

"I'm saying I let her die how she wanted to."

"But not how Aisling wanted?" was Jason's sharp question.

Lucas pressed both hands flat against the table, data streaming away from his fingertips. "Aisling doesn't concern you."

"Like hell."

Lucas ignored him. "Ciari knew what was at stake. Why do you think she did all this? Why do you think she gave me the four Strykers I needed in order to break the government's hold on you? Ciari knew exactly what she was doing when she was sane."

"What about when she wasn't?" Keiko demanded.

"You have Jael to thank for that, not me."

The Strykers Syndicate's CMO flinched with her entire body, but Jael didn't protest his accusation.

"Ciari set all of you free," Lucas said, gaze sweeping over everyone. "She made it possible to get the neurotrackers taken out of your heads. She made it possible for me to have a child not beholden to the rules that run my family. Be grateful for that. I know I am."

"So is that it?" Aidan asked. "We're free and we let the registered humans leave without a fight?"

"No," Threnody said. "We're not letting them leave."

"Why not?" Keiko asked. "Let them have Mars Colony. They can't touch us anymore."

"Maybe they can't, but their descendants might."

"You're seriously going to force a fight over something that might happen?"

"Lucas isn't working on a timeline beholden to *might*," Jael said, speaking up. Her hazel eyes were steady as she stared at Lucas. "Are you?"

Lucas ran a hand through his pale blond hair, shaking his head. "I should have known you couldn't kill your curiosity."

"It's my job to look after the collective health of Strykers."

"I am not a Stryker."

"No, you're simply taking over for Ciari, whether we like it or not."

"I'm not going to live long enough to rule you people."

"So you're leaving it to your daughter?" Jael frowned in his direction. "How can you be sure she'll be strong enough for the job? She won't be a high-Classed psion. We breed low on the scale when psions breed at all. We need corrupted human DNA to build off of."

"It's rare, but it happens." Lucas pointed across the table at Jason. "My genes are stronger than most. My daughter will be a Class I triad psion, she just won't have my exact attributes. Jason is changing her Class and her telekinetic power."

"Into what?"

"Into a more stable version of what I am," Jason said. "I'm a microtelekinetic, remember? I can manipulate cellular structure on the atomic level. Do you know what that means?"

Jael didn't have to think too hard on the answer. Her words came out in a raw whisper. "We could live a human lifetime."

"If we find psions before they're born, then yes. Not only that, but we can work on cleaning up this planet," Lucas said. "It might take a few thousand years, but we have the means to do it now, both in technology and genetics. The humans left behind will need guidance. We're losing so many people who had knowledge on how this world works that we psions will have to pick up the slack. The registered humans who didn't make the launch won't take kindly to psions taking over, so what better way to prove our right to lead than to show them what we're capable of?"

"They used us without a second thought," Quinton said. "They can work with us to rebuild or find a bunker near a deadzone to live in for all I care. We don't need to prove anything to them."

"Hating them isn't going to help us," Threnody said.

"Then let it benefit the next generation of psions. I don't give a damn about those people. I'd rather worry about the ones in the street."

"They aren't the only ones you have to worry about," Lucas said. "What we're planning won't last if we let Nathan leave with everyone on those shuttles."

Jael tapped her fingers slowly against the table. "Aisling told you that, didn't she?"

"No," Threnody said. "She told me."

Quinton jerked his head around to stare at his partner. "Come again?"

"Aisling said if we let them leave, they would come back, and we wouldn't win that fight. Nathan's Warhounds have more higher-Classed psions than we do, courtesy of the Silence Law. Even if we give it a decade and they return, we'll still be at a disadvantage. Nathan is filling half those shuttles with people not in the Registry. He'll have the means to breed psions on the *Ark*, if not Mars Colony."

"Are you certain?" Keiko said.

"Aisling is a precog," Threnody said slowly. "I believe in what she said."

"So she's alive?"

"No," Jael said with a sigh as she folded her hands together on the tabletop. "Aisling Serca died during the Border Wars. Her death is in the Registry, ancestral genetic proof that the Serca family's DNA was supposedly clean. They wiped most of the psion markers from her genome, but a few remained for me to note the distinction between Aisling and her older brother."

"Matthew Serca wasn't a psion," Lucas said with a sharp smile. "He only carried the genetic capability for it, and that capability showed up in his descendants as triad psions. Matthew followed his sister's orders and hacked her medical records when she was committed for therapy and experimentation by her government at the time. Aisling was the first psion and Matthew made sure we wouldn't forget her."

Jason rubbed hard at his face. "Fuck. Are you serious?"

"Serious enough to believe in what Aisling says. Mars Colony isn't the answer." Lucas closed his eyes, an unreadable expression crossing his face. "It never was, at least not for us. I was willing to let the government leave Earth, but that won't solve our problems. They'll only return somewhere down the line, and I needed Threnody to see that. Stopping the launch is our only option."

"How?" Aidan said. "Shuttles are still flying to Paris, and the military is still patrolling the skies over that country. How are we going to stop it?"

Threnody carefully pressed her hand against the case. The thick metal was cool to the touch. "With this."

"Do I even want to know?" Keiko asked.

"It's a nuclear bomb," Lucas said, opening his eyes. "Hard to believe our ancestors could make them so small, but they seemed to excel at destruction on many different levels."

Everyone except Lucas, Threnody, and Kerr shoved themselves away from the table and put their backs against the wall.

"Holy shit, are you *insane*?" Jason snarled.

Threnody dropped her hand away from the case and looked over her shoulder at Quinton. "Sit down. It hasn't been activated yet."

"We wouldn't be alive if it were activated," Quinton felt the need to point out.

"Do you think I would have agreed to this if I thought there was any other way?"

The two stared at each other, becoming the center of everyone's attention. Quinton shook his head in denial, a pleading look filling his face. "Thren, this is—we can't do this. It makes us no better than the people who started the Border Wars."

"How is that any different than the one we'd be heading into if Nathan gets all his Warhounds into space?" Threnody asked quietly. "Nathan's people will return wanting what we're trying to rebuild and we'll be left repeating history. The old countries fought for their fair share, so how is this different?"

"Because it's *wrong*."

"And I'm not saying it's right. I'm saying it's our only option."

For a moment, no one moved. Then Quinton took a step forward, heels dragging against the floor. With jerky motions, he pushed his chair closer to the table and sat back down.

Slowly, everyone else did the same.

[THIRTY-EIGHT]

SEPTEMBER 2379
TORONTO, CANADA

Samantha's feet hit the floor of the Strykers' arrival room in the medical level with a heavy thud, Kristen landing right beside her out of the teleport. The empath smiled widely at her brother.

"It's a madhouse back there," Kristen reported cheerfully.

"I know," Lucas said. "It's almost as bad here."

Samantha dropped the bag she carried on the arrival platform before stepping off, eyeing her brother. "Why are you wearing that?"

Lucas tugged at the collar of the Stryker uniform he wore over his insulated skinsuit. "Easier to tell Strykers apart from Warhounds and humans if we're wearing a uniform. I doubt Nathan is going to have his people in field uniforms when they board those space shuttles."

"Which means they'll just find it easier to target us."

"The Strykers are used to the risks that come with this uniform. What Warhounds remain on Earth will stand their ground. Nathan won't back down from this fight."

Samantha curled her lip at his attire. "I suppose you'll want us to wear it as well."

"You aren't an exception anymore, Sam." Lucas gestured at them to follow him. "Let's go."

He led them to a decontamination room, where he waited while they washed off any lingering taint of radiation. They had ditched the skinsuits in the generator room back in Paris, but this was standard protocol when returning from a deadzone.

When they were clean and wearing a new set of skinsuits and uniforms, Samantha and Kristen met with Lucas out in the busy hallway. Samantha tapped a finger to her temple, damp blond hair sticking to her skin. "I've got what you need for Paris."

Lucas pulled her into a psi link and let Samantha dump the information straight into his mind. It was already mentally sorted, information practically choking his thoughts. Grimacing, Lucas pressed a hand to his forehead. "Nathan isn't in Paris yet?"

"He's scheduled to arrive tomorrow," Samantha said. "He's busy hailing himself as the only one who can replace the World Court, and people are listening, judging by the conversations we overheard. Did you kill them?"

"No. He did."

"The world press is blaming psions for their murders."

"Of course they would. Better the monsters they know than the ones they don't."

Samantha covered her mouth, yawning. "You have the security information. What else do you want from me and Kristen?"

"For you to get some rest," Lucas said. "I'll find you in a few hours. I need both of you clearheaded for what's going to happen next."

"I don't know the layout of this Syndicate. Where are we sleeping?"

The two were abruptly teleported into a room that looked to house four people at a time, but was currently unoccupied. The beds looked as if no one had slept in them in a while.

Sleep, Lucas said into their minds. *When you wake up, I'll brief you.*

Samantha didn't feel like arguing, even if Kristen did. She pushed the younger girl to the lower bunk on one side of the room. "Listen to him," Samantha said firmly. "Close your eyes and sleep."

Kristen shrugged and curled up in a ball on the bed, promptly dozing off. Samantha didn't remember her head touching the pillow. She knew she must have slept, but the hand on her shoulder that pulled her back to consciousness sometime later was unwelcome.

"I could still sleep," Samantha grumbled.

"We all could," Lucas said. "Get up. Your shuttle is scheduled to depart soon."

Samantha sat up slowly, careful not to knock her head on the bunk above. Kristen was already awake and seated cross-legged on the other bed, eating her way through a ration bar. Samantha took the handful that Lucas offered her, all of them already torn open. She ate them mindlessly.

What's the plan? she asked.

I'm sending you and Kris to London. Lucas bent his head so he could look her in the eye. *Not to the Serca Syndicate, but to the outer city zones. You'll be traveling with most of the telepaths here, and others will meet with you in London. Jael is already there, getting things sorted.*

Samantha kept chewing. *Why am I not going with you to Paris?*

Because London is closer than Toronto for what I need from you and the Strykers. They don't know how to merge, Sam. Keiko is the only one I had the time to teach, and her understanding of it is shaky at best, but I need her in Paris with the telekinetics.

I'm perfectly capable of watching my own back in the field.

I know you are, but the merge I'm asking you to help hold together is too massive for you to concentrate on anything else. You'll be a liability in the field.

If that's the case, why are you leaving Kristen with me?

She won't be in the merge. Lucas nodded in Kristen's direction. *Her job is different.*

If I'm handling the merge, then what is she doing?

"I'm making sure Lucas doesn't feel a thing," Kristen said, her manic glee tempered by her brother's desire to see this through to the end.

Samantha cleared her throat. "I hope you know what you're doing, Lucas."

"This isn't how I thought we'd finish it, but I'm not going to argue how we're choosing to fight. It's something Nathan never understood," Lucas said.

"What? How you saw the world?"

Lucas shook his head. "Choice. Marcheline showed me that, Sam. I didn't care for her programming or Nathan's, but at least she showed me what it meant to control my own mind."

"What about my choice?"

"Do you really need one?"

She didn't have to think about her answer. "No."

Lucas smoothed back her hair with one hand. His mind tangled against the edge of hers and something resonated deep in her thoughts. She couldn't find its origins, but a part of her would always wonder if the answer came from herself or from Lucas's subtle, subversive mindwipe. Samantha supposed she would never know.

"Nathan never believed in humanity. Humans make their own mistakes and he despised them for that. Like everyone else in our family, he felt he was above them. That he deserved better," Lucas said. "We can't blame humanity for their errors when they made us through their faults."

"Is this how you save them? Through some preemptive strike?"

"It doesn't matter how I save them, just that I do."

Samantha leaned away from his touch, picking up her last ration bar. She didn't look at him when she said, "You told me to trust you. To follow you. I should hate you, but I don't. I think that's all you, but I'll follow your orders if that's what you need from me."

"It is." Lucas straightened up. "Your shuttle is getting prepped. Let's get you to it."

They walked instead of teleporting, needing to conserve their strength. Lucas led them to a lift that took them four levels down to one of the enclosed walkways. It connected to the landing docks, which protruded from the sides of the city tower. A large group of Strykers was already boarding. Most of them looked back warily at the three Serca siblings who approached. The only ones who didn't were Threnody and Kerr.

"You're flying with us dressed like that?" Samantha asked them.

Both Threnody and Kerr wore expensive outfits over skinsuits. They looked strange out of uniform or the grimy clothes of the street that they'd worn all their lives.

"We're being dropped off at one of the city towers in London," Threnody said. "Jason hacked our names into a passenger manifest using the information you brought back from the Command Center. We'll be flying into Paris with registered humans, so we need to look the part."

Between Threnody and Kerr sat a heavy-looking carrying case and two bags that looked as if they held clothes. Kerr leaned down to grab the handle on his side of their cargo. "See you on board."

The two followed the rest of the Strykers onto the shuttle. A quick scan showed Samantha that the majority of the Strykers traveling with them were telepaths, but quite a few telekinetics, pyrokinetics, and electrokinetics were in the mix as well.

Psychometrists and most of the empaths won't be accessing the mental grid, Lucas said. *We've ordered them into field positions to coordinate Stryker movements across the continents. I've allocated some 'kinetic-oriented psions for defense, so you'll be protected.*

You're putting a lot of trust in psions who hate us.

They know what's at risk. Now do your job.

Lucas walked away, leaving Samantha and Kristen alone to face down people who were once their enemies. The two boarded the shuttle last, strapping into seats near the front next to Threnody and Kerr. The shuttle wasn't built with luxury in mind, geared more toward transporting large groups of people. The seats weren't all that comfortable, but they settled as best they could. Samantha wrapped her hand around Kristen's wrist and closed her eyes as the shuttle unlocked from the anchoring arms of the docking cradle.

Close your eyes, Samantha told her sister. *Rest your mind.*

They slept on the flight to London, only waking when the pilot announced over the comm system that they were descending into a city tower. Samantha opened her eyes and yawned, trying to wake up. Kristen hadn't changed position at all during the flight over, though she was no longer sleeping, even if her eyes were closed.

Samantha turned her head to look at Kerr. "See if you can't mindwipe your pilot into landing in the rear of the launch area, behind the Command Center. It's the area with the least amount of security feeds, though that's not saying much."

Kerr nodded as the shuttle locked into a docking cradle with a heavy shudder. "We'll take that under consideration."

He and Threnody were the only ones to disembark, leaving the confines of the shuttle with the carrying case held between them. Samantha watched them leave until they were out of sight. The hatch closed again and ten minutes later the shuttle got the all clear to depart.

Whatever hack Jason was able to perform, it must have been good. They weren't challenged at any point during their flight across London. When the shuttle finally landed with a heavy shake on the cleared street, everyone undid their harnesses and got to their feet. The group disembarked in an orderly fashion, with Samantha pulling Kristen after her. Jael greeted them outside in the street.

"Can't say I'm happy about this," Jael said as the pair stepped off the shuttle.

"Considering what's going to happen, no one really should be," Samantha said as she studied their location.

The Strykers had taken over a single block of tenements in an outer city zone. It was night and the streets weren't lit. The building they were working out of had light escaping around the edges of badly boarded-up windows. A quick scan of the place told Samantha no humans were in the area. A lot of psions were, however, and she frowned at the way all those Stryker minds pinged on the mental grid.

"Right, first thing I'm doing is teaching you lot how to read like humans on the mental grid," Samantha said. "We don't need to be advertising our presence to the Warhounds still here."

"Lucas said all the telepaths involved in this merging venture aren't to exhaust themselves," Jael said as she gestured for the two younger girls to follow her.

"This trick of the mind is fairly simple and needs to be done if we're to stay safe."

"We're using the street as an arrival area for those telekinetics in Paris and the ones nearby to pull the wounded out of the way. We've got 'kinetic-oriented psions guarding the area along with empaths and psychometrists. We'll be safe."

"Against a city dead set on burning itself to the ground?" Samantha shook her head as they walked into a musty-smelling building. "No, we can't take any chances."

"The riots won't reach here. We won't let them."

Samantha still retained her uneasiness. Blinking her eyes to adjust to the bright interior, she took in the space that was their safe house for the time being. Strykers wearing the white scrubs of doctors and psi surgeons milled around inside, handing out bunks for the telepaths assigned to London. Samantha declined a bed or couch, not liking the looks of the ones she passed, and instead took up position in the kitchen. She and Kristen claimed a small table with four chairs. Kristen immediately folded her arms over the tabletop and rested her head on them, body canted at a sharp angle.

She gave her sister a sharp smile before closing her eyes. "It'll be brilliant, Sammy-girl."

Samantha sat down under Jael's watchful eye, not protesting when a nurse started to hook her up to a monitoring machine. "Remember your orders, Kristen."

"Don't worry. Lucas won't feel a thing."

PART EIGHT

ASCENSION

SESSION DATE: 2128.02.17
LOCATION: Institute of Psionics Research
CLEARANCE ID: Dr. Amy Bennett
SUBJECT: 2581
FILE NUMBER: 160

"Should we fear you?" the doctor asks.

The child shrugs and picks at the lace on her white sock. She is kneeling on the chair and hooks a finger beneath the strap of one shiny black shoe as she stares around the room. "I think you already do."

"This is only a precaution. Do you consider yourself dangerous, Aisling?"

She wrinkles her nose at the doctor. "I'm four."

"You don't act it sometimes."

Aisling shrugs again and settles more comfortably on the chair, her feet swinging freely through the air after she shifts position. "I can't help that. I can't help what I see."

The woman settles a hand over her datapad, leans forward, and offers up a smile. It doesn't reach her eyes, barely curls her lips. "You're the first person we've found who has a one hundred percent accuracy rating. We need that. We need you."

Aisling tilts her head to the side, the way any inquisitive child would. "You don't need me, you need my dreams. But they aren't for you."

THIRTY-NINE

SEPTEMBER 2379
PARIS, FRANCE

Nathan was in the launch command room, in the middle of a conversation with the head of operations, when the security grid around Paris pinged with numerous threats. The chatter in the command room picked up, growing louder with every second that passed.

"Those aren't confirmed routes."

"Sir, no one is answering our hails."

"Someone get those jets scrambled!"

Nathan took one look at the targeted mass of dots drifting closer to the ruined city on the hologrid map before abruptly turning on his feet and leaving the room. The hallway that separated the command room from the rest of the boarding facilities of the building was filled only with scattered government employees. It wasn't private, but it was empty enough for what he needed to do.

The four Warhounds masquerading as soldiers in a quad followed him out and stood guard when Nathan put his back against the wall. He closed his eyes and sent his mind skimming across the mental grid, picking up Warhound telepaths and dragging them into a merge. Bolstered by external power, Nathan allowed himself to reach for the cluster of buzzing thoughts that were getting closer with every second that passed. A morass of psi signatures hit his leading mental shields, and Nathan abruptly pulled back, retreating in a way that snapped pain through his head when he opened his eyes.

"Sir?" the Warhound to his left asked. "What's wrong?"

"Confirm the numbers we have on-site for Warhounds," Nathan said in a low voice.

"The last groups are still flying in. They number a little over one hundred. On-site? We've got two hundred Warhounds still waiting to board and about fifty already on their assigned space shuttles. Everyone else is already en route to the *Ark* or on board the colony ship."

Nathan calculated the odds. Three hundred of his Warhounds, half of them higher-Classed psions, were already in space and unavailable for this fight. Nathan had staggered the exits of Warhound teams, knowing that things would be going to hell during such a shortened transfer time frame. He ground his teeth, exhaling sharply through his nose as he picked through his options.

"Get them off those space shuttles and out of this building. I want them on the streets and ready to fight *right now*. That's Lucas flying in with Strykers and we need to be ready." Nathan gestured at the hallway they were in. "Send me all the Class VI and higher telepaths and empaths we have on-site. Tell them to prepare for merging."

One of the Warhounds nodded sharply at the order, and Nathan headed for the command room. He pulled his suit jacket straight as he walked back into chaos. The grating static of human thoughts beat against his mental shields as he took up his post next to the command terminal manned by the head of operations.

"Jets are confirming no response from those shuttles, sir," someone told the man in charge. "We're starting to lose uplinks with the jets as they approach the targets."

"What do you mean we're losing uplinks?" the government officer demanded.

"They're disappearing from the security grid."

"Do we have a visual?"

"Negative."

"Why the hell not? Get me that goddamn visual!" The assistant ran off to obey and Nathan took his place. The officer didn't look up from his terminal. "You shouldn't be here, sir. Grab a quad and have them take you to the space shuttle we're readying for launch. We need to get you off this planet."

"I can't leave just yet," Nathan said.

"If I have to haul you onto that space shuttle in cuffs, I'll do it. We need you alive, sir."

"Yes, but that won't happen if those incoming shuttles aren't stopped. You have no clue who you're dealing with."

The officer scowled and waved over a quad. "I don't have time to listen to politicians. They're taking you to a shielded transport shuttle and putting your ass on the next space shuttle in the launch queue."

The first soldier to lay a hand on Nathan got his arm broken, and the breaking didn't stop until the screaming man was a mutilated mass of pulpy flesh and shattered bone lying on the floor. It took only a minute for the man to die, but it seemed like eternity to those watching. Nathan stared disdainfully at the dead man and tugged his suit sleeve straight.

"Don't presume to tell me what to do," Nathan said, raising his eyes to meet the officer's shocked and uncertain gaze. "I don't take orders from humans. Not anymore."

Words died on the man's lips as Nathan telekinetically broke his neck. Another body hit the floor and Nathan tossed it aside, clearing the way for him to take control of the command room. He could feel the rising panic in the large room, fear meshing into a ragged mob mentality that would have left him short of needed people for the controls.

The Warhound telepaths and empaths that entered the command room took care of that for him, brutally mindwiping the humans of their fear and panic. The mindwipe kept the basic pattern of human thoughts intact, leaving them with the ability to still function and do their duty. They were essentially puppets now, with bodies going through directed motions, all except Dalia.

She rose from her seat and crossed the room to take the second-in-command position one terminal down from Nathan. "Bringing up the visual you wanted, sir," she said crisply, hands flying over the controls in front of her.

Nathan nodded, hands resting on the edge of the command terminal as his eyes flicked across the vidscreens and hologrid. The Warhounds settled themselves where they could, minds sliding into a pulsating merge that hovered near the back of Nathan's mind.

A visual finally came up, taken from a security feed two kilometers away. The remains of fighter jets burned in the broken streets of Paris, smoke curling black and ugly into the sky. Strykers were already on the ground, moving around the wreckage. Nathan licked sweat off his upper lip before merging with the waiting Warhounds, taking the apex position in that grouping of minds and power.

Don't let them near the launch area, he said. The order burned across the mental grid, reverberating and branding itself into every Warhound mind he could reach. *Our priority is protecting the space shuttles. We can't let them gain access to even a single one.*

"Dalia," Nathan said. He stared through the information scrolling across his terminal, feeling sweat sliding down the back of his neck, following the curve of his spine. "Keep the launches going. I want—"

He broke off as a familiar mind spiked on the mental grid, the psi signature one he didn't think he'd ever feel on this planet again. Nathan jerked his head around, staring in anger and shock as Gideon leaned against the side of the command terminal, face calm.

"Nathan," Gideon said.

"Why the *hell* aren't you on the *Ark*?" Nathan demanded. "I need you off this goddamn planet, Gideon."

"I have what you need."

Nathan stared at him in disbelief, noting the soft silver gleam that stained his son's dark blue eyes. "Lucas nearly burned out your mind. You've got holes in your memory. You don't even know what to look for."

"Lucas didn't destroy everything." Gideon slid a hand through his hair and pulled, the action one of Kristen's habits. "There's an echo in my head. Where Samantha used to be."

Nathan didn't ask for permission before entering his son's mind, sifting carefully through broken thoughts for the scar that was left of the psi link Gideon once shared with his twin. Tangled through its raw layers were pieces of memory, transferred from Samantha in that moment when she saved Gideon at the Strykers Syndicate. Nathan saw it and carefully mapped out a large fragment of a psi signature that didn't belong to either of his children.

"How did I miss this?" Nathan said.

"We're twins. We can't remain apart forever." Gideon smiled slowly, the curve of his mouth tight and forced. "You always did fear insanity, but it's all that's left for you now."

Nathan couldn't deny that fact. "Suit up, Gideon. You're right. I'm going to need your help to stop Lucas."

[FORTY]

SEPTEMBER 2379

PARIS, FRANCE

The shuttles landed in the streets of Paris, between the remains of bombed-out buildings and away from the wastewater that flowed through the Seine. It was as close as the Strykers could get to the launch area without running up against Warhound telekinetic shields. If the Strykers didn't land, they risked ending up like the military jets, blown to pieces after hitting a barrier their instruments couldn't pick up.

The rest of the fighting was taking place on the ground, in the middle of a deadzone with toxicity levels that were still dangerous, even to psions. The two-pronged push came from the west and the north, both Stryker groups filled with telekinetics, pyrokinetics, and a few dozen telepaths not drafted into the Stryker merge.

They outnumbered the Warhounds by a decent margin, but that didn't mean anything. Most of the Warhounds were higher-Classed psions than the Strykers, and all of them knew how to merge. The crushing telekinetic blow that slammed into the Stryker ranks coming from the west tore through weaker shields, throwing people to the ground with bone-breaking force.

Jason anchored his telekinetic shield with all his Class 0 strength against the Warhound merge. His shield wavered beneath the heavy weight of foreign power, but didn't break. Swearing, Jason shoved his power forward at breakneck speed to clear the street ahead of them. Beside him, Quinton had a fireball formed, the crackling flame joined by dozens of others as pyrokinetics prepared to attack.

"Dropping shields," Jason shouted. *"Go!"*

A firestorm ripped down the street, riding gas and burning through debris to add fuel to the fire. The pyrokinetics forced the fire to burn white-hot on its way to their targets. They came up short against telekinetic shields, but the fire served as a needed distraction. The Strykers had numbers on their side, and the hundreds of mental strikes started to slowly bog down the merged Warhound telekinetics. Some shields caved, sending Warhounds to their knees on the street, screaming from severe psionic overload in their minds.

The Strykers kept searching for weak spots, struggling to find a way into the center core of that power. They found some with Lucas's help, his guidance enabling them to shatter pieces of the merge and, with it, some of the Warhounds' concentration. The telekinetic shields in their immediate area disappeared and the fire consumed Warhounds.

Screams echoed in the air, along with the stench of burning human flesh, but the Strykers ignored both on their push forward. Quinton looked over his shoulder to where Lucas ran, dark blue eyes like holes in his face behind the helmet of his skinsuit. Blood slid out of his nose in a thin trickle. He was skirting a line of mental damage far beyond psi shock by being here on the ground, but he had no choice. Lucas was commanding this battle, and if he was on the field, Nathan wouldn't be looking for an attack anywhere else.

"Can you handle this?" Quinton asked as he adjusted the grip on his pulse-rifle. The strap was slung across his chest; he'd let the rifle go in order to use his power.

"Don't question my judgment," Lucas said.

"I'm not. You got us this far, but if you're dead, we're fucked."

Lucas waved at Quinton. "We have to keep moving."

Quinton took him at his word and lengthened his stride as Jason picked up the pace, pulse-rifle gripped in both hands. Everyone was loaded down with weapons for this fight, but half the Strykers on the field treated them as an afterthought. Telekinetics were guilty of that mind-set more than others, used to relying on the physical force of their power over the guns in their hands.

The sun beat down on them through a partially cloudy sky, smoke warping their line of sight. Telekinetics wrapped layered shields around everyone as they double-timed it down the street. The mental grid was like a warzone beyond every Stryker and Warhound shield, telepathic and empathic strikes ripping against hundreds of minds. The constant mental attacks wore down everyone's defenses, with shields slipping beneath the weight of focused power. Once those shields slipped, the minds behind them were torn to pieces. Lucas's merge of telepaths was holding off a good many Warhound strikes, but the distance between London and Paris put them at a disadvantage.

You should have let us onto the field, Samantha said through the psi link that tied her to Lucas. *Here, catch the next layer.*

Power slid through his mind, bolstering his Class I strength, burning against the edges of his shields. The faint hint of pain was caught by Kristen and locked down somewhere that Lucas couldn't reach. His sisters were like twin spots of brightness buried in his mind. Kristen's presence was chaotic and distracting, her empathy pulling at his mind in ways it didn't want to bend, but had no choice but to accept. Samantha was a mental bridge between Lucas and the Strykers in London, linked beyond that to other Strykers across the planet. A web of psionic power spanned the world, and she was slowly spinning it all together, feeding him the power. Her own Class II strength was barely enough to guide the Strykers into the merge and help Lucas hold it together.

Lucas was the apex of that merge, the only one who could have carried the load and survived. Nathan made it a point to target him first.

The next telepathic strike caused Lucas to stumble in midstride. Jason caught him with one hand, keeping Lucas upright as they ran. Jason didn't look at him, all his attention focused on the street ahead. "Lucas?"

The crushing pressure of merged minds weighed down on Lucas's shields, echoed in the drag of his feet against the ground. He blinked black dots from his vision. "Let's start teleporting."

Telekinesis wrapped around everyone, dozens of Strykers picking up their fellow teammates and teleporting across the distance ahead in short-distance 'ports. They judged the distance as best they could using binoculars to get a visual, putting kilometers behind them in seconds rather than minutes or even hours. The Strykers came out of the last teleport into a hail of enemy gunfire, energy darts and bullets slamming into telekinetic shields and Warhound telepaths struggling to break their minds as their feet hit the ground.

The Strykers in the scattered group spread farther out. Some telekinetic shields fell beneath Warhound attacks, forcing Strykers to find physical cover behind broken cement foundations. Some weren't quick enough and took bullets in the back, collapsing to the ground. They didn't remain out in the open for long. Telekinetics pulled the wounded out of fire range, teleporting them back to London with the help of telepaths who provided up-to-date visuals.

Quinton dragged Lucas down behind a crumbling wall with Jason's help, watching Lucas's back while he watched over their minds. Lucas let his head fall back, helmet scraping against a cracked cement wall. His breath came rapidly, the oxygen coming out of his tanks clean, even if it tasted like copper on his tongue.

The sound of gunfire filled the air, screams echoing every once in a while over the shouted orders coming from both sides of the fight. Voices echoed down dozens of psi links, the mental chatter buzzing in the back of everyone's mind. Beyond the Warhounds and conscripted human soldiers, the launch platforms were visible with their space shuttles, sunlight glinting off fuselages.

"They've got a space shuttle on the launch ramp," Quinton said as he ducked down to reload.

"Lucas, who's on it?" Jason asked.

"Unregistered humans," Lucas said after a moment, the telepaths in his merge bringing him the information. "Some Warhounds."

"What about Nathan?"

"No. He's still on the ground." Lucas coughed, trying to catch his breath. "We can't let that space shuttle launch."

"Then we won't."

Quinton looked over Lucas's head at Jason. "You pulling back your cover?"

"No other choice," Jason said grimly. He handed Quinton his gun. The Strykers ranged around them moved to compensate for his loss. Jason slid down beside Lucas and put his back against the wall, closing his eyes. "Can't let the Warhounds have a gene pool to breed from. Besides, this will buy Threnody and Kerr some more time."

Lucas nodded tightly. "They're almost in position."

"Good to know," Quinton said as he focused on the enemy. "We'll watch your backs."

Lucas pulled Jason into the merge, reaching through him for Keiko. She was on the other side of the city, having come in from the north, her group of Strykers closing in on the launch area. Lucas's mind pressed against Keiko's shields and she dropped them.

The merge had mostly been filled by telepaths. Samantha anchored the 'path-oriented psions as Lucas rolled through Keiko's mind, pulling the telekinetic into a secondary merge that began to meld with the first. Keiko knew every last Stryker in the Syndicate, both those in Paris and the ones left scattered across the world. She gave up those psi signatures to Lucas, their locations sparking across the mental grid for Lucas to see.

He reached for them, searching out the psions that read to his touch as telekinetic, and pulled the ones he could spare from the fighting into the merge. It was difficult for the Strykers to give up control, to cede their power to someone else completely. In the face of a changing world, they succumbed to Lucas's mental order reluctantly, and he felt the merge strain beneath hundreds of psion minds. This merge held more power and more minds than any other Lucas had ever created, and its strength scorched through his own power, nearly shattering his concentration. Pain crept through his awareness, pricking at his thoughts.

That's not for you to feel, Kristen said, his sister suddenly there in the center of his mind.

She turned off the pain, the safety function that enabled a person to know when something was dangerously wrong going dormant. The body needed pain, needed to know what was wrong with itself, as did the mind. Lucas couldn't know, not for this. Kristen locked down all the pain synapses in his head and body, her empathic manipulation a mental block not even Lucas could break down.

Through the jumbled eyes of too many people, the Strykers in merge saw the space shuttle launch, saw it streak down the long length of the curved ramp as it was propelled into the sky. Engines fired with a roar, the vapor trail streaming behind the space shuttle, thick and impossible to miss in the late-summer sky as it fought gravity to leave the planet.

Jason, Lucas said, his thought echoed by hundreds of others. *Take point.*

The bottom seemed to drop out of the merge, every single one of Jason's shields falling. His power exploded on the mental grid as a novalike burn, channeling into the merge. Through Lucas, Jason linked to every telekinetic in the Stryker ranks they could spare from defense on the field, drawing on their strength to bolster his own as he telekinetically reached for the space shuttle with a crushing mental grip.

Lucas nearly lost Jason in that rush of power, struggling to hold on to the other man's mind in the sheer massiveness of the merge. It took Quinton to find him, the bond between the two stretched taut, but it held. The backlash rolled through Quinton's mind, springing back down the bond in a never-ending loop that threatened the pyrokinetic's sanity. Lucas threw up a telepathic shield around Quinton's mind, struggling to keep the other man from succumbing to madness. Quinton's thanks was wordless and desperate.

In the sky, the space shuttle hit the upper atmosphere. In Lucas's mind, the merge was a glimmering monstrosity. Jason was somewhere in the thick of things, his Class 0 strength straining everyone's connection. Despite the Warhound merge striking against their minds, driven by Nathan's angry desperation, the Stryker telekinetics still managed to grab the space shuttle and wrench it off course. The broken angle of ascent was helped along by way of merged telekinesis. The space shuttle shredded apart as it fell back to earth.

NO!

Dozens of Warhounds minds screamed the word through the mental grid as the aborted launch—so close to its goal of escape—ended in hundreds of fiery fragments that streaked across the sky like meteorites. Silence stretched across the mental grid where the space shuttle fell, the static of human minds diminishing. They died in Earth's atmosphere, burning up as gravity pulled them home.

Nathan's merge ripped through the frayed mess on the mental grid, aiming for Lucas's merge. The mental grid tore beneath the clash of so many minds slamming together, so many minds breaking apart and dying, threatening to take neighboring minds with them. Then Samantha was there, cutting and tearing the Stryker merge apart from the inside out. She reassembled it into something that would hold, struggling to keep it stable.

Lucas's mind momentarily blanked out beneath the weight of the merge, thoughts and power twisting with something he couldn't identify, some emotion that Kristen refused to let him experience. In that moment where it seemed his mind would tear out of his body, Nathan slammed through his thoughts, fracturing everything.

Lucas's mind didn't break, though it took every bit of skill he had to force it to remain together. He borrowed strength from the merge itself, taking power pulled out of the willing minds of hundreds of Strykers. Aisling had seen this symbiosis years ago, lifetimes ago, in a white room bombed to ashes during the Border Wars. The disparate pieces of a world struggling to realign themselves into something new.

Somewhere, in the space that existed between two heartbeats, in the possibilities that festered in the human mind, Lucas saw it all. In the bottom of his mind, in memories too numerous to count, Lucas thought he could hear her.

Tell me that they're worth it, Lucas remembered saying once as a child as he gripped his future in his hands, knowing even then that it was too late to back out. Too late to give up. *Tell me that what's left of humanity is worth the future you're trying to give them.*

Silence was his only answer then, same as it was now. He'd heard all her excuses before anyway.

He was the means. His daughter was the end.

In the here and now, none of that mattered, not when the only thing that everyone was striving for was survival.

The sound of a gunshot, too close for comfort and too loud to ignore, jerked Lucas's attention out of the merge, instinct pulling up a telekinetic shield around himself. The split-second distraction lasted long enough for him to recognize the voice that started screaming, to feel Jason wrench himself free of the merge. Jason's abrupt exit ripped too many minds apart in the process, ruining the network Samantha had built through Lucas's mind.

Lucas opened his eyes, the world gone bright and liquid as his mind overloaded. He saw a familiar figure standing in front of them, gun leveled at someone else. Lucas watched Gideon smile.

"You couldn't hide Jason forever, Lucas," his younger brother said. "You didn't mindwipe me deep enough. I still had his psi signature in my memories."

The crack of displaced air from a teleport broke his tenuous concentration, and Lucas spiraled downward into a fraying merge that Nathan was taking apart one mind at a time with lethal, focused intent.

At the bottom of that tangled mess, Lucas found a way out.

[FORTY-ONE]

SEPTEMBER 2379
PARIS, FRANCE

With the help of a telepath, Gideon used the eyes of a dying Stryker for his visual and teleported in behind the Strykers' defensive line. Quinton never saw him arrive, but he felt it when Jason got shot. The crack of the gun going off drowned out the sound of the teleport. The bullet slammed into Jason's chest at close range with telekinetic help. The sudden agony was shared between them. Quinton doubled over screaming as Jason's mind exploded through his own, the trauma nearly incapacitating him.

Jason, tied deeply in the merge, was forcibly yanked out of that connection, his mind ripped away from the collective whole. His eyes snapped open, the world spinning around him with a suddenness that made him sick. He choked back the bile that crawled up his throat, not wanting to vomit inside his helmet. He thought he heard Quinton yell a name, maybe his, as he struggled to breathe.

Blood bubbled past his lips. The hand that suddenly pressed down on his chest pulled a scream out of him that showed up in sound waves and light, in the blood that rushed through Quinton's face and veins and skin. Jason blinked, his power fluctuating in ways it wasn't supposed to—or maybe it was. Around him, he could see a glittering blanket of light, of energy, that flowed back in a connecting line to a body of cells and bones and breath. The connection hummed in his ears, against his skin.

Is this what our powers look like? Jason thought in some distant corner of his mind. *Do we all burn like this?*

His telekinetic shields went down beneath his shattered concentration. Everything hurt, the pain worse than when Kristen ripped open his natal shields. The world was shifting, Quinton pulling him back into the spectrum that they lived in, his mind impossible to ignore through the bond. Jason blinked, and blinked some more, until he was looking up into Quinton's pale face behind his helmet. Quinton's eyes were wide from shock and fear, blood leaking from his nose and ears. The pyrokinetic was leaning over Lucas in order to reach Jason.

"Jason," Quinton said, voice breaking on the name. "Damn it, Jason. You need to hold on."

"I am," Jason gasped out. He lifted a hand to Quinton's shoulder, fingers skittering over rough synthfabric. Jason left streaks of blood behind where he touched, the shape of hemoglobin in his sight swallowing him whole. "I am."

Jason felt the tug of foreign telekinesis pull at his body, like the shock of a defib machine on a heart. Gideon was trying to teleport him off the field. Jason closed his eyes and anchored his power in the only thing that mattered if he was going to survive—Quinton. Jason held on to the pyrokinetic through the teleport, forcing Gideon to bear the extra weight.

They landed hard on a cold metal floor, in a room filled with shouting voices and the steady hum of machines. Jason choked on blood, Quinton's hands yanking at the flak jacket strapped over his uniform to get to the wound beneath. Neither man cared about the guns trained on their bodies; Quinton only cared about Jason, because if Jason died, then so would he, along with the rest of the world. With shaking fingers, Quinton undid the helmet of Jason's skinsuit, pulling it off.

He fumbled at his own, communication lost with the comm link wired into the helmets. He tossed both aside, pressing his hands down harder over the sucking wound in Jason's chest, fingers digging against synthfabric and torn flesh, blood slicking his own skin.

"I wanted him alive, Gideon," Nathan said from somewhere behind them.

With Jason slipping away beneath his hands, Quinton ignored everyone. "Don't do this, Jays," Quinton said raggedly as he leaned his weight against the wound, eyes riveted on Jason's bloodless face. "Don't you fucking die on me. Threnody and Kerr would never forgive you."

Lashes flickered over Jason's eyes.

"That's it. Come on, do what you did for Threnody. Fix yourself."

"No nanites" came the near voiceless reply.

Quinton shook his head fiercely, one hand moving to slap Jason's face lightly to keep him awake. "You don't need it. You never needed it. They were just a goddamn crutch. Now fucking *look* at me and fix yourself."

Jason's protest was soundless, blood bubbling bright and red from his lips. The bubbles popped on a wet breath, and Jason jerked beneath Quinton's hands, still drowning.

"Please," Quinton begged, feeling the bond begin to fray in the back of his mind, starting to give way. He could feel cracks in his own mind at that anchor point, the painful stretch of his thoughts beginning to unravel. "*Please.* Goddamn it, don't do this."

Jason forced his eyes open, black pupils having swallowed the hazel of his irises. He struggled to bring the face above him into focus, Quinton's expression frantic.

"Okay," Jason said, lips barely moving.

He closed his eyes, forced his power to sink into his own body. Down, down, until he saw his own cellular makeup against the back of his eyelids, all the possibility of life held in the double-helix coil of a DNA strand. No need for nanites and a biotank, just the code that defined his body. Just the power found in the genetic makeup of a Class 0 psion.

Jason dragged his power through his veins, through muscle and tissue, the fragile sponginess of his lungs, looking for what needed to be fixed. Tear by tear he healed himself from the inside out, fixing the hole the bullet had torn through him. The blood loss was something he would have to fix later. He didn't have time to remake pints of the stuff by coaxing at his bone marrow, not when Warhounds wanted to peel him off the ground and take him into space.

Jason hacked up sticky globules of blood, spitting until nothing was left in his lungs but air. A metallic taste saturated his mouth as he gripped Quinton's arms, needing an anchor. The bond between them shuddered in their minds. It couldn't block the headache pounding through Jason's head or the shaky weakness in his limbs. Pain burned through his nerves, impossible to ignore.

"Oh, man," he gasped. "I feel like shit."

Quinton was abruptly wrenched away, the pyrokinetic slammed down to the floor beside him. Jason felt that same telekinesis pin his own body to the floor. Weakly, he tried to fight it, but his mind hadn't stabilized yet, even if his body mostly had. He needed time to focus.

Nathan wasn't going to give him that.

Kerr did.

The telepath slid into Jason's mind with an ease that came from a lifetime of living in each other's head. Jason didn't fight him as Kerr focused through his eyes. Kerr soaked up the details of the room and used that visual to teleport in by way of merged Stryker telekinetics, mind cutting through Jason's bruised and battered thoughts without apology.

Jason—shield!

[FORTY-TWO]

SEPTEMBER 2379
PARIS, FRANCE

The pilot landed the shuttle hard, one of the last civilian shuttles allowed to come to ground. The Command Center had ordered everyone else to stay clear of Paris until the current problem was dealt with.

"Could he not get us killed prematurely?" Threnody said as she glanced at Kerr. "That's the worst landing I've gone through in months. Matron is a better pilot than he is."

Kerr undid his harness before grabbing his helmet and putting it on. "Let's just be happy we got here at all and get the hell off this shuttle."

Threnody stood up. "Couldn't agree more."

The fifty-person shuttle was packed to the bulkheads, the pilot having ignored weight restrictions. They didn't have enough fuel to make it back to London, which was the only reason the Command Center allowed them to land. Kerr mindwiped every passenger and crew member on their way out, erasing their memories of himself and Threnody.

"Maintenance hatch is in the galley," Kerr said. "Let's get below."

They reached the galley and knelt on the floor. The latch was embedded in the decking; Kerr undid it and the hatch dropped down. First Threnody, then Kerr slid into the cargo bay of the shuttle. He locked the hatch behind them.

The space was full of cargo trunks. Heavy-duty straps kept everything held down, with a small aisle between the two sides of the cargo bay. They found the carrying case still secured where they'd left it with their bags. They freed their bags first and stripped out of their clothes in favor of the nondescript workers' uniforms and tool belts Samantha had stolen for them. Then they freed the carrying case from the anchor straps.

"Two options," Kerr said, pointing at the dimly glowing signs bolted to the side of the shuttle at the rear from where they stood and farther ahead. "Loading hatches, or another maintenance hatch."

"Where's the maintenance hatch down here?"

"Decking."

"We'll come out beneath the shuttle?"

"Yes."

"Then we want that one."

It took them five minutes to find it. The wide floor hatch was cordoned off near the rear of the shuttle. They got it open and found themselves staring at the smooth metal launchpad. It was a good four-meter drop, an impossible descent with what they carried.

Threnody lifted her head and looked at Kerr. "Trunks?"

He nodded. "Trunks."

They worked quickly to undo the safety harnesses and ropes that kept the nearest cargo trunks in place, pushing several onto the platform. The noise the trunks made was drowned out by the noise of dozens of transport shuttles sitting with their engines running.

Kerr jumped down to stack the trunks, arms straining to move them. Once they were stable, he climbed on top and waited as Threnody carefully pushed the carrying case over the edge. She grunted as the weight swung from the end of her arms, joints aching, but she didn't let go. She saw Kerr get his shoulders beneath it and some of the tension eased in her arms as he took most of the weight. Threnody quickly pitched herself out of the shuttle and onto the platform.

She landed loosely, letting her body absorb the impact, and steadied herself with her hands. Then she moved to help Kerr. From beneath the body of the transport shuttle, they could see the rear of the Command Center, the squat building taking up most of the view. Technicians raced about, most heading for an emergency exit. Whatever their orders, Threnody and Kerr couldn't hear them. They weren't tapped into the comm channel being used, so they couldn't eavesdrop on the chatter.

"Shit," Threnody said as she stared out at the launch area. "This place is bigger than I thought."

"Let's head for those doors."

They ran as fast as they could, trying not to jostle the dangerous contents of the carrying case. A brief touch of telepathic power on unsuspecting human minds caused the workers to ignore them. They couldn't do anything about the security feed, but hopefully the bioware on the recognition points of their faces would trip up the computers long enough for them to get inside.

The supervisor on duty let workers through the emergency exit in small groups. Threnody and Kerr made it inside within five minutes, the door closing behind them. They waited impatiently inside a small decontamination chamber, the process agonizingly slow to them. Once they were cleared to proceed, a second door slid open and they walked into a hallway crowded with workers. Threnody and Kerr paused only long enough to unlock their helmets and take them off. They breathed in recycled air that stung their noses. The emergency alarm going off hurt their ears; the strobe lights nearly blinded them.

Best place to put it would be on one of the upper levels, Threnody said as they pushed their way through the crowd. *Setting it up in one of the support columns would effectively put it belowground, and that's not going to help us.*

The further up we go, the more Warhounds we're going to encounter, Kerr warned. *I can feel them on the mental grid. They're merged with Nathan and it's not pretty. Their attention might be outside this place, but I can guarantee you that if we're spotted, they'll turn all that power on this building to try to find us.*

We need to stay aboveground.

Then let's find somewhere on the next level. It's the safest place we can use.

They took an access stairwell up, and appropriated the first empty room they came across. The pair set the heavy carrying case down once inside. After locking the door, they tossed their helmets aside. Threnody looked around the storage room at the half-empty shelves and dented walls.

"Let's figure out where to put the bomb," she said.

They wrestled the carrying case to the rear of the storage room before opening it. Strapped securely inside was a second, smaller case that, when opened, revealed the components of a nuclear bomb. Wires protruded from it, connecting to an external receiver, the remote detonator strapped securely beside it. Threnody pried the remote detonator free and set it down on a nearby metal shelf.

"Okay," she said, letting Kerr take her spot. "Let's hope Novak did this right."

Kerr removed the flashlight hanging from his tool belt and propped it up at an angle on the open carrying case to get more light. He then carefully slipped the receiver out of the case and set it down on a shelf. Having grown up with a hacker for a partner, he knew what to do better than Threnody, but that didn't mean he was an expert. Halfway through the setup, Kerr let out a sharp gasp.

"Tell me you didn't just set the timer," Threnody said, trying to keep the fear out of her voice. "We're not ready, Kerr. Everyone's not off the field yet."

Kerr looked over his shoulder at her, face gone gray beneath the harsh lights. "No. Lucas just ripped apart a space shuttle with Jason's help."

Threnody curled her hand around his forearm. "Focus on the bomb."

They wanted to be out on the field with their partners, but instead they were here, finishing what Lucas had started. The two former team leaders of the Strykers Syndicate understood that failure wasn't an option, even if the plan was built through the shady gray areas of morality.

Kerr was plugging in the command codes that Novak said would connect the remote detonator with the receiver when agony exploded through his mind. He bent double beneath the pain, stumbling away from the shelves. Threnody grabbed him, giving Kerr support before he collapsed. He leaned heavily against her, forehead pressed into the curve of her neck as he bit down on his bottom lip against the scream wanting to leave his lungs. She felt something wet slide between the collar of her skinsuit and her throat: Kerr's blood.

"Kerr," Threnody said, voice tight. "*Kerr.* I need you to focus."

Jason's been shot, came the shaky words. *Feels like he's dying.*

They didn't share a bond anymore, but Threnody would never believe that meant Kerr gave up crawling into Jason's mind whenever he felt like it. Shoving the taller man upright, Threnody forced Kerr to look at her. The haunted look in his eyes made her stomach knot.

"Go save him," she said fiercely. "I'll give you five minutes to distract the Warhounds. You better make damn sure Jason has you shielded from anything metal. Understand? I don't care if you have to hold his mind together to do it, you make sure he shields you."

Kerr stared at her. "You're not coming."

"One of us has to finish this. Now go."

"I'll find Lucas," Kerr said as he pulled away from her and ran for the door. "I'll let him know we're almost ready."

She felt Kerr dig his power into her mind so hard and deep that for a moment all she saw was brightly colored spots. *I'll keep you hidden,* Kerr said, and then he was gone.

Kerr hit the hallway running, telepathy spanning the damaged mental grid for the only minds that mattered to him. He found Jason and Quinton first, their tangled thoughts weak and getting weaker. He couldn't find Lucas, but the Stryker merge still held against Nathan's focused attacks. Lucas was alive—somewhere—and all Kerr had to do was find him. But with all the telepathic power in the world tangled up in everyone's mind, Kerr only had one chance.

Using his empathy, he skimmed through the ravaged and dying minds around him, fighting the overwhelming urge to vomit in midstep as the horrendous feeling of hundreds of people dying overwhelmed him. He had to fight to regain his balance and continued running down the lower-level hallway, his footsteps echoing against the metal walls.

He felt Kristen first, her dysfunctional power like a hole in the mental grid that threatened to swallow Kerr's sanity. Keeping his distance would have been the smart thing to do, but he didn't have time to think about his safety, only about what needed to be done. Kerr snapped a telepathic psi link between them, Kristen's thoughts swirling through his mind.

I need Lucas, Kerr said.

He can't hear you, Kristen told him, the usual manic cheer gone from her mental voice. In its place was some emotion he couldn't identify, not in the context of her power. Kristen wasn't the sort to feel fear.

Then find me a telepath who can link with me.

Kristen gave him to Samantha, and Kerr almost lost himself to the merge. He had to claw his way back to a balanced mind, with Samantha dragging Kerr behind his shields to keep him from getting sucked into the pulsating mass of power that was the merge. Samantha was barely managing to hold it together, and he could sense the brittleness in her mind.

Make it quick, came Samantha's strained voice. It echoed, as if she was speaking from far away.

We're almost ready. Start clearing the field.

Understood.

He could feel her pulling away, layers of his shields peeling off as the magnitude of power bruised his mind. Kerr still reached for her. *Wait! I need a teleport.*

Visual?

It wasn't her voice alone this time, but dozens. Stryker telekinetics reached for him with their power through the psi link while others sought to hold off the Warhound merge. Through them, Kerr felt the strikes that

Nathan was orchestrating against the apex, Lucas succumbing to agony, even if he could no longer feel it. Samantha was a conduit between the Strykers and her brother, with the Strykers giving Lucas their powers while still struggling to understand how it all worked. Their lack of knowledge was crippling him.

We need a visual, the voices said again.

Kerr struggled to come back to himself, to keep his focus, reaching for the familiarity of a mind he would know anywhere. Years spent hiding behind Jason's mental shields meant it was simple for him to slide into the microtelekinetic's thoughts, to look through someone else's eyes and see where he needed to go.

Samantha's telekinetics saw through Kerr's mind and out through Jason's eyes, their resolve coalescing into a teleport that broke through the telekinetic shields surrounding the Command Center. Kerr arrived in the command room with a heavy stumble, nearly falling to his knees, surprising everyone. Kerr tightened the psi link between himself and Jason, calling out a warning.

Jason—shield!

Kerr got his balance back and slammed his fist straight into Nathan's face, even as Lucas struck at his father's mind. The physical attack briefly broke Nathan's concentration, head snapping back from the blow. It was enough of a distraction for Jason to slide his telekinesis around them in the strongest shield he could create. He was just in time.

The sudden tearing shock that ripped through the command room rode the back of an electrical storm. It exploded out of every terminal, ripping through the metal structure of the building itself, burning through everything it could. Half the Warhounds in the command room died, burned beyond recognition by electricity surging under psion control.

FORTY-THREE

SEPTEMBER 2379
PARIS, FRANCE

Threnody descended into the depths of the Command Center. She wasn't the telepath and Kerr wouldn't remain undiscovered for long, not with the core of the Warhound merge in the levels high above them. They both knew it, Lucas had known it.

You'll only get one chance, he'd said back in Toronto. *Make it count.*

She planned to.

Threnody ran down the hallway, counting down the seconds in her head. She held a gun in one hand and the remote detonator in the other. She kept her weapon out of sight when passing people. Most were talking frantically into personal comms, too focused on the emergency to pay her any attention. Psionic interference, she thought. She could distantly feel Kerr through the psi link, his concentration a pressure in the back of her skull that faded in and out. It made her ears ring. She swallowed to make them pop as she dodged into an access stairwell.

Threnody's knees started to ache with every impact her feet took on the way down to the bottom level. The schematics Samantha had stolen were downloaded into the datapad hanging from Threnody's tool belt. Threnody had them memorized, the layout pressed indelibly into her mind. She had one goal and it lay at the very bottom of a support pillar— where the generator room Lucas had teleported them into on their way to pick up Novak in Antarctica was located.

She slammed her way out of the access stairwell, stumbling into a short hallway. The alarm seemed louder down here, the flashing emergency lights hard on her eyes. Threnody looked up and came face-to-face with a pair of soldiers blocking her way. She didn't think the soldiers were a quad since there were only two of them. The door she needed was located right behind them. Threnody headed for it, acting as if she had every right to be there, but one of the soldiers grabbed her arm.

"What do you think you're doing?" the man snapped.

"Do you hear that alarm? Do you know what's happening out there?" Threnody said. "I've been ordered to do a manual check of the generators."

"A manual check was done an hour ago."

"Now the brass wants another one. You can help me with it."

She spun, lightning quick, slamming her elbow into the man's throat hard enough to crush his trachea. She dropped the remote detonator and shoved him against the wall, one hand pressed over his mouth and nose, cutting off his air as she shoved her electrokinesis into his body. With her other arm, Threnody aimed her gun and fired twice, one of her bullets finding its mark in the other soldier's face. Quinton was a brilliant teacher. She would never reach his level of expertise with firearms, but he had ensured she would survive a gunfight.

Breathing heavily, Threnody bent to pick up the remote detonator and headed for the door that led to the generator room below. She stepped on blood, feet skidding on slick wetness. When she reached the door, she discovered it was locked. Threnody smacked one hand against the control panel, frying the system. The door shuddered in its casing and she had to wrench it open, muscles straining against the weight. Her goal was within reach, the one place in the heavily shielded structure where she could start a chain reaction and guarantee it would affect the entire Command Center.

Threnody squeezed through the opening and stumbled onto a cramped landing. Several flights of stairs led down to the confines of the generator room. She started down them and was two steps up from the generator-room floor when she caught movement out of the corner of her eye. A lifetime of training saved her from getting killed, but not from getting shot. Pitching herself over the metal railing, Threnody took the bullet high in her right thigh instead of in the chest.

Threnody landed hard, heartbeat pounding loudly in her ears. She managed to keep her grip on the remote detonator. Adrenaline masked the agony in her body, long enough for her to get a shot off at the two soldiers advancing on her position. One soldier took her bullet in the shoulder.

"Wasn't fucking thinking," Threnody gasped. "Two soldiers don't make a goddamn quad."

She smacked her bare hand down on the floor and called up her power. Bright blue electricity erupted from her skin, the metal the perfect conductor. The two soldiers died almost instantly, their nervous systems overloading. They collapsed as the alarm changed pitch. For one frantic moment, Threnody thought the Warhounds had located her.

A merged telepathic strike exploded on the mental grid. Her shields nearly didn't hold. Only Kerr's telepathic maneuvering saved her. He shoved her thoughts further beneath static human minds so hard that her vision swam, or maybe it was the blood loss. She could sense the rest of the Stryker merge behind Kerr's mind, the power crackling across the mental grid. Threnody rolled onto her back, gasping from shock and pain. She pressed one hand over the wound in her leg, blood flowing over her fingers.

"Fuck," she breathed. "*Fuck,* that hurts."

Numb fingers fumbled at her tool belt. She unclipped all her tools and yanked the belt free. Methodically, Threnody wrapped it high around her thigh. She pulled the belt as tight as she could to form a tourniquet, choking back the yell that threatened to rip out of her lungs. Teeth tore through the thin skin of her bottom lip, slicing it open. Blood filled her mouth. She swallowed it, gagging on the taste. Lying there, the metal floor electric-warm beneath her, Threnody tried to breathe.

"You can do this," she told herself, voice raspy and hitching from pain. "You have to."

Threnody rolled to her good side and reached for the handheld laser saw nearby. Gripping it, she got her left knee under her and shoved herself to her feet, using the railing to take her weight when she stumbled. Putting weight on her right leg almost caused her to vomit.

"I fucking hate getting shot."

She hobbled forward. It was hot down here, despite the specialized shielding in place to keep out the radiation taint in the ground. Sweat trickled down her back and neck. She looked around, seeing only machinery beyond the walkway railings. She limped down the length of one generator, looking for the control panel.

When she found it, Threnody set the remote detonator on the floor and gripped the laser saw in shaky hands. She used it to cut through the metal paneling and let it clatter to the floor. She pressed a hand to the side of her head as pain throbbed through her temple. Kerr must have sensed her discomfort because he strengthened her shields with his telepathy. Threnody let him do whatever he needed to keep her under everyone's radar. Taking a deep breath, Threnody stared at the interior of the control panel.

For the first time in years, she thought of Atlanta. Of the scorching summer heat and the muggy feel of the air. Of the acid storms and the churning hurricane that came to shore when she was only three years old. She remembered the night when her natal shields broke in the middle of that screaming storm of wind and rain and ocean salt. How she accidentally fried the generator that supported environmental controls for two blocks of slum tenements, too young to comprehend the damage she had inflicted. Her first use of electrokinesis forced dozens of families out into that raging storm when air no longer flowed through the packed rooms.

Threnody remembered how everyone else in that storm died and how she didn't—saved by the Strykers Syndicate and destined for a life of slavery.

Except Lucas had shown her another way, and maybe it wasn't the best way or the right way, but it was better than how she'd lived under the government's control. Freedom always came with a price. This was hers, and she would pay it.

Panting, Threnody stuck her hands into the cavity before her, wires and motherboards scraping against her bare fingers. She was elbow deep in a piece of the sealed Command Center's complicated wired interior, fingers wrapped around what was, essentially, a computerized nervous system.

It could die.

"One chance," she whispered.

Threnody hoped she had given Kerr enough time to do what needed to be done. She hoped he had saved Jason and Quinton. Closing her eyes, Threnody tapped into her electrokinesis.

Electricity exploded from her nerves with no restriction, bursting through the Command Center. Threnody poured everything she had into the overload she was desperately trying to create. She didn't have lightning this time to fall back on, just sheer desperation.

A deep, cracking groan echoed through the structure, the generators shuddering as they overloaded and died. Electricity burned through the wiring embedded in the walls and floor of the Command Center. Threnody's electrokinesis pushed the damage further, tearing through circuitry until it found the command room itself with explosive, deadly results.

[FORTY-FOUR]

SEPTEMBER 2379
PARIS, FRANCE

Kerr stared through the too-bright electric power as it crawled over Jason's telekinetic shield. Nathan's rapidly swelling face stared back at him from behind Gideon's own telekinetic shield. Around them, humans, telepaths, and empaths fell over, bodies jerking through electrocution. Kerr could sense both Sercas trying to restructure the Warhound merge through those deaths.

"Kerr," Jason said weakly as Quinton helped him sit up. A thick red stain was spread across his chest, tiny bone shards sticking to his torn skinsuit.

For a second, Kerr ignored him, reaching through a different psi link for Threnody. He shoved aside the pain, whispering apologies into her mind even as he pulled a visual for teleportation through her eyes.

'Port here, Jays, Kerr said as he pulled Jason into the psi link and shared the visual, then added a second one of the storage room below. *Don't worry about me, I'll be all right.*

You lying son of a bitch, do you really expect me to leave you behind?

You don't have a choice. You've only got enough strength left for two teleports, three if two of those are short, and one of those 'ports has to get you and Quinton to London.

Kerr—

Jason. Kerr drowned out his partner's thoughts with desperate words, seconds ticking away as the spark of Threnody's power faded. *I knew when Kristen broke your shields Quinton would come first from here on out. He has to if you're going to live.*

Kerr could feel Lucas and the merge at the far reaches of his mind, the mental grid lighting up with the thoughts of those who had survived the battle so far.

A hand grabbed at Kerr's leg, fingers twisting around his uniform. He knelt down, prying Jason's hand free and gripping it hard in his own. *You don't have much time.* Kerr looked over at Jason, at the blood on his face and the panic in his partner's eyes, and smiled gently. *You'll have to learn to follow someone else after this, Jays. Don't hate them because they're not me. Now go.*

I could stay, Jason said. *I'm the one Nathan wants.*

That's not how this works. You know that.

Slowly, Jason nodded, eyes filled with pain and regret, his mind brimming with countless thoughts and emotion that washed over Kerr. Jason never looked away as he teleported out, taking Quinton with him, his hand disappearing from Kerr's clenched fingers. His telekinetic shield stayed standing.

Kerr turned and pressed his hand flat against the invisible power of Jason's telekinesis, the hard, layered shield all he had left now. The psi link that connected him with Jason was a faint spark at the bottom of his mind.

Nathan's diminished merge was already regrouping and stabilizing. Those dark blue eyes didn't look away from Kerr's face as clarity returned to them.

This ends here, Nathan said, his words riding a wave of desperate power.

Of course it does, Lucas said, slamming into and *through* Kerr's mind with enough force to black out the world. *But you'll never see the* Ark, *Nathan. You'll never see Mars Colony.*

Kerr's strength flowed through the Stryker merge, filling the cracks and smoothing out the jagged edges that had been torn into it. Lucas let him mend what Samantha couldn't, giving up more and more space as other minds extracted themselves from the merge. First one, then two, then a dozen psi signatures disappeared—not dead, but teleported out, carrying Strykers who weren't kinetic-oriented with them. Kerr kept his hand pressed hard against Jason's shield, the support grounding him as Warhound telepaths dug hooks into the merge and his own mental shields.

The Stryker merge kept growing smaller, seemingly beaten into submission by Nathan's. Warhounds started to outnumber Strykers on the mental grid. Kerr felt the strain of the merge start to build up in his own mind as Lucas transferred more and more control over to him. The weight was something he could handle better than Lucas at this point, having been inactive during the majority of the battle. Out of every 'path-oriented psion in the Stryker ranks, Kerr was the only one left who could take Lucas's place.

I thought I could pull you out, Lucas said.

I know, Kerr said. *But the future always changes.*

It's not supposed to.

Maybe. But you did. And I don't blame you for that.

It was Kerr's job now to keep Nathan's merge anchored in this moment and to Kerr's mind. If those connections broke, they would lose this fight and all the rest waiting to start in the coming years.

Kerr held up as best he could, but against a Class I triad psion with years of practice under his belt, it was only a matter of time before Kerr started to buckle. He struggled to shore up all the Strykers' shields until those, too, started to disappear.

I can't hold it any longer, Lucas said, thoughts a fractured, broken mess. Kerr could barely sense Samantha or Kristen in the maelstrom that was Lucas's mind.

Kerr did what he was trained to do, what he had promised to do. He stood his ground.

Let me have the rest of the merge. Jason's telekinetic shield was still solid beneath his touch. Gideon kept hitting it with merged telekinesis, but couldn't break through. *Don't worry about me, Lucas.*

Lucas exited Kerr's mind, leaving behind a gaping hole in Kerr's thoughts that was filled with a myriad of minds from Nathan's merge. Kerr held on to the Stryker merge for a few moments longer, holding up the façade, until everyone else let go and all he could feel were two last people lingering in his mind.

Jason and Threnody.

For a second—Kerr lived a lifetime.

Jason's shield disappeared. Kerr cut the psi link between them. Merged Warhound telekinesis, once held at bay, now slammed into Kerr. He was thrown back by the force, the punch a harder hit than anything he'd ever before experienced. He crashed to the floor, felt his bones shatter from the inside out, felt the deep ache of organs tearing apart. All he tasted now was blood.

Merged telepathy curled deeper into his mind, stripping his shields down to their last layer, down to where his Class IX empathy mingled with his Class II telepathy. It wasn't enough to save him. Not this time.

Kerr blinked, struggling to breathe. Emptiness clawed at the edge of his mind and brightness interfered with his vision. He could see sunlight glinting off the space shuttles through the plasglass observation windows of the command room, everything shining with false halos.

He felt Nathan digging through his mind and Kerr couldn't stop him, didn't even try as the Warhound merge got lost in the maze of his psyche. He let all those minds find anchor points in his own thoughts, tying them down. Blood and clear fluid slid out of his nose and ears, pouring out of his mouth, choking him. He sensed Threnody's determination through the tenuous psi link that still ran between them. Kerr closed his eyes, feeling some distant sort of satisfaction as Nathan found, too late, what was hiding in his mind.

No, Nathan said, his telepathy a ragged, bright line of thought knotted deep in Kerr's mind. *You Strykers would never do this. It goes against everything you are.*

That's why you never saw it coming, Kerr said, thinking of Lucas.

With the last of his strength and every mental trick Lucas had taught him, Kerr held tight to the faded imprint of the merge, trapping Nathan and the merged telepaths and telekinetics there with him on the ground. The Warhounds struggled to get free of the deep holes in Kerr's mind, and maybe some did, but Kerr didn't know how many of them survived. All he knew was the shock that colored everyone's thoughts, their shared horrified, frantic disbelief. In that last hectic instant, Kerr heard them, heard them all as they died screaming.

FORTY-FIVE

SEPTEMBER 2379

PARIS, FRANCE

Threnody felt, distantly, when the last motherboard burned out, the spark of exploding circuits cascading through her brain. Or maybe it was something else, something more immediate. Threnody didn't know, couldn't care, as she collapsed to the floor, struggling to stay conscious.

Everything seemed distant until Kerr's voice whispered through her mind. Threnody could barely understand his words, but it didn't matter. All he needed were her eyes, so she focused on the generator room, everything blurry to her sight. Then it sharpened, brought into perfect clarity not by her, but by someone else. The connection overwhelmed her traumatized system and she passed out for a few seconds. She came back to herself slowly, hearing someone calling her name.

"Thren, please. Wake up," Quinton said, his voice a ragged, painful plea in her ear.

It took effort to open her eyes. She was barely aware of her surroundings, of the person holding her up so she could breathe. She coughed, her lungs burning. She tried to move, but the agony in her body made her choke out a cry.

"It's okay, it's okay," Quinton said, sounding desperate. He shifted her in his arms, one hand resting above the bullet wound in her thigh. "I know it hurts, but we'll fix you up in no time. I promise."

Only one emergency light was still working, whatever power source it ran on spared from the damage she'd caused. It cast an eerie glow over the two men gathered around her. Threnody opened her mouth to speak, but no words came out.

Quinton's shaking hand touched her face. "Jason, get us out of here."

Threnody blinked, the room changing shape with a crack of displaced air as Jason teleported them not to safety, but to the storage room she had left behind for the generator room. A single emergency light burned over by the door. The Command Center must have had a separate emergency backup system that she hadn't been connected to. There still wasn't enough light to see by.

"Flashlight," Threnody rasped out. "Near the case."

"Jason, we don't have time for this shit," Quinton snarled. He still grabbed the flashlight and turned it on. The bright light hurt Threnody's eyes.

Threnody coughed and looked down at herself. Her arms were black husks streaked through with scorched red, her uniform and the skinsuit burned off. Pieces still remained, melted into muscle, mixing with plasma. She could move her fingers, barely, but she couldn't feel a damn thing. Her head felt strangely weighted down.

"The case?" she managed to ask.

"Bomb's still active. The insulation in the carrying case protected it," Jason said in a hollow voice. "The shelves were metal. Receiver is nothing but slag. I can't find the remote detonator."

Threnody let out a choked little laugh. "Had it with me. Left it on the lower level."

She could hear Jason swallow. "Then it's probably slagged as well."

Something wet hit her face; tears, maybe. Or blood. She couldn't smell the difference, couldn't smell anything. Threnody focused on hands that she couldn't feel anymore, muscle memory ingrained in a way the brain couldn't forget. Quinton always said that even after he'd lost his arms or hands to his power, somehow he always thought his limbs were still there. Phantom sensations that his nerves remembered, would always remember.

Hers remembered.

"How much time?" she said.

Quinton's arms tightened around her. The pressure nearly sent Threnody spiraling back into unconsciousness, and she let out a pained noise. Quinton loosened his grip. She squeezed her eyes shut.

"Kerr and Lucas can't hold Nathan back for much longer," Jason said. "Three, maybe four minutes. Everyone else has teleported out. It's just us."

Threnody opened her eyes. The darkness seemed strangely bright to her. "Leave me."

"*No.*"

Quinton ground out the word. Threnody felt his entire body jerk in protest at what she was telling him to do. She struggled to lift an arm, bumping a ruined hand against the line of his jaw, refusing to let the pain pull her under. A roaring sound filled her ears, but she didn't know what it was and couldn't care.

"No choice." She smiled, struggling to form it. "Bomb needs to go off."

"I'll do it," Quinton said, burying his face against the top of her head, his teeth catching on her hair. "Jason can teleport you to London, then come back for me."

She caught sight of Jason's face and the bitter regret in his eyes. "I've only got enough strength left for one more teleport," Jason said. "I can't—"

Save you. The same way he couldn't save Kerr. She didn't need to be a telepath to hear those unspoken words.

Threnody drew in a short breath, finding it hard to breathe. She felt cold. "The world needs Jason. He needs you, Quinton. There's no one left to do this. Just me."

Quinton clutched wordlessly at her uniform, pulling at it.

Threnody felt Jason's hand on her shoulder, his grip shaky. His voice wasn't much better. "We're running out of time."

Quinton picked her up with arms that shook, but his hands were gentle as he cradled her close for the last time. He sat her up against the back wall of the storage room, Jason dragging the black case within easy reach. The glow from the flashlight showed Threnody everything around her, everything that mattered.

Quinton framed her face with his hands, fingers warm against her skin as he looked at her, his eyes searching hers out in the dark as they'd done countless times before.

"Hi," Quinton said, voice breaking.

"Hi." Threnody leaned forward, pressing her forehead against his. "I wanted to see it."

"I know."

"Live it for me. As long as you can." He tried to say her name, but nothing came out, just the shape of it on his lips. Threnody smiled, refusing to look away. "It's okay, Quin. Don't be afraid."

Jason teleported them out in a crack of displaced air and Threnody was left alone, the ghost of Quinton's touch on her face. The flashlight was angled to spotlight the open black case and the shape of the nuclear bomb that rested inside.

Threnody reached out with a shaking hand, ignoring the pain that came with movement, until her ruined fingers hovered over the arming switch near the base of the warhead. The tattered psi link between her and Kerr was held together by mental whispers, and then not even that.

She sobbed out a breath, biting down hard on her torn bottom lip until blood flowed over her tongue. She still couldn't taste it, but she remembered the metallic flavor, and her life, and all the decisions that had brought her to this moment.

Threnody flipped the switch.

The world burned hot and white for an instant. The mental grid dipped. Pulsed. Flattened.

In her mind and Kerr's, everything was quiet.

[FORTY-SIX]

SEPTEMBER 2379
LONDON, UNITED KINGDOM

Telepaths were dying beneath her hands, beneath her power, and Jael could only let them slide away as the merge ate through their minds. Nothing she could do would keep them alive long enough for her to stabilize their minds. She couldn't save most of them, so Jael settled for a few, two of them being Lucas's sisters. She kept a careful mental touch on Samantha and Kristen as she worked on the Strykers she could help. Jael judged the state of the fight by the state of those two Sercas and how damaged their minds were becoming.

Only when telekinetics started teleporting into the street in droves did Jael realize how many Strykers they were going to lose. She was inundated by the spiraling death throes of too many minds, and they threatened to take her down with them. Even her shields weren't enough, the mental shrieks of the dying clawing at her mind. For the first time since she'd dipped into a person's mind for psi surgery, Jael closed herself off to their thoughts and pain, trying to find her balance again.

The telepaths who were purposefully held back from the merge to be available for the fallout couldn't have known what was coming. They couldn't have foreseen that Strykers would be dying in the streets, slumped over one another, bleeding in the gutter, minds tangled together in a knot that no one could undo.

Then the cause of the whole damn mess teleported into the street, legs crumpling beneath him as he appeared. Someone screamed for Jael, but she was already running, stumbling over bodies to reach Lucas. The Stryker merge that had hung over the mental grid for so long finally broke down completely, the Serca siblings losing the viselike grip they had on everyone's minds. Lucas, for all his immense power, was so far gone, wrapped so tight and stretched so thin, that he never even felt it when his mind broke.

Samantha did, but she could do nothing, had nothing left to reach for him with that could help. Her telepathy was as shattered as the merge, and Kristen was no longer present to help pull Lucas out of the mental abyss that threatened his sanity. Kristen was already gone, mind broken beyond repair and shutting down, one dying spark in a wave of many. Try as she might, Samantha couldn't find Lucas in the mess that was the mental grid, and Jael felt the girl slip away somewhere deep inside herself.

Jael crashed to her knees beside Lucas's body, yanking at the lock of his skinsuit helmet and prying it off. She cushioned his head with one hand, letting her fingers catch the weight of it rather than the street. At the touch of her mind to his, Lucas's eyes snapped open, pupils tiny black pinpricks in a sea of dark blue, blood leaking out of the corners like tears.

"Lucas," Jael said, heart pounding in her chest. *Stay with me.*

He focused on her, or seemed to. Recognition was there, but Jael knew, somehow, that it wasn't of her. She would never know what he saw in that moment.

He opened his mouth and choked on words. "I—"

Breath stuttered in his chest. Jael felt his mind fall through the mental grid.

She couldn't catch him.

Jael felt the massive, gaping hole in Lucas's ravaged mind—all that was left of him after the merge—swallow everything in the wake of the trauma he'd inflicted on himself. Jael was effectively shut out, clawing at his mind and not even touching shields, just empty space.

"Lucas," she whispered, staring blankly down at his unconscious form and the slow rise and fall of his chest. Jael needed to transport him to the Strykers Syndicate immediately, but she wasn't sure if any telekinetics were left who had the strength to teleport.

A shadow drifted over her and Jael looked up, staring at Jason and Quinton. Jason had his arm slung over Quinton's shoulder, letting the other man take most of his weight. An ugly rip was torn through his uniform and skinsuit, blood having saturated the area, but his chest seemed whole. The grief they exhibited rubbed against the raw places in her own mind. Quinton was staring down the street with a dead look in his eyes, seemingly unaware of his surroundings.

"It's over," Jason said, eyes bloodshot, voice raw and wounded. "Threnody detonated the bomb. Kerr made sure Nathan and his Warhounds couldn't leave the explosion radius before everyone else teleported out of range."

Jael closed her eyes, her mind still searching for Lucas's. "And the people already in space?"

Quinton spoke, but he didn't sound like the man Jael knew. "Let them die out there."

PART NINE
TABULA RASA

SESSION DATE: 2128.09.28
LOCATION: Institute of Psionics Research
CLEARANCE ID: Dr. Amy Bennett
SUBJECT: 2581
FILE NUMBER: 881

The doctor kneels before the girl, one hand gripping the cascade of wires that hangs from bruised skin. Those bleached-out violet eyes seem sunken and they no longer look at the camera. They look elsewhere.

"Aisling," the doctor pleads. "We can't survive like this."

The girl is still and quiet, one hand clutching a white card. After a long moment, she unclenches her hand and lets the card fall to the floor. "Thank you," she whispers.

The doctor picks the card up, turns it around to see the shape on the underside. "We don't want your thanks."

"I know." The girl smiles and leans forward, the effort making her gasp. She presses a kiss to the woman's forehead, like a benediction when it isn't, not in her prison cell. "I wasn't thanking you."

The doctor drops the card to the floor and reaches out to help the child lean back in her seat. Behind them, the machines click and hum and whine, a nonstop sound that has been a constant companion to them both.

"What do we do?" the doctor whispers. "What do we do next?"

"Anything you want, Lucas." Aisling smiles, eyes wide and glazed and looking at things no one else can see. "Anything at all."

FORTY-SEVEN

OCTOBER 2379

TORONTO, CANADA

t never changed.

Jael wondered about that, the first time she went down into the static of Lucas's mind to try to anchor a psi link. She gave up analyzing it on the tenth try. The vibrancy was gone, the brightness normally there on the mental grid missing. Nothing remained but an echo, a negative imprint that she couldn't hold on to.

Not a memory, exactly. Not really a dream. Just the seam of his mind and the spaces in between that he'd fallen through. Just that last, drawn-out moment before the permanent end he hovered over, unable to let go, because psions were incapable of forgetting. Dying quick was always preferable to dying slow. Bleeding out in the mind happened like this, in increments. Searching for Lucas was like trying to find one clean drop of water in an ocean of toxic mistakes. Impossible without belief, without help.

Jael stared across the medical bed where Lucas lay, at a hollow-eyed Samantha, who swayed on weak legs, Marguerite standing worriedly behind her.

You won't find him, you know, Samantha said, the psi link between them quivering on her end as she struggled to hold on to something that only Jael was generating. *Not how he was. I don't know why you brought me in here.*

I'm not expecting to find sanity in his thoughts, Jael said as she curled a hand around Lucas's lax one. *I'm only interested in what's left behind. We need your brother.*

Samantha hunched her shoulders, the rigid line of her body bending into a brittle curve. *Do you, Jael? You need something he no longer is.*

Samantha could feel him, here in his mind, damaged as they both were, when all the times that Jael had tried before she only felt that vast,

605

echoing emptiness; only seen a flatline on the EEG and supporting machines, despite the heart beating in his chest. Jael had been in and out of both their minds for weeks on end, struggling to find the pieces of two shattered personalities and coming up achingly, bitterly short.

Jael was a Class III telepath. She would never be able to reach far enough to find Lucas, but Samantha *could*. She could find him, when no one else had the ability to, because Lucas always led her to him. It took nearly a month for Jael to realize why, of days spent holding Samantha's thoughts together while the telepath screamed her throat bloody and raw beneath makeshift mental shields that wouldn't hold. Permanent shields weren't an option, not yet, not until they found Lucas.

Samantha was as whole as Jael could make her, something far less than what the girl had been born to be. Jael could see the fragility in the blonde, in the tiny mental threads that held her together. All Jael's work and all for nothing, the Stryker thought tiredly.

Jael pressed her telepathy against the edge of Samantha's mind and the old scar of the mindwipe that had Lucas's touch all over it. All over his sister. Samantha's mind had never been her own. It had horrified Jael when she'd figured out what the scars pressed into Samantha's thoughts meant, yet it also relieved her. Here was the shape of Lucas, in Samantha's mind, the mold he needed to fill. Here was their salvation, as fractured as it was.

Jael stared at Samantha as their minds plunged deeper into the void that was seemingly all that remained of Lucas. Then she closed her eyes and Jael dug her telepathy into Samantha's battered thoughts with precise pressure.

I'm sorry, Jael said, *for what they did to you. For what I need to do.*

Samantha's screams echoed in the room, in their thoughts, bouncing off the jagged edges of a broken mind and against her shields, as Jael stripped Samantha of the mindwipe. The last piece of who she was—torn from everything that had made her into what Nathan and Lucas forced her to be. Jael cut the psi link between them, and Samantha, no longer anchored, slipped away, collapsing unconscious in Marguerite's arms.

Jael wondered who Samantha would be, if she would be anything at all, when she woke up.

The pattern was in Jael's thoughts now, a delicate thing that only a higher-Classed psion could possibly create. Borrowed, for now, as she spread the mindwipe through Lucas's mind, the mental grid humming around her.

We need you, she thought fiercely as that pattern of himself Lucas gave up so long ago seeped back into his thoughts. Some errant shard of a forgotten whole sparked and sputtered in her power, forming into a knotted, twisted psi signature she didn't recognize.

It always came back to that simple, selfish demand that drove humanity forward.

Need. Want. Some distant, half-formed idea of world integration beneath a clear blue sky.

Just some child's impossible dream.

Lucas, please.

. . . Jael.

What seemed like hours later, when she opened her eyes and came back to herself in a medical room at the top of a city tower, Jael was greeted by the soft, rhythmic noise from monitors tracking the synaptic pulse of Lucas's damaged mind, his hand weakly squeezing hers.

[FORTY-EIGHT]

NOVEMBER 2379

TORONTO, CANADA

Here's your weekly update," Jason said as he handed over a datapad to Jael before easing himself into a chair. "The major fallout from Paris stayed inside that country's borders. Winter winds will spread the radiation particles, but whatever damage it might do where it falls won't rate much. The radiation is mostly going to hit deadzones."

"I could wish that was the last time a nuclear bomb is detonated on this planet," Jael said as she scrolled through the report. "Somehow, I doubt it."

"If it happens again, we won't be around to see it."

But they were seeing the political fallout and it wasn't going to be easy to navigate a world where fear of psions might never fade.

"Oh, before I forget." Jason pulled a small fruit out of his jacket pocket and set it on Jael's desk. "That's for you. Courtesy of Matron. Carried it with me when I brought in the latest shipment of seedlings."

Jael looked up from the datapad in her hand and eyed the orange fruit as if it were something dangerous. "You sure she didn't poison it?"

"That woman barely lets people near her garden. You think she'd knowingly allow poison?" Jason shook his head. "Try it. She said it's called a kumquat."

Jael stared at the tiny, bite-size fruit before her with the healthy hesitation that a lifetime of wariness had gifted her. Eventually, she picked up the fruit and popped it in her mouth. The skin was sweet; biting into it was a different story. The taste shifted from sweet to sour on her tongue, the flavor shocking her taste buds.

She made a face and swallowed the pulp as fast as she could, spitting out the seed. "I don't know about that one. You sure you didn't mess up the seed growth somehow?"

Jason scratched the back of his neck, shrugging. "Maybe? Thought I had this tree down. I guess Matron will have to wait on her pears."

"What in the world is a pear?"

"It's another fruit. I think."

Jael set aside her work, wishing she had a glass of water to wash away the taste. "Where is she putting that bush?"

"Tree. Pears grow on trees, and she's thinking of putting some greenery into Kensington Gardens."

"Kensington Gardens is full of transients. What's she going to do? Order them to move?"

"If she wants us to clear it out, we'll clear it out." Jason slouched a little in his seat. "She's just taking what's owed to her. I'm willing to let her experiment, but winter's coming soon and nothing grows in the cold."

"Maybe wait until spring."

"Maybe," Jason echoed, tipping his head back to stare at the ceiling.

The silence in the office was heavy, but neither of them felt the need to break it. Nearly two and a half months since the world almost ended again, and things were still changing. There was an orchard in St. James's Park that people visited, or talked about visiting. It was overseen by Matron and her scavengers, the group having appropriated a building abandoned during the riots. No one in London fought her on her claim that she owned that bit of land, not even the drug cartels. Matron was only human, but she had psions on her side, and that was enough to make anyone pause these days.

Jael ran a fingertip over the line of her teeth, the tartness from the fruit still stinging her tongue. The amount of new food that was growing in Toronto's SkyFarms and others across the world was heartening, even if their stomachs couldn't handle it yet. A lifetime of bland GMO food had prepared no one for the shock that came with taste. Adjusting to the new diet was going to take time. Her people had enough of it for now.

"Does it ever feel weird?" Jason said, his voice jerking Jael from her thoughts. "Sitting in this office?"

"Always," Jael replied, trying not to hunch her shoulders. Leadership was always so much easier when someone else was doing it.

The door to Jael's office slid open, causing Jason to twist around in his chair to see who it was. He stood up as Samantha's thin figure stepped inside. The young woman crossed the office with measured strides, holding herself rigidly, as if she were afraid she would take one wrong step and break.

Samantha wore the soft, comfortable clothes those in recovery were given, though she no longer had a room in the medical level to call her own. Jael had upgraded her physical condition weeks ago to discharge, though Samantha's mental state was still in doubt   she was still at risk for suicide. Jael thought a change of scenery would be helpful; better than being sequestered in a white medical room with machines that constantly showed what she was missing, even if her new room came with twenty-four-hour surveillance.

Psions didn't mutate postnatal. Their Classification, however, could change. Samantha's telepathy was, for the most part, nonexistent now. The merge and Jael's psionic interference had broken her mind down to a Class IX, more human than psion, her telepathic reach no stronger than the softest whisper within her own thoughts. Samantha never used her power anymore, too aware and too prideful of what she had once been to accept what she had become.

Maybe it would have been better, more merciful, if she had died like Kristen. Jael hadn't been able to save Samantha's sister. If she was honest with herself, she hadn't tried very hard. Kristen's mind had torn itself apart during the merge, pain finally overcoming the empath's power. There hadn't been much left for Jael to save, and she didn't regret letting the teenager die. Keeping Samantha from doing the same was a full-time job on some days.

Samantha flicked Jason a wary look. Jason, for his part, made sure his shields were locked down tight. "If you need to speak with Jael in private, I can leave."

"No," Samantha said, her voice raspy. The weeks she'd spent screaming in the medical level during her recovery had permanently ruined her once-pretty soprano voice. "I need the latest report on survivors. There's a press conference tomorrow and I'm better at writing speeches than the people you've assigned to public relations."

Jael picked up a datapad from the pile on her desk and pushed it toward the edge. "It's right here."

Jason took a careful step back, giving Samantha room to take the datapad and not feel as if he was invading her personal space. She took it and hugged it to her chest.

"Latest world population count puts us at over a million by about fifty thousand," Jael said quietly. "Give or take a few hundred. The Registry only told us who was going into space, not who was left behind, and we lost tens of thousands in the riots. The census will take maybe another year or so to complete, but you can report on the rough findings. I think that will satisfy the public."

"And the count for psions?" Samantha said, sounding as if the question was difficult to ask.

"Around six hundred or so, if we're being generous. There's talk of a child or two in the Americas that show signs of being psions." Jael hesitated before saying, "Telepaths, according to the bioscanners. I'm sending out a team for retrieval."

Samantha's entire body flinched. She bit her lip, looking away from Jael and out at the view of Toronto instead. "We need those. There are so few telepaths and telekinetics left."

"I know."

This is all we've got, Jael thought as she watched Samantha turn around and head for the door. *Just the remains and nothing more. We've got to make it worth something.*

Keiko and Aidan were dead, as were nearly 85 percent of the Strykers' telepaths and 50 percent of their telekinetics. The worldwide merge Lucas had led in the assault on Paris had decimated the Strykers Syndicate's ranks. Empaths, pyrokinetics, electrokinetics, and psychometrists outnumbered the other two kinds of psions now, those that survived the riots at least. Prior to that, they had lost roughly 250 psions through the World Court's mass termination. Whoever was brought back from the retrieval mission would never know the feel of a neurotracker in his or her head.

It was a start.

The door slid shut behind Samantha. Jason was kind enough to wait until she was gone before tipping his head in Jael's direction as a silent good-bye and teleporting out. Jael sighed and leaned back in her chair, rubbing wearily at one shoulder. She ached in a way she never had before, body running through the last dregs of life in her cells. Jael knew the signs better than most; she just didn't know how long she had left. Maybe a year, maybe less, maybe more.

"So much to do, so little time," Jael murmured to herself as she got to her feet.

She was never much good at leading beyond the confines of the medical level. Whoever succeeded her would have to be. The Strykers Syndicate couldn't show weakness to the world, but neither could it show the same rigidity the old government had ruled with. It was a delicate balancing act, and she thought only one family could actually pull it all off. Pity the one they all needed wasn't even born yet.

Jael left the office, nodding at the handful of aides working in the area beyond her doors. "I'll be on the medical level if anyone needs me."

She headed for the lift, rubbing at her temple, wishing the headache she had would go away.

FORTY-NINE

NOVEMBER 2379
LONDON, UNITED KINGDOM

Jason crossed two continents and an ocean, arriving in London after two days' worth of work back west. His feet hit the floor of the small arrival room with a dull thump. Toronto was five hours behind and still working through its late afternoon. It was evening here. Sighing, Jason stepped off the wooden arrival platform. The room was painted white, but even the paint job couldn't hide how worn-out the place looked.

The door opened manually and he left the room behind, heading for the faint sound of people on the ground level. Matron and some of her scavengers were finishing their evening meal when Jason walked into the communal kitchen. The rest of her crew were still down in the southern hemisphere, cataloguing the seed bank on Antarctica. The shift change wouldn't happen for another week.

Matron looked up from the conversation she was having with Zahara in between bites of stir-fry. "You're back early. Jael like the fruit?"

"No," Jason said.

"She just don't know what tastes good." Matron jerked her thumb in the direction of the tenement's entrance. "If you're looking for Quinton, he's outside."

Matron only meant one place when she said outside. Jason nodded and headed out into the chilly, late-autumn night. He was glad for the warmth of his coat, but the wind still found places to blow through, making him shiver. He crossed the cracked street for the dry expanse of St. James's Park, ducking his head against the wind. The park was a fallow patch of earth that once provided homes for transients, but not anymore. The squalor had forcibly been removed, leaving behind swathes of hard dirt and a barren lake bottom.

Jason cut west across the area. He didn't join the crowd that always gathered around the motley growth of trees and bushes that hugged one small, raised plot of dirt within the perimeter of the lake bed. Glancing over his shoulder, Jason could see the light that played across the tree branches with their brittle red-gold leaves. People were more interested in what Matron was growing with his help than the news streams that slid over the hologrids surrounding the park area, lighting up the night with neon.

Jason wasn't interested in anything except the person sitting on the worn-out cement steps surrounding a cement pillar at the other end of the park. A statue had sat on top of it once, according to records, but it was lost to history now. Jason climbed the steps at an angle, moving around the people gathered there. Everyone ignored him, which Jason appreciated as he went to sit beside Quinton. The older man nodded faintly, the only greeting Quinton gave. Jason got comfortable, watching the crowds pass them by on the street, quads mingling to try to keep the peace on the Strykers Syndicate's orders.

They didn't speak right away. They didn't need to. The bond that linked them had been cut even deeper into their minds during the fight in Paris, a casualty of the merge. It had strengthened the psi link to such a degree that not even a Class I telepath would be able to sever it now. Jason's power hummed down the length of the bond when he used his microtelekinesis, needing Quinton's mind as a stabilizing anchor.

It wasn't going to be enough in the long run; they both knew it. The stronger the psion, the shorter the psion's life, and Jason knew he had only a couple years left if he was lucky. It was the trade-off for what he could do—reconstruct everyone else's life at the cost of his own.

Despite the bond, the two couldn't read each other's mind or emotions, but they understood each other better now because of it. The antagonism that had been there months ago upon joining up for that fateful mission in the Slums of the Angels was gone, buried beneath shared experiences and shared grief.

"You have a headache," Quinton said after a while, staring at the low skyline of London beyond the razed area where a palace once stood. It got turned into a night market over a century ago, and the cacophony of people coming out for an evening of street entertainment reached their ears.

"Same one from this morning," Jason said. "I don't know how to block you from getting feedback."

"It's fine."

Gas hissed as it was released from the biotubes in Quinton's arms. He snapped his fingers, lighting it, letting the ball of fire grow to a decent size as it hovered in the air between them above their knees. The heat made the chill bearable, even if it made everyone else around them draw away out of fear, giving them space. Jason pulled a pack of cigarettes from his pocket and pried one out, lighting it off Quinton's fire.

People around them weren't discreet in the way they gave ground to the pair of psions sitting on the steps. Without uniforms anymore to distinguish psions from the rest of the population, everyone looked human. It was hard to see the differences now that the old laws no longer applied.

Quinton tilted his head back, staring up at the cloudy sky. Jason followed his gaze, blowing smoke up into the air. "Think any of them made it?"

"I don't know," Quinton said, mouth thinning into a flat line. "I hope not."

In the weeks since the nuclear destruction in Paris, the Strykers Syndicate had been focused on Earth, not the stars. If any of the space shuttles made it to the *Ark*, if the *Ark* made it out of cold-dock, maybe the people who fled had survived and were headed to Mars Colony. Maybe not. The Strykers Syndicate only had access to a few working satellites, and even those could only tell them so much. Most of the government's codes and knowledge had been lost when The Hague was half-destroyed and the Peace Palace burned to the ground.

Popular opinion leaned toward abandoning The Hague. Too many memories were left behind in that city, memories no one wanted. The psychometrists who scoured the rubble there said the memories were too corrosive, too strong, to ever really fade. It wasn't worth rebuilding over the lies buried there. But the bunkers and tunnels below were still viable for people to call home. Even if the government left that city behind, civilians wouldn't.

The Strykers Syndicate was still functioning. Most of the Strykers who survived had opted to stay and work rather than leave. Despite their newfound freedom, they had nowhere else to go. Some still left once they recovered from wounds incurred in Paris or in any number of riots that filled the world's streets during that time. Problems were reported from time to time of psion attacks against people, sometimes by ex-Strykers, sometimes by Warhounds. Not all of Nathan's people had died in Paris; they just didn't know how many survived.

Security was an issue that Strykers excelled at, but they weren't doing it for free. If the world wanted stability, it would have to pay for it. The cost seemed high to the registered humans still living—psions wanted equal decision-making authority with whatever government was being cobbled together in London—but most people in the streets weren't as discriminatory, despite the Strykers' use of a nuclear bomb. It hadn't been directed at them, but the registered elite.

"Hell of a way to go, dying on some other planet." Jason took another drag on his cigarette. "I hope they die slow."

Quinton barked out a laugh, the smile on his face humorless and all teeth. "You and me both."

The sound of London at night filtered through the air, the city towers only half-lit. For all that the city towers were open to everyone now, people on the street were still hesitant to enter them. They weren't abandoned, not how some city towers had been in other parts of the world. No one was certain of the whereabouts of those registered humans and probably never would be, even with the oncoming census set to document everyone's identities to create a Registry of humans and psions alike. The old government didn't exist anymore to deny people access based on damaged genetics. That didn't mean old habits were easy to let go.

"We should leave soon," Jason finally said as he stubbed out his cigarette. "Lucas is expecting us."

Quinton didn't move. "I hate Toronto."

"I know."

It was why they lived here now, in London, with Matron and her scavengers. Maybe things would be easier if they moved back to the city tower they'd spent most of their lives working out of, but other Strykers kept wanting to pull them back into a fold they'd left months ago in a broken-down cathedral on America's western shore. While survivor's guilt was shared by all of them, almost every Stryker back in Toronto and those residing in outposts in various cities hadn't experienced what they had.

The loss might be similar, but it wasn't the same.

"I miss her," Quinton said quietly.

Jason's mouth twisted, grief a bitter taste on his tongue, even after all these weeks. He pressed one hand against the edge of the cement step, thinking he could still feel Kerr's hand in his. Thinking maybe, if they'd had just a little more time, he could have saved them. Both of them.

"I'm sorry," Jason whispered.

Neither knew whom he was apologizing to.

Quinton let his hand hover over the fire, his power slowly fading. When the fire was gone, he got to his feet and Jason did the same. Taking a breath in London, they let it out in Toronto, Jason's teleport bringing them to the arrival room on the medical level.

They stepped off the platform, nodding at the Stryker on duty before heading into the hallway. They made their way to Jael's private lab in silence. The door was locked, but Jason had the override. Lucas knew better than to keep them out of the lab. When they walked inside, they could see Lucas standing before the gestational unit, one hand resting against the warm side of the machine that held his daughter. Jael stood beside Lucas, watching him.

"Lucas," Jason said in greeting as he and Quinton crossed the lab space. "Jael."

"Didn't expect you back so soon," Jael said, lifting her hand in a half wave. "Hello, Quinton. Haven't seen you in a while."

"There's a reason for that," Quinton said.

"I know." Jael didn't bother to hide the sadness in her voice. "But you're always welcome here. You know that."

Quinton ignored her words. Jason shrugged at Jael, not willing to apologize for their choice of distance over reunification. "How's the kid?"

"Doing exceptionally well," Jael said as she picked up a datapad and handed it to Jason. "She's got the genetic markers of a triad psion, but I think we can conclusively say her telekinesis is going to be like yours."

"I should hope so. After all the effort I put in to make her into what we needed, she better be like me."

They all knew that the power Jason had engineered Lucas's daughter into having would change the course of history as surely as nuclear war had. Jael no longer hated Ciari for the closely held orders that woman had given, at Lucas's urging, that set them all on this road. She regretted, uncomfortably so, that she never told Ciari that while she still lived. Not forgiveness, nor regret, but a thank-you. Jael liked to think Ciari would have accepted it.

"We'll have to figure out a way to keep engineering this power," Jael said, gazing at the monitors, voice thoughtful. "It's going to take so long to fix this world, even with the terraforming machines, that we can't let this power die out."

"What about when the world is fixed?" Quinton asked as he braced himself against a nearby lab table. "What then? What happens to our kind?"

"If we're going by rates of half-life, psions are going to be around for the next several thousand years, no worries," Jason said, studying the medical information on the datapad. "Maybe by the time we shrink some of the deadzones, what we can do won't be considered a disease. Maybe we'll all be human, able to live an entire human lifetime, but still have these abilities. Maybe it won't take bad genetics to give birth to a psion."

"That's a lot of maybes."

Jason shrugged. "Who knows? It might happen."

"Let's just stick with what we do know," Jael said. "Someone else can figure out the future."

"Someone already did," Jason reminded her, glancing at Quinton. "Aside from not having a death switch in my head, I'm still not sure I like it."

Empty spaces existed in their lives now, silence where another person once lived. The two still grieved the losses of Threnody and Kerr, and always would, no matter how many years they had left to live. They still kept looking over their shoulders for two people who were no longer there, who would never again be there.

Jael tilted her head in acknowledgment of their unsaid words. "That's your prerogative. I'm heading out. Don't keep Lucas in here for too much longer. We need him to get better, not backslide."

"Do you?" Lucas said, his voice quiet, empty.

She'd only allowed him out of his recovery room this week, and he had spent every waking hour in this lab, watching his daughter's heartbeat on the cardiac monitor. Jael stared at his profile, at the bruises still marring the skin beneath his dark blue eyes; those would fade. The bruising in his mind would be with him until death.

Genetically, Lucas would always be a triad psion, but his telepathy wasn't much stronger than Samantha's now, and his telekinesis was completely broken. He couldn't teleport at all. The mess of his emotions, of his pain, was Kristen's legacy. The ruination of his mind was self-inflicted. He would have to live with it, for however long he had left.

"I'm not made to rule," Jael reminded him after a brief pause. "I'm a Stryker, not a Serca."

"You're the OIC."

"I was the last possible choice and you know it. You and Ciari both did."

Jael left the lab on quiet feet, the door sliding shut with a soft hiss. Jason set the datapad down on the table Quinton was leaning against and drifted over to Lucas's side. Jason pressed his hand against the gestational unit, let his power drag him down into amniotic fluid that washed the world out in a sea of proteins, lipids, and other nutrient structures that kept the baby growing. Jason followed the coils of her DNA in his mind, assuring himself that the genes that would make her a microtelekinetic were still holding up strong.

Jason blinked rapidly when he came back to himself, the world solidifying into hard lines with Quinton's distant help through their bond. "Have you chosen a name yet?"

"No," Lucas said.

"You've got a few months until she's born. There's still time."

Lucas splayed one hand over the top of the machine. "Will she have it?"

"I'm not a doctor, Lucas. I wasn't taught medicine. I followed what Korman and Jael showed me would be the best genetic course, but genes don't always stay true to DNA. I think she'll live longer than you or I will. How much longer, I don't know."

"Your daughter's survival for the sake of humanity doesn't absolve you of your actions, you know that, right?" Quinton said, coming to stand by Jason.

"You mean *you* won't," Lucas said, not looking up.

Quinton rubbed his fingers together, the sound of metal on metal grating on their ears. "You didn't need Threnody to change your mind about the launch, to keep everyone on Earth instead of letting them go into space. You could have figured that out on your own."

"No," Lucas said. "I don't think I could have. I needed someone to believe in. Threnody showed me how."

"You had Aisling for that."

"I simply followed orders where she was concerned and Aisling is dead. Threnody wasn't." Lucas lifted his head, meeting Quinton's gaze, seeing the sharp grief that still existed in the other man's eyes. "Your partner helped me see what needed to be done. I couldn't do that on my own. I wasn't raised with the ability to believe in someone other than myself. It's why Aisling told me to find her."

"Threnody wasn't a precog."

"The thing about precogs is that they see so many futures. They have to choose the best end result they can find. In order to do that, they have to build the future that will become our history. That takes a lot of steps, a lot of people, and a lot of time. One wrong move, one wrong choice by any single person, disrupts that goal and forms a new future." Lucas smiled bitterly. "There are linchpins that precogs find who need support, places where the future turns. Threnody was mine. You were Jason's."

"And Kerr?" Jason asked sharply. "What about him?"

"Kerr did what he was supposed to do. He made sure Threnody had time to do her job." Lucas looked away from them, back at the machine that housed his unborn daughter. "We all did what we had to do."

Quinton shook his head. "I don't count this as a win."

Lucas choked on a hollow laugh. "It's never been about winning."

"What if we made a wrong choice?" Jason said. "Somewhere in all this mess that happened, what if we didn't do something right? How do we know?"

Lucas didn't answer, only stared straight ahead.

"We don't," Quinton said as he walked to the door. "That's the problem."

Jason followed Quinton out of the lab, locking the door behind them. Alone, Lucas mentally reached with everything he had for the datapad that sat on the other work counter, mind stretched to its limits, struggling to locate a power that was nothing more than the ghost of a memory.

The datapad did not move.

Lucas stayed where he was, counting heartbeats.

PART TEN
EPITAPH

SESSION DATE: 2128.01.30
LOCATION: Institute of Psionics Research
CLEARANCE ID: Dr. Amy Bennett
SUBJECT: 2581
FILE NUMBER: 99

The doctor holds up the card, the back of it smooth and white where it faces the girl, the side facing her holding a single shape. The child knows this game. It bores her, and it shows. The electrodes attached to her skull and chest and arms itch, the machines she is connected to beeping a familiar cadence into the quiet, white room.

"Let's try again," the doctor says, a strained expression on her face. "What do you see, Aisling?"

She blinks bleached-out violet eyes slowly, a child playing at a grown-up game.

"What do I see?" The smile she offers is more than enough to make the doctor flinch as pupils contract to pinpricks in a sea of bleached-out violet. "I see—"

The machines behind her scream.

"There is a child, a girl, tiny against the backdrop of a ruined city, of a broken world. She wears a jumpsuit, durable little boots that carry her over a cracked street that stretches out before her, green grass shoving up through the dusty ground here and there and there. Her hair is honey brown, her eyes so dark a blue they're almost black. Her mind is wide and open, power burning hotly through the synapses of a triad psion's brain."

A breath. Then another. The cadence of her singsong words never wavers, sounding so much older than the handful of years she has lived.

"A voice calls out to her from behind. Deep. Exasperated. Not her mother, because her mother is dead. Not her father, because he cannot teach her what she needs to learn. But one of the two men behind her are important to her life. The little girl who does and does not listen to her minders skips farther away with a teasing laugh, flowers blooming bright and colorful and alive in the footsteps she leaves behind."

Aisling convulses on her seat, bitten-down nails digging scratches into her skin.

"The world is waking up. Or she is waking the world."